Three delightful love stories from Harlequin's Romance library, memorably written by Flora Kidd

If Love Be Love...Nancy Allen was free at last to make her own plans. Now that her brother was contentedly settled, she dreamed of a suitable marriage for herself. But that was before she met the Laird of Lanmore—a man who proved to be a most unsettling influence. (#1640)

The Cave of The White Rose...To Juliet, alone and jobless, the position of secretary to a woman author was heaven-sent. Admittedly Lance Crimond had been intolerably high-handed in pushing her onto his famous mother, but Juliet had to agree the arrangement was perfect—until she discovered Lance's plans for her also included marriage! (#1663)

The Taming of Lisa...Lisa was ready to do battle with Fraser Lamont, the newcomer, when she learned he wanted her family's property. But meeting Fraser in the flesh and blood came as a pleasant shock. Though not the unscrupulous man Lisa had expected, he determinedly rejected all her efforts at friendship. (#1684)

**Another collection
of Romance favorites...
by a best-selling Harlequin author!**

In the pages of this specially selected anthology are three delightfully absorbing Romances—all by an author whose vast readership all over the world has shown her to be an outstanding favorite.

For those of you who are missing these love stories from your Harlequin library shelf, or who wish to collect great romance fiction by favorite authors, these Harlequin Romance anthologies are for you.

We're sure you'll enjoy each of the engrossing and heartwarming stories contained within. They're treasures from our library...and we know they'll become treasured additions to yours!

The first anthology of Harlequin Romances by

Flora Kidd

Harlequin Books

TORONTO • LONDON • LOS ANGELES • AMSTERDAM
SYDNEY • HAMBURG • PARIS • STOCKHOLM • ATHENS • TOKYO

Harlequin Romance anthology 59

Copyright © 1977 by Harlequin Enterprises Limited. Philippine copyright 1982. Australian copyright 1982. All rights reserved. Except for use in any review, the reproduction or utilization of this work in whole or in part in any form by any electronic, mechanical or other means, now known or hereafter invented, including xerography, photocopying and recording, or in any information storage or retrieval system, is forbidden without the permission of the publisher, Harlequin Enterprises Limited, 225 Duncan Mill Road, Don Mills, Ontario, Canada M3B 3K9.

All the characters in this book have no existence outside the imagination of the author and have no relation whatsoever to anyone bearing the same name or names. They are not even distantly inspired by any individual known or unknown to the author, and all the incidents are pure invention.

These books by Flora Kidd were originally published as follows:

IF LOVE BE LOVE
Copyright © 1972 by Flora Kidd
First published in 1972 by Mills & Boon Limited
Harlequin Edition (#1640) published November 1972

THE CAVE OF THE WHITE ROSE
Copyright © 1972 by Flora Kidd
First published in 1972 by Mills & Boon Limited
Harlequin edition (#1663) published February 1973

THE TAMING OF LISA
Copyright © 1972 by Flora Kidd
First published in 1972 by Mills & Boon Limited
Harlequin edition (#1684) published May 1973

ISBN 0-373-20059-5

First edition published as Harlequin Omnibus in June 1977
Second printing April 1982

The Harlequin trademark, consisting of the words HARLEQUIN ROMANCES and the portrayal of a Harlequin, is registered in the United States Patent Office and in the Canada Trade Marks Office.

Printed in Canada

Contents

If Love Be Love 9

The Cave of the White Rose 201

The Taming of Lisa 391

If Love Be Love

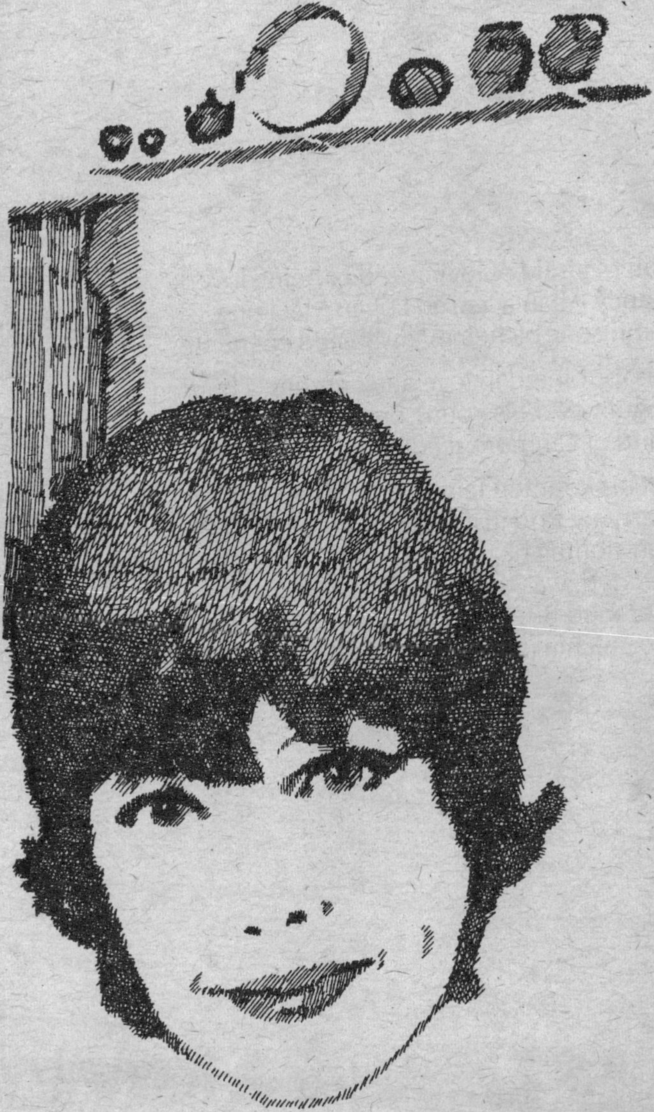

"You're afraid of loving and of being loved," Nancy Allan accused Logan Maclaine during one of their many heated encounters.

Disappointed in love and carrying a burden of guilt over his young brother's death, the Laird of Lanmore readily agreed.

Yet his counterclaim—that Nancy was marrying Rod just for security—left her questioning her own motives. Logan, she decided, was the most disturbing man she'd ever met! But was marriage the best way of proving him wrong?

CHAPTER ONE

"How do you spell 'ancestral,' Nancy?" Linda Allan asked her sister, who was sitting in the front of the car next to her brother, Don, who was driving.

"What do you want to know for?" asked Don scornfully. "Surely you're not writing your diary at this time of the day in the back of a car. I thought you'd be too excited."

Linda, a lively fifteen-year-old whose present ambition was to be a distinguished writer, gazed at the back of his head, a pitying expression on her freckled snub-nosed face.

"That's the whole point. I want to convey my excitement through words immediately, or I'll lose the whole effect."

"I always thought the best writers produced their greatest works when working in peaceful surroundings long after the incidents or conversations they were describing had happened," observed Nancy mildly. "Why ancestral, Lin?"

"We're going to find our ancestral home, aren't we? You told me that the Allans had all lived on Lanmore until daddy left. And they were our ancestors, so it must be our ancestral home," explained Linda with exaggerated patience as she enjoyed playing her favorite role of misunderstood genius, a pose she adopted when her sister and brother handed out criticism. Then, forgetting her part, casting dignity aside, she exclaimed, "Oh, I wonder what it will be like? Do you think it will be like Dunvegan castle, or perhaps a ruin like Duntulm?"

Don snorted with derision.

"To hear you talk you'd think the Allans had been clan chieftains! They were only crofters. I expect the house is small, only two or three rooms, and possibly it has a tin roof. It's the land I'm interested in. Evidently the Lanmore peninsula is one of those outcrops of sedimentary rock that occur in the Highlands, providing fertile soil and good grazing, and it's unapproachable from the landward side because there's no road through the mountains there. Do you know, Nancy, I can hardly believe this is happening to me, of all people."

Nancy glanced at him. His brown eyes were bright. Enthusiasm sparkled in his thin angular face as he stared at the road in front of him. He leaned over the steering wheel, as if by doing so he could reach Lanmore faster. Urgency and excitement were expressed in every feature and every limb.

She looked away through the windscreen at the winding ribbon of gray tarmac that was the old road north, the road from London to Scotland, parts of which followed the original Roman road once known as Watling Street. It was almost eight o'clock on a dull April morning and soon they would be in Newcastle. Then they would turn west to drive along the road that linked Newcastle, on the east coast of England, to Carlisle, on the west coast.

They had left Dulthorpe, the north Yorkshire industrial city where the three of them had been born and where they had lived until today, at six o'clock, after saying goodbye to a rather tearful Aunt Win.

"Aunt Win seemed quite sorry to see us leave, didn't you think so?" said Nancy.

"Well, we've lived with her for five years, and she's known us since we were babies," murmured Linda.

"Five years too long," grunted Don. "I bet she and Uncle Arthur were glad to see the back of me."

The touch of bitterness in his voice made Nancy look at him again. She hoped that this adventure on which they had embarked was going to provide a few answers for Don. Ever since the fire that had robbed them of both parents five years previously, Don had been a headache. After his last stormy two years at school he had left with a handful of mediocre O-level results, a reputation for unreliability and a great dislike for the industrial society in which he lived. However, a certain native hardheadedness and a sincere desire to be independent made him accept a job as a sampler in the chemical works for which Dulthorpe was famed. The job had been obtained through the influence of Rod Ellis, an acquaintance of Uncle Arthur's.

If Love Be Love

That had been three years ago and had brought Rod, tall and handsome, an up-and-coming executive in his mid-thirties, into their lives. He had taken an interest in the Allans' affairs, often offering advice in his crisp methodical manner and showing admiration for Nancy in her efforts to ensure that Don and Linda were guided in the way that she thought her parents would have wanted. Now she and Rod were engaged to be married and the date for the wedding would be set as soon as this pilgrimage to Lanmore was over.

Lanmore—a peninsula on the rugged sea-indented coast in the northwest of Scotland, the place where their father had been born and where a few months ago their grandfather had died. They had seen the old man only once because their father had never taken them to Lanmore to visit him and had never spoken of his family. But their grandfather had come to Dulthorpe, traveling the long distance by ferry, bus and train to attend the funeral of his only offspring when Aunty Win had written to him. Five years later he had remembered Don in his will, leaving him two thousand pounds. In the letter informing Don of his legacy, Mr. Roberts, the Glasgow lawyer, had also drawn attention to the fact that the Allan croft on Lanmore could be Don's, too, in the time-honored way of the passing on of crofts, since his father was dead, and if he wished to claim it and to pay the annual rent, Mr. Roberts had suggested that Don should make his claim soon, because the laird of Lanmore, Mr. K.L. Maclaine, wished to know. Apparently a croft that was not claimed could be rented these days to a party who wanted the use of it.

To say that the letter completely changed Don's attitude to life was an understatement. He was almost ecstatic.

"This is it, Nancy!" he had crowed. "This is what I want—a chance to get away from this dump and its clockwork routine, its 'where there's muck there's brass' outlook on life. I can go and live in a place that is mine, grow my own food and be completely independent."

"But supposing you don't like it? You haven't seen it."

"I'm going to see it. And so are you. We'll take six months off and go. You've nothing to keep you here."

"Only my job...and Rod."

"You know you can stop work anytime, just as I can. It isn't as if either of us will be missed."

That was true. When Nancy's parents had died she had left school, giving up all idea of studying pharmacy at a university, and had gone to work as a sales assistant in the Dulthorpe branch of a well-known chain of pharmacies. She had done so because she wanted one of them to be independent of Aunty Win's generosity. Another reason had been a desire to stay near Don and Linda during their formative years, a responsibility that she had taken very seriously. But although the work had been pleasant it had not satisfied her any more than Don's had satisfied him.

"As for Rod," Don had continued, "I'm sure he'll agree if he thinks the move is going to get me out of his hair for a while."

Indeed, Rod had been most understanding. With a small flash of rebellion Nancy thought she would have liked it better if he had been annoyed, had said he couldn't bear the thought of her leaving and had insisted on marrying her immediately to prevent her from going. Instead he had agreed with the whole idea and had even helped them to pack the secondhand car they had bought to take them to Lanmore.

At her leave-taking he had kissed Nancy in his usual brisk way, had said that he would write regularly and that he might take a week of his annual holiday in August to join them and to see how Don was coping with his croft.

Scarcely loverlike behavior, Nancy thought now, as they drove through the shopping center of Newcastle on their way west. But perhaps she expected too much. Perhaps that was all there was to love, mutual respect and a feeling of general kindliness. Instead of wishing that Rod's behavior was more exciting she should be glad that someone as highly thought of and as responsible as he was wanted to marry her. She wasn't much of a matrimonial catch with her troublesome appendage Linda. She wasn't good-looking, or particularly blessed with social graces. Her hair was red—not a nice becoming chestnut but more the color of new copper, and it was dead straight so that she wore it short in an urchin crop and it fell forward in a spiky fringe under which her dark brown eyes twinkled with mirth or blazed with outraged pride according to how she felt.

Newcastle was behind them and as they drove along the road to Carlisle at a steady speed Nancy began to feel the first stirrings of excitement. Now at last they were breaking new ground and she was seeing places she had not seen before. Linda, who had been unusually silent, came to life again and on looking at the road map discovered to her delight that if they digressed to the right they could visit the remains of the Roman town of Corstopitum, which were situated near the little town of Corbridge.

Don, who could not get to Lanmore fast enough, refused to give in to Linda's request that he should turn off to Corbridge, and went on to the gray-stone market town of Hexham. All the time Linda agitated, muttering that he had no romance in his soul, until eventually he stopped in a lay-by and looked at the map while they ate their packed lunch.

After due consideration of the mileage involved he agreed to turn off the main road at Bardon's Mill and cross the country to join the road that followed the line of Hadrian's Wall so that they could visit the remains of the famous fort of Borvicium, more commonly known as Housesteads, the name of the nearby farmhouse.

By this time the sun had struggled through the gray clouds and was shining benignly on the rolling border countryside. It was possible to see for miles. Cloud galleons sailed above the wavelike ridges of the fields that sloped gradually upward to the north. The short grass was pale, lifeless after the long winter, and the clusters of tall elms that were silhouetted against the sky were still leafless, although a pinkish brown blur smudging their outline indicated that their buds were swelling.

Looking out at the seemingly endless flow of land, crisscrossed by dry-stone walls where there was no visible sign of habitation, Nancy experienced again a wonderful sense of freedom. The feeling was replaced by one of awe when they reached the road that followed the line of the ancient wall and she saw straight ahead of her situated at the top of the last gently sloping ridge the excavated walls of the Roman camp.

There was only one other car in the car park because it was early in the season for visitors. The car was low-slung and aggressive, making the Allans' old Rover seem very sedate. Naturally it attracted Don's attention and after informing his sisters that it was the most recent development in sports cars he began to peer at it closely, the efforts of the Romans completely forgotten as he admired the product of modern genius.

Nancy and Linda, both under the spell of the past, set out without him to explore the camp. On the way up the windy slope they passed the farmhouse hiding among its clump of trees. Behind the house was the museum, where various artifacts discovered during the excavation of the site were displayed. They did not linger there long because Linda, intent on seeing all she could, went ahead of Nancy, guidebook in hand, to examine the walls of the camp. Nancy followed slowly, enjoying the silence, the sharp sting of the wind in her face and the tangy smells of the reawakening earth.

By the time she reached the excavated remains of the granaries Don had caught up with her and together they admired the ingenuity of the Roman builders as they looked at the system of ventilation. Between the buttresses that supported the outer wall, there were spaces that acted as ventilators, allowing free access of air beneath the floor, which in this case had been made of lengthwise planks laid on crossbeams resting on upright pillars. Only the pillars remained, but for a while they stood and stared, imagining the whole building; the wind sighed around them and the feeling of the past was so strong that Nancy could fancy she heard a centurion shouting orders to his men.

"Time we were on our way," stated Don. "Where's Linda?"

"I don't know. She went ahead without me."

"And now I suppose we'll waste another half hour looking for her."

"Why the rush?" queried Nancy. "We've plenty of time, Don. This is the first holiday we've had for ages. Let's make the most of it and see all we can."

"We haven't plenty of time. We have to be in Glasgow

If Love Be Love 15

by tomorrow to see Mr. Roberts. And have you forgotten we must show that we want the croft or the laird will take it over?"

"We'll be there in time, don't worry. And Mr. Maclaine, the laird, will soon find he can't prevent us Allans from claiming what's ours."

Don grinned as he recognized the fighting spirit that had kept the last of the Allans with their heads in the air during the past five years.

"All right. I thought we'd get to Dumfries tonight. It isn't on the fastest route to Glasgow, but it'll interest you and Linda, and we can stay in the youth hostels there. What's the betting Linda is lost or has fallen into a ditch somewhere?"

They moved away from the granaries and started to search for Linda. She wasn't very far away, and she wasn't in a ditch. She was sitting on the well-worn steps of what remained of the great hall, and she was with a man.

As far as Nancy was concerned the situation was worse than if Linda had fallen into a ditch and ruined her clothing. Time and time again she had warned Linda against her propensity for talking to complete strangers, who were usually men. Very conscious of her responsibility for her young sister, Nancy had developed a rather exaggerated fear of strange men. The sight of Linda sitting close to the dark-haired stranger, gazing up at him, apparently enraptured by what he was saying, roused all her protective instincts, and she marched forward.

"Linda! What d'you think you're doing? We've been looking everywhere for you. How many times have I told you not to talk to strangers!"

Her hair ruffled by the wind into a crest that resembled a cock's comb, her brown eyes snapping dangerously, she glared down and encountered a pair of gray eyes set under thick straight dark eyebrows. The eyes considered her coolly, almost insolently, and then looked back at Linda.

Linda said, "Don't take any notice. Go on, finish what you were saying. *She* is my sister, Nancy."

"Your sister, is she?" The voice was quiet and had an attractive lilt to it. "I thought she was one of the hens from the farm...so much clucking and so many ruffled feathers."

The mockery as well as the way in which he ignored her reduced Nancy to unaccustomed speechlessness, and she could only glare down at a head of thick longish dark hair while he continued to talk to Linda.

"As I was saying, one of the gods they worshipped was Mithras...the Persian sun-god. He found special favor with the Roman army in the third century. He exacted high standards of conduct. Knowledge of the ritual attending his worship was only attained by grades of initiation. Men who wished to join the cult had to pass physical and psychological tests that were very difficult. For this reason the cult was secret and it excluded women."

"How mean!" exclaimed Linda, jumping to her feet in her usual restless manner.

"Personally I think it was an excellent idea to exclude women, and if I'd been a Roman I think I'd have worshipped Mithras," replied her teacher. He stood up, too. He wasn't much taller than herself, noted Nancy, possibly about five foot ten, and he was compactly built. He was dressed in finely checked trousers, a white woolen round-necked sweater and a brown leather jacket. He looked elegant and expensive like the car in the car park.

"I'd like to see the place where the temple used to stand," said Linda hopefully, looking at him with bright expectant eyes.

Nancy recovered her voice and her wits and said sharply, "There's no time. Go straight to the car at once, please."

Linda tossed her head mutinously and stood her ground.

"No. I want to see everything. I might never come here again." She turned to the stranger with a complete change of tone and of facial expression, a change that irritated Nancy so that she spoke again.

"Linda...."

"You can see it quite easily on your way to the car park," said the stranger smoothly as if Nancy hadn't spoken. "It's below the farmhouse and it's marked by a single upright post. Now off you go. Goodbye, Linda."

If Love Be Love

Linda smiled, her sudden sweet smile that crinkled her freckled nose and made her brown eyes dance.

"Thank you. Goodbye, Mr.—er—I don't know your name."

"Linda..." started Nancy threateningly.

"Nor are you ever likely to know it," said the man. "I'm not in the habit of revealing it to every schoolgirl I meet."

"Then I shall call you Mr. Mithras," retorted the irrepressible Linda. "Goodbye."

Without a glance at Nancy she tripped off and out of the hall.

"But you are in the habit of speaking to schoolgirls, even when you don't know them," accused Nancy acidly, giving expression to her indignation at last. Everything about him irritated her. His longish hair, the bold arrogance of his nose, the startling lightness of his gray eyes against the sallowness of his complexion and the downward curve of one corner of his mouth as he gave her an oblique glance over his shoulder.

"I did not speak to her. She spoke to me. Your warning about the undesirability of her accosting strange men seems to be totally ineffective. Good afternoon."

He turned on his heel and walked away with a quick determined stride, his hands thrust in his jacket pockets, his shoulders slightly hunched. The desire to go after him and explain to him all her difficulties in restraining Linda's exuberant behavior was so strong that Nancy had taken a few steps after him before she realized the folly of doing such a thing. She turned to follow Linda instead.

But by the time she had reached the post marking the site of the Mithraum or temple of Mithras, Linda was already loping across the wide windy field to the car park. As she reached it, the rakish car left it with a roar of exhaust and headed west. Linda stopped running to wave to the driver.

When Nancy reached the Rover, Don and Linda were already sitting in it and the engine was running.

"Come on, hurry up," chided Don impatiently. "You should have seen the fellow who owned the other car. Talk about posh! His clothes must have cost a fortune, never mind the car. It's the type that won the Le Mans last year, only it has two extra seats at the back. I wish we had his horsepower. We'd soon be in Lanmore if we had."

"We did see him and talk to him. I found him. He was all alone and looking so sad that I just had to speak to him," said Linda as they chugged at a steady forty-five miles an hour westward.

"Sad?" exclaimed Nancy, her feathers still ruffled. "That's the last word I would use to describe him. He was... he was...." She searched for a word to describe the cool authoritative manner of the stranger. "He was insolent," she said lamely.

"Well, you were rude to him. You made out that he was one of those horrible men who pick up young girls and strangle them or something, and naturally he was annoyed," accused Linda.

"For all I know he could have been," defended Nancy. "I'm always telling you to be careful about strangers."

"Yes, I know. As if I hadn't more sense. I knew he was all right. I knew I could trust him. I'm going to put him in a story. My adventure with Mr. Mithras. I think he must be a history teacher."

"Huh, with a car like that?" gibed Don. "Don't be daft. No teacher could afford a car like that. I can't help thinking I've seen him somewhere. His face was familiar."

"Why do you think he might be a history teacher?" asked Nancy.

"He knew so much about the wall and the camp," replied Linda dreamily, her mind already busy with her story. "Or perhaps he was a ghost... the ghost of the Roman commandant of the camp."

"You're nuts," remarked her brother unkindly.

"Judging by his clothes, his car and his hairstyle it's more likely that he's a pop singer or a TV actor, which would account for your thinking he seemed familiar," said Nancy. "Anyway, whoever he is I'm glad there's no possibility of our meeting him again."

Don slanted an amused glance in her direction.

"He's roused you all right. What happened, Nancy? Didn't you win?"

Nancy compressed her lips and tilted her chin.

If Love Be Love

"I've no wish to discuss the man anymore," she replied haughtily, her manner making her brother grin more widely. "It was an unfortunate meeting that I shall proceed to forget."

DURING THE REST OF THAT DAY and the whole of the following day it wasn't difficult to forget the meeting with the stranger because they were all too busy absorbing the sights and sounds of the journey.

They spent the first night at Dumfries, the old county town with its houses of red sandstone crouched beside the swan-scattered waters of the Nith. After a good night's rest they were up early and at Linda's insistence they inspected the house where Robert Burns spent the last years of his life and found the plaque that marked the site of the church in which Robert the Bruce had murdered Red Comyn in the struggle for the throne of Scotland.

Having paid their respects to history they had to hurry along the road to Glasgow and were half an hour late arriving at the lawyer's office. Mr. Roberts, a thin sharp-faced man with a voice like rustling leaves, informed them that Mr. Maclaine, who had cut short a visit to London especially to come north and meet them before they set off for Lanmore, had been unable to wait any longer to see them. The laird was rather concerned about Don taking over the croft, said the lawyer. He had no wish to see it deteriorate through incompetence and had hoped to persuade Don to give up his claim.

A roused Don hotly assured the lawyer that he had no intention of giving up what was his until he had seen it and had tried living there. Pursing his lips and shaking his head, the lawyer reluctantly handed over the key to the cottage as well as a check for two thousand pounds. As he shook hands with Don he wished him luck and added warningly, "Mr. Maclaine has a bad impression of you already because you were late for the appointment, so don't be surprised if you receive a poor welcome from him."

With this cold comfort they left the city and drove out toward Loch Lomond, reaching Balloch at the southern end of the loch as rain began to fall in the late afternoon. For a while they pushed on, but soon the rain was so heavy that it blurred visibility and the narrow lochside road became so slippery that they decided to stop for the night and stay at a small hotel.

Next morning there was a hint of sunshine behind the gray clouds that hid the mountains from view. The water of the loch was flat and inert. But in spite of the cloudiness and the discomfort of traveling along the winding road, the spirits of all three suddenly soared and they sang cheerfully all the Scottish ballads they knew with frequent repetitions of "Loch Lomond" and "The Road to the Isles."

The dour barren stretch of Rannoch Moor reduced them to silence for a while. Although the sun had struggled through it did little to relieve the desolation of the moor, so that they were fully prepared for the strange and terrible atmosphere of Glencoe.

Nancy was glad when they left that haunted place and had crossed Loch Leven on the Ballachulish ferry. They followed the comparatively straight road beside lovely Loch Linnhe, a long arm of the sea, which dimpled and glittered in the mellow light of the afternoon sunshine. The steeply sloping banks of the loch were thickly covered with pine, birch and oak and the succulent luscious green of rhododendron, evidence of the mildness of the climate created by the invasion of the land by the sea.

Although Linda wanted to look in the many gift shops, they did not stop in the busy town of Fort William. As Don pointed out, it was Saturday and the ferry to Lanmore, the only means of access to the peninsula from the south, did not run on a Sunday. If they did not reach the ferry point at Glenarg by six o'clock they would have to spend another night in a hotel which they could not afford.

Don was determined to sleep in his cottage that night, so taking over from Nancy who had been driving, he put his foot down on the accelerator and drove as fast as he dared along the road to Spean Bridge, refusing adamantly to stop and let the girls look at the memorial to the commandos who had trained there during the Second World War.

Along the side of Loch Lochy they sped, watching carefully all the time for a signpost that would show them the

If Love Be Love

way to Lanmore. When it appeared they almost missed it, because its pointing white finger was half-hidden by the drooping branches of a tree and the entrance to the narrow road was scarcely noticeable.

It was as if Lanmore was reluctant to draw attention to itself, as if it did not wish to be invaded by persons from the world of commerce and industry. This impression increased as they drove carefully along the road. Up and up it climbed, a switchback that hung at times over precipitous banks screened by a thick scrub of hazel and birch and oak. Far below shadowed lochs gleamed wanly, linked together by silvery snakes of rivers, while above them towered rugged bracken-clad hillsides down which waterfalls cascaded.

The road was rough and took its toll of the car as they bumped along. They reached the top at last, had a brief glimpse of the sun shining on the sea and then they were plunging downward, twisting and turning on a road that was not much wider than the car.

But there were no complaints about the discomfort of the journey. Nancy was too fascinated by the wild landscape. Don was happy because he was nearly at Lanmore and Linda was too enthralled with the idea that it was possibly in this type of country that Bonnie Prince Charlie had hidden when in flight from the battleground of Culloden.

"Just think, Nan, it must be the same as when he was alive. He might have hidden behind that boulder there, or behind that screen of birch. One of the first things I'm going to do is visit Skye and see the place where he sailed from."

"Don't you believe it," scoffed Don. "When you get to Lanmore you'll have to work. The house is probably in a mess and needs cleaning. No trips to Skye or anywhere else until you've done your stint of work!"

At that moment the car, which had been behaving rather erratically for the last few miles, gave an ominous cough, stopped momentarily and then moved on jerkily. It coughed again, stopped and went on again.

"What's the matter?" asked Nancy. "Have you run out of petrol?"

"Of course not. I filled the tank at that petrol station this side of Fort William," replied Don.

"Hadn't we better stop here where there's a passing place?" suggested Nancy. "We can't stop in the middle of the road, we'd block it completely."

Limping and spluttering, the car jerked on a few yards as Don guided it into a small space carved out of the hillside. These spaces occurred at regular intervals to enable cars to pass on the narrow road. They had hardly reached it when the car engine stopped altogether, and although Don tried several times to coax it to life it remained silent and unresponsive.

"Of all the fiendish luck, when we've only another eight miles to go to the ferry!" moaned Don.

"Maybe someone will come by and stop and help us," said Linda, who was always optimistic.

"I shouldn't think anyone ever comes this way," commented Nancy. "I have an unusual feeling that we've entered a place that doesn't really exist and from which we'll never return."

Her brother and sister regarded her with surprise, because Nancy was the most practical and realistic of the three of them and she never romanced or indulged in flights of imagination.

"It exists all right, although I'm half expecting the wee folk to appear any minute," laughed Linda. "Maybe there's a demon in the engine. Let's get out and look."

They got out. The air was cool and smelled slightly of the sea. Sunlight dappled the purplish rock of the hillside where the passing space had been gouged out of it. Don opened the hood of the car and looked in. There was no demon. The engine appeared to be normal, if a little overheated by its exertions.

The only noise in that place was the occasional twitter of a bird; but suddenly they became aware of another noise, the drone of a car engine.

"Someone's coming!" cried Linda delightedly. "The way we came. I'll wave and stop them."

"Be careful. Don't step out or you'll be knocked down," cautioned Nancy.

If Love Be Love

The sound grew louder, the unmistakable roar of a high-powered engine. A car appeared around the bend. Linda waved frantically. It passed them, screeched to a stop beyond them, and then reversed slowly. It was dark green, low-slung and aggressive-looking.

"It's Mr. Mithras!" screeched Linda excitedly.

"What on earth is he doing here?" murmured Nancy, more and more convinced that she was living in a dream and aware of a strange feeling amounting almost to fear as she watched the door of the green car open and its driver step out.

"He's going to be our Good Samaritan," said Linda with complete disregard for her mixture of religions.

Anyone who looked less like a sun-god or a kindly do-gooder it was hard to imagine, thought Nancy as she watched the stranger of Housesteads approach them. With his dark hair and sallow complexion he was more like Pluto, the god of the underworld.

"So it's you again," he said quietly to Linda, but it was Nancy who received the slightly disdainful glance of his heavy-lidded gray eyes. Then, turning to Don, he asked politely, "What's happened? Can I help you?"

"I don't know," muttered Don, grudgingly, not willing to admit his ignorance. "The engine just stopped and it won't start again."

With an expressive twitch of his eyebrows and the corner of his mouth their Good Samaritan managed to convey that he thought very little of people who did not know why their car had stopped; and ignoring them all proceeded to make a thorough inspection of all that was under the hood.

Linda and Don leaned into the hood with him watching everything he did, occasionally offering comments to which he did not bother to reply. Wishing heartily that it could have been someone else who had come to their aid, Nancy leaned against the side of the car and watched the shadows grow longer down in the deep glen as the sun sidled down the sky, hoping by her detached attitude she would show him that she wished him far away.

His inspection made, the man took the rag offered to him

by Don with which to wipe his oily hands and to Nancy's annoyance came to lean beside her.

"You're admiring the scenery?" he queried. "Tearlath's country."

"Tearlath? What does that mean?" questioned Linda.

"Bonnie Prince Charles to you, little southerner... our brave, valiant and so romantic prince. I'm sure he's the only character in Scottish history in whom you're interested."

There was an undercurrent of amusement in his voice as if he was making fun of them, which irritated Nancy. But his claim to Prince Charlie as his prince surprised her and before she could check her interest she exclaimed disbelievingly, "Are you a Highlander?"

A faint smile revealed his appreciation of her disbelief.

"Insomuch as I was born in the Highlands, and now make my home here," he replied indifferently as if he satisfied her curiosity reluctantly, and immediately she decided that she would not be trapped into asking any more personal questions.

"Why did you buy this outdated machine?" he asked curtly, slapping the side of the car with a derogatory hand.

"It was all Don and I could afford to buy," she answered stiffly, looking him in the eye.

"Do you realize you've been swindled? It isn't fit to take on the roads."

"It has a recent certificate of roadworthiness, and I was sure that the fellow who sold it to us was honest," defended Don hotly, reacting violently as usual to implied criticism.

"I expect he put on an act of being honest," commented the stranger. "Didn't you take anyone with you who had experience of cars when you went to buy it?"

"Rod offered to go with you, Don, but you wouldn't let him," put in Nancy.

"He knows as much—about cars as I do," snorted Don. "Do you know what's wrong with it?" he asked, rounding on the other man.

"Yes. The petrol pump has packed up, and the fan belt isn't in very good shape." He spoke quietly with that touch of authority that put paid to argument.

If Love Be Love

"Oh!" Don sounded thoroughly disappointed.

"But what are we going to do?" wailed Linda. "We can't stay here all night. I'm getting hungry and it'll soon be dark."

"Where are you going?" asked the man, turning to Nancy again.

"To Lanmore." She wondered where else they could go along this road.

"It's a peninsula, almost an island. You can only reach it by ferry," burst out Linda. "Do you know it?"

The stranger did not answer at once but gazed at each of them in turn as if summing them up.

"Yes, I know it," he replied at last. "There's a garage at Glenarg where the ferry is. They do repairs there and they have a towing truck. Leave your car here and I'll drive you there. I doubt if they'll tow your car in this evening. And then tomorrow is Sunday, truly a day of rest in these parts, except in the summertime when there's money to be made from the tourists. So it will be Monday before they move it."

He was amused again and Nancy felt her pride stiffening her attitude toward him. What right had he to be amused at their plight?

"But where shall we stay?" Don asked. "I hoped to be at the cottage tonight."

"Which cottage?"

"The cottage on my croft at Lanmore."

Again they were all subjected to a searching glance and as if realizing that the stranger wished to know more Don introduced himself and his sisters.

"We're just on our way to take up possession of the croft to show the local laird he can't have it," he asserted.

The stranger did not offer to introduce himself. In fact he looked as if he was regretting having played the part of the Good Samaritan, as if he wished he hadn't become involved with them. Immediately Nancy's pride went into action.

"There's no need to tell Mr.—Mr.—all our business, Don," she said sharply. Then, turning to the stranger, she gave him her haughtiest glance and said coolly. "If you would be so good as to give Don a lift to the garage he can make some arrangements with the proprietor to come and tow the car in."

The unusual heavy-lidded eyes surveyed her dispassionately for a couple of seconds.

"And meanwhile, what will you do?" he inquired politely.

"Linda and I shall wait here with the car."

"Oh, no, Nancy, that's not fair! I want to have a ride in Mr. Mithras's car. It looks very fast," said Linda uncooperatively.

"You'll have a long wait, I'm thinking. Your brother will not be back until Monday, unless my knowledge of Duncan Macrae is badly astray," replied the man. "No, you will all come with me. There's enough room in the car, although it will be a tight fit. You can speak to Duncan and then I shall take you to your cottage."

"Would you really? That would be fine. Thanks very much," accepted Don cheerfully.

"A real Samaritan," cooed Linda, gazing up at her new idol with adoring eyes.

The sight of her adoration made Nancy more annoyed than ever and she put in quickly, "Oh, no...no, thank you. It's very kind of you to offer, Mr.—"

"Mithras," he supplied with a sudden grin that she might have found disarming if she had not been so confused.

"You don't have to take us to the cottage. Glenarg will be far enough. We shall wait there until the car is mended. We don't want to impose on you and take you out of your way."

Another long cool stare that made her feel as if she was hopelessly foolish.

"You will not be taking me out of my way," he said. Then as if that statement settled the argument he turned to Don and said, "If you would like to take out of your car the minimum you'll require for the night we'll stow it in mine. Although you may have to nurse some of it on your knees."

When he saw the amount of luggage they had brought with them he whistled softly.

If Love Be Love

"You seem prepared to stay for a long time," he commented, as they pulled out their sleeping bags and a small holdall in which they had kept their overnight things for the journey.

"We've brought all we own," replied Don. "I intend to stay on the croft and live on it as grandfather did."

"Do you know anything about crofting?" inquired the stranger, as he pushed the sleeping bags into a small space at the back of the rear seats of his car.

"No," admitted Don. "But I'm willing to learn. Nothing could be worse than living in a city doing a job you loathe."

Linda and Nancy sat in the two small cramped seats at the back of the car in order to give Don the benefit of the small amount of legroom at the front. Don seemed quite at ease with the stranger and talked away happily, telling him of the miseries of his work in Dulthorpe. In fact with Linda's help he was telling the stranger far too much, thought Nancy furiously, although it was difficult to make out whether the man was listening or not because he said nothing and seemed more intent on his driving.

Of course he was going far too fast for the state and type of road on which they were traveling, and perhaps she should tell him. On second thoughts there was nothing wrong with his driving. In fact he drove at speed better than Don drove normally. So she said nothing. Soon they topped the final rise and saw the white cottages of a small village strung out beside a narrow strait of water that glimmered in the last of the evening sunlight. Beyond the water were gently sloping wooded hills rising up from a foreshore of flat salt marsh. Lanmore was in sight at last.

At the garage and petrol service station Duncan Macrae was not at all keen to take his towing truck out when told by Don about the plight of the Rover. But he promised he would go out to look at the car on Sunday and that he would tow it to his garage on Monday without fail.

"And when I haf it here, and haf ben lookin' at it, I'll be speakin' to you on the telephone to tell you how long it will take to repair it," he said courteously in his lilting voice, the sound of which kept Linda spellbound and silent. "Now, if you would be leavin' me your name and address...."

"Our name is Allan," said Don proudly, "and we shall be at our croft on Lanmore."

The tall towheaded man with the bright blue eyes stiffened slightly and it seemed to Nancy that when he spoke again his courtesy was less spontaneous, but he made no comment beyond murmuring, "Just so. There is no telephone at the house. I will ask my brother Ian to call on you and tell you when the car is ready, then."

"Perhaps we can save you the trouble, Mr. Macrae," put in Nancy quickly. "If you could tell us of somewhere where we might stay until Monday.... You see we have no means of reaching Lanmore without our car."

"Ach, himself will be taking you, surely," said Duncan, jerking his head in the direction of Mr. Mithras, who was leaning idly against his car talking to the ferryman.

Nancy's mouth set in a determined line.

"He said he would, but we have no wish to take him out of his way. And how would he get back to the mainland if the ferry stops running at nightfall?"

Duncan's bright eyes narrowed under his shaggy eyebrows as he glanced in the direction of the dark green car and its owner.

"If he hasn't told you himself, miss, it isn't for me to be sayin'," he answered strangely. "And there is no house in the village where you could be stayin', whatever, and I cannot promise that the car would be ready by Monday. Now, if you would be excusin' me...."

With a polite nod of his head he walked away across the yard, which was littered with old oil drums and bits of ancient cars.

"What a lovely voice," breathed Linda. "However am I going to describe it?"

"He wasn't very friendly," asserted Don as they walked down the slope toward the green car and the ferry. "Did you notice, Nan?"

"Yes, I did," said Nancy. "As soon as you mentioned our name." The famed Highland courtesy was a good facade behind which to hide hostility, she thought. Outwardly Duncan had remained polite, but antipathy had been there. Mr. Mithras Pluto also had the same polite manner. You couldn't really fault him on courtesy, but under the surface there was a similar hostility, as if he resented them for some unknown reason. And they were still dependent on him to take them to Lanmore.

To be under an obligation to someone who did not like them irritated Nancy. A further irritant was that Duncan Macrae had quite obviously recognized Mr. Mithras and yet had not seen fit to inform her of his identity. He had seemed to think it enough to refer to the stranger as "himself" assuming that the Allans knew him.

By the time she reached the green car Linda was already settled in the back seat and Don had also taken his place. They had apparently accepted the stranger's offer without any hesitation.

"Well, Miss Allan, are you staying the night in Glenarg or are you going to accompany your sister and brother and me to Lanmore?"

The politeness was still there. It was so cool as to be almost icy—an icy film behind which all sorts of emotions could be hidden. Now that she had heard Duncan Macrae's Highland speech she realized the Mr. Mithras possessed the smallest suspicion of Highland sibilance in his quiet voice. Quiet, polite... and yet an impression of insolence.

"I don't seem to have much alternative," she answered coolly. "It seems that there's nowhere for us to stay in Glenarg. In fact Don and I have a distinct impression that we're not welcome. I wonder why?"

"You will not be long in finding an answer to your question," he replied noncommittally, dodging an issue in much the same suave way as Duncan had.

"But if you're going to take us across the ferry, how are you going to get back? The croft isn't near the ferry and it's almost dark now."

"Afraid that you might have to put me up for the night, Miss Allan?" he queried mockingly. "Let me set your mind at rest. I shall not stay at the croft a moment longer than necessary. And now I think we'd better get aboard, otherwise Davie will be going without us."

If it hadn't been for Linda and Don the crossing of the narrow strait and the rest of the journey might have taken place in dead silence. But they were both so excited at the thought of landing on Lanmore that they chattered inconsequently the whole time, exclaiming at the view to the west of a satin smooth sea on which small islands floated, black silhouettes against an orange sky.

As the car rolled off the ferry onto a slipway that was in far better condition than the one at Glenarg, Mr. Mithras wound down the car window and shouted something in a strange language to the ferryman.

"Gaelic," exclaimed Linda triumphantly. "What did you say?"

"Don't be rude, Linda," cautioned Nancy. "Maybe it was something private."

"I said '*Oidhche mhath mata*,' which means 'Good night, then.' That's all. Nothing very private," said the stranger, and again there was amusement in his voice, as if he found Nancy's intervention ridiculous.

She resolved to say no more. His attitude toward her was far different from his attitude to Linda. He seemed to like Linda and answered her forthright questions without any hesitation so that they were all now knowledgeable about the fact that he had driven all the way from Glasgow that day. With Don he was offhand but not unpleasant. He talked to him as man to man, and this Nancy knew would endear him to her brother, who had often been resentful of Rod Ellis's condescension.

The road crossed a no man's land of salt marsh. It was well surfaced, better than the road they had traveled to Glenarg. On either side pools of water glinted in the fast-fading daylight. Ahead the hills of Lanmore were melting into the darkness. Soon the road was among the hills, losing its level straightness as it twisted and turned in a westerly direction. Twin shafts of headlights picked out the dry-stone walls behind which dark trees crowded. A whitewashed cottage loomed toward them and was passed. Farther on a white signpost bearing the words Lanmore Lodge pointed west, and Nancy thought of Mr. K.L. Maclaine, the laird whom they had just missed meeting at the lawyer's office. She assumed that it was his wealth that ensured that the slipway and the road were kept in good condition.

If Love Be Love

After several more twisting miles they turned left off the road on to another narrower road. They passed open fields bare of trees. The road descended, jumped over a bridge and turned left again, and there was the sea smoothly reflecting the last gray streak of light.

The car stopped beside a stone wall in which there was a gate. Don and Linda were out of the car and through the gate before Nancy could move. She spoke stiffly to the man who still sat in the driver's seat.

"Thank you very much. We're very much in your debt."

"And that will be bothering you, of course," he murmured. "Have you the key to the house, because it looks as if your brother hasn't."

"Come on, Nancy. What are you waiting for?" urged Don. "We're here. I hope you haven't lost the key."

"Of course I haven't," she retorted as she moved over and, pushing forward the back of the seat that Don had vacated, extricated herself from the car.

She dug in her handbag for the key, but no matter how much she groped she could not feel it. It was impossible to see into the bag, so she walked around to the front of the car and bent down before the headlights in an attempt to see into it. Behind her Don was muttering sarcastically about women and their inability to keep keys.

"I shall soon be thinking that you are not the rightful owners of the croft," said Mr. Mithras close beside her. "I have a torch here. Empty the contents of your bag on the seat of the car."

A torch! The one thing they had not brought, thought Nancy wildly. Supposing there was no light in the house? Supposing they had to grope in the dark in order to make a meal before they went to bed? Suddenly she realized how hungry and tired she was and how much she would have to do before she would be able to go to bed, and her already lowered spirits plummeted to zero.

The emptying of her bag and the search among its contents under the watchful steady beam of the torch did not reveal the key.

"I must have lost it," she said dully.

"Oh, Nancy!" wailed Linda. "I'm so tired and hungry. What shall we do?"

"I should have guessed you would lose it," said Don impatiently. "I told you to give it to me."

"As if you're any better with keys than I am!" she snapped back. "Don't forget it was you who so cleverly locked the car keys in the boot the night we stayed in Dumfries."

She realized it was dark again in the car. The torch and its owner had gone. "Where is he?" she whispered to Don.

"At the front door with Linda," he whispered back. Just then Linda came skipping toward them.

"The door's open, Nancy. Mr. Mithras has opened it. I think he must be a magician, or perhaps a genie, like the one Aladdin had. He always seems to be around when we need help."

"Not a genie... merely knowledgeable about the people who live in the Highlands. There was a key hidden on a ledge above the porch door. It's common practice to leave a key handy in case someone comes home and wants to get in. And now if you would like to take your sleeping bags and other belongings out of the car I'll take you into the cottage and show you how to light the lamp," said the stranger.

"Lamp?" chorused the Allans.

"Isn't there any electricity?" quavered Nancy.

"I thought all the Highlands were served with electricity nowadays," added Don.

"You're quite right, but not this cottage," answered their magician.

As they took their sleeping bags out of the car and walked after him into the cottage Nancy couldn't help wondering how he knew all he did about the cottage. Was it possible that he lived hereabouts? But where? He didn't look like her idea of a crofter or a shepherd and he was too young to be the laird.

The cottage had a damp musty air that made her shiver as she entered, following the torchlight. There was a tiny paneled entrance hall off which two rooms opened one on either side. Their guide turned into the one on the left. It

If Love Be Love

was furnished with a large table on which stood an oil lamp.

"If you'll hold the torch I shall show you how to light it," said Mr. Mithras, handing the torch to Don and picking up the box of matches that lay handily close to the lamp.

He took the glass chimney off the lamp and laid it on the table. Then he picked up the brass base of the lamp and shook it, and they could hear the gurgle of oil within it. Putting it down on the table again, he turned a small knob fixed to the neck of the container and turned up the wick.

"Looks dirty," he commented laconically. "Shine the torch over here."

He moved to the fireplace. The beam lit up the heavy wooden overmantel that was laden with numerous pieces of dusty china ornaments. He searched among them and apparently found what he wanted, because he returned to the table and proceeded to clean the wick with the object.

That done, he struck a match and applied it to the wick, which began to burn with a strong yellow light. When it was burning well he turned it down a little and fitted the chimney over it. In the chimney there was a white gauze mantel. This immediately incandesced and a brighter light spread through the room until it was full of a mellow glow that cast deep shadows in the corners.

"Oh, what a lively light!" said Linda. "It's just as if we were living years and years ago. I wish we always used lamps like this. They're much better... much more cozy than electric light."

"You may not think so when you find you have to clean and fill them every day, one for each room," commented Mr. Mithras dryly.

Nancy glanced around the room. Its walls were lined with painted wooden boards and the floor was covered with linoleum that was bright red and covered with a jazzy black and white pattern. Red seemed to have been Grandfather Allan's favorite colour, because the frames of the windows and the doors were painted bright red. As well as the table, there was an old brown dresser against one wall on which blue willow-patterned plates were arranged. On either side of the black range there were two big wheel-backed chairs.

There were no chairs at the table, but a bench was pushed under each side of it.

Nancy's gaze came around to the fireplace and range again and she stared at it with an odd feeling of dread.

"How will we cook?" she asked, knowing full well what the answer would be and bracing herself to meet the amused glint that she guessed would be in Mr. Mithras's gray eyes when he answered.

She was right. The glint was there, although his mouth remained serious.

"As you have guessed," he replied. "On the range."

"Oh, Nancy, just think! Homemade bread from a coal-fired oven!" enthused Linda, who was still entranced by the old-fashioned facilities of the room.

"A peat fire," put in Mr. Mithras softly, almost wickedly.

"That's even better," said Linda.

"But doesn't it take ages to light?" complained Don. "I'm absolutely famished. It's hours since we last ate."

"Yes, it does take a long time to light it if you haven't the knack," murmured Mr. Mithras, "especially when the house has been empty for some time and the chimney is damp and cold. And you should never let it go out once it has been lit, unless of course you're leaving the house for a long period."

It seemed to Nancy that he was relishing pointing out all the inconveniences of the place, as if he was trying to put them off, and at once her pride asserted itself. She turned and smiled brightly at him.

"Well, I expect we shall manage very well once we get the hang of it. We mustn't delay you any longer. Thank you very much for all your help," she said with a jauntiness she was far from feeling. Once this man was on his way she would be able to relax and it wouldn't matter how many mistakes she made because he wouldn't be here to laugh at her. If only she didn't feel so tired! If only she could get rid of the sense that the presence of the Allans at Lanmore was not welcome. The red paint didn't help her spirits at all. It was probably daubed all over the house and it would take her and Don all summer to get rid of it.

She became suddenly aware that the stranger was ignor-

If Love Be Love

ing her suggestion that he should leave and that he was removing his jacket and pushing the sleeves of his sweater above his elbows.

"I shall light the fire for you before I go," he said. "There are dry peats in a box beside the hearth. Meanwhile, Don, if you go through that door over there you'll find a scullery. In the cupboard I think you'll find a small Primus stove that will do for you to boil water on."

Don, followed by the enthusiastic Linda, went through the door at the back of the room taking the torch with them. Mr. Mithras knelt before the hearth and cleaned out the old ashes. Then, selecting some peats from the pile stacked beside the hearth together with some chopped wood sticks, he began to arrange them in the hearth.

Nancy looked down at him with something like respect dawning in her mind.

"This is very kind of you," she began stiltedly.

"If that's all you have to say may I suggest that you keep quiet and hand me the matches," he remarked coolly, and once again she was aware of the icy barrier of politeness keeping her at bay.

She handed him the box. Their fingers touched and she withdrew hers quickly.

"You must be a genie," cooed Linda as she came back into the room. "There's a Primus and some paraffin oil and some methylated spirits. Don is getting it going and we'll soon have a cup of tea. You'll have some tea, won't you, Mr. Mithras?"

"No, thank you, Linda. As soon as this fire is going I must be on my way." He glanced at his watch. "I was expected for dinner at eight."

To Nancy's surprise his fire was beginning to burn slowly with more smoke than flame.

"Don't touch it. It will burn," he asserted as he shrugged into his leather jacket. "And when you put more peats on make sure you build them around the glow. Bank it up well before you go to bed and it will stay alight until morning. You'll be all right now."

It was a statement rather than a question, and he looked directly at Nancy as he spoke. His glance was no longer lazy and dispassionate but wide open and intent, making him seem an entirely different person—a person who was interested and concerned and who knew she was tired and disenchanted. "Don't be worrying," he added softly. "Everything will look different in the morning."

He turned and walked to the door. Don appeared from the scullery and they all crowded into the small dark hall.

"You haven't told us your name. We can't go on calling you Mr. Mithras. It's ridiculous after all the help you've given to us," said Don.

The stranger opened the door and stood for a moment outlined against the starlit sky.

"My name is Logan Maclaine," he said reluctantly. "Good night." He was gone and the door was closed before they had time to catch their breath. The car started with a roar and a cough and then whined away into the night.

"Maclaine? That's the name of the laird, our landlord, the fellow who wanted us to give up our claim to the croft," muttered Don as they returned to the kitchen where lamp and fire glowed and flickered, giving the room a cozy welcoming appearance.

"Logan," mooned Linda, in the throes of an attack of hero worship. "A beautiful name. It is music in mine ears."

"Honestly, Linda, he must have thought you were nuts, with your Mr. Mithras and all your soppy questions," snapped Don. "It's a wonder he helped us all he did. You're enough to frighten the most sympathetic person away."

"It was because he liked me that he helped us," retorted Linda spiritedly. "It was obvious he didn't like Nancy. I suppose because she's a woman; and remember he said at the fort he liked the religion of Mithras because it excluded women. I suppose," she went on dreamily, "he's been badly let down by a woman and he's since avoided their society. Yes, that's it. That's why he looked so sad when I first saw him. What a wonderful idea for a story! I shall start writing it at once. Where did I put my pad and pencil?"

"You left them in our car," snapped Nancy, finding that she was annoyed at Linda's suggestion that Logan Maclaine had not liked her.

"Which is a good thing, because you can just set to and

If Love Be Love

help me to make a meal. He can't possibly be our landlord, Don. He doesn't look like a farmer for one thing, and I don't think he's old enough to be the laird," said Nancy. But to her own ears her arguments sounded completely unconvincing as she tried to stave off a growing suspicion that the dark stranger who had helped them was in fact the man whom Mr. Roberts had described as being a stickler for punctuality and who had already a bad impression of the Allans.

"Then he's probably K.L. Maclaine's son," returned Don equably. "Come to think of it, if he was the laird he wouldn't have treated us so kindly, if what old Roberts said about him was true. Logan Maclaine," he reiterated slowly. "It has a familiar sound, and I still have a feeling that I've seen him before, in a photograph in a newspaper. Maybe it will come to me soon."

IT RAINED IN THE NIGHT. That was when Nancy discovered that the roof leaked. She and Linda had chosen to sleep together in their sleeping bags on the big old-fashioned bed in the room at the top of the stairs. It had been impossible for them to air the beds because they had been too tired to heave the mattresses down the stairs to the fire and they had no other means of airing. After feeling the bedding, Nancy had decided that they would come to no harm if they stripped off the blankets and lay on the beds in their sleeping bags.

Although she was tired she did not sleep at once. She lay curled up, envying Linda who had gone to sleep as soon as she had lain down. At first when she closed her eyes she kept seeing the winding road through the mountains coming toward her. Then she began to think of the coincidence of their meetings with Logan Maclaine. He must be the laird. It all fitted in so neatly. Hadn't he told Linda that he had driven up from London the day they had met him at Housesteads? Then today he had driven from Glasgow. He had been known by Duncan Macrae, who had referred to him with respect. He had known about the key above the porch door, about the oil lamp and the Primus stove. And he had known how to light a peat fire. And what was so exasperating, he had known he would not be going out of his way if he conveyed them to the cottage because his own house was a few miles away along the road.

Nancy ground her teeth with embarrassment. How he must have been laughing at them, at her in particular. But why hadn't he told them who he was?

Rain pattered on the roof and the windowpanes. Raising her head, she looked at the uncurtained window. The stars had gone, obliterated by cloud.

"Everything will look different in the morning," Logan Maclaine had said, as if he had guessed she was fed up with the oil lamp and the peat fire. He had been offering comfort in his own way, she supposed, and yet Linda had said he didn't like her. Was dislike the reason for his insolent attitude toward her? Not that it mattered, because the dislike was returned in full measure. She didn't care at all for men with heavy-lidded eyes who kept their emotions hidden behind a facade of icy politeness and who didn't think it necessary to introduce themselves. He was probably sufficiently arrogant to assume that they recognized him. But why should they recognize him? Nancy's thoughts grew muddled as sleep began to claim her.

Plop! In a second she was wide awake again, convinced she had felt something wet on her cheek. She waited tensely and it happened again—right on her nose, this time. She reached for the torch that Logan Maclaine had left for their use, clicked it on and shone it at the ceiling. It lit up a brown mark that she recognized as a damp patch. As she stared at it a globule of moisture formed and dripped onto the bed.

"Nancy!" Don's hoarse whisper from the direction of the door made her jump. "The roof leaks."

"It leaks in here, too. Better move your bed so that you aren't under the drips. I'm moving closer to Linda."

"I wanted to tell you that I've remembered who he is." Don went on as if prepared for a midnight talking session.

"Who...who is?" groaned Nancy. "Oh, please save it till morning, Don. I'm terribly tired."

"Logan Maclaine," he persisted. "He is, or rather he was, a racing driver. There were two Maclaines who raced—

If Love Be Love

he and his brother. They used to drive in Grand Prix races as well as rallies. Then two years ago the brother was killed. This one pulled out of racing, and everyone said he'd lost his nerve." Don yawned noisily. "I'm glad I've remembered. Couldn't sleep until I did. Good night, Nan."

CHAPTER TWO

EVERYTHING DID LOOK BETTER in the morning. The rain had given way to clear pale blue skies. Across Loch Arg four mountain peaks presented a variety of colors, ranging from sandy brown that merged with rose pink to sage green and lavender gray. The water of the loch was still and smooth, reflecting every detail of the mountains and of the dark pines and white cottages that nestled at their feet.

A little breeze rippled the water and the reflected mountains shivered and blurred. The movement roused Nancy from her reverie. She was standing on the narrow shingle shore below the cottage. Allan croft was situated on the favorable southwest tip of the peninsula. It was protected from the onslaught of wind and sea in bad weather by a long rugged island that ran out from the end of the peninsula across the entrance to the loch.

Slowly Nancy turned her back on the magnificent views of mountains and sea and walked across the rough spiky grass to the small green gate set in the dry-stone dike that ran around the garden of the cottage. The house was neat and unpretentious. It had a plain front door set in a little porch that was built at right angles to the main building. On either side of the porch were plain sash windows. Above, two dormer windows perched on the slate roof. Behind the house stretched the land that formed the croft, four fields stretching upward toward the low craggy hills. To the right was the byre that had once been the original "black house" or thatched crofter's house. It was small and squat and hugged the ground.

It was the garden that amazed and delighted Nancy. She realized that it must have been created by her grandfather. It gave an impression of being entirely natural, but she guessed that every bush and shrub had been planted care-

If Love Be Love

fully and had been tended with love. Now it presented a tangle of winter-bleached grass through which crocuses had recently struggled to bloom and where now a drift of wild daffodils nodded their pale heads. A group of rowan trees crowded in one corner of the garden and a shrubbery made of rhododendrons darkened another. Gooseberry bushes, gnarled and spiky, were grouped above a rockery that separated one part of the garden from another. Below the bushes were three gray beehives around which Nancy skirted carefully as she made her way to the front door.

Even though it was only April the garden was warm and sheltered, and Nancy decided to bring the bedding out and hang it on the clothesline to air. While she hung blankets she noticed another white house similar in style to the Allan house, set on a green knoll to the right. There was no wall around it and no garden. In the field behind it two brown Highland cows grazed and higher up where the fields sloped to gray boulders there were white blobs of sheep and lambs.

It was quiet, not just the quietness of Sunday but the quietness of a land empty of people. Yet people had once been there—the ruins of the cottages on the crofts beyond the house to the right were evidence of that. And Nancy had the oddest feeling that the spirits of the people who had once lived there lingered among the hills and hovered over the limpid sea.

The throb of a car engine broke the silence. Nancy tensed, but the sound was different from that made by Logan Maclaine's car. She watched the narrow road where it crossed the burn beside another whitewashed cottage. A blue station wagon appeared, turned the corner and stopped in front of the garden gate. A tall angular woman with blue-rinsed gray hair got out of it. She was neatly dressed in a heather-colored tweed suit.

"Good morning," she said in a crisp, decidedly English voice. "I'm Mary Maclaine. You must be Nancy Allan. When Logan told me why he was late for dinner last night I was quite annoyed to think he had allowed you to come here to sleep on damp beds in an unknown house. I told him he should have invited you to stay at the Lodge for the night...and he gave me one of his stares and said, 'If you had met Nancy Allan you would know why I didn't invite them.'"

Nancy was astounded by this speech. Whatever could Logan Maclaine have said about them? He must have given a bad impression of her in particular.

"I beg your pardon?" she said haughtily.

Mary Maclaine smiled, a sweet, faintly mischievous smile. "Did you look at him like that, and speak to him like that?" she asked. "He didn't invite you to stay at the Lodge, so he told me, because you would have refused. So I just had to come and see you—to see the one woman who could refuse Logan. By the way, I'm a cousin by marriage. My husband is Keith Maclaine, cousin to Logan's father. How do you do." She thrust out a hand and shook Nancy's heartily. "Now that I've straightened that out I'll give you the food I've brought over. Logan said your car broke down and that you were only able to bring a few things in his car."

Rather bewildered by this managing but likable woman, Nancy was persuaded to accept two dozen eggs, a piece of bacon, a joint of beef and several pints of milk that she was assured had come from the Allans' own cows.

"They've been kept at the Lodge farm since your grandfather died. Logan is bringing them over this morning," explained Mary. "The hens will have to come in the Land Rover some other day. No one works on a Sunday, you see. That's why Logan is bringing the cattle himself. You'll need this butter, too—and these potatoes and vegetables, I expect."

"Don and Linda, my brother and sister, have set off for the Lodge to see if anyone knew anything about the cattle and to collect them if possible," said Nancy.

"Well, they haven't got very far, I can tell you that. I saw them exploring the old broch."

"Oh, how typical of Linda!" commented Nancy. "What is a broch?"

Mary frowned a little and then said, "That's a good question, and it would be better if you asked Logan. He's very good at history. He once told me, but I can never remember details. All I know is that the people who built them lived in this round building, animals and all. Can't say I'd have

If Love Be Love

liked it—most insanitary. You know, I'm rather glad you've come here."

Nancy blinked. It was the first sign of welcome she had received since she had arrived at Lanmore.

"It's very nice of you to say so. Last night we were beginning to feel as if no one wanted us here."

"Hmm, I can imagine. Did Logan try to freeze you? I know he was concerned about your brother coming to live on the croft. He had a feeling that someone from a city would be no earthly use and would let the land deteriorate, and he wants to stop that from happening. You'll be company for him."

Again Nancy blinked. Mary Maclaine's abrupt statements were somewhat confusing.

"In what way?" she asked.

"It will be good for him to have young lively people around who need his help when he lives here. When he stays in London it's a different matter because he has his racing friends there... and then there's Anya. But when he's here he's alone in that big house, and I think he broods about the accident still. You know about that, of course?"

She shot a bright blue glance in Nancy's direction and Nancy, who was by now completely swamped by the information that was pouring out of her garrulous visitor, shook her head.

"No, I'm afraid I don't. My brother said something about recognizing Mr. Maclaine...."

"Call him Logan, dear. Everyone does and it makes it easier for me. Logan is his second name, his mother's maiden name. His first name is Kenneth, like his father. Silly notion, calling boys after their fathers—always leads to confusion. His mother is Deirdre Logan...the poetess, you know. She lives in Jersey, in the Channel Islands. Has been there for years. She and Kenneth didn't hit it off, so they separated. She let him have the upbringing of the boys, which is just as well, because she hadn't a maternal instinct in her. Now, what was I going to tell you?"

"About the accident."

"That's right. Logan has been mad about cars since he was seventeen. Raced whenever he could, much to his father's annoyance. Kenneth thought that Logan, being the eldest, should concentrate on being a good landlord and farmer. It might not have been so bad if Angus, Logan's brother, hadn't followed in his footsteps. Strange, isn't it? Very often brothers do the opposite to each other. But Angus always had to try and go one better than Logan. They were very close friends, as well as being close in age. I always have a feeling that Logan considers himself guilty of Angus's death."

"How did the accident happen?" asked Nancy.

"Their cars collided during a race. Angus's was thrown down an embankment and it burst into flames. Logan tried to free him and was badly burned. Angus died on the way to hospital. It shocked Kenneth, and he never really recovered. He died last year. I don't think he ever forgave Logan, either."

But what was there to forgive?" exclaimed Nancy.

"Logan lived, but Angus the favorite didn't. If Logan hadn't taken up racing Angus would not have raced, either. Kenneth was a rather hard man. Angus was his soft spot. Anyway, he died and Logan inherited all Lanmore, one of the biggest farms in the Western Highlands, as well as quite a fortune. He's a very wealthy man."

Again she shot a bright inquisitive glance in Nancy's direction as if she expected this piece of information to bring forth a comment. But Nancy had never been impressed by wealth and instead she said, thinking of the death of a disappointed old man, "How sad!"

"Yes. And what was worse, Angus was married...to Anya. For a while we thought it was going to be Logan and Anya, because Logan met her first. But he always said he would never marry while he was racing, so it was Angus who married Anya. They had six years together and one child. Now I'm wondering if it's going to be Logan and Anya after all. He's been going to London quite a lot recently. She's an actress—Anya Baron. You may have seen her on TV."

Nancy had a fleeting memory of someone blond and athletic with a deep guttural voice who had escaped from difficult situations in a recent mystery serial by using judo technique.

If Love Be Love

"Of course you can never tell with Logan," continued Mrs. Maclaine. "He hasn't a very high opinion of marriage because of the failure of his parents to make a go of it. Heavens, I must fly! I promised Keith I'd take a sandwich to him. He's fishing the North Loch, you know."

Nancy didn't know, but she smiled and nodded as if she did.

"I'll see you before we return to Edinburgh, dear. Keith is in law, you know. Goodbye for now."

Still smiling, Nancy watched the station wagon reverse, shoot forward and disappear over the bridge. Then she went into the house to put away the food. It had been kind of Mary Maclaine to bring it. She decided she had better cook the beef as the best way of keeping it since there was no refrigerator, and that made her look at the fire.

It was almost out. Hurriedly she crossed to the stack of peats and choosing several, she began to place them around the small glow. Then she swept the hearth.

"Hello, anyone at home?" She recognized the voice at once, but although she stiffened she did not turn around or stop sweeping as she called out, "Yes. Come in. I'm in the kitchen."

There was the sound of someone dropping rubber boots on the stone step and then the soft slither of stockinged feet on the linoleum.

"Never in my wildest dreams have I imagined Cinderella with red hair," commented Logan Maclaine.

Although surprised by his remark, Nancy did not show her surprise. She hung the hearth brush on the hook provided for it, rose to her feet and after regarding her visitor for a moment replied, "Nor have I ever imagined a Prince Charming wearing a kilt, but then I don't believe in fairy stories."

He was leaning against the doorjamb. A dark turtlenecked sweater emphasized the darkness of his hair and eyebrows and contrasted with the red and green of his kilt. He glanced down at the kilt and murmured, "I wore it specially for the benefit of your romantic sister, but she doesn't seem to be here. I hope the smell of mothballs isn't too strong. It's some years since it's seen the light of day."

Nancy couldn't help laughing at his honesty in admitting that he did not normally wear a kilt, and he showed his appreciation of her mirth with his charming crooked grin.

"Linda and Don have gone to see you, to collect the livestock," she said. "Your cousin has just been here. She brought us some food. She told me you were on your way with the cows."

"And the goats."

"You shouldn't have bothered."

"So Mary came. I thought she might out of sheer curiosity."

"Why didn't you tell us your name, who you are, when you stopped to help us?"

His glance was enigmatic.

"Sometimes it's more interesting to remain anonymous. Would it have made any difference if you had known?"

"Yes, of course it would."

"In what way? I suppose, knowing you, you would have been less forthright, less honest."

"Not at all. But it would have made everything more... more understandable. As it was...."

Nancy paused, realizing that what she was about to say bordered on the personal and was really the result of knowledge about him that Mary Maclaine had imparted to her.

"As it was?" he prompted.

"I'm not going to tell you."

"You see," he accused triumphantly, "already you're being careful about what you say. What have you been doing to that fire?"

With a colorful swirl of his kilt he swung across the room and knelt down at the hearth.

"I've mended it," defended Nancy. "I want to heat the oven to cook the meat."

He looked around and found some old bellows with which he blew up the fire. Then he showed her how to adjust the damper so that the heat from the fire was directed toward the oven.

Nancy watched him and wondered. "He's a very wealthy man," Mary's words whispered through her mind. Then

If Love Be Love

what was he doing in her kitchen mending her fire? Prince Charming come to seek out Cinderella? Nancy shook her head slowly as she looked down at his dark head.

"Not a bit like Prince Charming, nor like Mithras. Much more like Pluto," she murmured, speaking her thoughts aloud as she remembered a book of myths she had possessed as a child in which there had been a drawing of the dark king of Hades.

He glanced up sharply, his gray eyes wide, unveiled.

"Who is Pluto?"

"You're like him. You're dark and...and...." She searched vainly for the right word.

"Dour," he offered dryly as he stood up and faced her. "Perhaps you fancy yourself as Proserpina. Are you expecting me to kidnap you and take you to my dark and gloomy underworld to spend the winter there, or is that another fairy story in which you don't believe?"

For a tense moment he was very close to her and she was mesmerized. There was a strange tight feeling in her breast and her heart was beating unusually fast. Fear plus excitement, she diagnosed. Fear because he had her almost believing in his underworld, and excitement because she was intensely aware for the first time of his attraction. He wasn't handsome in the accepted sense like Rod, but the combination of swarthy irregular features and light farseeing eyes plus a compact muscular physique made him a person she could not dismiss easily.

Warm blood crept into her cheeks and she looked down quickly. She had thought she could stand her ground with anyone, but now she was actually turning pink, and she wasn't given to blushing normally.

"The roof leaks," she squeaked. Anything to break the tension.

"I know."

"Oh. You knew last night and you didn't warn us."

"I didn't think it would rain. Did you get wet?"

"Yes. And so did Don. It was then that he remembered where he had seen you before—in the newspaper, after the crash."

His face closed immediately. It became a polite mask that

covered all expression. He moved away from her toward the door.

"I'll go and look at the ceilings in the bedrooms," he said curtly and left the room.

Why, oh, why couldn't she hold her tongue? Why did she have to blurt out tactlessly, hurtfully?

She followed him upstairs and into the first bedroom. He stood in the middle of the room and stared up at the ceiling.

"It doesn't do, you know," she said. "To brood, I mean, about what's happened. Especially about accidents. It wasn't your fault anyway."

He turned to look at her.

"How do you know?"

She didn't know, of course. She only knew what Mary had told her that morning and what Don had said last night.

"Mary," he guessed, and contempt grated in his voice. "You will oblige me by forgetting anything she may have told you. It's none of your business anyway. I'll send someone to mend the roof tomorrow. That is, if you're still thinking of staying."

"Why shouldn't we be staying? We haven't come all this way just to go back again. This croft is Don's by right of inheritance as long as he is able to pay the rent. Mr. Roberts the lawyer said that you wanted to persuade Don to give up his claim. I suppose you want the land for yourself, although what four acres can possibly mean to you when you already own umpteen, I can't think."

He folded his arms across his chest and looked at her in a rather pitying way that did nothing to quelch her temper.

"You have it all mixed up," he said softly. "I don't want the land. As you so succinctly put it, I own umpteen acres already. It's Ian Macrae who wants it. He's brother to Duncan at the garage and he's young and ambitious. He's taken over several abandoned crofts. When the old people die the young ones don't usually want to come back from the cities to claim the crofts, so they deteriorate and the cottages fall into ruins. It is better if the unworked crofts are taken over by people like Ian who are willing to stay and work on the land. Gradually he will have enough land to make a farm. This particular croft has been decaying for several years be-

If Love Be Love

cause your grandfather could not work it anymore. With the arrival of your brother, Ian has lost the opportunity to gain another soum."

"That's why Duncan Macrae resented us?"

"Exactly."

"But whatever is a soum?"

"The number of sheep a crofter has a right to put on the common hill grazing. Your grandfather had the right to two hundred, but in the end he had only twenty. It's difficult for an old man to keep sheep, and I'm wondering if your brother can do any better."

His voice was cold and abrupt. The expression on his face was stern and Nancy had the impression of deep concern for the land and little liking for those who did not treat it with respect.

Accustomed to defending her brother, she faced Logan fiercely across the expanse of the old faded patchwork quilt that covered the bed. "Why shouldn't he? He's always wanted a place of his own. He hates the town and the rat race of industrial life."

"A dropout, is he?" The words were loaded with scorn.

"No, he is not! Oh, how can you understand? Don was only fourteen when our parents died."

"What happened to them?"

"A fire. We all escaped, but dad remembered something he wanted to save and he went back into the house. Mother went after him. We didn't see either of them again."

The expression in his face softened slightly.

"I see. And you've tried to be mother ever since," he remarked quietly. "I gather that Don has missed having a father at an important time in his development. Didn't your grandfather ever visit you?"

"He came to the funeral, that's all. My father never talked about him or Lanmore. I always had the impression that he had quarreled with his father and that he had left home as a result."

A faint smile quirked Logan's mouth.

"It was not difficult to quarrel with Hector Allan," he commented dryly. "On the other hand, your father may have rebelled against the crofting way of life, for it is a way of life. A crofter has security and a home, but he can't make money unless he does what Ian has done, and that has only been possible recently. You will find that most crofters these days have a sideline as well as their crofts. Some do seasonal work like road mending, others like Ian and Duncan are motor mechanics or carpenters. Some have shops in the village."

"Perhaps Don could find some sort of job."

"What can he do?"

Nancy did not answer at once. Don could do very little, but she had to make it clear to this man, who was far too observant, that although Don might not seem very dependable, he was good and kind and that placed in the right environment he would flourish.

"The town was stifling him. When the letter came about the croft it made such a difference to him. He likes animals and he loves the countryside. Living here in this lovely place, working with animals close to nature is surely the answer for him. It has to be," she added quietly, almost desperately. She turned away to look out of the window in order to hide her feelings. She was not normally the confiding type, but in her attempt to convince Logan that Don must have his chance on the croft she had unconsciously revealed the burden she had carried since her parents had died.

"You've had a difficult time these past few years, haven't you?" he remarked. Surprise spun her round. He was watching her in the same way as he had last night when she had been so tired. It was almost as if he could see into her mind. Inherent pride coming to her aid, she was able to return his stare coolly.

"I admit it hasn't been easy, but I've managed to keep the three of us together and to preserve the feeling of family. The chance to come here has made all the difference to Don and I won't let anyone part him from this croft until he's had time to find out if he likes living this way. You needn't think you're going to put us off. You tried yesterday through your lawyer and then not warning us about the leaking roof. It will take more than that to drive us away. We'll manage to live here even if we aren't used to oil lamps and peat fires!"

If Love Be Love

This fiery speech made no impression on him. He continued to survey her in a maddeningly knowledgeable way, as if he was observing the antics of a species with which he was extremely familiar.

"There are oil lamps because your grandfather was too stubborn to have electricity. He said he couldn't afford it," he replied smoothly. "The roof leaks because the last gale lifted some of the slates off and I wanted to be sure someone was going to inhabit the house before repairing it. You don't have to use peat. Coal can be delivered if you're prepared to pay for it. Alternatively once electricity is installed you might prefer to have an electric cooker and fire, provided of course you can afford them. Your grandfather could not... and I'll tell you why. The money that he left to Don he saved by doing without. I suppose he intended originally to leave it to your father, to whom he had not spoken for years. That's pride for you. How often it's allowed to spoil what should be the best of human relationships."

There was a touch of bitterness, as if he had experienced the effects of too much pride in his own life. Nancy had nothing to say, and after a quick amused glance at her haughty face, he added thoughtfully, "I can see you have inherited more than your fair share of Allan pride, too, as well as the red hair and temper. And that in spite of the arrogant off-putting behavior of the local laird, you intend to stay."

"I didn't say you were arrogant," gasped Nancy.

"No. But you implied it."

"Well, you weren't exactly welcoming," retorted Nancy, bouncing back. "Come to think of it, perhaps you're worried because Linda and I are here as well as Don. Well, you needn't worry. We shall stay only for a few months to help Don settle in. He asked me to come and I'm glad I did. Already I love the place... the stillness and the silence, and the spirits of the past."

"Wait until a westerly gale lifts more slates off the roof. It won't seem so still and silent then," he remarked cynically, but his narrowed glance was sharp. "As for the spirits of the past, they can be strangely disturbing to one who's not accustomed to them."

Nancy felt the hairs on the back of her neck tingle, but before she could ask him what he meant he turned toward the door as if impatient to leave the room, asking over his shoulder, "So you're going to sacrifice some more of your life for your brother."

"Four months only," replied Nancy sharply. "I shall return to Dulthorpe at the end of August, as I intend to marry in the autumn."

"Another form of sacrifice," Logan murmured. He leaned against the doorjamb and looked back at her. "Have you no desire to lead your own life, go where you please and do what you like without reference to any other person?"

Nancy tilted her head to one side, a habit she had when she was thinking.

"I suppose because you've always lived like that yourself you find it difficult to understand that for some people life is being involved with others. I don't think I'm sacrificing myself because I want to help my brother or because I'm going to marry a man I respect."

"You're right. I don't like getting too closely involved with other people."

"Isn't that rather cowardly?"

"In what way?" he asked sharply, and she suddenly remembered Don saying that Logan Maclaine had been accused of losing his nerve when he had given up racing. Perhaps he had been called cowardly before.

"You're afraid of loving and of being loved. Love makes demands," she replied.

"I know," he said quietly, and his quietness rebuked her. "But how do you know you're not making a mistake in promising to marry this man whom you respect? Tied to Linda and Don as you have been you can't have had much opportunity for the normal pleasant pursuits of youth. Will it be wise, do you think, to tie yourself down before you've achieved a measure of freedom? Are you sure it isn't fear that is motivating you, too?"

Nancy was bewildered. She hadn't known fear until she had met this man.

"Fear of what?" she asked.

If Love Be Love

"Fear of being left on your own when Don and Linda don't need you anymore."

She had not considered this view of her acceptance of Rod's proposal. It made her feel slightly uneasy. But she wasn't going to betray her uneasiness. Tilting her chin in the air once more, she asserted grandly, "I wouldn't marry for such a despicable reason. I'm marrying Rod because he's good and clean and decent... and has helped us a lot."

"A father figure who offers security," interjected Logan rather scoffingly, and she found it difficult to return his sardonic glance. "It will be interesting to see whether you'll be able to leave Lanmore at the end of the summer to marry your 'perfect gentle knight,'" he added obscurely, and Nancy felt an odd touch of alarm as the story of Pluto and Proserpina sprang into her mind. Pluto had kept Proserpina in his underworld for six months of every year. Quickly she shook it out of her mind as being a ridiculous and uncharacteristic flight of fancy. Lanmore and Logan Maclaine certainly affected her peculiarly.

"Nancy, where are you?"

A strident shout from Linda was a welcome intrusion. Relief caused Nancy to relax visibly and it lilted through her voice as she called, "Upstairs, Lin!"

She crossed the room to the door. Logan did not move. His smile revealed his appreciation of her relief.

"Linda to the rescue," he commented as she tried to pass him.

At that moment Linda arrived at the top of the stairs. She was breathless and disheveled. Her shoes were caked with mud and her hair was sliding out of its confining band and slipping forward over her face.

"Oh, what a gorgeous kilt!" she exclaimed immediately.

Nancy, suspecting that her impetuous sister was about to bend down and examine the kilt more closely, rapped out, "Look at your shoes! Wherever have you been?"

"We found a most odd building, or ruin of a building. It was made of stone, like the walls around here, with no mortar to hold them together, and it was circular. We met a lady and she said she was Mrs. Maclaine. She told us the building was a broth—"

"Broch," corrected Logan quietly.

"That's right. She can't be your wife; she's too old. Are you married?"

"Linda!" warned Nancy.

"No, I'm not married," answered Logan calmly, seemingly quite unperturbed by Linda's question.

"I'm so glad," cooed Linda. "It makes it much easier for me to write my story."

"What story?" asked Logan curiously. He was still blocking the doorway and Nancy was imprisoned in the bedroom.

"I'm writing a story, and you're the hero," explained Linda.

Logan laughed. "I'm afraid I'm not the stuff of which heroes are made. Couldn't you find someone better?"

Linda shook her head.

"No. Anyway, what are you both doing up here in the bedroom?" she asked.

"I've been examining the leaks in the ceiling," he replied gravely.

"Did you bring the cows and goats? Mrs. MacLaine said you were coming over. Nancy, I'm famished. Aren't we ever going to have food? I mean real food?"

"Yes, of course," replied Nancy, who had at last managed to squeeze past Logan. "I'll make a snack lunch and put the beef in the oven. You go and look at the cows and goats and—"

"No. Linda will make the lunch, while you and I go and look at the cows and goats," said Logan.

Linda turned a wide surprised gaze in his direction.

"But I don't know how," she said.

Then it's time that you learned. Your sister will not always be at your service," he replied firmly. "And you should know how to make a meal by now. You can't really go wrong with eggs, bread and butter and fruit. I shall be staying to lunch because I want to talk to your brother and give him some advice, so do your best. Come on, Nancy, and make the acquaintance of Jamie the billy goat. From the sounds I hear coming from the garden Don has met him already."

If Love Be Love

In a curious trancelike state induced by his calm firm handling of the situation Nancy followed him downstairs. Behind her Linda continued to grumble about making the lunch. When they all reached the little hallway Logan spoke curtly, cutting across the grumbles.

"You'll find everything you need on the table in the kitchen, Linda. Put the trivet over the fire and place a pan of water over it to boil the eggs. I expect you know where the pans are kept by now. I like my egg boiled for four minutes. Call us when everything is ready. We'll be at the byre."

Linda stamped one foot on the floor, her usual form of expressing her annoyance, and Nancy braced herself as she expected an explosion of defiance. But the explosion did not occur and to her surprise Linda swung on her heels and went into the kitchen.

Nancy turned to Logan, who was about to open the front door.

"I'd better go and show her what to do," she said, "I'll look at the goats later."

"No. You'll be doing as I tell you... and so will Linda," he replied sternly. "It's very obvious that she requires discipline. She will soon be completely unmanageable if someone isn't firm with her. You're not consistent enough."

"Oh!" Nancy could only gasp as he opened the door and stepped into the rubber boots that he had left in the porch. Before she could gather her wits and retaliate sudden laughter transformed his dark face as he looked into the garden.

"At the moment it looks as if Don is more in need of your help than Linda," he observed.

As she followed Logan into the garden she saw Don running toward the house. One hand clutched the back of his trousers. Behind him the billy goat, its head lowered threateningly, horns at the ready, rushed after him.

Red-faced and panting, Don reached them and immediately placed himself behind Logan.

"It butted me!" he blurted.

"And there was your sister telling me you have such a way with animals," remarked Logan softly. He bent swiftly to pick up the tethering rope around the goat's neck as it rushed past him. A strong jerk on the rope and the goat stopped at once, pulled onto its haunches. For a second or two it pulled from one side to the other in an attempt to break free, but as it realized its freedom was over for the day it dropped its head and began to munch quietly on the grass.

"Why did you untether it?" asked Logan.

"It seemed a shame that it should be tied up."

"Jamie will be better tied up until he's grown used to you, and you don't want him to be wandering away. Go and change your trousers and come out again. I'm taking Nancy to see the cows. You come with us and I will be telling you how to milk them, and how to feed them."

Caught and held captive by her awakening interest in Logan, Nancy followed him to the tethering post in the rough grass of the garden and watched him hitch the rope around it. As he straightened up he laughed again and she noticed how the sudden change of expression lightened his face, breaking the polite facade, replacing it with warmth and gaiety.

"Your neighbors will be appreciating that little entertainment although they will not outwardly approve of such behavior on a Sunday," he said.

"Where are they? I haven't seen anyone this morning," said Nancy.

"Over there are Ian and Meg Macrae." Logan jerked his head in the direction of the trim white house on the green knoll. "And in the house across the bridge lives their aunt, Agnes Macrae. You won't have seen them today because they don't go out on a Sunday except to the meeting in the church later. But they'll have been watching, peeping through the curtains at the heathen newcomers."

"But don't they consider you a heathen, too? I can't imagine you staying in all day."

"Yes. My family is past all redemption," he replied with a slight ironic smile. "My great-grandfather returned to Scotland from the Far East, having made his fortune planting tea. He bought Lanmore Lodge and the estate from the rather impecunious clan chieftain who once lived here."

If Love Be Love

"Then you're not descended from the original owners of the estate?"

"No. Does that disappoint you?" The amusement that had irritated her yesterday was back in his voice and in his glance, but today she was more able to appreciate his mockery.

"Not as much as it will disappoint Linda. She has it all worked out that your family has lived here since the thirteenth century and that you must be a clan chieftain."

"I thought she might. You'll have to break it to her gently. Perhaps if you tell her that my great-grandfather was feared by the crofters because he'd learned all sorts of black arts in the East that he practiced on his return she won't mind so much."

Although she realized he was still making fun Nancy shuddered. She wanted to ask more, but he had turned away and was walking toward the byre. She followed him. The two great golden-horned cows looked fierce, but were quite placid. Don joined them, and he and Nancy listened carefully while Logan instructed them about feeding the cattle and about milking times. All the time she was listening Nancy's mind was busy wondering about the enigma of Logan Maclaine. She was surprised that he was so knowledgeable about farming. He was no more like her idea of a farmer than he was of her idea of a Highlander. He surprised her perpetually—a characteristic that attracted her while at the same time she was repelled by his cool authoritativeness.

After lunch, which was unexpectedly successful, Logan took Don off to inspect the fields. Linda, her liking for him restored, went with them, and Nancy, left to herself once more, continued to air the bedding, rearing the mattresses up against the windows so that the sun could warm them. It was while she was doing this that she saw a man and woman walk past the house. They were fairly young—she guessed them to be in their late twenties. The man had crinkly brown hair and a thick brown beard, and the woman was small and dark. They looked neither left nor right and as they crossed the bridge over the burn they were joined on the other side by an older woman dressed all in black. They set off at a brisk rate along the road, presumably to the chapel.

Logan stayed until milking time so that he could supervise Don's efforts to milk the cows. Apparently satisfied with what he had seen and with the talks he had with Don, he looked into the kitchen where Nancy was busy preparing the dinner.

"I'm going now. I've told Don what to do. It's time he was setting the early potatoes, and you and Linda will have to help him. Ask Ian about the tractor. He'll be across tomorrow, I expect, to offer his advice. You'll find the Macraes will treat you well as long as you don't try to lord it over them. You would like to have the electricity?"

"Yes, if it isn't any trouble."

"No trouble. The poles are up and the other crofts have it. It's only a question of bringing a line across and wiring the house. A telephone would be advisable, too. You know about the school bus?"

"School bus?" repeated Nancy rather vaguely.

"Of course. You weren't thinking of letting Linda miss a whole term of schooling, were you? The school is over there." He pointed through the kitchen window at the dark pines and white buildings across the glittering sea loch. "School starts tomorrow as the Easter holidays are over now. If you haven't registered Linda you'd better go with her." A frown pulled his heavy eyebrows together and he gave her a sharp assessing glance. "No. Perhaps a better plan would be for me to pick her up and take her across and explain everything. It will be easier that way."

"Why?" asked Nancy, all prickles again because he was taking over, and managing her.

His grin was disarming.

"She won't argue with me," he announced with exasperating authority.

"She doesn't want to go back to school and I'm not sure whether I want her to go back, either," she retorted with a final flash of spirit.

Logan raised his eyebrows slightly and his disdainful glance told her what he thought of her decision.

"If she doesn't go you'll be breaking the law, and she'll

If Love Be Love

miss an important experience. Besides," he paused and his smile appeared suddenly, "there'll be less skin and hair flying if you two are separated for part of the day at least."

Nancy gasped for breath and then burst out, "You haven't a very high opinion of us!"

"That's not the way of it at all. I merely know the temper of a redheaded Allan. Good night."

He went from the room before she had time to reply. Suddenly remembering her manners, Nancy ran after him. He might be exasperating and overbearing, but he had accepted them and had gone out of his way to help them today instead of trying to freeze them out. By the time she had passed through the front door into the garden he was already opening the garden gate and walking into the road.

"Good night, Logan," she called. "Thank you."

He looked back and waved in acknowledgment, crossed the road and vaulted the stone dike into a field. Nancy watched him cross the field until he was out of sight.

LINDA WAS NOT PLEASED when Nancy told her that school started the next morning and that it would be a good idea if she attended. After the usual passage of hot words between them that accompanied any proposition that tended to frustrate Linda's desires, the girl burst into tears.

"But you said I needn't go anymore once we came here. You promised and now you're going back on your word. I hate school, you know I do! I won't go," she sobbed.

Nancy sighed wearily, wishing that she hadn't mentioned the subject.

"Look, Linda, I know I promised, but when we were in Dulthorpe I didn't realize that there would be a secondary school here and I thought it would be simpler if you stayed at home. But Logan says there's a bus that takes all the children from Lanmore over on the ferry. He also said that if you don't go we shall be breaking the law, which is true. He said he'll come for you in the morning and take you over to register."

The transformation of Linda from a tearful slumped bundle of frustration into a smiling, shining-eyed, pretty girl was almost miraculous.

"He did?" she breathed. "That makes all the difference. If he thinks I should go then I'll go. I'd better go and get my school clothes ready."

Her head aching after the clash of wills, Nancy felt slightly disturbed by her sister's reaction to the news that Logan would take her to school. She hoped that Linda's tendency to hero-worship was not going to cause any embarrassments between the Allan family and the laird. Coping with Linda's tantrums was exhausting enough without any further complications being added to the already difficult relationship she had with her sister.

NEXT DAY they were all up early becase there were cows to be milked. At half-past eight Logan arrived and whisked an obviously delighted Linda away with him. Nancy watched them go with a twinge of uneasiness, but she had little time to wonder how her sister fared at school because she had hardly cleared the breakfast dishes when Ian Macrae arrived. After shaking hands with her and with Don he said authoritatively, "You'll be wanting to set the tatties. I'll be helping you. I'll away to get the tractor."

By the time he returned with the tractor, a Land Rover had arrived driven by a hatchet-faced man dressed in tweeds who introduced himself as Harris, factor of the Lanmore estate. He had brought with him two other men who were slaters, and they unloaded their ladders and proceeded to inspect the roof. Meanwhile, Harris himself unloaded a wire basket that contained several clucking hens and a cockerel. After releasing the fowl, which began to peck among the grass at the roadside, Mr. Harris asked Don if he was interested in taking another job besides farming his croft.

"They're needing an extra hand in the forest over on the north side. There's a lot of fencing to be done to keep the sheep out. You'd be picked up at the road junction every morning at seven and you'd be brought back at four-thirty in the afternoon. Plenty of time to do your own jobs in the long summer evenings. You can be telling me later in the day when I come to collect the men if you want the work."

Mr. Harris had hardly left when Ian was back with the tractor and the rest of the day was spent following him

If Love Be Love

around the field and setting the seed potatoes in the furrows that he plowed. Halfway through the morning, just when Nancy thought her back would break, Meg Macrae arrived, bringing a flask of tea and some buttered scones that they all shared sitting against the dry-stone dike looking down the newly plowed brown earth to the misty blue sea and the faint shapes of distant islands.

Far from being resentful that the Allans had come to claim their croft, as Nancy had expected, the two Macraes were very friendly. Ian, who was stockily built, had a forthright way of speaking, quite different from his brother who kept the garage.

"I'm not saying I wasn't disappointed when Maclaine told me ye were coming," he admitted, "and like him I was a wee bit worried in case ye were just coming to squat like some of the younger townspeople we've been hearing about. But I can see ye're not like that at all, and we're glad ye've come, aren't we, Meg? It'll be fine having young neighbors. Most young people go away from the crofts."

"I wonder why," asked Nancy. "It's so beautiful here. How can they possibly prefer the towns?"

"They are looking for an easier way of life with more amenities," said Meg, who was small and dark with shy secretive brown eyes.

"You have to love the place to stay and ye have to be prepared to make haste slowly," explained Ian. "I have eight crofts now and three hundred sheep. Every time a croft is abandoned I ask if I can take it over so that I can get more sheep on the hill. With six hundred sheep I'd have a fairly decent living. At the moment both Meg and I have to do other work. But we've been lucky here in having good lairds. The Maclaines brought electricity to Lanmore a long time ago. They know how to farm, too, and how to conserve the land and make the most of it. They haven't let the sheep have their own way. They've fenced and reforested and they've kept the heather. Ye won't find anyone burning heather on Lanmore after the end of April."

"But why is it so important to keep it, and why do you burn it?" asked Don.

"Ach, I can see ye have a lot to be learning," said Ian

with a grin. "Ye have to burn it because it grows so well here and makes such a close carpet that regular burning has to be done if a good crop of heather is to be kept going for grouse and sheep. So it's burnt every ten to fifteen years. But if ye burn it after April it's too late, and instead of new growth appearing the place of the heather is taken by moor grass and bracken."

As Ian had said, there was a lot to learn and from that first day the Allans were all busy learning. Surprisingly enough Linda settled down in the school and had soon made friends with the other children who traveled from Lanmore to the school at Glenarg. Don took the job offered to him by the factor and left every morning to travel to the north side of the estate to work in the new forest.

Nancy found that she had very few spare moments because with Don away she was responsible for the hens and the other animals, although he did the milking every morning and evening and they both worked in the fields in the evening if there was any hoeing to be done. But if Nancy had been asked to describe her memories of the first six weeks on the croft she would have had difficulty in drawing a clear picture, because her memory was a jumble of impressions, of soft Highland voices greeting her when she went shopping in Glenarg, of sunlight glittering on the sea, of sudden sharp squalls of wind and rain that swept in from the sea and blotted out visibility and made the waves hiss as they tumbled on the shingle beach. There was the memory of the weekly ceilidhs or informal meetings of friends at the Macraes' cottage and a vivid portrait of Agnes Macrae, Ian's aunt, tall and angular with a strangely raddled face and a heart of gold. And all memory of this time was accompanied by the smell of paint with which Nancy systematically covered up the red that her grandfather had daubed all over the cottage.

By the end of six weeks the electricity had been installed and so had a brand new cooker. Coal had been delivered, and although the days were often warm, a fire was needed in the evenings.

The trees in the garden were now in full leaf. The rhododendrons had bloomed, red, white and violet, and so had the other shrubs. Clumps of perennials had pushed through the dark soil of the borders and the rose that clambered around the porch door was already showing pale pink buds.

Nancy was constantly amazed by the mildness of the climate in the sheltered southwest corner of the peninsula and by the peace and quiet of the garden. She often wondered why her father had left such a place of beauty to go and live in Dulthorpe. Surely the scenery and the timeless way of life were sufficient compensation for the lack of amenities.

Before she had come to live at Lanmore she would never have believed it was possible to spend the whole day doing housework, feeding animals and gardening and to feel contented, too. But she was contented and she looked forward to every day as each morning brought its share of new experiences. Some of her contentment, she realized, was bound up with the fact that Don was happy, too. He had done the right thing returning to the land of his forebears. Linda also seemed happier and there had been fewer tantrums during the past weeks.

Lanmore had cast a spell on the three of them, thought Nancy fancifully. It was another fine June day, slightly warmer than usual, and to her consternation one of the hives of bees had swarmed, rising in a dark cloud and making off over the dike toward the little clump of trees that encircled a small hillock in a field across the road.

Don was working, so she would have to go after the swarm herself because she knew he would not want to lose it. Ever since that first day when Logan Maclaine had talked to him about bees and had given him instructions on how to look after them Don had been a keen beekeeper. Nancy remembered vaguely Don mentioning something about a basket called a skep. He had said that when the bees swarmed you must go after them, make them enter the basket and then take them back to the hive.

Swallowing her fear at the thought of having to face so many bees, Nancy found the skep together with a hat and thick veil and tough leather gauntlet gloves that she had seen Don wear when he had been working with the bees. Dressed in the hat and gloves and carrying the skep and a clean white cloth, she climbed over the wall into the field and made for the copse.

The sun beat upon her back and under the close heavy veil she felt stifled. As she walked she remembered that this was the direction in which Logan Maclaine had gone the day he had stayed with them for lunch. It was, she had learned from the Macraes, a shortcut across the fields and moors to the Lodge. Although she had seen most of the other houses on Lanmore by now she still hadn't seen the Lodge, which was on the western tip of the peninsula, and although they were such near neighbors they hadn't seen Logan once since he had taken Linda to school. There was no doubt in Nancy's mind that he didn't know how they were progressing, because everyone knew what everyone else did on the peninsula, but she felt faintly hurt that he had not shown any further interest in them. Presumably he thought he had done enough to help them and that any future assistance from him could come to them through Harris.

At last she reached the copse that consisted of a few windswept pines and a couple of small rowan trees. A humming noise assured her that the bees were there and she found them closely encircled about one of the rowans. They resembled a close black collar around the slim trunk of the tree.

The whole operation depended on being able to get the queen bee into the skep, Nancy remembered. Once that was done the rest of the bees would follow. The queen should be in the middle of the swarm. But how could you tell which was the middle of this swarm?

Approaching cautiously, she began to sweep the bees into the skep with the small brush that she had found with the basket. The bees buzzed angrily and perspiration beaded Nancy's forehead. Suddenly one got under the veil and stung her on the cheek. At that moment the queen flew off and the whole swarm followed, leaving Nancy hot and bothered with an empty skep.

The swarm did not go far. After making a short reconnaissance around the copse it attached itself to a branch of the other rowan and hung downward, a giant dark globule.

If Love Be Love

Nancy eyed it apprehensively. The sting on her cheek smarted. Who was it who had told her recently that swarming bees rarely sting? Ian Macrae, who else? He who was so adept at handing out advice. Well, tonight when she saw him at the ceilidh at his house she would prove him wrong!

She had also been warned that bees sense fear and that they know when the person approaching is afraid of them, so marshaling all her courage she moved toward them with a display of confidence.

"What are you doing?"

The childish voice startled her, making her jump so that she dropped the skep. Turning around, she encountered the bland gaze of a small thin boy who was standing a few yards away.

For a few seconds they stared at each other in silence. Nancy was silent because she was surprised to see a child of that age. None of the people she knew living on Lanmore had any children under ten. He was painfully thin, his legs looking like matchsticks and making his gray shorts seem too wide and baggy. He was also extremely pale and his large gray eyes seemed to be too big for his thin wedge-shaped face.

"I'm trying to collect a swarm of bees," replied Nancy gently.

"You do look funny in that thing, and I can't see your face properly. Why are you wearing it?"

Nancy removed the hat and veil from her head.

"To protect my face from the bees," she explained. "They might sting me, because they don't like anyone trying to make them go back into the hive."

"Then why try to make them?"

"Because I don't want to lose them. They belong to my brother and he wants to keep them so that he can have their honey."

"I think that's horrid, taking the bees' honey. It's like stealing. What's your name?"

Nancy told him and with similar youthful directness asked him the same question.

"I'm Neil Maclaine. I'm five, nearly six, and I've run away from my wickeduncleLogan."

He said the last three words as if they were one long word and it was a second before Nancy was able to make out what he meant. Keeping to herself the surprise she felt on hearing that the boy was Logan's nephew, she asked, "Why do you say he's wicked?"

"My nanny always said he was wicked because he wanted to take me away from her and my mommy. Nanny went away and I had some other nannies, but they weren't as good. Then I was ill and wickedunclelogan came and brought me here to con...con...."

He stumbled in his speech as he tried to pronounce a word he had often heard but had never spoken. Nancy smiled sympathetically.

"Convalesce," she supplied softly, and was immediately rewarded with a sweet smile.

"That doesn't sound very wicked to me," went on Nancy. "This is a lovely place and you'll get better faster here than you would in London."

"Oh, do you think so? I hope so. I'm tired of being ill. Wickedunclelogan says it's because I've been neg...neg—"

"Neglected," offered Nancy.

"That's right. I heard him tell mommy. Is your hair really that color or is it painted?"

Taking the change of subject and the question in her stride, Nancy answered him seriously.

"It is really this color. Awful, isn't it?"

He considered her silently for a moment and then shook his head in disagreement.

"No. It makes you look like a marigold. I've seen marigolds, they're orange and bright. My mommy has fair hair like me and she's much prettier than you. Aren't you going to collect your bees?"

Amused by his childishly honest comments, Nancy turned to look at the gently humming bees.

"Yes. I've never collected a swarm of bees before and I'm not sure I'm doing it right. But don't you think it's time you went back to your uncle? He'll be wondering where you are."

Neil's face crumpled pathetically and tears glinted in his eyes.

If Love Be Love

"I didn't really mean to stay away from him. I meant to go back, but I couldn't find my way back. He was fishing in a burn, and I don't like fishing, so I thought I'd go for a walk and maybe he'd come after me. I'm lost," he wailed.

Touched by his distress, Nancy knelt on the ground before him. She put her arms around him and drew him against her and smoothed his shaking shoulders.

"Don't cry, Neil. You can stay with me while I collect the bees. You can help me and then I'll take you to my cottage and you can have a biscuit and a drink; then I'll ring up the Lodge and tell your uncle you're here with me and he can come and fetch you."

He seemed comforted by her words because gradually his sobs stopped and he knuckled his eyes to dry the tears. He leaned against her shoulder and Nancy's arms tightened around him as she reacted to his obvious need for love. Silently she reviled Logan Maclaine for being so engrossed in his fishing that he had not noticed his nephew's boredom.

"Wickedunclelogan will be cross with me. I don't like him when he's cross," whispered Neil. "He frowns and speaks very quietly."

"Don't worry. He won't be cross when he finds you're here with me," said Nancy, with more confidence than she felt.

She stood up and became aware immediately that someone was approaching the copse across the field of tussocky grass. It was Logan and he was making straight toward them.

Grasping Neil's small warm hand in hers, she whispered, "Here's your uncle now. I wonder how he guessed you were here?"

"He's very clever at guessing," said Neil.

If Logan was cross there was no sign of anger on his face, which wore its usual expression of cool politeness. He stopped in front of them and his heavy-lidded glance rested on Neil. Nancy felt the little boy's hand clutch at hers and gave it a reassuring squeeze while she tried to deal with the sudden speechlessness and breathlessness that attacked her on meeting Logan face to face again. He was dressed in a blue-and-white finely checked shirt, dark trousers and the thick-soled rubber Wellington boots that he had worn the last time he had visited and that Nancy had learned the hard way were essential footwear for walking the fields.

He glanced from Neil to her and said gravely, "Good afternoon, Nancy Allan. Do you make a habit of talking to small boys?"

Although his reference to their first meeting at the Roman fort when she had reprimanded him for speaking to Linda surprised her and slightly undermined her confidence, Nancy looked him straight in the eye and retorted, "I didn't speak to him. He spoke to me first."

A slight lift to the corner of one eyebrow showed his acknowledgment of her retaliation and he looked down at Neil again.

"Why did you run away? I thought I told you to stay near me. You'll never learn to fish if you aren't patient."

He spoke quietly, but even so Nancy felt the tremor that shook Neil. Still holding her hand tightly, Neil looked down at the ground and stubbed with one rubber-booted foot at the grass.

"I don't like fishing," he muttered obstinately.

Logan's heavy eyebrows lowered in a frown and for a moment Nancy thought he might retaliate unkindly, but the frown was quickly displaced by the usual urbane polite mask. With a slight shrug of his shoulders he turned away from the child and looked at the rowan tree.

"Yours?" he inquired, pointing to the swarm.

Nancy nodded. "They collected around another tree and I tried to get them into the skep, but they swarmed again. I was wondering what to do next when Neil came up to me."

"I see you've been stung. Swarming bees rarely sting. You must have annoyed them in some way," he asserted coolly and authoritatively, making her feel as usual as if she was ignorant and inept. But she had no chance to retort because he picked up the skep and went toward the swarm. While Neil and Nancy watched from a safe distance he persuaded the swarm to move up into the skep

If Love Be Love

which he placed above the cluster of bees. Once the bees were in the basket he covered it with the cloth and set off immediately down the hill in the direction of the cottage.

CHAPTER THREE

STILL HOLDING NEIL'S HAND, Nancy urged the little boy to accompany her and together they followed Logan down the hill and across the fallow field to the cottage. By the time they had climbed the garden wall Logan was already shaking the bees out of the skep on the floorboard of the frame hive that Don had prepared in case there was a swarm.

Watching him working silently with the bees, Nancy recalled the last time he had visited the croft, that first Sunday more than a month ago when he had talked and laughed as he had shown Don and her how to deal with the goats and cows. This afternoon there was no sign of the warmth and gaiety he had shown then. He was once more the withdrawn stranger of the journey north.

The bees were gradually entering the hive.

"I'm glad Don took notice of my instructions and prepared a spare hive," murmured Logan, "otherwise we'd have been in trouble. Look, Neil, they like the hive because there's wax in there, all ready for them. Come closer and look at them."

He held out a hand to the boy, who shrank against Nancy and blurted out loudly, "No. I don't like them. They'll sting me!"

"Only if you show your fear," replied Logan patiently, although the heavy frown had darkened his face again.

"Neil will look at them another day," Nancy intervened swiftly, sensing the tension that existed between man and boy. "He's had a rather harassing afternoon. He meant to leave you for only a few minutes, but he got lost and couldn't find his way back to you."

"He shouldn't have left me," replied Logan coldly, giving her one of his supercilious glances that told her clearly that he resented her defense of Neil and her interference.

"Maybe he shouldn't, and perhaps he wouldn't have done if you'd paid him more attention. You can't expect a small boy to stand waiting for a fish to bite in the same way that a man can," retorted Nancy.

"I used to when I was six. And my brother Angus, Neil's father, was even younger when he first went fishing."

"But you and he were born here and grew up here. Neil has been living in a city and isn't accustomed to animals and country life. Give him time," pleaded Nancy.

"You seem to know a lot about him already," was the dry response, accompanied by another disdainful look.

Nancy could not help the flush that stained her cheeks at the implication that she was a busybody, concerning herself too much with the problems of the Maclaine family, and all the original dislike she had felt for Logan came surging to the fore. She tossed back her head and her eyes sparked with anger as she stood her ground.

"Poor little boy, he's exhausted after walking so far. I'm going to give him a biscuit and some milk. You can wait for him."

Suddenly she realized she was being rather rude and added belatedly, "Thank you for taking in the swarm. I think I'd have lost it if you hadn't come, and then Don would have been furious with me."

"I think you'd have lost it, too," he agreed with maddening equanimity, "because you're also afraid of bees, otherwise you wouldn't have been stung. I'll look at the sting while Neil and I are having those biscuits and milk you've just mentioned."

The glint of amusement in his eyes disconcerted her; she would have been able to deal with more disdain better. But when he laughed at her she felt confused. With a muttered excuse she fled into the house to prepare the milk and biscuits.

When she returned to the garden Logan was lounging on the bench that was set against the cottage wall under the kitchen window and Neil was perched beside him, his skinny legs looking more pathetic than ever as they hung downward too short for his feet to touch the ground.

Neil ate and drank quickly and asked for another biscuit.

Then, noticing the rope swing that Linda had arranged to hang from the branches of an old tree in the corner of the garden, he asked if he could go and swing on it. Since Logan did not seem to hear the request—for he neither refused nor assented—Nancy took the little boy to the swing, helped him to climb onto it and stood for a while pushing him. He wanted her to stay, but she hadn't finished her own milk, so after telling him to play for a while on his own she went back to the bench to sit beside the silent Logan, who seemed to be lost in thought.

Drinking her milk, Nancy did not attempt to break the silence. Her eyes wandered past the gently swinging child to the sun-hazed expanse of water, to the shimmering roll of mountain and moor, gray green and dappled with purple shadows.

"Who's been gardening?" asked Logan idly.

"I have."

"It looks better... and yet you've managed to preserve its naturalness. Your grandfather would be pleased with your efforts. It was his great consolation."

He eased his shoulders against the wall behind him as if trying to relax and then said softly, musingly, "'Here, where the world is quiet.' The quietness is really the only aspect it has in common with Swinburne's Garden of Proserpina, for everything seems to grow here, whereas in that other garden only the green grapes grow 'whereout she crushes for dead men, deadly wine.' Do you know the poem?"

"No, I don't. It sounds rather morbid and dismal."

He laughed. "I suppose it is. And yet sometimes I've found in it an echo of my own thoughts when 'I am weary of days and hours... and everything but sleep.'"

Nancy turned to look at him in surprise. Seemingly relaxed now, he leaned against the sun-warmed wall and watched Neil swinging. Nearer to him than she had ever been before, she was able to study him closely. "Dour" he had described himself in a moment of self-mockery, and certainly the combination of dark hair and eyebrows, a sallow complexion and a rather beaky nose did give an impression of harshness. But she noticed that his mouth was

If Love Be Love

well-shaped and had sensitive lines graven at its corners, hinting at severe control.

He turned his head suddenly and looked at her. Annoyed at being caught staring, Nancy flushed for the second time that day and her annoyance increased as she noted a knowledgeable gleam in his eyes. Immediately she looked away down the garden at Neil.

"You see, he's quite happy now. All he needs is time and a place to play in his own way. Do you know he's afraid of you and calls you 'wickedunclelogan'?"

"That's because he has been taught to be afraid of me, not because I have ever frightened him," he replied concisely, and showed no inclination to pursue the subject. Instead he placed a hand on either side of her head and tilted her face so that the right side was toward the sunlight. "The sting is still there," he murmured. "Don't move while I take it out."

Taken completely unawares by his action, confused by the feel of his hands against her face, Nancy kept still while her heart pounded and her skin felt hot. Furious with herself for reacting so violently to everything he did or said, she kept her eyes averted while he removed the beesting.

"A first sting is always the worst, and being tender-skinned you'll feel it more. It's a good thing you had no more or you'd have had some bad swellings."

"Thank you," she replied stiltedly, hoping he had not noticed her confusion, glad that he had moved away. "Neil says that he's been ill and that you've brought him here to convalesce."

"That's right. I was down in London on business and I called in to see him and Anya, my sister-in-law. She's an actress and her household arrangements, to put it mildly, are somewhat chaotic. Neil had had a bad bout of measles in the middle of which the latest nanny had left in a tantrum. To cut the story short, he developed bronchial pneumonia and had to be rushed to hospital. When I arrived he had just been released, so I brought him here thinking the country air and the regular routine of the Lodge would help him to recuperate. For once Anya didn't try to stop me. She was in such a muddle she was glad to see him go."

The faint smile that curved his mouth was a blend of triumph and cynicism and Nancy, recalling Neil's reference to his nanny's description of Logan as "wicked" because he had tried to take Neil away from his mother, felt the hairs tingle on the back of her neck.

"Have you tried to bring him here before?" she asked.

He seemed rather surprised by her question and for a moment she expected one of his setdowns. But instead he answered simply and directly, "Yes, I have. You see, my brother made me Neil's legal guardian and wanted him to grow up at Lanmore."

"But surely his mother is his guardian."

"No, not in this case. Neil is heir to Angus's estate, which is quite considerable, and my brother for once in his life showed some foresight in realizing that his wife was and is incapable of administering it on behalf of Neil until he reaches twenty-one."

While he spoke he continued to lean against the wall, his arms folded on his chest as he watched the swinging child with half-closed eyes. Again alarm tingled through Nancy's veins. The expression on his face was so grim that she fancied he was thinking of a way in which he could rid the world of Neil Maclaine.

"What happens to the estate if anything should happen to Neil?" she asked, speaking her thoughts aloud.

He glanced at her and she had the usual feeling that she had asked too much.

"That's none of your business, Nancy Allan," he replied coolly. "I know what you're thinking. It didn't take long for you to catch on to the wicked-uncle bit, did it? Well, in spite of what Neil might have told you and in spite of what you're imagining I have no intention of removing Neil from this life. My brother gave me the responsibility of taking care of his child and I take that particular responsibility seriously insofar as I've been allowed. Neil has been neglected because his mother has put her career before him. You can see for yourself that he needs care and attention."

"And love," put in the irrepressible Nancy. "Can you provide that when you've admitted that you dislike being involved? I doubt it. Fancy taking a small boy fishing and then forgetting all about him! He'd be better with his mother. She must surely have some natural feeling for him."

She seemed to have hit a sore spot, for he interrupted her sharply.

"Anya has only ever loved herself. She should never have been a mother, but it was the only way she could...." He stopped abruptly as if he realized he was telling her too much. The polite mask descended. He stood up. "It's time Neil and I were leaving," he said quietly.

"Oh, you can't—you don't intend to make him walk all the way back. He'll never make it. He'll be exhausted," exclaimed Nancy, getting to her feet.

He turned on her so abruptly that she was forced to take a step backward.

"You seem determined to point out the error of my ways to me this afternoon," he began.

"I seem to remember that you had no hesitation in pointing out how I mismanage Linda, last time you were here," she retaliated.

"I have no liking for interfering, inquisitive females," he threatened.

"And I can't bear arrogant managing males."

His sudden smile transformed his face as a shaft of sunlight slanting across dark moors relieves their brooding melancholy.

"You're never at a loss for an answer, are you?" he observed. "All right, how do you suggest that Neil gets back to the Lodge without walking?"

"Surely there's someone at the Lodge who would drive over to collect you. I was going to ring up if you hadn't arrived. I'd drive you over, but I'm afraid our car isn't working again. You were right about that. It wasn't the bargain we thought it was."

"I'm always right about cars," he replied with maddening superiority. "But it's magnanimous of you to admit it. Now tell me where your phone is and I'll call Harris."

At that moment Linda arrived, disheveled and mudcaked as usual after her walk from the bus. When she saw Logan she almost threw herself at him, demanding why hadn't he been to see them, why wasn't he wearing his kilt, who was the little boy and were they both going to stay for tea.

Logan seemed pleased by her energetic and enthusiastic welcome and pointed out that he and his nephew had not been invited to stay to tea and were about to leave.

"Oh, you can't go yet," complained Linda, "I've lots to tell you. I thought he must be some sort of relation because he looks a bit like you. And you must stay and see Don. They can stay to tea, can't they, Nancy?"

She turned on her sister aggressively, almost accusingly, as if she expected Nancy to refuse. Neil, who had been attracted by the appearance of Linda and had come across the garden to stand beside her, said solemnly, "Another marigold lady. I'd like to stay to tea, please."

"There, that settles it!" exclaimed Linda triumphantly, glaring at Nancy and Logan in turn. "Neither of you dare refuse to do as he asks." After asking Neil his name and promising she would take him to see some kittens when she had changed out of her school clothing she ran into the house.

Nancy glanced ruefully at Logan, wondering whether he was annoyed by Linda's arrangements, and murmured diffidently, "Do you want to stay to tea?"

He gave her one of his strangely penetrating stares before replying, "Like Neil, I'd like to stay, please."

THE REST OF THE AFTERNOON possessed a dreamlike quality. Everything went smoothly and happily. When Linda reappeared dressed in jeans and shirt and Wellington boots she took Logan as well as Neil with her. Nancy went back into the kitchen to prepare the meal and as she worked she thought back over the curious conversation she'd had with Logan in the garden. He was such an enigma. He seemed to want to keep people at bay and yet he was obviously lonely and had accepted the invitation to stay to tea without hesitation. Perhaps if she could read the poem to which he had referred she would understand him better.

"I am weary of days and hours... and everything but sleep," he had quoted, and it was true he did look as if he

If Love Be Love

and sleep were strangers. But why should he feel like that? What caused his unhappiness? Was it possible Mary Maclaine had been right when she had said that she thought he brooded about the accident in which his brother had been killed?

If that was the case, thought Nancy compassionately, she was glad that Linda had suggested that he and Neil stayed for tea. The only way to deal with a person like Logan was to ignore his reticence, which was after all only a cover for unhappiness, to turn a deaf ear to his supercilious snubs and to treat him as if he was normal and happy. Look at the way he had responded to Linda's infectious greeting, to her own lively retorts. He laughed at them, and when he laughed he was such a different person.

There was a lot of laughter at teatime when Don came home and they sat down to tea and described their various experiences with the animals and the neighbors. Logan listened attentively and although he said little Nancy had the feeling that he was relaxed and completely at ease with them.

After tea he went with Don and Linda on their usual fishing expedition in the old wooden dinghy that had belonged to Grandfather Allan. Between the three of them they persuaded Neil to go, too, and they rowed out to the middle of the calm loch.

When she had finished washing up Nancy walked down to the beach to watch them return. Golden evening light lingered on the still water and on the steep curves of the mountains. Blue shadows collected in the hill recesses and slanted across the fields. Only the lap of water against stone, the occasional cry of a pewit and the voices from the dinghy carrying clearly across the water broke the trance of silence, the essential silence of the Highlands.

The four fishermen came ashore triumphant because they had caught three small haddock that they proposed to have for breakfast. Logan said it was time he and Neil returned to the lodge. Neil immediately clutched Nancy's hand and muttered that he didn't want to go.

"But it's your bedtime, darling," said Nancy, kneeling to comfort him as she had that afternoon. "Your uncle will phone for a car to take you both back, and perhaps he'll let you come to see us again."

"I want to stay here for the night, with Lin and Don and you."

"He could do that. He could sleep in the spare bed in my room," suggested Don brightly.

"That's a good idea," cried Linda. "I'll be at home tomorrow because it's Saturday. Perhaps he could stay until Sunday. It would be like going away for the weekend."

"Would you let him stay with us?" Nancy asked, looking at Logan. The polite mask was in place, hiding any emotion he might be feeling.

"If it's what he would like, and you think you can manage him, he can stay with you," he replied smoothly, and there was no way of telling how he felt about the proposition.

"You... you could come and see if he's all right tomorrow," offered Nancy, suddenly thinking that he might be hurt by his nephew's obvious preference for their company.

"I could," he agreed, "but I won't. What will he wear for pajamas?"

"Oh, we'll soon fix something up. That's all part of the fun of staying," said Linda with juvenile enthusiasm. "Come on, Neil, say good-night to your uncle and then we'll go and find something for you to wear. I know, I'll bath you. I've some marvelous stuff for making bubbles and when you're in bed I'll read a story to you."

"Will you really? Nanny used to read stories... I mean one of my nannies did. Mommy doesn't have time, and wickedunclelogan doesn't know any. What will the story be about?"

"About Noggin the King and the Omruds."

"I've never heard of them before. Who are they?"

"I suspect they're some relatives of Linda," suggested Logan. "Good-night, Neil."

Neil said good-night and walked away hand in hand with Linda and Don. He did not look back at Logan, and Nancy had an urge to explain that the little boy had not intended to hurt anyone's feelings.

"You mustn't mind about him wanting to stay with us,"

If Love Be Love

she said consolingly. "Children don't always realize that adults have feelings that they can hurt."

He swung around slowly to look at her and she had the impression that he was rather puzzled by her observation.

"Now what on earth makes you think that he has hurt my feelings?" he asked. "On the contrary, I'm very glad he's met someone he can trust. It might stop him from pining for London—the one place where he's not really wanted. He's still wary of me because, as I've pointed out, he has been taught not to trust me."

Nancy tried not to feel as if she had been brushed off like a rather irritating pest, but it was difficult and she could think of no answer to his very reasonable explanation.

"And one thing you must learn," he continued, "is not to credit others with your own feelings. You might have been hurt if Neil had been your nephew and had so patently preferred a stranger's company. But please don't attribute those feelings to me, and don't offer pity where it's not wanted." His voice softened slightly, amusement robbing it of its habitual coolness. "As a matter of fact, I'm rather relieved to get rid of him for a couple of days, as I can go down to Oban to live it up with some yachting friends of mine who have invited me for the day. Now I shan't have to think up ways of entertaining Neil, something which I've found increasingly difficult to do during the past week so that I've often found myself regretting having brought him here."

"Oh, what a terrible thing to say!" blurted Nancy, her anger at this confession making her blind and deaf to the amusement on his face and in his voice as she failed to realize he was making fun. "Oh, you selfish beast! I thought you said that Neil is the one responsibility you take seriously."

"It is," he assured her. "So seriously that when I come across the ideal baby-sitter by accident, practically on my front doorstep, can you blame me for using her? I'm glad Neil got lost today and that the bees swarmed. You're welcome to cosset my unangelic nephew for two nights and a day. I'll come for him on Sunday. Thank you for the meal. Good night."

THE SENSE OF OUTRAGE that she experienced on learning that Logan had used her interest in Neil for his own selfish ends stayed with Nancy all next day. How easily she had been deceived into thinking he was unhappy and lonely! How foolish she had been in attributing to him feelings he did not possess. Looking back over the whole episode from the time he had found her and Neil together, she thought she could see how deftly he had manipulated her, rousing her compassion both for himself and for Neil with well-placed words. She remembered suddenly that Mary Maclaine had come to see her originally because she was interested in meeting "the one woman who could refuse Logan." Now she knew what it was like to be placed in a position in which it would be difficult to refuse Logan. For if he had asked her after tea on Friday to mind Neil for him while he went away she knew that she would have agreed. He hadn't had to ask because Neil had asked for himself.

But next time he asked she would be on guard. No matter what he suggested she would say no.

Linda was so good with Neil that by the time Saturday night came Nancy was ready to admit that having the boy to stay with them had solved one of her problems temporarily, which was how to keep Linda entertained during a wet weekend when she couldn't spend the whole time out of doors and there was no TV set and no cinema around the corner.

When he got bored or restless with the particular game they were playing she was never at a loss for something else to do. She rigged up a makeshift easel so that he could splash paint on paper and when he tired of that she made puppets for him out of scraps of material.

Sunday was not as wet as Saturday had been, but the wind was blustery, sending squalls of rain across the gray sea that were immediately followed by patches of bright blue sky and brilliant sunshine.

Logan arrived after lunch, driving up to the gate in the blue station wagon that Mary Maclaine had used. There were dark lines under his eyes, which seemed even sleepier than usual. He was extremely polite, asking without any spark of interest if Neil had slept well and if he had behaved himself. At once Nancy found herself wondering about his

If Love Be Love

politeness. Not only was it a facade behind which he could hide his emotions, but possibly it was a cover for boredom. Still annoyed by his behavior of Friday, she was ready to think badly of him. If he was bored by Neil why had he been so cruel as to take the little boy away from his mother? If he was bored by the Allans why did he bother to make conversation with them?

She watched him as he turned away from her and spoke to Linda, and her resentment reached boiling point as she noticed how differently he treated her sister. He obviously enjoyed the hero worship she ladled out to him and went out of his way to praise the efforts Linda had made to entertain Neil. Nancy had often heard how grown men were susceptible to the attention of teenage girls, but to see it happening and to know that it was her own sister who was involved disturbed her so much that when Logan turned back to her and invited them all to go back with him to Lanmore Lodge to have tea with him she declared uncompromisingly, "No, thank you."

"Oh, Nancy!" wailed Linda. "Why shouldn't we?"

Struggling with a wave of new and violent emotion, aware that Logan was watching her with suddenly wide-awake observant eyes, Nancy searched vainly for an excuse and found none.

"I...we..." she began, and stopped. Logan raised an eyebrow and looked amused, and she plunged into speech, saying what she thought, regardless of the consequences.

"Mr. Maclaine is only being polite. He doesn't really want us to go and take tea with him. He thinks that because we've looked after Neil for him and because he has eaten here, he owes us hospitality."

"Nancy!" exclaimed Linda in shocked tones.

"Don't you think that's going a bit too far?" cautioned Don.

"It's true, though," said Logan surprisingly. "I am being polite. I do owe you hospitality. I can't accept it without returning it."

"But you don't really want us, do you?" persisted Nancy. "You're asking us only because it's the right thing to do and not because you want our company."

"Whether I really want you to come or not has no part in it. I have accepted your hospitality; now I must repay it," he replied coldly, and Nancy experienced a queer little tremor at the thought that for once she had annoyed him. "You and Linda will now go and change into more suitable clothing," he ordered firmly, his glance sweeping over her rather disreputable jeans and striped cotton sweater. "Neil and Don and I will wait for you in the station wagon."

His arrogance brought more defiant words to Nancy's tongue, but on encountering the expression in his eyes she bit them back. Instead she said in mimicry of his own polite phrase, "As you wish. Come on, Linda."

TREMBLING A LITTLE, slightly appalled by her own bad behavior but at a loss to account for it, Nancy dressed in a plain green dress. Its brief skirt revealed her well-shaped legs clothed in pale stockings. For the first time since she had arrived in Lanmore she used makeup skillfully in the way she had been taught when she had served on the cosmetic counter at Green and Selby's, the pharmacists where she had worked. She brushed her hair until it shone like an orange silk cap.

Linda had already joined the others in the station wagon so after locking the front door Nancy walked down the path to the car, whose engine was running.

"You may sit in front with me, Miss Allan." There was a touch of irony in Logan's voice as he opened the door for her. Unsmiling, Nancy sat down beside him and closed the door. Wondering why he didn't engage gear at once, she looked at him and encountered a glance that made her want to shout for help.

"I see that you've found it necessary to put on war paint. Does this mean an end to preliminary skirmishing? Should I take it as a declaration of war?" he drawled, as he released the hand brake and the car slid forward.

Unnerved by his glance as well as by his words, Nancy could not reply and she kept her head averted during the short journey. To her relief Logan did not pursue the conversation with her but contented himself with answering Linda's impetuous questions as they drove over the hump-

If Love Be Love

backed bridge and onto the main road. There they turned left and after a mile of bends came to two stone gateposts through which they entered. They went up a long tree-lined driveway that ended before a white house.

The Lodge was quite different from what Nancy had expected. Influenced possibly by Linda's descriptions of Scottish castles and her references to Dunvegan, she had expected a severe turreted building. Instead she was pleasantly surprised to see a low rambling whitewashed house. The Lodge was, in fact, a simple Scottish house with a slate roof and dormer windows, to which additions had been made in the form of two wings built at right angles to the original building.

Inside the house parquet floors gleamed and Indian carpets glowed. Choice pieces of antique furniture were arranged effectively among well-designed twentieth-century pieces. In the lounge, a high-ceilinged austere room, Nancy noticed a glass-fronted cabinet full of ornaments from the East that she assumed had been collected by Logan's great-grandfather.

Logan showed them the whole of the ground floor, explaining that the right wing of the house was used by his cousins Keith and Mary Maclaine and their sons during their regular visits to Lanmore. He led them eventually to the kitchen, where a blue-eyed, dark-haired woman called Mrs. MacFadyen, who was the housekeeper, was preparing tea.

"You can bring it to the lounge," Logan told her.

"Oh, no," objected Linda. "Can't we have it in the room you call your office? That's the best room by far. Please, Logan."

He looked at her in surprise, and then said politely, "As you wish. May I ask why?"

"Because it's your room," replied Linda simply.

Linda was right, thought Nancy, as she looked around the bright westward-looking room. It was the best room in the house because apart from the kitchen it was the only room they had seen that had a lived-in atmosphere. It was paneled with a golden-hued wood and was furnished with an old but beautiful Indian carpet, a large oak desk, some wheel-backed chairs with cushioned seats and a very large comfortable settee. It was full of books and pictures, and in one corner there was a stereo record player and a stack of records. Its French window opened onto a small stone terrace.

Nancy went to stand beside the window. A lawn sloped down to the rough grass that bordered the shore of Lanmore Bay. Out at sea the islands looked like half-submerged porpoises in the water. A small squat boat with two masts swung at a mooring in the bay.

"Is that your brother, in that photograph?" she heard Linda say behind her.

"Isn't that a picture of the car you drove at Le Mans?" she heard Don ask, followed by the murmur of Logan's voice as he answered their questions politely.

"Don't you miss the racing?" Don asked next. "I can't understand why you gave it up."

"Whose boat is that?" asked Nancy loudly, cutting in at the end of Don's words, hoping to divert the conversation into less personal channels.

Her ruse worked. Ignoring Don, Logan came to stand beside her.

"That's *Vagabond*, my father's old cruising boat, very old but very reliable. We used to go cruising in the Outer Hebrides during the summer. My father was a very keen amateur naturalist and he liked observing the birds in their island sanctuaries. One year my brother and I stole the boat and set out to look for the island of Rockall by ourselves."

"Did you find it?" asked Don.

"No. We soon got bored with looking at each other and with going up and down in the same waves, so we turned around and came back."

"How old were you then?" asked the curious Linda.

"Seventeen. Angus was fifteen."

"Don't you go cruising now?"

"No. At least, not much. My cousins use the boat, and I've used her to do some scuba diving around the coast. But I haven't been out this summer. It isn't sensible to dive alone."

"Scuba diving?" echoed Linda. "You mean in a skin suit with a mask and air tanks?"

Logan's smile was indulgent as he looked down at her.

"That's right. Are you interested?"

Linda's eyes blazed with enthusiasm and delight.

"Of course I am. And so is Don. We've always wanted to do it, but we haven't had much opportunity and we couldn't afford the equipment." She sent a withering glance in her sister's direction. "Besides," she added, "Nancy wouldn't let me go. She thought it was too dangerous and that I might have an accident."

"Would you like to come with me?" asked Logan. "We have several wet suits and I think there's one that would fit you that my cousin used last year. Can you swim well? You have to be able to float or tread water for at least half an hour, and to be able to swim at least three hundred to four hundred yards on the surface."

"Swimming is about the only thing I did well at school— and the one reason why they didn't kick me out. I used to bring home the county freestyle trophy from the annual swimming meet," put in Don dryly. "If you need company while you go diving I'll be glad to come with you."

"He's not the only one who's won trophies for swimming," added Linda swiftly. "I have, too. But if you want me to come I expect you'll have to ask Nancy." She sighed exaggeratedly and rolled her eyes in a manner that made Nancy long to retaliate. "She never lets me do anything I *really* want to do."

"That isn't true," Nancy defended herself. "I only try to stop you from making a nuisance of yourself." She looked at Logan, trying to assess his real feeling about the subject, but as usual his expression was bland. "You can't really want to take Linda diving with you," she said hopefully.

"Why not?"

"She's too young."

"Oh, Nancy, you spoil everything!" moaned Linda.

Logan looked at Linda appraisingly.

"I don't think she is," he announced at last. "But would it make you feel any better if I invite you to come along, too? You can look after Neil and keep watch for us on the boat."

"You can't say no this time, Nancy. Can't you see he isn't being polite? He can't go diving unless he takes someone with him," urged Linda.

Nancy hesitated for two reasons. One was that she resented the fact that Logan seemed to want Linda's company and in order to have it he was prepared to put up with herself as baby-sitter for Neil. He hadn't invited her to go diving and since she was as good at swimming as both Don and Linda she was just as interested in diving. The resentment worried her because she had never felt like this toward Linda before. It was almost like jealousy and seemed closely bound up with her other reason for hesitating.

A spark had been ignited between herself and Logan this afternoon and it had made her very aware of him. His reaction to her "war paint" had unnerved her. He had hardly spoken to her during their tour of the house and she had said very little to him. But the many times she had glanced at him when she had thought he was not looking at her she had been surprised by a bright alert stare from eyes that were no longer sleepy; a stare to which her senses had responded in the most disturbing way.

So she hesitated, wondering if it would be wise to agree to a suggestion that would bring not only Linda into closer contact with Logan but also herself.

"Nancy, pleeease!" urged Linda.

"Give her time," said Logan softly. 'She's thinking whether her intended will approve or not."

"Her intended?" gasped Linda, and went off into peals of laughter. "Oh, what a good description of Rod!"

"I'm thinking nothing of the sort," flashed Nancy. She hadn't thought about Rod for days and the mention of his name gave her a slight jolt of guilt.

"Then why the hesitation?" persisted Logan. "Is it fear of the water or of the company you'll have to keep?"

"Neither," lied Nancy. "I'm just as good a swimmer as the other two, and I'm certainly not afraid of you or of Neil. All right, I'll come. But you must be honest with us. As soon as you're tired of taking us you must say so."

She could not look straight at him as she felt that amusement would be lurking in his eyes.

If Love Be Love

"It shall be as you wish," he answered politely, making her wonder why she had made such a fuss.

"Goody!" yelled Linda, and the door opened and Mrs. MacFadyen walked in with a tea trolley laden with a silver teapot, a fine china tea set and plates of homemade scones and biscuits.

"Maybe Miss Allan would like to pour for ye," she suggested with a gentle smile in Nancy's direction as she left the room, closing the door after her.

Logan placed a hand on Nancy's shoulder and guided her toward the trolley. To her consternation she shivered in reaction to his touch.

"Will you pour, please. You see I'm not in the habit of inviting people to tea," he said quietly.

"There, I knew you were only being polite!" she pounced. "How I hate people who extend invitations only because it's etiquette and not because they want to!"

"Hate?" he queried as she picked up the teapot and began to pour the tea. "That's a very strong emotion. I should take care about indulging in it, if I were you. By the way, is it normal to pour the tea until it overflows into the saucer?"

After that verbal engagement Nancy determined to say no more directly to Logan and she concentrated on pouring tea properly and on handing around the scones and cakes. Contrarily she was rather annoyed when he made no further attempt to talk to her or even to include her in conversation, allowing Linda to monopolize his attention to such an extent that Nancy decided to put an end to their visit by abruptly rising to her feet when they had all eaten and drunk and saying that it was time they returned to the cottage because Linda had homework to do.

In spite of Linda's protests Logan rose politely to his feet and said he would drive them home. On the way back to the cottage arrangements were made that he should take them all diving the following Saturday if the weather was suitable, and Nancy found herself secretly hoping, for no valid reason, that the weather would not be suitable because she was doubtful about the wisdom of becoming too involved with Logan Maclaine.

A FEW WEEKS LATER Nancy sat in the cockpit of *Vagabond* untangling Neil's fishing line. It was a placid Saturday afternoon at the end of July and the boat was moored in the middle of a small bay on one of the islands. Looking across the water, she could see the white mass that was Lanmore Lodge set among the dark green of its surrounding pines. Behind it rose the gentle hills of Lanmore and behind them was the more rugged outline of the mountains of the mainland.

Nancy threaded the end of the line through the last tangled knot, wound it around the reel and handed it back to Neil with a warning that he should not get it tangled again. The little boy thanked her with a smile and walked away to the bow of the boat to try his luck again.

Watching him walk with confidence along the side deck Nancy thought how much better he looked than he had a bare month ago when she had first met him. She could not help feeling pleased that his recuperation was due in some part to the attention she had given him. He had lost his dislike for fishing, and instead of being a person he distrusted, his uncle was now his hero from whom he did not like to be parted for long.

Nancy sighed suddenly. The doubt that she had felt originally about becoming too involved with Logan had increased gradually, fed by the numerous intrusions that he had made recently into the life of the Allan family.

It had all happened so naturally that it had been difficult to stop. Having extracted a promise from Nancy to baby-sit Neil while he took Don and Linda diving, Logan seemed to assume from then on that she was willing to baby-sit at other times, too. During the week following the tea party at Lanmore he had turned up one morning at the croft with Neil and had asked her to mind the boy for the day. She could have asked him why his housekeeper could not mind the child or she could have refused. But she had done neither because Neil had been so happy to see her again. Logan had returned just as Linda had come home from school and had invited the girl to go fishing with him and Neil that evening. He had told Nancy she could come, too, if she wanted to, but he didn't want her to think she had to come just to be polite. The offhand invitation had been extended in a certain tongue-in-cheek manner that had infuriated her, and of course she had gone fishing, not only that day but on other days, too.

The first time they had gone diving Logan had taken them to a shallow bay and had insisted that all three of them tried with snorkels first. Having satisfied himself that they were quite competent the next weekend he had shown them how to use the tanks of compressed air in conjunction with face masks and regulators and for the first time in her life Nancy entered the strange fascinating underworld of the sea, an underworld that she would always associate with Logan, who in his black wet suit, mask and fins reminded her more than ever of the mysterious Pluto, as he guided her with hand signals through the translucent water on a tour of his kingdom beneath the surface.

The Allans enjoyed diving so much that they had no hesitation in accepting Logan's invitation to go with him every weekend, weather permitting. Nancy soothed her doubts away by deciding that if their contact with him was limited to weekends there wasn't much danger.

But after the second weekend she found herself minding Neil for two days in succession. On both days Logan returned from where he had been after school was out, and on both days Neil had gone on some jaunt with Linda. So Logan had sat down on the bench under the cottage window to wait for his nephew. He accepted politely the tea and biscuits Nancy had offered him, and gradually his politeness had melted; he had relaxed and they had talked. Their conversations, it was true, often resembled boxing matches because they tended to circle around each other verbally, feinting and withdrawing, testing each other and occasionally landing a shrewd blow, which would be followed by a brief silence while they reassessed each other.

By the end of July, with Linda on holiday from school, both diving and baby-sitting had become almost habits, and Nancy knew she would have been disappointed if a week had passed without two or three visits from the boy and his uncle. She knew the boy benefited and she had a secret hope that the man did, too, although after over four weeks of seeing him almost every day Logan was still as much as an enigma to her as he had been when she had first met him. Some days he was so polite and distant that she was hurt and bewildered. Other days he was amusing and good-humored, making them laugh with stories about their grandfather and of the mischief Logan himself and his brother Angus had done during their boyhood at Lanmore.

With Don he was always patient and encouraging, giving the younger man the benefit of his own farming and fishing knowledge. With Linda he was an indulgent listener, giving the girl far more attention than Nancy thought she ought to receive. It seemed often that it was only in the hope of seeing Linda that he sat and talked to Nancy in the "quiet world" of the garden, thought Nancy with a frown.

"Nancy, I've caught a fish! Quick...quick! Come and take it off the hook," demanded Neil, who had not yet mastered the technique of removing the hook from the mouth of the fish.

She went to the bow of the boat and gently unhooked the small codling he had caught.

"Is it enough for breakfast for uncle and me?" he asked. "Or shall I catch another?"

Nancy suggested that he should catch another and together they baited the hook once more and he let the line over the side.

She looked around at the islands, the sea and the mountains. It was such a lovely place and she had been fortunate to see it in summertime. What would it be like in winter? Nancy shrugged and made her way back to the cockpit. Why should she care? By the time winter came she would be settled in Dulthorpe as Mrs. Rod Ellis.

She put her hand in the pocket of her jeans and pulled out the letter she had received the previous day from Rod, and which she had brought with her to reread.

He had decided to take ten days of his annual three weeks' holiday to visit her at Lanmore. There was a lot for them to discuss. He had been to look at a new house in a suburb of Dulthorpe. The house was next to the one bought by the Unwins—Nancy would remember them, a nice couple who would make good neighbors. Anyway, they would talk about it when he arrived in Lanmore.

There was no word of love in the letter and no suggestion that he was missing her. It seemed as if he had chosen the house where they were going to live after they were married without her seeing it. He had everything planned, and she should feel pleased. But she didn't.

There was a disturbance in the water near the boat. A head surfaced and then a smooth black figure wearing a weighted belt and carrying two air tanks on its back appeared. Nancy knew it was Logan because he was not as tall as Don. He sat on the side deck, pushed the mask up and began to unshackle the harness that held the two tanks on to his back.

Forgetting her letter that fell into the cockpit, she went to help him.

"Where are the others?" she asked.

"Trying to catch a lobster. I doubt if they will. It looked old and wily to me. I feel thirsty. Is there any beer?" he said.

While he removed the flippers from his feet she went below into the cabin for a can of beer. When she returned to the cockpit he was sitting in it. He had removed the black hood from his head and his hair was tousled. The top part of his wet suit was unzipped to the waist to reveal his bare thickly muscled chest. In his hand he held the envelope that contained her letter.

"A love letter?" he queried. "Judging by the postmark it's from your intended."

She almost snatched the letter from him as she handed him the beer.

"Yes, it is. He's coming to stay with us at the end of next week."

He drank some beer and stared silently across the water at the island, apparently wholly uninterested in her reply. Deciding he was in an unapproachable mood, Nancy stood up, intending to go and see Neil. At once her hand was caught and held.

"Don't go," he commanded.

As usual she overreacted to his touch and shivered. As usual he noticed and dropped her hand immediately.

"Will you go back to Dulthorpe with him when his stay here is over?" he asked her.

"I might. Although I had intended to stay until the end of August. Rod has found a house he likes, so I might go back to see it."

"He must be very sure of you if he's decided already where you should live."

"Why shouldn't he be sure? I promised to marry him."

"Do you always keep your promises?"

"I try."

He took hold of her left hand. By sheer effort of will she controlled her reaction and didn't allow herself to shiver. He inspected it and then released it.

"He can't be sure of himself, though," he murmured thoughtfully. "He didn't give you a ring."

"That was something we decided we could do without. After all, an engagement ring is an old-fashioned idea, and an unnecessary expense," replied Nancy coolly, hiding her surprise at his comments. Logan was not usually so personal.

"I don't think it is," he disagreed. "If I asked a girl to marry me I'd want to make sure she was wearing my mark, to remind her when she was far away that she had promised to be mine."

His possessive attitude surprised her. Possessiveness was one quality she had not attributed to him.

"But then the question will never arise, because you prefer a way of life that excludes women," she taunted dryly, feeling that she must get her own back for his implied criticism of Rod.

He raised his eyebrows. "When did I say that?"

"The day we first met you, at Housesteads."

"I remember. I was in a sour mood that day, with good reason." He made no further explanation, finished his beer, put down the can and stood up.

"Here are the others. I'll go below and change," he said, then added with a faint smile, "You must make sure your intended sees all he can while he's here. The Games will be on in Portree. They're worth a visit. The end of August. Summer will be almost over then, although we often get good weather in September. Will spring begin in Dulthorpe, I wonder, when you go back there?"

He swung down the companionway, leaving her to stare after him and to ponder on his strange comment.

When they landed at Lanmore Logan surprised them all by inviting them to the Lodge to have dinner with him. Usually after the Saturday outing in *Vagabond* the Allans returned to the croft after having made arrangements to meet him again the next day if the weather was fine.

Ignoring an inclination to refuse, giving in to Linda's and Neil's enthusiasm for the idea, Nancy accepted and the Allans returned to the cottage to change their clothes.

It was a pleasant meal and Logan was an exemplary host. Neil enjoyed the whole affair thoroughly, but eventually his head drooped and after extracting a promise from Nancy that she would put him to bed and read a story to him he went up the stairs with her quite happily.

She read one of Edward Ardizzone's stories about Tim that Logan had bought for him. It was fairly long and she had to finish it, because Neil was a stickler for hearing a story in one reading. She had reached the last page when the door opened and Logan entered the room. He waited quietly until she had finished reading.

"Time you were asleep, Neil," he ordered. "Nancy has done quite enough for you for one day."

"Nancy's kind. I love her," said the boy, and flinging his arms around Nancy's neck, he kissed her. "Now you kiss me," he demanded.

Laughing at his peremptoriness, Nancy kissed him.

"Good night, Neil. Sleep well."

He beamed sleepily, happily.

"Good night, Nancy. Good night, Uncle Logan. See you tomorrow."

Logan went through the door first and when Nancy closed it behind her he turned on her suddenly and said, "I don't see why Neil should do all the kissing."

Before his words really penetrated her understanding he pushed her against the wall and kissed her roughly. To Nancy's annoyance with herself her body quivered at his touch and she experienced a strong inclination to respond by holding him close and returning the kiss, but exerting all her willpower, she pushed him away and said in a loud whisper, "What do you think you're doing?"

"Behaving like a child," he retorted wickedly. "Now you kiss me."

More disturbed than she cared to reveal, Nancy said loudly and clearly, "No!"

She hoped he would move aside and let her pass, but he didn't move.

"Why not?" he asked.

"Because you're not a child," she flashed, recovering slightly.

He laughed appreciatively and to her relief turned and went down the stairs. Nancy followed, slowly conscious that her heart was pounding loudly and her throat was dry. She had a great urge to run across the hall and out through the front door and down the drive; to run away before it was too late. But Don and Linda would think she was crazy if she did such a thing, so she swallowed hard and went into the lounge where she expected to find them with Logan.

The beautiful high-ceilinged room was full of rose-colored light that slanted in through the window from the sunset. Logan was the only person in the room. He was standing by a low table and the light glinted on the glass he was holding in one hand and struck bubbles of color from the facets of the cut-glass decanter that he was holding with the other.

"Will you have a drink?" he offered politely.

"No, thank you," answered Nancy, equally polite. "Where are Don and Linda?"

He finished pouring liquor into the glass, placed the decanter on the table and replaced its stopper before answering her.

"I was telling them about the dance in the village hall tonight and they decided they wanted to go to it. All Lanmore will be there, including Mrs. MacFadyen."

Disconcerted by his reply, Nancy could only stare at him as he sipped from the glass, apparently quite unconcerned. Don and Linda had gone without her, without even con-

If Love Be Love

sulting her, without bothering to find out if she would have liked to go, too.

It was then that she noticed the silence of the house, the lack of human sound and movement. All Lanmore was at the dance, including the staff from Lanmore Lodge. All Lanmore except herself and Logan.

"I must go," she said urgently. Then, realizing that she must sound rather rude, she added by way of explanation, "Linda shouldn't have gone without me. She's too young."

"She's with Don. He'll look after her. She'll enjoy it," he replied smoothly.

"Oh, you don't understand. He has no control over her. She's never been to a dance before. She won't know how to behave."

"Then it will be a good opportunity for her to learn," he remarked seriously. He put down his half-empty glass on the table and came to stand in front of her. "What are you trying to do to her? Inhibit her, so that when she grows up she'll be incapable of behaving normally? Just because you did not have a normal adolescence why deny it to her?"

The unexpectedness of his scathing attack had a peculiar effect on Nancy. She remembered the struggle she had had with Linda during the past five years and the efforts she had made to curb her own natural high spirits in order to set a good example to her younger sister, and she had a sudden desire to burst into tears. Instead she sought refuge behind a stinging retort.

"You seem very interested in Linda. It's a wonder you haven't taken her to the dance yourself. Perhaps you'd like to go now—I'm quite willing to baby-sit!"

She could tell by the corner of his mouth turned down and the way his eyebrows met above the bridge of his nose in a frown that she had landed a blow and she prepared to face his anger. But as usual his reaction was different from what she had expected.

"That was unworthy of you, Nancy," he rebuked her quietly. "Sour grapes. Could it be that you're resentful because Linda is having the fun you would like for yourself?"

"That's not true. I don't resent Linda," blurted Nancy as he touched a tender spot. And this time the tears would not be held back. She was not sure really why she wanted to cry. It had something to do with Logan thinking so badly of her. He would think even worse of her if she broke down and wept. But she couldn't help it.

"Oh, you don't understand," she wailed, and burst into tears.

She wasn't quite sure how it happened, but she found herself sitting on the settee and she was crying into Logan's shoulder; hot wet tears and body-shaking sobs that brought miraculous relief. She hadn't cried since she was a little girl. There had often been times when she had wanted to, but pride had always kept her going; the fierce Allan pride that Logan had condemned at their second meeting. Now, here in his house, with her head against his shoulder and his arm around her, her pride was in ribbons and she must apologize.

She raised her head and said through her nose that was still blocked with tears, "I'm sorry."

The rose-colored glow was fading and the room was full of blue shadows. A single lamp, which must have been lit when she entered the room but which she noticed now for the first time, shed a yellow light in one corner.

"Why apologize for behaving in a perfectly normal way, even if you have soaked my shirt collar? I should be the one to apologize for taunting you. I understand much better than you think, but you have to admit that though you're able to cope satisfactorily with the kindergarten state, when it comes to dealing with an adolescent girl you're hopeless. You have to let Linda go and do things on her own so that she'll learn. If you shelter her too much she'll make the most disastrous mistakes when she's older."

"But she's so impetuous and ... and stubborn."

"So are you, particularly the latter," he responded dryly. "Rushing into marriage with the only man who's ever proposed to you!"

Nancy giggled suddenly.

"It's not exactly a rush affair. I've known Rod for three years and I promised two years ago that I would marry him," she said.

Logan groaned.

If Love Be Love

"It's worse than I was thinking, then," he murmured. His hand moved up to her shoulder and he pulled her back against him again. Nancy lay quietly, almost exhaustedly, thinking how natural it seemed to lie there. His shoulder was flat and hard under her cheek and his hand was warm on her bare arm. His breathing was quiet and regular. Quiet, polite Logan who sometimes forgot to be polite and said what he thought with devastating effect.

"Why is it worse than you'd thought?" she asked. "What's wrong with my marrying Rod?"

"It's worse because it's obvious that you've accepted marriage to him as a fait accompli for two years. You've never attempted to compare him with anyone else. How do you know he's right for you if you've never known anyone else?"

"When you meet him you'll realize..." she started to explain, but he interrupted her roughly.

"I don't need to meet him. I can guess. He's tall and handsome and keeps to the straight and narrow, and he's never made love to you."

Rather disturbed by the roughness of his speech, Nancy tried to sit up again, but his arm tightened around her and she was unable to move.

"You're quite right about him being tall, and he is quite handsome," she admitted. "He's very highly thought of at his work, but I don't know why you think he's never made love to me. He kisses me every time we meet and when we part."

Logan snorted scornfully.

"That isn't exactly what I meant," he said. "Have you ever sat with him like this... and has he ever kissed you like this?"

He put a hand under her chin, tilted her face upward and kissed her.

Nancy's eyes closed. She was sinking down into an underworld filled with rose-tinted green light. It was pleasant to let herself sink, but dangerous, too, because she might drown.

Quickly she opened her eyes as Logan raised his head.

"I must go and find Lin," she said desperately, using the

first excuse that came into her head, trying to pull away from him.

"Cluck, cluck, little hen," he mocked. "Your chicken will be all right."

"Please let me go," she urged.

"As you wish." Even the polite answer seemed to mock her as he released her. "Now tell me what's wrong. Why the sudden panic?"

Once free she stood up quickly, smoothing down her skirt and straightening her ruffled hair.

"I'm waiting, Nancy Allan, for you to tell me what's wrong," persisted Logan.

"I...I think you're playing some sort of game and I don't like it," she replied. "And I don't know the rules."

There was laughter in his voice as he answered, "I could teach them to you."

"I've decided I don't want to learn them, thank you. I have my own rules and one of them is this: I don't let another man make love to me when I'm engaged to be married."

"I hadn't noticed that you offered much opposition," he remarked. Nancy's face flamed and he had the grace to apologize immediately. "I'm sorry, I shouldn't have said that."

"You took advantage of me," she accused.

"In what way?"

"First you made me cry, and then—"

"Has the respectable Rod ever seen you cry?" he challenged.

"No. But I don't see what that has to do with—"

"He's going to get a shock, then, when after a couple of weeks or perhaps even after only a couple of nights of marriage you treat him to a wholly feminine display of tears, as you will. It's inevitable. Women always weep when criticized or when they can't get their own way."

"For a bachelor you seem to be very knowledgeable about women," she sniped back.

For answer he gave her one of his cool stares and then rising to his feet he asked politely, "Where would you like me to drive you? To the cottage or to the dance?"

If Love Be Love

For a moment Nancy stared at him, not knowing what to say. The change in his manner was bewildering. When bewilderment had passed she recognized his smooth polite offer for what it was. With his usual impeccable courtesy he had suggested to her that she was not welcome anymore, that he would like her to leave.

The cottage would be lonely without Linda and Don, so she would be better going to the dance. But first her pride had to step in.

"There's no need for you to drive me," she replied coolly. "I can walk. Anyway, you're baby-sitting Neil."

He glanced at her feet. She was wearing high-heeled shoes.

"You can't walk in those shoes. Neil will be all right for the few minutes it will take me to drive you. But first of all you must decide on your destination."

Never had she known anyone who could be so polite and yet so insolent. But why the sudden change in manner? Why had he withdrawn? A few minutes ago they had been talking as good friends might talk. But that had been before he had kissed her.

"The dance, please," she answered. Then as he turned away and walked to the door she came to a decision and said,

"Logan, wait!"

Hand on the door knob, he looked back at her, his eyebrows raised in polite inquiry.

"Well?"

Nancy took a deep breath, knowing that the decision she had just reached was going to hurt herself as much as anyone.

"Linda and I won't come diving anymore. And I would prefer it if... if you didn't bring Neil to the cottage to stay with me. I don't know whether you've heard, but there's been some gossip among the crofters, and...."

"I see." His light eyes were diamond bright and about as hard.

"And naturally you would prefer not to be gossiped about because you're engaged and because you're expecting your fiancé to visit you. I understand perfectly. Although I've no doubt that both Linda and Neil will be disappointed, it shall be as you wish. And now if you're ready I'll take you to the village hall."

CHAPTER FOUR

TIME THAT HAD PASSED SO QUICKLY ever since she had arrived at Lanmore dragged slowly all the next week. Nancy tried to convince herself that the weather was to blame. It was cold and blustery, making the performance of outdoor work difficult and uncomfortable.

By keeping her mind on the forthcoming visit of Rod she managed to get through the days without too many backward glances at the evening she had been alone with Logan at the Lodge. By Friday lunchtime, however, she was ready to admit she was losing the battle with her pride and that not only was she missing Neil, but she was also missing Logan and the quiet moments they had spent together in the garden.

As she washed up the lunch dishes she wondered why the most disturbing thoughts occurred when she was doing the most mundane jobs. Here she was at the kitchen sink and the memory of Logan's kiss had to catch her unawares. She rattled the dishes with unnecessary vigor as she assured herself that the memory would fade as would the memory of his gentleness when she had cried. Meanwhile both were vivid, and the thought that she would experience neither again left her with a strange aching feeling of sadness.

"The weather is clearing up," announced Linda, coming into the scullery, as usual too late to be of much help. "I hope we'll be able to go diving tomorrow. Logan hasn't been to see us all week. Do you think he's away?"

"I don't know. But I might as well tell you now, we shan't be going diving with him again and he won't be bringing Neil here again."

Incredulous dismay puckered Linda's forehead and caused the corners of her mouth to droop.

"Why? Is he tired of us?" she asked.

It would be the easy way out to let her believe that had happened, thought Nancy, but it would not be fair to Logan.

"No. I asked him not to take us diving and not to bring Neil here anymore."

"I don't understand. Why should you do that?" asked Linda. "I thought you enjoyed the diving as much as Don and I did. I thought you liked looking after Neil."

She stared at Nancy, puzzlement clouding her brown eyes. Nancy said nothing and started to put away the dishes she had washed and dried.

"You did it deliberately," blurted Linda suddenly. "To spoil my fun. Oh, isn't it typical!"

"That wasn't the reason at all, Lin," said Nancy patiently. "I've been doubtful all the time about our becoming too involved with Logan. I didn't think he would come to see us so often and I didn't think there would be gossip about—"

"Gossip?" exclaimed Linda. "I don't care a hoot about gossip. I bet Logan doesn't, either."

"Well, I do. I've had enough of Ian Macrae's sly digs about the laird's interest in us. Apart from that I happen to be engaged and Rod will soon be here, and I wouldn't like him to be upset by anything the neighbors might say. You know how they talk to complete strangers about everyone else's business."

This characteristic of their neighbors had amused the Allans at first. Now Nancy was very much aware of how it might affect Rod when he came. "You mean the crofters think that you and Logan... well!" Linda went off into shrieks of laughter. "That's really funny, especially when we know he doesn't particularly like you."

Although she was glad that Linda's anger had been changed to laughter Nancy could not help feeling hurt by her sister's comment.

"How can he like you when you're always arguing with him?" went on Linda. "Men like Logan dislike bossy women."

"How do you know what men like and dislike?" snapped Nancy, thoroughly nettled by the implication that she was bossy.

If Love Be Love

Linda gave her a slow infuriating sidelong glance.

"I bet I know more about what men like than you did at my age," she said slyly.

"You don't know what you're talking about," riposted Nancy rather weakly.

"Yes, I do," asserted Linda with a toss of her head. "But you needn't worry, I can take care of myself. And now I think I'll phone Logan to tell him that I would like to go diving with him, no matter what you say. After all, I'm not engaged."

"You will do nothing of the sort!"

"Why shouldn't I? I'm not afraid of gossip."

"If you phone him you'll make yourself look ridiculous, a girl of fifteen chasing a man who's twice her age."

"I don't care," replied the defiant Linda. "And I'm nearly sixteen."

She went through to the kitchen and picked up the receiver. Nancy followed her, although short of snatching the instrument from Linda there was nothing she could do. She could only hope that Logan's common sense would lead him to give Linda the setdown she was asking for. On the other hand there was always the chance he might be flattered by Linda's interest. Nancy closed her eyes and groaned at the thought.

At that moment there was a knock at the front door. To her dismay her heart leaped at the sound as she thought immediately that it might be Logan tired of his nephew's company and looking for someone to entertain the child.

Linda must have thought the same because she put down the receiver and ran out into the little hallway and flung wide the door.

"Hello, dear. Is your sister at home?" asked a silvery, unmistakably English voice. "Neil wants to see her. He's been bored to tears, poor child—the weather, you know— so I thought we'd pop over to see how you all are."

It was Mary Maclaine. Pink-cheeked and smiling, not a hair of her blue-rinsed coiffure out of place, her pleated tweed skirt and thin woolen twin set ideal for the cool August day, she was a welcome intrusion. Beside her Neil clung to her hand, but when he saw Nancy he ran forward and flung his arms around her and burst out, "Wickeduncleiogan said you didn't want to mind me anymore and I thought you didn't like me. You do like me, don't you?"

Silently Nancy reproved the absent Logan for being too honest with the little boy and for causing him unnecessary hurt. She ruffled the child's blond hair and smiled down at him.

"Yes, I like you, but it isn't always possible for me to look after you. It's nice to see you, Mrs. Maclaine. Do sit down and we'll make some tea. Linda, would you put the kettle on, please."

Linda glowered sulkily and went out into the scullery while Mary settled in a chair by the fire and Neil rummaged in a drawer for the paints and paper he knew were kept there for him.

"That will be very pleasant," said Mary. "I'd have come sooner if it hadn't been for Logan saying that on no account was Neil to bother you. You're very popular with the child and I hear that he and Logan have been seeing you often recently. I hope they haven't been making a convenience of you?"

"Oh, no, I liked looking after Neil. He's no trouble," said Nancy vaguely. "And Logan has been very kind to us all."

"Yes, he can be generous when he wants." Mary sighed a little.

"It's all as well to remember that when he behaves selfishly. Keith and I had hardly arrived with the boys on Sunday—we found him in a very sour and restless mood—when he announced that he was off to Europe immediately and that he'd be glad if I would look after Neil until Tuesday when Anya would arrive. I expect he told you she was coming?"

"No, he didn't mention her," replied Nancy slowly. "I didn't know you were coming, either."

Her grand gesture of deciding not to go diving with Logan, of not looking after Neil anymore, of cutting all contact with Logan, had been wasted after all. With the arrival of the rest of the Maclaine family it was doubtful if the Allans would have been invited to go diving again and certainly Neil would not have wanted to stay with them when his mother arrived. How amused Logan must have been by her grand airs! She felt suddenly deflated.

"Didn't you? Well, I suppose there was really no reason why he should tell you. Keith and I always come a few days before the twelfth, to get settled in before the shooting starts."

"The shooting?" repeated Nancy vaguely.

"Oh, Nancy!" exclaimed Linda disgustedly. "The grouse shooting." She had returned from the scullery and was sitting contentedly with Neil. "Don't you remember Logan asking Don if he would like to be a beater, to rouse the grouse out of their hiding places on the moors?"

Mary Maclaine smiled at her.

"I can see you are getting to know the Highland customs," she commented. "Now where was I? Oh, yes. Logan said Anya would arrive on Tuesday. On Monday she rang up from London and asked to speak to him. I had to tell her he had gone to Austria to a race for sports prototypes and she said in her strange abrupt manner, 'Damn, I forgot the Grand Prix. I won't come north tomorrow. I'll fly over to join him and Stan. I'll travel back to Lanmore with him.' Then she rang off. Not a word about the child."

"Who is Stan?" asked Nancy.

"Stan Black, the racing-car designer. He designed the cars Logan and Angus used to race in. You know, I hope Logan isn't thinking of taking up racing again. I have a feeling he hadn't intended to go to Austria... that something had upset him and that he'd decided to go on the spur of the moment. Anyway, Keith is furious with both him and Anya, says neither of them give a thought for anyone else. Now tell me about yourselves. You've made a difference to the house."

They chatted, the kettle boiled and tea was made. Outside the clouds lifted and pale yellow sunlight appeared. It was almost four o'clock. Rod would be preparing to leave Dulthorpe. He would be setting out in his little car, heading west, taking no chances, cutting no corners, cautious and careful as ever.

And what would Logan be doing? The thought sprang

unbidden into Nancy's mind, sweeping the image of Rod away. Would the Grand Prix still be taking place? She realized suddenly that she was completely ignorant about car racing. It was true she had heard Don talking about Formula One and sports prototypes, but she really hadn't any idea what either meant. She hadn't known there was a race held in Austria called a Grand Prix. She must ask him later what sort of cars raced in it and whether he thought Logan would go back to racing. And then thinking of the danger involved she found herself hoping fervently that he would not.

ROD ARRIVED at five o'clock the next day. Fortunately the sun had shone all day and the scenery looked its best, the mountains clear-cut, every ridge and cranny defined, the water of the loch smooth and shining.

Tall and fair, neatly and conventionally dressed in a tweed sports jacket, dark trousers and a blue shirt and tie, Rod looked his best, too, and at first Nancy was glad to see him. He was a known quantity. She knew where she stood with him and could predict, or so she thought, his reactions and consequently knew what to say to him.

After a brief embrace he walked with her through the garden to the cottage, his narrowed blue gaze roving over the bee-loud, flower-scented borders and the shaggy shrubbery.

"Hmm. You don't seem to have the garden in very good shape, Nancy," he observed in his clipped crisp voice. "You'll have to do better than this when we get our own house."

His critical comment surprised Nancy. She had not known that the town-bred Rod was interested in gardens. Here was a reaction she had not predicted and as a result she was defensive immediately.

"Oh, don't you like it? I do... and Logan loves it."

The last words were said without thinking and she was surprised again, this time at her own imprudence.

"Logan... Logan?" repeated Rod in his quick staccato fashion. "Sounds Irish to me. Who is he anyway?"

"Not Irish in this case. He's the laird and owns all the

If Love Be Love

land on Lanmore," replied Nancy, and even to her own ears she sounded cool and reticent as if regretting the mention of Logan's name.

"Oh, you mean the chap who didn't want Don to take over the croft. Isn't it odd for him to be on visiting terms? You never mentioned him in your letters."

Rod's voice was sharp and his eyes inquisitive and Nancy wished she had kept silent on the subject of the garden and Logan. How unlike her it was to behave so foolishly!

"Didn't I?" she said brightly. "That just shows how unimportant I think he is. I'm sure you must be hungry and tired of driving. We'll have a meal and then I'll take you to meet Miss Macrae. You'll sleep in her house and have your meals with us, except for breakfast. I hope the arrangements will suit you, Rod."

"I hope they will, too. It's nice to know you have everything organized as usual," he said, with one more critical glance at the garden.

After a few days Nancy was beginning to wish that Rod had never made the comment about her having everything organized, because everything that could go wrong with his holiday had gone wrong. In the first place he had taken a dislike to Miss Macrae.

"I can't think why you thought I would be comfortable in her house," he complained one morning when he arrived after breakfast. "Every time I turn over the bed creaks. I've inspected it carefully because I'm convinced it's going to collapse with me in it one night."

Linda gurgled with unrestrained laughter.

"Oh, what a joke if it did!" she said, unthinkingly.

"You may find it funny, but I don't," said Rod, frowning at her repressively. "And another thing—I believe your precious Miss Macrae is a secret drinker."

"Whatever makes you think that? She seems perfectly normal to me," said Nancy, who was having difficulty in suppressing her temper.

"Maybe she does, but you don't visit her late at night. Every night when I've left you and gone over there, she's come out of her kitchen and invited me to have 'a wee drop' as she calls it. Each time she's been very charming but a little on the talkative side. Then last night when I went in there were three men and two other women sitting there. She introduced me and then sat down at her harmonium and began to play it—and not very well at that—and she began to sing in Gaelic."

"I'm told that when she was young she sang very well and won medals at the Mod," murmured Nancy.

"What's that?" asked Rod.

"A singing competition for choirs and individual singers. It's held every year at places like Oban and Inverness and people from all over Scotland enter for it."

"Well, after she had finished the others sang, too—no words, just sounds."

"*Port a beul*...mouth music," exclaimed Linda proudly, showing off her newly acquired Gaelic pronunciation. "She made a ceilidh for you. You should feel honored, Rod."

"Should I?" was his sardonic remark. "All the time the whiskey bottle was going around. I went to bed, but they were still singing after midnight...and this morning she wasn't up and I didn't get any breakfast."

"I'm sorry," said Nancy, making an effort not to laugh. He sounded so put out. "You'd better come and stay with us. I'm sure Don won't mind sleeping down here and letting you have his room."

"No, no, that wouldn't be right from the point of view of propriety, as I said in my letter."

"What has propriety to do with it?" asked Linda, mischief dancing in her eyes.

"Never mind," said Nancy. "It doesn't matter, Rod. Don is here and everyone knows we're going to be married."

"No." He was quite adamant. "I stay where I am."

"I could ask Meg Macrae," persisted Nancy. "She would let you sleep there, but I know Miss Macrae would be terribly hurt if I do. She's so kind, and was very grateful when I asked her if she could put you up. Evidently she used to take in summer visitors and then gradually they stopped coming."

"I'm not surprised if they had to sleep in that bed, and if they discovered her drinking habits. Honestly, Nancy, I'm

If Love Be Love

not joking. I opened a cupboard on the landing upstairs and it was full of empty bottles."

"I hope you don't go snooping through our cupboards," Nancy retorted, her irritation with his complaints getting the better of her. "You might find something in them that you don't approve of."

"I was not snooping, Nancy!" he declared indignantly.

IT WAS ONE of the many little frictions that occurred between them. It seemed to Nancy that he found nothing right in the Highlands. He criticized everything, even the natural beauty of the landscape, saying that it didn't compare with anything he'd seen in the Mediterranean. He did it to such an extent that one day Linda was roused enough to say it was a pity he hadn't gone there for his holiday. After reprimanding her for bad manners he left the room and went into the garden where Nancy found him, spade in hand, about to dig up a lovely clump of forget-me-nots.

"No, no, leave them, Rod. Please don't touch anything. It may not be as tidy and as productive as you would like a garden to be, but it's natural and lovely, a quiet place that the birds visit."

He leaned on the spade and looked down at her, his blue eyes speculative.

"Too quiet for me," he remarked. "And Lanmore isn't the sort of place I would normally take my holiday. I can see that you and Don like it. You like the eccentric characters, the silence, the 'God's own time' atmosphere. I must say I'm surprised, though, that anyone as active and with as much initiative as you have should have stayed here as long as you have."

His glance was probing and she looked away and said lightly, "Perhaps I'm reverting to type. You must remember my father was born here and before him his father and grandfather, going back for generations, so I'm bound to feel at home."

He did not seem entirely satisfied with her answer because he murmured, "I wonder if that's all. It does seem as if it's right for Don, though, which is a blessing. There's only Linda, now. Have you any idea what she wants to do?"

Nancy drew a sigh of relief. This was the familiar Rod, interested in her plans for her sister, willing to give his co-operation. Whatever she decided he would not tell her that she did not understand the adolescent stage.

"Shall we ask her later?" she suggested.

"Good idea," he agreed.

But the talk with Linda went wrong, too. It took place while they were all having tea. Don and Linda had been to some sheep sales in Oban and they were talkative and excited.

"And who do you think turned up while we were there?" asked Linda.

"I haven't a clue," returned Nancy carelessly.

"Logan, with Neil and Neil's mother. Nancy, did you know that she's Anya Baron, the film actress?"

Nancy nodded, trying to appear disinterested, although with the mention of Logan's name her heart had begun that peculiar pounding again.

"She's absolutely fabulous," went on Linda. "But she didn't like the sheep and complained about the smell of the animals, so they left, although Neil wanted to stay with Logan. By the way, Neil wanted to know when he could come and stay with us again. Logan explained to him that he couldn't come to stay while you had a visitor and that seemed to satisfy him."

"Who is Neil and why should he want to stay with you?" asked Rod.

Linda explained and he frowned.

"It's rather strange, don't you think, for a man in Maclaine's position to bring his nephew to stay here. Surely he can afford to employ someone to look after the child?"

"But the whole point is that Neil liked coming here. So did Logan," said Linda impulsively. "He took us diving every weekend before you came and hardly a day passed when we didn't see them both. Logan liked to sit in the garden."

"I'd think more of him if he'd tidied it up for you. It will soon be choked with weeds and nothing will grow," commented the fastidious Rod.

"They're not weeds," objected Nancy. "They're wild

If Love Be Love

flowers. And everything grows there because it's so warm and sheltered."

"Whoever heard of a garden of wild flowers?" scoffed Rod. "Also, I'm not sure whether I approve of your going diving. Did you go, Nancy?"

As she had suspected, he did not like the idea of her having dealings with another man, and if it hadn't been for Linda saying too much he might have never known.

"I went to mind Neil and to keep a watch on the boat while the others dived. I dived, too," she said quietly.

"But you know nothing about boats," objected Rod. "It seems to me all of you have been very ready to do anything this man Maclaine has asked you to do."

"Logan has been a very good friend to us," growled Linda ominously. "He's helped Don enormously. Anyway, you shouldn't pass opinions on people you haven't met."

With these defiant words she flounced out of the room leaving her meal half eaten.

"She is really growing very impertinent," said Rod. "You realize, Nancy, I hope, that it's you I'm concerned about. You have quite enough to do looking after Linda without having someone else's child thrust upon you."

"It's over now," replied Nancy soothingly. "I shan't be minding Neil again now that his mother is here."

"I'm glad to hear it."

The matter of what Linda wanted to do when she left school remained unsolved because next day to her delight she received an invitation from Meg Macrae, who was going to visit her mother who lived at Dunvegan on Skye. Knowing that Linda was interested in the castle, she told Nancy she would be pleased to take the girl with her as she would be company for the two younger Macraes.

"You won't say no, Nancy," Linda pleaded.

Nancy didn't say no. Ever since Logan had criticized her management of Linda she had tried to let the girl do more on her own. This was the first time Linda had been invited to go anywhere by another family and it was a good opportunity to let her off the leading rein in the company of someone as kind and as sensible as Meg. Also it would allow Nancy to have more uninterrupted time with Rod.

Without Linda it was possible that there would be less friction and they would be able to discuss their plans for the future more constructively.

Linda went off to Skye and a day later Rod and Nancy followed her, not to visit Dunvegan but to watch the Highland Games at Portree.

As they drove along the road to the Kyle of Lochalsh where they would catch the ferry that would take them to the island, they discussed what they would do when Nancy returned to Dulthorpe.

"I'll take the rest of my holiday in October, so we could be married then. That will give you a month to prepare," stated Rod. "I daresay Linda could stay with your aunt while we're on our honeymoon."

"I'm sure she could," murmured Nancy, to whom the thought of a honeymoon with Rod seemed suddenly strange.

"I hope that by then she'll have recovered from this infatuation she's developed for Maclaine," said Rod.

Nancy was surprised. She hadn't realized he had noticed.

"I think it's a sort of father fixation," she observed musingly. "After all, he is almost twice her age, and...."

She stopped, appalled by what she had just said. Rod at thirty-six was twelve years older than herself. Was it possible she had been attracted to him originally because he had, in his time, represented a father figure for her?

"Of course Linda is extremely romantic," she continued in a rush, hoping that Rod hadn't noticed the pause. "That's why Logan, with his interesting background, attracts her. She makes up all sorts of stories in which he has the part of the hero."

While she was speaking she had an uneasy feeling that she was using this explanation of Linda's infatuation as much to convince herself as to convince Rod.

"I suppose that I should be glad that you're not romantic," commented Rod. "If you were I might have cause for anxiety, since Maclaine has apparently so much in his favor."

Sensing his irritation, Nancy did not reply. She gazed out of the window at the clouds that brooded over the moun-

If Love Be Love

tains, and thought of all that Logan had in his favor. A lovely home, the accumulated wealth he had inherited from his father, the apparent time and ability to do anything that took his fancy and a quiet polite manner with a touch of arrogance. It was enough to attract any romantic female.

But she wasn't romantic, so she wasn't attracted. For a while she and Logan had formed an odd kind of friendship based on their common concern for Neil and Linda, and on the mutual liking for an old man's garden. She had learned that behind the polite manner there existed a person of warmth and gaiety who could be tender. Logan had tried to take the friendship further, but she had been unable to go with him because of her promise to marry Rod; and so Logan had withdrawn and the friendship had ended abruptly.

They were approaching the Kyle of Lochalsh and Nancy thrust all the disturbing thoughts about Logan away. Across the narrow strait of water she could see the ramparts of blue mountains whose summits were hidden by thin gray clouds. Soon the car was following a line of other tourist cars on to one of the British Railways car ferries that carried them over the water to Kyleakin. The road to Portree ran close to the sea, skirting by the Red Hills near Broadford and following the sea loch Ainort inland and out again. At the head of Loch Sligachan, a deep indentation into the towering Cuillin Mountains the road left the coast, and followed Glen Verragill. The sun appeared and shone mistily for a while, brightening the green moorland that sloped upward on either side of the road, but as they approached Portree the cloud came down again.

"I hope it doesn't rain," grumbled Rod, as they parked the car outside the entrance to the site where the games were being held. "Nothing much to do here if it does, I suppose, except visit the gift shops and take tea in a hotel. We'll go to Majorca in October and treat ourselves to some sunshine and all the best a good hotel can offer."

Again Nancy said nothing. So many times during the past few days she had felt irritated by everything Rod had said. She kept reminding herself that it was natural for him to behave differently when away from his home environment, that he wasn't usually fussy and hypercritical. But deep down she was beginning to wonder whether he wasn't always like that, only she hadn't noticed before because she had not known anyone with whom she could compare him. "How do you know he's right for you if you've never known anyone else?" Logan's words seemed to mock her because now she was comparing Rod with Logan himself.

The Games were held as always in a natural amphitheater outside the town. It was a perfect circle hollowed out of the rock by nature, covered by green grass and sheltered by clustering trees.

When Rod and Nancy arrived a fairly large crowd was already watching young girls dressed in bright kilts and black velvet jackets performing the sword dance to the music of the pipes. Finding a space among the crowd, Nancy spread her raincoat on the grass and sat down. After standing looking about him and wondering in a rather loud voice if there were any chairs to be hired, Rod sat down beside her.

The dancing came to an end and the spectators clapped. The awards to the best dancer were made. Another group of dancers arranged themselves upon the platform, the pipes started up and the dancing started again.

Fascinated by the intricate foot movements, dazed by the pipe music, Nancy sat, unaware of Rod's restlessness until he groaned, "Oh, not another lot! I'm going to stretch my legs."

She didn't prevent him from going nor did she join him. She was too absorbed in the movement and music. The skirling of the pipes stirred her blood and she felt a strong urge to get up and dance.

When it was over and the platform was removed she looked around for Rod, wishing that Linda was with her so that she could have shared the excitement with her. All around her the spectators were eating sandwiches and consuming soft drinks. Here and there a dancer would join a family group and would be praised for her prowess.

Rod came back and they shared the sandwiches she had brought, although he said he would have preferred to go into the town and to have lunch at a hotel.

"But we might miss something," said Nancy, to which

If Love Be Love

he replied that if it meant missing more dancing and piping he was not adverse to going.

There was no more dancing and the athletic competitions, including the throwing of the hammer—a feat of strength and precision that created great interest in the crowd—filled the rest of the time. It was quite obvious that the crowd had its favorite throwers, some of whom were local lads and some of whom had come from other parts of Scotland to participate. One of the throwers, Nancy was informed by a loquacious spectator sitting beside her, had been in the Olympic trials and had almost qualified for selection.

But as the afternoon wore on and the rain threatened more seriously, Rod's boredom became very noticeable. Although he always gave in to Nancy's entreaty to stay and watch just one more competition she was very conscious of his increasing impatience. The clouds grew blacker and the rain fell more heavily. The spectators began to move toward the exit and eventually the competitors left the arena and it looked as if the Games were over for the day.

"Come on, we'll go and see if we can find a decent place to have some tea. That place back along the road with the unpronounceable name looked as if it had a first class hotel," said Rod urgently. "What a washout! It was a waste of time coming and now it looks as if we're going to get soaked."

"What would we have done if we hadn't come?" countered Nancy. "You must remember there are no entertainments laid on at Lanmore that you like either. At least you've set foot on Skye, and you've seen the Cuillins."

"Have I? All I seem to have seen are heavy clouds and patches of bog," remarked Rod with heavy sarcasm.

Nancy tied her head scarf firmly under her chin, put her hands in the pockets of her raincoat and trudged after him. She had looked forward to seeing the Games and she had hoped that the day alone with Rod would have held pleasure and contentment. Instead it was dreary. There was no communication between them at all. All lines were dead.

Seeing the umbrellas and brightly colored head scarves in front of her through a blur of rain, she became aware of a wave of contrary movement through the crowd, as if someone was trying to force a passage against the flow of people toward the exit.

The person immediately in front of her moved to one side and there was Logan standing before her, his rain-soaked hair hanging in tails across his forehead, the collar of his damp tweed jacket turned up, his eyes wide open and intent, brilliant against the sallowness of his skin.

"Have you seen Neil?" he asked.

There was a shock in the sudden meeting, the shock of gladness. All around her sound was muted. Other people ceased to exist.

"No," she whispered, unable to take her eyes away from his gaze.

"I've lost him."

"Again?"

His mouth quirked in amused appreciation of her mocking question.

"He knew you were here. We saw you arrive. I thought perhaps he'd wandered off to find you."

The movement and sound of people that had stopped when they met started again like a cine film when another person joined Logan—a person whose long blond hair hung casually to her shoulders and curled slightly in the rain, and whose white-and-blue checked elephant pants fitted and flared in all the right places.

"Who is this?" asked the apparition in a low guttural voice with the slightest suggestion of a foreign accent.

Two more people appeared, a big friendly-looking man who had nondescript thinning brown hair and smiling eyes, and a small rather sulky young woman who was also dressed in the height of fashion in elephant pants and a belted high-necked raincoat patterned in psychedelic colors.

"This is Nancy Allan—Anya. My sister-in-law—Nancy," he said in his most polite manner.

"Oh. You are Neil's marigold lady. I am so glad to meet you. Neil is forever talking about you, and your sister—Lin, is it?"

The smile was charming and the attitude of pleasant interest just right.

If Love Be Love

"What are you doing, Nancy?" Rod, who must have gone on without her, had returned to find her, and he sounded impatient. "This is hardly a suitable time to be passing the time of day. You'll get drenched. Come along."

Logan swung around to stare at him and then thrust out his right hand.

"You must be Rod Ellis, Nancy's fiancé. *Failte d'on du-thaich,"* he said politely. "I am Logan Maclaine."

Looking rather nonplussed, Rod shook hands and muttered, "How do you do."

Anya laughed, a low exciting sound that Nancy suddenly decided was artificial.

"Don't mind Logan," she purred. "He's only showing off. He's welcoming you in Gaelic, Mr. Ellis. I am pleased to meet you too. I am Anya Baron, and this is Stan Black and Polly Martin."

Interest had chased the impatience from Rod's face. His blue eyes sparkled and his brilliant white smile appeared.

"Not Anya Baron, the actress?" he said, and there was a mixture of awe and admiration in his voice that was not lost upon the actress.

"The same," interposed Logan swiftly. "Only here she is Anya Maclaine, and my sister-in-law. And now we must find Neil."

No one seemed to take any notice of him as Rod, turning to Stan Black, revealed that he was not ignorant when it came to racing-car designers either. A hubbub of talk and laughter began, and the rain that still dripped down and formed puddles at their feet was ignored. Logan stood a little apart, his glance roving over the amphitheater that was now almost deserted.

"Logan," Anya called to him, "Rod has a wonderful idea. Why don't we all go and have tea at a hotel and get dry?"

"We must find Neil first," he replied stubbornly.

She pouted up at him, a well-known pout that drew attention to her full lower lip.

"But I'm soaked, darling. Rod will take us in his car and he's offered to take us back to Lanmore, so that we won't have to go back in that dreadful old boat."

"I'd be only too pleased, Maclaine," said Rod, who was obviously enjoying himself as the rescuer of Anya Baron.

"It's the best idea to date, Logan," laughed Stan. "None of us can say that a life on the ocean wave appeals to us, can we, Polly?"

The small sulky girl gave a wholly dramatic shudder and said, "Give me a car anytime!"

Logan shrugged his shoulders and said politely, "As you wish. I shall go back on *Vagabond*. I can't leave the boat here. But first, Anya, we must find Neil. After all, he is your child."

"And your responsibility as much as mine," she said sweetly, putting a hand on his arm. "I know you wouldn't like him to have an accident while he's in your care, especially when you know he is accident-prone like his father."

Logan's face went white. He shook off her hand, turned on his heel and walked away, hands in his pockets, shoulders hunched.

"What extraordinary behavior!" observed Rod into the uncomfortable silence.

"You must excuse Logan," said Stan. "He's an extraordinary character, but he always does what's right. Let him look for the child. Am I glad we met you! It'll be great to go back in comfort. Let's go and have that tea we talked about."

They all moved down the path to the exit as Rod said diffidently, "Well, it won't be exactly comfort. It'll be a bit of a squeeze with five of us."

Anya pushed a hand through the crook of his arm and laughed up at him. "Who cares? I rather like a squeeze," she said. "With the right people."

They reached the roadway. Nancy could see Logan walking up the hill in the direction of the town and she came to a sudden decision.

"I won't come with you to the hotel, Rod. I'll go and help Logan look for Neil. One person looking isn't enough."

As she started up the hill she heard him say, "But, Nancy, where shall we...."

The rest of his words were drowned in the noise of a

If Love Be Love

passing car. No one came after her to stop her. All the walking she had done at Lanmore had put her in good condition and she took the steep slope easily.

When she reached the top Logan was standing on the edge of the pavement looking lonely and rather desperate, as if trying to decide what to do next.

"I'll help you," Nancy said at his elbow. He looked at her silently. Rain ran from his hair down his nose and dripped off the end of it.

"You don't have to. I can manage," he replied distantly.

"Oh, stop being silly and... and uppity, Logan Maclaine!" she snapped. "Have you any plan, or any idea where he might be?"

"None. All I know is that when Anya said she didn't want to go back on the boat, he objected and said he intended to go back that way. It was because of him that we came by sea; also it's slightly quicker, being more direct. But I'm afraid the weather wasn't really suitable. As you've heard, my guests are not good sailors."

"Then he might have gone to the harbor," mused Nancy. "Or he might be in the police station. It would be a good idea to go there and tell the police you've lost him. You go there while I go to the harbor. When you've finished with the police you could meet me at the quayside and if neither of us has had any luck we can decide what to do next, then."

He stared across the street at a shop window as he considered her plan. Nancy waited. The rain had soaked through her head scarf and her hair felt wet. Her fringe dripped water onto her face and she wiped some of it away with her hand. But for all the discomfort she felt contented. The dreariness of spirit that she had felt earlier had gone completely.

Logan turned his head and looked at her again. His glance rested on her wet fringe. He smiled and murmured, "You're a very wet marigold. As you suggest, I'll go to the police station and you go to the harbor. I'll meet you there."

Without another word he set off across the road. Nancy watched him until he turned a corner and was hidden from her sight, then she set out to find the harbor.

It wasn't difficult to find. She went down another steeply sloping street bordered on one side by a row of houses and cottages. At the bottom of the street she turned left and saw the beach at the head of the sea loch that formed the harbor. She walked along the road that bordered the right-hand side of the loch, passing a few shops that sold postcards and other attractions for tourists. Beyond the shops were the harbor buildings.

Rain blurred the distant entrance to the long loch and wind still ruffled the surface of the water. *Vagabond* was the only boat at anchor, blue and squat, her bow pointing seaward as she rode the incoming tide.

Nancy walked the full length of the quayside but saw no sign of Neil or anyone else. The whole place seemed deserted, which was not surprising on such a wet day. She walked back in the direction of the town and took shelter in the doorway of one of the shops, occasionally peeping out to see if Logan was coming down the steep hill from the town.

It was a good half-hour before he appeared and to her relief a wet, bedraggled Neil was clutching his hand. She stepped out of her shelter and went toward them. Neil greeted her quietly with none of his usual abandon. In fact he looked rather sulky, and with his lower lip stuck out she could see he had a strong resemblance to his mother. She guessed that Logan had been scolding him for getting lost.

"You were right, he was at the police station. They'd just dug the information out of him about who he is and where he lives when I walked in. Now we'd better find the others. Do you think there'll be room in Ellis's car for all of you?"

"But I don't want to go back by car. I want to come with you," objected Neil.

"You'll do as you're told," commanded Logan briskly. "Which hotel did they go to for tea?" he asked Nancy.

"I...I don't know," she confessed weakly. "I left them before they had decided."

His eyebrows pulled together in a frown and she expected a setdown as sharp as the one he had given Neil, but before he could say anything Neil piped up again, "Nancy could come with us on *Vagabond*."

"How do you know she would want to come?" said Logan. "She came to the Games with someone else and probably wants to go back with him. You aren't the only male in her life. We'll try the Royal. I expect Anya will have taken them there as she knows it's the hotel the family usually uses when in Portree."

"Male? What's male, Uncle?" asked Neil.

Logan's explanation lasted up the hill and as far as the hotel entrance. They went in and were eyed severely by the receptionist, who was obviously not impressed by the three soaked people whose clothing dripped water onto the carpet. But a few words from Logan assured her that they were satisfactory, and she went on to suggest that the party they were searching for might be in the dining room.

As soon as they had set foot in the dining room Neil said loudly, "I'm hungry. Can we have tea?"

"They're not here," murmured Logan after looking around the room, "but perhaps it would be a good idea for us to eat."

Nancy agreed with him. She removed her head scarf and raincoat and Neil's soaked Windbreaker and hung them on the clothes rack. Logan removed his jacket too and hung it up.

They had hardly sat down when Logan said, "I wonder if they've gone to another hotel."

"I'm going to have baked beans," asserted Neil. "Baked beans on toast."

"Supposing it isn't on the menu," countered Logan absently. He was still frowning and Nancy guessed that he was disturbed by the absence of the others and wished she had had the sense to ask where they had intended to take tea.

"What's menu?" asked Neil.

Logan didn't answer, obviously deep in thought. Fortunately a waitress arrived at that moment with the menu and Nancy was able to explain to the child and to discuss with him what he might have to eat.

Logan put his menu down abruptly and rose to his feet.

"Order the mixed grill," he said. "It's always good. I'll

go and see if they're in the bar. If they're not, I'll phone the other hotels and find out if they're at one of them."

By the time he came back cups and saucers and a pot of tea had been brought and Nancy was feeling warm and relaxed. One look at Logan's face, however, made her sit up.

"They haven't been here, nor have they been to the other hotels. I think I can guess what's happened. And what annoys me most is I didn't foresee it happening. I was so concerned about Neil. I'm sorry, Nancy."

"Why?"

"Because it looks as if Anya has persuaded Rod to go back to Lanmore, leaving you to return with me."

"But why should she do that?"

"To annoy me."

"But what about the others—Mr. Black and Miss... Miss Martin? Wouldn't they be troubled about being rude? I mean, it isn't really the sort of trick you play on your host."

He smiled.

"Isn't it? Maybe not in your world, Nancy, but in theirs self always comes first. I'm not concerned about them being rude to me, after all, I did say I intended to return on *Vagabond*. It's their treatment of you that annoys me." He sighed and then smiled again rather ruefully and added, "I can't say it's been the most successful of days."

"Not for me," sighed Nancy in sympathy, thinking of Rod's numerous complaints, the way his face had lit up when he had been introduced to Anya. He must have been very impressed by her to have allowed her to persuade him to leave Nancy behind with Logan.

The food arrived. Neil received special attention from the homely waitress, who was quite smitten by his angelic blond appearance. Conscious of the admiration, the boy played up for all he was worth, much to Nancy's amusement. But her amusement soon faded when she realized Logan was watching his nephew coldly, as if he didn't like his behavior.

They ate for a while in silence. As Logan had said, the mixed grill was good and Nancy thought that if it hadn't been for the little niggling worry about the departure of the

If Love Be Love

others she would have been enjoying herself thoroughly for the first time for days.

"If Mommy and the others have gone back to Lanmore, Nancy can come with us on *Vagabond*, can't she, Uncle Logan?" said Neil complacently, almost triumphantly because he had got his own way after all.

"Yes, she'll have to," agreed Logan absently. He didn't sound particularly keen on the idea, thought Nancy whimsically. A heavy frown still marred his face and she suspected he was still annoyed by Anya's behavior, and possibly suffering from jealousy. It probably wasn't pleasant for him to have to acknowledge that the woman whom he hoped to marry preferred to drive home in someone else's company, leaving him with her child to look after. Almost as unpleasant as it was for her having to acknowledge that the man she hoped to marry preferred to drive off with a beautiful actress whom he had just met, leaving her to be taken back to Lanmore by a rather reluctant Logan.

The humorous side of the situation struck Nancy suddenly and she giggled.

"What's the joke? Tell us," commanded Neil.

Logan's frown disappeared as he added, "Yes, tell us. I could do with something to laugh at."

"It isn't exactly a joke. It's—oh, the whole situation is so funny, almost farcical."

"Far... far... what's that?" asked Neil.

"Another word for funny," replied Logan. "And I wish you'd pipe down. You're always joining in other people's conversations. Go on, Nancy. What is so farcical?"

With a sympathetic glance at Neil, who scowled at his uncle's sharp but necessary rejoinder, Nancy went on, "We—I mean, my fiancé has gone off with...." She remembered with a sudden shock that Neil might not know of any arrangement between his mother and his uncle to marry and that, in fact, all she knew was a vague reference to the possibility of their marriage by Mary Maclaine. So she said no more.

"Not so funny, after all," said Logan softly. She shook her head and whispered, "No."

He frowned again.

"Poor Nancy, what a way to end your day out. Never mind, we'll soon put it right," he said consolingly. "Now if you have both finished eating we'll go aboard *Vagabond* immediately and if we're lucky we might reach Lanmore before the others."

Feeling frustrated because she had been unable to explain her real reasons for laughing because of Neil's presence, realizing that Logan had misunderstood, Nancy was quiet on the way to the boat. The rain had abated a little and the wind had dropped. They rowed out to the squat two-masted cruiser in a sturdy varnished dinghy that Logan hauled out of the water with the davits that hung over the stern of the yacht.

Going below, they all dried their wet faces and hair on towels that Logan produced from a locker. He found some oilskins for Nancy and an old sweater for her to wear under them. For Neil there was an old raincoat several sizes too large. After dressing in oilskins himself Logan started the engine, instructed Nancy to hold the wheel and then went up to the bow to winch up the anchor. When he had done that he returned to the cockpit, took the wheel from her and turned *Vagabond*'s bow toward the entrance of the sea loch.

The visibility wasn't very good and all that Nancy saw of the island of Raasay was a looming gray shape on their right as the boat sped swiftly south with the tide under her. Soon the rain increased again and Logan ordered her to take Neil into the cabin where she attempted to entertain him with stories and guessing games. She was just wondering what to do with him when she could think of no more games when the engine coughed and sputtered ominously and stopped. Immediately Logan called to her, asking her to go up into the cockpit.

"What's happened?" she asked, her mind going back to the time the car engine had stopped on the narrow road to Glenarg.

"Water in the petrol," replied Logan unconcernedly, as if it was a common occurrence on *Vagabond*.

"Can you do anything about it?" she asked anxiously.

"Yes. But I'll hoist a sail first to keep the boat from drift-

If Love Be Love

ing. There's a faint breath of wind now and that should keep us moving slowly while I fix the engine. Do you think you can steer?"

Nancy looked around at the gray water, at the gray islands. They were in a narrow strait of water and she realized that if the boat was allowed to drift it might go aground on one of the bleak deserted shores.

"I'll try," she answered faintly.

Neil was quite excited at the thought of using sail and he wanted to help Logan to hoist it. However, Logan ordered him to stay in the cockpit, explaining that while he and Nancy were both busy, the boy had to take the responsibility of looking after himself. Neil accepted this argument without complaint and sat as close to Nancy as he could while he watched his uncle pull up the fluttering white sail.

Under the wide old-fashioned cotton sail *Vagabond* moved slowly but surely between the intimidating shores of the islands of Raasay and Scalpay into the wider water of the inner sound.

"Can you see those two humps over there?" asked Logan, pointing into the gray murk.

Nancy could barely make out the faint outlines of what seemed to be two rocks jutting up out of the sea.

"Yes, I can," she replied.

"Then steer in that direction. It's a straight run from here with the wind behind us. But you won't have to sail for long. I'll soon clear the water out of the carburetor and the engine will start again," Logan asserted confidently.

The engine did start again and once more *Vagabond* pushed through the water toward the two humps. The sail was left up, although it did not help at all because with the thrust of the engine the slight amount of wind was soon shaken out of it.

Fifteen minutes later the engine stopped again. Nancy took the wheel and steered. The clouds were growing darker in color as the night approached, but she could still see the two humps that had grown larger and had changed shape. Logan tinkered with the engine and put in new plugs, muttering something about Ian Macrae not having done his job properly the last time he had overhauled it.

It started again, ran sluggishly for a short time and stopped. Logan went below again, but not for long. When he returned to the cockpit he took the wheel from Nancy.

"While this wind holds we'll try and make it to the islands," he said. "We can anchor between them. It's quite sheltered there. Then I'll empty the petrol tank. It's the only way to get rid of all the water. I have a spare can of petrol on board that should be free of water."

"It's going dark," moaned Neil, "and I'm tired."

"Then you shall go to bed," said Logan. "How would you like to sleep in a hammock in the fo'c'sle, in a sleeping bag, like a real sailor?"

Neil thought that it might be a good idea and asked if his daddy had ever done that.

"Often," was the reply. "In the same hammock."

This answer satisfied the boy and Nancy had no difficulty in persuading him to go down into the cabin and then through to the smaller cabin in the bow of the boat. There he climbed into the sleeping bag quite happily and snuggled down. For a few minutes Nancy told him yet another story, but she wasn't required for long. Tired out by his adventures and the sea air, Neil was soon asleep.

When Nancy returned on deck she found that the two humps were much closer and that they had now become two separate islands. Logan was guiding the slowly moving boat directly at the narrow strip of water that divided them. The entrance was so narrow that Nancy had difficulty in believing that *Vagabond* could get through without going aground or without touching the rocks, but the old boat slid past gently, the strip of water widened into a bay and Logan was able to turn the boat into the wind so that the sail flapped and it came to a stop. Then, leaving Nancy to hold the wheel steady, he went forward to let down the anchor.

The light was fading fast and all Nancy could see of the island was a slightly tilted plateau of rock that afforded protection from the wind and rain. Behind her the other island was similarly tilted and would provide the same sort of protection if the wind should change.

Logan stepped down into the cockpit beside her.

"We shall stay the night here," he announced firmly.

"Visibility is bad and it's now dark. I would prefer not to take any risks with you and Neil on board. I hope you understand."

There flashed into Nancy's mind a picture of his white face when Anya had made the gibe about Neil being accident-prone like his father and she said simply, "I understand."

"We shall motor home in the morning," he said, paused and then added rather hesitantly, "I'm sorry, Nancy, for the second time today. I should have hired a car in Portree and taken you and Neil back to Lanmore in a civilized way."

"But if you had, Neil and I would have missed this adventure," she answered cheerfully. "You must remember I'm used to engines breaking down and being stranded."

"So you are... not that I'd forgotten our second meeting. Now you'd better take one of the sleeping bags and turn in."

"No, I shan't," she replied. "I'm going to search in the lockers to see if I can find anything with which to make us a hot drink."

He lit the Tilley lamp for her and then disappeared into the cockpit, saying he would empty the fuel tank and fill it with fresh petrol from the spare can.

Nancy knew from her previous visits to the yacht that the food locker was well stocked with canned goods and she soon found a tin of evaporated milk that she poured into a pan, added water and placed on the Primus cooker to heat through. When it was hot she poured the liquid into two mugs and spooned powdered chocolate into them.

By that time Logan was back in the cabin and trying to start the engine again. It did not start. He accepted the mug she offered to him and sat on a settee berth to drink it. He sat in silence staring all the time at the casing that covered the engine. When he had finished his drink he thanked her absently and handed her the empty mug, then began to remove his oilskins. He opened a locker and brought out a tool box, then, pushing back his sweater sleeves, he began to remove the engine casing. He worked silently, completely absorbed in what he was doing, examining parts of the engine. And Nancy sat on the settee berth behind him watching and waiting, wondering why it was she could sit so patiently doing nothing, saying nothing.

Eventually Logan fitted the last piece back on the engine, replaced the casing and pressed the starting button. The engine started at once. He turned around and grinned at her.

"A case of patience being rewarded, I suppose," said Nancy.

"And knowing a little about engines," he replied, stopping the engine and coming to sit beside her on the berth. "It was the distributor that was sooty and so the electrical parts were not working properly. There was water in the petrol, too."

"You seem to know such a lot about so many different things—sheep and bees and how to milk cows, and now how to repair engines," commented Nancy.

"My knowledge is all the result of a misspent youth and no shortage of money, of which I'm sure you really disapprove," he said facetiously. "I expect your intended is much more knowledgeable than I am, and he's probably better educated, too."

"I wish you wouldn't call him that," retaliated Nancy. For the past few hours she had forgotten Rod.

"It's what he is... your intended husband."

"I know, but you say it to make fun," she accused.

"There are times when I have to make fun, to make life bearable," he murmured obscurely. "You realize, I suppose, that our absence from Lanmore tonight is going to cause consternation?"

"You mean that your sister-in-law won't be pleased?"

"No, I wasn't thinking of Anya particularly. After all, if she had come with me to find Neil and to look after him, she would have been here with me instead of you, so she has only herself to blame if she's worried," he remarked.

And he probably would have preferred Anya's companionship to hers, thought Nancy.

"She's very lovely," she said, speaking her thoughts aloud.

"Yes, she is," he agreed. "More lovely now than when I first met her eight years ago, when she was an unknown

If Love Be Love

actress in repertory." There was a brief silence and then he added, "I wish I'd never introduced her to Angus, my brother."

"But he would have met her anyway."

"Not necessarily. I didn't introduce everyone I met to him."

"I suppose if you hadn't you might have married her yourself."

He turned to glance at her.

"Might I? Whoever put that idea into your head?"

Nancy flushed at the implication that she had been gossiping about him.

"Mary has really gone to town when she has talked to you, hasn't she?" he said dryly. "I wonder what it is about you, Nancy Allan, that makes people want to confide in you?"

"Well, I certainly haven't inspired you to confide in me," she retorted defensively. "How can you expect anyone to understand you if you never say anything about yourself?"

His mouth tightened and he looked away from her.

"What do you want to know that you haven't learned already?" he asked in a low voice.

"Why do you feel so responsible for Neil?"

"I've told you, I'm his guardian."

"That isn't the only reason," she persisted, thinking of the way he had flinched at Anya's cutting remark that afternoon.

"It's because I was to blame for Angus's death. I killed him. Isn't that reason enough?"

He turned on her as he spoke and his voice was harsh. Nancy swallowed and asked quietly, "How?"

For a moment he looked at her as if he hated her, and she would not have been surprised if he had refused to answer her question. Then he leaned against the back of the berth, folded his arms across his chest and began to speak in a cold flat monotone.

"Someone suggested to my brother that Anya was having an affair with another man, and implied that the man was me. The suggestion was made just before the start of a

Formula One race at Silverstone over two years ago. Angus and I were competing as teammates in cars designed by Stan. He came to me and accused me five minutes before the race was due to begin."

"Was there any truth in the suggestion?" Somehow it was important that she should know the answer to that question.

He shrugged as if he couldn't have cared less.

"There might have been, but the man wasn't me."

"Did you tell your brother that, or did you look at him and through him as if he was a fool?"

He turned to look at her again and surprise widened his eyes.

"Have I done that to you?" he asked curiously.

"You often do it...to everyone. It's...it's infuriating!"

"Possibly I did because I didn't see why I should have to deny such an accusation. He should have known me well enough to have realized that I wouldn't have an affair with his wife. As it was I said nothing because I wasn't going to argue with him just before the race. He was worked up enough as it was, and was too emotionally disturbed to race. I said as much to Stan, who tried to stop Angus from participating—without any luck."

"And what happened?"

"Don't you know? I thought it was common knowledge. If Mary hasn't told you, surely someone else on Lanmore has enlightened you," he said bitterly.

"Logan, please understand. No one has said anything about it. Mary and Don have only ever mentioned that there was an accident and that your brother was killed. You don't have to tell me any more. I think I understand now about Neil," said Nancy gently.

"No, you don't. You can't until I tell you the rest. I might as well go on," he answered flatly. "I was in the lead. After a bad start Angus came up behind me. I knew he would try to pass me, but I thought he would wait until we were on the straight. Instead he pulled out to pass as we were going around a bend. Then he cut in in front of me too sharply. I couldn't brake fast enough and the front of my machine hit the back of his, turned it off the track and down an embank-

If Love Be Love

ment. He died on the way to hospital. I was with him and I think a bit of me died with him. He spoke to me once only and that was to ask me to take care of Neil."

He paused and there was silence in the cabin broken only by the sputtering of the Tilley lamp.

"It was my fault. I didn't brake soon enough. I gave up racing because I'd caused an accident," he added in that cold flat voice.

"But couldn't it have been his fault? Didn't he cut in too sharply? Isn't it possible that his jealousy of you impaired his judgment?" said Nancy urgently, suddenly distressed to realize how much the accident had affected him. Mary had been right when she had said he brooded about it. "Jealousy is a very powerful emotion."

"Is it?"

He was suddenly very remote and polite and she guessed he did not like her suggestion that his brother could have been at fault. So she said no more and stared at the Tilley lamp.

The boat rocked gently and waves lapped at its hull as a slight breeze disturbed the water. It was a peaceful setting for the violent story she had just heard, a story that had opened another world up where temperament was an important factor and often meant the difference between life and death. Probably if Angus Maclaine had possessed a different temperament he would have been alive today, and Logan would not have been the lonely aloof person that he had become.

She glanced at him. He was still leaning back. His eyes were closed and there was a smudge of engine oil on one high cheekbone. She had a sudden longing to put her arms around him and comfort him as she had often comforted Neil. Shaken by the urge, she looked back at the lamp quickly. The bright light hurt her eyes, so she closed them tightly. It was a good way to prevent the tears that had gathered from falling too.

The feel of a hand touching her hair made her stiffen slightly. The hand was removed immediately and Logan drawled, "Your hair is still very wet. If you'll pass me the towel, I'll rub it dry for you."

Startled by his suggestion, she put a hand to her hair. It was wet, but it would not be wise to let him dry it. That would involve too much close contact and under the circumstances she didn't think she could trust her own reactions.

"Oh, no, thank you," she replied lightly. "I can dry it myself."

He smiled sleepily at her, stifled a yawn, stretched his arms above his head and then without any warning leaned forward and placed a hand on either side of her face as he had done when he had taken the sting from her face. Held captive, Nancy could only gaze at him wonderingly.

"I've missed you," he murmured.

"That's a tall tale, if ever there was one," she countered shakily. "You couldn't have missed me. You went away with your friends."

"Even so, I missed you. Did you miss me?"

All she could see was her reflection in the dark pupils of his eyes.

"That's rather a leading question," she replied, still trying to keep the whole situation on an even keel. "You don't really expect me to answer it, do you?"

He did not reply. His gaze went deliberately to her mouth and she guessed his intention.

"No, Logan, I didn't miss you," she said clearly, and saw his mouth quirk with amusement.

"I think differently," he mocked. "And I still have to thank you for helping me to find Neil."

Did he know that it was impossible for her to move when he held her that way?

"I did very little."

"It was more help than I've ever received before from anyone, and so I must thank you properly," he said softly. He kissed her gently and briefly on the mouth, then moved away and stood up so quickly she had no time to respond.

"Neither you nor anyone else could call that taking advantage," he observed mockingly. "Nor should it offend your principles. And to make sure you'll be able to inform your intended quite truthfully that we observed the proprieties—because I've a feeling he'll want to know every detail of our nocturnal adventure—I shall sleep up forward with Neil. Good night."

It was the longest night Nancy had ever known. She tried to convince herself that her sleeplessness was caused by the fact that she was lying on a narrow bunk in the darkened cabin of a boat that possessed its own strange noises and movements. But she found that no matter how hard she tried to find a new position in which to relax, and no matter how hard she tried to make her mind a blank, the memory of the moment when Logan had appeared in front of her at the Games kept leaping into her thoughts.

Why had she been so glad to see him? What had the upsurge of happiness she had experienced meant? Had it been merely associated with the recognition of a friend in a crowd of anonymous people? Or was it possible that the spontaneous delight that she had felt on meeting him unexpectedly was based on something deeper than friendship?

She hastily buried the betraying thought, reminding herself sternly that Logan did not belong to her normal way of life. He belonged to Lanmore, and after September Lanmore would be only the place where her brother lived and which she might visit occasionally in the future.

He belonged to an entirely different world from hers; a world of large estates, of wealth, of fast cars and beautiful actresses. And if it hadn't been for a child who persistently lost himself she would probably have never come into close contact with him.

CHAPTER FIVE

EVENTUALLY SLEEP CLAIMED NANCY and she slept deeply. It was the throbbing noise of the engine that awoke her. For a while she lay with her eyes closed, reluctant to face a day that she knew would be complicated by explanations and suspicion. How lovely it would be if she did not have to return immediately, if she and Logan and Neil could cruise among the islands for a few days. She let her imagination roam and saw herself with Logan walking hand in hand on the white sands of some remote Hebridean beach. She saw them diving into the cool shadowy underworld of the sea where the tall weeds were wafted by currents and the silver fishes drifted by.

She opened her eyes and sat up. Whatever was the matter with her? Such imaginings were pure escapism, romantic fantasy in which she never normally indulged. She left that sort of thing to Linda. Noticing that the sun was shining brightly, she struggled out of the sleeping bag and pulled on the skirt and sweater she had been wearing the day before, thinking how peculiar it was to be on a boat wearing a skirt instead of trousers.

Going forward, she used the small washroom and then pushed open the door that divided the boat into two cabins. Neil was still fast asleep, flat on his back, his arms flung out on either side of him, his blond hair tousled. Moving quietly, Nancy went back into the main cabin and looked through a porthole. Under a blue sky the sea shimmered with rose-dappled golden light and she could see high mountains, the Cuillins of Skye glowing pink against the sky beyond the green island of Raasay.

The urge to see more made her hurry up the short companionway into the cockpit where Logan greeted her with a cool, polite good-morning.

If Love Be Love

"What a lovely morning," she replied, gazing around at sea, island and mountains. "Oh, we're almost home!"

Ahead of the boat she could see Lanmore Bay and the white of the Lodge nestling against the dark green trees.

"Home," echoed Logan. "Is that how you think of Lanmore?"

She turned to smile at him.

"While I live there I do. Shall I wake Neil?"

"No, leave him. He had quite a tiring day yesterday."

"You should have wakened me when you wanted to set off. I could have helped," she said.

"I didn't waken you for the same reason that I didn't waken Neil—you were sleeping soundly. Only children and those with a clear conscience sleep like that."

The thought that he had observed her while she was sleeping made her glance at him sharply to see if he was making fun of her. Above the turtleneck of his dark blue sweater his chin was dark with stubble. There were lines under his eyes as if he hadn't slept much and his hair needed brushing. His appearance was not exactly prepossessing and yet she would not have preferred any other companion on that serene morning. It seemed to her that they were the only two people alive and awake in a colorful, beautiful world.

"Are you ready to face the storm that is bound to break about our heads?" he asked, with an ironic twist to his mouth.

"What storm?"

"I may be mistaken, but I think your fiancé might be a little displeased by your nocturnal absence, and the fact that you spent the night aboard *Vagabond* with me."

"He might be worried," conceded Nancy, "but he can hardly be displeased. Once he realizes that it was accidental, that we couldn't help being delayed, he...." A sudden thought occurred to her and she broke off abruptly, then asked an urgent question. "It was accidental, wasn't it?"

"It was," he agreed gravely.

"And I hope," continued Nancy, her mind at ease once more, "that Rod knows me well enough to know that I wouldn't..." she hesitated.

"To know that you wouldn't kiss another man while engaged to him," Logan put in with a mischievous grin. The grin faded and he remarked seriously, "Complete trust. Is that what there is between you? I hope so, because:

> "In love, if love be love, if love be ours,
> Faith and unfaith can ne'er be equal powers.
> Unfaith in aught is want of faith in all."

Nancy looked away over the dimpled water. They were passing a small rocky islet, one of a string that guarded the entrance to Lanmore Bay. As they passed she noticed the heads of several gray seals bob down under the water, and on the rock other seals basked and played in the sunshine.

What would Logan say if she told him it was she who was beginning to have doubts about her relationship with Rod, and that already a rot had set in and she was beginning to wonder if she knew what love was?

But she said nothing of her thoughts. Instead she commented idly, "You seem to like poetry. Who wrote that?"

"Tennyson. Not one of my favorites, but he sometimes provides the right word at the right moment. Poetry is so often the quintessence of thought or feeling. Don't you know any?"

"A little. I haven't had much time to read any. I wouldn't know where to start."

"Then when winter comes...."

He didn't finish the sentence. The wheel turned under his hands and *Vagabond* altered course slightly. Nancy waited for him to continue, but he did not speak, nor did he look at her. He seemed to have forgotten what he was going to say and she was just about to question him when he said tersely, "Wake Neil now. We're almost there."

Puzzled by the brief conversation and even more puzzled by his withdrawal, Nancy went and woke the boy, who was full of questions and who seemed quite disappointed when she told him they were almost at Lanmore.

"I wish I could stay on the boat forever and ever. I like being with you and Uncle Logan. He isn't cross when you're with us," he said.

If Love Be Love

"I'm sure he's never cross," said Nancy.

"Yes, he is. He gets cross with Mommy. Yesterday he was rude to her."

"I can't believe that. Your uncle is always very polite."

"I know he was rude because Mommy told him not to be," replied the child stubbornly.

Logan angry enough to be rude. Logan shaken out of his cool manner. Logan expressing violent emotion with violent words. Anya was capable of rousing him, as Nancy had seen, by his reaction to her spiteful words about accidents when Neil was lost in Skye. And why could she rouse him? Nancy could find only one answer. It was because he was in love with Anya that she could hurt him.

Nancy's spirits plummeted suddenly, causing her to be silent as they came to the end of their voyage. Silently she obeyed Logan's instruction and went up to the bow with the boathook to pick up the mooring buoy.

Sitting in the dinghy opposite Logan as they went ashore she stared over his shoulder at Lanmore Lodge, at the two figures that waited at the water's edge. While she had been on *Vagabond* she had been happy because she had been with the person she had wanted to be with most. As soon as they touched land again they would be parted by people, by problems. With her usual honesty in facing up to reality Nancy faced the truth squarely, but for the first time in her life her courage wavered, causing her to bite her lip and to frown.

The oars stopped their rhythmical movement. A hand was closed over hers where they rested on her knees and she heard Neil say from the bow of the dinghy, "Why have you stopped, uncle? I can see mommy. She's waving to me."

Then Logan's deeper voice said quietly, "Don't be worrying, Nancy. I shall do all the explaining."

She looked at him. His eyes were bright and intent. They stared at each other and once again time stood still, as it had when they had met the previous day at the Games. And in that timeless moment Nancy realized that it was possible she was in love with Logan and not in love with Rod. Realization came as a shock and her first reaction was to reject the idea as ridiculous. That sort of thing did not happen to practical, realistic people like herself. Annoyed with herself for behaving no better than Linda, she pulled her hands from under his in a gesture of rejection and said coolly, "I'm not worried. I have nothing to worry about. I can explain for myself. Rod will understand. You'll have enough explaining to do to your sister-in-law."

Her words did the trick. They broke the spell. He began to row again, and the timeless moment of wonder was over. Logan's face wore its customary closed polite expression. He said lightly with an indifferent shrug, "As you wish."

At once Nancy felt painful stirrings of remorse. Thinking that she was very concerned about Rod's reaction to her nocturnal escapade, Logan had offered to shoulder the full responsibility for the explanation. He wanted to shield her from blame and she had rejected his offer curtly in her effort to hide her confusion. Again she looked at the bulky blue ramparts of the familiar mountains on the other side of Loch Arg and tried to pretend that their clear outline was not blurred by unexpected tears.

Within minutes the dinghy was beached and she was being helped to step ashore by Stan Black. Anya greeted her son effusively, kneeling on the sand to embrace him, crooning over him in her deep guttural voice.

"Don't overdo the anxious-mother act, Anya," gibed Logan nastily. "He's been perfectly all right."

Anya, who was as lovely in the early morning as she had been in the rain of the previous afternoon, released Neil, and kneeling back on her heels, looked up.

"But I have been anxious, darling—about you, too." She scrambled to her feet and added with a winning smile, "Oh, is that why you're sour? I did not say so...and you are jealous."

Going up to Logan, she flung her arms around his neck and kissed him. "I was very anxious," she repeated in a low voice, then, turning to look at Nancy, she said, "About you too, Nancy. You have come to no harm, I hope?"

Nancy smiled. Her face felt stiff and she had never felt less like smiling.

If Love Be Love

"I'm fine, thank you. We had a very peaceful night in a perfect anchorage."

"A very peaceful night," repeated Anya with irony. "That is more than we can say, isn't it, Stan?"

"I can't say I lost much sleep," grinned Stan. "I had a feeling Logan would turn up sooner or later. He always does."

"Were you really anxious, Anya?" Logan's voice was still sharp. Anya's embrace did not seem to have pacified him.

"Of course. I was thinking of my little Neil." She fondled the child's blond hair.

Neil immediately spoiled the effect by acting perfectly naturally, jerking his head away from her caress and saying, "I'm hungry. I want my breakfast. Can I go and see Aunt Mary? She had lovely cereal for breakfast. Can I, mommy, can I?"

"It's a pity you didn't show more anxiety yesterday, then, when he was lost. Why didn't you stay in Portree until we had found him?" asked Logan in that same caustic way.

Anya pouted at him and linked an arm through his in a manner that Nancy found familiar. Anya had behaved in the same way toward Rod the previous day. Perhaps she hoped by physical contact to allay Logan's anger.

"You are in a foul mood, darling. Maybe, unlike Nancy, you did not have a peaceful night. Come and have breakfast and you will feel better and then I shall explain."

"You can tell me now why you didn't wait in Portree for Neil and Nancy."

Anya's smile had a seraphic quality very reminiscent of Neil's.

"I believe you are really jealous this time. I forget why we did not wait. Do you know, Stan?"

Stan looked rather troubled and muttered, "Someone had said something about the hotel at Sligachan, so we went on there."

"That's right," said Anya as if she found it a satisfactory explanation. "We thought you'd send Neil and Nancy to Lanmore in a taxi. We didn't think you'd take them on *Vagabond*. Poor Rod, he has been terribly worried about Nancy."

"Why?" Logan's voice was ominously quiet.

"Well, you have to admit it was rather disconcerting for him. His fiancée walked off, then disappeared into the blue with another man and didn't turn up all night. Don't you think so?"

Anya's gaze roved over Nancy's crumpled skirt and sweater and in spite of her efforts to remain calm and unconcerned Nancy could feel her temper rising. Anya's description of what had happened was insinuating and it was quite obvious that she wanted to lay the blame for the whole episode on Nancy.

"If you had remained in Portree until we had found Neil or had even offered to help me find him the situation would not have arisen," replied Logan. "It seems to me that you're playing a strange game."

Anya's glance wavered under his direct stare, but not for long. Her smile was bland and beautiful as she retaliated, "But not as strange as yours, darling. Were you hoping to make me jealous, too?"

Exasperation with this comment darkened Logan's face. Without a word he flung off Anya's hand and turned and walked away as he had the day before. Pleased that someone had at last shown an interest in moving toward the house and food, Neil ran after him shouting, "Wait for me, wait for me!"

"You will excuse me, Nancy, Stan, while I go and see if I can placate Logan. He is difficult to manage, that one, and always I say the wrong thing."

She went off, running lightly and gracefully. Side by side Nancy and Stan began to walk after her.

"For a person who's been at sea all night you're looking remarkably none the worse for wear, which is more than can be said for Logan," remarked Stan affably. "What happened out there?"

Nancy explained briefly and he nodded.

"Quite feasible. Logan wouldn't have so much of that trouble if he installed a diesel engine on that tub, as I was telling him yesterday. Anyway, your reason for not turning up is a much better one than ours for having deserted you and for having left you to Logan's tender mercies. We're all

If Love Be Love 141

to blame, but Anya more than the rest of us. She fairly dazzled your fiancé so that he didn't know whether he was coming or going. I can't make out what she hoped to achieve, unless it was to make Logan jealous as she suggested. She's hoping he'll propose marriage while she's staying here."

"Do you think he will?" asked Nancy.

"I'm hoping he won't. But Anya has a big pull with him in the person of Neil."

"In what way?"

"The child needs a father, and Logan knows that. The fact that Neil is Angus's only son weighs very heavily with him."

"Yes, I realize that. Why are you hoping he won't propose marriage? If he marries Anya the problem will be solved," asked Nancy, who was puzzled by his offhand statements.

"Because Anya and I have an arrangement that I don't want spoiling."

Nancy blinked.

"Then why don't you marry her?"

"I don't want to be a father... not even a stepfather," he replied with a rueful grin. "I'm not cut out for it any more than Anya is to be a mother. I'm far too selfish and engrossed in my career. Anya and I make a good couple because neither of us expects too much of the other. It would suit me very well if Logan took over the upbringing of Neil and left me with the task of looking after Anya."

Feeling bewildered by his unusual attitude to life and by his frank admissions, Nancy asked another question.

"Mr. Black, I wonder if you could tell me something about Logan. You must have known him for a long time."

"Ten years. I'll try. And the name is Stan, Nancy."

"Do you think he was responsible for the accident that killed his brother?"

Stan took his time. They were close to the house and he stopped walking and turned to look back at the view. Nancy stood beside him waiting.

"I guessed that it had been on his mind," he said at last. "I take it that he told you that was the way of it, did he?"

Nancy nodded.

"And I suppose that's the way most people looked at it at the time, especially when he decided to give up racing altogether," continued Stan. "But those of us who knew both brothers well knew that Logan was the better driver of the two and the one least likely to make a mistake. He's always been calm and extremely disciplined. He never did anything that might cloud his judgment when he was racing. He didn't marry because he felt that not only would it be unfair to his wife when his way of life was so dangerous but also because he felt that the emotional involvement might affect his driving. While racing was his love no woman stood a chance with him, although that's not to say that he didn't like the opposite sex."

Stan wrinkled his brow as if wondering how to go on. Nancy prompted him, "And Angus?"

"Very different. Brilliant and unstable and as jealous as hell of Logan. Used to take unnecessary risks. We were always warning him. His greater mistake was in marrying Anya. He was never sure of her and I suppose you could say that it was she who was responsible for his death. He was suspicious of her and in a bad state just before that race. Wild enough to take chances when he shouldn't; and he was determined to beat Logan because he had had a series of poor races while Logan had been successful."

"Then he could have made a mistake by cutting in too sharply," said Nancy.

"That's exactly what he did. A grave error of judgment. No one driving behind him could have missed hitting him. But it had to be Logan."

"Yes, it had to be Logan," repeated Nancy sadly, as she thought of Logan's version of the accident and the way in which it had affected his attitude to life.

"Have I told you what you wanted to know?" asked Stan, glancing at her shrewdly.

"Yes, thank you. It's a pity that Logan still thinks he was entirely to blame."

"I suppose it is, but I think he's recovering. This place has helped." He waved an arm toward the house and the land surrounding it. "It's absorbing his interest now. And

If Love Be Love

that reminds me—there's just one flaw in Anya's plan to marry him. He wants to live here and she doesn't. She prefers London, quite naturally. That's all. Think about it. And now you'd better go in and have some breakfast."

There was no time to think immediately about Stan's suggestion, because as soon as they entered the house Mary Maclaine appeared.

"Now, my dear," she said to Nancy, "you must be longing to have a wash and something to eat. Let me show you where the bathroom is and then you must come to the morning room. Logan has phoned your brother. Don said he would come around straightaway with your fiancé."

In the well-appointed bathroom Nancy washed her hands and face and brushed her hair. Looking at herself in the mirror it seemed to her that her face was thinner, its expression was more controlled, and her reflected eyes did not meet her gaze quite as frankly as usual.

"You look like someone with a secret," she murmured critically, as she tried to look herself in the eyes. But it was no use. She could no longer face herself because she was afraid of what she might read in her own eyes.

She turned away from the mirror quickly and, leaving the bathroom, made her way to the morning room, hoping that Don would not be too long. She would be very glad to see one of her own kin again. She was not so sure about meeting Rod, however.

Neil was sitting at the table with Mary Maclaine. He was spooning up cereal and chattering about his adventure to her. Anya was prowling up and down the room, her hands on her shapely hips. She was smoking, holding a long cigarette holder between her lips.

As Nancy entered the room Mary looked up and then stood up.

"Now I'm sure you feel much better. Sit down here while I serve you," she said warmly. "Would you like cereal and fruit juice first? Logan said I was to look after you and see that you had an adequate meal."

"Nancy is well able to look after herself, I should imagine," drawled Anya. She stopped prowling to stand by the table opposite to Nancy and stared down at her with narrowed hostile eyes. The hostility jolted Nancy, who stared back while she answered Mary.

"I should like cereal, please, and tea if there is any," she said.

Anya leaned her arms on the back of a chair and continued to stare. The smoke from her cigarette rose upward in a straight gray stream. Behind her the curtains at the open window stirred slightly. Through the window Nancy could see the curved branches of larch trees.

"I'll go and get fresh tea," said Mary, and left the room, followed by Neil who was still chattering to her.

"Have you been living on Lanmore long?" Anya asked.

"Since the end of April," replied Nancy as she scattered sugar on her cereal. She started to eat, conscious that Anya was still staring at her.

"Do you like it?"

"Yes, very much."

"I wonder whether it is the place you like... or the laird?" There was a wealth of insinuation underlying the seemingly harmless question and Nancy looked up quickly. Anya's beautiful tawny eyes were still hostile as she drew on her cigarette.

"You are surprised by my question?" continued Anya silkily. "You have no need to answer it. Your feelings were clearly expressed on your face when you and Logan met yesterday at the Games."

Nancy drew in her breath sharply and put down the spoon she was using. She could eat no more. She wished fervently that Don would arrive and that she could leave the house.

"Not hungry?" asked Anya mockingly. "Mary will be disappointed. I'm sorry if I spoilt your appetite, but I thought I must make it clear to you that it would be unwise for you to develop a grand passion for Logan."

Nancy's pride awoke and came to her rescue. Head held high, her brown eyes ablaze, she answered, "I'm not the sort of person who develops grand passions for men I scarcely know," she flashed. "And you seem to have forgotten an important point: I'm engaged to be married. Might I suggest that instead of concerning yourself about my affairs and the state of my emotions you would do better to pay more attention to your child?"

Anya's face hardened as she stubbed out her cigarette in an ashtray.

"You are presumptuous," she said coldly.

"No more than you are," retorted Nancy, who was beginning to feel better. "And in answer to your question as to whether it's the place I like or the laird, I can answer that it's the place. Logan Maclaine means no more to me than the...the—" she searched for a comparison and came up with a wild one "—than the moon!" she finished.

"An interesting comparison, because that is exactly how I feel sometimes—like the man in the moon, on the outside looking in." Logan's voice was light and whimsical as he approached the table.

Nancy cringed inwardly. How long had he been there? How much had he heard of the conversation? Across the table Anya's eyes gleamed triumphantly. She turned to Logan and said, "Darling, at last! Do you feel better now? What can I get for you? Mary has gone to get more tea for Nancy, but there is coffee in the percolator."

"Coffee will do, and whatever there is that's cooked," he replied carelessly as he sat down opposite Nancy. "What are you going to eat, Nancy?"

She looked at him. He had bathed and shaved and had changed his clothes. His hair was damp and it curled a little. He was wearing a blue checked shirt and a red neckerchief was knotted around his neck inside the open collar of his shirt. As usual he looked casually elegant and his eyes were blank and impersonal under their lazy lids.

"I'm not hungry, thank you," she replied.

"I can see that Anya has a reason for dieting, but not you. Finish your cereal and then have some bacon and eggs or whatever else there is on the hot plate."

He must have heard the conversation, Nancy decided, and now he was being deliberately and coolly polite, behaving as if nothing unusual had been said.

Anya set a full plate in front of him with a housewifely air especially created for the occasion.

"I'm not going to force Nancy to eat if she doesn't want

to," she said. "And you are very unkind about my diet, darling."

She stood beside Logan, a hand resting lightly but possessively on his shoulder, all part of her wifely act. Nancy ate the rest of her cereal. It tasted of chaff.

The sound of voices heralded the reappearance of Mary Maclaine carrying a teapot. She was followed into the room by Don and Rod.

"Here's your tea at last, Nancy. Sorry to be so long. Would you like a cup, Don, and Mr., er, Ellis?"

"Yes, please," said Don. "Hello, Nancy. Are you all right?" He sounded very brotherly and quite unconcerned as he grinned down at her and Nancy had a strong inclination to hug him. Instead she smiled back and said, "I'm fine."

"There, I told you, Rod, that there was nothing to worry about," said Don, in his best "I told you so" manner.

Rod, who had been staring at Nancy intently, ignored Don's statement and asked, "What happened, Nancy? Where have you been?"

"On *Vagabond* with Logan and Neil," she replied shortly. She had told Logan she could do her own explaining, but now, faced with Rod's searching suspicious gaze, she found she did not want to explain.

"Now do sit down, both of you, and be comfortable," said Mary as she placed two cups of tea on the table.

Rod and Don sat down obediently one on either side of Nancy.

"Is that all you have to say?" persisted Rod. "I don't call it a very satisfactory explanation."

"It's the truth," she retorted.

"Maybe it is, but there must be more to it than that. It doesn't take all night to cross from Skye to the mainland. Perhaps you have something to say, Maclaine?"

Logan finished what he was eating, placed his knife and fork carefully on his plate and wiped his mouth on a table napkin before replying. Then he gave Rod one of his disdainful stares and said laconically, "Water in the petrol. We had to anchor while I cleared it. By the time that was done it was dark and I decided not to risk coming across without navigation lights. Now perhaps you would be good enough to explain something to me. Why didn't you wait for Nancy in Portree?"

Rod shifted in his chair and looked uncomfortable. He looked at Anya as if hoping she might come to his aid.

"I wasn't sure what Nancy intended to do, and Mrs. Maclaine said..." he began reluctantly.

Anya moved away and flounced into a nearby chair.

"Why make such an issue of it, darling?" she interrupted. "It was my fault. I persuaded Rod to take us for tea to Sligachan. We were all enjoying ourselves so much we forgot the time. Then we decided you must have found Neil and had sent him and Nancy back to Lanmore in a taxi." She tilted her head and sent a sidelong glance across the table at Nancy and winked slowly. "You know, Nancy, I think we should both be pleased we have such jealous menfolk."

Logan pushed back his chair from the table and stood up. His black frown had descended and when he spoke irritation rasped in his voice.

"If Ellis found pleasure in doing what you asked I'm sure he was very welcome to your company, Anya. If you'll excuse me, please, I must go. I promised my cousin and Stan I would go fishing with them."

He nodded politely at all of them and strode toward the door. With a lithe movement Anya was on her feet immediately and hurrying after him.

"But you can't mean to leave me here all day alone," she complained.

"You have Polly and Neil for company," was all they heard of Logan's reply as he went out of the room.

ALTHOUGH ROD MADE no more reference to her absence until he and Nancy went for a walk after supper later that day, and although she hoped that he had accepted Logan's brief explanation of what had occurred to cause her absence, she was aware that he was strangely silent and that he was watching her. Fortunately Linda returned from her trip to Skye and was full of stories and descriptions about Dunvegan and Meg's parents and their croft and how different it was from Lanmore; otherwise the atmosphere might have been noticeably strained.

Even so, Nancy was glad when Rod suggested they go for a walk. It was a lovely evening, calm and golden. *I should be happy,* she thought, *completely and gloriously happy, because here I am in a beautiful place on a perfect evening with the man I'm going to marry.*

She looked across the water at the rugged island stretching out into the sea from the corner of the peninsula. That morning she had been on the other side of the island, passing the small rocky islets where the seals had been basking. The morning had been perfect, full of color, and she had been gloriously happy for a few stolen moments alone with a man she was not going to marry.

Rod's voice cut suddenly and sharply across her thoughts.

"For the life of me I can't understand why you went after Maclaine yesterday in Skye. In the first place it wasn't your business, and in the second place why didn't you tell me what you were going to do? I've studied it from all angles and I can't find a satisfactory answer. Why did you go?"

The question was too searching. He was suspicious of her after all. He had not accepted the explanation. She supposed he had a right to be suspicious but she was rather disappointed to find that he was.

"I knew that he was worried about Neil and I had to offer to help," she replied frankly. "Wouldn't you have offered help to a friend in the same situation?"

He looked at her with narrowed eyes. Nancy stared up at him. Her hopes that he had decided to attach no importance to the events of the previous night were fading fast.

"Are you sure that is all he is to you?" questioned Rod sternly.

"What do you mean?" challenged Nancy shakily.

"I mean that perhaps Anya's suspicions are not unfounded after all. She suspects that you and Maclaine have been having an affair this summer. He told her himself that he's seen a lot of you."

"And of Don, and of Linda," Nancy spoke hotly. "And you believed her. Oh, you don't trust me...." She broke

If Love Be Love

off sharply and then continued more quietly, "I suppose we could have had an affair, but I didn't because I put you first, because I remembered that I am engaged to you."

Rod's eyes avoided hers and he kicked at a pebble, finally dislodging it from the rest and sending it through the air to fall with a small splash into the still water of the loch, where it created a circle of ever widening ripples. Rod watched the ripples for a moment and then glanced down at Nancy. The expression on his face was one of shame.

"It was wrong of me to doubt you. I'm sorry, Nancy. Shall we try to forget the whole business?" he said quietly. "After all, tomorrow is my last day here, and we have many more important subjects to discuss."

Nancy accepted his apology and they continued their walk. But there was a constraint between them and it persisted throughout the next day. It was caused for Nancy by the knowledge that he had doubted her, that he had not had complete trust in her. The small rift in their relationship caused by his dislike of Lanmore had been widened by his demonstration of unfaith. If he really loved her he would never have doubted her, she argued. And apart from this troubling thought Nancy was bedeviled by a feeling that Rod had been disappointed when she had denied having an affair with Logan. She had the oddest suspicion that he would have preferred her to have admitted having become emotionally entangled with another man. But why? It was all extremely puzzling, to say the least.

They had just finished supper, and Linda and Don had gone fishing on the loch, when Rod broached the subject of the house he intended to buy in Dulthorpe.

"I've an option on it until the end of August. I'd like you to see it, so why not come back with me tomorrow?"

Taken by surprise by his suggestion, Nancy stalled for time.

"But I promised Don I would stay until September."

"I know you did, but he doesn't need you anymore. Anyway, the end of August is only two weeks away. It would be much more sensible for you and Linda to come back with me. You'd save two rail fares." He sounded almost desperately urgent.

"But I don't want to go back to Dulthorpe yet." The words surged through Nancy and she bit them back just in time. Instead she said, "Tell me more about the house."

"You've seen the Hargreaves' house, haven't you? Well, it isn't unlike that." Suddenly enthusiastic, Rod produced a plan of the house from his jacket pocket.

Nancy stared at the lines on the paper and tried to rake up some interest.

"I'd be just as happy in a flat for a while," she murmured. "It would give us time to look around and find something better."

"Better?" exclaimed Rod. "There's nothing better being built in Dulthorpe at the moment. These houses are being snapped up. Everyone at the works is buying them. I had the greatest difficulty in persuading Tom Lawrence the builder to let me have an option."

Nancy frowned. If everyone from the chemical works was buying the houses on this particular estate, living there would be like living at the works.

"Rod, couldn't we wait, please, before choosing? I'd rather like to live outside Dulthorpe, in the country. There are some lovely old cottages in the villages on the moors."

"Do you realize how long it would take me to commute from one of those places? Thirty minutes at least," he snapped exasperatedly. "Probably forty-five, at rush hour. Dead time, wasted time. And some of those old houses are drafty and cold in the winter. No, I'm settling for central heating and all the modern conveniences we can get. Living on the moors would be like living here, miles from anything."

"It would be pleasant and peaceful, and we could get a lot of pleasure out of modernizing a cottage," said Nancy wistfully.

"And spend a lot of money unnecessarily. Look, Nancy, from Greendale where these houses are being built it will take us only a few minutes to reach the center of town. And for entertaining they're ideal, with the dining room leading straight out of the big living room. I can't understand why you're hesitating. If you would only agree I could give Tom the go-ahead. I could sign the contract when I return."

Nancy was silent. How could she tell him that she was hesitating because she was not sure whether she wanted to marry him? Her sense of fairness told her that she should not let him go ahead and buy a house in which it was possible that they would not live together.

Rod leaned toward her and said urgently, "Don't you trust me to do the right thing?"

She wanted to say, "You didn't trust me, so why should I trust you?" But it was true she didn't trust him to choose a house she would like. In fact the more he talked about the house and its position the more she disliked it. And wasn't it important to their future relationship that she should like the place where he wanted to live?

"I don't know, Rod. I'm not sure."

"Then come with me tomorrow," he argued. "Once you're back in Dulthorpe and you've seen the house, you'll feel better. You'll be sure again." He spoke with unusual jauntiness, as if he was trying to convince himself as much as her.

Go back to Dulthorpe. Leave Lanmore and return to the rat race of the city. Faced with the decision once more, Nancy realized she had been dreading the end of August for some time.

"I don't want to go back to Dulthorpe." She didn't attempt to bite back the words this time.

"What do you mean?" exclaimed Rod. "If you and I are going to be married you'll have to go back. What's the matter with you, Nancy? You're behaving as if you're bewitched!"

"Maybe I am," she replied slowly. *Now is the time to tell him,* she thought. *But how?*

She got no further than the thought because at that moment she heard the sound of a car stopping at the gate. She went to the window to see who was coming.

"It's Anya Maclaine," she exclaimed in surprise. "I wonder what she wants."

Glad that Anya's arrival would put an end to further discussion with Rod and would give her time to sort out her incoherent thoughts, she went into the hall and opened the door before Anya had a chance to knock.

Brilliant long-lashed eyes gazed at her assessingly.

"You look surprisingly glad to see me," drawled Anya with a touch of mockery. Her glance slid past Nancy to Rod, who stood stiffly in the kitchen doorway. "Don't tell me I've interrupted a lovers' quarrel," she added.

"Please come in," said Nancy politely.

"Not for long, I hope," returned Anya as she swept past Nancy and walked after Rod into the kitchen. "The expression on your face, Rod, is positively thunderous. Perhaps my suggestion will change it."

Graceful and tantalizing, she swung around and leaned against the table to face them. Her blond hair glinted in the shaft of sunlight that slanted through the window. She was wearing black bell-bottomed pants topped by a black tunic that had a mandarin collar and that ended at the top of her thighs. A belt of heavy gilt chain emphasized her waist, and gilt earrings glimmered in her luxuriant hair. She looked complacently sure of herself as she smiled challengingly at Rod.

"I wondered whether you would both like to come out for the evening. To be frank, Lanmore Lodge is driving me crazy. It always did. I can't imagine why anyone wants to live there... or anywhere else in the Highlands. When Angus was alive and we used to come and visit his father we relieved the monotony of our stay by going over to Port Ban on the other side of Loch Ort. There's a good pub there and it's a friendly place this time of the year, full of summer visitors from the south. There's also a growing artists' colony over there. Are you interested in coming? You needn't worry about the ferry. There's a special late one at ten o'clock to bring back the pub crawlers."

Nancy could tell by Rod's face that he was interested and she thought herself that an evening spent among other people might do both of them good, relieving as it would the strain that had been growing between them.

"Like you, I feel the limitations of a place like Lanmore," said Rod enthusiastically. "I'd like to go with you. How about you, Nancy?"

"Yes, I'd like to go."

"That's fine," drawled Anya. "May we go in your car, Rod? I'll take the station wagon back to the Lodge when you are both ready. You can follow me there."

She lit a cigarette and sat down in a chair to wait for them. Rod went over to Mrs. Macrae's to change and Nancy ran up to her bedroom.

She was the first to return to the kitchen. Anya eyed her short green linen dress, gleaming red hair and well-applied makeup with deliberation.

"Quite a transformation," she commented. "You're not such a country bumpkin after all."

"Considering I've lived in a city all my life, that's hardly likely," retorted Nancy. "Are Stan and Miss Martin and Logan going to Port Ban, too?"

"Oh, no. If they were I wouldn't be searching for company. Polly left yesterday. She couldn't stand the place any longer, and I couldn't stand her. Logan has taken Stan off to an agricultural show somewhere. Oh, I'm so bored! Neil has been driving me distracted and Mary and Keith have ignored me. They've never liked me."

"Why didn't you go to the agricultural show, then?"

"Me? Go to a cattle show? My dear girl, Logan knows better than to ask me to go to one of those affairs."

"Well, if this place bores you so much why come and stay here?" asked Nancy honestly.

Anya's glance was oblique and mocking.

"The answer is quite simple. I am out of work and I have nowhere else to go. There is a big attraction here—my brother-in-law, who incidentally holds the purse strings. My beloved husband left all his wealth to Neil and made Logan his guardian. That, in a nutshell, is why I am here. And if I can only get Logan to myself for a short while I'm hoping to persuade him to return to London when we are married. After all, his presence isn't necessary to run the farm. He employs other people to do that."

At that moment Rod returned to the kitchen. He looked extremely amiable and he clapped his hands together and exclaimed jovially, "All set to go? Then what are we waiting for?"

Anya slid off her chair and going up to him slipped her hand through the crook of his arm in that semiproprietorial way that she had.

"For the company of the most congenial man at present visiting Lanmore, of course," she murmured flatteringly. "What a pity I didn't know of your existence a few days earlier. Think of all the fun we've both been missing!"

THE PUB WAS SMALL. It consisted of only two rooms in a traditional village house. The back room was considered by everyone to be reserved for local people only. Anya told them that she had been in it once when she had first visited Lanmore before she was married. It had been in the winter time when the front room was closed because of the small amount of customers at that time of the year.

The front room on that summer evening was full of people who were all summer visitors, judging by their clothes, their accents and their carefree manners. Anya had hardly stepped through the door when she was greeted by a bearded individual who was wearing a kilt. It wasn't long before she was the center of an admiring group. She was clever enough not to forget her companions. Introductions were made, drinks were bought and handed around, and Nancy and Rod were made to feel part of the group.

It made quite a pleasant change, Nancy found, to sip beer, to talk hard and fast to a strange young man who informed her that he was an artist and that he had just moved to Port Ban to be near Ewen MacKay, who was the man with the beard and who was fast gaining recognition as a leading Scottish artist. The easygoing jovial atmosphere of the pub made her forget her immediate problems and she found herself being silently grateful for Anya having appeared when she had and for having invited Rod and her to go out with her.

The young man, who was called Sandy, took her empty glass and struggled toward the bar to get another drink. Rod, his fair face flushed by the warmth of the room, was busily engaged in a three-sided argument with Anya and the bearded gigantic Ewen, and he was obviously enjoying the company. Watching him, Nancy felt a return of all her

If Love Be Love

liking for him. Perhaps he was right, she would see everything in better perspective if she went back to Dulthorpe with him tomorrow. Maybe she should go. She was sure Don didn't need her help anymore.

She turned and looked toward the door and then blinked rapidly, wondering whether her imagination was playing tricks. Just inside the door Logan was leaning against the wall quietly, unobtrusively. He was staring at Anya and the expression on his face was not pleasant, reminding Nancy of the way in which he had watched Neil at the table in the hotel on Skye.

She felt apprehensive. She did not like the way he was watching and waiting; his manner held a threat that was all the more dangerous because it was under strict control. The threat might be directed at Anya. On the other hand it might be directed quite erroneously at Rod. In that moment Nancy wondered whether Anya's apparently innocent invitation and encouragement of Rod had an underlying motive, and that was to make Logan jealous, as Stan had once suggested.

She must speak to Logan before he exploded into speech or action. She was considering edging her way through the crowd in his direction when she realized he had seen her and was making straight for her. As he stopped in front of her the expression on his face was no longer unpleasant. The polite mask was in place.

"How long have you been here?" he asked, and he spoke so quietly that she could hardly hear him through the hubbub of voices.

"Since half-past eight."

"Was Anya here when you arrived?"

"She invited us to come here with her," she explained, and then screwing up all her courage, risking a cool setdown, she blurted, "Logan, please don't blame Rod. She's used him...and me. She said she didn't want to come alone."

He seemed puzzled.

"I would never think of blaming you, or your intended. I know Anya's tactics very well."

"But you're angry with her."

"I am. Not for the reason you're thinking," he murmured, glancing over her head at the animated group of people surrounding Anya. "I've decided that the time has come for a reckoning between Anya and me. She left Neil alone in the house to come here."

Nancy was appalled.

"Oh, I didn't know. She didn't say...."

He looked at her and a faintly cynical smile curled his mouth.

"Why should she say? She'd guess that a person like you would assume that she had made arrangements for a baby-sitter. You would never leave a child as young as Neil alone, would you?"

"No. I thought that Mrs. MacFadyen or your aunt would be with him."

"Mrs. MacFadyen usually has every evening off unless I ask her to stay, and Mary informed Anya as soon as she arrived at Lanmore that she did not intend to baby-sit for her. He was asleep, but he must have woken and found he was alone, because he was shaking with sobs. I left Stan with him and came over. Anya had left a note so that I should know where she was."

"How could she leave him alone like that, to come and enjoy herself?"

"I think I've told you before that Anya should never have been a mother. She is completely selfish and thinks only of her immediate desires."

"Then how can you..." Nancy started, then checked herself. This was not the time or place to ask him how could he love Anya knowing she was so selfish. Anyway, wasn't loving a person accepting them for their faults as well as their virtues?

Someone pushed past her, knocking her against Logan. For a brief moment she felt his hand on her arm steadying her. The person, a tall man with a shock of reddish hair whom she had noticed in the group surrounding Anya, turned to apologize, saw Logan and slapped him on the back.

"Hello there, Logan. Haven't seen you in here for a long time." He eyed Nancy speculatively and added, "It's glad I

If Love Be Love

am to see you in circulation. Rumor has it that you'd become something of a hermit since Angus—"

"Rumor is wrong." Logan's voice had a bite as he interrupted. He turned his back deliberately on the man and said to Nancy, "Let's go outside and walk, where the air is fresher."

Before Nancy could object and tell him that someone was bringing her another drink he had seized her by the hand and was pulling her after him through the crowd. Together they surged through the door and into the rose-tinted evening light.

The air was like velvet, soft and smooth to the skin. Above, a pale greenish rose-shot sky was already scattered with faint stars. In the semicircle of the bay the smooth water reflected the pink of the sky.

"Poor man," commented Nancy. "He must be feeling very squashed. You're very high-handed when you want your own way. You didn't even ask me if I wanted to go for a walk. I happened to be waiting for a very pleasant young man called Sandy to bring me another drink."

The touch of mockery paid off. The painful grip on her hand was relaxed and Logan grinned.

"I apologize. I'd forgotten that I mean no more to you than the moon."

The reference to her unfortunate remark brought the blood to Nancy's cheeks and a flash to her eyes.

"That isn't fair! You weren't intended to overhear. I was trying to make it quite clear to Anya that she had no reason to fear that I was...."

Again Nancy checked herself in mid-sentence. How could she explain the reason for her remark? But he was looking at her inquiringly, so she continued rather breathlessly, "That she had no reason to be jealous because I had spent the night with you on *Vagabond*."

His heavy-lidded eyes watched her, their expression enigmatic, as he considered her admission.

"Do you know I'm beginning to wish that Anya and your intended had good reason to be jealous," he drawled slowly. "Perhaps we behaved too circumspectly after all. Think of the pleasure you and I denied ourselves in their interests...to no effect."

The implication that lay behind his words made Nancy's pulses leap, but before she had time to assess his meaning he asked politely, "Will you walk to the end of the village and back with me, please?"

"But I thought you'd come for Anya?"

"I've decided not to pander to her liking for a scene in front of a ready-made audience. What I have to say to her is for her ears alone, so I'll talk to her when we can be alone, after closing time. Meanwhile you and I could take a walk. Unless you would prefer to return to your fiancé or to the young man called Sandy."

Nancy did not hesitate. The current was back, that warm flow of feeling between the two of them, and she was sure he was as much aware of it as she was.

"I'll walk with you," she agreed.

"Thank you."

They walked past the squat village cottages out toward the single detached houses, each one set on its separate sward of unfenced green grass. There were other people walking about enjoying the mild air of the late summer evening. On the narrow seaweed-strewn shore children were still playing and the noise of their shouts and laughter echoed back from the hills behind the village. The whole place had a leisurely holiday atmosphere. No one hurried. Tomorrow would come soon enough, and when it did it would be such a day as today, slow to start and slow to end.

"Has Rod enjoyed his stay here?" asked Logan. He was being polite again. She could tell by the lack of expression in his voice.

"Not as much as I had hoped," she replied frankly. "He's used to staying in a good hotel in a place where there's plenty of entertainment."

"Surely he came to be with you, and not for entertainment," he remarked critically. "When does he leave?"

"Tomorrow. He wants me to go back with him."

"Will you go?" The question was sharp.

"I think so. It seems to be the sensible thing to do."

"But I thought you intended to stay until September?"

"I did. However, Rod has chosen a house for us to live in and I would like to see it before he buys it."

If Love Be Love

They had reached the end of the houses. A rough road led onto a rocky promontory that jutted out into the sea loch. At the end of the rocks a small white beacon was perched. Already its warning red light was flashing, coloring the water beneath it with a baleful red. Across the slate blue sea the sun slipped down behind the tall dark peak of a distant island mountain, leaving the pale sky suffused with pink light.

"So you don't trust him to choose a house you would like," probed Logan softly as they stopped to stand beside the beacon. "Having doubts?"

With unerring accuracy he had pinpointed the problem that was uppermost in her mind, but her stubborn Allan pride would not let her admit to him that he had. Ignoring the insinuation that she should have more faith in the person she was about to marry, she replied coolly, "The house is in the suburbs of Dulthorpe and I would prefer to live away from the city in a more rural area."

He made no immediate comment, seeming to be more interested in looking out to sea at the lights that flashed at regular intervals from unseen lighthouses and beacons on the islands. Nancy watched, too, and as always the ineffable silence created a dreamlike tranquillity in her mind. But this evening the tranquillity was shot through with yearning. Time was running out, and this was probably the last time she would talk to Logan.

"Why don't you admit that you and Rod are incompatible?" The harsh critical question jolted her out of her tranquillity.

"We ... we're not," she stammered defensively.

"Yes, you are. It stands out like this red beacon, a warning of danger. I noticed it at the Games, which you enjoyed and he did not. You like Lanmore and he doesn't. He wants to live in suburbia and you don't. Is that the way to start a marriage? If you really loved him you wouldn't care where he wanted to live. You'd let him choose your home. You'd live anywhere—in two scruffy rooms, in an attic, in a basement, you'd be so happy to be with him."

His bitter attack left her temporarily speechless. He had implied criticism of her relationship with Rod before, but always there had been a touch of amusement underlying his comments, as if he had only been teasing her. This time there was no doubting that he was serious.

"You'll go through an outmoded ceremony with him only to discover that you're not suited to each other after all and that you're headed for the divorce court," he continued harshly.

Hurt by his comments, already troubled and on the defensive, Nancy took refuge again behind her pride.

"What do you suggest, then?" she retaliated. "A trial marriage? One of those affairs where we would live together to find out if we like it?" She tried to speak gibingly, but her voice trembled uncontrollably.

"I'm merely trying to help you as any other friend might. I'm trying to prevent disaster," he replied rather wearily. "But perhaps I should save my breath. Like the rest of the stubborn Allan tribe you don't like advice."

Nancy wondered if he knew he was hurting her and if he was taking pleasure in doing so, and out of her own hurt came an urge to strike back.

"I'm surprised to hear that you despise marriage, since apparently you're going to go through that outmoded ceremony yourself. Yet you and Anya are scarcely compatible, according to your own definition. She loathes Lanmore and wants to live in London, while you prefer to live here," she sniped.

He turned sharply to look at her. In the fading light it was impossible to read the expression on his face, but she had an impression that he was surprised.

"Who told you that Anya and I are going to be married?" he asked. The harshness gone, he was polite once more.

Surprised in her turn by his question, Nancy did not answer. Was it possible he had not known that Anya was willing to marry him? Had Anya been playing hard to get? And now in her anger she had told him what he wanted to know most. There was a certain irony in the situation, but Nancy felt far from laughter.

"Nancy, will you answer my question, please." It was the quiet authoritative manner that he used with Neil when the

If Love Be Love

boy was stubborn. There was a subtle threat in it and it never failed to defeat Neil as it defeated her now.

"Anya herself... tonight," she admitted reluctantly.

Water swirled and swished in the rock pools as the tide encroached once more upon the land. The distant flashing light grew brighter as twilight deepened into night. Nancy was aware that Logan was still looking at her closely.

"You're sure she said that?" he asked.

"Quite sure. She said that she hoped to persuade you to live in London once you and she are married because she doesn't like Lanmore."

He was still and silent, looking out at the flashing lights again. Nancy was silent, too, miserably so, wishing that their conversation had taken a different course, wishing that her pride had not blinded her into saying the wrong thing. Yet something must have driven Logan into speaking as he had done. He had said he was advising her as a friend. But his advice had hurt more than it should and she could not think why.

"Now I know what to do," Logan muttered more to himself than to her. "Let's go back."

He turned and walked away. Nancy watched him go. He had withdrawn and the warm feeling had gone. He was walking away from her to Anya and tomorrow she would probably leave Lanmore with Rod.

She hurried after him past the houses with their windows bright with yellow light in the purple dusk. The stars were brilliant now, twinkling in the clear dark sky.

By the time Nancy caught up with Logan he had almost reached the pub, which was obviously closing because there were people coming out and standing about outside to talk. As they approached Rod came toward them and in the light streaming from a cottage window she could see the worried expression on his face.

"Where have you been?" he asked her. He glanced sideways at Logan, who paid him no attention but walked straight past, in search of Anya.

"For a walk with Logan," she replied woodenly.

"I see," he said very quietly.

"Darling! You came, after all!" Anya's rich voice greeted

Logan and she came to stand beside him. "You are just in time. Ewen... you remember Ewen, don't you? Well, he has invited us all over to his studio for a ceilidh. Rod and Nancy are to come too—that is, if we can find Nancy. She disappeared."

"Nancy is here," said Logan. "It's very hospitable of you, Ewen, but not this evening. I'm wanting to talk to Anya... alone."

He put a subtle emphasis on the word "alone" and the burly, bearded Ewen laughed appreciatively.

"Ach, Anya, in the face of an invitation put like that I am withdrawing mine. I shall be seeing you another evening. You also, Logan. It is a long time since we had the pleasure of your company." He continued in Gaelic that Logan answered briefly and politely. There was a chorus of goodnights. People faded away leaving Anya, Logan, Nancy and Rod standing in the shadowed roadway.

"I'm so glad you came, darling," purred Anya. "I have wanted so much to be alone with you. Always there have been people this holiday."

He did not answer her, but turning to Rod and Nancy, said politely, "You will excuse us, please. I will drive Anya home. Good night."

THEY MADE THE SHORT JOURNEY to the ferry in silence. In front the rear lights on Logan's car glowed a brighter red as he braked going down the slip to the gangway. They followed and stopped behind the sports car and the ferry began to creak its way across the narrow strait of water. On the other side the ferry had hardly touched land when the car in front moved forward, streaked up the slipway and disappeared into the night as if anxious to reach its destination.

As they trundled ashore and took the slipway cautiously Nancy wondered vaguely whereabouts in the Lodge Logan would have his "reckoning" with Anya. Would they talk in the high-ceilinged gracious lounge as they sipped drinks from cut-glass tumblers? Or would they prefer the comfortable intimacy of Logan's office? And what would Logan say

If Love Be Love

to Anya? It wasn't difficult to guess. After berating her about leaving Neil alone in the house he would ask her to marry him and Anya would agree.

"Well, it would seem that Anya got what she wanted tonight," said Rod shrewdly. "An evening out with her friends here and a ride home with the laird. I wonder if there's anything serious between those two?"

"Yes. They're going to be married," stated Nancy flatly.

"Oh." He sounded almost dumbfounded and said no more on the subject. They had almost reached the cottage when he spoke abruptly.

"I've been thinking, Nancy, that there's no need for you to come back with me tomorrow if you don't want to. Stay another two weeks, and by then I think you'll have had enough of this romantic Highland atmosphere and will be ready to return to city life."

He sounded like the familiar kindly Rod she had always known and she felt a stronge twinge of conscience to think that she had ever doubted him.

"But what about the house?" she asked.

"I'll try and persuade Lawrence to extend the option. If he won't then I'll let it go. There'll be other houses. And I'm beginning to think that perhaps it would be a good idea if we rented a flat while we look around for a house. Well? What do you think?"

His change of attitude was puzzling. He sounded almost eager to fit in with her earlier suggestions just when she had decided she would give in and go back with him. And Logan had said she and Rod were incompatible!

"If you don't mind my staying a little longer I'll stay. It would have been rather a rush having to tell Don and Linda the change in plan, and then having to pack tonight," she said.

"That's what I thought," he said matter-of-factly. "There are one or two things I want to clear up before you return to Dulthorpe so that when you do come we can concentrate on preparations for the wedding. After all, it's a big step we're going to take, Nancy."

"I expect you're right," she murmured.

"That's settled, then." He sounded very cheerful, better than he had since he had arrived on Lanmore, as if he was glad to be going without her.

They stopped at the cottage and he got out of the car to open the door for her. For a moment they stood together and looked out at the smooth water and the dark mountains.

"I expect this place is entirely different in winter. It must be bleak and lonely," observed Rod. "And I should guess that when winter comes Maclaine departs for warmer climates, and that his tenants and employees see nothing of him."

"When winter comes...." Only yesterday morning Logan had started a sentence with those words. He hadn't finished the sentence, and now she would never know what he had meant to say.

CHAPTER SIX

MIDNIGHT WAS NOT THE BEST TIME to take stock of a situation, thought Nancy ruefully as she lay in bed and deliberately reviewed all that had happened since she had come to Lanmore. Every incident became blown up, exaggerated possibly beyond its importance. Every emotion experienced became more deeply felt, more intense.

But she had to take stock sometime in order to reach some conclusion about her own feelings, so she calmly went over every meeting she'd had with Logan, trying to be as objective as possible. Then she tried to assess her emotions, and this was where doubt stepped in again.

Whom did she love? Rod, whom she had known for three years, or Logan, whom she had known for only a few months? Common sense asserted that it should be Rod. It wasn't sensible to discard a person she had known for a long time in favor of someone else she had just met, especially when that someone was considering marriage with another woman.

Yet, did she really know Rod? Hadn't his stay in Lanmore, a place where people were still very dependent on each other for company and entertainment, revealed faults in his character she had not known before? Could she accept those faults and still love him? Or would they irritate her more and more after they were married? Were she and Rod incompatible as Logan had suggested?

Nancy puzzled until her head ached and she had to get up and take some aspirin. On the way back to bed she paused by the window and looked out. Stars still twinkled in the sky. The sea gleamed faintly. The scents of the garden rose upward and tantalized her nose. All was quiet and it was difficult to imagine that places like Dulthorpe, through which heavy traffic rumbled all night, existed. In a few weeks she would be back there and her summer at Lanmore would be no more than an episode that she would remember occasionally. That was the only way to think of it sensibly. It had been an episode in her life when she had been bewitched by the romantic Highland atmosphere and for a short while had imagined herself to be in love with Logan Maclaine.

Having reached a conclusion Nancy went back to bed and went to sleep. The next morning was fresh and cool and she felt calm and practical as she made breakfast for herself and Don after they had milked the cows.

She told him of the evening out at Port Ban and mentioned that Rod would be leaving that morning.

"You could go with him if you want," said Don. "I can manage here now."

"No, I shall stay until the end of the month as we arranged. It would be too much of a rush to leave today; there's too much to pack. Anyway, he doesn't want me to go back with him."

"You're talking just as he does," Don scoffed. "Cut-and-dried, nothing left to chance. I bet he's never been late for work or for anything else in his life. He doesn't like it here, does he?"

Nancy shook her head.

"I thought not. The pace is too easy for him, and people behave as if they're human beings and not like machines. They have feelings, and that's something Mr. Computer can't understand. Emotions can't be programmed," Don remarked gibingly.

"Oh, Don... that's unkind. Rod isn't as bad as that," Nancy exclaimed.

"He's not far short of being like that, which makes me worry about you. Do you think you're going to stand his way of life after being here?"

"I've promised to marry him," replied Nancy with dignity, "and I don't break promises."

"That's what I'm afraid of," murmured Don. "Even if you did experience a change of feeling you wouldn't let on; your pride wouldn't let you. Look, Nan, you don't have to marry him. You can stay here. I know I said the other day that there wasn't any room for anyone else to live on the croft... that was for Lin's benefit. But if it's a case of marrying Rod because you feel you have to—oh, darn it, I'm getting all mixed up—because you feel you have nowhere else to go...."

Nancy smiled at him and went to his rescue.

"It's nice of you, Don. I know what you mean. I can assure you I'm not marrying Rod because I have nowhere else to go. I can always go back to Aunt Win and work at Green and Selby's again. No, I'll stay with you as we arranged. By then the summer will be almost over here and I'll probably be dying to get back to the hustle and bustle of Dulthorpe."

"Well, rather you than me," grinned Don. "I've escaped and nothing would make me go back."

"Coming here was right for you, wasn't it?" said Nancy, glad that she could divert him from further discussion of herself.

"Perfect," he conceded. "I can't understand why dad ever left the place."

"Circumstances must have been different for him. He had to live here with his father. And remember that grandfather was strict and possibly a little mean. You have no restrictions like that. You're master in your own house here. Dad had to go away to achieve his independence and to be free."

Don shook his head slowly, disbelievingly.

"I'll never understand. For me freedom will always be where I work out of doors close to nature, among simple people. It will never be in the city tied to an industry. If I hadn't had this chance, Nan, I'd have been in trouble—bad trouble. You know that, don't you?"

"Yes, Don, I know. That's why I'm so glad it's worked out well for you."

Rod's leave-taking was as brusque and as businesslike as his arrival had been. As she watched his car disappear over the bridge Nancy touched her mouth, which he had kissed briefly before leaving. He hadn't made love to her once during the whole time he had stayed on Lanmore. At one time she would not have found the thought strange, but now she wondered.

She walked slowly through the garden. Another strange thought followed the first. She wasn't sorry Rod had gone, in fact she was relieved. He had been the stranger here. He had not fitted in. He had disturbed and detracted from the way of life she had made for herself here.

Now that he had gone she could take her time again. She could stand and stare at the sea, at the mountains for as long as she liked without being told she was wasting time. She would be able to sit on the bench in the sunshine and listen to the bees and the birds.

Almost defiantly Nancy sat down on the bench, easing her back against the sun-warmed wall. She closed her eyes and relaxed. But relaxation did not last for long. It was impossible, she realized, to sit on the bench for long without wishing that Logan was beside her, teasing her in his quiet way or sitting in silence, sharing the quiet world of the garden.

She must accept the fact that the moments of sharing with Logan were over. Last night he and Anya must have come to an agreement just as she and Rod had. The romantic episode was over for both of them. It had finished with hard hot words between Logan and herself, words with which they had hurt each other. Nancy could not help but feel sad that it had ended that way, yet it was probably for the best.

Linda seemed determined to make the most of the last two weeks she would spend on Lanmore. Since her trip to Skye she had been much easier to deal with, and Nancy could only conclude that Logan had been right yet again when he had suggested she would have less trouble with Linda if she allowed her a little freer rein. So when her sister asked if she could go visiting at a croft the other side of Lanmore where one of her new friends lived or if she could go fishing with Malcolm Macrae, eldest son of Duncan Macrae of the petrol garage at Glenarg, Nancy always agreed provided Linda made her bed or helped with the dishes or the feeding of the hens before she went. The result was a much sweeter-tempered Linda who did her chores willingly and even did a little extra without being asked.

She had just left the house on an errand to the village one morning two days after Rod's departure and Nancy was just putting on her Wellington boots to go and round up some sheep for Don when she noticed the blue station wagon from the Lodge stop outside the cottage. The garden gate opened and Anya, dressed as usual with expensive extravagance, came up the path. She was alone.

"I wasn't sure whether you were still here," she said when Nancy opened the door to her knock. "Logan told me that you were leaving with Rod the day after our outing to Port Ban. Then I thought I saw your sister yesterday—at least Neil said it was your sister when we passed her near the ferry."

"Please come in," invited Nancy politely.

"No, thank you. As a matter of fact, I'm in rather a rush. We're leaving for London in about an hour and we can't find Neil. Knowing his fondness for you I wondered if he had come down here to say goodbye to you."

They were leaving for London. Had Logan capitulated, then? Had Anya won her point? A stab of disappointment thrust through Nancy. She had not thought Logan would give in so easily. But of course, as Stan had remarked, Anya had a big pull in the person of Neil.

"I haven't seen Neil since Sunday," she replied. "He isn't here."

Anya looked thoroughly exasperated.

"Oh, the little devil," she sighed wearily. "He's been terribly trying the past few days. He must be hiding in the house somewhere. When are you leaving Lanmore?"

"Not until the end of the month. Rod and I decided it wasn't necessary for me to go back with him."

"But you and he are still engaged to be married, I hope?" asked Anya. "You haven't changed your minds?"

"Oh, no."

"I'm so glad." The sultry voice was sticky with pretended gladness. "I had a feeling the other night when we went to the pub that you and he were not quite hitting it off. Then you disappeared and someone said they had seen you go out with Logan, and Rod was anxious. But all's well that ends well. I'm sure you'll be very happy together. I think you are admirably suited to each other."

"Thank you," said Nancy distantly, and then had to ask a question. "Is Logan taking you to London?"

Anya sighed again and looked desolated.

"No, worse luck. He's busy here just now, or so he says. It will soon be harvesttime and he wants to be here, although I'm convinced they could manage perfectly well without him. But he'll follow, have no fear, because I'll have Neil with me. I'd have stayed longer and waited for him, but I've been offered a part in a new play. It's a chance to get back into the theater, the chance I've been looking for, so I daren't pass it up, no matter what Logan says."

"Doesn't he want you to go back to the stage?"

"Well, you know how he is about this place. But as long as I have Neil, he'll come and he'll continue to pay the rent of the apartment."

"Poor Neil," murmured Nancy.

"Why do you say that?"

"You are using him as a pawn. No wonder he's a bundle of nerves. He's just settled here and you're going to snatch him away again. And I suppose Logan will follow you and try to bring him back here and it will go on until one of you has the grace to give in."

Anya's magnificent eyes flashed with an anger that was quite sincere.

"You have no right," she growled, her guttural voice several notes lower than usual.

"No, I haven't. I've no right at all," agreed Nancy. "I shouldn't have said what I did. I hope you find Neil. Please say goodbye to him for me."

She went back into the house and closed the door and leaned against it. She discovered that she was shaking. She had spoken her mind on the subject of Neil to the person who should have had his welfare close to her heart. She hoped a little of what she had said had gone home and would have some result.

The problem of Neil stayed with Nancy all day, nibbling at her peace of mind. She kept thinking of his wide appeal-

If Love Be Love

ing gray eyes, of the mischief that often bubbled up from within him, of the way he loved to play up to an audience. He was no concern of hers, but the fact that he had hidden when his mother was about to take him away from Lanmore to London meant only one thing to Nancy, Neil had not wanted to go.

It was grocery day and the traveling shop called as usual in the afternoon, stopping outside Miss Macrae's house. Its blaring horn warned everyone on the crofts that it had arrived. Linda went with Nancy to choose the food they required and as usual the whole business became a social occasion when they met the other crofters and passed on the gossip.

As they returned to the cottage with their box of purchases Nancy noticed a movement among the bushes at the end of the garden. Through the dark greenery she thought she detected the gleam of blond hair, then she decided it was a trick of her imagination. She had Neil on her mind so much that she was seeing him in the places where he had liked to play hide-and-seek.

She went into the house and put her box down and went outside again. There was no sign of blond hair by the bushes, but it seemed as if one of them was moving slightly.

"Neil!" she called, feeling rather foolish. "Neil! Are you there? There's no need to be frightened. You can come out."

Nothing happened. Practical Nancy ridiculed imaginative Nancy.

"Don't be silly. It's the Highland atmosphere playing tricks again. Go back into the house and start making that tart you promised Don for his supper," she said to herself.

The bush moved again and the sunlight glinted on fair hair. This time she did not call out but went straight to the bushes. Gray eyes, solemn under a fall of blond hair, stared back at her out of a wedge-shaped face.

"I didn't want to go back to London with mommy, so I ran away," blurted Neil.

Nancy put out her hand. Without hesitation he put his in it and she drew him out from behind the bushes.

"That was a very naughty thing to do, Neil. Your mother must be very worried," she admonished him.

His face crumpled and tears welled in his eyes.

"She's gone," he cried. "I hid in the woods near the house and watched her go. I didn't want to go to London. I want to stay here. Uncle Logan said I could. He said I could go to school here like my daddy did."

Nancy felt bewildered. There was more to what he had said than he was able to explain. He might have sufficient inherent independence of spirit to take action on his own behalf, but to explain what had driven him to that action was beyond his powers. At the moment she could see that all he required was comfort. The way in which he had put his hand in hers showed how much he trusted her plus the fact that he was here in the garden, and she must not betray that trust.

"Shall we go into the house and have some milk and biscuits?" she said. "I've some new ones from the grocer. Linda will soon be here and I expect she'll play with you or read a story to you."

He smiled joyfully and she knew she had said what he wanted to hear. They went into the kitchen where he helped her to put the groceries away and had his milk and biscuits. By the time that was done Linda was back. Nancy explained briefly to her what had happened. Linda listened with wide eyes, but when she would have questioned Nancy in her usual forthright fashion Nancy cut her short with, "Don't ask questions now, there's a love, because I can't answer them. The main thing is to keep him happy. Take him out to play with him and I'll telephone the Lodge."

Linda obeyed and within a few minutes Nancy was talking to Mrs. MacFadyen, who informed her that Mr. Maclaine was away for the day to Oban with Mr. Black and that Mrs. Maclaine had left for London.

"She took Master Neil with her, miss. She said there had been a change in the arrangements, whatever, and that he was to go with her."

"I'm afraid he didn't go with her after all, Mrs. MacFadyen," explained Nancy. "He ran away and he's here with me."

"Och, ye're never saying so, miss." Mrs. MacFadyen sounded thoroughly flustered. "His mother never said a word about him being missing. Och, whatever will himself be saying to me? You'd better send him back here at once."

Nancy thought of Neil's troubled gray eyes. Mrs. MacFadyen, in her state of anxiety about Logan's reaction, did not sound the best person for the child to be with.

"I think it would be better if he stayed here until his uncle is back and can come to get him," she said decisively. "I'll give him his tea. Now be sure to tell Mr. Maclaine where Neil is and to say that he has come to no harm."

"I'll be doing that, miss, but it may be late when he comes."

"That will be all right. No matter how late it is tell him to come and fetch Neil."

"Och, I will. Whatever will himself be saying?"

Nancy cut Mrs. MacFadyen's complaint off with a curt good-afternoon and thought to herself grimly, *It's what I will be saying to himself that matters.*

IT WAS LATER than she had expected when Logan came. Neil, his good spirits restored, had enjoyed a hilarious bath-time with Linda and had gone to bed in Don's room quite happily. After fishing in the loch for an hour Linda and Don had returned with their catch and Don was cleaning the fish in preparation for the next day's breakfast when they all heard the roar of a car's engine being revved before the ignition was turned off.

"Logan!" exclaimed Linda, jumping to her feet.

"Sit down," ordered Nancy crisply. "I want to speak to him alone." She had reached the porch door before he was able to knock and walk in, and surprised him with his hand already raised to knock. The sight of him disturbed her as usual and she lost her initial advantage as she struggled to control the feeling of delight that surged through her.

"I received your message," he said cooly. "Neil is here?"

"Yes. He's in bed." Her heart was resuming its normal beat and with a great effort she was able to look him in the eye and say crisply, "I want to talk to you."

His thick eyebrows tilted sardonically and he inclined his head politely.

"I'm honored," he murmured. "Do we talk here?"

"No, in here." She waved a hand in the direction of the "room," the parlor that no one ever used.

He grimaced and shook his head.

"No, thank you. Remembering the last time you talked to me I think I shall feel safer in the garden."

There was something about his attitude, a facetiousness that was unusual, which roused her suspicions. She stepped closer to him and sniffed. The smell of whiskey was unmistakable.

"Where have you been? What have you been doing?" she asked. In the light streaming from the porch she could see the gleam of mockery in his eyes.

"Stan has been celebrating a success and I've been drowning a sorrow. It's his last evening here, so we went over to Port Ban to have a drink. Now what do you want to talk to me about? I'm surprised you're still here. I thought you'd shaken the sand of Lanmore from your feet and had returned to Dalthorpe to enter into that life of bliss known as marriage."

"Will you be serious, please," pleaded Nancy.

"I do not wish to be serious. I'm glad you haven't gone because that means there is still time."

"Time for what?"

"Time to... take Linda diving again."

She could tell that he had not said what he had intended to say, that he was teasing her. When he behaved like this it was impossible to reprimand him.

"Why is Neil here?" he asked with a sudden change of manner. "Mrs. MacFadyen was not exactly clear in her explanation."

"That's what I want to talk to you about, but... but...."

"But I won't be serious. I can see that we Maclaines are a great trial to you. There's no need for you to think that you must make yourself responsible for us all the time, you know. You could have sent him straight back to the Lodge."

"I couldn't when you weren't there. He was upset and—Logan, I must talk to you about him."

If Love Be Love

"Then let's sit in the garden, on the bench."

Taking her by the hand, he flicked off the porch light and darkness took over. He drew her into the garden and closed the porch door firmly. In the dark silence of the garden his nearness was disturbing, and pulling her hand out of his Nancy walked to the bench and sat down. He followed and sat beside her, close beside her. She moved slightly along the bench, putting space between them, and he laughed.

"I'm waiting, Nancy," he said.

The trouble was that his unexpectedly facetious behavior had scattered her wits and she was having difficulty in remembering the fine scornful phrases she had rehearsed to say to him. She had been going to berate him for using Neil as a pawn as she had berated Anya, but he had diverted her from her intention, as if he had guessed what it was.

Once more she was aware that he had more experience in dealing with her sex than she had in dealing with his and that he had no compunction in using that experience in avoiding trouble or in getting what he wanted. Out there in the scented garden, listening to the lap of the water against the unseen shore, she was no longer annoyed with him.

"Have you been struck dumb?" he asked teasingly.

Nancy drew a shaky breath and said "No." Then she launched into quick explanation of Anya's morning visit and of how she had found Neil hiding. When she had finished he said nothing, so she took another breath and came out with her condemnation.

"I think both you and Anya should be ashamed of yourselves, using a little boy in this game you're playing with each other."

"I am not playing any game with Anya or anyone else," he replied coldly. "I am merely trying to carry out my brother's wishes. Angus wanted Neil to go to school here as he and I did until we were old enough to go on to school in Edinburgh. Even when he was alive that was his plan for his child. It's Anya who's been using Neil for her own ends. She and I had it out the other night and came to an arrangement that seemed to satisfy her at last. I told you I was going to have a reckoning with her."

"Then why did she want to take Neil to London with her?"

"She was trying to slide out of the arrangement," he replied bitterly. "She wasn't supposed to be leaving until tomorrow when she was to have traveled with Stan. This is the first I've heard about a new play. When we talked the other night she had no future prospects at all."

Nancy sighed. It was all very puzzling.

"I'm afraid I don't understand. You once said that you regard marriage as a form of sacrifice and the other night you called it an outmoded ceremony, and yet you're prepared to go through with it for Neil's sake."

"You surprise me all the time," he murmured. "Whom am I going to marry this time?"

"Anya, of course. You said you'd come to an agreement with her and I know she wants to marry you."

"But I didn't say at any time that I wanted to marry her," he put in patiently. "I've never wanted to marry anyone. I thought I made that quite clear. Anya agreed at last to let me keep Neil here and to supervise his schooling in return for a settlement out of Angus's estate, a regular annual income that Angus should have arranged in his will if he had been thoroughly wise. Unfortunately he made his will when he was furious with Anya about something and cut her out completely. He always let his emotions govern his actions."

"And you never do?"

"Occasionally I'm like other humans. I have...I do," he replied quietly.

"Then when Anya tried to take Neil away with her today she was breaking the arrangement she had made with you. Neil guessed that she was, but he couldn't say so. He could only act, so he ran away."

"Yes. It seems he has more Maclaine in him than I'd hoped. Anya was doing exactly what you said. She was using him as a pawn to get me to marry her. God knows why."

"Because she loves you," suggested Nancy, and he laughed scornfully.

"Don't let that be fooling you, Nancy Allan. Anya loves only herself, and her career. Sometimes she wants badly

If Love Be Love

something she can't have. I was attracted to her once, on a purely physical level, but she demanded too much. My love at that time was racing and I wasn't interested in marriage, so she seduced Angus. It was our potential wealth that attracted her." He paused, then said rather bitterly, "It's difficult to be sure when you have wealth and possessions, to be sure whether anyone likes you for yourself."

Understanding came to Nancy in a flash. Why hadn't she realized that the icy barrier of politeness, the often stiff reserved manner was his protection against people he was not sure of, against the hangers-on and the fortune hunters?

"Have you a love now?" she asked.

She could tell by his silence that she had surprised him. She had surprised herself by daring to ask him such a personal question and she decided it was the influence of the quiet dark garden.

"I'm not sure," he said at last. "Sometimes I think I have, and then.... You're very curious tonight."

He moved closer to her again, but she did not bother to move away. Nor did she pull her hand from his when he lifted it from her knee and held it between both of his.

"It's because there's so much I don't understand, and time is running out."

"On Tuesday morning when I woke up I told myself that it had run out... that you had gone," he said softly.

Nancy held her breath. It was fantastic. Here was Logan Maclaine admitting that he had thought of her in his wakening moments!

"Why didn't you go with Rod?" he asked.

"We decided that it wasn't necessary for me to go immediately. I shall go back as I intended at the end of the month."

"Ten days. Time enough," he muttered obscurely.

The porch door opened and light streamed across the garden. Linda called, "Nancy, Nancy... where are you?"

"I'm coming in a minute!" she called back.

"Neil had better stay the night with you. I'll come over and pick him up in the morning. I must thank you again for looking after him."

He pulled her toward him, framed her face with both

hands and his mouth found hers in the darkness with unerring instinct. At his touch the desire that she had held in check for so long exploded in Nancy and she returned his kiss with interest. It was only when she realized that his hands were on her shoulders and he had moved closer to take advantage of her response that she remembered she was not free to enjoy being kissed by him.

"No!" she whispered fiercely. She pulled away and felt his fingers grip her shoulders painfully.

"Those principles of yours are becoming a nuisance," he mocked gently. "Aren't they a little out-of-date?"

"Out-of-date or not, they're all I have and I'm not going to change them now," she replied desperately. This time it was very difficult not to give in to him.

"Not even for me?" he challenged.

"Not even for you," she answered shakily.

His hands slid from her shoulders and he stood up.

"Then I shall not be wasting any more of your time. Goodbye, Nancy," he said quietly, and walked away into the darkness.

IT REQUIRED A GREAT DEAL OF EFFORT next morning to muster sufficient self-possession to meet Logan again face to face. Then when she had made the effort he didn't come for Neil after all, but sent Harris instead.

Although she had been worried about meeting him again when he didn't come Nancy felt deflated. He must have meant that he didn't intend to see her again when he had said goodbye so politely. And why should he see her again? Hadn't she repulsed him in every way she could think of? Hadn't she made it obvious to him that she did not go in for dalliance because she was engaged? Such arguments might bolster her morale temporarily, giving her a sense of righteousness, but they did nothing to ease the awful aching sense of regret that gnawed at her heart.

The memory of his lovemaking flooded her mind suddenly, making her throat ache. Immediately she scoffed at herself. Such thoughts proved that the attraction was a purely physical one. Time enough, he had said. What had he meant? Time enough to finish the romantic episode

If Love Be Love

with a summer visitor. Well, she had finished the episode for herself. She could see that now. He had asked her to change her principles for him and in doing so had asked her to give up Rod. In refusing to give up her principles she had refused to give up Rod and Logan had apparently accepted her decision as final.

But why had she refused? It would not have been difficult to have agreed to his suggestion. Why was she stuck with this overdeveloped sense of loyalty to Rod? The golden days of late August slipped by. The heather blazed on the hillsides under pale cirrus-streaked skies. Fields turned from green to ocher as oats ripened. But the beauty was unnoticed by Nancy as she struggled with her conscience and the time to leave Lanmore came nearer, and she realized unhappily she did not want to leave not because she loved the place but because she loved Logan. It was useless now she knew to say that she would forget when once she was back in Dulthorpe. No matter where she was or who she was with her mind would reach out to his across the miles. And she knew that in refusing to change her principles for him she had made the biggest mistake she had ever made.

Rod's letter arrived on a perfect morning. Limpid water reflected lilac-tinted mountains. White houses at Glenarg across the loch gleamed in the sunlight. Nancy sat on the bench in front of the cottage to read the letter while she had her elevenses; the haunted bench where she had rejected Logan for the last time.

She turned the letter in her hand, putting off opening it. Its arrival jolted her into reality, the reality of marriage to Rod. Tomorrow she and Linda would pack in readiness to leave. The day after, Ian Macrae would take them to Mallaig where they would catch the train to Glasgow. They would spend the night in the city and continue their journey the next day by way of Carlisle, arriving at Dulthorpe in the late afternoon when Rod would probably meet them. She guessed that the letter would contain the arrangements for that meeting and also the latest news about the housing situation.

Nancy sighed, and slit the letter open. After the usual

preliminaries of asking after herself and inquiring about Don and Linda, Rod went straight to the point.

"I have decided that for you and me to marry would be a mistake. I'm sure that you are aware as much as I am that my stay with you was not a success. But it was a visit that had to be made in order that both of us might learn that we are not suited to each other. I was beginning to have doubts before you ever left Dulthorpe because I had already met Shirley and had discovered that she and I had much more in common, including age, than you and I ever had.

While you were away I found myself seeking and enjoying her company more and more and, in fact, I took her with me when I went to look at the house. You will guess that she liked it immensely.

However, I was not prepared to go back on my word to you until I had seen you again, as I realized it was not sensible to believe I had fallen in love with someone I had known only a few weeks.

I think it was when you went after Maclaine in Skye that I began to think that possibly your feelings for me had undergone a change, too, and I began to wonder if they had ever been particularly deep. Here I must be honest and tell you that when I proposed it was out of a sense of duty and pity, and at the time it is possible that you were too young and inexperienced to know any different.

At Lanmore I began to see that you preferred and enjoyed many pleasures that leave me cold, and that you were attracted to a younger man.

It occurred to me then that that sort of situation might arise after we were married, with unpleasant consequences.

I should have told you all this before I left, but I still did not have the courage to let you down. I had to come back alone to think things out, and to see Shirley again. It was when I saw her again that I knew I must take this step, not only for my own happiness and hers, but ultimately for yours, too.

I feel sure you will be glad because I have relieved you of the onus of having to break the engagement."

The letter finished with his best wishes for her future.

Jilted. The harsh unkind word flashed through Nancy's mind and made her laugh. The first time she had laughed for days. She had been jilted in a good old-fashioned way and she didn't care. She raised her face to the sun and smiled. She was free, thanks to Rod, who in the end had possessed the maturity to assess the situation in his methodical way and to act accordingly. She must write and thank him and wish him happiness.

A car stopped outside the gate. It was the station wagon from the Lodge. Mary Maclaine, neatly dressed in an expensive tweed suit, entered the garden and walked up the path.

"Enjoying the sunshine? How wise of you, dear, since you won't be here much longer. You know I once passed through Dulthorpe. How anyone can live there is beyond me."

She sat down beside Nancy, her inquisitive blue eyes going to the letter.

"I've called to say goodbye. Keith and I are going to stay with some friends near Ullapool and Logan tells me you are going at the end of this week, so you won't be here when we return. It's rather a sad occasion because you're leaving, but a happy one, too, because you are going back to marry that nice fair man—Ron, or was it Rod?"

"Rod," murmured Nancy, and smiled seraphically. "But I'm not going to marry him. He's just jilted me, by letter."

"As she expected Mary Maclaine looked a little shocked.

"Oh, really? How dreadful! I am sorry. But you don't seem a bit concerned."

"I'm not. I'm relieved."

"Relieved?" An expression of impatience tightened Mary Maclaine's face and Nancy guessed she was saying to herself, "Tut, these young people... behave most peculiarly." Actually she said, "I'm afraid I don't understand."

To tell Mary was to tell Logan, Nancy was sure, and once he knew the changed circumstances he would come to see her and then perhaps they could take their friendship a little further. Her heart hammered at the thought and her hands curled around the crisp paper of the letter. Without any hesitation she plunged into a description of her relationship with Rod from the time she had met him, pointing out how he had been an acquaintance of her uncle's who had helped her and who had offered to marry her out of a sense of duty and whom she had accepted because he had offered security. She told of the tension created during his stay at Lanmore, and of her own difficulty in breaking promises and going back on her word.

When she had finished Mary was silent for a few minutes as she considered the story. Then she observed shrewdly, "He must be a very good man. I hope you realize that, Nancy."

"He is. I do. He is too good for me—too competent and capable. I prefer someone who needs me."

"I can see what you mean. You, too, are competent and capable and organized. I hope you'll find someone who needs you, and I'm glad it has turned out right for you. It could have been otherwise, I can see that now. But what will you do?"

"I'm not sure yet. I have to think of Linda. She wants to go to college and train to be an infant teacher. That's the result of us staying here. She's been very interested in Neil."

"Yes. I noticed when I visited you the last time. Which reminds me, I cannot understand why Logan has taken on that child, and I'm sure he's beginning to regret it. It's either that or he has had a setback of some sort."

"Why?" asked Nancy, suddenly anxious. "What's the matter with him?"

"Moody," said Mrs. Maclaine succinctly. "Silent one minute, making the most biting sarcastic remarks the next. I know it can't be anything to do with Anya, because he told me that he isn't going to marry her, and that he has no intentions of marrying anyone and never had any intentions of marrying anyone. He said it all as if he thought I went around telling everyone his business. Of course, there could be some perfectly simple explanation to do with the stock market. Maybe some of his shares have taken a tumble. Anyway, I told him that he'll have to hire someone to help with the child. Mrs. MacFadyen is useless."

"What did he say?"

"Told me very politely to mind my own business. You know he can be polite and you are left wishing that you hadn't opened your mouth."

"I know," replied Nancy with a faint smile.

"That would be an ideal job for you," announced Mary brightly, pleased with her sudden idea. "If you looked after Neil it would mean you could stay here with your brother. I'll mention it to Logan, if you like."

"Oh, no," gasped Nancy. "You mustn't. I couldn't. Please don't, Mrs. Maclaine. I wouldn't like the position."

To her horror she began to wonder if she had protested too much, because Mary tilted her head to one side and considered her with shrewd blue eyes.

"I wonder why?" she murmured thoughtfully. "Well, seeing that you are dead set against my making the suggestion I won't although I can't help thinking that it would work out rather well for all concerned."

To Nancy's relief she stood up and said she must be going, and after wishing her good luck for the future she left.

Linda and Don took the news that she wasn't going to marry Rod after all with a calmness that surprised her.

"Of all the good turns Rod has done for you that's the best," said Don. "Now remember what I said the other day, Nan. There's no rush for you to leave here. Take your time to decide what you want to do."

Nancy smiled at him gratefully.

"It's good of you, Don, but I think we'll return to Dulthorpe just the same. You can't afford to keep the two of us on the croft and there's no work that I could do here. All our savings are used up and Lin wants to take some O-levels now and go to college, so I think it would be better if we go on Friday. Aunt Win will have us, I know, and I can get my job back."

He looked rather dubious, but did not argue and went out to see Ian about harvesting the oats.

"You're really glad you aren't going to marry Rod, aren't

you?" commented Linda as they washed up the supper dishes together.

"I must admit to having had doubts about the whole business," answered Nancy.

"You could marry Logan now," suggested the irrepressible Linda.

"Linda! I've never known anyone like you for jumping to conclusions. I thought you'd reserved him for yourself," retorted Nancy.

"I never considered marriage with him," replied Linda seriously, then added loftily, "One should never marry one's hero."

"Why not?" asked Nancy, trying to stifle her laughter at her sister's superior attitude.

"Think how disappointing it would be to discover that he had feet of clay and wasn't a hero after all."

"I suppose you have a point there. But why should I marry him?"

Linda shrugged her shoulders carelessly and said airily, "It was just a thought that passed through my mind. I saw him kiss you in the garden the other night."

"You couldn't have seen. It was too dark," countered Nancy, her face flaming suddenly.

Linda laughed gleefully and did a little jig on the spot.

"I was right, I was right!" she chanted. "I couldn't see, but I noticed that you stopped talking and that there was a long silence. Was it nice?"

"Linda!" threatened Nancy, snatching the first weapon to hand which happened to be Grandfather Allan's knitted tea cozy. "You should know better. People who kiss don't necessarily marry. Besides, Logan isn't the marrying sort. He's said so often enough."

"Isn't he?" queried Linda, and gave some thought to the subject as she finished drying a plate. "He might be if he found the right person, if someone kind and gentle who would help him when he had problems came along. I guess you aren't that type, though, Nan. You're too bossy. All right, I'll stop," she added laughingly. "You shouldn't blush, Nancy. It doesn't go with your hair."

Laughing, she raced out through the door and closed it

just as the tea cozy that Nancy had hurled at her sailed through the air.

THURSDAY BROUGHT A CHANGE in the weather, but no Logan. If Mary Maclaine had relayed to him the news of Nancy's broken engagement it had made no difference to him. Which meant that he had not been particularly serious in his feelings for her, thought Nancy, as she snapped the locks on one of her suitcases.

Rain beat on the windows and the wind howled in the chimneys all night and when Friday dawned the crops of oats in the fields were flattened and sodden. The wind-tossed stretches of gray water looked desolate. "As desolate as I feel," thought Nancy as she wandered around the garden and mourned over the battered plants and scattered leaves, which had had no time to change color before being hurled from the trees.

Everything was ready for departure. The baggage was standing by the porch door. Ian would come for them at ten o'clock. Meanwhile Linda was saying goodbye to the younger Macraes after both she and Nancy had been over to see Miss Macrae.

It was surprising how docile Linda had been about leaving Lanmore, mused Nancy, as she kept nostalgic thoughts at bay by thinking about her sister, and how much she had changed and developed mentally and physically during the past few months. No longer was she given to emotional outbursts when her will was crossed, no longer did she go in for fantastic daydreams. Instead she was full of plans for the future and was actually looking forward to the beginning of the school term so that she could start her course of study for the examination that would take her to college.

Don had changed also for the better. As his remarks to her about her own future had revealed, he had grown up, and with the measure of self-reliance that he had achieved while tilling his own land and caring for his own animals, he had become more observant and more considerate of others.

Nancy supposed she had changed, too, though whether for the better or not she could not say. Certainly she had slowed down considerably and had ceased to push people so much. She realized now how much she had used to nag at Linda, how much she had "mothered" Don and how much she had been afraid of changing the familiar security offered by her engagement to Rod for the uncertainty of an association with Logan.

Now she had lost both. She had only herself to blame.

The familiar sound of a sports car's powerful engine froze her in her tracks. Mesmerized, she watched the low green car race over the bridge, swerve around the bend and shudder to a stop in front of the gate. Still dazed, she watched Logan open the gate and stride toward her, hands in pockets, shoulders hunched. The expression on his face reminded her of their first meeting at the Roman fort on Hadrian's Wall. Sour, he had called his mood then and sour he looked now. That he had been suffering from sleeplessness she could tell by the telltale dark lines under his eyes.

"Is Neil here?" he asked.

"No, of course not. I haven't seen him since Harris came for him last week."

He was looking past her at the cases by the porch door and he was frowning.

"I thought perhaps he had come over to say goodbye to you and Linda. He was talking about it yesterday, saying he wanted to come."

"And you wouldn't bring him," she accused in a low hurt voice.

He rubbed a hand over his forehead in a weary gesture and muttered, "I couldn't."

Once again he looked lonely and a little desperate as he had that day in Skye and once again the impulse to help him sprang up in Nancy, overcoming pride and vanquishing pain.

"Do you think he's lost again?" she asked.

"I'm afraid so. He must have set out quite early. Mrs. MacFadyen didn't miss him until she went up to his room at eight-thirty to see if he was ready for breakfast. Even then she wasn't alarmed, thinking that he must be somewhere in the house. But I looked for him and he wasn't."

"Oh, how could you be so careless as to lose him again?" blurted Nancy. "If you had done as he asked he would

If Love Be Love

never have tried to come and see me on his own. It would have been quite easy for you to have sent him with Mr. Harris. You didn't have to bring him yourself."

His eyebrows lifted in a supercilious expression and when he spoke he was urbanely polite.

"You are right," he agreed. "Why didn't I think of that for myself? On the other hand it would have been quite in order and possibly kinder for you to have come to the Lodge to say goodbye to him. You needn't have been afraid you'd have seen me. I don't spend all day with Neil, and yesterday I wasn't at home."

As Mary Maclaine observed, when Logan spoke to you in that polite and yet scathing way you wished you had not opened your mouth. Incapable of answering, Nancy stared at him. What he said was true. She had been afraid to go to the Lodge to say goodbye to Neil in case she had met Logan and in case he had thought she was pushing in where she was not wanted by him.

He turned away and said, "I'd better be looking for him, since he's not here."

In spite of the setdown he had just given her she followed impulsively.

"I'll come with you."

"I don't need any help, thank you."

Shades of that wet afternoon in Skye! He had often criticized her Allan pride, but his was no better. It was a barricade he threw up as a shield when he most needed help.

"Yes, you do," she asserted. "Don't try to put me off with your supercilious manner; you have no idea where to look for him. You haven't even started to think about what you're going to do."

Her impetuous words had results. Instead of continuing on his way he turned and looked at her properly. Their eyes met and time was of no account. His were no longer blank and impersonal.

"You'll miss the train," he murmured, and she wondered how he knew she was on her way to catch a train. "Then your intended will be anxious when you don't arrive at Dulthorpe at the right time."

"He won't be there to meet me," she replied. "And he

isn't my intended anymore. He's broken off the engagement. Didn't Mary tell you?"

He shook his head slowly from side to side negatively, like a man who could not believe what he had heard. He moved a step toward her and her pulses leaped in response to the expression in his eyes. Then, apparently changing his mind, he looked away and the strange breathless moment ended.

"Where shall we start looking?" he asked, and there was only the slightest suspicion of a tremor in his voice.

"I think he would try to come through the woods and over the fields because he has been that way twice before. But I can't understand how he could get lost. Unless he's had...." She found she could not say the word accident to him anymore because she was too sensitive to the effect it had on him.

"Unless he's had an accident," he finished for her grimly, and for the first time she noticed the lines of strain and anxiety around his mouth. She knew then that she had done right to offer him help and to force him to accept it. Logan needed her, not because he was helpless and incompetent, far from it, but because she was the person who could break through the barriers that he had erected around himself.

"We'll try the fields first, then," he said.

They crossed the road and climbed the dike into the tussocky field where she had met Neil when the bees had swarmed. The ground oozed water and the burn was swollen and noisy. They crossed over the wooden bridge and walked up the hillock to the little copse of trees that crowned it. Although it wasn't raining anymore water still dripped from the branches and Nancy felt the raw damp air nipping at her cheeks and striking through her raincoat. She looked down at her shoes. They were caked with mud and she wished she'd had the sense to go back to the porch for a pair of rubber boots before setting out. Logan, she noticed, like the knowledgeable Highlander that he was, had come prepared and was wearing his boots.

"He could be anywhere," he sighed as he looked down from the hillock across the field to the old broch, the gray

If Love Be Love

ruin of a mortarless circular building close to the road opposite Miss Macrae's house. Turning slowly, they searched the fields with their eyes, following the line of trees that marked the edge of the woods surrounding the Lodge.

"We can't do it alone, Nancy," announced Logan decisively. "It would take all day, and even then we could miss him. I'll have to round up some of the crofters to help. I'll go back to the cottage and use your phone to contact Harris."

Without waiting for a reply he set off immediately down the hill. Nancy stayed where she was and thought of Neil, trying to put herself in his place. She could imagine his determination to see her before she left Lanmore and she was touched by his thought for her. He would set off through the woods following the path that he knew. She hoped he had remembered to wear his boots and suitable clothing, but she feared that he hadn't. Determined little boys setting off in a hurry on an adventure seldom thought about clothing.

She walked down the hill and across the field in the direction of the broch. She had always intended to look at it closely, but somehow had never done so. She looked at her watch. It was five minutes to ten. There would be time for a quick look before she had to return to the cottage to meet Ian Macrae. Logan would not need her anymore if he was going to get the help of the crofters. For a moment, in the garden, she had thought that he had been about to declare his need of her. When she had told him that Rod had broken off the engagement his eyes had seemed to blaze with joy. But perhaps she had imagined it.

Nearing the broch, she looked up at the mossy stones, each one set carefully upon another, fitting snugly together without mortar. She knew now that it had been built by an ancient race possibly as a defense against an enemy. She knew also that such buildings were found only in the northern part of the Highlands.

This particular broch had been well preserved and there was a plaque set into the wall explaining what it was and when it had been built. Nancy walked through the shored-up entrance into the circle of wet green grass that grew inside.

"Hello, Nancy. Look where I am!"

The childish voice floating down from somewhere on high startled her. She looked upward to the narrow galleries that were built into the thickness of the sloping circular walls. The galleries were not very high, offering evidence that the people who had lived in them had been small. From one of them a blond head appeared.

Quelling her annoyance that the child seemed quite oblivious of the anxiety he had caused, she said calmly, "Hello, Neil. How did you get up there?"

"There are steps in the wall. I climbed up them." He sounded triumphant.

"I think you'd better come down now. Your uncle is looking for you."

"Oh. Is he cross?"

"No, not cross. Just very worried."

She found the rough staircase in the wall. A plaque on the wall spelled out the word Danger. She waited for Neil to come down. He came slowly and cautiously, never slipping on the wet surface of the steps. When he stood beside her he looked up, his gray eyes at their widest and most appealing, and again Nancy had to squash an urge to spank him. She was beginning to realize that Neil had a great future before him as an actor.

"Why did you run away again?" she asked.

"I didn't run away. I wanted to see you. Uncle Logan wouldn't bring me. He said he and I weren't wanted over here, so I came by myself. He's been cross for days."

"But why didn't you come straight to the cottage? Why did you hide in the broch?"

His eyes slid away from hers.

"I wanted to see what it was like," he muttered sulkily.

"Well, that was very unkind of you. Your uncle thinks you've had an accident on the way here. We'll go and find him now. He's at the cottage phoning Mr. Harris to organize a search party for you."

She took the boy firmly by the hand and began to lead him out of the broch.

"What's a search party?" asked the ever inquisitive Neil.

"A lot of people looking for someone who is lost."

"Are you cross, too, Nancy?"

"Yes, I think I am."

"I'm sorry I've made you cross," he said in his most charming way. "I wanted Uncle Logan to come and see if I was at your cottage. I'm glad I hid in the castle."

"It isn't a castle, it's a broch," corrected Nancy absently, her thoughts busy with his pleasure at the way everything had turned out. It sounded as if he had planned it all deliberately for some reason. He had dressed properly after all, she noticed, in Wellington boots and raincoat, so it had not been a sudden whim that had brought him all the way from the Lodge.

"Coooeeee!"

The call was from Linda, who was standing by the dike waving. Nancy looked at her watch. It was ten-fifteen. If they were to catch the train Ian would have to drive very fast.

As she helped Neil over the dike, Linda said excitedly, "Where was he? Logan has just finished talking to Mr. Harris. Ian's getting impatient."

They crossed the road and met both Logan and Ian at the garden gate. At the sight of his uncle's frown Neil half hid behind Nancy.

"Where have you been?" rapped Logan. The boy didn't answer, so Nancy replied for him.

"He was in the broch. He wanted to look at it."

Exasperation twisted Logan's mouth and made him swear softly, "I'll have to phone Harris again and stop the search."

As Logan swung around to walk back to the cottage Ian said in his lilting voice, "If we are to reach Mallaig before the train leaves I shall have to be breakin' the speed record for the distance, Nancy. I'm doubtin' ye'll catch the train today. Howeffer, if ye would be gettin' into the car I'll be doin' my best for ye."

"No!" The word seemed to explode out of Logan as he turned back. "Nancy won't be leaving. Neither will Linda," he added rather belatedly.

They all stared at him. He stared back arrogantly. Ian's tufted eyebrows almost disappeared into his thick curly hair as he registered surprise.

"Ach, I suppose since it's yeself givin' the orders we'll be doin' as ye say, although I'm thinkin' that Nancy should be decidin' for herself whether she is leaving or not."

"Nancy is going to stay, aren't you, Nancy?" piped up Neil, his courage rushing back.

"She'll be havin' to stay another two days, whateffer, if she isn't decidin' soon. My car isn't one of the world's fastest like some I know," remarked Ian dryly with a sly sidelong glance at the green sports car.

"Of course. We can't go tomorrow," chipped in Linda, "because it's Saturday and the trains to Dulthorpe from Carlisle don't run on a Sunday. Hurry up, Nancy, make up your mind!"

Nancy, who had been staring at Logan ever since he had said "No" and trying to understand his sudden interference in their plans, muttered dazedly, "I don't know."

"You are staying here," asserted Logan brusquely.

For once his authoritative manner did not rouse any antipathy in her. He had commanded her to stay, so she would stay.

"Now whatever would you be wantin' her to stay for?" asked the inquisitive Ian, his shrewd blue eyes going from one to the other, his long nose almost quivering as he sensed a juicy piece of gossip.

Logan smiled suddenly and answered him in Gaelic. Immediately Ian let out a wild Highland yell. Logan did not wait to be questioned but hurried away up the path into the cottage.

"What did he say, Ian?" demanded Linda. "Oh, do tell us!"

"Ach, no, it is for himself to be tellin' ye. I'm away to tell Meg. Ach, we'll be havin' a grand celidh tonight, I'm telling ye!"

He flung back his head and let out another yell, did a brief Highland fling, went out through the gate, threw himself into his old battered car and drove away up the road to his own house.

Nancy and Linda stood in the wet garden and stared at each other.

"Do you know why Logan wants you to stay?" asked Linda.

If Love Be Love

"No. But we'll find out. It may be only for a day or two. I'm longing for a hot drink and I know Neil must be famished because he hasn't had any breakfast. Would you like porridge, Neil?"

"Yes, please... the way you make it."

Logan had just finished speaking into the phone as they entered the house.

"We're going to give Neil some breakfast," said Nancy. "Would you like some tea to drink?"

"Yes, please. But Linda must do the cooking and the tea making. I want to talk to you... in the garden."

Nancy followed him outside again. It seemed as if she had no will of her own. He commanded and she obeyed. Although she did not think the garden the best place to talk on a damp day she sat on the bench beside him. It was quiet apart from the patter of water dripping from the eaves and the trees and the soft shush of the waves on the shingle shore.

On the grass a lone thrush, plump and spotted, tugged at a worm that was reluctant to leave the warm moist earth.

"You will stay, won't you, Nancy?" He didn't sound so arrogant now.

"I don't see how I can. It isn't fair to Don for Linda and me to live on the croft. He may want to marry someday. And there isn't any work that I can do around here. There aren't any pharmacist's shops on Lanmore."

"But you would like to stay?" he probed.

"You know I would. Remember you said once that it would be interesting to see whether I would want to leave Lanmore once September came. Well, I don't want to leave Lanmore, but I have to earn my living."

"I know of a way to make it possible for you to stay."

He was going to suggest she stay and act as a nanny to Neil. She couldn't bear the thought of it and she had to stop him before he made the suggestion.

"If you're thinking of offering me a position in your household as Neil's nanny, don't bother, because the answer is quite definitely no."

"The thought never entered my head," he replied coolly. "I was thinking that the way for you to stay on Lanmore would be for you to marry me."

Marry him! Marry Logan Maclaine who regarded marriage as an outmoded ceremony and as a form of human sacrifice! She couldn't believe her ears.

"Surely you don't mean that? Why, only last week you told me that you had never had any intention of marrying anyone. And Mary told me that you still had no intention of marrying."

His grin was rather rueful.

"Did I say that to her? Put it down to one of my sour moods. I haven't been the best person to live with since you refused to change your principles for me. And I haven't been on good terms with Mary because I felt she had been talking too freely to you about my past affairs. Certainly I had no intention of marrying anyone until I met you, Nancy Allan, and here I am proposing to you because it's the only way I can think of to prevent you from leaving Lanmore—and me—short of kidnapping you and carrying you off to the Lodge to keep you there under lock and key, which you must agree is not a civilized way of behaving."

"But why do you want me to stay?" she asked breathlessly.

"Because I love you. What other reason could there be? I've loved you ever since you stood in the lamplight in the kitchen and wouldn't admit defeat in spite of the damp dusty cottage and the thought of having to light a peat fire. I loved you because you didn't care who I was or what I had done. I loved you and I tried to make you love me... but always there was Rod in the way to block my progress."

Nancy sat tensely, not daring to look at him. Then she felt his fingers in her hair.

"Look at me, marigold lady," he murmured.

She turned her head and at once he framed her face with his hands.

"Don't you believe me?" he questioned softly.

She believed him because love was there in his eyes and on his lips as he kissed her gently.

"I am thinking you are not far from loving me, either," he taunted tenderly as he released her.

"I've been in love for days... for weeks... with you," she answered, "but I couldn't believe it was possible. I

If Love Be Love

hadn't known you for very long and I'd known Rod for years."

"And nothing I said or did would move you in your loyalty to him. I guessed you were bewildered and unhappy and like you I wasn't sure whether I loved you enough to change my way of life, to risk marrying you. You see, Nancy, my parents' marriage and my brother's marriage were not shining examples and have made me rather overcautious and perhaps a little cynical."

"If you're not sure..." she began uncertainly.

"What are you going to suggest?" he cut in with a mischievous grin. "A trial marriage?"

"I'm willing if you would prefer it," she replied seriously.

He laughed and shook her gently by the shoulders.

"Oh, Nancy, if ever I wanted convincing that you love me that's done the trick," he said. "No trial marriage for us. I've learned recently that I'm just as possessive and jealous as the next man. I want everyone to know that you're mine, and the best way of advertising that is to marry you with all the necessary pomp and ceremony. And now I'm wanting badly to kiss you."

"Here?"

"What better place is there?"

"But the neighbors...."

"I told Ian Macrae that I intended to ask you to marry me, so they will have been watching and waiting."

They kissed, and Nancy forgot that her feet were cold and damp in her mud-caked shoes. Around them in the quiet garden the birds twittered. On the hillside a sheep bleated and out on the gray loch the sea gulls cried.

"Tea's made!" called Linda. "Oh, I didn't know you were busy."

Logan raised his head and smiled at her.

"You can get used to us being busy, as you call it, I'm going to marry Nancy."

"Another hero falls from his pedestal," mourned Linda dramatically.

"Does that mean Nancy is going to stay?" asked Neil, nudging close to his uncle's knees.

"I hope it does," said Logan.

"Yes, I'm staying, Neil, and you won't have to say goodbye," said Nancy.

"Then I won't have to get lost anymore," Neil smiled seraphically as they all looked at him with puzzlement.

"Do you mean to say you've been getting lost deliberately?" asked Logan, and there was menace in his voice.

"Not the first time, but all the other times. In Skye 'cos I wanted to go back on the boat. Last time 'cos I didn't want to go to London with mommy. And this time 'cos you were cross and I knew you would come to ask Nancy if I was here... and you're never cross when you're with Nancy, and I didn't want her to go away."

The explanation of his motives was becoming all too complicated for Neil, so he stopped and stared up at his uncle appealingly.

Nancy and Linda couldn't help laughing at his confession, but Logan frowned at his nephew, who took a few steps backward in haste. Linda grabbed him by the hand and still choking with laughter said, "I think you've done enough for one morning, you little manipulator! Come and have your porridge."

They went into the cottage. Logan muttered through his teeth, "Manipulator is too mild a word to describe that child. He's nothing less than a blackmailer. He'll always get people to do as he wants by fair means or foul."

"But without him getting lost that first time, we might never have known each other really well," whispered Nancy.

"Don't you be believing that," he admonished softly. "I'd have found a way. Once you stepped onto the soil of Lanmore you were lost to the rest of the world, and when winter comes and we're sitting together in the long dark evenings I shall be telling you why."

THE CAVE OF THE WHITE ROSE

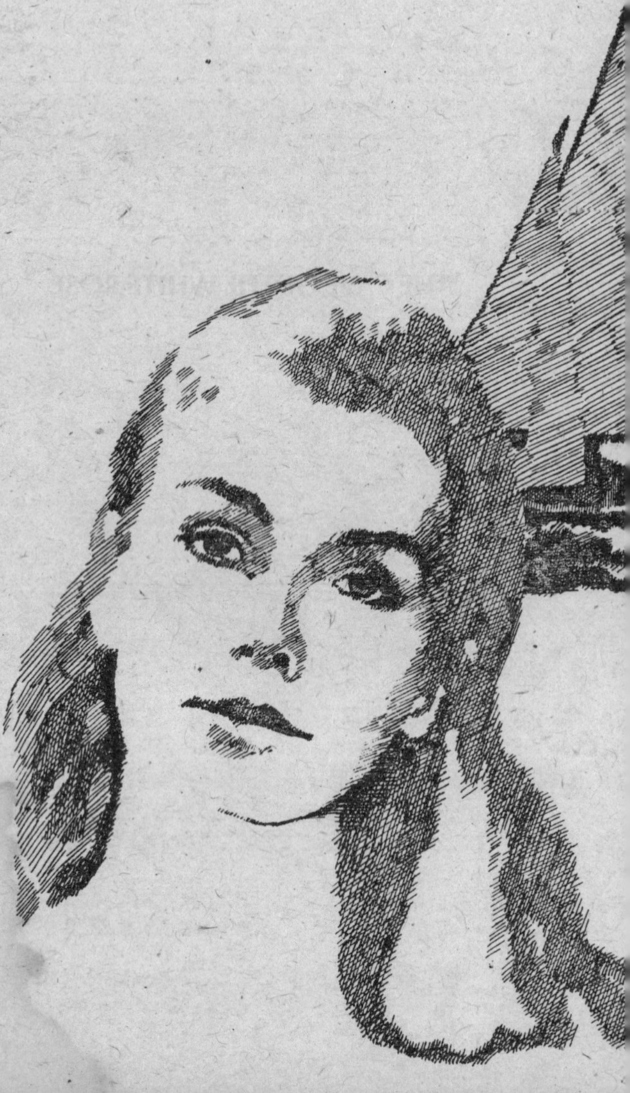

The Cave of the White Rose

"Lance will do anything for his family," an old friend had told Juliet. But her own experience privately led her to disagree.

Lance Crimond was insensitive and intolerant of the weaknesses of others. Didn't he show a total lack of sympathy for his crippled brother, whose wife's death was rumored to be Lance's fault?

Furthermore, he displayed only a callous disregard for Juliet's own feelings. Lance seemed determined to control every member of his household—including Juliet herself!

CHAPTER ONE

THE BRIDE AND BRIDEGROOM were going away. Juliet Grey stood on tiptoe and tried to see over the broadcloth-covered shoulder of the man who stood in front of her and who was effectually blocking the front doorway of the Ring o' Bells, the old coaching inn where the wedding reception was taking place.

It was useless. He was too tall and too wide. He took up all the space. He was deaf, too. She'd asked him twice to move and let her pass him so that she could join the laughing, joking group of relatives and friends who were saying goodbye to the happy couple, but he hadn't heard her.

She should be there out in front to wave to Hilary, her lively good-natured cousin who had married Ian Munro that afternoon in the thirteenth-century church on the other side of the village green. Coming from the Highlands of Scotland, quietly spoken and a little shy, Ian had come to work for Hilary's father more than a year ago. Perhaps it was his native reserve and his obstinate refusal to be stampeded by his boss's gay daughter that had appealed to Hilary, mused Juliet romantically, for she knew that her cousin had fallen head over heels in love with the young, highly qualified engineer.

Now they were going away together for a honeymoon in Europe and Juliet was determined to wish good luck to the cousin who had remembered her and had invited her to attend the wedding.

"Excuse me, please." She spoke as loudly as she could. "I'd like to see them go."

This time the man in front of her heard. He turned. She was strangely and tinglingly aware of the cold glitter of light eyes, deep-set under dark eyebrows, of a broad chest only just confined by the severe tailoring of an impeccable morning suit, and then she slid past him, graceful and cool in her sea-green dress.

She was only just in time. Ian had started the engine of the car and Hilary was giving her parents a last kiss and hug before getting into her seat beside her husband. Juliet had to push a little before she was able to get anywhere near the car, and then at last she was standing beside her other two cousins, Hilary's twin sisters, Anthea and Sylvia.

Before the car moved away Hilary opened the window on her side and threw her bouquet of red and white roses toward the group of young women. Her sweet, infectious smile lit up her face.

"Here," she cried, "whoever catches it will be the next to marry!" Juliet wasn't conscious of striving to catch that bouquet. Like her cousins she held out her arms, but having always been a butterfingers she didn't think she would catch it, so that no one was more surprised than she when her hands closed around the sweet-smelling bunch of flowers with its long trailing ribbons. She gazed down at them in a bemused fashion, only half aware of her cousins' envious comments.

The car was going to the accompaniment of waves and cheers. Aunt Faith, Hilary's mother, superbly elegant as always in navy blue and white, was dabbing at her eyes with a lace-edged handkerchief. Uncle Clive, short and vigorous, his expansive smile a more studied masculine counterpart of his daughter's, was informing the guests that the party wasn't over yet and that there was plenty of champagne left.

And then suddenly everyone had gone back into the inn, and Juliet was alone in the afternoon sunshine that filtered through the leaves of the sycamore trees edging the green, and she was looking down through a mist of tears at the bouquet of roses.

Still blinded by the tears, she turned and walked reluctantly into the dim interior of the inn. Now that Hilary and Ian had gone her interest in the wedding waned. She would have liked to escape from the reception, but she knew that if she didn't join the party, comments would be made about her by Aunt Faith, and she wasn't having that.

The Cave of the White Rose

It had been a lovely wedding, she thought. Hilary had looked almost regal in a simple dress of white lace. Sunlight had mellowed the gray stonework of the church, which was famed for the brasses set into the floor of its aisles. From the carved oak choir stall the voices of the boys had soared heavenward in perfect harmony, backed by the throbbing sound of one of the finest organs in the country. The reception after the service, held in the elegant paneled dining room of the eighteenth-century inn, widely known for its excellent cuisine and cellar, had gone off without a hitch.

In fact it had been everything a wedding should be, as Aunt Faith had intended it should be; a wedding that the county would not forget in a hurry, as Aunt Faith had intended it should not; a wedding that had been as much a testimony of Aunt Faith's severely conventional outlook and brilliant powers of organization as it had been the crowning ceremony of Hilary's and Ian's love.

Crash! Juliet's thoughts splintered in all directions. She had walked into something rocklike and resistant. The tinkle of glass warned her that something had broken, and a faint feeling of dampness in the vicinity of her knees made her realize that whatever had broken had contained liquid, which had spilled on her dress; her beautiful dress on which she had spent all her savings.

Shock drove the last glimmer of tears from her eyes and alerted her. Her glance traveled up, over a pale gray waistcoat fastened with pearl buttons, past a pale gray cravat to the edge of a square chin. Above the chin a contradictory mouth was curved into a faintly contemptuous smile. The mouth was contradictory because its long thin upper lip hinted at sternness and possibly cruelty, whereas the full lower lip hinted at generosity and a love of life.

Juliet didn't allow her glance to go any higher than the contradictory mouth.

"I'm sorry," she muttered to the crushed bouquet in her hand, which looked distinctly forlorn after its contact with that formidable physique. "I wasn't looking where I was going."

"You can say that again!"

The voice was a surprise, as was the expression he used. It was quiet and edged by a crispness of accent she couldn't place.

"Were you blinded by tears, perhaps?" he added, and there was a sarcastic taunt implicit in the words.

But Juliet was impervious to that kind of taunt. Astonished that he had been able to guess so accurately, she looked higher into pale gray eyes bright and observant between thick dark lashes. Above the eyes a lock of dark hair had slid forward onto a lined forehead. It seemed to her to be completely out of keeping with the rest of his immaculate appearance, a symbol of rebelliousness against conventional surroundings.

"Supposing I was?" she replied earnestly. "People always cry at weddings. They were tears of happiness. Hilary is my cousin and I'm happy because she's happy."

"And what about the groom? Are you happy for him too?"

"Oh, yes, of course I am. Hilary is one of the nicest people I know. Ian can't help but be happy with her."

"You astound me," he gibed softly, but didn't say why. "So you're the cousin of the bride—and incidentally, the only unmarried woman who hasn't been introduced to me yet by my very attentive hostess." His gray eyes flickered sardonically in the direction of Aunt Faith, who was busy talking to Sir Humphrey Bartlett, chairman of the group of engineering companies of which Uncle Clive was the managing director. "I wonder why she left you out?" This time the gray eyes subjected her to their all-assessing glance.

"I expect it's because I'm not very important," Juliet replied in all sincerity. "I'm only Juliet Grey, the poor relation. If you'll please excuse me I'll find someone to sweep up this mess." She indicated the smashed champagne glass on the floor.

"There's no need. Someone is already coming to do that," he said.

His hand was gripping her arm above the elbow and she was unable to move away without pulling in an undignified manner. She looked up inquiringly.

The Cave of the White Rose

"You don't dress poor," he remarked. "That outfit must have set you back a bit." His bright gaze roved over the sea-green gown with its deep U-shaped neckline, its high waist and long full sleeves, edged with embroidered white roses.

"Yes, it did," she replied equably. "All my savings. I wanted to look my best for Hilary."

"Even though the coffers were empty and the prospects were nil?" His astuteness took her breath away.

"How do you know?" she asked sharply, her eyes wide and wondering.

He touched the fine bones that showed through the white skin where her neck joined her shoulders. The tips of his fingers were slightly rough and their touch embarrassed her and she tried to draw away. But his other hand still held her arm firmly.

"Too thin," he remarked. "And I watched you eating earlier."

"Oh!" The knowledge that those brilliantly lit observant eyes had been watching her when she hadn't noticed startled her.

"Don't think I don't understand what lies behind your effort to put on a brave show. I once did the same, and turned up at a wedding all correctly dressed, without a penny in my pocket," he said, and the undercurrent of laughter in his voice mocked himself. "It's odd what youthful pride will drive us to do. But your beautiful dress is stained. You must let me pay for the cleaning of it."

"Oh, no, I couldn't! I mean, I don't know you, and it wouldn't be right. It was my fault and I...."

"Yes," he agreed aggravatingly, "come to think of it, it was your fault. Then come and drink champagne with me and I'll introduce myself, if you insist on being conventional."

She had the oddest feeling that she was being swept off her feet by a ruthless force that would push her along remorselessly in the way it wanted her to go, irrespective of any feelings she might have on the matter.

She considered the recalcitrant lock of black hair and

then the bright glitter of the gray eyes and came to a conclusion.

"No, thank you," she said. "You've quite obviously had more than enough already."

He was puzzled. "Enough what?"

"Enough champagne. Now, please let go of my arm."

By way of answer he let out a shout of laughter, which caused every head in the room to turn in their direction.

This time she felt anger scorch through her.

"Oh, now look what you've done! Everyone is looking at us," she hissed at him.

"Including your aunt, and her expression is one of disapproval, but of you, not me," he answered with a wickedly attractive grin. "So you think I've had more than enough champagne? That's a pity, because I was looking forward to drinking the happiness of the newlyweds with you and at the same time becoming better acquainted with you. You see, I saw your mother dance when I was a boy. It was before you were born. She was dancing the part of Juliet in Lambert's ballet of *Romeo and Juliet*. I guess you were named after her favorite heroine." He tipped his head to one side and studied her. "You're not unlike her. Do you dance, too?"

"No, I don't. Oh, do tell me about her," she urged, forgetting that she wanted to escape from him.

"Only if you promise to drink champagne with me."

She promised, and from then on he took over. Not that he wouldn't have done anyway, she thought ruefully, as she sat on the cushioned window seat that curved under a bow window at one end of the big room. He was the sort of man she detested, typical of the big business executives with whom Uncle Clive associated; the sort who would always manage to get his own way using any means available to him. But she would sit with him for a while because she wanted to hear about her mother.

When he came with two glasses of champagne he presented hers with an amused tilt of his dark eyebrows.

"With the compliments of your uncle. He's very pleased that I'm entertaining his niece, even though his wife frowns upon us and would prefer to see me entertaining one of her daughters."

Juliet sent a quick anxious glance in the direction of her aunt. It was true, Aunt Faith was watching her, a faint frown of irritation on her usually blandly smiling face, which meant she didn't like what she was seeing.

"Why should uncle be pleased because you're entertaining me?" Juliet asked, raising innocent eyes to his face. "Who are you?"

"If you're the poor relation of the Greys, I suppose I might be considered the wealthy relation of the Munros, so watch out, you'd better not offend me," he remarked with a laugh. "I'm Lance Crimond."

Juliet was really none the wiser. The name Crimond meant nothing to her.

"Lance for Launcelot?" she inquired.

"Yes, but spelled with an *a* only. Your turn to laugh and to tell me that you've never met anyone less like a knight in shining armor than I," he replied, and his wicked white grin was in evidence again.

"Although Lancelot was the warrior whom King Arthur 'loved and honored most' he didn't always behave himself," murmured Juliet, recalling the stories she'd read of the Arthurian legend. "He broke a few rules."

The quick upward glance of his gray eyes was as bright as a flash of lightning against the darkness of a thundercloud.

"And you think I'm capable of doing the same?" he queried with dangerous softness.

"Not only capable, but probably you have already," she answered coolly. The lightning flash was brighter and she quailed a little at her own temerity. But he didn't retaliate. Instead he laughed again and once again heads were turned curiously, and she wished she hadn't agreed to sit and drink champagne with him.

"We're forgetting our toasts," he said easily, raising his glass. "To the happy couple, to Hilary and Ian."

"To the happy couple," repeated Juliet, and sipped the sparkling wine.

She glanced at the crushed roses on her lap. "Whoever

catches them will be the next to marry." Would it be her turn next? Would she ever meet anyone who would love and cherish her? Would the loneliness she had known for so long ever come to an end?

"Will you be the next to marry?" said a quiet crisp voice beside her. Now she was convinced he had magical powers.

"You should have been called Merlin, not Lancelot," she said sharply.

"Nothing magic about it. You looked down at the bouquet and it was easy to guess what you were thinking from the expression on your face. Will you be the next?"

"How do I know? I have no magical powers and can't see into the future."

"Does that mean you're not in love with anyone?"

"Can't you tell by the expression on my face?" she countered acidly, and his grin appeared again.

"I wondered when you'd show your claws. So you're not in love. For that I'm glad, because it will save complications later on."

What on earth did he mean by that? She was about to burst into speech when he held up his hand and said quickly, "I know, I know, don't say it. I'm infuriating, and I've had more than enough champagne. But what else is there to do at a wedding if you're not the bride or the groom except to keep on drinking their health?" He twisted his empty glass in his hand and added somberly, "Last time I went to a wedding I vowed I would never go to another."

"Whose wedding?" asked Juliet, her interest caught by his unusual statement.

"My brother Gareth's," he replied brusquely.

It was incredible. First Lancelot and now Gareth. Was it possible that Gareth's wife was called Lynette? Juliet longed to ask, but a certain grimness about the set of her companion's mouth suggested that the subject of his brother's wedding was forbidden ground.

"Then why have you broken your vow and come here today?" she asked instead.

He considered her slowly and deliberately before he answered.

"To look for a wife," he replied, and cocked a quizzical eyebrow at her. "Interested?"

Again anger scorched through her like a flame. She gathered the bouquet in her hand and stood up.

"Now I'm sure you've had more than enough!"

His hand grasped her elbow again and she was forced to sit down on the cushioned seat.

"You'll have everyone looking at us again if you behave like that," he cautioned derisively, "and you know how much you dislike drawing attention to yourself. Besides, I haven't told you about your mother yet."

Out of the corner of her eye Juliet could see that Aunt Faith was gradually approaching the window seat, stopping every so often to talk graciously to guests.

"Relax," murmured her companion. "I'll behave, and I'll deal with your aunt when she comes."

He noticed too much, she decided, but she leaned back and fiddled with the bouquet. The petals of one rose fell suddenly and lay like crimson drops of blood on the aquamarine sheen of her dress.

"Was my mother a very good dancer?" she asked diffidently.

"To my ten-year-old eyes she was the perfect Juliet, slight and graceful with a cloud of fair hair," he answered soberly. "It was my first visit to the ballet—or to any theater for that matter. My mother is an English-literature buff, as you might gather from the names she gave to her three sons. My youngest brother was christened Tristram. That year she decided to take Gareth and me with her on her annual pilgrimage to the London theater. The ballet was thrown in for good measure because it was *Romeo and Juliet*, and also because she knew your mother. They both came from the same part of Wales. Did you never see her dance?"

"Not that I can remember. I was only five when she died. How did you know I'm her daughter?"

"Your uncle told me. When I saw you come into church this morning I thought I was seeing things. You resembled her very much, and I was sure you must be related to her.

So at the earliest opportunity I asked Clive about you and he told me the whole sad story, how both your parents were killed when they were staying with friends on a seagoing yacht at Monte Carlo. I believe it was a gas explosion, wasn't it? He also told me that he'd brought you up as if you were one of his own daughters."

"Yes, Uncle Clive has always been very kind. He has a great sense of family," she replied woodenly.

"More credit to him then. But why did you leave his home to fend for yourself?"

How could she tell him of the unhappy years she had endured living with Aunt Faith? How could she describe Aunt Faith's subtle forms of cruelty to her, which were the outcome of jealousy of the beautiful unconventional Norma who had married the equally unconventional Lawrence Grey, music lover and critic for a leading newspaper?

"Have you ever felt rebellious?" she asked.

"Not only have I felt rebellious but I've rebelled many times during my life. But you don't look as if you have an ounce of rebellion in you." He glanced at Aunt Faith and his eyes twinkled wickedly. "I gather you rebelled against the establishment and ran away. It must have taken a lot of courage."

"All I had," she agreed, and experienced a strange warmth because for the second time he had understood and appreciated her feelings.

"Where did you go?"

"To London, to see my mother's old ballet teacher. I'd always longed to dance ballet, but neither Uncle Clive nor Aunt Faith encouraged me. When I left school I was sent to a secretarial school. It was taken for granted that I would go to work in uncle's company in gratitude for being given a home and having my education paid for. But when I'd finished my training and I realized what lay before me... something burst inside. I couldn't stay any longer with them."

"So what did you do?"

"Madame Follet told me I was too old to train as a dancer. She ran a rather select ballet school, and she took me on as an assistant to her overworked secretary." She paused a moment, then added in a sad little voice, "I was there until Madame Follet died quite suddenly three weeks ago."

"What happened to the school?" His voice was sharp, interested.

"It's been closed. I've been trying to find another similar position, but it isn't easy. I'm not really a secretary type of person, but I enjoyed the work at the school because being involved with ballet made it seem worthwhile."

She was aware of a flash of navy blue and white. Aunt Faith was on her way toward them.

"Mr. Crimond," she whispered urgently, "please don't say anything to my aunt or my cousins about my not having a job. I have reasons for not wanting them to know."

He nodded absently as if he was thinking of something else, and the warmth she had felt faded. He had lost interest in her problem and she was out in the cold again, on her own.

"Where do you live?" The quick question startled her.

"London — Earl's Court. I moved there when the school was closed."

"Living in a grimy little bed-sitter, no doubt," he remarked scathingly. "How would you like to live in a castle...?"

"Called Camelot," she couldn't resist saying.

"I'll drive you back to town and tell you about it."

"Oh, no, I couldn't! I wouldn't dream of imposing on you," she began.

"Now, Julie, you mustn't monopolize Mr. Crimond," Aunt Faith's throaty voice oozed sweetness. "I'm sure there are many other people here whom he would like to meet. Remember always, Julie, that it's good manners to circulate at a party. That way no one ever gets bored with your brand of conversation. Don't you agree, Mr. Crimond?"

While Juliet cringed over the poor wilted bouquet, Lance had risen politely to his feet. He regarded Aunt Faith with cold eyes.

"No, I don't," he said curtly. "Juliet and I have had a

most interesting conversation. I'd like to continue it and I want very much to drive her back to town, but so far I've been unable to persuade her to come with me. I wonder if you'd be good enough to assure her that I'm sober, in my right mind and come from a highly respectable and respected family?"

The devil! The infuriating devil! What did he think he was doing? Now she was sure to receive a lecture from Aunt Faith on how not to treat an honored and respected guest. Her sea-blue eyes flashed angrily and her pale hair belled out as she swung around to face him. But on meeting his steady gaze the hot words that trembled on her lips remained unsaid.

To her amazement she heard Aunt Faith saying, "How could you think such things, Julie? Of course you must go with Mr. Crimond. I can certainly vouch for his respectability. But must you leave so soon, Mr. Crimond? Clive and I were hoping you would come back to our home for dinner. Julie could come, too—after all, she is one of the family, and you could take her up to town later."

"Thank you for the invitation, but I'm afraid I can't stay any longer. I've promised to meet some business acquaintances tonight. It's my only chance to see them, because I'm off to Germany in the morning," replied Lance coolly.

"So disappointing," cooed Aunt Faith, "but I understand. Perhaps next time you're down this way. Just give Clive a ring. We'd be delighted to see you. Now are you quite sure you want to take Julie? She can always go back by train, you know."

But he was quite sure, and once again Juliet was conscious of being swept along by an irresistible force. This time it swept her through farewells to her uncle and her cousins, out of the inn and into a dashing dark green car, which soon was nosing its way through the village out onto a road that wound between leafy hedgerows and past pale stone farmhouses.

"We'll have dinner in town," said Lance crisply. "Will that suit you?"

The Cave of the White Rose

"I wonder you bother to consult me," she returned tartly, and he chuckled.

"I guess I hustled you a bit, but I knew that the time had come for me to leave and I had a feeling you didn't want to stay much longer. Was I right?"

"Yes," she admitted with a sigh. "You like to be right, don't you?"

"I do, and I am right, nine times out of ten. How long did you work for Madame Follet?"

"Four years. That makes me twenty-two. Is that what you wanted to know?"

"You look and behave younger," he replied bluntly, and for a while there was silence between them.

Juliet watched the elegantly tailored Oxford countryside roll by the window. Tall trees cast long shadows over green fields. Little more than an hour ago Hilary and Ian had come along this same road on their way to Heathrow, yet because of the strange turn of events it seemed hours since they had left. She glanced sideways at her companion and wondered what he had in store for her next. She had to admit he'd handled Aunt Faith very well.

"The last thing Aunt Faith wanted was for you to drive me into London," she murmured.

"I know. The invitation to dinner was produced very slickly."

"And I suppose the business acquaintances you have to see tonight are fictitious."

"Not at all. They're staying at the same hotel. They're really friends over from British Columbia, three wild miners on the spree in the swinging city. I promised I'd have a last game of poker with them tonight. They return to Canada tomorrow."

Canada. Now she was beginning to place that elusive intermittent accent.

"Are you a Canadian?" she asked.

"No. I'm British born and I was reared in Scotland like Ian. But I lived in Canada for the best part of nine years. Does it show?"

"A little. Sometimes in your speech, the expressions you use, and you have a slight accent."

"And sometimes in my manners, perhaps," he put in dryly. "Life on a construction site in the wilds can be pretty rough."

"Why did you come back?"

"My father was ill. I came back to help him in the family business."

"What sort of business?"

"Do you mean to say you don't know, that you've never heard of Crimond Civil Engineering or my grandfather Alexander Crimond who designed the Kawali Dam and the Fraser Bridge?" His voice shook with incredulous laughter.

"No, never. Should I have done?" asked Juliet innocently. Now she understood his association with Uncle Clive, whose company supplied equipment to construction companies.

"Oh, this is priceless," he was still chuckling. "Tess is going to love you."

"Tess?"

"My mother. She's a sort of elderly hippie. She's always scorned big business and money-grubbing. She lives in a prepetual daydream and prefers the simple life as long as someone is willing to foot the bill. She writes... romantic thrillers, I think they're called. Perhaps you've heard of her even if you haven't heard of my illustrious grandfather. Her pen name is Tessa Dean."

Juliet, who had recently read the latest offering by Tessa Dean, was enthralled by this piece of news.

"I loved her last story. It was fascinating. It was called *Sounding Brass*. But why is she going to love me? I'm not going to meet her."

"Yes, you are. You're going to have dinner with her, and with a bit of good luck you're going to be her secretary-companion and live in a place that isn't called Camelot."

Juliet took a deep breath. Somehow she must make an effort to battle against this inexorable force that had entered her life and had taken her over, before it swept her in a direction she didn't wish to go.

The Cave of the White Rose

"Mr. Crimond—" she began firmly.

"If you're going to object you may as well save your breath," he said curtly, "because I'm not going to listen. There's the motorway ahead. I like driving fast, but I find it safer if I'm not involved in an argument at the same time."

After several miles of tight-lipped, fist-clenched silence, Juliet's temper began to simmer down. She wasn't normally a quick-tempered person, but Lance's calm assumption that she should do as he dictated had roused the independent spirit that slept beneath her docile appearance, and it took her some time to control the urge to attack him verbally. By the time she had decided there was little use in speaking to him if he wasn't going to listen and if he wasn't going to retaliate, which for some reason was even more irritating, they were speeding along the motorway toward London, and she was saving her breath.

Save your breath to cool your porridge. The old saying flashed through her mind. Did they eat porridge in the place that wasn't called Camelot? Since it was in Scotland it was quite possible that they did. He had said he would tell her all about the castle while he drove her into town. In fact that had been the bait that had enticed her to come with him, she thought crossly, conveniently forgetting that she had had no choice in the matter but had been hustled into coming with him. And now he was sitting there silent and relaxed, not telling her anything, while the car hurtled along at seventy miles an hour.

Perhaps she would learn more about the castle from his mother, who was Tessa Dean, the novelist, with whom she was going to have dinner. Alarm struck. How could she have dinner in a London hotel in this dress on which champagne had been spilled? She leaned forward to see if the stain was bad. It was quite faint and might not be noticed by others, but she knew it was there and she would be conscious of it all the time and it would worry her.

Juliet's eyes gleamed mischievously. Here was her excuse not to go to dinner with Lance Crimond's mother—a way of thwarting this man who thought he had taken over. When they were nearer London she would ask him to take her to Earl's Court so that she could change. Once she was in her own place she would refuse to go on with him, and short of abducting her with physical violence there would be little he could do.

As the sprawling suburbs closed in around them she brought up the subject of the dress.

"I can't go to dinner in this dress," she announced clearly.

"Why not?"

"It's stained, and it isn't very suitable."

He flicked a sidelong glance in her direction.

"As an excuse to get out of dining with my mother that's very poor," he gibed. "You must know how elegant and mysterious you look in it."

Elegant and mysterious? That wasn't how she saw herself. She was so interested and puzzled by the different image of herself, wondering how she could possibly have achieved it quite by accident, that several more miles passed before she saw his comment for what it was, a way of diverting her from her intention.

"I must change it," she insisted. "It won't take long. I live quite near the Exhibition Hall and I can direct you from here."

"Nothing doing, Juliet. You're fine as you are. My mother isn't a stickler for etiquette like your Aunt Faith, and she probably won't care what you're wearing. Ten to one she'll be in tweeds and beads herself."

After that she gave up and sat in passive silence trying to pretend to herself that she wasn't excited at the thought of meeting Tessa Dean, and that the possibility of becoming her secretary wasn't enticing. If only the opportunity hadn't come her way through this domineering, infuriating man!

Mrs. Crimond wasn't staying in the same hotel as her son. She preferred the slower, more conservative ways of an old-established hotel in Bloomsbury to the streamlined, efficient American-style amenities offered farther west, which were his choice.

At the reception desk they were told that she had already gone in to dinner and had left a message for Lance saying

The Cave of the White Rose

that he was to join her in the dining room. Attacked suddenly by shyness, Juliet excused herself to go to the ladies' room to freshen up before going to the dining room.

"You can go if you promise not to try and escape by the window," said Lance sternly.

"Having come this far I'm not going to be done out of a meal," she retorted a little shakily, lifting her chin.

"That's better," he said, and glanced down at the dilapidated bouquet that she was still carrying. He took it from her and examined it. Only one rose seemed to have escaped being squashed. It was a white half-opened bud. Lance pulled it out, stared at it for a second and then to Juliet's surprise tucked it behind her ear.

"I think you might call it symbolic," he remarked. "See you here in a few minutes."

Slightly bemused by his action, Juliet stared at herself in the mirror in the ladies' room. There was a flush on her usually pale cheeks and her eyes were sparkling. The white rosebud looked untouched and curiously innocent against the swath of her pale hair. Symbolic, Lance had called it. What had he meant? She knew the white rose was one of the Scottish symbols along with the lion rampant and the thistle. Had he meant she should wear it because with a bit of good luck she might go to Scotland as his mother's secretary? Or had he meant something deeper? Who could guess what went on in the mind of a man like Lance Crimond? He was too complex a personality for her to understand. Nor did she wish to understand him.

But even as her hand was raised to remove the rose from behind her ear and to throw it into the wastebasket she experienced a sudden bewildering change of mind, and left it where it was.

They found Mrs. Crimond sitting alone at a table for two, peering through a pair of owllike spectacles at the menu. She was a slim straight-backed woman with a mass of wavy white hair. As Lance had said, her attitude to dress was careless and she was wearing a nondescript skirt and blouse that Aunt Faith might have considered suitable for supervising the cleaning of the house. Around her neck were row upon row of multicolored beads of which any hippie would have been envious.

When they reached the table and Lance spoke to her she looked up and removed the glasses, and at once the initial impression of someone who was careless and slovenly was dispersed by the high forehead, clear-cut aquiline nose, fine sweep of cheek from temple to chin and the intelligent vivid blue eyes.

"Lance, how lovely! Are you going to dine with me after all?" Her voice was gentle with just the slightest suspicion of a lilting Welsh accent.

"No, but I've brought someone who is."

Juliet in her shyness had lingered behind him, hiding behind his broad shoulders, but as he spoke he reached out a hand, took one of hers and pulled her forward. Mrs. Crimond's blue eyes focused on her and surprise widened them before she transferred her gaze to Lance.

"The young Juliet," she murmured. "Where did you find her?"

"At the wedding. And her name really is Juliet—Juliet Grey. She's Norma Thomas's daughter."

"Oh, my dear!" To Juliet's amazement Mrs. Crimond stood up, grasped her by the shoulders and kissed her on both cheeks. "This is wonderful! I knew your mother well. Her death was one of the great tragedies. She still had so much pleasure to offer the world. Please sit down—here, near me. Lance, ask them to set two more places. This is a very important occasion and should be celebrated accordingly."

"Then you shall celebrate it with Juliet. I need to change out of this lot," replied Lance, indicating his morning suit. "I promised Eddie and Cal that I'd see them, as it's their last night in London."

A faint frown expressing supercilious distaste marred Mrs. Crimond's high white forehead.

"So you prefer a night out on the town with some of your more uncouth acquaintances to dinner with Juliet and me," she said with a touch of asperity, and Juliet glanced uneasily at Lance, expecting him to take offense. But he merely grinned affectionately at his mother.

"They're a wild bunch when they're let out on the spree, I admit, but I wouldn't call them uncouth. Rugged, hard-working and entitled to a gay time occasionally, but not ill-mannered," he murmured in defense of his friends.

Mrs. Crimond's frown faded and her eyes twinkled with understanding.

"All right, I'll let you off this time, but only because you found Juliet and had the sense to bring her to me," she said, smiling warmly at Juliet, who was immediately enslaved.

"I thought you might see it like that," said Lance. "But now that I've found her for you, can I trust you not to let her escape? She has quite a strong streak of independence. It just happens that she's out of work, and I think she's what you've been looking for."

Mrs. Crimond gave him a slightly puzzled glance.

"She types...and can do secretarial work," prompted Lance softly, and understanding dawned slowly in Mrs. Crimond's eyes.

"Is that true?" she asked Juliet.

"Yes. I've been working as an assistant secretary to Madame Follet for the past four years."

"I can hardly believe it! You look more like a ballet dancer to me," whispered Mrs. Crimond. "You know, Lance, she's like an answer to an oft repeated prayer."

"She's been conjured up by old wizard Merlin especially for you, Tess," he remarked mockingly. He touched Juliet briefly on the shoulder and to her consternation she shivered at his touch. "I'll say goodbye to you for now. See you in Camelot," he murmured, and there was a strangely cynical twist to his mouth as if he had noticed her shiver. He turned to his mother and added, "Bye, Tess, and remember what I said. Don't let her escape."

"Camelot?" repeated Mrs. Crimond as she watched her son leave the room, a shadow of anxiety deepening the blue of her eyes. "Why does he say he'll see you there?"

"He told me that you'd named all your sons after the Knights of the Round Table, so when he said you lived in a castle I asked if it was in Camelot. I'm afraid I was making fun because of his name," Juliet explained honestly.

The shadow was routed by the sudden warm smile.

"You're not the first to do that, dear," said Mrs. Crimond. "Although I don't think your own mother was any less romantic than I when she named you Juliet. You see I was brought up on the Arthurian legend. My father was a professor of ancient history and he used to spend most of his spare time searching for evidence of the city of Camelot. I used to dream that when I married and had sons I would call them after King Arthur's knights, hoping that they would grow up to be chivalrous and brave. And in spite of the fact that I married a hardheaded, practical Scot who had his own ideas on how his boys should be named, I kept that resolve. Robert finally indulged me in my whim, provided each of the boys was given a good honest Scots name as his first name."

"And have they grown up to be chivalrous and brave?" asked Juliet, who was enthralled by this story. Its silly romanticism was right up her street.

"I'm going to let you be the judge of that, dear. You've already met Lance."

"I think he's very arrogant," Juliet couldn't help saying. "I had no intentions of coming here, but he made me."

Mrs. Crimond chuckled.

"Yes, he's very like his father in that respect. That's why fur and feathers used to fly whenever they were together, especially after Lance went into the business after he'd qualified as a civil engineer. He thought he knew all the answers and quite naturally Robert took exception at being told how to manage by a young man just out of university. It was fortunate for all concerned that Robert's Canadian associates received a new contract to build a hydroelectric dam at that point and were willing to take Lance to work on the project as a junior engineer. He stayed with it for a while and then went on to work on other projects over there. I think he wouldn't have come back if I hadn't asked him to come three years ago."

Mrs. Crimond sighed suddenly and her eyes went blank as she looked into the past. Juliet busied herself with the menu. A waitress approached and Mrs. Crimond came back into the present again and they ordered their meal.

The Cave of the White Rose

Often afterward Juliet was to remember the hours spent in the old-fashioned dining room of the hotel. Mrs. Crimond was a skillful questioner and a sympathetic listener, so it wasn't long before she had heard all about Juliet's uncomfortable childhood with Aunt Faith, her slight rebellion and the pleasant years spent in the ballet school.

"What a waste!" sighed Mrs. Crimond. "You should have been a dancer. You are almost the exact replica of your mother, small but graceful, delicate yet resilient, with the air of untouched innocence that was so invaluable to her in the part of Juliet. But instead you're a typist, and above all things I need a typist, but not any typist. I need someone with sensitivity who won't mind living in an old fortified house built on a promontory in a Scottish sea loch; someone who likes young girls such as my granddaughter Maree; someone who won't be disturbed by the sight of a cripple, my son and Maree's father, Gareth."

"A cripple?" exclaimed Juliet.

"Yes. Didn't Lance tell you about Gareth? I can see he didn't. He thought he'd done enough by bullying you into coming to see me. Gareth was hurt while on a skiing holiday with his wife, Moira, almost three years ago. He survived, but only just, and he's paralyzed in one leg. Sometimes it's worse than others. Lance says...." She caught her lower lip between her teeth as if to stop herself from saying more. "But then Lance is often unkind," she added in an undertone. She looked directly at Juliet again. "Do you think you would like to come and work for me?"

Juliet felt she was drowning. Tessa Crimond's way of stating her case was as effective in its way as her son's high-handedness had been. It was going to be difficult to refuse this offer of a job. The castle, the girl, the cripple, all made their appeal to her romantic outlook on life. She wanted to take the job because she wanted to see them, to find out what they were like.

"Yes, I think so," she said, hiding her intense excitement under a matter-of-face facade. "Where is the castle?"

"Please don't think it's like an English castle, like Warwick or Ludlow. It's really only a house. It's called Castle

Ross—Ross is the Gaelic word for promontory. We found it, Robert and I, thirty years ago when on holiday on the west coast. It was roofless and empty, and for sale. Robert bought it and the surrounding land, mostly bare moorland and mountain, and he proceeded with his usual interest in anything to do with buildings to restore it and alter it. Its restoration became his hobby and was a great source of escape from the demands of business life. I only wish he had lived long enough to enjoy his retirement living there."

There was a little silence as Mrs. Crimond thought of what might have been and Juliet finished her dessert.

"I live there all the time now, but I've not been able to persuade anyone to come there as my secretary. Sometimes I think it's because the place is too remote, too far from the bright lights, and sometimes I think it's because Maree lives there with me."

"How old is she?"

"Just twelve. Gareth was only twenty-one when he married Moira. He and Maree have lived with me ever since Moira was killed last winter in an avalanche in the French Alps. I have to admit that I'm not the best of mothers, I get too absorbed in my writing, but I find Maree a handful—lovable, you know, but definitely a rebel. Of course, the best thing would be for Gareth to marry again and provide her with another mother, but as he says, what woman nowadays is going to saddle herself with a cripple and a child?"

The frown of anxiety had appeared again as a new thought occurred to Mrs. Crimond and Juliet waited patiently to hear more.

"Last time he was at the castle Lance, who as I've said can be very unkind to Gareth, suggested that while he was down here in London he should find a wife for Gareth in the same way that he found the last one."

Startled, Juliet sat up straight, recalling Lance's derisive remark that he had gone to Hilary's wedding to look for a wife and asking her if she was interested.

"Did he really find the last one?" she asked curiously.

"I suppose he did in a way. He met Moira first when he

was on a sailing cruise somewhere off the west coast. He brought her home just as he used to bring all his friends home. It was a case of love at first sight with Gareth. But sometimes I've wondered.... But there I go rambling on, when I should be making sure you won't escape. Are you going to come to Castle Ross and help me? I'd like you to come partly because you are your mother's child but mostly because I think you will enjoy living there. I think you'd fit into our way of life. You wouldn't find it strange as so many would. Having worked for Nina Follet all that time you won't be bothered by displays of temperament, and your experience in dealing with young ballet dancers should be a help in coping with Maree. Now don't commit yourself immediately. You're to think about it while we have our coffee."

There was really no need for her to think about Mrs. Crimond's invitation to go and work for her, thought Juliet, because she was caught, trapped in a spell cast by a wizard called Lancelot Crimond. When she had come to the hotel she had been determined to resist any persuasion on his mother's part. Her determination had its origin in a desire to prove to that arrogant man that he had been wrong in his judgment of her own personality and of his mother's requirements.

But he had been right, uncannily right. The situation at Castle Ross, as outlined by Mrs. Crimond, appealed to her. There was only one snag, as far as she could see, and that was the overbearing, enigmatic Lance, whose wisdom frightened her.

It was as if her thought communicated itself to Mrs. Crimond.

"I hope you won't let Lance's high-handed behavior this afternoon influence you too much against us. He's principally a man of action and is the most practical of my sons, and so often he appears ruthless and inconsiderate of others' feelings. But I think his intentions were good in this case. He would be thinking of me and wanting to help you so his main object this afternoon would be for you and me to meet. Once we met he was wise enough to leave us alone."

"Is Gareth like him?" Two like Lance would be too much.

"Not at all. He's eighteen months younger than Lance and has always been the gentler, more sensitive of the two. Until the accident took away his ability to move about easily he was a lecturer in political philosophy and was beginning to be recognized as quite brilliant."

The faint distressed frown appeared again. "He could have continued with his work, I'm sure, but the accident plus Moira's death had a very bad effect on him. He stays at the castle all the time and doesn't go out, as if he's afraid to venture into the world in case he gets hurt. But he's begun to write, to my great pleasure. History, of course, and it's just possible you might find yourself typing for him too...that is if you decide to come."

Juliet capitulated at once.

"I shall come. I can't help myself, and your high-handed man of action knew it."

"Yes," murmured Mrs. Crimond, gazing past her with blank eyes. "Lance is so often right...."

AFTER ARRANGEMENTS HAD BEEN MADE for Juliet to travel north two weeks later, she returned by taxi to the dingy, badly lit, shabby room in which she had lived since the Follet Ballet School had been closed. It was like returning to earth after a glimpse of heaven, and she was beset by a sudden irrational fear that perhaps she had imagined everything that had taken place since she had walked blindly into a complete stranger at Hilary's wedding reception.

Then she caught sight of herself in the mirror above the sink as she filled a glass with cold water. The white rosebud on its long stem was still tucked behind her ear. Slowly she pulled it out and placed it in the glass. It was a little droopy, but it still retained that look of purity and innocence.

An air of untouched innocence—Mrs. Crimond had said that. Juliet examined her reflection. A pale elfin face framed by pale blond hair and lit by wide and wondering sea-blue eyes that tilted upward slightly at the corners. Yes, she did look rather innocent. Was that how she appeared to Lance Crimond too? Was that why he had said the white rosebud was symbolic?

As she stared at the mirror her reflected face seemed to dissolve and its place was taken by another. Hawklike masculine features, a lock of dark hair sliding forward on a wide forehead, eyes that glittered with a cold brilliance, a contradictory mouth curved in a faint enigmatic smile. Juliet blinked rapidly and the image faded.

Hastily she turned away from the mirror and began to prepare for bed, telling herself that in spite of reports she had read in newspapers and magazines about modern witches and wizards, witchcraft belonged to the past, to myths and legends such as that written about King Arthur and his knights. She had only seen Lance Crimond's face in the mirror because he had been the most disturbing factor in a very eventful day. He had been disturbing because he had taken control of her life so easily, whisking her away from the elegant ritual of an English wedding to an old hotel, and an interview with his vague, romantic mother.

She pulled back the covers on the bed-settee, shook her pillow and lay down. She switched off the light and lay with her arms under her head watching the reflection from the street lamp outside on the ceiling.

A very eventful day. Looking back over it it seemed to her that when she had waved goodbye to Hilary she had also waved goodbye to a part of her life. Ahead was the future, shrouded in Scottish mist that swirled about the turrets of a fantastic castle inhabited by people with beautiful names—Tessa, Maree, Gareth, who was afraid to go out into the world anymore because his leg was paralyzed; Tristram who preferred to be known by his Scottish Christian name of Jamie; and Lancelot, who could be unkind to his crippled brother and who preferred actions to words.

HE WAS MUCH MORE A JAMIE than a Tristram, thought Juliet, as the youngest of Mrs. Crimond's three sons greeted her in the arrival lounge at Glasgow airport. About twenty-six years of age, slightly shorter than his eldest brother but possessing the same width of shoulder, he was a freckled-faced, friendly young man with placid blue gray eyes and brown crinkly hair, and he performed the chivalrous task of carrying her luggage out to his car cheerfully and effortlessly.

"I hope you're prepared for a long drive," he remarked as they settled into the front seats of the car. "The road from here to Castle Ross is tortuous to say the least. It's actually quicker to go by boat down the Clyde and up Loch Fyne and then overland from Tarbert, but since I'm going there for a few weeks' holiday mother thought it would be better if I met you and took you there. She had some funny idea that you might get lost on the way. So by road we shall go following the coasts of the great sea lochs as they delve into the mountains. It's a good day for travel...cool and clear."

They crossed the River Clyde at Erskine and followed the inland thrust of that long narrow arm of the sea, Loch Long. From Arrochar they turned left and drove westward along Glen Croe, under the formidable shoulders of a mountain called the Cobbler, so often shrouded in mist but putting in an appearance, as Jamie remarked cheerfully, especially on Juliet's behalf.

Although the road, as he had said, was tortuous, he seemed to know it well enough to keep up a flow of words, not only informing her about the scenery and place names but also managing to slip in a few facts about himself and the Crimond family.

It turned out that he was a geologist, or at least he was taking a postgraduate course in geology at Edinburgh University, lecturing and doing research at the same time. His hobby was speleology, the study of underground caves, more familiarly known as potholes.

"Did you know that the world under our feet is almost the only part left unexplored, and that in Scotland, in the northwestern part of the country, there is still an extensive cave system unopened?" Jamie didn't wait for a reply to his question but continued to tell her about what was for him a most important activity.

"I've just come from a meeting of the Caving Society in Glasgow. Incidentally, it was founded by my brother Lance and his friend Graham Lee some years ago. Graham is the president and a keen caver. Lance dropped out of the society when he went to Canada, although he's shown an interest since he returned, and last year he and I had a look at the one limestone thrust we have on the estate at Castle Ross, but it was rather disappointing. After a few weeks at the castle I'm joining Graham's new expedition to the valley of caves up in the north. This year we're hoping to get into the main system...."

He chattered on. Juliet found his impersonal manner relaxing and found she was enjoying the drive along the road through Glen Kinglas, around the top of another wide loch to the town of Inverary where they stopped for lunch.

She left Inverary with an impression of one wide street, of sunlit white paint everywhere and pleasant homey hospitality in the George, the old inn where they ate their meal. Traveling southward for a while they meandered beside the mighty Loch Fyne, placid and dimpling under the summer sun, with the hills of Cowal beyond alternately smiling and scowling as clouds chased each other above them.

After several miles they turned west again along a secondary road that wound among moorland scattered with sheep and outcrops of rock. As they twisted and turned Juliet expected to see another loch around every bend or after they had topped another hill, but it wasn't until almost four o'clock in the afternoon that she had her first sight of Castle Ross, romantically mysterious in the glow of afternoon sunshine, its square tower silhouetted on a promontory of rock, dark against the shimmering sheen of Loch Moy.

Then the car dipped down yet another hill between stone walls and the castle was lost to view as the road made a right-hand bend into the village of Lochmoyhead, a single street of whitewashed cottages, glinting in the sunlight against the blue green of the forest behind them.

Once through the village, the gray and dusty road wound its way some distance away from the rocky cliffs that bounded the eastern side of the loch. On the left-hand side of the road the land rose gently to the craggy ramparts of mountains, and it was planted with small mixed trees.

"Lance's pride and joy," said Jamie, waving a hand in the direction of the trees. "He's got a thing about reforestation, about paying back to the land what has been taken from it by man. Atonement, he calls it. He's spent a lot of money planting acres of trees on the estate."

"I thought the castle and estate belonged to your mother," said Juliet.

"No. Father left everything, on condition that my mother should be allowed to reside here for the rest of her life, to that unknown quantity, my eldest brother."

"Why do you call him that?"

"Because he is virtually unknown to me. I was fourteen when he went off to Canada, and all I knew of him before that were the vibrations that went through our home in Glasgow every time he came home from school or university and tangled with my father."

"But surely he used to come home occasionally from Canada, for Christmas and New Year, and you saw him then," suggested Juliet.

"Oh, he came home sometimes, but not for the festivities to which you refer. He came at other times and his visits were brief. I never saw him." He glanced at her curiously. "I'm told he found you. What does it feel like to be selected from the masses by one of the wealthiest men in this part of the world?" he asked.

"I'd no idea he was as wealthy as all that."

"No?" There was a touch of unexpected sarcasm in his voice. "Are you sure? Isn't his wealth the attraction? Isn't that why you've taken the rather nebulous position of secretary-companion to my mother?"

"No, it isn't," denied Juliet hotly, appalled by his accusation that she was chasing Lance Crimond because he was a wealthy bachelor. "I've taken the position because I like your mother and because I need a job. It has nothing to do

The Cave of the White Rose

with your brother's attractions, financial or otherwise. I don't like him."

Jamie's chuckle was an infectious sound.

"Well, you're frank enough. I'm sorry if I hurt your feelings, but you see since my father died and left most of his wealth to Lance, my brother has been subjected to that sort of pursuit from various young women. Not that he hasn't been able to take care of himself. He has. In fact you may have noticed that he has certain inhuman qualities."

"Inhuman? What do you mean?" demanded Juliet.

She noticed they had turned off the road into a narrower one, which curved between spruces, tall and straight, forming a narrow tunnel into which the sun did not penetrate.

"Perhaps I used the wrong word," explained Jamie, who didn't seem to be at all disturbed by the gloom or by the strange image of his brother that he had evoked. "Extrahuman would be better, as if he possesses powers beyond those supplied to ordinary mortals."

Juliet's blood seem to freeze as she recalled the vision of Lance Crimond's face in her mirror.

"You mean... like Merlin, the magician in the stories about King Arthur?" she whispered.

Jamie's crack of laughter was like the sunlight into which they now drove, warm and cheerful dispersing the chilly gloom.

"You're as bad as mother! Full of romantic, fantastic fantasies. I suppose that's the Welsh blood showing. No, Lance isn't a wizard in the strict sense of the word and he'd be very scornful if you attributed his abilities to witchcraft. But he's right so often about people and events that it's damned uncomfortable having him around at times."

"I think I understand," said Juliet, feeling a little easier. "Does he often come to Castle Ross?"

"I suppose you're hoping you're going to escape his eagle eye," said Jamie, sending her an amused yet sympathetic glance. "Then I'm afraid you're in for a disappointment. He comes as often as his business commitments allow him and he arrives when he's least expected and puts everyone into a tizzy. He likes to keep an eye on the estate and also on mother and Gareth. Not that I blame him for watching them. They're both so vague and scatterbrained when it comes to money and business matters that it's no wonder dad left the administration of their inheritance in Lance's hands. He doles out their allowances. Well, here we are, Juliet, at the enchanted castle where, as in the case of Camelot, you'll find that nothing is as it seems."

At close quarters, in the warm hazy light of afternoon sunshine, the castle lost much of its mysterious romanticism. It consisted of a strong stone tower, three stories high, to which had been added an L-shaped wing. That afternoon, basking in warmth, surrounded by a garden of green shrubs, rose beds and deciduous trees, with a creeper winding its way up its gray stonework, it looked pretty and idyllic rather than majestic and aloof.

Jamie took Juliet in through the main door, a rather grand affair set in the wall of the L-shaped wing. It was built in the Jacobean style, he told her carelessly, with curved corners to its square arch and a family crest, carved in the stone, set above it.

"Not ours," he added with a cheeky grin, pointing to the crest. "It belonged to the previous owner who lost his life at the battle of Culloden. We come from more plebeian stock."

The hallway was wide and had paneled walls and a high ceiling decorated with ornate plaster work. Jamie put down her luggage and let out a yell.

"Anyone at home? Mother... Gareth... Vinnie? We're here!"

No one came immediately in answer to his call, so he took her into a room on the left. It faced westward and the only word Juliet could find to describe it was gracious. Long velvet curtains moved slightly at the open French window through which she could see a small stone terrace.

"Sit down and make yourself comfortable while I go and find mother," said Jamie. "I expect you'd like a cup of tea. I could do with one myself. The last part of the drive is exceptionally tedious."

When he had gone Juliet looked around the room and

The Cave of the White Rose

once again was struck by the mixture of comfort and elegance. It was a room in which to take afternoon tea and yet it was also a room in which to read or sew. There were several watercolors on the walls, mostly depicting scenes of mountains and lochs, and over the fireplace there was an oil painting of a man dressed in clothes of the Edwardian era, who possessed a pair of remarkably piercing gray eyes. Going over to the picture, she read on the gilt plaque beneath it...his name, Alexander Crimond. Glancing up at the painted face again, she decided that there was no doubt at all as to his relationship to Lance Crimond.

Tempted by the open window, she went across to it and stepped through onto the terrace, and had her breath taken away by the view. Below was the loch, that long water, island scattered, opening on the distant glittering deeps of the sea. Ahead was a dark bank of hills above which the misty disk of the sun shone.

She stood quietly absorbing the tranquillity of the scene spread before her.

"Admiring our view?" inquired a pleasant voice behind her. "You'll find none better anywhere in the world."

Startled, she swung around. A man stood in the window frame, and as soon as she saw him the words from Tennyson's *Idylls of the King* came into her mind.

> The last tall son of Lot and Bellicent,
> And tallest, Gareth....

He must be Gareth, not the last son of Tess and Robert Crimond, but the last one for her to meet, and certainly the tallest and most handsome. Brown hair, darker than Jamie's but not as dark as Lance's, waved back from a lean, fine-boned face to which suffering had added its own distinction.

He moved and the impression of lithe grace was destroyed immediately as the stick he used became evident and he dragged his right leg stiffly.

"You must be Juliet," he said softly, and held out a hand to her. Speechless, Juliet nodded and put her hand in his and felt the warmth of his grasp.

"I'm Gareth Crimond," he added. "I believe my brother Lance found you, and as usual I'm astonished by his good taste. Welcome to Castle Ross. I've been looking forward to your coming here."

Bewitched by his voice as much as by his words, Juliet looked up into eyes that were as deeply blue as parts of the loch, and drowned willingly.

CHAPTER TWO

JULIET AWOKE EARLY, disturbed by the sound of a bird's cry, a long-drawn-out wistful wail. She blinked sleepily at the square of window. It framed a patch of blue sky across which a wisp of white cloud trailed. Slowly she looked around the room, her glance lingering on the pretty antique furniture. Although she had been at Castle Ross almost three weeks she hadn't yet become used to the pleasure of waking in this small room tucked away under the roof of the square tower, and comparing it with the room she had left in London.

Lying there, comfortably drowsy, safe in the knowledge that she wasn't expected to rise for at least another hour, she let her mind drift back over the time that had passed since she had first set foot in the castle and had met Gareth Crimond. The days that had followed that meeting had possessed a curious dreamlike quality as she had gradually adjusted to the slow pace of life at the castle. No demands had been made on her, because Mrs. Crimond didn't require her to type just yet as she was still immersed in the composition of the first chapter of her new book, and because Maree, Gareth's daughter, was away staying with friends of the family in Ayrshire.

At first idleness had worried Juliet and she had mentioned her worry to Mrs. Crimond. The novelist had looked at her vaguely and then had smiled kindly and told her not to worry.

"Think of this time as a holiday, one that you've needed, dear," she said. "Relax, explore the estate, talk to Gareth. He'll be glad of the company. There'll be plenty for you to do later when I've got my story off the ground, and when Maree returns."

So Juliet had wandered at will about the castle and its grounds and along the shore of the loch. Sometimes Jamie would walk with her and talk about the geology of the area or tell her about caving, but she had the impression that he accompanied her only because his mother had told him to do so. She much preferred the occasional accidental meetings she had with Gareth when he emerged from his study on the ground floor of the wing of the castle, to lounge on the terrace or in the room behind it.

It required only a little shy prompting on her part to make him tell her some of the fascinating legends about the castle and the surrounding district, and she listened attentively, watching the play of expression on his face, her heart full of pity because such a handsome and intelligent person as he was had chosen to become a recluse.

As the days drifted by and he began to realize he had a willing and sympathetic audience, it seemed to her that he did not stay in his room quite so much and that he deliberately sought her out. Every evening at dinner, the only time the family assembled together, he would sit across from her looking at her with deep blue eyes whose expression caused the blood to pound excitedly in her ears as they made her aware for the first time in her life of herself as a woman.

Juliet sighed and stretched luxuriously, and wondered, not for the first time since she had come to Castle Ross, if she were in love. Had love winged, with the darting swiftness of a summer swallow, into her heart at last? How else could she account for this longing to stay there whatever might happen, to help Gareth in any way she could to alleviate the pain and frustration that had been his since the accident that had deprived him of the proper use of his leg?

Gentle and gallant, he fitted exactly her own romantic image of the man whom she could love. If she had ever had any doubts about coming to the castle they had been chased away completely by her growing friendship with him. It had been right for her to come, right for her to meet him. Dared she look further and hope that they might love each other?

Even the arrival of Maree last night could not dispel Juliet's anticipation of another enchanted day, because Maree was part of the enchantment. She was tall for her age with russet-colored hair and exceptionally clear gray eyes. Maree had shown no signs of the rebelliousness to which Mrs. Crimond had referred. Pleased to be back at the castle, she had been happy at dinner, answering her grandmother's questions about her stay in Ayrshire enthusiastically. The friends she had visited apparently owned horses and now Maree wanted nothing more than to own a pony or a horse and to learn to ride.

Yes, thought Juliet, she was looking forward to meeting Maree again this morning. It was most important that she should be friends with Gareth's daughter.

"Miss Grey, are you awake?"

The girl's voice coming from the direction of the door startled her, coming directly as it did after her thought, and she sat up in bed suddenly. Just inside the door, which she must have opened very quietly, stood Maree, her square-shouldered boyish figure dressed in long blue pants and a striped cotton T-shirt. Her short hair stood on end spikily, the result of having pulled the shirt over her head, and under her thick dark eyebrows her eyes were very clear and unwinking.

"You're up early," said Juliet, as the girl advanced rather shyly into the room.

"Are you really wide awake?" she asked seriously.

"Yes, I am now."

"I want to show you something. Please will you get dressed and come out with me into the hills?"

"It's very nice of you to ask me, Maree, but before I agree I think I'd better ask your grandmother if she needs me this morning to do some typing for her."

Maree shook her head slowly from side to side.

"No, she won't. Not in the morning. Anyway, she's not awake yet. There's only you and me and Vinnie awake."

"Then where is this something you want to show me?"

"It's a secret. If you'll get up and get dressed I'll take you to see it."

As she had already decided that it was important for her to nurture friendship between herself and the girl, Juliet agreed to get up, and having achieved what she wanted Maree grinned happily and slipped out of the room.

Once out of bed Juliet discovered that the morning, although sunny, was cool, so she dressed in jeans and sweater. A peep from the window high up in the wall of the old tower showed her the loch crisp with white-topped waves that had been churned up by the brisk northerly wind, and down in the small bay formed by the curve of the promontory the yacht that belonged to Lance Crimond tossed and tugged at its mooring as if wanting to be free.

In the passage outside her room Juliet found Maree waiting for her and as soon as she appeared the girl slipped a firm hand into hers and led her to the fascinating curved stairway known as a wheel stair, which in olden times had been the chief means of access from the main hall of the castle to the stories above it. The main hall itself had been converted into a small suite of rooms for Mrs. Crimond and himself by Robert Crimond, and was shut off from the wheel stair by a stout oak door. Below the suite of rooms on the ground floor the big vaulted storerooms had been converted into a morning room and an up-to-date kitchen. All the other rooms were in the three-story wing, which, Juliet had learned from Gareth, had been added during the seventeenth century.

Maree took Juliet into the kitchen where Mrs. McVinn, who was cook and housekeeper, had already started her day's work. A plump brown-haired woman who moved with brisk confidence about the kitchen, she had impressed Juliet as being a kindly, motherly sort of person. Now she greeted her in her lilting Highland voice.

"You're up early, miss. What would you be liking for your breakfast? The porridge is simmering and then there's ham and eggs, or perhaps you'd like some of the haddock McVinn was after catching last night? Fried in oatmeal they're very good."

Ever since she had come to Castle Ross Juliet had been trying to avoid eating the heavy breakfasts that Vinnie cooked, but so far she had failed. That didn't stop her from trying again.

"Oh, no, just toast and some tea will do. I can get it ready myself."

"Ach, that's no sort of breakfast for a day like today when the wind is fresh. As for getting it ready yourself, that will never do." Vinnie's sharp black eyes glinted fiercely. "No one cooks in my kitchen, not even Mrs. Crimond. Not that she'd be wanting to. She likes to have her meals prepared for her, and she likes them on time, too."

"Uncle Lance sometimes cooks in your kitchen," said Maree. "When he's been fishing. He says trout have to be cooked as soon as they're caught to taste right."

"Ach, so he does." The black eyes softened slightly. "But then he's the master here now."

"But he told me he used to get up in the morning before everyone else when he was a boy, even before you, Vinnie, and cook his own breakfast," argued Maree.

"Aye, and then he'd be away for the rest of the day, a bag of biscuits in his pocket, roaming the hills or sailing his wee dinghy on the loch, and only coming back when it was dark, and not always then. The Lord knows what he did all the time," said Vinnie. "And he's no different today when he comes here."

"Daddy says Uncle Lance always likes to live on the edge of danger," said the informative Maree. "What does that mean? Do you know, Miss Grey?"

"Please call me Juliet, Maree. I suppose it means that your uncle likes doing things that take him into dangerous places or situations, like climbing hills or sailing."

"Or caving. That's dangerous, too, and Uncle Jamie does that."

"Aye, and he's another who's never happy unless he's worrying your grannie. Both of them are tarred with the same brush, never giving her a minute's peace. And you're no different, Maree. A madcap, that's what you are." Vinnie's glance at Maree was wholly affectionate. "And where are you off to this morning, I'd like to know?"

"It's a secret," replied Maree coolly.

"You and your secrets!"

"It's all right, Mrs. McVinn, I'm going with Maree. I'll

see that she doesn't do anything dangerous," put in Juliet, and Maree flashed her a grateful glance.

The housekeeper looked relieved.

"Then that's just fine," she said. "Now away with this blethering. Sit down at the table and I'll be cooking the breakfast I was talking about. Which is it to be? The ham and eggs, or the haddock?"

Once the meal was over Maree lost no time in leading Juliet out of the house into the cool fresh morning air across the green lawn at the back of the building and straight into the natural woodland of oak and birch that covered the lower parts of the hillside. Through the woods they followed a path that gradually grew steeper and more rocky. Soon they burst out of sweet-smelling sun-shot gloom onto the bare hillside.

Juliet, who by now was out of breath, sat down on an outcrop of rock.

"Let's rest awhile, Maree. I'm not used to climbing hills so early in the morning," she said.

There was a certain amount of scorn in Maree's sidelong glance.

"You're not used to climbing hills at all," she said bluntly. But she sat down too and together they gazed down at the world spread at their feet; at the squares and oblongs of the castle and its outbuildings; at the swathe of blue water sprinkled with brown rocky islands, widening out to the sea; at the loom of other darker higher islands on the distant horizon.

"Grannie says your mother was a ballet dancer and that you used to work in a ballet school," said Maree abruptly. "I think ballet is silly. I'd rather do gymnastics and play games like hockey and basketball, and I'd like to learn to ski, like my mother did."

"You may think ballet is silly, but you have to be just as physically fit to do it as you have to be to participate in sports. In fact skiing isn't unlike ballet. You can't do either successfully without having exercised properly first," replied Juliet quietly.

Maree looked at her with a certain amount of respect dawning in her eyes.

The Cave of the White Rose

"Could you show me how to dance?" she inquired.

"I wasn't a teacher of ballet, only a secretary in Madame Follet's school."

"But you must know all about it. You must have watched her teaching. You must know the steps."

"Yes," admitted Juliet hesitantly, thinking how well she knew them.

"Then you could show me. I must learn everything I can," said the determined girl. "Good, that's settled. Come on, we've rested long enough."

It was astonishing, thought Juliet, as she followed Maree along a sheep path across the shoulder of the hill. Here was the same refusal to take no for an answer, giving her the same feeling that she was being swept along by an irresistible force that she had known when she had first met Lance Crimond. Judging her by her clear gray eyes and her manner Maree might be Lance Crimond's daughter.

Whatever was she thinking? Maree wasn't Lance's daughter. She was Gareth's. Children often resembled uncles or aunts or grandparents more than their own parents. When she looked closely at Maree she would see other characteristics that she had inherited from her mother's family. It was just that on first impression she seemed to be all Crimond.

But instead of having fantastic thoughts she should be watching where Maree was leading her so that she would be able to find her way back to the castle. Looking about her she noticed that the scenery had changed. They were now following the course of a gaily chuckling burn that tumbled over its rocky bed. Ahead the sharp edge of a mountain peered down the glen formed by the burn. Everywhere boulders and stony debris were scattered, and underfoot the grass was short and very green.

As they followed the burn deeper and deeper into the hills, enticed possibly by that sharply outlined mountain, Juliet also noticed a change in atmosphere. Although the burn still chuckled there was something mocking about its laughter, and Juliet, whose imagination was extremely active, had a feeling that if they continued to follow the bubbling water it would lead them to their doom. So strong was this impression that she decided that when she caught up with Maree around the next outcrop of rock she would ask how much farther they had to go before they reached the secret.

But when she eventually rounded the next outcrop of rock the burn disappeared suddenly and dramatically, and all that could be seen was a deep gash in the hillside. Standing near the gash among the mass of boulders and scree where the burn had disappeared was Maree, a triumphant grin on her face.

"I found it before I went away to Ayrshire," she announced. "This is the place that Uncle Jamie calls the Cauldron and grannie calls the Hollow Hill. I daren't tell anyone I'd found it because daddy said I wasn't to go any farther than three miles from the castle. This is really out-of-bounds for me."

Completely mystified, Juliet stared at the rough rock of the hillside. The gash or fissure was long and deep and had obviously been made by the fast-flowing water of the burn as it had worn away the rock until it had caved in.

The word *caved* was a clue. This must be the limestone thrust about which Jamie had told her.

"I'd love to go into the crack and see if I can find a way into the passage that leads to the caves under the hill," Maree went on excitedly. "It isn't fair of them to keep it to themselves."

"Them?" queried Juliet, sending her an alarmed glance.

"Uncle Lance and Uncle Jamie. They explored it last summer, but they weren't able to get into the main cave because the passages were too narrow and because there was danger of falling rock. Uncle Jamie wanted to blast, but Uncle Lance wouldn't agree because he was afraid the whole hill might come tumbling down if they did. Uncle Jamie was very disappointed, and I don't blame him. If they'd brought me with them I might have been able to get farther than them because I'm smaller." Her eyes lit up with a reckless gleam. "Juliet, do you think that while you're here I could squeeze into the crack and see if I can find the entrance to the passage?"

The edge of danger. Oh, yes, she could see very well what Vinnie had meant when she had said that madcap Maree was every bit as bad as her uncles. Juliet stared at the deep fissure in the rock toward which Maree had pointed and her imagination leaped ahead. Supposing Maree was able to squeeze into the crack and crawl into a passage? Supposing she reached the cave, an echoing place with slippery walls? Supposing she slipped and fell into the rushing water of the underground stream?

Juliet closed her eyes and shook her head. Really, this place was bad for anyone with imagination. She opened her eyes again to find Maree was staring at her.

"Are you all right, Juliet?" she asked sympathetically.

"Yes, I'm fine, thank you, and the answer to your question is no, you are not going to squeeze into any crack while I'm here to watch you. We're going to turn right around and go back to the castle *now*."

The gray eyes clashed with hers. It was a tense moment for Juliet, a battle of wills that she had to win or she might as well leave Castle Ross immediately. She had to vindicate the trust that she realized, with a slight qualm of uneasiness, had been placed in her by Mrs. Crimond. Even at the risk of losing the girl's friendship she had to show her who was in authority.

It was a great effort not to let her gaze waver, but she managed to maintain an outward calm and to outstare the willful girl. At last Maree lowered her eyes, kicked at a pebble and muttered sulkily, "All right, I won't. But I thought you'd be a better sport."

"It's not a question of being a sport, Maree. Surely you're intelligent enough to realize that while you're with me I'm responsible for you, and that your father would never have forbidden you to go this far away from the castle if he didn't have a reason."

"He thinks it would have been better if I hadn't been born."

Juliet gasped at the bitterness of the girl's unexpected outburst.

"It's true," continued Maree. "I overheard him saying

so once to grannie the time I got lost on the moors and they had to organize a search for me. He doesn't really want me. Nobody has wanted me since mommy died."

Juliet's annoyance with the girl faded and died, as the words touched a chord in her memory. How often she had experienced the same feeling of rejection after her parents had died. How often she had reached the edge of despair, only to be rescued by Hilary's kindness and humor.

She touched the girl gently on the shoulder.

"I'm sure that isn't true, Maree. I'm sure there must be somebody who wants you and cares for you. I expect your father does really, and there's your grannie—"

"She cares only for her silly books!"

"That's not so. I know she cares very much for you and for your uncles, too. And both of them must care for you."

"Uncle Jamie hardly notices me. When I ask him if I can go caving with him he always says I'm too young."

"And he's probably right, Maree. You are," said Juliet patiently. "What about your Uncle Lance? Doesn't he notice you're here?"

"Yes, sometimes. Last summer he took me sailing one day in his boat." Maree's eyes brightened as a treasured memory was recalled. "We were gone for the whole day. We landed on one of the islands and had our lunch there. It was a bird sanctuary and Uncle Lance told me all about the birds. He knows about everything. Then we sailed right out to sea." Her eyes clouded. "But daddy spoiled it all. He was awfully cross when we came back. He said Uncle Lance had no right to keep me out so late."

"Doesn't that show your father cares for you if he was anxious about you?" said Juliet, quick to point out that concern for the safety of his only child had probably been at the root of Gareth's anger.

Maree shook her head slowly.

"No. It's difficult to explain. He wasn't cross because he was worried about me, he was cross because I'd been with Uncle Lance. If I'd been with anyone else he wouldn't have said a word."

The Cave of the White Rose

This time Juliet had no argument ready because Maree had touched on a subject that was unknown to her, the relationship between Lance and Gareth. She longed to ask questions, but realized that it wasn't wise or right to pump Maree. Nor should she believe everything Maree told her about her father. The girl's view of Gareth was bound to be colored by her own overpowering sense of rejection.

"Look, Maree," she said comfortingly, "when I was young, younger than you, I lost both my parents in an accident and I had to go and live with relatives. There were many times when I used to feel exactly as you do, that no one wanted me. But I had, and still have, a cousin called Hilary, and when I was down in the dumps she used to tell me not to be silly because she wanted me and needed me, even if it was only to tease me and have a pillow fight with me. And as I grew older I began to realize there's always someone who wants you somewhere."

"It must be nice to have a cousin," said Maree. "Is she older than you?"

"Yes, and she's not long been married to a distant cousin of your father's."

"Oh! Who is that?" asked Maree, all curiosity. "Did you go to the wedding? Please tell me about it. I've never been to a wedding."

Juliet told her about the wedding as they retraced their steps down the glen and by the time they reached the castle they were on very good terms, having discovered they had a common love of wild flowers and a liking for rolling down grassy banks.

As they approached the castle Jamie came out of the main door and put some cases in the back of his car.

"Hello. Where have you two been?" he asked casually.

"Maree has been showing me the Cauldron and the Hollow Hill," replied Juliet honestly, having decided that honesty must be her best policy if she had to answer such a question.

He glanced at Maree.

"Oho, mischief, so you found your way there, did you? I might have known you wouldn't rest this summer until you had!" He turned back to Juliet and asked, "What did you think of it?"

She shuddered, remembering the eerie atmosphere of the place.

"It gave me the creeps," she admitted.

"I can see your imagination rivals mother's," he scoffed. "But now Maree knows where it is you're going to have your work cut out keeping her away from there. If you don't Lance won't be any too pleased. He's convinced the place isn't safe."

"Oh, I think Maree has enough sense not to go there and try caving on her own," replied Juliet calmly, and Jamie's eyebrows shot up in surprise as he glanced again at his niece.

"I hope you're right," he murmured, "because Maree has a tendency to do just what she's been told not to do, and remember, caving should never be done without the company of an experienced speleologist like myself or Lance. Now I'm off to Elstone to join the expedition up there."

"Oh, I wish I could come with you," cried Maree.

"What would I do with you if you came?" asked Jamie mildly, as he opened the door of his car.

"I could help you. I could get to places where you can't. Oh, please, Uncle Jamie, let me come!"

"Another time. When you're older," he answered carelessly, and getting into the car, he slammed the door shut as if determined to cut off any more appeals. He switched on the ignition, the car started with a roar, gravel chippings spat out from under the wheels as he left at speed, with a grin and a wave of his hand.

"See what I mean?" said Maree almost choking with fury. "It's always the same. How am I ever going to do everything that mommy did if no one will take me anywhere and teach me?"

Swinging around, she ran off and disappeared around the side of the house. Juliet hesitated, wondering whether she should go after the girl and talk her out of her frustration. Then reluctantly she decided that this time Maree would have to get over her disappointment alone because

Mrs. Crimond might be looking for her new secretary.

Entering the house, she paused as she passed the open door of the lounge and looked inside, thinking that perhaps Mrs. Crimond might be in there. The room was just as it had been all the other mornings, quiet and sunlit. The French window was open and the curtains swayed in the breeze. Someone must be on the terrace.

As she approached the open window Gareth spoke from the terrace, having seen her coming.

"Good morning, Juliet. I was wondering when I would see you again. Last night when I couldn't sleep for the pain in my leg, I thought of you."

His unexpected greeting made every nerve in her body tingle and brought a delicate tinge of pink to her cheeks. She sidled through the open window with a sort of diffident eagerness, longing to see him again and yet shy of meeting the very personal gaze of his blue eyes.

He was lounging full length on an upholstered chaise longue. He was dressed in light fawn trousers and a navy blue casual shirt that was open at the neck. Sunlight glinted on the hairs on his bare forearms and picked out the reddish tints in his thick wavy hair. In one hand he held a book and in the other a pipe, but when he saw her he laid them aside on a table close by.

His lazy glance took in her slight slim figure and she was suddenly aware of how untidy and windblown she must appear after her tramp into the hills, and the pink on her cheeks deepened.

"You were up and out early," he remarked. "I saw you leaving with Maree. You mustn't let her make too many demands on you. She possesses a kind of feverish energy and must be going somewhere or doing something all the time. She's very like her mother in that way."

It was the first time he had ever mentioned his dead wife and Juliet watched an expression of sadness darken his eyes, and once again her soft heart was touched with pity. But when he glanced at her again the sad look had passed.

"Please sit down," he said, "and I'll ring for Vinnie and ask her to bring us some coffee."

"Oh, no!" she blurted quickly. His eyebrows rose in an expression of hauteur and she rushed to explain why she was refusing. "I must find Mrs. Crimond. I'm afraid I'd no idea how far Maree intended to take me. I didn't mean to be so long. I've done nothing for almost three weeks and I'm sure it's time for me to be doing some work. After all, that is why I came here."

The expression of hauteur was replaced by an expression of indulgent amusement.

"Work? What's that? None of us really works at Castle Ross. It isn't a place that induces one to work. Even Lance relaxes when he comes here. No one is expecting you to work hard, least of all my mother. I expect she's still in her room indulging in her usual form of escapism, pushing her characters around, making them go where she wants, which is something she can't do with her sons. So please be good enough to press the button in the wall over there, and then sit down."

He broke off abruptly and a frown of frustration marred his handsome face.

"Dammit," he muttered between clenched teeth, "I can't even get up and move a chair for you!"

His outburst went straight to her heart and the seed of pity already set there and which had begun to grow in that warm and tender environment attained full growth—pity because Gareth, who must have once been quick and active, could no longer perform without difficulty the simple but naturally chivalrous action of placing a chair in a convenient place for a woman.

"Oh, please don't worry about it," she said. "I can manage very well, thank you."

She went across to a basketwork chair that had been set near the balustrade of the terrace.

"Bring it here...close beside me," he ordered.

He tried to push the table aside, but it overbalanced and books and papers scattered in all directions.

"Blast!" exploded Gareth, and Juliet set the chair down hurriedly and darted over to pick up the table. Then she went down on her hands and knees to collect the fluttering papers together.

"I suppose I shall get used to being a helpless, useless hulk one day," he ground out. Then with a change of tone he added, "You must forgive me, please."

The softly spoken request astonished her. Looking up, she discovered he was leaning toward her and that their faces were on a level.

"What is there to forgive?" she whispered.

His eyes widened and their expression changed from despair to intense excitement.

"My impatience and bad temper, my disability," he murmured.

Mesmerized by the intensity of his gaze, she swayed slightly on her knees as she was shaken by a strong desire to drop the papers and to put her arms around him in an attempt to ease away his bitterness. The papers actually slithered to the floor unnoticed, and her hands were reaching out when she heard a discreet cough come from the window behind her.

"Were you after needing something?" asked Vinnie.

Brought back to her senses, Juliet half turned, wondering how much the housekeeper had seen and heard. The bright black eyes were unrevealing and the plump pink face wore a bland and surprisingly servantlike expression. If Vinnie had seen anything she wasn't going to betray her reaction by the flicker of an eyelid.

"Some coffee, please, Vinnie, for Miss Grey and myself," said Gareth. "We've just had a little accident. My clumsiness, of course."

"Of course." Even Vinnie's voice was devoid of expression as she turned away and was swallowed up into the depths of the lounge.

Juliet bent again to pick up the papers. Then she collected the three books and put them on top of the papers on the table. She picked up the pipe. Hardly had she laid it down than a hand descended on her wrist and still on her knees she was pulled around slightly to face Gareth.

"Juliet, look at me," he ordered.

She looked up. She was so close to him she could see the flecks of darker blue radiating outward from the pupils of his eyes.

"Why did you drop the papers?" he asked.

Still troubled by her violent urge to offer comfort to him, she was unable to reply with certainty.

"I'm not sure," she said, sidestepping the issue. He smiled, and she had an impression that he knew as well as she did why she had dropped them.

"I've been needing someone like you, Juliet, to help me," he said softly.

A shadow fell across them, blotting out the sun. A voice in which a certain crispness overlaid the Scottish lilt cut sharply across Gareth's softer tones.

"Well, well, you aren't wasting much time, are you, Gareth?"

Juliet snatched her hand out of Gareth's grasp and jumped to her feet. She clasped her arms around her waist in a defensive action while her wide shocked gaze turned to the balustrade, fully expecting to see no one because she believed that she had imagined the shadow and the voice.

But this time he was there in the flesh, wide shouldered, bold featured and cold eyed. He was dressed in a conventional dark suit and a white shirt, clothes that did more to draw attention to his powerful physique and unusual, rather saturnine looks than a more colorful style of dress would have done. He must have come up the steps from the garden and approached very quietly.

Having recovered from the start that Lance's sudden appearance had given him, Gareth spoke sharply and rather petulantly.

"Why do you always have to walk so damned quietly?"

"I wasn't walking quietly. You were so intent on making an impression that you didn't hear me," returned Lance with a grin. His light gray eyes raked over Juliet insolently.

"How are you, Juliet?" he inquired politely. "Taking to life in the country quite quickly, judging by the leaves and

The Cave of the White Rose

burrs in your hair and the rent in your pants. Have you been walking with Maree?"

Juliet's hands went first to her hair and then to the tear in her pants, but as the meaning of his last question penetrated she stopped feeling to stare at him.

"How do you know?" she asked in an awed voice.

"Maree is the only one here who would take you for a tramp in the woods and possibly even farther afield, to a place where a burn disappears underground."

How did he know? Panic struck at Julie for a moment and she almost turned and fled into the house away from this disturbing man. Then noticing that he was looking at her feet she glanced downward. Her brown brogues were covered with a film of dust.

She looked up. There was no glint of amusement in the gray eyes. They were ice-cold as they met hers.

"Oh, for heaven's sake, Juliet, sit down," said Gareth irritably. "There's no need to stand there dithering because my omniscient brother has guessed you and Maree have been out-of-bounds this morning. Why are you here anyway, Lance?"

Wishing she could think up some excuse to leave, Juliet sank down slowly on the edge of her chair, her arms once more clasped about her waist as if she were cold. There was no doubt about it, Lance Crimond was a disruptive force who had already irritated Gareth and had made her feel foolish and incompetent.

"Why shouldn't I be here? It's my place."

His abrupt arrogance was offensive and Gareth was duly offended by it.

"How you love to rub that in, don't you," he retorted rather wearily. "If it wasn't for this useless leg of mine I wouldn't stay here. I'd leave now, today."

"Would you?" Lance's voice had a sardonic edge to it. "Isn't that going a little too far? Where else would you find such comfort and ease without having to lift a finger and without having to pay? No one wishes your leg was better more than I do. But just think of the problems you would have to contend with if it were."

Juliet gasped audibly. Here was an example of the unkindness Mrs. Crimond had told her about. Horrified, she watched Gareth's face contort with anger.

"Shut up, you devil!" he spat at Lance.

"Are you afraid that Juliet will start thinking badly of you? I shouldn't worry. She's very tenderhearted and I expect she's already on your side and hating my guts, aren't you, Juliet?"

The rattle of china being carried heralded the approach of Vinnie with the coffee and saved Juliet from having to make a reply immediately. Contenting herself with what she hoped was a contemptuous glance in Lance's direction, she moved the books and papers on the table to one side so that Vinnie could place the tray on it.

As soon as the housekeeper saw Lance her face lost its bland expression as she smiled warmly at him.

"Ach, 'tis yourself then. And why weren't you after telling me you were coming?"

"I wasn't sure I could get away until late last night. I left Glasgow at five this morning," said Lance.

"And will you be staying long?"

"Ten days, perhaps longer. It depends on business."

"Heaven forbid," groaned Gareth, with typical brotherly directness.

"Now that isn't a nice thing to be saying," said Vinnie, rounding on him. "He's needing a holiday, I can see that with my own eyes, and what better place is there for him to be having it than here among his ain folk?"

"There are times, as you should know, Vinnie, after all these years, when his 'ain folk' can do very well without him. And one of them is now," replied Gareth testily.

To Juliet's surprise Lance laughed.

"A truly brotherly sentiment," he remarked. "I know I'm a thorn in your flesh, Gareth. But if I didn't come to prick you now and again you'd soon degenerate into a loathsome mass of frustration and self-pity."

"Aye, that's so," said Vinnie, nodding her head and glancing at Gareth with an expression of motherly solicitude in her eyes. "Shall I be bringing another coffee cup?"

The Cave of the White Rose

"No, thanks," replied Lance. "I'm going up to see mother in a few minutes. Is Jamie here?"

"Ach, no. He was away to Elstone this morning. 'Tis sorry he will be to have missed you."

"I may go up there next weekend to see how the expedition is making out."

Vinnie went away and there was silence on the terrace. Realizing that she was expected to pour the coffee, Juliet picked up the coffeepot, her hand shaking a little as she was conscious of Lance watching every move she made.

"I brought a neighbor of ours to her home this morning. She used to be a good friend of yours," Lance said suddenly to Gareth.

"Oh? Who is she?" Gareth sounded lethargic and indifferent.

"Alison Coates."

There was another silence, but this time it seemed to Juliet it was loaded with tension.

"And what did she have to say for herself?" Gareth still sounded casual, but Juliet sensed that his indifference was counterfeit.

"Quite a lot. She's just back from working in a hospital in the south of England. She's going to stay at home for a while. Apparently her mother has been ill. She said she'd call in to see us. I suggested she might be able to give you some advice about your leg, and—"

"You what?" exploded Gareth irritably. "Why can't you leave me alone? Why must you be forever suggesting remedies and cures?"

"Alison is a physiotherapist," said Lance smoothly, as if Gareth hadn't interrupted him. "She has a great deal of experience in your kind of problem. She might be able to suggest some new exercises."

"I've had enough of physiotherapy, or any other therapy," said Gareth forcibly.

Lance shrugged his shoulders.

"Okay, forget it. When she comes over she doesn't have to see you at all, if that's the way you want it."

The crispness had gone from his voice and it sounded

strangely flat and weary. Juliet glanced cautiously at him. He was gazing at Gareth, who was looking down at his coffee as he stirred it. The expression in Lance's eyes surprised her. They were shadowed with anxiety, and she felt an odd tug at her heart. It wasn't pity this time. It was almost a twinge of conscience as if she had been guilty of condemning someone unheard.

Then Lance pushed away from the balustrade and the impression was destroyed. On his way to the house he passed behind her chair and she stiffened involuntarily as she heard him pause. His touch was light on her head as he tried to disentangle a sticky burr from her hair, but even so her scalp tingled in reaction.

"I'd stay and remove the others," he muttered unexpectedly, "but I must go and see mother. Here's a job for you, Gareth. It should keep you occupied for the next quarter of an hour and help you to get even better acquainted with Juliet. But why should I be telling you that? I guess you don't need any advice in that respect. See you later."

He went as quietly as he had come. Gareth put down his cup and saucer on the table and swore softly under his breath. The expression on his face was withdrawn as if his mind had gone wandering down paths unknown to her.

"I wonder why he's decided to take a holiday now," he muttered suddenly.

"Most people take a holiday in the summer months," replied Juliet.

He gave her a kindly but skeptical glance.

"But not Lance. He's not like other people. He does things because he wants to, not because it's the time to do them. He makes his own rules. He'll have some dark and deep reason for wanting to be here just now, and I'm wondering if it has anything to do with Alison Coates. Ah, well, only time will tell." He sighed and moved restlessly. "Now, what were we talking about when he arrived?" he asked lightly.

"You were saying how much you needed someone to help you," said Juliet shyly, and pink stained her cheeks again.

"So I was. Now, I know you're here principally to help mother and to keep an eye on Maree and see that she doesn't get into mischief, but I've been wondering whether you'd also do some typing for me. It would be a great help. I've started to write a book, a political history of Scotland, and...."

His voice went on, but Juliet hardly heard. She knew it was silly to feel disappointed, but she couldn't help it. She was sure he hadn't meant he had been needing someone to do typing for him when he'd said he needed help from someone like her. His eyes, his voice, his hand holding hers had conveyed much more than that.

But now his eyes avoided hers, his voice had lost its compelling vibrancy and he made no attempt to take her hand again. She put the blame for his change of attitude on the arrival of Lance and as a result found herself sharing Gareth's feelings regarding his brother's decision to stay at Castle Ross for a few days. She wished Lance Crimond hadn't come. They could do very well without him.

This feeling was increased when she carried the coffee tray into the kitchen a few minutes later and discovered a tearful, subdued Maree eating her lunch at the table.

She had hardly set the tray down on the table when Maree burst out, "You told Uncle Lance where we went this morning!"

"No, I didn't."

"Then how did he know?"

"He looked at my shoes and guessed."

Maree looked at the offending shoes. "Oh, I see. He would. He knows everything," she muttered.

"Was he very angry with you for going there?"

"Not thunder-and-lightning angry like daddy. He just made me feel mean and small."

"But how? What did he say?"

"He said I'd deliberately taken advantage of you being new here and not knowing about the Cauldron being out-of-bounds for me. He said that if he were in your place he wouldn't want to be friends with me because I'd taken advantage of you, but... but..." Maree's eyes filled with tears and her mouth trembled. "I didn't mean to take advantage of you, Juliet. You will be my friend, won't you?"

"Of course I will." Juliet was quick to answer the appeal. She could feel her annoyance with Lance growing. The fact that he had guessed she could be taken advantage of, especially by lonely vulnerable people like Maree, rattled her almost as much as his unkindness to Gareth had aroused her protective instincts.

"And when I ask you to come for a walk with me again you won't think I'm taking advantage of you, will you?" persisted the troubled girl.

"No, I..." began Juliet, and then stopped as she realized that whenever Maree sought her company in the future she would be a great deal more cautious and would ask a great many more questions concerning their destination before agreeing to go with her. But Maree was staring at her, her gray eyes wide with hurt as she sensed the hesitation. "I'm sure you aren't going to take advantage of me, are you, Maree?" she went on quickly, touching the girl's hand in a gesture of friendliness. "Promise?"

The gray eyes blinked once.

"I promise," muttered the girl. "Oh, Juliet, I'm so glad you came here."

At that moment Vinnie came into the kitchen and informed Juliet that Mrs. Crimond, who was now having her lunch in her room as usual, expected to see her in half an hour.

"So you'd better be having your lunch quickly and then be changing your clothes and making yourself look tidy instead of sitting there blethering with Maree," she added sharply.

A little taken aback by the housekeeper's changed attitude, which was indicated by her grimly disapproving glance and her critical words, Juliet ate the meal put before her in silence and then scurried up the wheel stairs to her room.

Truly nothing was as it had seemed at Castle Ross anymore, she thought with a regretful sigh as she tried to disentangle burrs from her hair. What a mess she looked, with her hair tangled and her face windburned and her pants torn! So much for behaving like a twelve-year-old and rolling down the hillside. No wonder Mrs. McVinn had looked disapproving.

But was her untidy appearance the only reason for the change in the housekeeper's manner? Or had Lance Crimond something to do with that too? Jamie had said Lance had a way of turning up unexpectedly and putting everyone in a tizzy. Well, he'd certainly done that this morning in the short time he'd been here.

Oh, how she wished he hadn't come. For the past three weeks everything had seemed perfect. Castle Ross had seemed an oasis of pleasant gracious living, an impression created not only by the building and its surroundings but also by the highly civilized behavior of the people living in it. But now she was aware of strange undercurrents of feeling and everyone had changed.

Gareth no longer seemed a quiet gentlemanly person bearing with fortitude the cross of his disability, but had shown he could be peevish and possibly even cowardly in his refusal to go out into the world. Maree no longer seemed to be a lovable madcap whose wildness was due only to lack of attention but had been revealed as capable of taking advantage of others to get her own way. And Vinnie no longer seemed the kindly motherly body to whom nothing was too much trouble but had shown that she could be vindictive and critical of a fellow employee.

It was as if a cold wind had swept through the house whipping away the warm cover behind which everyone had been hiding, and with a shiver Juliet wondered if the wind had reached Mrs. Crimond's room too.

It had. Although when she entered the big comfortable room, which Mrs. Crimond used as a combined study and private sitting room, she thought the novelist looked as usual, a leisurely person with plenty of time to stand and stare at a window. But when Mrs. Crimond turned to see who had entered the room Juliet could see that her face was creased by lines of worry and that she twined one hand nervously in one of her strings of beads.

"Oh, there you are, Juliet. I've had a most difficult morning. Basil wouldn't behave at all, so I'm afraid I've wasted reams of paper." She waved a hand in the direction of the floor, which was scattered with screwed-up sheets of yellow copy paper.

Juliet knew that Basil was a character in the new book Mrs. Crimond was writing and that he often gave his creator problems. Feeling that she should make herself useful, she moved forward and bent to pick up some of the paper to put it in the wastebasket.

"No, don't touch anything, please," commanded Mrs. Crimond. "You see, dear, there might be the germ of an idea in one of those pieces of paper—which one I can't be sure. Lance says I have no system, and he's quite right. But we can't all be as methodical as he is and I've never been able to work any other way." She glanced anxiously at Juliet. "You've seen him, of course."

"Yes."

Mrs. Crimond swallowed nervously, and once again Juliet felt her annoyance rising as she realized the eldest Crimond had upset his mother as well as everyone else in the house.

"It was too bad of Maree to take you to the Hollow Hill," murmured Mrs. Crimond apologetically. "And I feel it's my fault for not having warned you. I just didn't think she would do anything like that or that she even knew how to get there."

"Oh, I do hope Mr. Crimond hasn't blamed you for what happened this morning," Juliet blurted out impulsively.

"Not entirely, but he did suggest that I should have told you more about the area and pointed out the dangers of wandering so far afield. I can see now that it was very thoughtless of me... if there'd been an accident. Oh, it doesn't bear thinking about!"

"But there wasn't an accident, and we didn't get lost," said Juliet gently. "And if Mr. Crimond hadn't come this morning he'd never have known that Maree had taken me there and then there wouldn't have been all this fuss about nothing."

Mrs. Crimond regarded her thoughtfully for a moment and then smiled with relief.

"Perhaps you're right, dear, although Lance never makes a fuss, he just has a rather unpleasant way of telling you what he thinks that makes you feel...."

"Mean and small."

"That's it exactly. I hope he hasn't been unpleasant to you."

"Not yet, but Maree told me how he'd made her feel."

"Well, in a way I'm glad that's how he made her feel because she needs to be put in her place. It was Lance who suggested to Gareth that she should not be allowed to wander at will on the moors, but of course she's very willful, and very like her mother in that she knows no fear. Moira was a wonderful athlete. She used to go rock climbing, aqua-diving, sailing and skiing and she was as good if not better than many men. In fact, I often used to think she went out of her way to show the opposite sex how much better than they she could be. I remember one year I went with her and Gareth to Chamonix. It wasn't the usual holiday I take at that time of year, much too cold, but I wanted to get background for a story. I used to watch her come gliding down the slopes leaving poor Gareth far behind. It was while he was trying to catch her that his leg was hurt, and then she had to go skiing alone or with Lance when he came back."

The blue eyes became vacant and once again Juliet found herself waiting while Mrs. Crimond looked into the past. This time she hoped more information about the athletic Moira might be forthcoming, but the clock on the mantelpiece struck the quarter and Mrs. Crimond returned to the present.

"Good heavens!" she exclaimed. "It's time I was leaving. I'm going to drive over to see a neighbor of ours, Janet Coates—Lance tells me she isn't well. Now, I think I've reached the point where you can help me. You can work quite undisturbed up here. I want you to make three copies of chapter one. You'll find there are some alterations scribbled in here and there, but I think you'll understand them all."

As soon as she was quite sure Juliet had everything she needed in the way of paper and that she understood the intricacies of the old-fashioned typewriter, Mrs. Crimond left the room and all was quiet except for the ticking of the clock.

Glad at last to have some work to do, Juliet soon became absorbed in what she was doing and the time slipped by unnoticed as she typed out the opening chapter of the story, which contained all the usual touches of suspense one expected in a novel by Tessa Dean.

She had just finished typing chapter one when Mrs. Crimond walked into the room.

"Do you know, dear, it's almost time for dinner. I didn't expect you to work all this time. Always stop at five no matter how much you've done, or Lance will be telling me I'm a slave driver next. Now, run off and make yourself pretty for dinner. Gareth does enjoy having a pretty girl at the dinner table."

The mention of Gareth brought back the conversation she had had with him on the terrace that morning, and her heart began to beat excitedly as she started up the wheel stair to the floor above. She was looking forward to seeing him again and seeing his blue eyes light up with appreciation as she entered the dining room. How good it made her feel to know that he liked the way she looked. It made her want to make an effort with her appearance.

Now, what should she wear? She hadn't much choice really. All the other evenings she had worn alternately a full black skirt and off-the-shoulder Gypsy blouse or a simple green summer dress. Dared she wear the sea-green dress she had worn for Hilary's wedding tonight?

"Where do you think you're going?"

Lance's voice startled her. She looked up. He was standing at the top of the stairway, his hand on the curving handrail, in readiness to descend.

"To my room," she replied stiffly.

"Who gave you a room up here?"

"Mrs. Crimmond. She said she wanted me to be near her."

"I see. Well, I suppose that's reasonable enough. I hope you won't mind sharing a bathroom with me."

"Oh, do you ...?"

"Yes. In the other room up here. When I was younger I wouldn't let anyone else come up here. I used to consider the whole of this top floor as my aerie...."

"From which you kept an eagle eye on everything." Strange to think that this cold practical man had indulged in fantasies of that sort.

"How did you guess?" he said, and his lopsided grin appeared. There were times when he looked very attractive, thought Juliet, and this was one of them. Over an open-necked white shirt he wore a thin charcoal gray sweater that matched his trousers. The white collar of the shirt contrasted sharply with the darkness of his hair and eyebrows and seemed to find reflection in his clear eyes. He had obviously bathed recently, because his hair was damp, sleek as a raven's wing, except for the rebellious lock that slid forward on his forehead.

He leaned a broad shoulder against the whitewashed wall of the stairway, making room for her to pass.

"Aren't you coming up?" he inquired. "There isn't room for two to pass on these stairs."

Realizing she had been staring at him for some time, Juliet went pink.

"Anyway, it's unlucky to pass on the stairs," she countered as coolly as she could, and began to mount the steps.

"I might have known you'd be superstitious as well as hopelessly romantic," he mocked, and as she gained the top stair where he stood he reached out and caught her by the arm so that she was unable to go on. "Are you sorry you came here?" he demanded.

She glanced deliberately at the hand holding her arm and then tried to move it from his grasp. It was impossible. As at the wedding he had caught her and now he held her with casual ease.

"I haven't been, but I might be now that you've come," she answered, and felt the hand tighten remorselessly.

"That isn't the sort of thing you should say to your employer, little white rose," he threatened softly.

The air was cold and sharp in her mouth as she gasped, "But I thought Mrs. Crimond...."

"It was my idea for you to come here and work for her and I pay the shot, as I do for everything else around here. And that reminds me, Miss Grey, you slipped up badly this morning, so badly that I'm wondering whether it was a good idea to bring you here at all. You're supposed to keep Maree out of mischief and danger, not lead her into it."

"I didn't lead—" she began, then decided that wasn't the right way to defend herself or Maree, so she added, "How was I supposed to know the place was dangerous?"

"You weren't to know unless someone told you, and I've already dealt with those who knew for not telling you. Now I realized when I met you that you were a little wet behind the ears, but I didn't realize you were so green as to let a twelve-year-old girl lead you by the nose. Vinnie tells me she tried to find out from Maree where you were going, but you stepped in and said that Maree would be all right with you."

Silently seething at his insolent taunts, Juliet flung back her head and glared up at him.

"And she *was* all right with me. When I saw the place and she told me that she would like to try and squeeze into the crack in the hillside I wouldn't let her, and I made her come back. I'm not entirely witless and irresponsible."

"I'm glad to hear it," he commented dryly. "But you'll not deny you're very trusting and easily put upon. Children often have a way of finding a person's soft spot. And you're soft, aren't you, Juliet? Soft and tenderhearted, and already a little bit in love with Gareth."

He had dealt with the others and now he was dealing with her, punishing her with a series of taunts. He wasn't angry. She would have preferred anger to this cold approach, which like the cold wind penetrated into the most protected parts of her heart so that now she hated him for having noticed how she felt about Gareth.

"Since you find me so unsuitable perhaps you would like me to leave?" she said shakily, and was mortified when he merely grinned at her.

"Not so fast," he murmured. "I didn't say you were un-

The Cave of the White Rose

suitable. I was only exercising my prerogative as an employer to see that I'm getting value for my money. You might be interested to know that when I learned you were looking for a job I couldn't help thinking how suitable you would be to fill the need here and how good you'd be, not only as a secretary to Tess and a companion for Maree, but also how you might be able to help Gareth. I'm still of that opinion. The accident in which his leg was hurt coupled with the unexpected death of his wife damaged his self-esteem and went a long way to making a recluse of him. He needs someone to make a fuss of him. You were doing pretty well this morning on the terrace, so I've no criticism on that score."

To her consternation Juliet's face flamed, and she couldn't meet his eyes.

"But on the subject of Maree, I think perhaps you need a little guidance," he continued. "She doesn't need yet another person over whom she can ride roughshod. She's done that already to Tess, and to Vinnie. As a result she has little or no respect for them and they have no control over her. Gareth only stirs himself occasionally to berate her and then sinks back into his lethargy. Her willfulness could lead one day to an accident, and there have been enough accidents in this family recently. Do you understand?"

"But why should you be concerned about her? She isn't your child," she said, looking up at him. His eyes were cold and crystal clear as the burn she had followed that morning and they gave no indication of his feelings.

"Everyone living here is my concern in some way or other," he replied quietly, and once again she felt that strange twinge of conscience as if she had been guilty of prejudice.

"Because you pay the shot?" She couldn't resist flicking the barb and should have known he would react unpredictably. Instead of retaliating he laughed and released her arm.

"You can think of it that way if you wish, it makes no difference to me," he murmured, and watched her rubbing the place where he had held her arm. "That's all I have to say for the time being, and unless you make another mistake you'll hear no more criticism from me. Do what you came here to do—type for Tess, take an interest in Maree so that she has no reason to wander and throw in some attention for Gareth by way of good measure and you'll earn every penny of your wages and I think you'll find life quite pleasant. But," he paused as if to add emphasis to what he was going to say, "anything beyond those duties is not your concern. Do I make myself clear?"

Juliet nodded. He meant that she wasn't to step beyond the limits he had just imposed and get involved with anyone else other than the three people he had just mentioned, and it wasn't until he had gone down the stairs that she realized she had just received a warning to keep her nose out of Crimond family affairs.

CHAPTER THREE

WHEN JULIET REACHED HER BEDROOM she found she was trembling. If every meeting with Lance Crimond was going to do this to her, she thought with a wry smile, she would be a nervous wreck by the end of his ten-day holiday. And as if his presence in the castle wasn't enough, he had to have his bedroom on the same floor as hers, right across the passage. At night they would be the only two up here in the aerie to which he wouldn't allow anyone else to come when he was a boy. However was she going to sleep knowing he was there? The very thought made her shudder again.

His remarks about herself and Gareth had destroyed the zest with which she had been looking forward to dressing for dinner. She dressed absentmindedly, automatically putting on the black skirt and Gypsy blouse, her eyes avoiding the sea-green dress, which Lance had once told her made her look elegant and mysterious, her subconscious instinctively drawing back from anything that had associations with him. She made no attempt to arrange her hair differently as had been her intention, but after brushing it let it hang loosely to her shoulders.

But by the time she took her place at the table in the dining room her poise had returned, restored by Gareth's warm greeting as she had entered the room and the pleasure that lit his eyes as they lingered appreciatively on her slim waist accentuated by the broad band of the skirt, and on her white-skinned throat and shoulders as revealed by the wide scooped neckline of the blouse.

Maree, her hair brushed until it shone, wearing a blue-and-white striped knit dress whose short skirt revealed her sturdy tanned legs, sat down next to Juliet and Lance took his place at the head of the table facing Mrs. Crimond.

As on previous evenings Mrs. Crimond and Gareth carried on a light and stimulating conversation designed, Juliet was sure, to inform herself and Maree on all manner of subjects and to give them both a chance to participate. Lance contributed nothing, but occasionally his bright observant glance would flick from one face to another, and Juliet had the impression that he didn't miss one word that was said. Certainly she found his presence at the table a restraint, causing her to choose her own words with care when she had something to say, so it was with a feeling to relief that she saw him toss his table napkin down when he had finished his dessert, and rise to his feet with a muttered excuse.

"Oh, Uncle Lance, are you going fishing? May I come with you, please?" pleaded Maree impulsively, also rising to her feet, obviously just as eager to leave the table as he was.

"Not this evening. I have something else to do," he replied, his smile glimmering briefly as he turned in the doorway. "But if you can be up early in the morning and ready about six o'clock you could come with me then. I'm going to fish the Black Pool. McVinn tells me that the trout offer a good fight up there."

"I'll be up," answered the girl, her eyes flashing with excitement.

"Maree, you will do nothing of the sort," said Gareth curtly. "You are not to go fishing with Lance."

Lance flicked a cold but slightly derisive glance at his brother.

"Juliet could come, too, to act as watchdog if you're worried in case something might happen to Maree while she's with me. She took good care of her today," he said quietly.

The atmosphere in the room twanged with tension. Mrs. Crimond's left hand began to twine nervously in one of her necklaces. Gareth's eyes darkened and his mouth went taut as he tried to control his easily roused temper.

Aware of antagonism between the two brothers, Juliet

felt rebellion rising within her. Nothing, not even the threat of the sack, would make her go with Lance tomorrow, just to look after Maree. She looked across at Gareth hoping he would continue to refuse to allow Maree to go fishing with her uncle.

"I'm sure Gareth isn't thinking that anything might happen to Maree while she's with you," protested Mrs. Crimond nervously.

"And I'm sure that he is," said Lance. "Well, Gareth? Will you let her come if Juliet comes, too?"

In answer to the question in Gareth's eyes Juliet shook her head slowly, trying to make the action as imperceptible as possible, hoping that Lance wouldn't see it.

"As a matter of fact I was hoping Juliet would be available to do some typing for me in the morning," said Gareth lightly. His gaze was steady as it met Juliet's and she smiled her thanks. In return she received a warm sympathetic smile.

"Wonders will never cease," gibed the hateful man in the doorway. "I wouldn't want to be responsible for coming between you and work, Gareth, so of course Juliet must stay. Sorry, Maree. Your luck's out this time. Try another day."

He went out of the room. The tension snapped as Maree turned on her father with a howl of disappointment.

"Why will you never let me go with him? Why? Why?" she raged. "He's the only one who ever wants to take me anywhere, and you'll never let me go. Why?"

Seeing tears brim in the girl's eyes, Juliet felt suddenly guilty. After all, she was here to take an interest in Maree. That had been the second on her list of duties that her employer had enumerated on the wheel stairs less than an hour ago, and helping Gareth had been only third. Perhaps she should have made an attempt to show she was willing to go fishing so that the girl could go too. If the fisherman had been anyone other than Lance, she would have done so, she argued with herself, but the thought of having to spend a whole morning, possibly a whole day, in his company, frightened her.

"Maree, you're behaving in the most ridiculous manner," said Gareth sharply. "I just don't want you to go, and that's reason enough."

"It's because of mummy, isn't it?" shrilled the girl. "It's because she was with Uncle Lance when she was killed, isn't it?"

Gareth and Mrs. Crimond spoke together, one ordering the girl to go to her bedroom and stay there until she could behave herself, and the other remonstrating with more gentleness and suggesting that Maree didn't know what she was talking about. At that moment Vinnie entered the room to say she had put the coffee tray in the lounge and to comment that it was a fine evening and that the wind had gone down at last. She clucked her tongue at the sobbing girl, put an arm around her and spoke in the motherly way that had impressed Juliet when she'd first met her.

"There, there, bairn, what's the good of carrying on like this? You'll only exhaust yourself. McVinn will take you fishing this evening on the loch." She looked over the girl's head at Gareth. "You'll be letting her go with him?"

Gareth assented rather wearily and Maree went with Vinnie willingly. With a sigh of relief Mrs. Crimond stood up and drifted out of the room. Gareth attempted to rise to his feet, only to subside into his chair again, a rather bitter expression on his face. Pity turning like a knife in her heart, Juliet hurried around to his side.

"Can I help?" she asked.

His smile was rueful.

"I'm afraid it's one of those days when my leg seems remarkably useless. I'll try again."

This time he managed to stand, but when he moved forward at her side he placed his free hand on her shoulder as if seeking support. Under his touch the half bare skin seemed to burn.

"You're very understanding, Juliet," he murmured as they went out into the hallway.

"I could say the same for you. I... I didn't want to go fishing," she stammered truthfully, "but now I'm wondering whether I should have said I'd go for Maree's sake."

"Nonsense. She can go fishing any time with McVinn. She doesn't have to go with Lance."

"But she must be feeling very disappointed and miserable."

"It's her own fault. She shouldn't behave so badly."

"She's only a child...."

"I know, and I'm a rotten father because I don't take sufficient interest in her and in what she wants to do. But how can I when all she's interested in is climbing hills, fishing, sailing, exploring underground caves, and I can't do any of those things anymore?"

"Did you ever do them?"

His grin was a little self-disparaging.

"Not much. I'm not really the outdoor type. I used to ski a little to try and keep up with Moira."

"What's wrong with your leg?"

"It's apparently paralyzed, something to do with pressure on a nerve."

"Isn't it possible to have an operation?"

"All avenues have been explored in that direction and I've been told that nothing can be done," he replied curtly. "Some days it seems better than others. Some days like today it seems to stiffen up completely."

His voice was cool, setting her at a distance, making it obvious that he didn't like to discuss his leg, and she was quick to respond.

"I'm sorry, Gareth," she murmured. "So terribly sorry."

His eyes crinkled at the corners as he smiled at her.

"I meant it when I said that I wanted you to type for me tomorrow morning," he said. "It wasn't just an excuse to get you out of going with Lance, although I realize that what I want wouldn't weigh with him if he insisted that you go. He calls the tune around here."

"So I'd noticed," said Juliet dryly, remembering her recent interview on the wheel stair. "But is it necessary always for you to dance?"

He gave her a surprised glance.

"No, it isn't, but it takes a lot of effort to defy him...and then he makes it difficult because he's so damned generous. Sometimes I think that perhaps he's trying to make amends for what happened, but I don't know, I just don't know." He smiled down at her. "But you don't want to be burdened by our family problems. Let's go out on the terrace while there's still some light in the sky."

Longing to know more but very conscious still of the warning Lance had given her on the stairs about anything beyond her work being none of her concern, Juliet suppressed the questions that clamored to be asked and went with Gareth through the shadowy lounge out onto the terrace where Mrs. Crimond had taken the coffee tray.

The evening was still and tranquil and above the opposite hills the pale green sky was streaked with rose-tinted feathery clouds, the colors of which were reflected in the smooth loch below.

"Do you like your coffee black or white, Juliet?" asked Mrs. Crimond. "I'm afraid I've forgotten already. White? Sugar too? Yes, I'm really becoming very forgetful these days. Even Janet noticed this afternoon. Poor dear, she's not been at all well—a slight heart attack. I'm not surprised. How often have I told her that she rushes around too much? Now she has to rest. That's why Alison is home, Gareth. And such a change in her. She's quite sophisticated, although underneath I'm sure she's still the good-natured girl we all used to love."

"Did we?" Gareth raised his eyebrows haughtily. "I seem to remember loathing her because her hair was so red and she had a temper to match it."

"Oh, not loathe, Gareth, surely?" chided Mrs. Crimond absently, as she placed his coffee beside him. "Anyway, I think Lance has gone over to Glenavon to see her this evening. He and Alison have been meeting in Glasgow quite frequently."

"Have they now? That's interesting," murmured Gareth.

"Isn't it?" crowed Mrs. Crimond, who was obviously delighted. "Both Janet and I think we can hear wedding bells at last. I'm so glad Lance is showing an interest in a woman and that she's someone with a similar background who would fit into the family perfectly."

Gareth moved his good leg restlessly and crossed it over his stiff one.

"Mother, stop being naive. Lance has always shown an interest in women. Wasn't there some talk of Alison being engaged to a surgeon? If she's broken off her engagement in favor of Lance ten to one he'll lose interest in her and go off hunting in some other direction."

"That isn't a very nice thing to say about him," remonstrated Mrs. Crimond, and the shadow of anxiety was back in her face. "You'll shock Juliet, and she'll think he's only interested in women who are already engaged."

"Or married," put in Gareth bitterly. "I'm prepared to bet Juliet knows a few things about Lance that aren't nice already. It may not be nice, but it's near the truth, mother, as you should know."

Mrs. Crimond's hand twined in her necklaces.

"You're thinking of Moira," she said, "but I'm sure he was only trying to help both you and her, in his own way. You know how frustrated she was after your injury. I think Lance thought he was helping by taking her out of your way for a few hours."

"Sometimes it was days," growled Gareth.

"Oh, surely not!"

"That time they went up to Aviemore and said they couldn't get back because they were snowbound in one of the lodges, they were away three whole days together."

"But there were other people stranded with them," objected Mrs. Crimond.

"So Lance said," replied Gareth, with a cynicism that surprised Juliet. "I often think that if I hadn't let her go with him that last time she might have been alive now," he added in a low voice, and Mrs. Crimond looked startled.

"Now, dear, it doesn't do to keep brooding about it," she said soothingly. "If you don't mind I'll leave you because I've had an idea about Basil. I must go and write it down before I forget it. I'll see you tomorrow, Juliet. You type beautifully, by the way, and you seem to have deciphered my squiggles very well. I think Gareth is going to find you a great help to him in his work."

"I know I am," murmured Gareth, smiling at Juliet as his mother went into the house, and Juliet whose thoughts were a little chaotic after the recent interchange between mother and son, which had shed an entirely new light on that unknown quantity called Lance Crimond, stood up and walked over to the balustrade to gaze at the rose-tinted water of the loch, shimmering between dark hills. She could see a lone rowing boat in which two people were sitting silhouetted against the sky and water and beyond the boat on the distant horizon a light flickered in and out at regular intervals. She supposed it was a beacon or lighthouse on a far-off shore and was fascinated by the fact that though she could see the light no land was visible. When she looked in the other direction several lights twinkled at her from the houses of the village, which curved round the head of the loch.

"Has your mother ever had a secretary before?" she asked, putting into words at last the problem that had been in her mind ever since she had started typing that afternoon.

"Once. A Miss Reid, but she didn't last long. She couldn't stand mother's vagueness. Why do you ask?" said Gareth lazily.

Juliet turned and leaned back against the balustrade. Gareth was lighting his pipe and the smell of tobacco wafted toward her, pungent in the soft clear evening air.

"I'm trying to find out why I've been taken on as her secretary. She doesn't need anyone to type her stories for her. She's a perfectly good typist herself."

Having got his pipe going Gareth removed it from his mouth and stared at her as he considered her statement.

"Don't you like being here?" he asked.

"Oh, yes, I like being here very much, only...."

"Only someone has disturbed you today and started you off questioning motives," he suggested softly. "I should leave well alone if I were you, Juliet. Although my mother doesn't need a typist as such, she does need help in other ways. She gets very tired and bewildered sometimes. She hasn't a daughter, and I think she regrets the fact that she hasn't a daughter-in-law. You noticed, I expect, her delight at the thought that Lance at last might be serious about Alison." He paused and took a puff at his pipe, then added more lightly, "And if you think you haven't enough to do just wait until tomorrow morning. Mother may be a good typist, but I am not, and I need your help very much. So stop questioning, Juliet, and be glad you're here, and for goodness' sake don't let him frighten you away."

"Him?" she queried.

"Lance. He'll only be here for ten days, two weeks at the most, and when he's gone everything will be as it was before he came."

BEFORE SHE WENT TO BED that night Juliet went to the kitchen to make her peace with Vinnie. She realized that if she was going to be comfortable during her stay at Castle Ross she must be on good terms with the housekeeper. Being of a gentle disposition she was quite ready to admit that it was her fault that Vinnie had been hauled over the coals by Lance Crimond that morning.

"Ach, don't be worrying your head about that," said the black-eyed woman. "I'm used to being told my place by himself, and I'd think less of him if he didn't do it. He was right. I should have warned you about how easy it is to get lost on these moors and about the Cauldron. But you seemed so confident this morning it didn't seem necessary."

Yet for all the housekeeper's apparently good-natured dismissal of the incident Juliet was still conscious of the woman's withdrawal, and was sure that Vinnie disapproved of something she had done that day. Even a close analysis of the day's events while she lay sleepless in bed later gave her no clue as to what she had done to earn disapproval.

Suddenly exhausted, she turned on her side and closed her eyes. All the other nights she had slept soundly, dreamlessly, lulled into a sense of security by the smooth effortless rhythm of life at the castle. But today that rhythm had been broken by the arrival of one man.

A board creaked in the silence of the night and she shot

up in bed, quivering. Her straining ears caught the sound of a doorknob being turned quietly. It was followed by the sound of water running through pipes. She relaxed on her pillows and tried to quell the frightened pounding of her heart. She had forgotten that Lance's bedroom was opposite hers and that he would be using the same bathroom.

He must have returned from his visit to see the red-haired Alison whom he had been meeting frequently in Glasgow and whom Mrs. Crimond hoped he might marry. Her mind drifted on, recalling the rest of the conversation between Gareth and his mother concerning Lance's association with Moira, Gareth's wife, and Gareth's low-voiced regret that he let Moira go with Lance that last time.

She turned again and punched her pillow to make it more comfortable. Whatever was the matter with her? She must keep her curiosity under control and not allow herself to be swayed by chance remarks about her employer. She must remember that although she had her doubts about the job she had been offered to do here, she was being paid to type for Mrs. Crimond, who didn't need a typist, take an interest in Maree, and give some attention to Gareth. Anything beyond that was not her concern and that "anything" presumably included Lance's relationship with his late sister-in-law.

In the week that followed his arrival she found it easy to do what Lance had said she should do, and gradually a routine developed, although she could never have complained of being overworked.

Every morning she typed for Gareth and listened to his pleasant voice as he dictated information he had unearthed about the family that had built Castle Ross and had played a prominent part in the rather chaotic political scene at the time of Mary, Queen of Scots. From his mother he had inherited an ability to tell a story, and this, added to his meticulous attention to historical fact, brought the past vividly alive.

In the afternoon she transferred from fact to fiction as with Basil and Anita she tried to unravel the secret of an old house set in the middle of a bleak and windy moor somewhere in Scotland.

When she wasn't required by either Mrs. Crimond or Gareth she showed Maree how to exercise for ballet or went walking along the loch shore with her. By unspoken mutual agreement they kept away from the hills and the moors, although there were days when the sun shone out of a cloudless sky and every summit of every mountain was revealed and Juliet felt the pull of those distant places. On such days, too, she would feel the pull of the sea, which heaved and glinted at the mouth of the loch as she watched Lance's boat apparently flying over the foam, its white sails translucent in the sunshine.

To her relief she saw little of her employer, a circumstance that pleased her because it meant she didn't have to take much avoiding action, since she had decided that the less she saw of him during his holiday the more she was likely to keep her employment there. If he wasn't sailing he was fishing, and if he wasn't doing either of those things she presumed he was visiting Alison.

But if she saw little of him, she heard him a great deal, for every morning between the hours of six and seven she would be awakened by his powerful baritone voice as he sang to himself in the bathroom. The first time she heard him she had not believed it was he who was singing but had thought he had a record player in his room upon which he was inconsiderate enough to play records early in the morning. But as she was just considering remonstrating with him the song had stopped in the middle and for a while all that she had heard was the swishing of water, followed by a rather muffled rendering of a different song of which he apparently didn't know all the words, because the singing gave way to humming and whistling before he went out of the bathroom and returned to his bedroom.

She supposed she would get used to it eventually, she thought, on the seventh day of waking early. Turning over lazily, she considered dreamily this unusual aspect of the domineering man who had bullied her into meeting his mother and as a result of that meeting in coming to Castle Ross.

The songs he sang were a mixture of British and American folk songs, many of which she had learned herself at school, with the occasional modern ballad thrown in. Sometimes he even attempted an operatic aria. To sing with such lighthearted abandon at that hour of the morning he must be a truly happy man. But then, when she thought about it, hadn't he everything to make a man happy? He was wealthy, he owned a beautiful castle on a fine estate, and it looked as if he was about to marry the lovely Alison Coates.

For Alison Coates was lovely, with that fine-boned fine-skinned beauty that so many Scottish women seemed to possess. Her hair glowed like beech leaves in the autumn and her eyes were the color of topazes. Juliet had met her only once, on the previous day, when Alison had called to see Mrs. Crimond. She had arrived on an old bicycle, which she had thrown down on the drive before coming in by way of the kitchen. Vinnie had greeted her as if she had been the long-lost daughter of the house and Alison had gone through and up the wheel stair as if sure of welcome.

"Who's that?" Maree had demanded.

"Miss Alison Coates," Vinnie had replied.

"Oh, she's Aunty Janet's daughter. I've never seen her before."

"She hasn't been here for a long time, more's the pity," Vinnie had said, with one of her disconcertingly vindictive glances at Juliet.

"She's pretty," Maree had remarked. "I'm going to wait here until she comes down from grannie's room so that I can see her again. Will you tell her who I am, Vinnie?"

"Well, now that'll be depending on how you're behaving."

Alison's visit to Mrs. Crimond lasted no more than half an hour and when she had appeared again in the kitchen she had gone straight up to Juliet and had held out her hand.

"You must be Juliet Grey," she had said in her forthright way. "Tess said I was to send you to her at once. I'm afraid I've prevented you from getting on with your work, but I had to give her a message from my mother."

She had looked then at the girl sitting beside Juliet and had smiled down at her, "And you must be Maree. I've been hearing all about you from your grannie. How would you like to come back with me to Glenavon? Have you a bicycle?"

No one could expect the girl to resist the warmth of Alison's approach, thought Juliet, as she turned restlessly on her bed. She couldn't herself. Everything about Alison proclaimed her to be generous, outgoing, strong and competent, and one day she would be the wife of Lance Crimond.

Deciding suddenly that she could lie in bed no longer, Juliet flung back the covers and searched for her slippers. No noise from the bathroom indicated that Lance had finished washing. Taking her dressing gown from the wardrobe, she slipped it around her shoulders and snatching up her toilet bag from the dressing table, she opened the door and stepped out into the passage just as Lance stepped out of his room.

"Oh!" gasped Juliet in surprise, pulling her dressing gown around her and backing into her room.

"Good morning," he said calmly. "You're up early." He closed his door and leaned against it as if he had all the time in the world to stand and talk. "Couldn't you sleep?" he added.

"I defy anyone to sleep when someone is roaring out the Soldiers' Chorus from *Faust* in the next room!" she snapped crossly.

"I'm complimented to know that it was actually recognizable," he returned imperturbably, his eyes busy noting the two plaits of hair which hung on either side of her face, the frill at the neck of her Victorian-styled nightdress, the line of her limbs showing through its flimsy material, the pale dancer's feet in the mules peeping below and then coming back to her face.

"What do you intend to do today?" he asked abruptly.

"Today?" she was puzzled.

"It's Saturday. Had you forgotten? I'm not such a grim

taskmaster that I expect you to type your fingers to the bone all day and every day. You are entitled to have the weekend off, you know."

She had forgotten it was Saturday. On other Saturdays she had walked to the village and back and on Sundays she had gone to church with Vinnie.

"I hadn't made any plans," she replied.

"The wind's in the west and I'd thought of sailing up north as far as Oban. I'll be leaving in about three-quarters of an hour. You're welcome to come with me if you'd like to. You'd get a different view of the land and see some of the islands."

The invitation was so unexpected and answered such a deeply felt desire that she was silent for a few seconds.

"Could Maree come with us?" she managed to say at last, knowing how much the girl longed to go sailing again.

"I believe there is already something laid on for her entertainment today. She's going visiting with Tess and Gareth," he replied smoothly. "Anyway, think about it while you're dressing and let me know if you want to come when you come down for breakfast."

Juliet thought about it, not clearly and concisely, but in a state of turmoil. Her first muddled thoughts, which were dictated not only by her dislike of Lance but also by convention, urged her to refuse. But her second equally muddled thoughts were more adventurous and liberal. How many times had she wished recently that she could board a sailing boat and skim over the water under billowing sails to those enticing islands. The opportunity to go had been offered and it might not come her way again. There was no one to frown and tell her she shouldn't go. Perhaps this was a case when second thoughts should be followed and let the devil take the consequences.

Quickly, before she could change her mind, she dressed in slacks, shirt and sweater and rubber-soled canvas shoes. When she entered the kitchen she found Lance alone at the table eating his breakfast and reading the previous day's newspaper, which he had propped against the teapot. His quick all-seeing glance flicked over her.

"I take it you've decided to come," he murmured. "Your breakfast is in the oven keeping warm."

There was no sign of Vinnie. The kitchen was quiet and sunlit. Lance continued to read the newspaper, moving it only to pour some tea for her. *How odd,* she thought, *to be sitting here with a man I dislike, eating the breakfast he must have cooked for me.* Then the domestic intimacy of the scene struck her. Anyone coming in unexpectedly would think that she and Lance had been taking their breakfast together like this for years, like a married couple, so in tune that they didn't have to speak to each other.

"It makes fantastic reading," drawled Lance, and she jumped. Looking up, she encountered his eyes above the edge of the newspaper. How cold and clear they were, icy pools fringed with black.

"W-what does?" she stammered, fully expecting him to quote from some article in the paper.

"Your face. Would you like to be married?"

She had forgotten his magical ability to read the expressions on her face. She would really have to be more careful in guarding her thoughts from him.

"Not to you," she retorted, hoping to put an end to such personal probing, and then was immediately surprised by the little leap of pleasure she felt when his rare and unexpected smile appeared.

"Point conceded," he said good-humoredly. "But remember you're the next to marry in your family. You caught the bouquet. Would Gareth suit, do you think?"

Rather bewildered by his question, she stared at him trying to guess what lay behind it, but no matter how she stared he remained unperturbed, returning her wide-eyed gaze steadily.

"I haven't known him very long, so I can't tell you," she replied eventually.

"You surprise me," he mocked. "I thought it was a case of love at first sight. But you do find him attractive even though he has a gammy leg, hasn't a job and at the moment is wholly dependent on his allowance out of my father's estate?"

"A man doesn't have to be sound in limb, or fully employed, to be attractive. Gareth has a gentle, kindly disposition as well as a very fine intellect. Who could help but like him?" she said gravely.

"Do you know, that's exactly what I thought you'd say, little white rose," he remarked with a touch of dryness. "Now, if you've finished your breakfast you'd better go and fetch a warm jacket, if you have one. Sometimes it can be cool on the water and we may not get back until late tonight."

Her doubts about him aroused by his recent remarks, Juliet hesitated as first thoughts came crowding back. Perhaps she shouldn't go sailing with him after all.

"Oh, but I don't think... I mean, do you think we should stay out late?" she stuttered as confusion reigned in her mind once more. His sardonic glance made her feel even more confused.

"One of the most exciting parts of going sailing is not knowing what will happen on the way or when I arrive at my destination, and also in now knowing whether I'll be coming back the same day. It's the not knowing that makes it exciting," he replied, and as she met the challenge in his eyes she felt a faint flicker of affinity with him. But convention had to have its last fling.

"Won't Mrs. Crimond wonder where I've gone?"

"I'll leave a note with Vinnie. She'll tell her. And now unless you've changed your mind, go and get that jacket and meet me down at the boathouse."

Lance's boat wasn't big by yachting standards, so he told her. It was small enough for him to handle alone, and was sturdy enough to stand up to the rough weather often encountered among the Hebridean Islands. He had bought it to provide himself with a sure means of escape when he had realized the weight of responsibility he had inherited when his father had died.

"Sometimes I think the old man left me a heavy load as a way of punishing me for the trouble I caused him when I was younger," he told Juliet, with a laugh.

"But wouldn't coming to stay in Castle Ross be escape

enough?" she asked innocently, a little surprised by his confession. The boat heeled suddenly as it moved forward out of the shelter of the bay in which it was usually moored, and into the open water of the loch where the wind was fresh. Feeling a little apprehensive at the sight of the water creaming along the side of the boat so close to the deck, she leaned back against the cockpit coaming and braced her feet against the opposite seat to prevent herself from sliding forward.

"No, it's only part of the load," said Lance crisply. "I don't enjoy being my brother's keeper or acting as my mother's treasurer. There was a time in my life when I wanted to live at Castle Ross all the time, but now...." He broke off and shrugged. "Enough of problems. We've come sailing to forget them, and as soon as we've cleared the entrance to the loch I'm going to give you your first sailing lesson. Meantime you can help with the jib when we have to tack, by freeing that rope over there and then pulling this one in on this side, when we've gone about."

When eventually he decided to go about Juliet did her best to obey his orders but managed to get the rope she freed fouled around the mast so that she couldn't pull in the rope on the other side. Leaving her to hold the tiller, Lance went forward to free the fouled rope. Filled with trepidation, she hung on to the wooden tiller, not sure what to do. The swish of the water around the hull, the loud cracking sound of the sails, the flick of her own hair pulled out of its ribbon by the tormenting wind, against her face and eyes, all unnerved her. For a few minutes everything seemed out of control.

Then Lance freed the rope and he was back in the cockpit pulling in on the other rope with jerks of his big shoulders. The boat heeled violently and water cascaded into the cockpit. The tiller was snatched from her hand and she was shoved roughly out of the way, the boat steadied as the rail came out of the water, and surged forward again.

Juliet rubbed the funnybone in her elbow, which she had banged against the edge of the cockpit when she had been pushed aside and gave Lance an alarmed glance. His grin was a white slash and his eyes glittered like diamonds.

"Did you get bruised?" he asked. "I'd forgotten you're a sensitive plant unused to the rough-and-tumble of outdoor life. If I hadn't pushed you out of the way we might have taken more water over the side."

She could tell by his grin and the glitter of his eyes that he had enjoyed the brush with danger and was pleased that he had been equal to dealing with it, and she suddenly understood why he liked sailing or any other activity with an edge of danger to it. He was much more suited to dealing with crisis situations when he was sailing or caving or even working on a construction site than he was to sitting in an executive's office or lounging on the terrace at Castle Ross. As his mother had once said, he was principally a man of action and not of words.

He hadn't cared about her being bruised or about her being scared silly by the contortions of the boat when she had held the tiller. In her imaginary sail down the loch the boat had skimmed over the water smoothly and silently with none of the jerking, plunging motion that was now threatening to bring up her breakfast.

But she mustn't be seasick, not yet, when she'd only been on the boat about half an hour, and certainly not in front of this tough self-contained man who hadn't an atom of chivalry in his character, and who had definitely been miscalled Lancelot!

So she swallowed her nausea and indignation, and hanging grimly with both hands to the side of the cockpit she turned her face to the bow of the boat, which chose that moment to plunge down into a deeper than normal trough in the waves and to rise up again sharply, sending a cascade of spray slap into her face.

Hair drenched and face dripping, she turned to splutter her objections to Lance and was immediately irritated to find that he was sitting completely relaxed, watching the mainsail. He was dry except for a sprinkling of water on his hair and she realized that she had sheltered him from the worst of the spray.

His gaze came down from the sail to her face and he made no attempt to hide his amusement at her appearance.

The Cave of the White Rose

"There's a towel down below, and an oilskin jacket and sou'wester. You might find them all useful," he suggested.

She turned and looked at the hatchway. Like the rest of the boat it was tilted at an angle. To reach it she would have to leave her present fairly secure position and start on a perilous journey on which she might suffer more bruises. Then she would have to negotiate the steps down into the cabin, and once there... Juliet's stomach heaved slightly as she imagined the movement down there. She couldn't go. She would have to stay wet. She looked quickly once more in the direction of the bow and received another salty slap in the face that left her gasping.

"Never mind," comforted Lance. "There won't be much more of this. It's the westerly wind that has caused this violent swell in the loch. Once we're clear of it and going north on the reach, you'll find it's all been worthwhile."

Juliet gave him a withering glance, which he returned with one of his tantalizing grins.

"Wishing you hadn't come, little white rose?" he taunted.

"Wishing you wouldn't call me that!" she snapped.

"Think of it as a compliment. There aren't many women of your age these days who manage to retain such a look of innocence. Even Maree has more knowledge of the ways of the world than you appear to have. How come you're so trusting?"

"What makes you think I am?" she countered uneasily, aware that she had always to be on the defensive against him.

"Watching you this past week."

Watching her! Where had he watched her? With whom had she been when he had watched her? With Gareth? No, that was impossible. When she had been with Gareth, either in his study or on the terrace, Lance had been far away inspecting the estate, sailing or fishing, or over at Glenavon visiting Alison.

"And what have you seen when you've been watching?" she countered lightly, trying to disguise the irritation she felt at the thought that he could watch her and remain unseen.

"Some things that perhaps I shouldn't have seen," he said tantalizingly, and her eyes, sea green and alarmed, flicked to his face. It was as usual cold eyed, impassive, and in the brilliant clear light created by the reflection of sunlight on an expanse of water she could see lines she hadn't noticed before; lines etched by laughter at the corners of his eyes, long creases from the corners of his bold nose to the corners of his contradictory mouth, furrows plowed across his wide forehead by thought and concentration. Everything he had done had left its mark on his face, she thought, and she felt again that strange tug at her heart that she had felt before. Perhaps she had been, and was still, guilty of condemning him unheard.

But he had said he had seen things that perhaps he shouldn't have seen. In her behavior, perhaps? Her mind searched wildly into the recesses of her memory to discover anything she might have done during the past week to give rise to such a remark, and found nothing unusual, except the growing intimacy between Gareth and herself, which had reached a climax the previous evening when he pulled her close to him, as she had wished him good-night, and had kissed her on the moonlit terrace.

Again her alarmed glance flickered to Lance's face. This time his eyes met hers directly and they glinted with derision.

"I've been accused before of walking too quietly," he observed, and she knew he had seen the incident on the terrace.

A wave of scarlet color swept over her face as she wished suddenly and fervently that Gareth hadn't kissed her and that Lance hadn't seen.

"You seem to be making good progress in that direction," continued Lance, still with that touch of derision.

"Well, isn't it what you wanted?" she retaliated. "Isn't that why you invented a job for me as secretary to your mother, because you thought I might be a suitable wife for Gareth?"

It was out and lying between them, the suspicion that had been planted in her mind by a few stray remarks.

"And where, may I ask, did you get that idea?" he asked blandly.

"I've been told that you found his first wife and that you once boasted you would find him another while you were visiting London. And at Hilary's wedding you said you were there to look for a wife," she replied as coolly as she could.

"So I did, and you took exception to my remark and attributed it to my having drunk too much champagne," he said calmly as he began to loosen the mainsheet so that the big white mainsail eased out slowly, the boat stopped plunging and its speed increased. Then he leaned forward and freed the jib sheet so that the foresail bellied out.

The sails trimmed correctly and to his satisfaction, Lance turned and smiled at her in an indulgent, curiously avuncular fashion.

"Your notion is a romantic one, but if you like it I have no objections to it. Anything that will help Gareth recover his self-confidence is okay by me," he drawled. "Now we're on the reach, which is a much faster point of sailing. If this wind keeps up we should get to Oban by this afternoon."

The change in the movement of the boat and the fact that she hadn't suffered a drenching recently made Juliet look about her. They had left the loch and were sailing past a rocky shore backed by wooded slopes. Looking ahead she saw a shimmering swirling stretch of water that seemed to suck the boat forward, and having seized it, swept it past a group of islands and out into a wider stretch of water across which she could see the towering bulk of a mountainous island.

Fascinated by the swift steady movement, by the glint of yellow light on the white-laced blue of the water, entranced by the brilliant greens, delicate violets and mysterious purples of the distant hills, she was silent, making no attempt to question Lance's faintly amused approval of the situation between Gareth and herself. She was still in the dark as to whether he had invented a job for her just to get her to Castle Ross to meet Gareth, but somehow out here on the sea among the islands it didn't matter anymore, and she understood why sailing was considered such a good escape from problems associated with the land.

Eventually she was sufficiently roused from her fascinated contemplation of the seascape to ask, "Where are we?"

"We've just come through the Sound of Luing and are now in the Firth of Lorne," replied Lance. "That's the island of Dana over there, an isle of delight, although that description could be applied to most of the Hebridean islands."

"It's beautiful," she murmured. "Could we go there?"

"Would you prefer to go there rather than go to Oban?" he asked.

"What is there at Oban?"

"Good shops, pleasant hotels, a fishing fleet...."

"I think I'd prefer the island. After all, I can see shops and hotels any day in other towns, but I may not have the chance of visiting one of the islands again. It must be lovely to anchor in a sheltered bay, miles away from the mainland. It's something I've always wanted to do."

He stared at her thoughtfully, his eyebrows raised in slight surprise. Then he glanced up at the sky. He looked at her again and smiled enigmatically and her nerves twanged suddenly with suspicion. After all, she knew so little about him and what she knew didn't endear him to her, yet here she was trusting him to take her across the sea to an isle of delight.

"If it's something you've always wanted to do then we shall do it," he said, and his eyes glittered with excitement. "Come hell or high water, we shall go to Dana and you shall anchor in a sheltered bay."

It wasn't hell, but the crossing to Mull wasn't entirely comfortable and there were times when Juliet, unused to being at sea in a small boat, found it both exhilarating and frightening.

At first they made good progress even though they had to alter course and beat into the wind again. But soon the wind

The Cave of the White Rose

died away altogether and the sun shone down on the idle boat as it drifted with the tide, its sails slatting. Lance made the most of their becalmed state to leave Julie at the tiller while he went below to prepare some lunch, which they ate in the cockpit.

While they were eating, cloud began to spread across the sky from the southwest and the sun lost its bright glare. Gradually the distant mountains lost their distinct violets and purples and became a uniform dull gray. A breeze sprang up, blowing out of the increasing cloud and Lance trimmed the sails accordingly so that soon the boat was running under widespread white wings of shimmering terylene directly toward the dark bulk of the isle of delight.

The wind strengthened and soon waves were building up under the hull and lifting the bow of the boat out of the water so that it seemed to surf. The effect was exciting but a little disconcerting because there were times when the boat came down off the crest of a wave and it seemed temporarily out of control, and Juliet held her breath, wondering if it was about to plunge bow first under the heaving surface of the sea, to be seen and heard of no more.

At other times when she happened to glance behind her toward the stern she gasped audibly on seeing a big wave with curling fangs higher than the boat bearing down on them and was sure that it would pour into the cockpit and swamp it completely. But always the wave collapsed just a little short of the stern and rolled under the hull.

Lance appeared not to suffer from such anxieties and controlled the movement of the tiller with little effort. He talked little, answering her questions briefly but adequately, and allayed her occasionally expressed fears with a few calm words. And gradually it occurred to her that he was an essentially uncommunicative person, quite unlike Gareth who talked incessantly about his thoughts and his feelings.

Toward the middle of the afternoon they reached a small bay where they found shelter from the swell and the wind behind a group of rocky islands. After being alone on the wide rolling sea exposed to every buffet of wave and wind, the bay was an oasis of calm pale sunlight and clear green water backed by a semicircle of light sand-colored cliffs.

Lance looked across at the high stone walls.

"The cliffs look interesting. I wonder if there are any caves," he remarked. "Shall we go ashore and explore?"

Juliet agreed eagerly, enticed by the deep green of a glen that ran inland as much as by the cliffs. The place had a romantic fairy-tale atmosphere. There was no sign of any habitation and she could readily believe that it was visited by the wee folk and the merfolk and all the other strange mythical creatures about whom Gareth had told her.

Gareth! How she wished he was there with her in the dinghy, rowing her to the shore instead of Lance. He wouldn't sit silently. He would tell her some legend associated with the place. But Gareth couldn't have brought her here, because he was lame, paralyzed by an accident while he was trying to keep up with Moira. Not for the first time Juliet found herself wondering what sort of a woman Moira had been and what had been her relationship with the man sitting opposite to her in the dinghy.

She glared at Lance, watching his averted face as he looked over his shoulder to make sure he was going the right way. Did he save all his conversation for Alison Coates whom he would marry one day if Mrs. Crimond had her way?

Alison! Why wasn't she here with him? Why hadn't he invited her to come sailing with him today? Had they quarreled? Or had Alison been unable to come because she had had to stay with her sick mother and he had had to find a substitute.

A substitute for Alison. That was all she was today? Oh, well, Alison's loss was her gain. If the lovely red-haired woman had been able to come sailing Juliet Grey would have missed not only several drenchings by spray but also the experience of coming to this island.

Still, there was something about being regarded as a mere substitute that troubled her.

"I shouldn't let it bother you," said Lance, unexpectedly, and she jumped. He'd been watching her again and she'd forgotten to be on guard.

The Cave of the White Rose

"Shouldn't let what bother me?" she challenged, flinging her salt-caked, wind-tumbled hair behind her shoulders.

"Being here with me," he answered smoothly, and then grinned at her as she gasped in an exasperated manner.

"I wish you'd stop watching me, like...like an eagle watching its prey!" she retorted.

"Why shouldn't I watch you? Your face is very pretty as well as being expressive. During the past few minutes you've looked wistful as if wishing I were someone else; then you glared at me as if you'd have liked to push me overboard; then you frowned and bit your lip, and most interesting of all, for a few seconds your eyes went quite green and you looked ready to spit and claw at the object of your jealousy. Then you looked frightened. But you often seem frightened when you're with me. Why?"

At that moment the dinghy bumped against the old stone pier. Lance shipped the oars and held on to an iron ring set in the wall of the pier. Instead of pressing her for an answer to his question he ordered her out of the dinghy.

"Be careful you don't slip on the steps," he added. "They're slimy through lack of use."

Glad of the chance to get away from him for a while, Juliet mounted the steps carefully. Once at the top she didn't wait for him but ran along the derelict pier until she came to a rough road that struck off westward, curving above a small beach of dark sand. Beyond the beach the road continued around the narrow grass-covered shore under the sheer cliffs.

She thought she heard Lance call her name, but she didn't look around to see if he was following her because a sudden impulse to annoy him, to shake his superb self-confidence, urged her onward. The impulse was natural, the eternal feminine urge to irritate the arrogant male who thought he knew her better than she knew herself, and who considered her naive and innocent. She had no doubt she rated as "safe" in Lance's mind. She was someone whom he could invite to go sailing with him without having to make much effort to entertain her and without annoying his future wife. Possibly he had even told Alison last night that he had considered taking his mother's young secretary with him, and Alison had condescendingly agreed to the arrangement, knowing that there couldn't possibly be any competition.

Well, she would teach him a lesson. She would hide somewhere, and when he couldn't find her he would be worried.

She plunged on along the upper margin of a beach of boulders, sometimes following ankle-twisting tracks just above the high water mark, and sometimes scrambling across recent rock slides. Light on her feet and well balanced, she moved quickly, flitting from rock to rock until she came to an area of flat stone just around the corner of the headland.

Above the flat plateau there was a wide opening in the cliff. Juliet entered the opening and found herself in a huge cave. Near the entrance there was a large boulder. She ducked behind it, and completely hidden from the view of anyone looking into the cave she sat down.

As her eyes gradually grew accustomed to the dim light she could see carved into the rough stone of the wall above her crosses and other symbols, sure signs that the cave had once been used as shelter by man. The wall on the other side was damper and was covered with moss, and from the roof of the cave on that side near the entrance water dripped in a steady stream.

Turning her back to the boulder and hugging her knees to her chin, Juliet decided she would stay there until Lance arrived. She was sure he would come and that he would call her name. She wouldn't answer straightaway, just to tantalize him. She had never tantalized anyone in this way before and it gave her a curious sense of power plus excitement. He would be anxious in case she had an accident, because accidents happened to people when they were with him.

Her thoughts pulled up short. Where had she got that idea? From the curious conversation that had taken place the day Lance had arrived at Castle Ross when Gareth had refused to let Maree go fishing with Lance and the girl had accused her father of not letting her go with her uncle be-

The Cave of the White Rose

cause her mother had been with Lance when she had been killed. Where and how had Moira been killed, and why had she been with Lance?

Too many questions and too few answers, thought Juliet disgustedly. She ought to ask Lance himself. But he would only tell her in that icy way of his not to concern herself with anything beyond her work.

She realized suddenly that she had been sitting behind the boulder for some time and he hadn't come. No voice had called her name. Supposing he hadn't seen her enter the cave? Supposing he had gone straight past along the shore?

The cave was echoing with the sound of the sea smashing against the rocks. It seemed much noisier than when she had entered. The tide must be coming in and covering the plateau of rock outside. It was time for her to move if only to ensure that she could get back along the shore to the pier.

Feeling slightly disappointed because she had not been able to tantalize Lance, she went to the entrance of the cave. She was greeted by a sight that sent icy prickles of panic chasing up and down her spine. The flat area of stone was covered by greenish gray swirling water and as she gaped a wave reared up and crashed over the edge of the plateau and greedy fingers of water spread right into the cave. It was followed almost at once by another wave, and looking beyond the spray and spume, she saw the whole sea was a heaving mass of white-topped waves being pushed against the land by the wind, which had increased in strength and was now moaning eerily in the hollows of the cliffs.

Gingerly she inched forward and peered around the edge of the cave entrance. The path she had followed under the towering wall of cliffs had disappeared under tossing water, which flung itself against the foot of the headland. She was cut off, imprisoned by angry hissing water that looked as if it might invade the cave.

> "Break, break, break,
> On thy cold gray stones, O Sea."

The voice spoke behind her. For another wild moment of panic she thought she was imagining it, then a hand touched her shoulder and she knew with a strange quiver of relief that Lance was really there in the cave with her. But how had he got there without her seeing him? Anger that he had walked in silently and unseen shook her, and with a wriggle of her shoulders she broke free of his hold and whirled around to face him. She spat out furiously:

"And I would that my tongue could utter
The thoughts that arise in me."

He laughed appreciatively.

"You're much quicker on the draw than one would expect from looking at you," he remarked. "I've often wondered how that verse ended. But I don't suppose Tennyson's thoughts were at all like yours are at present. I guess you're angry with me."

"Yes, I am. How dare you creep up behind me like that and frighten me!" she fumed. "How did you get in here without me seeing you or hearing you?"

"I walked in the same way that you did. I walk quietly—remember?"

"Then why didn't you call my name and tell me you were here?"

He stood, hands in his trouser pockets, considering her thoughtfully, that faint enigmatic smile curving his mouth.

"Well now, that's hard to explain," he drawled. "I had the impression that you were deliberately hiding from me when I came into the cave, and I remembered how irritated I used to get when I was a boy if I'd found a good hiding place and I was found too soon. So I thought I'd let you enjoy your hiding place and let you stay hidden for a while. Also I thought it would teach you a lesson for running off the way you did."

Teach her a lesson! Her own words concerning him. Juliet gritted her teeth. He was making fun of her, treating her like a child with whom he'd condescended to play a game of

The Cave of the White Rose

hide and seek. He hadn't been worried about her one little bit.

"How long have you been here?" she asked.

"A few minutes less than you. And now it's my turn to ask a question. Why did you run away and hide?"

Still furious at the treatment handed out to her by him, she had no answer ready because she no longer understood her own impulse to annoy him—an impulse that had landed them both in their present predicament.

"I...I don't know," she muttered, just as water ugly and edged with white foam swirled about her feet. "Oh, what shall we do? The water is going to flood the cave. Where shall we go?" she exclaimed.

He took her arm and pulled her back into the darker recesses of the cave.

"It won't come any farther than the entrance," he said calmly.

"How do you know?" she asked.

"There's a line of seaweed where the high water stops. Beyond that the floor of the cave is fairly dry."

"How long do you think we'll be here?"

"About an hour...maybe a little longer. It depends on the weather. It's deteriorating and the wind tends to keep the tide pushed in for longer than normal."

"But there was no sign of a storm when we left the boat."

"Yes, there was. There've been signs of storm all afternoon in the sky. I've been watching it grow."

"You didn't say anything," she accused.

"I'd no idea then that you were going to go exploring on your own as soon as we came ashore," he remarked dryly. "I called after you to suggest you didn't go far because the tide was coming in. But you weren't listening."

"And now we're both stuck here until the tide goes out, and it's my fault," she moaned. "Oh, you must think I'm very foolish."

"And trusting."

"Wet behind the ears, you said the other day."

"Did I? Not very polite of me, but truthful. More truthful than your answer to my question a few minutes ago. Why did you run away, Juliet?"

In the half-light of the cave he seemed big and overpowering. She guessed he was capable of forcing an answer out of her, but the spark of rebelliousness that had made her run away from him was still alight. Flinging back her head, her face and hair pale blurs in the dimness, she looked up at him and retorted, "Perhaps because I'm not so trusting after all. I don't trust you."

"You expect me to believe that?" he said scornfully. "Since you don't trust me why did you come sailing today? Come on, now let's have the truth. Why did you run away?"

"I wanted to teach you a lesson," she muttered.

"That makes two of us. But why should you want to teach me a lesson? What have I done?"

"You take me for granted. You're so smug, especially back there in the dinghy, making out that you know me better than I know myself, so I thought I'd hide somewhere and then when you couldn't find me you'd be worried in case something had happened to me!" she burst out, then as she realized he was beginning to laugh at her, her temper seethed and she went the whole way and added, "You wouldn't want an accident to happen to me while I'm with you, would you?"

That stopped his laughter and she saw his shoulders stiffen. But when he answered her he was still coolly in command of himself.

"Naturally I wouldn't want you to have an accident whether you're with me or whether you're not. I'm not the sort of person who goes around wishing accidents on others out of petty spite."

"But people tend to have accidents when they're in your company, don't they, because you like to take risks. You like living with the edge of danger and you're contemptuous of those who can't or who won't... like Gareth."

The silence that followed her words was so fraught with tension that she began to wish she hadn't spoken so boldly.

"I suppose I have him to thank for this load of drivel,"

he remarked rather wearily at last. "What has he told you about accidents happening to people who go with me?"

"Nothing really," she admitted reluctantly. "But Maree said that her mother was with you when she was killed and I heard Gareth say to Mrs. Crimond that if he hadn't let Moira go with you she might be alive now."

She waited hopefully for his reply, because now was his chance to tell her how Moira had died and possibly clear up the doubts in her mind about his relationship with his sister-in-law.

"And consequently your curiosity was aroused,' he murmured. Then with a quick change of manner, his voice icy, he added, "I thought I'd told you that anything beyond your work at Castle Ross was not your concern."

"Yes, you did, but I couldn't help hearing what was said," she whispered, backing away from him.

"And now you know that Gareth blames me for Moira's death," he said, following her slowly, looming over her, a threatening shadow. "And you've believed him, haven't you?"

She couldn't answer because her throat had dried up. She tried to back away from him again, but he was too quick. He tucked two fingers inside the turtleneck of her sweater and pulled her gently toward him.

"Haven't you, Juliet?" he persisted.

"Yes," she admitted.

"Then you'll realize that because he believes what he does about me and because he feels the way he does about you he's going to go through hell tonight wondering where you and I are and what we're doing together."

"I... I don't understand. I thought we were going back to the castle."

"There's no way we can reach Castle Ross before tomorrow. Tonight you and I shall sleep aboard the boat. That is, if we ever get back to it."

CHAPTER FOUR

LANCE'S VOICE was a low murmur and his breath fanned her cheek as he bent his head close to hers. Juliet closed her eyes. She hoped that when she opened them she would find herself back in bed at Castle Ross, and all that had happened since she had woken that morning would recede into the depths of her subconscious; a dream, nothing more.

But when she opened her eyes she was still there in the sea-echoing, dimly lit vault and Lance's fingers were still in the collar of her sweater, warm and rough against the skin of her throat, sending an uncontrollable tingling sensation through her body. She was so close to him that she could see the glint in his eyes as he looked down at her.

"We must get back today," she insisted rather wildly. "What will they think when we don't return?"

He released her sweater and plunged his hands into his pockets again.

"You should have thought of that earlier," he said coldly. "You realized surely that you threw away any possibility of our returning to Castle Ross today when you asked if we could come to Dana when there was a storm in the offing. If we'd gone to Oban instead you'd have been able to leave the boat and return to Lochmoyhead by bus. A phone call from there would have brought McVinn out to pick you up in the station wagon. As it is, the situation in which you now find yourself is really of your own making."

Juliet couldn't remember having felt so angry in her life. It seemed to her that he was actually blaming her for the predicament in which they now found themselves.

"How was I to know that?" she exclaimed. "Oh, you're no better than Maree! You take advantage, too. You've taken advantage of my ignorance about sailing, about distances and about storms. You could have refused to bring me here."

As usual he didn't retaliate to her furiously flung words but took time to consider what she had said, his head bent as he kicked idly at the stony debris on the floor of the cave, and his calmness made her even more cross.

"True," he admitted at last, "I could have refused, and what would you have thought of me then? I brought you here against my better judgment in order to grant your wish to see one of the islands while you had the opportunity. Seems to me you're very hard to please, Juliet."

While she was still gasping he moved away from her into the back of the cave, leaving her to ponder his words. He had granted her wish because it had been in his power to do so and for that she should be grateful instead of accusing him of taking advantage of her. The now familiar tug at her heart made her aware that once again she had been guilty of misjudging him. This time the urge to apologize to him was strong.

But he was nowhere to be seen.

"Lance!" she called tentatively, moving toward the dark wall of rock at the back of the cave.

"Over here," he answered. "I've found somewhere to sit. Sandstone is very obliging—it provides ledges for sitting on; this one is rather narrow, but it serves. I must bring Jamie here some day. He'd be interested in the rock formation."

His cool matter-of-fact voice relieved her, but also made her hesitant about offering an apology. He must have decided to dismiss their recent confrontation and she decided against reviving it. She stood uncertainly before him, and he put out a hand, gripped her arm and pulled her forward.

"Come and sit down," he ordered.

She obeyed. There wasn't much room and her shoulder and knee brushed against him as she balanced rather precariously on the stone seat. He put an arm around her waist to keep her from falling off. The warmth and strength of his body struck through her, sending alarm signals in all directions. She stiffened involuntarily, but his arm didn't relax.

"There's scarcely room for two," he murmured, "but like this we'll be fairly comfortable for the next half hour or so."

Little shudders ran through her body. Hoping to divert his attention from her shaking, she burst into speech.

"Do you know any stories about the cave or about this part of the island?" she quavered, and her voice sounded unnaturally high.

"All I can tell you is that the area of sandstone in front of the cave is what is known as a tidal quarry and has probably been used for centuries and even quite recently. Slabs of stone can be detached by driving wooden wedges into the horizontal cracks. Seawater does the rest of the work by forcing the stone apart."

"Where would it be used?" she asked, interested and forgetting her fear of him.

"For ornamental carvings in Iona Cathedral, which isn't very far from here, and also in the doors and window facings of old chapels on the island. Some of the carving must have been done by the monks and the craftsmen years ago in this cave. Did you notice the symbols carved into the wall?"

"Yes, I found several crosses and something that looked like a windmill and some leaf designs rather like a shamrock."

"They're probably the trademarks of individual workmen. I found a carving of a rose, so I think I'll give the cave a new name."

"What is its name?"

"I believe it's called Uamh nan Cailleach, which is Gaelic for the Cave of the Old Woman, but I'm going to call it the Cave of the White Rose, because I found myself having to put in an hour or two with you here."

She knew he was teasing her, but his mention of the white rose made her aware of him again and she tried to move away from him, but couldn't.

"Don't move so violently," he warned. "You'll fall off. I'm sorry my story telling isn't up to Gareth's standard. My abilities tend to be on the practical side."

"A man of action," murmured Juliet, in retaliation for the white rose. "Your mother told me that you preferred actions to words and that often made you seem ruthless, and inconsiderate of the feelings of others."

Almost at once she wished she had kept her mouth shut, because his arm tightened around her waist ominously.

"So that's why you're afraid of me," he mocked.

"I'm not afraid," she denied weakly.

"Then why have you avoided me all week? And why are you shaking now? Is it possible that you're afraid of the next action I might take?"

There was a dangerous edge to his voice. The palm of his hand slid against her cheek as he forced her face around. She closed her eyes and willed herself to ignore the fire that scorched through her veins at the touch of his hand on her skin.

"Now, what happens next?" he said, and once more laughter threaded its way through his voice. "Useless for you to scream here, because there isn't anyone to hear you. You could slap my face, I suppose."

Outraged and bewildered by his easy mockery, Juliet tried to free herself. Then, unable to break that steellike grip, she searched for words to fling at him.

"You...you...you're..." she spluttered, and then words failed, too.

"I know," he replied accommodatingly. "I'm unkind, inconsiderate, shameless. But no more shameless than you are for believing that I break rules."

"Gareth says you make your own rules," she flung at him, stung into replying because he had guessed so accurately why she was afraid of him.

"Perhaps I have in some cases, but I've never broken any where innocents like you are concerned, and I'm not going to start now."

He released her suddenly and slid off the ledge, and walked away. Unable to keep her precarious position on the ledge without his support, Juliet slid off, too.

"Where are you going?" she inquired timidly, as her anger dissipated.

"To see if the tide has started to go out," he said carelessly over his shoulder and she felt suddenly cold as his interest was removed from her. Not wanting to be left alone she followed him to the entrance of the cave.

The force of the wind sent her hair streaming back from her face and flung stinging, salty spray into her face. Flying spindrift had reduced visibility to a greenish gray blur in which it was impossible to distinguish sky from sea. Waves were still pounding on the sandstone plateau, but the insidious spreading fingers of water no longer reached as far as the new line of damp dark seaweed that curved at her feet.

"It's on the turn," observed Lance, "but it will be some time before we'll be able to make our way along the shore. You can see now why it's impossible for us to sail back to Castle Ross today. The risk would be too great."

"But I thought you liked taking risks."

He turned a narrowed gray glance on her.

"Seems to me you've thought a lot about me," he gibed, and in spite of the cool spray, her face felt hot. "Yes, sometimes I do take risks, just as I'm capable of making my own rules. But ever since I made its acquaintance as a boy I've had a great respect for the sea. When it's in this mood it's safer to stay on the shore."

As she stood there beside him watching the monotonous advance and retreat of the waves, feeling completely isolated from the rest of the world, it occurred to Juliet that he had been in a similar situation before when he had been snowbound in the Cairngorms with Moira, and Gareth had gone through hell wondering where they were and what they were doing. Had he been granting Moira's wish by taking her skiing when a blizzard was imminent?

Her thoughts rankled and she turned back into the cave in an attempt to change their direction. Going over to the west wall, she stared at the carved symbols. With one finger she traced the outline of a simple cross, then a shamrock, then a letter W and on until she came to the unmistakable carving of the flower of a wild rose, and suddenly she was standing again in the busy entrance hall of a London hotel and Lance was tucking a long-stemmed white rosebud be-

The Cave of the White Rose

hind her ear and saying, "You might call it symbolic." Now she knew he had meant the rosebud had been symbolic of her innocence—and he had just told her that he didn't break rules concerning innocents like her.

The outline of the rose blurred a little and her finger shook. In spite of what he had said she was still afraid of him, but not because of any action he might take. She wasn't afraid of what he might do but of her own reactions to him; afraid of the effect he had on her emotions.

She glanced over her shoulder fearfully, remembering his strange ability to guess at her thoughts. He was still leaning against the wall of the cave just inside the entrance watching the sea, so still and absorbed he could have been in a trance. But as she looked he moved and stepped out of the cave. In a few seconds he was back and calling to her.

"Come and look outside."

She went, following him out onto the wet stone and looking where he pointed to the cliffs down which waterfalls were descending only to be checked by the strong wind, which blew them back like smoke to the rim of the cliffs high above.

"I've heard that that could happen, but I've never seen it before," said Lance, excitement crisping his voice.

"'A land of streams! some, like a downward smoke, Slow-dropping veils of thinnest lawn, did go,'" murmured Juliet, staring fascinated at the white mist.

He turned to her with a quizzical lift of his eyebrows.

"More poetry?" he queried.

"Tennyson again," she replied.

He eyed her narrowly again, and then his mouth twisted cynically.

"No wonder you and Gareth deal well together. You must enjoy quoting poetry to each other," he gibed, and turning away he pointed to the path that was just appearing, a series of puddles winding under the cliff. "It won't be long now before we can leave this place."

He sounded as if he would be glad to leave it, and the gibe about her and Gareth hurt, reminding her that he was unkind and unpredictable. She wanted to tell him that she didn't quote poetry to Gareth for the simple reason that Gareth talked so much when she was with him that she didn't get a chance. She wanted to tell him that only here with him, encouraged by his own deep-voiced utterance earlier and now by his obvious delight at the sight of the windblown cascades of water, had she felt the need to quote poetry in an attempt to reach out to him and to show she shared his delight.

"Are you hungry?" he asked suddenly, and she blinked, more than a little bewildered by her surprising thoughts.

"Yes, I suppose I am."

"Then I think it's time we made a move. The going will be rather soggy underfoot, but if you keep close behind me and follow in my footsteps you should be all right." He sounded impatient now, and she guessed that he had had enough of being alone with her in a cave. A man of action, he disliked being inactive. "Supper will be out of cans," he added, "but I can safely promise you fresh trout for breakfast."

The walk back was wet and uncomfortable and by the time they reached the pier they were both wet and chilly, a state that wasn't improved during the journey back to the yacht in the dinghy.

Once aboard Lance ordered her to go below and came down himself after checking the anchor. He showed Juliet where the canned goods were stored and then busied himself lighting the Primus cooker. The meal wasn't exciting, but it was filling, and the heat from the cooker and from the Tilley lamp that Lance had lit soon thawed out the chill in Juliet's bones.

After they had eaten she washed up the dishes while Lance went once more to inspect the anchor. He came back to inform her that he had decided to put out a storm anchor to ensure that the boat wouldn't drag out of position during the night. From the shelter of the cabin she watched through a porthole as he rowed out in the dinghy, a big fisherman anchor propped up in its stern, which was attached by a stout line to the bow of the boat. When he had rowed far enough away from the boat he stopped and stand-

The Cave of the White Rose

ing up in the dinghy heaved the anchor overboard, then came back.

Satisfied that the boat was safe for the night, he joined her in the cabin again and producing a pack of cards suggested that they played gin rummy. It was warm and quiet in the cabin and the gentle swinging movement of the boat had a soporific effect on Juliet so that she had difficulty in keeping her eyes open long enough to concentrate on her cards.

"Are you sleepy?" asked Lance.

She looked up and nodded.

"Then go to bed," he said gently.

Bewildered, she looked around the cabin, wondering how and where she was to go to bed.

"Here's a sleeping bag and a pillow," he said, producing them out of a locker behind him. "If you'd like to go and wash up for'ard I'll get your bed ready for you."

In the forecastle she did her best with her tangle of hair, and rinsed and dried her face, which glowed after its exposure to the elements. When she returned to the cabin Lance had gone and she could hear him moving about on deck. On the berth on which she had been sitting the sleeping bag had been arranged and unzipped and the pillow placed at one end. Juliet slumped down for a moment on the berth. The long day in the open air plus the strain of being on the defensive with Lance had taken their toll. She longed for bed, but wondered when once she was in the sleeping bag curled up on the bunk whether she would sleep knowing that he would be there lying on the opposite bunk!

Slowly she removed her sweater and shoes, climbed into the bag and zipped it up. For a few seconds she lay blinking drowsily at the flaring lamp and listening to the creak of the boat as it swung in the gusts of wind that shook it. Her eyes closed involuntarily and she slept at once.

THEY BREAKFASTED on fresh trout as Lance had promised. He had caught them from the burn that hid among the tall trees in the green glen. He had caught them by hand by a method he called "guddling." Juliet wished she had been with him to see him do it, but he had gone ashore early, long before she had wakened.

She ate every morsel of her succulent fish and even enjoyed the tea without milk. She had a wonderful sense of well-being, which surprised her. It was all to do with having slept soundly and having woken to the sight of golden light shimmering on the ceiling of the cabin and the smell of the trout being cooked.

After opening her eyes she had lain still for a while and had watched Lance as he had bent over his cooking, his jaw blurred with dark stubble, his hair slipping forward on his forehead, and she had thought how pleasant it was to know that someone capable was in charge of everything; that for once she didn't have to do the planning and be on the alert for all eventualities. And a new and startling thought had leaped through her mind. How lovely it would be if it could always be like that!

Then Lance had turned his head. His cold clear eyes had looked at her, through her and had dismissed her, and she'd known a strange sense of loss because he didn't share her thought.

When breakfast was over they made preparations for departure. Lance went out in the dinghy and hauled up the big anchor, brought it aboard and stowed it away. Then he hoisted the mainsail. It flapped idly because there was little wind in the bay behind the islands. Telling Juliet to keep the boat pointed in the direction from which the wind was blowing, he went forward and pulled up the other anchor, then returned to the cockpit to take the tiller from her. The mainsail filled with the slight wind and the boat moved out of the anchorage.

As she looked back at the green glen and the towering cliffs Juliet knew she would never forget Dana. As they cleared the entrance to the bay she could see the opening of the cave above the plateau of sandstone. The Cave of the White Rose. It was there that she had clashed with the enigmatic man who had brought her sailing. It seemed to her that she understood him less than before because, although she had been so close to him both physically and mentally

The Cave of the White Rose

for a short time, she found now that he had withdrawn behind a film of ice that she had no way of cracking.

The sail back to Loch Moy, although not as exciting as that of the previous day, provided its own color and breathtaking views. It was a day of alternating cloud and sunshine with a steady wind, which made it possible for them to reach Castle Ross in the early afternoon.

Leaving the boat at its mooring, they walked up the path from the shore and approached the terrace. A tall figure limped out of the lounge, and Lance broke his long silence.

"Your gentle knight awaits you," he mocked. "Didn't I say he'd be anxious? Anxiety has actually brought him to his feet!" He sounded pleased, almost complacently so, and Juliet glanced at him in surprise. He was watching Gareth and the cold assessing light in his eyes caused a return of all the dislike she had ever felt for him.

"Juliet, are you all right?" Gareth's voice was harsh with anxiety. He was hobbling down the steps and he was without his stick. She had never thought she would see him move so quickly. Above him on the terrace there was a movement. A bright green dress topped by red hair glowed against the mellow stone of the castle as Alison moved forward to wait and watch by the steps.

Gareth took hold of Juliet's hands. His blue gaze roved over her and then flashed to Lance.

"What happened? Where have you been?" he rapped autocratically and for a brief moment there was a faint resemblance between him and his older brother.

"You know," returned Lance easily, almost insolently. "I took Juliet sailing."

"That wasn't all. Why didn't you come back last night?"

"We went to Dana Island."

"In that storm?" Gareth's voice expressed disbelief.

"We arrived before the storm broke. There was no way we could come back until it had blown out, and by then we had our heads down and were fast asleep."

A dull red stained Gareth's thin face and an ugly glint appeared in his eyes. His hands tightened painfully on Juliet's.

"That sounds a familiar story. It's time you thought up another, Lance," he remarked.

Lance chose to ignore the sneer as Alison came down the steps.

"Hello, Alison," he said, and a warm smile lit his eyes. "Have you been offering comfort to the anxious?"

"No, she hasn't," interjected Gareth. "All she does is nag, nag, nag about my leg. She hasn't given me a minute's peace all weekend. As if I didn't have enough of her yesterday when we went visiting to Glenavon she has to come over this afternoon. Why don't you go home now, Alison? Lance is here at last, and I'm sure he'll be only too pleased to drive you."

Alison's topaz-colored eyes were puzzled as she glanced at him.

"I shall go in a few minutes," she said coolly. "But Lance doesn't have to take me because he's going to be busy. Your mother has just received a phone call from Elstone. There's been an accident."

"Jamie," said Lance quietly.

Alison turned to look at him, her eyes widening slightly.

"How did you know?" she asked.

His big shoulders lifted and dropped.

"I don't know. I've had the feeling all morning that I shouldn't have gone sailing, that I should have gone up there yesterday. Is he trapped?"

"Yes. Your mother has all the details. The leader of the expedition rang up. He wanted to speak to you. I think you'd better go and see her, Lance. She wants to go up there."

He didn't wait to listen to any more but sprang up the steps and disappeared into the house.

Alison turned to look at Juliet. Her glance took in the tangled pale hair, windburned face and creased clothing and a faint, slightly patronizing smile curved her mouth.

"I expect you're feeling in need of a bath and a change," she said. "Lance should never have taken you so far."

"No, he shouldn't," put in Gareth. "A sail down the loch and back would have been enough. But then he has

The Cave of the White Rose

never considered anyone else's feelings. I suppose he decided on the spur of the moment that he wanted to and you had to go too whether you wanted to or not."

"I asked him to take me to Dana," said Juliet quietly, feeling the time had come for her to take the responsibility for the previous day's events.

"You asked him? Why?" exclaimed Gareth.

"It seemed to be an interesting place to go, and it was. We found a cave in the cliffs and saw the wind blowing the water back up the cliffs just as it's described in 'The Lotus-Eaters,'" she replied, wanting to share with him the pleasure she had known, sure he would understand at once. But the blue eyes held no warmth for once as they met hers.

"I don't understand why on earth anyone would want to go all that way on an afternoon like yesterday afternoon just to see a cave," he replied.

"Well, evidently Juliet thought it was worthwhile being knocked about on the boat and having to sleep in her clothing," murmured Alison. "I can't say I'd enjoy such an outing. And it isn't done, you know, my dear," she said with a touch of condescension, "to stay away all night with one's employer. The family might understand, but just imagine what Vinnie and the other people on the estate must be saying and thinking about you! Everyone knows you went with Lance because Mrs. Crimond was so upset when you didn't return that she wanted a search party organized."

Whatever had given her the idea that Alison was a warm, kindhearted person, thought Juliet miserably. Spite had flickered out of every word the woman had just spoken.

"But she must have known I'd be all right with Lance. You must have known that," she said appealingly to Gareth.

"I know no such thing," he returned coldly. He tried to move forward and then winced. "Damn, I forgot my stick."

"I'll go and get it," said Alison, and swept gracefully up the steps.

"Don't bother. Juliet will help me," said Gareth. His hand came down on Juliet's shoulder, reassuring her, comforting her in the face of Alison's spite, and she smiled up at him gratefully.

As they mounted the steps slowly Alison watched them.

"A very touching sight," she remarked with a touch of sarcasm. "But you know, Gareth, you went down those steps as if nothing was wrong with your leg apart from a little stiffness due to misuse. Regular exercising would cure that. I think Lance is right when he says your lameness is purely psychosomatic. You're only lame because you've been made to think you're lame. You've worried yourself into being lame."

"Go home, Alison!" he answered through clenched teeth. "I've had enough of your advice."

"All right, I'm going. Don't let him lean on you too heavily, Juliet," she added. "I know you mean well, but Gareth is much stronger than you in many ways and he'd soon wear you out."

With a swirl of her green skirt and a toss of her red hair she went into the house, while under his breath Gareth called her a rude name.

"Take no notice of her, Juliet. She loves to think she can boss everyone around. She and Lance are well suited." He lowered himself onto the chaise longue and looked up at her. "I hope he treated you well."

"Yes, he did. He granted my wish. Now please excuse me. I must go and change my clothes and go to see Mrs. Crimond. She must be very worried."

"She was distracted last night wondering what she would do if Lance were drowned, and I... well, I don't mind admitting I went through hell too. Juliet, you must know...."

"Juliet," the crisp voice spoke from the French window. Lance was there, still in his sailing clothes, his face still unshaven, its expression grim. "My mother would like to see you."

It was an order and she obeyed, flitting past him without looking at either him or Gareth, concerned only with what Mrs. Crimond might say to her. Would she reprimand her for going with Lance? Would she say what Alison had said, that it wasn't done to stay out all night with one's employer?

The Cave of the White Rose

But as soon as she walked into the study she knew that Mrs. Crimond was thinking nothing of the sort, because the novelist greeted her with outstretched arms and held her closely for a moment.

"I'm so glad to see you safe and sound. It was naughty of Lance to take you away like that, and I've told him so."

"I asked him to take me to Dana," said Juliet quickly.

"But even so he should have known better than to take you so far. I don't know what he was thinking of. Thank heaven he's come back in time. Have you heard about Jamie? There's my poor baby trapped in an underground cave now."

"Yes, Miss Coates mentioned it."

"Dear Alison! Such a tower of strength in time of need. What a comfort she's been. But now you're back and I want you to come with me and Lance to Elstone this afternoon. It will help me to have you there while waiting for news. Lance will, I expect, want to go and help with the rescue. So as soon as you can change and pack a few clothes we'll set off. Oh, to think of poor Jamie trapped underground! Why will these boys have such dangerous hobbies? Why do they never learn what anxieties they cause me?"

On the way to her room Juliet met Lance coming up the stairs again. He followed her to the top landing where she turned to speak to him.

"Is it really necessary for Mrs. Crimond to go to Elstone?" she asked.

The curl to his mouth wasn't pleasant.

"You don't want to go. You'd prefer to stay with Gareth and hold hands," he accused.

"No, no, it isn't that. I just wondered what use she could possibly be up there. Won't it task her nerves even more than they're tasked already?"

"She wants to go, and I think that provided she has you there for company she'll be better there close to Jamie than sitting here and fretting. For one thing she'll understand better what's happening, and for another her being there will help Jamie."

"Are they in contact with him?" she asked.

"Yes. I've just talked to Graham Lee, the leader of the expedition. They know where he is and they can hear him when he speaks to them. He says he's broken an arm. There's a girl trapped with him." He pushed the hair back off his forehead with an impatient gesture. "You take the bathroom first, and hurry," he ordered tersely.

Suddenly it was important that he shouldn't think badly of her, that he should know she didn't want to stay with Gareth and hold his hand, that she wanted to help if she could.

"If you really think it will help your mother if I go with her I'll be glad to go," she said urgently. "And I'm sure it will help Jamie a great deal to know that *you* are going to help rescue him."

He swung round, surprise and puzzlement breaking up the usual impassivity of his face. Then he grinned.

"Why, Juliet, could it be that you're beginning to appreciate my worth after all?" he mocked softly, and her face went pink. With a quick change of tone he snapped, "Now, hurry," and went into his room.

ON THE JOURNEY NORTH Juliet sat in the front of the car next to Lance. He said that he hoped to reach Inverpool, a fishing port on the northwest coast, by seven o'clock that evening. As the crow flew the distance was only ninety-five miles, but looking at the route they would have to follow in order to avoid impassable mountains and that took them first to Oban, then to Ballachulish Ferry and on through the Great Glen right across to the east coast of the country before they could start approaching the port, Juliet thought he was overoptimistic. However, they made fairly good progress on an afternoon in which sunshine and cloud alternately highlighted and dimmed the landscape.

Gradually the Highlands unfolded before her fascinated eyes. In turn she admired the lovely Loch Linnhe, a blue slash of water between emerald and bottle green shores, noted the simple whitewashed elegance of small towns and villages, looked with awe at mysterious majestic mountains,

The Cave of the White Rose

some gray and forbidding in the shadow of clouds, others purple and warmly enticing in the sunlight. When they approached the east coast the flatter, more arable land came as a surprise before they turned northwest into a forest of mountains and deep glens.

As usual Lance had little to say except to make an occasional derogatory remark about the narrowness of the roads. At one point he said to his mother that he should have invested in a small light airplane instead of a sailing boat.

"But I couldn't have come with you in a plane," objected Mrs. Crimond. "No, Lance, a car is quite fast and dangerous enough."

"Not in an emergency like this when you want to travel directly and not on an everlasting switchback," he growled, as he pulled the car around yet another hairpin bend.

"Your trouble is that you got too used to fast travel when you were in Canada. Think of all the beauty we would have missed this afternoon if we'd come by plane. Aren't you glad you came, Juliet, or do you find the journey as frustrating as Lance does?"

"Oh, no. I think the glens and the mountains are beautiful. I'd no idea that there was so much natural wild scenery in Britain," replied Juliet.

"Then you might spare a thought for the conservancy people who are making sure it's kept natural and wild—and remember that a few good roads wouldn't spoil it in any way," said Lance.

They reached Inverpool just before half-past six. A rainbow curved over the white houses, its spectrum of colors brilliant against the blue black of sky and mountain. From there it was only a few miles to Elstone, the small town where some of the cavers were staying, and they passed through more wild romantic country dominated by the evening silhouettes of two towering mountains against a sky that had changed to lemon color. But as they dropped down a hill into the town Lance pointed out a change in the landscape in the distance. In the evening light the sharply edged outcrops of some hills were milky white, and at once Juliet recognized a similarity to the hills surrounding the Cauldron, near Castle Ross. They had come at last to the country of the underground caves.

They went straight to the small gabled country hotel where some of the cavers were staying and where two rooms had been reserved for them. The leader of the expedition, a tall man called Graham Lee, was there to greet them and to assure Mrs. Crimond that Jamie was alive and cheerful.

"But I'm glad you came, Lance, because I'm thinking we'll have to blast the rock to get to him and I'll be glad of your help. Morley is up there now and laying the charges, Jamie'll be glad to hear your voice, I'm thinking, so if you wouldn't mind coming up to the site now...?"

"Yes, I'll come straightaway," replied Lance readily.

"Lance, you'll be careful, please," pleaded his mother, but her plea fell on deaf ears, for he was already walking away with Graham.

Mrs. Crimond's glance was rueful as she looked around the homey hotel lounge.

"You see what I mean, Juliet," she sighed. "We've hardly arrived and he has to go rushing off to the caves, leaving us to take care of ourselves. And it isn't just the thought of Jamie that is taking him there but the prospect of the danger involved in rescuing him. He could have seen us settled in before going up there."

"I don't think so," replied Juliet, who found it difficult to imagine Lance overseeing the settling in of two women into a hotel while other people tried to rescue his brother. "You wanted him to be like that, you know, a lion in battle. You wanted all your sons to be adventurous or you wouldn't have called them after King Arthur's knights."

"Yes, I know. But remember that the knights were also gallant and gentle when in the society of women. Those characteristics seem to be totally lacking in Lance, whereas Gareth has them to excess and isn't at all adventurous."

"Not physically, perhaps," argued Juliet gently, rather surprised at herself, "but his mind goes adventuring into the world of philosophy."

The Cave of the White Rose

Mrs. Crimond stared at her with her brow creased in thought. Then she leaned forward and patted Juliet's hand.

"I'm so glad you understand Gareth. I used to feel that Moira didn't. She was so active, not in the least romantic, and I've often wondered if they were really happy together during the last few years."

The last few years when Lance had been back from Canada; when he'd taken Moira skiing and sailing, granting her wishes because it had been in his power to do so while his brother had been helpless. Why had he granted her wishes? Because he had loved her, had always loved her and should have married her, perhaps? Had that been the situation? And was it the reason for the antagonism between Gareth and Lance now? Had Lance lost Moira to Gareth originally because he lacked gallantry and gentleness?

So wondered Juliet, trying as always to solve the enigma of her employer. Since last night she was finding it difficult to continue to dislike him. Although she agreed with Mrs. Crimond that he didn't show the obvious social graces as Gareth did, he had shown gallantry and gentleness to her in other ways. He had used his skill as a sailor of small boats to take her to an island of delight. He had calmed her fears when they had been cut off by the tide in the cave. He had seen that she was warm and comfortable before she slept. He had caught and cooked fresh fish for her breakfast. Oh, yes, there were many ways in which a man could show gallantry to a woman, and they weren't always obvious.

There wasn't much spare room in the hotel, the proprietress explained as she took them upstairs, and she hoped they wouldn't mind sharing a room. She had put up a temporary bed in Jamie's room for Lance. She was sure they must be hungry after their long drive and when they had washed and freshened themselves a little they would find a wee bite of supper in the dining room.

The "wee bite" consisted of a mixed grill, home-baked scones and jam, and an enormous pot of tea. While they were eating, Mrs. Robertson, the proprietress, brought in a young man who had just come down from the caves and who was able to give them a firsthand account of how Jamie had been trapped while he sat down to eat with them. His name was Eric Woodsworth and he explained that he was also a diver.

"But why is it necessary for you to have diving experience?" asked Juliet.

"Well, at the moment we're only investigating the entrances to the system of caves, and since there's a considerable flow of water in the passages a lot of exploring has to be done underwater."

"Have you had any success this time?"

"We were doing fine. Laura—that's Laura Penny who is trapped with Jamie just now—managed to wriggle into a crack in the rock that we knew must lead to a bigger cave. She reported that there were no further large openings, so we decided to blast. That's what we've been doing most of the week."

"Surely blasting is dangerous," said Mrs. Crimond. "No wonder there was a rockfall."

"It is dangerous, and very small quantities of explosive are used, just enough to enlarge a crack to remove obstruction so that a good caver can worm his way through."

"So I gather you made a way and that good caver who wormed his way through was Jamie," said Mrs. Crimond with a touch of dryness.

"That's it," said Eric with a sheepish grin. "Jamie went first and I went after him. We discovered a distinct flow of water under a low roof and some space beyond. We decided to dive. It took us ages to get the gear down there. We found there was enough draft to show that there was space beyond the cavern, but that most of the channels were heavily silted up, which meant excavating and possibly blasting. Then Jamie found another crack, Laura wriggled through it and he followed. That was the last we saw of them. Some rock slipped and closed the crack. But they've found a big cave."

"Is there water in it?" asked Mrs. Crimond anxiously.

"Yes. But there's plenty of air space above it. Jamie says there's enough to last them a day or so."

The Cave of the White Rose

Juliet flashed him a warning glance as she noticed the sudden blanching of Mrs. Crimond's face and he added hurriedly, "Of course they'll be out soon. When I left they'd just started blasting."

"How long is soon?" asked Juliet.

"Oh, another hour or so. It takes awhile for the smoke caused by the explosion to clear so that we can see what's happened. And then someone will have to try and worm his way through to them, probably Graham or Lance."

It was in fact nearly half-past ten when Lance walked into the bedroom shared by Mrs. Crimond and Juliet to which they had both gone when Mrs. Crimond, tired of sitting and waiting, had decided to go to bed. His face and clothes were grimy, but he was smiling and he was closely followed by Jamie, whose clothes and face were even dirtier and whose left arm was in a sling. Behind Jamie came a small, equally dirty young woman.

"Mother, this is Laura Penny," he announced cheerfully. "I'm going to marry her. She's a fine wee caver."

His matter-of-fact announcement coming on top of the hours of waiting and anxiety had the effect of making them all laugh.

"Oh, Jamie, whatever will you do next?" exclaimed his mother, as she searched for a handkerchief in her handbag. "I've been nearly out of my my mind with worry about you while you've been doing your proposing in an underground cave, of all places. Couldn't you have waited until you and Laura had been rescued?"

"No, not really. It was while we were stuck down there that it occurred to me that there was no one I'd rather be trapped with than Laura and that there was no better place for one caver to propose to another than in a cave, with the water swirling around our feet and dripping down on us and the rock glistening in the darkness. Most romantic, don't you think so, Laura?"

The young woman smiled up at him shyly, obviously in agreement.

"I'm sure we're all very pleased to meet you, Laura," said Mrs. Crimond pleasantly, having more or less recovered. "This is Juliet Grey, my secretary. I'd ask you to sit down, but there's only one chair and Juliet has that... and your clothes do seem to be a little dirty."

"Oh, please don't bother," said Laura in a rush. "I'm going to have a bath and go straight to bed. I'm so tired, I'd have gone to my room, only Jamie wanted me to meet you."

"And quite rightly, my dear. I'm very pleased for you both. We'll see you again in the morning, when you're more rested, I hope meanwhile, you'll consider coming back to Castle Ross to stay for a few days, because you'll realize that there'll be no more caving for Jamie this holiday with that arm out of action."

"I'd like to come very much," replied Laura, and then escorted by a smiling and obviously triumphant Jamie, who said he would be back after he had washed, she left the room.

"Well, I'm sure I don't know what to say," sighed Mrs. Crimond, lying back against her pillows and closing her eyes.

"It's not often you're at a loss for words," remarked Lance dryly, and Mrs. Crimond's eyes opened immediately and she gave him a wary glance. He had sat down on the edge of Juliet's bed and now he leaned back on one elbow. His hair was disheveled and he looked rather tired.

"How was the rescue?" asked Juliet curiously, and he glanced at her briefly, impersonally.

"Tough," he replied. "The passage we managed to open up was very narrow. They were lucky to get out alive. Mother, I think you should know that Laura is only seventeen."

"Oh, dear," sighed Mrs. Crimond. "Then what is she doing here with Jamie, and why has he asked her to marry him?"

"You can ask him that when he comes back." He rose to his feet. "I'll go and wash and change too and give him a hand. The doctor in the village says it isn't a break, just a crack in the bone, but I think it should be x-rayed as soon as possible. Jamie's going to be in pain later tonight, especially

The Cave of the White Rose

when the anesthetic of having got himself engaged has worn off," he added rather sourly.

He went out of the room. Mrs. Crimond's frown of anxiety was once more in evidence.

"Now I wonder what is the matter with him," she murmured. "I thought he wasn't in a particularly good mood when he came to see me after you'd come back from sailing." She gave Juliet one of her disconcertingly sharp glances. "What did Gareth say to him when he learned that you'd stayed the night on the boat at Dana because of the storm?"

Juliet repeated the exact wording of Gareth's sneer, uneasily aware that Lance's "bad mood" had begun soon after he had left her sitting alone on the ledge of sandstone in the Cave of the White Rose and had nothing to do with anything Gareth had said. It was something she had done or said that had annoyed him, and for the life of her she couldn't think what it might be.

"Yes, Gareth was quite upset when you didn't return yesterday. In fact he was very irritable when he discovered you'd gone with Lance. Perhaps I should warn you, Juliet, he's very possessive about people he loves. I'm so afraid that he and Lance will quarrel, and that Lance will get fed up with us all and go back to Canada. I couldn't manage without him. You see, he looks after all my business for me." Mrs. Crimond's voice shook with distress, but Juliet had no chance to comfort her because the two brothers returned to the room.

Jamie went straight over to his mother's bed and sat down beside her while Lance propped himself against the wall beside the door. Looking at his dark withdrawn face, Juliet had the impression that he wished heartily that he wasn't there.

"Well, what do you think of Laura, mother? Isn't she a darling?" asked Jamie, who seemed none the worse for having been trapped underground for hours.

"I shall give you my opinion when I've seen her properly. You might have had more consideration for her bringing her in here looking like that. Poor girl, she must have felt most embarrassed," replied Mrs. Crimond.

"Not Laura. Nothing bothers her," said Jamie confidently.

"But what is she doing here with you, exploring caves? It's hardly an occupation for a young woman."

"Why not? Women make grand cavers because they're nimble. It's her hobby just as it's mine."

Mrs. Crimond shuddered delicately.

"I shall never understand the girls of today. This urge to do everything that men do, to explore under the ground. So claustrophobic!"

"But it isn't. There's too much to do, to worry about that, isn't there, Lance?"

"I agree," said Lance. "Although caving isn't the sort of thing a casual visitor can do. You have to work in groups for safety. How did Laura come to join your group, Jamie?"

Jamie's face changed color slightly.

"She's the sister of a friend of mine. She showed an interest and I invited her to join the society last year. Graham seemed to have no objections. She's quite mature for her age. But there's the rub. I doubt if her parents will agree to us getting married until she's eighteen."

"It won't do you any harm to wait." Lance's suggestion was made casually, but it seemed to strike a spark in Jamie.

"Look who's handing out advice!" he gibed. "What does a confirmed bachelor like you know about falling in love and wanting to marry?"

"Enough to realize that marriage isn't to be undertaken lightly," replied Lance equably, impervious to the gibe.

"I'm not undertaking it lightly," exploded Jamie suddenly. "I'm older than Gareth was when he married Moira, so I should know my own mind better than he did."

"And is Laura old enough to know hers?" asked Lance quickly.

"Ach, how I hate your cold-blooded approach to everything! Laura and I are in love and I want to marry her. Waiting won't harm us, but it isn't going to do us any good either," returned Jamie sulkily.

"Go carefully, dear," advised his mother gently. "It won't do to alienate her parents. And since you are several

The Cave of the White Rose

years older than her you mustn't encourage her to defy them. Be engaged for a while in a nice sensible fashion. That way you'll get to know each other a little better, and it will give Laura a chance to grow up. It will also give me a chance to know Laura and for her family to know you."

Jamie snorted with disgust and standing up began to walk about the cluttered bedroom.

"Families!" he exclaimed scornfully. "What does family have to do with two people who are in love and want to marry?"

"Quite a lot, dear," said Mrs. Crimond patiently. "As you should know."

"Oh, yes, I know all right," Jamie ground out, with a swift underbrowed glance at Lance who was apparently quite uninterested in the conversation. "But you can be sure, mother, I shan't let any member of my family come between me and my wife."

Mrs. Crimond's quick almost furtive glance in Lance's direction and her quiet "Shush, Jamie!" left Juliet in no doubt that Jamie's last remark was an oblique reference to Lance's association with Moira, and she also looked at him. To her embarrassment she encountered his bright gaze and knew by the faint smile on his face that he had guessed what she was thinking.

"Calm down, Jamie," he said. "No one is going to come between you and Laura, and if you're truly in love with each other I'm sure everything will work out to your satisfaction. But why not take mother's advice? You can't go wrong in observing the conventions in this case."

"We'll take Laura back to the castle, as I suggested," put in Mrs. Crimond, her frown disappearing as she took delight in making plans. "She can stay for a few days to recover from what I can only think must have been an unpleasant experience and we'll invite her parents over for next weekend. We'll have a little party, and if they agree, we'll announce your engagement."

After another uncertain, slightly puzzled, look at Lance Jamie went back to his place on the side of Mrs. Crimond's bed and putting an arm round her hugged her.

"Sounds fine, mother. Just what's needed," he said.

"We'll invite Janet and Alison over," said Mrs. Crimond, her eyes glowing with excitement.

"Alison Coates?" Jamie was immediately on the alert. "Where does she fit in?"

"Well, for all your description of Lance as a confirmed bachelor I've been hoping lately that he'll soon announce his decision to marry," said Mrs. Crimond.

Lance raised his eyebrows in an expression of mild surprise.

"I marry? Now why should I do that?" he drawled. "And whom should I marry?"

The expression on Mrs. Crimond's face changed from one of hopefulness to one of intense irritation.

"Alison, of course," she snapped. "Now, you can't deny, Lance, that you're interested in her. You've been over to Glenavon nearly every evening since you came to Castle Ross, and Alison herself told me that she'd met you several times in Glasgow."

"Which only goes to show what I've often suspected— that women love to exaggerate," murmured Lance aggravatingly. "I've been to Glenavon twice since I arrived at Castle Ross. All the other evenings I've been fishing or sailing. Alison and I met twice in Glasgow, once by accident at a cruising club affair, and the second time the day before I drove her home. Hardly enough basis for marriage, to my cold-blooded way of thinking," he added with a barbed glance in Jamie's direction. "And hasn't it occurred to you that she might have another interest?"

"I know there was a surgeon at the hospital in the south, but that's all over. She'd made a mistake. She told me herself."

"I wasn't thinking of him," said Lance quietly, but his mother didn't seem to hear him, for she went on rather plaintively, "You and she have been friends for years, off and on...."

"More off than on," he remarked dryly, "when you consider that until I bumped into her at that cruising club affair I hadn't seen her since Gareth's wedding."

The Cave of the White Rose

"And you'll see more of her," persisted Mrs. Crimond. "It's always been Janet's and my dearest wish that our two families should be joined by marriage. Oh, the plans we used to make when you and Gareth were boys! It's time you and Alison were married. Neither of you are getting any younger."

"I can't deny it. I noticed some gray hairs in my head only yesterday morning, and I believe Alison has taken to dyeing her hair," interrupted Lance wickedly, and Jamie nearly fell off the bed with laughing.

"Give up, mother," he advised. "Can't you see you'll never get him to tell you what he has in mind? If Lance ever marries I'll bet the family will be the last to hear of the arrangement. You're saying all the wrong things."

"I'm always saying the wrong things to all of you, so it seems," snapped Mrs. Crimond suddenly, as if at the end of her tether. "Juliet, you've met Alison and you know Lance. Don't you think they're well suited?"

Taken aback by this sudden appeal and attempt to draw her into a family discussion, Juliet went pink as both Jamie and Lance looked at her and waited for her reply. She found it was quite impossible to answer Mrs. Crimond's appeal while Lance was there watching her, much as she would have liked to help the older woman in her struggle to get her eldest son to commit himself.

Strangely enough it was Lance who came to her own rescue.

"You don't have to answer that one, Juliet," he said, and she sent him a grateful glance. "Aren't you being a little unfair putting Juliet on the spot like that, mother, when she's met Alison about twice and then only briefly, and as for me—"

"Oh, I know her opinion of you," interrupted Mrs. Crimond crossly. "She told me that the first time we met, and I'm fast coming to the conclusion that she was right. You're quite infuriating, and why you had to take her sailing with you when I thought you were in agreement with me that it would be ideal if she and Gareth...."

"Mother, mother!" Jamie's voice was choked with

laughter again. "Please spare Juliet's blushes. This isn't a novel you're writing. You can't arrange marriages in this way. Do you mean to say you asked Juliet to come and work for you in the hopes that Gareth would like her and would marry her?"

"It wasn't my idea that she should come and work for me at all," said Mrs. Crimond unwittingly, "it was Lance's. But when I saw how Gareth was reacting to her, how much he came out of his shell, the thought did cross my mind and I said as much to Lance—and he didn't disagree.... Now where are you going?"

Lance had already opened the door of the bedroom and was halfway through it. He looked back to answer his mother's sharp demand.

"I've had enough of this rather boring conversation, and it's embarrassing Juliet," he said coldly. "I'm going along to the hut that the rest of the cavers are using to have a drink by way of celebration of the finding of the entrance to the main system of caves and the release of Laura and Jamie."

"Wait for me." Jamie sprang to his feet.

"Oh, Jamie, you should be in bed, dear, resting," cautioned Mrs. Crimond ineffectually.

"Tomorrow," he grinned down at her. "I'm not missing a party for anything. You go to sleep. You're the one who's fatigued with worrying needlessly about your awkward brood. Why did you go sailing, Lance? I thought you were coming here on Saturday. I'd told everyone you were coming," he said as he walked over to the door.

"I gave in to impulse, something I rarely do, and as you can guess by the uproar it's caused, I'm fast regretting it," replied Lance. His cold glance drifted to Juliet, who was looking at him with suddenly troubled and accusing eyes. "I'd ask you to come to the party, Juliet, but as things stand at present between you and Gareth such an invitation might be misunderstood," he remarked acidly. His glance passed on to his mother and he inclined his head with an affectionate grin. "Good night, matriarch. Your suggestion concerning Alison is interesting. Maybe I'll think about it."

He closed the door behind him and Jamie, and Mrs. Crimond let out an exasperated sigh.

"Was there ever anyone so aggravating!" she complained, putting a hand to her head. "I'm very much afraid I've said the wrong thing, as Jamie pointed out. I should have had more sense than to mention marriage to Lance. He's always been touchy about it, ever since Gareth married Moira. But I'd hoped that he'd got over that disappointment by now. After all, twelve years is a long time and Moira has been dead almost one. Oh, what a difficult situation it was, almost nightmarish."

"In what way?" asked Juliet.

"Both my sons in love with the same woman. I've told you Lance brought Moira home, but Gareth fell in love with her at first sight and it was soon obvious that she preferred him to Lance. Then Lance went off to Canada, and while he was away Gareth and Moira decided to get married. Invitations were sent out, with one to Lance of course. We didn't know he was coming until he turned up at the last minute and told Gareth he was a fool to go through with the ceremony just before the poor boy was to leave for the church. Robert was furious with him, as you can imagine, and there were the usual fireworks. I can still remember the way Lance came to me and pleaded with me to stop the wedding. I could do nothing, so he went to Moira's home and tried to prevent her from going to the church. Quite naturally she didn't listen to him. He left and went back to Canada as soon as the ceremony was over, and I've never known since then what he'd really been thinking or feeling."

After she had gone to bed and had switched out the bedside lamp Juliet lay awake for a long time, aware of Mrs. Crimond's restlessness in the other bed.

She agreed with the other woman that Lance's answers to her suggestion that he might marry Alison eventually had been aggravating. He had obviously no intention of allowing his mother or anyone else to know how he felt about the red-haired woman whom he had known off and on for so long. But two things had been confirmed that evening.

Lance had been in love with Moira and he had lost her to Gareth. Yet in the end wasn't it possible that he had not lost her at all? That they had picked up where they had left off when he had returned from Canada to find Gareth crippled? It was that part about which Juliet couldn't be sure, and it was the part that bothered her the most for some reason. She couldn't bear to think that possibly Lance had deceived his brother.

She turned on her side and tried to sleep. But just as she was growing drowsy the other vital piece of information she had learned that evening and that had confirmed an earlier suspicion pricked her into wakefulness again to worry and tantalize her. Now she knew for certain that Lance had brought her to Castle Ross deliberately to carry out his boast that he could find another wife for Gareth, just as he had found the first one.

CHAPTER FIVE

NEXT MORNING Mrs. Crimond didn't feel well. She lay limp and apathetic against her pillows, her blue eyes drawn and shadowed, her thin ascetic face pale and haggard.

"It's no good, Juliet. I can't possibly travel back today," she said. "It would be too much on top of yesterday's journey and two very anxious nights. Lance will have to make arrangements for us to stay another night here. I'm sure Mrs. Robertson won't mind if I keep to this room today until I feel more rested. I won't have any breakfast, just a glass of milk. Perhaps you'd like to phone Gareth again and tell him why we won't be back; otherwise he'll worry about you. I hope you don't mind putting in the day by yourself. Did I disturb you during the night?"

"No, I was awake anyway, part of the time. Too much excitement yesterday, I expect," said Juliet, trying to be cheerful and alert.

"Then a nice quiet day won't do you any harm, either, nor Jamie and Laura for that matter." Mrs. Crimond frowned again. "It was past two o'clock when Jamie and Lance came back. I heard them, for all they tried to creep past the door."

Juliet had heard them, too, so when she went into the dining room she was surprised to see Lance already there, alone, eating his breakfast. She explained to him about his mother.

"I half expected it," he replied coolly. "She was very tired, and when she's like that she gets overexcited and talks too much; then she can't sleep."

"No thanks to you," she rebuked him sharply, knowing that it had been his remarks concerning Alison that had kept his mother wakeful. But she might as well have saved her breath, because he merely gave her a cold, slightly haughty glance that dismissed her comment as unnecessary.

"Jamie isn't feeling too well this morning, either," he said, "so I was going to suggest we delayed our return until tomorrow. Won't you sit down," he added politely. "The table is set for two and the waitress should be back soon."

He was firmly entrenched behind that film of ice that she had noticed yesterday whenever he had spoken to her, and once again she wondered what she had done or said to annoy him.

"I'd like to make a phone call first," she replied hastily, thinking it was a good excuse to avoid having to have breakfast alone with him again.

"Gareth?" he inquired accurately, and looked at his watch. "Too early. He won't be up yet, so you'd better wait. Sit down."

She was obeying his curt order before she realized it, lowering herself slowly into the seat opposite to him, watching him pour tea into one of the cups set on the table. He pushed a full cup across to her.

"You look as if you need it. Did you have a sleepless night too, no thanks to me?" he asked sardonically.

How unkind he was, deliberately and unpleasantly unkind. He went out of his way to torment people. Was it a form of self-defense to keep everyone at a distance so that they wouldn't inquire about his real feelings? Was it because he had once cared deeply about someone and had been badly hurt, and didn't want that to happen again?

Juliet stirred her tea reflectively, thinking of what she had learned about him from his mother the previous evening.

"You're doing it again," he cautioned crisply. "Wondering about something that is none of your business."

She met his clear cold gaze across the table, but this time she didn't let herself be put off by his apparent omniscience regarding her thoughts.

"You can't stop me from wondering. Mysteries have always intrigued me," she replied.

The film of ice was cracked for a moment as he laughed at her.

"But there's no mystery. You've been reading too many of Tess's books," he jeered.

She shook her head and her pale hair glinted in the sunlight that poured in through the window near which they were sitting.

"No, I haven't, and I don't agree with you. There is a mystery. You are the mystery."

For a brief moment he looked disconcerted, then his face stiffened and the crack in the ice closed up.

"So I'm a mystery and you'd like to solve me," he drawled. "Sorry, but it's against my nature to offer any clues. I guess your interest is well meant, but I think I've warned you before not to concern yourself with anything beyond the job you're paid to do."

"A job that didn't exist until you invented it," she retorted.

"Of course it did," he countered imperturbably. "Just because my mother says it wasn't her idea that you should work for her that doesn't mean to say she didn't need a secretary-companion. She's always needed one, but she was hopeless at choosing the right sort of person for the job, so this time I did it for her. From all accounts you're very satisfactory except for an unfortunate tendency on your part to be curious about matters that are not your concern." He paused, then added threateningly, "Keep off the grass, Juliet. You're not welcome."

The sharp rebuff hurt far more than it should have done, and she was trying to deal with the emotional upheaval he had just caused when the young waitress came in and apologized for keeping her waiting. Juliet gave her order in a low voice, then turned away to look out of the window because to her annoyance her eyes were filling with tears. How stupid to behave like this because a man she didn't like very much had rebuffed her! She felt like a child who, reaching out for and wanting friendship, had been rejected.

A chair leg scraped against the polished wooden floor as he rose to his feet.

"I'll leave you to have your breakfast in peace and go and see Tess," he said, and his voice sounded oddly flat and dull, causing her to look at him. He had half turned away ready to move toward the door when a thought seemed to strike him and he turned back. His eyes narrowed as they observed the slight droop to the corners of her sensitive mouth and the sheen of tears in her eyes.

"What are you going to do with yourself today?" he asked abruptly.

"I thought I'd go for a walk," she muttered.

He leaned against the back of the chair he had just vacated and stared at the table as if deep in thought. A lock of hair slid forward onto his forehead and he pushed it back impatiently, then rubbed the side of his face with his fingers. Juliet had the impression that he was hesitating about something, and was surprised. She had never had reason to consider him to be a hesitant person before.

"Would you like to see where the caves are?" he asked suddenly.

"Yes, I would."

"I'm going up there this morning to help bring back equipment. With Jamie and Laura out of action they're shorthanded. You could come with me, if you like."

If she liked. It was the same sort of invitation he'd issued on Saturday morning when he'd asked her to go sailing, and this time she was more suspicious.

"Are you sure you won't regret the impulse that prompts you to invite me?" she asked with a touch of acidity.

His glance was lightning bright and she braced herself for another rebuff.

"I might...later. But that's my affair, not yours," he said tersely. "Do you want to come?"

"Yes, I do, if you're sure such an outing wouldn't be beyond the limits of the job I'm paid to do," she replied coolly, and then wilted visibly when she saw his face darken ominously. But he didn't retort. Instead the film of ice cracked suddenly and he smiled at her.

"The rose has thorns," he mocked, coming around the table to stand beside her. "I deserved both of those pricks.

The Cave of the White Rose

Yes, I suppose I am behaving inconsistently and that the outing to the caves is beyond the limits of your job just as going sailing was, but I thought perhaps you'd prefer to see something of the countryside instead of moping about here all day on your own. Would you?"

In the face of this surprising show of consideration for her well-being she couldn't help smiling back at him.

"Yes, I would very much," she said.

"Then I shall see you in the entrance hall in about half an hour. That should give you time to eat and to phone Gareth. It might be a good idea to tell him where you're going and with whom, because if he doesn't hear it from you and someone else should tell him he might think you were being unnecessarily secretive and get some funny ideas. Oh, and one more warning. I'd appreciate it if you didn't try to solve mysteries on the way there and back. Do you understand?"

For a moment they stared at each other; sea-green eyes puzzled and a little hurt; gray eyes wary and watchful. Then Juliet inclined her head and whispered, "I understand."

LATER WHEN SHE PHONED GARETH his voice sounded warm and welcoming as he greeted her, and he chattered away happily, telling her about the work he was doing that morning and saying that he missed her very much.

"I'll give you three guesses why," he teased gently.

"There isn't time," she stammered as she noticed Lance walk past the kiosk in the entrance of the hotel and cock an inquiring eye in her direction. "We've already had more than three minutes."

"Lance is paying, so why should we care?" he chuckled. "Tell me why I'm missing you."

"Because you want some typing done."

"Right first time. So make sure you come back tomorrow without fail."

"I must go now," she said hurriedly. "Lance is waiting."

"Why?"

"We're going up to the cave to help bring down equipment."

"You don't have to go with him."

"No, but I'd like to see the caves."

"Don't go," he said urgently.

"Why shouldn't I?"

"Because you might get lost, or have an accident," he said seriously.

"No, I won't. I shall be quite safe."

"That's what you think!"

"Gareth, what's the matter? You're not making sense."

"Oh, nothing. It was just a thought I had. Goodbye, Juliet."

It was impossible to hide the puzzlement she felt as she stepped out of the kiosk, and Lance's all-seeing glance noted it. His mouth took on a sardonic curve as he remarked, "I gather Gareth was on form. Shall we go now?"

She nodded and he led the way out into the clear sparkling morning air.

The first part of the journey to the caves was along a rough road to a lonely white cottage set on the moors at the back of the village. As they drove along, rising steadily higher and higher, Lance pointed out the hut that was the cavers' headquarters and had once been a deer-stalker's bothy. He also drew her attention to the isolated mountain peaks of the area, which protruded above a wilderness of low hillocks and innumerable small lochs. Most of these mountains possessed very definite shapes, and Lance told her that one of them always reminded him of a fairy castle that had been pictured in one of his childhood books, perched on the top of steep slopes, and that another seemed to resemble a sugar loaf because its grayish quartzite boulders sparkled like sugar in the bright light. And gazing silently at the two mountains Juliet was surprised again that he was capable of such a fantasy.

When they reached the cottage Lance parked the car beside the Land Rover used by the cavers and went to the house to arrange to borrow the two small horses that were grazing on the hillside at the back. They were known as garrons, he informed Juliet, a species of horse indigenous to Scotland, which were nowadays used mostly for deer-stalking.

"Have you ever ridden a horse before?" he asked, noticing that she was eyeing the stocky, long-maned animals with a certain amount of apprehension.

"No. Do I have to?"

"Like sailing a boat, it's an experience you shouldn't miss. It's about four miles from here to the caves over rough moorland. We'll ride there and walk back leading the horses, which will be loaded with gear. I'll help you up onto its back."

"No saddle?" she queried.

"Bareback for fun," he replied with a grin. "Come on, there's nothing to be afraid of. They're quite docile and used to carrying novices."

She tried hard to heave herself up onto the back of the smaller of the two animals, but couldn't quite make it, and in the end allowed Lance to lift her up onto its back. He showed her how to hold the reins, then turned away to mount the other horse. He was far too big for it and presented a sight that tickled Juliet's sense of humor and sent her off into fits of giggles.

"What's so funny?" he demanded.

"You are, on that horse. You look like a giant on a pony. Your feet almost touch the ground."

"They do," he replied, showing her. "These horses used to be ridden by Highlanders to cross country in the past. They're capable of carrying a person for miles no matter what his height or weight. Are you ready?"

"I think so," she said dubiously.

He turned his horse and it trotted out through the gate of the yard onto the moorland path. Juliet tried to turn her horse to follow him, but it remained stubbornly in the same place. She pulled on the reins, clucked her tongue, but it didn't move, except to lower its head and start nibbling at a tuft of grass. Lance looked around, saw her predicament and came back.

"Kick with your heels and it'll move," he instructed.

She did, and the horse moved off obediently at a far

faster pace than she had anticipated. It had a peculiar rocking motion and she could feel the action of its back muscles beneath her. She kicked again, hoping to make it go faster so that she could catch up with Lance, and it broke into a lurching trot. Not being used to riding, Juliet didn't know how to move when a horse trotted, so she bumped up and down on its back, feeling sure that at any minute she would slide off sideways.

When she did go, it wasn't sideways. The horse stopped suddenly and she shot off over its lowered head, did an unexpected somersault and landed on her back in a bed of springy bog myrtle.

Bewildered, bruised and breathless, she lay and blinked at the sunny sky for several seconds, panic-stricken in case she'd broken any bones, remembering Gareth's concern about her, and his insistence that she shouldn't go with Lance. Then the thud of hooves on the ground told her that Lance was on his way back to see what had happened and she struggled onto her knees.

"What happened?" he asked, slipping off his horse and coming to help her to her feet.

"The silly thing stopped and I fell off, that's all," she replied shakily as she tested each leg gingerly before putting her full weight on either of them. Looking up as he released her arm, she saw amusement lurking in his eyes. He was laughing at her because she couldn't ride just as he'd laughed at her when she had got drenched with spray on the boat. She was suddenly angry. "I could have hurt myself badly," she accused hotly. "I could have broken an arm or a leg, or fallen on my head and cracked my skull and died."

"And that would have taught me a lesson, because accidents happen to people when they're with me. Isn't that how it goes?" he put in coldly. "I'm surprised Gareth didn't warn you against coming with me when you phoned him."

"He did," she retorted.

"Yet you came."

"Yes—after all, I'm not Moira."

Her hand went to her mouth and her eyes widened with

dismay as she saw his face go pale and a strange expression, it could have been pain, flicker in his eyes.

"No, you're not Moira," he agreed quietly. "She knew how to ride." Just as she'd known how to sail, how to ski, how to climb hills, how to do everything, thought Juliet miserably. How could she, who could only type, possibly compete with such a paragon? And on top of that question came another—why would she want to compete?

Confused and shaken, she looked around at the seemingly never-ending moorland where the heather was already purple, at the distant hills shimmering silver gray in the sunlight. It was a beautiful morning and she had started out with high hopes thinking that perhaps this might be one of those perfect days, a day to remember. A big golden bird appeared high in the sky flapping its wings lazily. Then gliding on a current of air it swooped downward and disappeared beyond the edge of the moor.

"A golden eagle," murmured Lance, half to himself. "Probably after a mountain hare, or a grouse."

Juliet shuddered. "Poor little prey!" she mourned.

"You feel an affinity with it, perhaps," he taunted, swinging around to look at her. "Only the other day you compared me to an eagle. You know, considering your opinion of me I'm surprised you wanted to come today. Well, do you want to go on or would you rather go back and sit in the car until I return with the others?"

For the second time that morning tears were very near. Her perfect day had already been spoiled and possibly would be remembered only for hard words, but she knew she couldn't bear to stay and sit in his car while he rode on to the caves. She had to go with him. She had to take up the challenge that going anywhere with him offered.

"I want to go on," she replied.

"Then get on the garron." He helped her up onto the horse's back and put the reins in her hand. "This time, stay put," he ordered. "And don't try to hurry. We have all day to get there and back. I'll ride beside you so that I can keep an eye on you. That way we'll avoid any accidents, I hope."

There were no more incidents and soon she began to enjoy the ride in the clear mountain air. The only sounds were the perpetual chuckle of a burn as it rushed down the hillside over pale stones, and the occasional mournful cry of a bird.

They kept close to the burn following its course through the narrow glen it had made. As he had promised, Lance kept beside her, occasionally reaching out a hand to grasp her horse's bridle to guide it around some obstacle he had seen and she hadn't. He spoke only once to point out the change in the landscape as the bog myrtle and sedge gave way to short green grass and small bushes with clumps of hazel and mountain ash trees. The hills had lost their rock-bun shape and were sharper edged, and she recognized a similarity to the area around the Cauldron on the Castle Ross estate. This was part of the big limestone thrust about which Jamie had told her on that day, so long ago now it seemed, when he had driven her from Glasgow to Loch Moy.

The burn disappeared underground where a long fissure made a ragged gash in a hillside.

"This is the outlet of this particular stream," said Lance as they paused to look down into the deep crack. "We'll find the others higher up the hill."

After a fairly steep climb up the craggy hillside they came to the place where the burn went underground on its way down from its source. Graham and his helpers were lounging beside the deep gash eating their lunches. Nearby three more garrons stood already loaded with the diving gear the cavers had been using.

The cavers greeted Lance cheerfully and stared curiously at the pale-haired girl whom he helped down from her horse.

"I see you've brought a fairy princess with you this morning," said Graham with a grin. "Good morning, Miss Grey. Have you come to see the scene of yesterday's little drama? If you'd like to be stepping this way I'll show you where we had to go and you'll hear the roaring of the water as it falls over a step of rock."

He led her to the edge of the deep fissure that was overhung by small bushes and creeping plants. It was wide and dark, and far below she could hear the sound of water.

"This is where we first tried to gain entry last summer," explained Graham, "but it led only to an impassable water trap, something like the one you'll find below a washhand basin. So we dug a pit between the accumulated scree and debris and the rock face over there until we found a crack." He pointed to the opposite side of the fissure. "That's the crack that Laura was able to enter last week."

"But it's only a few inches high!" exclaimed Juliet. "However did she get in?"

"Nine and a half inches, to be exact," replied Graham. "And she got in by lying on her back and wriggling about like a snake. Anyway, she was able to tell us that after a few feet it widened out into a small cave where there was another crack about seven inches high. We were all able to wriggle into that crack over there, but the seven-inch one defeated us and that's when we had to start blasting, and the trouble began. But at least we know now that our first guesses were right and that there's a big cave system under this hill that will rival that of Cnoc na Uamh."

"Where is that?"

"A few miles away."

"No progress this morning?" asked Lance, coming to join them.

"No. We need a bigger party to do some digging. At the moment the system is only passable for divers. We'll have to find another entrance. We explored some more potholes this morning, but we miss Laura and Jamie, so we'll postpone investigation for another year. Unless you'd care to try and wriggle into one of the cracks and report back some information to us, Miss Grey?" said Graham, turning to smile at her.

"Now go easy, Graham," warned Lance, and Juliet felt his hand grip her elbow and pull her back gently from the edge of the crack. "I brought her to see the place and to help with the humping back of the equipment, not as a replacement for Laura. She isn't my property, so I have to take great care she doesn't get lost or hurt or there'll be hell to pay back at Castle Ross."

Graham's shrewd gray eyes flicked from Lance's face to Juliet's and back again.

"Aye, I can imagine, but there are others ways of getting lost or hurt than falling down a pothole," he murmured obscurely. "If you were my property, Miss Grey, I wouldn't be letting you roam the countryside with this rogue." He jerked a thumb in the direction of Lance.

"Then what would you do?" asked Juliet, at once amused and fascinated by the strange turn in the conversation.

"I'd keep you locked up until he'd passed by."

"I'd no idea you had such a medieval outlook on life," said Lance with a laugh. "Now, tell us what you'd like us to load onto the garrons and after we've eaten our lunch we'll start back."

Juliet ate the packed lunch that Lance had brought from the hotel sitting beside the deep chasm. The noonday sun shone down out of a cloudless sky, and the only sounds were the muffled roar of the hidden water and the desultory conversation of the men. Feeling relaxed, Juliet leaned back on her elbows and gazed back down the glen up which she and Lance had recently come.

Difficult of access, devoid of any habitation, the place had a wild romantic beauty to which sunshine and shadow added their serenity and mystery. Amid such scenery it wasn't difficult to take seriously Graham's strange remarks about fairy princesses and rogues.

Her gaze slid down from contemplation of the summit of the hills to Lance where he sprawled on the ground beside Graham listening to the other man's slow voice. Her glance lingered on the strong, bold features of his face outlined against the pale rock behind him. Certainly he looked more of a rogue than a knight in shining armor. She assumed that Graham's description was based on a fairly close knowledge of Lance and it was the sort of thing that could only be said to a friend. Odd to find that Lance had a close friend. He seemed such a loner, a person apart, even from his family, difficult to know and understand—an uncomfortable person to have around, as Jamie had once said.

The Cave of the White Rose

And if, as Mrs. Crimond and apparently Lance himself wished, she married Gareth, Lance would be her brother-in-law.

The thought alarmed her and she sat up suddenly, clasping her arms around her knees. Up here in the hills of the northwest Gareth seemed very far away and insubstantial and she didn't want to think about marrying him.

A shadow came between her and the sun. She knew at once who it was and glanced up warily to meet the enigmatic glitter of light gray eyes.

"Graham thinks you should see Cnoc na Uamh while you're here, so we'll go around that way instead of going back the way we came," Lance said. "It's the long way and it will take us most of the afternoon to get back to the cottage."

She looked around in surprise. While she had been lazing and thinking the garrons had been loaded and the other cavers had already set off down the glen.

To reach the Hill of Caves they had to walk around the shoulder of the hill in a northwesterly direction, leading the loaded garrons behind them. On the way Juliet talked to Graham and she learned that he was a teacher of science in an Edinburgh school, and that he was married and had two children.

"Don't you bring them with you when you come caving?" she asked.

"Ach, no. It's my hobby, not theirs. And one advantage of being a teacher is that I can have a holiday with them and then take a few days off to go caving."

"How long have you been caving?"

"About ten years, perhaps more." He half turned to ask Lance who was walking behind them, "How long since we spent that holiday in South Wales?"

"More than twelve. The gray is beginning to show in your hair, too," joked Lance.

"What little I have of it," laughed Graham. "Aye, that was the beginning of it. We went potholing among the Welsh hills with a group from the university. It made a change from cruising in the Western Isles in someone else's yacht, which was our usual occupation during the summer months, and the bug bit me down there. Two years later a book was published about the underground caves of Scotland and that clinched the matter. I formed a society, with Lance's support. We got some experience with other groups down in Derbyshire, then we came up here, because although the main area of caves has been known for some time they haven't all been properly explored."

Soon they reached the arched openings in Cnoc na Uamh, which Juliet duly admired. Graham pointed out that most of the stalactite and stalagmite formations, the long needlelike formations hanging from the roofs or protruding upward from the floors, had mostly been removed by casual visitors to the caves, an act of vandalism that he deplored, as such formations were rare in Scotland.

When they set off down the hillside, going south this time, Juliet walked again with Graham, with whom she was on very good terms by now, and asked him if he knew that there was an underground stream near Castle Ross.

"Yes, but Lance says the stream isn't very big and that there would have to be a lot of blasting done, and he doesn't want that. Have you seen it?"

"Maree took me to see it."

"She's Gareth's child?"

"Yes. Do you know her?"

"I haven't seen her since she was a wee bairn. I knew her mother. Fearless as they come. Lance says the girl is very like her. A hard time her father will be having keeping her in order, if that's the case," Graham observed dryly. "You know how her mother died?"

"I know that there was an accident of some sort, that's all."

"Aye, when she was skiing abroad. She was warned not to go out, but she insisted on going when there'd been an avalanche warning. She was very willful, was Moira, and I know of only one person who could keep her in her place." He jerked his head backward in the direction of Lance, who appeared to be in no hurry to catch up with them.

The Cave of the White Rose

"But if that was so why wasn't he able to stop her from going out when there was a warning?" asked Juliet.

Graham flashed her a surprised glance.

"How could he? He wasn't there."

"But... but..." Juliet felt as if she were groping in a fog even though the day was very clear. "I've been led to believe that he was."

"Led to believe is right," remarked Graham caustically. "May I ask by whom?"

"Gareth. I heard him say that if he hadn't let Moira go with Lance that last time she'd be alive now."

Graham was silent as he turned this piece of information over in his mind.

"So that's the way of it," he murmured at last. "It would be interesting to find out who has been misleading whom, and perhaps we'll never know because Lance isn't one to discuss family or personal affairs. But I'm willing to bet he wasn't with Moira."

"But he often took her out, I've heard Mrs. Crimond say so. He thought he was helping Gareth when he was unable to get about because of the paralysis in his leg."

"Curiouser and curiouser. There seems to be a wee bit of a mystery here, don't you think?"

"Why do you say that?" she asked sharply.

"I knew Moira quite well. As I've said, she was willful and headstrong. If she wanted to go anywhere she would go. She wouldn't wait for anyone to invite her," he said with an air of authority. "I also know Lance better than most people do, and I can't believe he would invite her to go anywhere with him, because he disliked her."

"Disliked her? Oh, but Mrs. Crimond told me that he was in love with her and was very disappointed when she married Gareth."

"Aye, it looked that way at the time and maybe he was attracted to her for a while; after all she was interested in all out-of-door activities just as he was, but he soon forgot her when he went to Canada. It was when he came back and saw what she'd done to Gareth that he began to dislike her. You see, although it may not be very apparent, because he isn't a demonstrative man, Lance has very great affection for the members of his family. For them he would do anything, as he would for anyone he loved, and so...."

"Sharing secrets already?"

Lance had caught up with them, and Juliet glanced with alarm at him, realizing that in the last few minutes she had been very concerned with something outside the limits of her job. But the mockery in his eyes was directed at Graham, not at her.

"You certainly have a way with the lasses, Graham," he taunted with a grin. "You must tell me how you do it some time."

"Nothing to it," replied the tall Scot imperturbably. "When a lass is like a fairy princess and her heart is in the right place a man can't help confiding in her. Anyway, where have you been loitering?"

"The garron got a stone in its hoof and I've been removing it. It's limping a bit, so I think I'll unload some of the gear. I'll leave it here and perhaps Eric or Morley can come back and pick it up."

The limping horse slowed down their progress because Graham kept pace with Lance and Juliet could do no less. The conversation concerned mostly plans for caving the following year when Graham hoped that Lance would join the expedition.

When they reached the cottage they found Eric and Morley waiting there, and Graham sent Eric to get the gear that had been left behind before walking over to the car with Juliet and Lance.

"This isn't the end of our acquaintance, Juliet," he said with a smile. "There's a *ceilidh* on in the village hall tonight and I'm inviting you to come to it."

"A *celidh*?"

"Aye, a get-together of everyone in the village and the outlying district as well as people who are on holiday up here. There'll be some Scottish dancing and some singing, and I'm thinking you'd like it. We had a fine wee party last night, but it was strictly all male. Tonight I'm making up for that by asking you to come along. Will you?"

"I'd love to," smiled Juliet.

"Tut, tut," mocked Lance. "What would Helen say if she knew?"

"She'd approve," retorted his friend. "If she were here she'd be doing the inviting herself and telling you you're a proud stubborn oaf who can't see any farther than the end of his nose."

There was a funny silence as Lance stared at his friend and Graham returned the stare with narrowed eyes.

"Has it ever occurred to you that perhaps I can see farther, very clearly, and that I'm trying to avoid complications?" returned Lance icily.

"And making more as you do," countered Graham.

"Watch it, Graham!" It was a haughtily uttered threat.

"All right, it's none of my business, but I'm surprised at you, and it's time you started putting yourself first and be damned to your brother."

"Come on, Juliet," said Lance. "We'll leave this madman now, and hope that he'll have recovered from the touch of the sun he seems to have by the time the *ceilidh* starts."

As the car bumped down the rough road toward the village Juliet caught sight of the mountain, which looked like a fairy castle on the edge of a precipice; a castle where the princess would lie sleeping until the prince came to wake her with a kiss....

"Well, was it a good day?" asked Lance abruptly, breaking into her daydream. Roused from her contemplation of the mountain, she glanced sideways at him. He was frowning, and the creases from the corners of his nose to the corners of his mouth were very marked.

"Yes, it was, thank you," she said primly, thinking she must keep the conversation cool and conventional. "Graham is very interesting. I learned a lot from him."

"I bet you did," he replied savagely, and she looked at him again. Was it possible that he was angry, really angry? Even as she looked at him he jammed on the brakes and the car came to a lurching, crunching stop at the side of the road.

He turned in his seat to face her.

"What did you learn?" he rapped.

Still confused by Graham's remarks about Moira, which had given her a totally new view of Lance's relationship with his late sister-in-law, she shrank back against the door of the car, away from the anger that glittered in his eyes.

"I learned about stalactites and stalagmites," she quavered, and heard him swear rather wearily.

"That isn't what I meant, and you know it, mystery-solver. What else did you learn?"

His anger had passed as quickly as it had blown up. He turned away from her and leaned his arms on the steering wheel and resting his chin on them closed his eyes, and for the first time since she had known him he seemed to Juliet to be thoroughly human; a man who did what he did because he was prompted by pride, affection, anger and immediately all her fear and dislike of him faded to nothing.

"I learned that you disliked Moira for what she did to Gareth," she answered quietly.

He didn't move a muscle.

"Is that all?" he said warily.

"Yes."

"I thought I'd told you not to try and solve any mysteries."

"I didn't. We were talking about Maree and Graham asked if I knew how her mother had died and I told him I didn't...."

"And he decided to fill you in. Very obliging of him, I'm sure," he said sarcastically. "Well, for your information Graham knows nothing about the circumstances surrounding Moira's death. No one knows here, except me."

"But Gareth...."

"He knows what I decided to tell him. She went skiing with me. There was an avalanche warning, but she insisted on going out. There was nothing I could do to stop her. That's the story, Juliet, and I'd be glad if you'd leave it that way, and stop probing."

"And if I don't stop probing, what will you do?" she couldn't resist challenging.

"I don't know, but you can be sure it won't be pleasant," he grated.

"But I don't understand," she blurted rebelliously. "Why did you lie to Gareth...."

He moved quickly. His hand stung her delicate skin as he clapped it across her mouth so that she couldn't say any more.

"I warned you," he hissed. "Do you want to stay at Castle Ross?"

"I'm not sure that I can stay now," she answered, as he removed his hand and slumped back into his seat.

"That is of course entirely up to you," he said coldly as he switched on the ignition, started the engine and maneuvered the car back onto the road, and the rest of the drive back to the hotel was made in uncomfortable silence.

When they reached the hotel Juliet let herself out of the car with a muffled word of thanks and hurried inside. Her one aim was to be by herself to give way to the tears that were threatening. But she had forgotten she was sharing a room with Mrs. Crimond and her face registered her disappointment at finding the room occupied by that lady, who was sitting in front of the dressing table attending to her hair.

Too late Juliet tried to cover up. Mrs. Crimond had noticed her reflection in the mirror and swung around to look directly at her.

"Why, Juliet dear, whatever is the matter? You're quite pale and distressed-looking. There hasn't been...? Lance is all right?"

"Yes, we're both all right," whispered Juliet. "There's nothing the matter," and promptly burst into tears.

With a quick impulsive movement Mrs. Crimond was out of her chair and putting her arms around Juliet.

"Oh, my dear, what is it? Come and sit down and tell me."

Sitting on the side of her bed, Juliet tried vainly to recover, taking her handkerchief and blowing her nose and wiping her eyes.

"It's so silly," she hiccuped. "Nothing to cry about really, only...."

"Only what? You'd better tell me. Has that abominable son of mine done something to upset you?"

"No, I mean, yes. Well, he had every right to say what he did, but...." Fresh tears made it impossible for her to continue.

"But he could have said it more pleasantly, I know," sighed Mrs. Crimond. "It's the Crimond in him. Neither his father nor his grandfather were in the least tactful."

"He said I must stop trying to solve mysteries."

"What mystery are you trying to solve? Something to do with the caves?" Mrs. Crimond sounded completely bewildered.

"No. It's difficult to explain, and it's possible I'm imagining it. It's to do with Lance and Gareth and Moira, and now it's been made more complicated by what Graham Lee said this afternoon."

"What did he say?" asked Mrs. Crimond.

"He said he didn't believe that Lance was with Moira on that skiing trip when she was killed. He said that Lance disliked Moira."

"But he loved her. That was the trouble and has always been the trouble. It's that that has soured the relationship between him and Gareth," exclaimed Mrs. Crimond.

"That's what I thought—not because anyone told me but just from observing."

"And adding two and two together from the odd conversations that occasionally take place," said Mrs. Crimond sympathetically. "Yes, I can understand, because that's all I've ever been able to do. Lance has never confided in me. He isn't the type. And although Gareth makes a pretense of doing so, I know he withholds things. I've never really expected them to tell me everything, believing that once your children grow up you mustn't expect them to come running to you with their problems, but that hasn't stopped me from wishing secretly that they would. Oh, dear, what a muddle, but I'm sure you know what I mean, Juliet."

Juliet nodded, smiling a rather wobbly smile. Talking to Mrs. Crimond was helping her immeasurably. It helped to

The Cave of the White Rose

know that someone else who was close to the two eldest Crimonds was just as puzzled by their behavior.

"But on what grounds does Graham base his idea that Lance disliked Moira?" asked Mrs. Crimond.

"He seems to know him very well. They've been friends for years."

"You surprise me. I'd no idea that Lance had any close friends. Did he tell you anything else?"

"Only that Lance is very fond of his family and will do anything to help them."

"That I know to be true in my case and possibly in Jamie's, and even though he and his father argued many times he didn't hesitate to come home when Robert was ill and I believe he was sincerely upset when his father died. It used to be true also in the case of Gareth, especially when they were boys. Being the stronger of the two Lance tended to protect Gareth when they were at school, but lately I would say his attitude has fallen far short of affection, because there have been times when he's been downright unkind."

"I know," said Juliet. "But why?"

"Did Graham tell you why Lance disliked Moira?" asked Mrs. Crimond shrewdly.

"He was just saying that it was because of what she did to Gareth when Lance came up and accused us of sharing secrets, so of course Graham didn't say any more. But later when we were coming back here Lance was annoyed because he suspected Graham and I had been discussing him and he said...he warned me..." Juliet gulped and swallowed more tears.

"I see," murmured Mrs. Crimond, her eyes vacant as she stared at Juliet without actually seeing her, obviously thinking hard. "There is something that Lance doesn't want Gareth to know and he's afraid that if you find out about it you'll tell Gareth. There is a mystery after all, and I think Graham may be able to help us. What did Moira do to Gareth? I've no idea, apart from the fact that I suspected they weren't very happy during the last few years of their marriage. I wonder how we can find out?"

"We?" queried Juliet.

"Yes. You must see, dear, that I've been very troubled by the deteriorating relationship between Lance and Gareth, but by nature I tend to avoid anything unpleasant, so I've not questioned either of them. And then Gareth has never uttered a word of criticism of Moira. As far as he's concerned she was perfect. You must find out from Graham what he was going to tell you. Between now and tomorrow morning, when we'll be leaving, you'll have to pump him, Juliet."

JULIET HAD NO DOUBTS that she would be able to question Graham further about Moira when she attended the *ceilidh*. The thought of going to the party cheered her up and she felt much better when she had changed into a multicolored gathered skirt that sported a deep frill around its hem and topped it with a simple full-sleeved blouse. She tied her pale hair back from her face into a high ponytail from which it fanned out on her shoulders.

As she walked with him to the village hall Graham explained to her that the social gathering that would take place that evening was not a *ceilidh* in the true sense of the word, because that was usually an informal spontaneous affair held in someone's house. But the event that evening had been organized by the proprietors of the hotel for the entertainment of the many summer visitors to the area who usually came from overseas and who wished to see a little local color. There would be a four-piece band and local singers would show off their talent in singing Gaelic ballads and other well-known Scottish songs. The dancing would be varied, but there would be a preponderance of Scottish dances.

"They're very enjoyable when you get used to them. As long as you have a strong sense of rhythm and remember eight beats to every bar you'll be all right, because the steps vary very little from one to another," Graham explained as they stood at the edge of the floor watching a reel in progress. "It's the movements that sometimes get complicated. But I'll push you into the right place at the right time, and you'll find the other dancers in the sets only too glad to tell you. It's all good fun and we all help one another."

Delighted by the brisk regular footwork of the dancers and by the gaiety of the music, Juliet watched entranced, her feet unconsciously trying out the steps. A quick glance at the people present had told her that Lance wasn't there and she knew a sense of relief curiously mixed with disappointment. She hadn't seen him since she had left the car because he hadn't appeared to take dinner with his mother, Jamie and Laura. If he came to the social she had decided not to speak to him, although she found it difficult to subdue the flurry of agitation that she had always felt at the thought of meeting him and that she had once believed to be fear but was now beginning to recognize as excitement.

Soon she was joining the other couples with Graham in a fairly slow dance called Strathspey to the tune called the *Glasgow Highlanders*. That was followed by *The Gay Gordons*, and by the time that was over her cheeks were glowing and her eyes were sparkling.

The dancing had been so complicated and energetic that she had had no chance to talk to Graham and she realized that any conversation concerning Moira would have to be done between the dances when they either stood or sat at the side of the hall.

She was just about to ask him some leading questions on the subject as they stood getting their breath when Lance spoke behind her.

"You learn quickly, but that was to be expected since your mother was a dancer," he said.

She stiffened a little but didn't turn to look at him, while the annoyance that she always felt when she learned that he had been watching her unseen flooded through her, making her wary of him. At that moment a resounding chord from the accordion signaled the start of another dance and Graham turned toward her just as Lance slipped an arm about her taut waist.

"My turn, Graham," he said with his wicked grin. "You've done your bit for this evening by showing her how."

Graham's answering smile was indulgent as if he liked the idea of her dancing with Lance although he spoke with pretended disgust.

"Now isn't that just like you, you rogue, sidling up when a fellow isn't looking and taking over his partner. All right, have it your own way. I was thinking I should be asking Laura to dance, anyway. She's looking a wee bit wistful over there because Jamie can't join in. I'll be seeing you, Juliet."

She could have refused to dance with Lance. She could have wrenched out of his hold on her waist and walked away, but she didn't because she knew he would follow her. She knew also that he was careless of the opinion of others and wasn't above making a scene, whereas her shy spirit shied away from drawing attention to herself. No, it would be better to dance one dance with him, not speaking, not even looking at him, which should be easy enough if the dance was another reel or a Strathspey.

But it wasn't either, and as the strains of "Come O'er the Stream, Charlie" started up and he took her right hand in his they moved off into the three-four time of the waltz country dance. He was a good dancer, much better than Graham, who was inclined to be too gangling for coordinated movement, and she soon realized that she was enjoying herself. Although it was difficult she managed to keep her head averted, but all the time she was very aware of him watching her.

The dance ended without either of them having spoken, but as they walked to the side of the hall he didn't release her hand, and try as she might she couldn't disengage her fingers from his without the possibility of an undignified scuffle. They were joined by Graham, Laura and Jamie, and some of the other cavers. The conversation was cheerful and general, but there seemed to be no way in which she could approach Graham and speak to him. She hoped he would ask her to dance with him again and that at the end of the dance she would be able to get him by himself, but as the evening wore on her hopes proved fruitless, because he didn't ask her to dance again.

She danced only with Lance, and when they didn't dance

but sat watching the others or listening to the singers he was there at her side watching her like an eagle, waiting to swoop as soon as she betrayed herself by moving closer to Graham. And she began to realize, ruefully, when no one else approached her to ask her to dance, that she had been accepted as Lance's partner for the evening as he deliberately cut her off from contact with anyone else.

The hall gradually filled with more people. The dancing grew a little wilder and noisier, and the singing a little sadder. Juliet began to react differently to her unwanted partner. She found she didn't mind any longer if his arm lingered around her waist when they stopped dancing and that she had no desire to avoid looking at him. Indeed the expression in his eyes when they met hers, while they were dancing or talking to the others, was a mixture of challenge and invitation that fascinated her.

After one particularly energetic dance he led her out through the door of the hall to cool off outside. By this time Juliet was under a spell and had forgotten her suspicion that he had been using all his wiles plus a considerable amount of masculine charm to prevent her from talking to Graham. So she went willingly with him down the road, beyond the village lights toward the crumbling walls of a disused wayside chapel.

All around them the rock-bun hills were humped black against the starlit sky and above the distant sugar loaf mountain a crescent moon shone, casting silvery light over the curves and angles of the land. It was a beautiful night, a night for romance, for walking with a lover, thought Juliet dreamily, and she didn't think once of Gareth.

Lance was humming the tune of the last dance as he walked beside her, hands in his pockets, not touching her for the first time since he had appeared by her side in the hall. He stopped humming to tell her that the tune was called "Jock o' Hazeldean" and to ask her if she knew the poem by the same name, which had been written by Sir Walter Scott.

"No, I don't. What is it about?" she asked curiously, interested as always in poetry.

"I suppose it's about the triumph of true love over obstacles. In this case the obstacle is a marriage of convenience arranged between the girl in the story and a man called Frank of Errington. But in secret the girl weeps for another young man called Jock of Hazeldean. The wedding is arranged, the groom, the priest and the guests are waiting in the kirk, but the bride never arrives because, 'She's o'er the border and awa' wi' Jock o' Hazeldean.'"

He sang the last two lines softly.

"Come to think of it," he continued, "Scottish poetry is full of young women ready to defy authority for the sake of love. You'll have heard of Lord Ullin's daughter who preferred 'To meet the raging of the skies, But not an angry father' and consequently came to a sad end."

"It wasn't only the young women who defied authority," she replied. "The men did, too. Jock of Hazeldean reminds me of one of my favorites, Young Lochinvar, 'So faithful in love, and so dauntless in war, There never was knight like the Young Lochinvar!'"

"I might have known he would appeal to you more than Lancelot does," he remarked dryly, and at once the spell was broken, its gossamer-thin web torn to shreds. Tension was back between them, and upset by the change, Juliet stopped walking and turned to face him. The moonlight tangled in her pale hair and glinted on the granite wall of the old chapel building behind her, as Lance stopped too and looked at her inquiringly.

Wanting to be back within the warmth of the spell, wanting desperately to feel again his arm around her waist and the touch of his hand on hers, Juliet said in a low, almost apologetic voice, "Sir Lancelot only lost his appeal for me when I read of his entanglement with Guinevere, Arthur's wife."

"You must remember the story was written in the age of chivalry when it was considered the height of romance to love and worship a woman who belonged to another and who was beyond reach," he replied smoothly, giving nothing away.

"But was she beyond his reach?" she demanded. "It

isn't very clear in the story. In some parts it states that their love was sinful, and then it caused so much trouble, leading Arthur to doubt Lancelot's and Guinevere's loyalty to himself."

She knew she was treading dangerous ground, but she was daring to do so because she hoped she might prod him into telling her the truth about himself and Moira.

"They both did penance for it later, something of which I'm sure you approve, little puritan," he replied easily, shrugging off the issue. "But I'm inclined to agree with you. Lochinvar is much preferable to Lancelot. He knew what he wanted and he went after it."

He had stepped closer to her and she backed away and was brought up short by the wall of the chapel. The rough granite pricked her hands as she placed them behind her back, the palms flat against the wall to brace herself against his approach.

"What do you want?" she quavered as he stood over her.

"That isn't an easy question to answer," he murmured. "Up to this point in my life I've always gone after what I wanted, too...."

"Regardless of whom you've hurt?" she put in quickly.

"Whom have I hurt?"

"Gareth, perhaps, if you took Moira away from him."

"So we're back to that! I have to hand it to you, white rose, you don't give up easily, but you'll get no information out of me about Moira—nor out of Graham, for that matter."

Suspicion was back lying like a sword between them as Juliet realized that while she was out here in the moonlight with him the *ceilidh* would be ending, and Graham would be going back to the cavers' hut and she wouldn't see him to ask the important question: what had Moira done to Gareth? Anger rocketed through her at the thought that Lance had brought her out here deliberately to prevent her from learning more; anger that was spiced by the most agonizing disappointment she had ever experienced.

"Oh, don't think I haven't realized that you've done

everything you could this evening to keep me from talking to him. You didn't dance with me because you wanted to," she accused, thinking that if she sidestepped quickly she could dodge him and run up the road to the hall and find Graham before he disappeared into the night.

"Didn't I?" mocked Lance softly, and as if guessing her intention he put both hands against the wall on either side of her, imprisoning her. "That only goes to show how little you know about me—or even about yourself," he murmured softly, leaning over her. "Don't you ever look at yourself, Juliet? If you did you'd see why a man wants to dance with you. Your wide-eyed innocence is a temptation hard to resist. It tempts one to kiss you, to try and wake you up out of your lovely romantic dream where love is cool, remote and chaste, and to show you that it's nothing of the sort."

She couldn't have moved if she'd tried. Like a small animal hypnotized by the larger one stalking it she shrank back against the wall, knowing he was making love to her and half wishing that he meant what he said. But there was no avoiding him. His hands dropped to her shoulders. He pulled her forward and kissed her ruthlessly on the mouth.

For a few seconds her whole body went taut as she tried to reject his embrace, knowing instinctively that it was dangerous to her. Then she felt the warmth of his hands through the thin stuff of her blouse and her resistance to him started to collapse.

With a desperate effort she pulled away from him, raised an arm and swung at his face. As her hand connected, flesh on flesh, he released her suddenly, one of his hands going to his cheek. In that moment she was away, running lightly up the road in the direction of the village. Once she looked back, thinking he might have followed her, wanting to go back and apologize. But the moon-bleached road was empty, and she remembered why he had kissed her and went on.

When she reached the village hall she found the *ceilidh* was over and that people were swarming out into the fine moonlit night, laughing, singing and talking. As she min-

The Cave of the White Rose 351

gled with them she looked for Graham and the other cavers, but there was no sign of them. Her heart still beating crazily from the effect of Lance's kiss, she hurried along to the hotel, thinking that Graham had gone there with Jamie and Laura in the hopes of seeing her.

A light was on in the quiet entrance hall, but there was no one there. She went across to the lounge. Only Laura and Jamie were there, embracing in the dimness. Muttering an apology, Juliet backed out of the room. One hand against her bruised mouth, she began to walk slowly up the stairs, suddenly exhausted by her own emotions, wondering how she was going to explain to Mrs. Crimond that she had been unable to find out more about Moira and Gareth from Graham because Lance, with a deliberation that hurt more than anything else he had done or said, had prevented her from doing so by making love to her.

CHAPTER SIX

Two DAYS LATER Juliet sat on the terrace at Castle Ross with Gareth. It was past eleven o'clock in the morning and she had been typing for him since eight-thirty, and now they were enjoying the coffee that Vinnie had brought out to them.

It was a fresh sunny morning, and down on the sparkling loch, moving between two dark islands, she could see a white triangle of sail. It was the mainsail of Lance's boat. He had taken Alison sailing with him, and as Juliet watched the blue hull of the boat forging through the water she was shaken by a sudden longing to be aboard, to feel again the spray in her face, to be alone with Lance.

Biting her lip, she looked away from the boat at Gareth. He was lounging in his customary position on the chaise longue and was looking through a pair of binoculars at the boat. He looked as handsome as ever, and yet she sensed a change in him. She had been noticing it all morning. When he had been dictating to her there had been a new crispness to his pleasant voice and he had moved about much more, pacing slowly up and down the room without his stick. Looking at him now she could also see a different, more determined set to his mouth. There was a brightness, a sharpness about him that had been lacking before. It was as if he had been half-asleep during the previous weeks and now he had woken up to reveal his true vitality.

As she watched him, wondering what had brought about the change, he lowered the binoculars and turned to smile at her.

"Alison is at the helm," he said. "She'll be enjoying that. She loves to be in control, in the position of command. Do this, Gareth, do that. Ach, she was here on Monday and again on Tuesday, telling me how to exercise my leg." He gave a self-deprecatory laugh, and added, "And the annoying thing is I find myself doing what she says when she isn't here."

"With results," said Juliet quietly. "You're walking much better. I believe her intentions are good even if she does seem to be bossy. Like Lance, she would like to see you walking properly again."

He glanced at her sharply.

"You didn't get lost and you didn't have an accident while you were away, but something happened, because you're not the same," he accused gently.

"Yes, I am," she asserted vigorously. In what way had she betrayed herself? When had she revealed that since that moonlit night at Elstone she had changed too? "I'm still the same silly Juliet with a hopelessly romantic outlook on life. What makes you think I'm different?"

He gazed out at the boat again with a faint puzzled frown between his eyes.

"A feeling, a faint flicker of intuition, call it what you will, that I had when you walked in yesterday afternoon with Lance. You're more wary of him than ever, but you don't hate his guts anymore, to use his own inelegant phrase. What happened while you were away?"

She sat very still, aware that his attitude was quite different from the one he had shown on Sunday afternoon when she had returned from Dana Island. This time he wasn't angry, just puzzled and interested.

"Very little," she replied. "Graham Lee showed me the Hill of Caves and—"

But he didn't allow her to go on.

"Graham Lee?" he interjected. "His wife was a friend of Moira's at one time. They were students together. Moira used to visit her often when she went over to Edinburgh to shop. Sometimes she'd stay there overnight. But during the past few years she stopped going. I think they may have had a disagreement over something."

While Juliet was busy digesting this piece of information Vinnie bustled out onto the terrace and whipped the tray from the table, then turned around and snapped, "Don't think you're going to sit there all day sunning yourself, miss. I could do with Maree taking off my hands. She's a wee divil this morning, in and out of the kitchen stealing my scones and biscuits, upsetting a pint of milk on the floor. Ach, the child's wild about something."

"I'll come at once," said Juliet, starting to her feet.

"Wait," ordered Gareth. "Vinnie, you have no right to tell Miss Grey what she should be doing. She isn't a kitchen maid. She wasn't brought here to help you."

"Humph, I'm often wondering why she was brought here. It wasn't to work, I can tell you that," snorted the housekeeper, and flounced into the house.

"Lance is back and immediately everyone starts behaving in an irrational manner," complained Gareth irritably. "He's to blame for Maree's wildness. She wanted to go with him and Alison this morning and I was willing to let her go because Alison would be there, but he refused to take her. He said he wanted Alison to himself for a few hours and it was impossible while they stayed on land. At her house there's always her mother or her sister or the dogs, and here there's always some sort of interruption. For once I understood how he felt." He lifted the binoculars to his eyes and looked down the loch again to the distant boat.

"I wonder if he'll manage to find some way of keeping Alison out all night, too," he murmured more to himself than to her.

Juliet recognized the new shock that ripped through her as jealousy, nothing else—jealousy because Alison was alone with Lance on the boat and might not return tonight. Once again she sprang to her feet.

"I'll go and find Maree," she muttered.

But he didn't seem to hear her, being more intent on watching the boat, and as she went through the lounge she couldn't help thinking that before she had gone to Elstone he would not have let her leave the terrace so easily but would have found some reason for her to stay with him until lunchtime.

Maree was only too glad to help pack a picnic lunch and

The Cave of the White Rose

to take Juliet on a fishing expedition to the Black Pool. Having learned how to tie flies and to cast from McVinn she was delighted to have an opportunity to show off her knowledge to a complete novice like Juliet, and she carried the fishing rods and the box containing the flies willingly while Juliet carried the lunch in a small canvas haversack slung over her shoulder.

"Aunty Alison likes fishing, too," she said, as they walked through the woodland on the lower slopes of the hill at the back of the castle. "She says Uncle Lance taught her how to tie flies and how to cast when they were younger. I hope he marries her and then she'll be my real aunt. We had great fun with her while you were away. Even daddy was more fun. She makes him walk without his stick. She doesn't care what she says to him. At first he roared back at her, but then he began to laugh and we all laughed together. Do you think Uncle Lance will marry her?"

He's probably working on that just now, thought Juliet waspishly, but aloud she said only, "I know very little about them, Maree, and it isn't really any of my business. I'm only an employee like Vinnie."

Maree grimaced with disgust.

"That sounds horrid," she complained. "I don't think of either of you like that, and Vinnie isn't an employee, she's one of the family. She used to look after daddy and Uncle Lance and Uncle Jamie when they were boys. She told me she's been more of a mother to them than grannie, especially when they stayed here. She used to make them wash behind their ears, and change their wet clothes so that they wouldn't catch cold, and give them the right sort of food."

"But your grannie looked after them when they were in Glasgow."

"No, she didn't, because they went away to boarding school in Edinburgh. I'm going to boarding school next month." A fierce rebellious expression darkened Maree's face. "I don't want to go. I want to stay here with daddy and Vinnie and you and Aunty Alison."

"If your Aunty Alison marries your uncle she won't be here, because he doesn't live here all the time," said Juliet absently, wondering why the thought of Lance marrying Alison made her feel so wretched.

"I suppose not," sighed Maree regretfully; then with a quick change of mood, her face lighting up with a new idea, she added, "Perhaps daddy could marry her. They seem to like each other quite well even though they argue a lot." Another black frown chased away the light from her face. "But I suppose Uncle Lance wouldn't like that. Oh, dear, grown-ups are so funny. They never seem to see things straight. Everyone says I need a mother to look after me, and Aunty Alison would suit me fine. Here we are at last. Isn't it a perfect spot for fishing? I hope you've made plenty of sandwiches, because I'm awfully hungry."

There was no doubt that the Black Pool was a beautiful place to spend an afternoon. It was about forty yards in width, very deep and dark under bluffs of rock on one side but shallowing steadily to the middle where a ridge of rock stood well out of the water. On the near side it was no deeper than a foot or two and it shallowed to a few inches bordering the gravelly spit on which they stood.

On the steep slopes opposite there were larch and pine trees, a pattern of light and dark green, while over all arched the blue sky, specked with little puffs of white cloud. The whole place was full of warm, lazy, dappled light and Juliet felt remote and safe there in the wide hollow of the hills, as she concentrated on learning how to tie a fly correctly and how to cast it, so that it lay on top of the water, a small delicate smudge of color to tantalize the fish lurking in the shadowy depths of the pool.

The afternoon passed pleasantly and she forgot for a while the thoughts that had been tormenting her ever since she had left Lance by the old chapel in the moonlight, and it was not until she and Maree were returning downhill to the castle and she caught sight of the blue boat running up the loch under full sail, its striped spinnaker billowing out in front, that the turmoil started up again.

While she washed and changed for dinner she took herself to task. Why should she feel jealous of Alison Coates? Why should she be suffering this deep-seated envy? It

The Cave of the White Rose

wasn't as if she were in love with Lance any more than she was in love with Gareth.

Not in love with Gareth! Juliet sank down on the edge of her bed and stared at the sea-green ribbon that she held in her hand and was going to use to tie her hair back. It matched exactly the color of the dress she had worn at Hilary's wedding and had decided to wear in an effort to boost her spirits.

But now this strange thought coming out of the chaos of her mind made her pause. She wasn't in love with Gareth! For a while she had been infatuated with him, a quite natural development for someone as lonely as herself on meeting someone as charming and as handsome as he was. It had been a feeling similar to a schoolgirl crush. To her romantic mind he had represented a stricken knight, straight out of a fairy tale, who had required help and comfort, and she had been ready to give him both.

But the infatuation had died while she had been away at Elstone and she suspected it had begun to fade earlier, possibly in a cave on an island. She didn't love him and even if he asked her, as Mrs. Crimond and Lance both hoped he would, she couldn't marry him. She couldn't marry him because she couldn't bear to have Lance as her brother-in-law.

She made a little sound of distress and going hurriedly to the mirror she tied up her hair and fled from the bedroom down the wheel stair, her long skirt billowing out behind her, through the joining passage into the lounge, where the sound of laughter greeted her and she was no longer alone.

Everyone was in the lounge. Alison was there, her red head like a flaming torch against Lance's dark sweater as she laughed up at him. Laura and Jamie were there, trying to sit together in one armchair. Gareth was there, lounging on the settee, his eyes bright as he looked at Alison and Lance. Mrs. Crimond was there smiling happily, enjoying the unusual moment of harmony in her family and Maree was there, hair brushed, face scrubbed, linking her arm affectionately through Alison's.

It was a family gathering and for a moment Juliet, hovering inside the door, felt forlorn, left out. She didn't belong, and she wasn't needed now that they had Alison.

Then across the red hair Lance's eyes met hers. His cool glance swept over the sea-green dress and then back to her troubled face. He moved away from Alison and came across to her.

"The return of the white rose," he murmured. "I wondered where you'd gone. Come and join us. We're having a premature celebration of Laura and Jamie's engagement."

She ignored the hand he held out to her and walked past him, her face pale and taut, her head held high.

"Yes, come and have a drink," said Jamie, struggling out of the chair in which he seemed to have been tightly wedged beside Laura.

"Champagne, of course. Lance said nothing else would do for a celebration of this sort. I hope you like it."

"Yes, she likes it, don't you, Juliet?"

Lance was beside her again, taking the glass that Jamie had filled and handing it to her. When he had welcomed her into the room it had been the first time he had spoken to her since she had slapped his face and she found herself wondering suspiciously what lay behind his unexpectedly friendly approach. She made no effort to respond and didn't look at him as she took the proffered glass and murmured her thanks.

"Now that we're all here," said Mrs. Crimond, smiling warmly at Juliet and immediately dispelling that feeling of loneliness that had attacked Juliet on entering the room, "I should like to make another toast. First to Laura and Jamie, wishing them every happiness for the future, then to Alison and Lance, hoping they will soon follow the good example set by these two young people, and then to Juliet and Gareth, hoping that the hard work they are doing together in the mornings will result in a more lasting relationship."

Everyone laughed, raised their glasses and then sipped their drinks. Alison turned and smiled at Lance, then her glance drifted slowly to Juliet, who was still standing beside

The Cave of the White Rose 359

him. The smile still lingering on her mouth, she came across and deliberately stood between them as if to make sure they wouldn't talk to each other, while Jamie chaffed his mother affectionately for trying to push people around as she did the characters in her books.

"But I don't push them around," complained Mrs. Crimond. "They act of their own accord, but occasionally I have to restrain them and point out the way they should be taking."

"Which is what you've just been doing to all of us," he mocked, and immediately a lively argument started between the two of them.

"Maree tells me you've been fishing the Black Pool this afternoon," said Alison to Juliet, "and that you caught your first fish."

"Beginners' luck," taunted Lance, and Alison turned to him.

"I seem to remember you teasing me in just the same way years ago. Why don't we go there tomorrow?"

"Maybe we will, but I'm not promising anything," he replied easily.

"Lance wasn't the only one you used to fish that pool with," put in Gareth, limping up to them. He was without his stick and stood tall, taller than his brother, more handsome in his more colorful slightly flamboyant clothes, looking down at Alison as if they shared a secret. "Do you remember when you fell in the pool and I had to rescue you?"

"I remember," replied Alison, turning to smile at him, and it seemed to Juliet, who was suddenly aware of undercurrents of feeling, that the smile was warmer, more spontaneous when bestowed on Gareth, as Alison remembered another incident that had involved him years ago when they had spent their holidays together.

And all through dinner it was like that, Gareth at his best, his eyes vivid in his thin face as he recalled one escapade after another in which he and Alison, or he and Lance, or all three of them had participated when young. It was inevitable that with his gift for story-telling and mimicry he should outshine his elder brother, and he was really very attractive and very lovable, thought Juliet after laughing at one of the more amusing anecdotes, and one couldn't really blame Alison for giving him all her attention, turning away from Lance on whose left she was sitting.

But as Juliet watched Gareth and Alison share laughter from her own position across the table on Lance's right she became aware of Lance's silence. Normally she wouldn't have thought it unusual for him to be quiet because he rarely talked at the table, but tonight he had at first been more expansive than she had ever known him, so that now his withdrawal from the conversation was more noticeable.

She glanced sideways at him. He didn't seem to be paying much attention to the others at all and looked as if his thoughts were far away and judging by the frown that darkened his face they weren't very pleasant.

A cold chill swept over Juliet. It must have been like this when he had brought Moira home, she thought. He must have sat silently watching and hearing Gareth charm her and win her away from him... and she wondered whether the same situation could repeat itself in the same family. Was it possible that the two brothers were destined to fall in love again with the same woman? With Alison?

There must be something she could do to prevent Alison from hurting Lance as Moira had once hurt him. Perhaps if she made an effort she could draw Gareth's attention away from the lovely vivacious redhead. After all, even if she wasn't in love with him, Gareth had seemed attracted to herself. Acting impulsively she leaned forward across the table and spoke to Gareth, just as Lance roused himself and spoke to Alison, and from then on Juliet managed to hold Gareth's attention until the meal finished.

He walked with her to the lounge from the dining room leaving Alison to come with Lance, and Juliet felt a bittersweet satisfaction in knowing that she had helped Lance indirectly. But when Alison eventually stepped out onto the terrace to join the rest of them, she was alone. She informed them that Lance had been called to the telephone and would come later, but as the evening wore on he never

The Cave of the White Rose

came, and when Maree persuaded Alison to play the piano to her before she went to bed and they both went into the lounge, Gareth followed them.

Juliet knew that she should follow him, but since Jamie and Laura had also left the terrace to go for a walk her good manners wouldn't allow her to leave Mrs. Crimond alone. So she sat on watching the gloaming deepen to night, seeing the stars come out one by one to glitter in the dark blue velvet of the sky, listening with only half an ear to Mrs. Crimond's plans for the party she intended to hold at the weekend when Laura's parents would come to stay at the castle.

After a while she realized that the piano music had stopped. She guessed that Maree had gone to bed, and wondered why Gareth and Alison had not returned to the terrace. Mrs. Crimond rose to her feet.

"We've had a very pleasant evening, one of the best I've known for some time. I wonder where Lance is? It's time he took Alison home. Just peep into the lounge, will you, dear, and see if he's there with her and Gareth."

When Juliet looked into the room she found it dim and empty. Only one lamp was lit close to the piano.

"There's no one there," she reported back to Mrs. Crimond.

"Then Lance has taken her home. Strange that she didn't come to say good-night. Alison is usually so particular about little things like that, but perhaps he hurried her. Well, I suppose we may as well go to bed. Gareth must have gone up already. I think he enjoyed this evening, too. It's a long time since I've seen him so lively. There's such an improvement in him during the past few weeks, which only goes to prove that time is a healer—although I also think I have you to thank, my dear," She patted Juliet's cheek in an affectionate manner. "I'll just take a walk around the garden before going up. It's another beautiful night. The weather has really been remarkable for the last day or so."

She went off down the steps, and Juliet, feeling curiously flat as if she has just witnessed a play to which there had been no climax, went up to her room. Sleepy after her afternoon with the fish, she prepared quickly for bed, sure that she would fall asleep straightaway. But once she had lain down all the evening's events paraded before her and she could not sleep.

She kept thinking about Gareth and his deliberate attempt to monopolize Alison's attention. He had revealed himself to be quite as capable of tormenting others as Lance was. For once their positions had been reversed.

But had Lance been tormented? She hoped not. It was possible that he was too sure of Alison to be worried, and if Mrs. Crimond's assessment of Alison's feelings was correct there was no fear of Lance losing her to Gareth as he had lost Moira. Yet according to Graham Lee, Lance had ended up disliking Moira for what she had done to Gareth.

Juliet twisted restlessly. What was the use of her lying here racking her brains trying to solve a mystery that Lance had no intention of allowing her to solve? And why did it matter so much to her? It would be better if she followed Mrs. Crimond's advice given the other night in the hotel bedroom at Elstone after she had explained she had been unable to extract any more information from Graham about Moira. The older woman had sighed a little and then had said, "If Lance thinks you shouldn't know, then leave it that way. He's often very wise about this sort of thing, so please forget I asked you to find out."

Juliet turned again in bed. Since she couldn't sleep she might as well read. Reading would prevent her from tossing and turning and would perhaps provide her with a new mystery that she would be free to solve.

She swung out of bed, found her dressing gown and pulled it on, and crept barefoot into the passage. The light was still on. Had Lance forgotten to put it off on his way to bed, or was he still with Alison? She dragged her thoughts away from that disturbing direction and flitted silently down the wheel stair.

Lights were also burning in the passageway and in the lounge the light beside the piano was still on. Going straight to the bookcase, she searched the shelves for something that might appeal and eventually chose a light mystery novel.

On her way out of the room she paused to turn off the lamp by the piano and noticed that the curtains at the French window were swaying slightly. The window was still open. Wondering a little at Vinnie's unusual carelessness, to which the burning lights and the open window were witness, she went to close the window.

Outside she could see moonlight reflected on the still water of the loch and tempted by the serenity of the scene she stepped out onto the terrace. Crossing over to the balustrade, she leaned there for a moment, fascinated by the dazzling glitter of silver on the water.

The familiar creak of the springs of the chaise longue, the sound of something being set down on the side table brought her whirling around hand to mouth to stifle a spontaneous cry of alarm.

"Gareth?" she queried nervously.

"Sorry to disappoint you," Lance's voice was lazily sardonic. "Were you expecting to find him here?"

"No, I..." she began, and had to stop because the pounding of her heart made speech difficult. Whenever would she get used to finding him where she least expected him to be? "What are you doing here?" she managed to say at last.

"Sitting thinking," he answered carelessly. As she approached the chaise longue she noticed moonlight reflecting on the glass he had just set down on the table, the glint of his light eyes in his shadowed face as he looked up at her, even the lock of dark hair that had slipped forward. He had been lying on the chaise longue, but as she came near he rose to his feet automatically with those impeccable good manners that either Mrs. Crimond or Vinnie had drummed into all three Crimond brothers.

"Why are you flitting about the house, half-dressed, when you should be in bed?" he asked.

"I'm not half-dressed," she retorted defensively, curving her arms around her waist to hold her dressing gown closer to her body.

"I think you are," he drawled, and she was suddenly glad

there wasn't much light on the terrace. "You must be finding it chilly out here in your bare feet. Do you often wander through the house at night?"

"No, of course not," she snapped, wishing she hadn't seen the open window and hadn't been tempted to step out onto the terrace.

"Then if you haven't a secret assignation with Gareth and you're not walking in your sleep, what are you doing here? I won't flatter myself by thinking you've come down in the hopes of meeting me."

There was an insolent kick to all his comments that roused her temper.

"I don't make assignations," she replied haughtily. "I came to get a book to read because I couldn't sleep. I noticed the window was open, so I came to close it and was tempted to come out on the terrace to see the moonlight on the water."

"Another night for lovers, but a little wasted on you and me, don't you think? You don't like being kissed by me and I don't like having my face slapped," he remarked acidly, and her cheeks flamed at his reference to the last time they had been alone together in the moonlight. "So you couldn't sleep," he continued. "Because Gareth seemed to pefer Alison's charms to yours this evening, perhaps?"

What a foul mood he was in! She couldn't let him get away with a sneer like that even though she wanted to turn and run from his scorn.

"Perhaps it's because she seemed to prefer his charms to yours that you're here, sitting thinking," her glance went deliberately to the empty glass, and she added in mimicry of his own acidity, "and drinking."

But as usual he seemed to find her attempt to taunt him amusing. He put his head back and laughed making her want to slap him again.

"Well done," he mocked. "But you're wrong. My reason for sitting out here and thinking and drinking is not as romantic as you would like to think. Like you I was tempted out by the moonlight to enjoy an hour or so of peace. Unfortunately tonight business reared its ugly head and tomorrow I have to return to work. There are contracts to be signed and appointments to be kept."

"And money to be made," she put in tartly, and he laughed again.

"That too," he agreed, then added almost wistfully, "And just now I don't want to leave Castle Ross."

He didn't want to go because of Alison, she thought, but her own first reaction to the news that he was going away was one of immense relief. She would be free at last from the eagle gaze, and the castle would return to normal, become once again the oasis of peaceful gracious living that she had known before he had arrived.

But hard on the heels of that first reaction came another. He was going and she might never see him again.

"Do I sense a feeling of relief on your part?" he gibed. "Perhaps I ought to warn you that I'll be back later in September to take the boat around to the Clyde to have it hauled out for the winter."

"I shall be gone before then," Juliet replied, surprising herself as well as him. She wasn't sure when she had come to the decision that she must leave or why she had made it.

"Am I to regard that as formal notice of leaving your position as Tess's secretary?" he asked coldly.

"Yes, I think so," she replied uncertainly.

"You think so? You're not sure? Does that mean you spoke on the spur of the moment, acting on a silly impulse? You'd better be sure, Juliet, because I've no time for ditherers," he snapped.

"Oh, yes, I'd forgotten you're cold-blooded and businesslike and rarely give in to impulse yourself, so how can I expect you to understand?" she retorted. "Yes, I intend to leave."

"May I ask why?" He was scrupulously polite suddenly, having withdrawn behind that icy film.

Desperately she searched for a reason that would not betray her real feelings, about which she was in a state of confusion anyway.

"I don't get on with Vinnie," she said vaguely.

"You don't—" he began incredulously. "Good God, do

you really expect me to swallow that excuse?" he exclaimed, politeness cast aside. "Everyone gets on with Vinnie."

"Well, I don't—at least she doesn't get on with me. She dislikes me for some reason, and goes out of her way to make me feel unwanted and unnecessary here. Only this morning she said she couldn't understand why I'm employed here. There are times when I don't understand either. Actually there's very little for me to do and—"

"If Vinnie's attitude is all that's upsetting you," he interrupted coldly, cutting across her tumbling words, "I'll speak to her and get her off your back."

"Oh, no!" She was dismayed now and feeling a little shaky. She hadn't bargained for this sort of confrontation with him at this hour of the night, or rather the early morning, and was beginning to wish she had turned right around and left the terrace when she had discovered he was there. "Please don't take her to task. She resents it terribly when you do, although she says she doesn't. But I know she does because the whole household suffers as a result."

"Does it, indeed?" he commented dryly. "Then it will have to suffer, because I'm not having her thinking she can say what she likes to you, and I can't understand why she thinks you're not needed. Mother needs you, and Maree...."

"Maree has Alison now, and will be going to school soon. She doesn't need me."

He was silent for a second or two, looking down at her, trying to read the expression on her face, which was bleached by moonlight.

"Gareth needs you," he suggested quietly.

"I doubt it. Alison has done more for him than I have. She has made him walk."

Again he was silent. Then turning away he walked over to the balustrade and stood looking out over the loch.

"You said the other day that the decision to leave or to stay was mine," she said, in a small voice, aware that her last remark concerning Alison had gone home and had hurt him in some way.

He turned and leaned on the balustrade, his face in the shadow now and unreadable.

"That was because I was angry with you for probing," he replied flatly. "The decision still rests with you and always will, Juliet, but I think you would be very foolish to allow your jealousy of Alison to drive you away from here."

She should have been used to his ability to put his finger on the hub of her thoughts by now, but she wasn't, and her outraged gasp betrayed her. He pushed away from the balustrade and came close to her, his bulk blotting out the radiance of the moon, casting a shadow over her.

"There's no need for you to be jealous of Alison," he said swiftly, confidently. "That little performance put on by Gareth last evening was directed more at me than at you. He was getting his own back for Saturday night. He even went so far as to take her home."

"But how? He told me he couldn't drive, that his leg...." She stopped, bewildered.

"As I've always thought, Gareth's leg isn't paralyzed. He only convinced himself that it was and stopped using it, and indirectly you have helped him to use it. He was so wildly jealous because I kept you out all night on Saturday, quite unintentionally as it happened, and because you went with me to Elstone, that he forced himself to do things he hasn't done for almost three years, in order to get back at me."

"By making you jealous?"

"Exactly. You see there's always been a certain amount of natural jealousy between us, as well as some very healthy rivalry. When we were boys he always wanted what I had and when we grew older it began to apply to girls. I brought them home and he took them over. I think I've told you what a bad effect his accident plus Moira's death had on him. He became so unlike himself, so lethargic and self-pitying, I had to try to do something about it. But nothing I did seemed to have any effect, not even deliberately taunting him."

He paused and drew a deep breath, and she had the impression that having to explain to her was a chore he disliked heartily.

"When I came here to collect mother to take her to London a few months ago I was so disgusted with him that I lost my temper. Mother had suggested he should marry again and he was moaning that no woman these days would settle for a crippled husband who already had a willful wayward child, and I blew my top and told him that I'd find him another wife just as I'd found the last. It wasn't a very nice thing to say, but it got results. For the first time in years he seemed to be himself and he bet me I couldn't find anyone suitable, and it occurred to me that perhaps the one way I could shake him out of his miserable lethargy was to accept the bet and to bring home a girl."

"Me," whispered Juliet.

"Yes, you. The very fact that I'd found you made him interested in you from the start."

"But why me?"

"I must confess that by the time I attended that wedding I was beginning to think that I'd never find anyone suitable. Then I saw you and you looked right. I talked to you and found you were innocent and idealistic, ridiculously romantic in your attitude to marriage, and that seemed right too. I discovered you were out of work and that you were Norma Thomas's daughter. The rest I left to mother."

"Lance will do anything for the members of his family." Graham's remark came back to her. That anything had included selecting her as a suitable second wife for Gareth, persuading his mother to choose her as her secretary so that she could be brought to Castle Ross, and then depending on his brother's charm to do the rest. And it had succeeded, or almost.

"I suppose you think you've won the bet?" she challenged in a low furious voice.

"Not yet. I win only when he asks you to marry him and you accept."

"You're very sure of that happening," she seethed. "You can't make me stay and do that."

"No. I can only rely on my first impression of you. I thought then you had certain qualities, tenderness and a strong sense of loyalty, which would help you to stay the course. Now that I've told you that your reasons for leaving aren't very sound because Vinnie can be dealt with and Alison presents no real threat, I don't think you'll want to leave."

He thought he had trapped her, that he was, as always, right, but there was something over which he had no control.

"You've forgotten something in your calculations," she said on a note of triumph. "People don't fall in love to order just to help others to win bets."

"I'm well aware of that, but what has it to do with you and Gareth?"

"I'm not in love with him," she asserted firmly.

"Oh. Are you sure?" he drawled softly. "Then why are you jealous of Alison?"

The book slipped from her nerveless fingers. Suddenly she was without protection, exposed and vulnerable to his mockery. He bent and picked the book up and held it out.

"Go to bed, Juliet," he ordered quietly, almost kindly, with that sort of indulgent kindness one expected from fathers or grandfathers or uncles, making her want to stamp her feet and scream at him that she preferred his taunts. "None of us are at our best in the small hours of the morning. You'll see everything differently when you've slept. Goodbye for now. I'll expect to see you here when I come again in September."

She took the book from him and fled.

CHAPTER SEVEN

THE ENGAGEMENT PARTY held for Laura and Jamie the following weekend was a great success. Mr. and Mrs. Penny, being slightly overawed by the castle and by Mrs. Crimond, had no objections to their daughter becoming engaged to Jamie as long as the couple didn't marry until Laura had attained her eighteenth birthday. They took both Laura and Jamie back with them to Edinburgh, where Jamie hoped to get better treatment for the cracked bone in his arm.

With their departure coming so closely after Lance's silent and almost unnoticed exit, Juliet fully expected the way of life at the castle to return to the same leisurely pace she had known before Lance had arrived, and to a certain extent it did. Vinnie was pleasant and smiling again and not once did she give Juliet a disapproving glance or make any harsh remarks about her employment there. Mrs. Crimond's story progressed in leaps and bounds so that Juliet typed every afternoon, and Gareth had truly come to life. With the returning use of his leg he was walking more and more without his stick and becoming more independent, often going off by himself somewhere in the station wagon. He spent less time lounging on the terrace and actually talked of leaving the castle once Maree had gone to her boarding school in Edinburgh.

This last suggestion, which he made one evening at dinner, startled his mother.

"But what will you do? Where will you go?" she asked rather querulously.

"I shall go to Edinburgh, too. I shall rent a flat there," he replied confidently.

"All the teaching positions at the university will be filled now," said Mrs. Crimond, a little tremulously. "What will you do for a living?"

"Write," was the succinct reply.

"But you can write here. You are writing here."

"Not as well as I would if I were on my own. To do what I want to do I have to have access to records, government reports, museums. I can live on my allowance out of father's estate as long as Lance doesn't mind footing the bill for Maree's education for a while, until I start earning again."

The change in him was for the better, Juliet could see that now, and she began to understand why Lance had done what he had done, and with understanding came forgiveness. His intention had been good even if his way of achieving it had been a little strange. But as the days went by she realized that there was no chance of his winning his bet with Gareth because it was quite obvious to her that there was no room for her, or any other woman, as far as she could tell, in Gareth's plans for his future. In a way she was relieved because it meant that he wasn't in love with her any more than she was with him, so that there was no possibility of him asking her to marry him, much to Mrs. Crimond's disappointment.

"At one point I really thought you and he might make a go of it," she said. "So much for wishful thinking. I've always been guilty of it. I hope your feelings aren't hurt, Juliet."

"Oh, no. I think we were both attracted to each other at first. I'd never met anyone like him before and he went to my head a little."

"Mm, I understand, and I think you went to his, because for so long he'd cut himself off from the society of pretty young women. I'm glad you're not hurt, although there is something wrong, isn't there?"

"What do you mean?" asked Juliet warily.

"You're not quite the same as you were when I first met you. You're not untouched by the more violent emotions, not so innocent. You look as if someone has woken you up rather rudely."

At that moment the telephone rang. The caller asked for

Mrs. Crimond and Juliet was able to escape upstairs to her bedroom. For all that she seemed so vague Mrs. Crimond noticed far too much, she thought, as she peered out of her window. The weather was heavy and humid. Beneath low cloud the loch lay sullenly smooth, pewter colored. Already it was mid-September and in the few scattered fields the oats and barley had been harvested and stooked. Tomorrow Maree would be leaving for her hated boarding school and Gareth would be going to his flat in Edinburgh and she would be left with Mrs. Crimond to wait for the arrival of Lance.

She must leave before he came, but how? Acting on sudden impulse she left her room and went down to the lounge where she was sure she had seen a local bus timetable. If she could persuade McVinn to take her into Lochmoyhead without saying anything to anyone, she could catch a bus from there to Adrishaig and from there she could go on to Tarbert and get a ferry to Gourock, thence by train to Glasgow, and on to London.

It was while she was leafing through the timetable that she heard the sound of voices raised angrily, followed by the slamming of a door. One voice she recognized as Gareth's in one of his thunder-and-lightning moods, but the other hadn't sounded like Maree's, more like Alison's. Juliet frowned as she traced with her finger the times of buses leaving Lochmoyhead. They weren't very frequent. One every other day, in fact.

Hearing a sound, she looked up. Alison had come into the lounge and not noticing her had sunk down on the arm of a chair. She was blowing her nose and the tears were streaming down her face. Sympathy, a quality of which Juliet had a superabundance, surged up and flinging down the timetable she went across to the weeping woman.

"Alison, what's wrong? Is there anything I can do to help?"

Alison spun around. Her topaz eyes blazed through her tears.

"Oh, it's you! Yes, you can help—by going away, far away, back to where you came from before Lance picked

The Cave of the White Rose

you up. He has a tendency to pick up stray cats, you know, because he's sorry for them and wants to give them a home."

Although Juliet stiffened all over in reaction to the insult that had just been hurled at her she was determined to keep her cool, realizing that Alison was very upset.

"Why do you want me to go?" she asked mildly. "What have I done to harm you?"

"You've taken Gareth away from me," wailed Alison, "just as Moira did."

"But... but I thought you were in love with Lance and going to marry him."

"Me in love with that iceberg? No, never. Oh, I like Lance well enough, but I've always loved Gareth and we might have married if Lance hadn't brought Moira home just as he brought you, and I hoped when I heard that she'd died that there was a chance he might ...." Alison started to sob noisily and Juliet had to wait for the sobs to subside before she could make herself heard.

"Gareth doesn't love me," she said quietly, when Alison had stopped crying and was just sniffing.

"But you're going with him to Edinburgh," said Alison, her eyes wide.

"No. I'm staying here with Mrs. Crimond. I'm employed to work for her, you know."

"Yes, I know," muttered Alison, pulling at her handkerchief nervously, then with a fresh burst of tears she cried out, "Oh, what have I done, what have I done?"

"Alison, please, you'll make yourself ill," pleaded Juliet, who was really perturbed by the other woman's anguish. "You'd better tell me what you've done."

"I told him about Moira. I told him how she cheated and lied to him, how she used to say she'd gone to stay with friends when all the time she was with other men. I told him that it was her fault his leg didn't get better because it suited her to have him immobile while she could go and enjoy herself. I told him that she wasn't with Lance that time she was stuck for three days in the Cairngorms, nor was she with him when she was killed. He used to let her go when she said she was going with Lance, because he trusted Lance, and all those years he trusted her and she ended by destroying his trust in his brother."

"But how did you know all this?" asked Juliet.

"I knew because Helen Lee told me when I met her recently. When I met Lance he told me I wasn't to say anything to Gareth about it because Gareth still thought Moira was perfect and that it would break his heart to learn differently."

"Then why did you tell him now?"

"Oh, because he's going away, because he wouldn't take any notice of me, and because I thought I was afraid the same thing was going to happen all over again with you in Moira's place, because I know you don't love Gareth. It's Lance who fascinates you, isn't it? But like Moira you'd marry second best just to get a comfortable home."

"Alison, stop it. Please!"

Alison sniffed, looked up into Juliet's troubled eyes and apologized.

"I'm sorry, I shouldn't have said that. I'm in such a state I don't know what I'm saying anymore. Oh, my poor Gareth! His face when I told him. What am I going to do?"

"You're going back to him and you're going to apologize to him as you've just apologized to me," said Juliet firmly. "Tell him your own strong feelings for him carried you away, made you say unkind things. Tell him you love him, but for goodness' sake, go back to him now."

"Excuse me, miss," Vinnie spoke from the doorway, and it was quite obvious from the gleam in her black eyes that she had heard every word Juliet had just said, "have you seen Maree? It's getting late and there's a heavy mist on the hills. It's time she was in and packing her clothes ready for tomorrow."

"No, I haven't seen her. Have you, Alison?"

"She was with Gareth and me. We were talking about her going to school, and she suddenly jumped up and ran out of the room."

"That'll be the root of it, I shouldn't wonder," sighed Vinnie, and her plump face looked aged with worry. "She's

The Cave of the White Rose

run off because she doesn't want to go. Ach, I'm getting old and I can't be doing with tantrums and willfulness anymore. Would you mind going and looking for her, miss? McVinn is away to Tarbert all day or I'd be asking him. If she gets lost in the mist Mr. Gareth and Mr. Lance will never forgive me."

"Mr. Gareth should be going to look for his own child," said Alison, rising to her feet. "I'll go and tell him."

"I've been already, but he's not in a good mood. Ach, it's one of those days when a body can't be saying or doing the right thing."

"It's all right, Vinnie, I'll go," comforted Juliet. "I'll find her. She won't be far away."

"That's good of you, miss. There was a time when I was thinking you were another come to wreck yon man's peace of mind like the other one did, but now I know I was wrong." Then turning to Alison she said, "Aye, lass, you go along to him and tell him. He needs someone like you, Miss Alison."

As the housekeeper left the room muttering to herself Alison and Juliet stared at one another.

"Perhaps I'd better come with you to look for Maree," began Alison uncertainly.

"No, you go to Gareth. Only you can put it right. Don't you see, Alison?"

"I hope you're right. I do hope you're right. But be careful on the hills. Don't get lost. Maree knows her way blindfolded by now, I should think, but you don't. Make for the Black Pool. That's her favorite place, as it used to be for all of us when we were in trouble or unhappy."

JULIET REMEMBERED Alison's warning later when, blindfolded by the thick clinging mist, unable to see her way and unsure of her whereabouts, she stood ankle deep in bog myrtle and admitted to herself that she was lost.

When she had left the castle she had taken Alison's advice and had started off toward the Black Pool. At first she had had no trouble as only an occasional wreath of mist had twisted across the path as she had climbed higher and higher, keeping the sound of the tumbling river to her left. Every so often she had called Maree's name and had waited for an answer, until the thought had occurred to her that if Maree didn't want to be found she wouldn't answer.

What was the use of searching for the girl if she didn't want to be found? With her knowledge of the area Maree would have many hiding places where she could stay until hunger drove her down to the castle. Or was it possible that she had run away properly, walking to Lochmoyhead and taking the bus or hitching a lift somewhere, anywhere as long as she didn't have to go to the school in Edinburgh?

It was while she had been thinking that the mist had come down in earnest and she had decided then she had better go back to the castle, when she discovered that she had no idea which way she should go. She had thought she could hear the river's song to her left, and that if she walked toward the sound she could keep close to it, walk downhill and eventually come out on the road leading from Lochmoyhead to the castle. But she hadn't found the river again, so she had begun to walk downhill anyway, and as she had walked the stories Gareth had told her about people being lost for whole days and nights on the hills and of some who had never been found because they had walked into bogs came to haunt her. For a while she had been unable to go any farther, thinking that if she did she might step into one of those deceitful patches of green and become its captive.

A little later the mist had lifted helpfully and she had caught sight of the old bothy, which she recognized from the time she had gone fishing with Maree. The sight of it cheered her, and glad to have some sort of bearings at last, she had started down the hill again.

But the mist had come back obliterating everything. She had trudged on doggedly, tumbling over unseen tussocks of grass, turning her ankle painfully on a hidden rock. Her hair clung to her head damply and the lower part of her legs and her feet were soaking wet.

It was when she had heard, or had thought she had heard, a voice calling her name that she had stopped again. Had she heard it or was it her imagination playing tricks?

The Cave of the White Rose

Once more Gareth's stories crowded into her mind and she had recalled his advice not to move if the mist came down but to sit and wait. If something called to her she wasn't to move but was to stay still, for if she wandered in the mist, the mist would hang about her and she would never find her way. Never, never was she to obey voices that she heard calling.

So she had taken that remembered advice and had stayed put in the middle of a moor and had admitted she was lost.

Soon she began to shiver. If only, she thought, she had stopped when she had seen the bothy. And quite suddenly, as if in answer to her thought, the mist lifted uncannily and she saw the sky pricked with stars and the dark angular outline of the bothy ahead.

She didn't stop to wonder why it was in front of her and not behind her but hurried toward it while she could see it, hobbling a little because she had developed a blister on the back of one of her heels.

Reaching the door, she groped her way into the limewashed building, which consisted of a single room. When her eyes had become accustomed to the gloom she found that it was furnished by a table and two chairs and sitting down thankfully on one of the chairs she decided to stay there and wait.

By now everyone at Castle Ross must be wondering where she was and why she hadn't returned with Maree. Would Gareth organize a search party to look for them? Or would he be too unhappy, too sunk in misery to spare a thought for either her or his daughter? Not if Alison had been successful he wouldn't. How silly of her not to have noticed that Alison was in love with Gareth. Did Lance know she was, or was it a shock in store for him?

The intrusion of Lance into her thoughts set her moving. She had discovered during the past weeks that the only way to avoid thinking about him was to do something, anything. Now she hobbled to the door and looked out. The mist was back, blotting out the starry sky, reducing visibility to nothing.

Juliet hobbled back to her chair and had hardly sat down

when she thought she heard her name being called. It must be the voice of the mist calling her again. She wouldn't go to the door again. She wouldn't go out, because if she did she would get lost.

"There are more ways of getting lost than falling down a pothole." Graham had said that. He had also said that if she had been his property he wouldn't have let her go roaming the countryside with Lance. She knew now what he had meant. She had gone to Dana with Lance, had gone to the caves with him and had got lost forever.

"Juliet!" The voice was nearer, at the door of the bothy, and it sounded very irritable and very human. Juliet raised her head and blinked at the dazzling beam of a powerful flashlight. Behind the flashlight loomed the head and shoulders of a man.

"Lance!" she exclaimed, and rising to her feet hobbled toward him. "Oh, Lance, I thought I was lost forever!"

She was in his arms and sobbing against the tweed of his jacket, crying because she was glad to see him, because he had come to find her. He held her silently, saying no words of comfort or endearment, but she could feel his hand on her head and then his fingers stroking her hair back from her face, touching the tears on her face.

At last her sobs subsided and he pushed her away from him, making her stand by herself. The beam of the flashlight flickered around the bothy as he inspected it and he asked curtly, "Why didn't you answer when I called your name?"

"I thought it was the voice of the mist."

"Voice of the mist? What the hell is that?" He sounded very cross and tired and her heart began to sink.

"Gareth told me that the mist has a voice that calls people to destruction and that you mustn't answer when it calls, or try to follow it, but stay put until the mist lifts and you can see your way."

"Trust Gareth to have some nerve-racking tale like that to tell," he grumbled.

"But it worked. I stayed put when I heard voices calling, and if I hadn't you wouldn't have found me."

"I suppose that's one way of looking at it, but it would have been a damned sight quicker if you'd answered me. I've been calling you for the best part of an hour. I caught a glimpse of you when the mist lifted temporarily. Since then I've been following, or hoped I was following you. You have a hopeless sense of direction. You've been going around in circles. Let's sit down," he added practically.

"But aren't we going back to the castle?" she asked as he pushed her into a chair and then pulled himself up onto the table. He stood the flashlight on the table so that its beam shone on the grimy whitewashed ceiling and reflected some light downward. She could see him quite clearly, the bold nose, the contradictory mouth, the damp dark hair straggling over his forehead, and after several weeks of not seeing him she felt quite weak inside.

"Not yet. I'm tired and I notice that you're limping. Also the mist is still bad," he replied. "If we have to stay the night it won't be the first time we've stayed out together."

He slanted a sardonic glance in her direction, but she managed to keep her face expressionless.

"Also, while we're alone and undisturbed," he added, "I'd be glad if you'd explain what's been going on at the castle today. I arrived tonight after the worst drive I've ever had through the hills to find everyone in a state of flap. Vinnie seemed to have lost her wits and kept rocking herself back and forth and muttering about her poor darling Maree being lost and how she should never have sent you out after her. Alison looked as if she'd shed enough tears to fill a reservoir. Gareth was locked in his room and wouldn't come out. In fact mother was the calmest of all, but then she didn't know what had happened either. Then to make things worse, Maree walked in without you, so I came to look for you. Now tell me what's wrong with Gareth."

"Didn't Alison tell you?" she asked warily.

"No. Maybe she was going to, but I didn't stop to listen when I realized you were out on the hills and probably lost."

"She told him about Moira."

"Why?" he rapped.

"She was angry because he's going away to Edinburgh and she thought I was going with him. You see—" this was going to be the most difficult part of all, telling him "—she's in love with him," she added in a low voice.

He was very still and very quiet sitting there on his hands staring at the floor of the bothy and not seeing it.

"And are you going with him to Edinburgh?" he asked, rather diffidently, she thought.

"No. He and I...I told you people can't love to order," she said in a rush.

"So you did," he replied heavily. "I knew that he was going because he telephoned me. No one was more delighted than I was to hear that at last he'd come alive again. Does he know how Alison feels about him?"

"I don't know. I told her to go back and apologize to him for losing her temper and to tell him she loved him."

"Maybe she tried and he wouldn't let her in." He swore softly. "Alison has always had trouble with her temper and it's often led her into saying what she shouldn't. If she hadn't lost it years ago it's possible Gareth wouldn't have married Moira."

"Is it true what she said about Moira—about her being unfaithful and encouraging him to regard himself as a cripple for life?"

"Yes, it is." Again there was a heaviness in his voice as if he was tired of the whole business, and longed to be away like an eagle soaring freely on the wind. "And you have Alison to thank for unwittingly solving your mystery for you."

"Not all of it. I still don't understand why you kept the truth from him and let him think badly of you instead."

"You know I met Moira first and was sufficiently attracted to her to bring her home?" he asked.

"Yes. I suppose she was a stray cat."

"What's that?" he demanded roughly.

"Alison said you were always bringing home stray cats. She said I was one."

"It's a pity some women can't keep their mouths shut," Lance grated. "All right, I brought home a stray cat who turned out to be more of a tigress so that I wanted nothing more to do with her. But by then the damage was done and when my back was turned she went hunting Gareth. I was in Canada when the news came that she and Gareth were engaged. I wrote to him telling him he was a fool, but it had no effect. The invitation to the wedding came in the next post. Moira lost no time. I hadn't been working out there very long. I couldn't get leave, so I threw up my job and flew home, arriving on the day of the wedding. I tried to stop it." He drew a sharp breath through gritted teeth. "The foolish quixotic things one does in one's youth," he murmured, in self-disparagement. "Everyone got the wrong idea, including my mother. They all thought I was in love with Moira and that I was jealous because she was marrying Gareth. I went to the wedding, and then caught the next plane back to Canada to hunt for another job. I couldn't bear to stay and see him being made a fool of."

"But you came back later and helped to make a fool of him," she accused.

"That was how it looked," he agreed somberly. "That was how she arranged it to look. I was shocked by the bad effect his accident had on him, and I began to realize it was her fault and I was fool enough to take her out of his way once or twice in the hopes that he'd react. She didn't want him to recover. While he was disabled she could go off where she liked and with whom she liked—and believe me, she was never very particular with whom she went."

"Did you take her to Chamonix?"

"No. She told Gareth she was going with me. She'd been telling him she'd been going with me for some time, but it didn't dawn on me what she'd been doing until I arrived at Chamonix and met her there. She was with a man. They were staying at another hotel. She came to see me and tried to persuade me not to tell Gareth about her latest little affair, but I refused. Next day she went up into the mountains and while she was up there she went skiing in spite of a warning. You know what happened after that—Graham told you. I took part in the rescue operation and made arrangements for her body to be flown home. I was going to tell

Gareth everything, then I realized that he wasn't surprised I'd been there with her. She had told him she was going with me, and he trusted her with me. There was nothing I could say at a time like that when he was so grief stricken, so I left it."

"And let him go on believing she was perfect. That was why you didn't want me to find out what she'd done to him in case I told him."

"Yes, and yet I've often wondered since whether I should have told him, whether it would have been kinder in the end." Lance shrugged his shoulders. "Well, it's over now. Alison's spilled the beans and ten to one he'll blame me for not having told him before."

"I'm glad she spilled the beans," said Juliet.

"Glad, when you realize what Gareth must have gone through in the past few hours?"

"I wasn't thinking of him, I was thinking of you."

"I'm afraid I don't understand."

"Now you'll be able to put yourself first, you won't have to shield and protect Gareth anymore from the truth about Moira," she explained.

"I'm sorry, Juliet, but I'm not with you. Perhaps I'm more tired than I thought. The last weeks have been particularly hectic. I've been traveling a lot and I haven't caught up on my sleep. I was hoping that...but I guess I was mistaken...." He slid off the table and walked over to the door muttering, "I'll see if the weather is improving."

He had come hoping to have a few days' rest with Alison, and what had he found, thought Juliet. Alison in tears because she thought she had lost Gareth for the second time. Alison in love with Gareth and not with himself. What a blow to his hopes! No wonder he sounded dispirited.

But he hadn't stayed at the castle to comfort Alison. He had left her, and tired as he was, he had come through the mist to look for herself. She recalled the excited leap of her heart when she had recognized him standing in the doorway of the bothy. Was it possible she was in love too? In love with this enigmatic man who was so strangely quixotic in his own way?

"It's better outside," he said, coming back to the table. "Are you willing to risk it? Much as I'd like to spend the night here with you I'm concerned about Gareth."

"There you go again," Juliet blurted, suddenly angry with him. "Putting him first instead of yourself. If you'd really like to spend the night here with me, why don't you?"

Her heart was beating madly. Never had she thought she would say such a thing to a man before!

She could tell by the glance that Lance flashed in her direction that he was startled. But he wasn't at a loss for long. He half sat on the table and leaned toward her.

"Sounds as if you're trying to seduce me, Juliet Grey," he accused.

It was her turn to be startled. She hadn't realized how her suggestion might appear to him.

"I suppose it does," she replied shakily.

"And do you think that's the way a sweet innocent girl like you should behave?"

"Oh, you're worse than Gareth at putting people on a pedestal. What makes you think I'm so innocent?"

"The look in your eyes, the shake in your voice." He reached out a hand suddenly and touched her side under her left armpit. "The frantic beating of your heart. You've never behaved like this before, and I'm wondering why I'm the target."

"I thought you'd be able to guess, with those magical powers you have," she countered.

"It's difficult to read a person's face in a dim light," he mocked.

"There are other ways of finding out," she whispered.

"Juliet, do you know what you're doing and saying?"

"Yes, I know. Thank you for coming to look for me. I've never been more glad to see anyone than I was to see you."

It wasn't far to reach his cheek. Her kiss was featherlight, but it had the effect of dynamite.

"You mustn't do things like that," he warned roughly.

"Why not?"

"Because it's bound to lead to something like this," he

retorted, and once again she felt the ruthlessness of his mouth on hers as he leaned forward and kissed her. A little later he asked, dryly, "Are you going to slap my face?"

"No, because this time I think you mean it."

"I meant it then. I told you I wanted to kiss you. I'd been wanting to kiss you ever since we tangled in the Cave of the White Rose. I did my best to keep my distance, thinking that it wouldn't do for me to fall in love with you if you loved my brother and if he loved you, but after dancing with you I couldn't help myself—and was socked on the jaw rather violently as a result."

"Oh, I didn't mean to hurt you and I was sorry afterward— but you see I thought you were doing it deliberately to stop me from going back and finding Graham," exclaimed Juliet contritely. "How foolish you must think me!"

"So foolish that I don't think I can let you wander about the world unprotected anymore. You'll have to stay where I can keep an eye on you. You'll have to come and live with me."

She eyed him doubtfully.

"Do you think that would be right?" she queried, and saw him grin.

"Yes, it will be right because I shall marry you first," he replied. "Which proves I must be in love with you, because I've never considered marrying anyone before. Have you ever been in love before?"

"How do you know I'm in love with you now?" she parried.

"I thought you might be the last time we talked together when you were quite obviously jealous of Alison but admitted you weren't in love with Gareth."

"Oh, you!" she began furiously. "Then why didn't you tell me you had fallen in love with me?"

"Because the time wasn't right. I wasn't sure, and you were all confused and hadn't long left off disliking me—and my cheek was still sore after being slapped."

"Are you sure now?" she asked curiously.

"Yes, I wouldn't have set out to scour the misty moors in search of a white rose to take home with me, if I wasn't sure," he murmured, taking her hand and pulling her to her feet. "But let's stop beating about the bush. Will you marry me, Juliet?"

"Yes, I think so."

"Only think so?"

"Yes, you see I'm not sure how to recognize when I'm in love."

"It gets easier with practice," he said with a ghost of a laugh, pulling her into his arms and trailing his lips across her cheek to her ear, which he bit gently. "And I promise to give you plenty of practice. But now we must go back to the castle and try to help Gareth and Alison. I have a feeling he might turn to her eventually, but first he has to recover his self-confidence fully and enjoy a little freedom of movement. Do you understand?"

"I understand," Juliet answered soberly, and then suddenly she flung her arms around him and cried, "Oh, Lance, I do love you, and I want to stay with you forever."

"Good. You're catching on fast," he murmured, hugging her gently. Then taking her by the hand he led her out of the bothy into the soft starlit night in which there was no sign of mist, and down the hill to the castle.

THE TAMING OF LISA

The Taming of Lisa

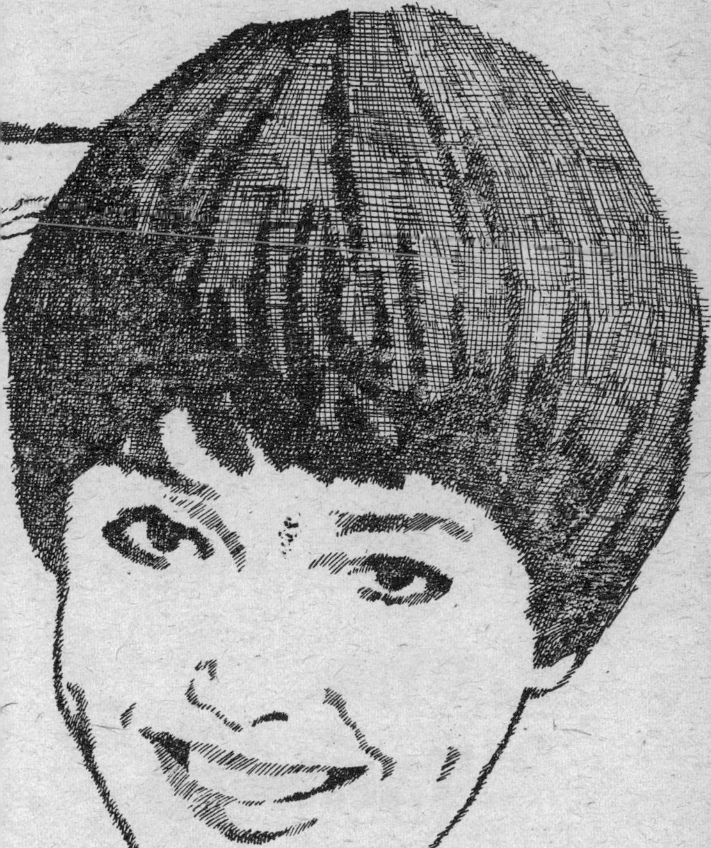

Lisa rushed to the aid of her elderly aunt, who claimed she was being harassed to sell her family home.

But Lisa soon discovered that Fraser Lamont, the would-be buyer, wasn't the archenemy she'd imagined. She was quick to see that within the tough, self-contained character was a proud and lonely man.

Now she was caught in a strange feud—and falling in love with Fraser only seemed to make matters worse.

CHAPTER ONE

ELISABETH ROY SMITH clutched her briefcase, a shopping bag and a bunch of chrysanthemums in one arm, and fitted the key into the lock of the door of the flat where she lived. The key turned quite easily, but as usual the door did not open until she had pushed a shoulder against it. Then it opened suddenly and she almost fell into the small hallway, landing with a crash against the wall.

"Is that you, Lisa?" called a voice from the living room.

"Who else?" she called back. Who else but she would make such a rowdy uncontrolled entrance?

Kicking the door shut with a backward flick of one shapely booted leg, she went into the big room and deposited her load on the old-fashioned round walnut table that was already cluttered with examples of handmade pottery. At the table sat a small fair-haired girl of about twenty-two. She was dressed in a multicolored smock and was bending over a classically shaped pottery jug on which she was painting a design with sure quick strokes of a thick brush. She looked up, saw the dark red shaggy blooms of the chrysanthemums, and her eyes widened.

"Who are those for?" she asked.

Lisa, who had been slipping off her long brown coat and tossing it carelessly over one of the armchairs, pulled off her emerald green crocheted beret, threw it on top of the coat and came across to the table. Picking up the flowers, she presented them to the fair girl with a theatrical flourish.

"For you. I thought they might cheer you up. Also, I couldn't resist the color. Aren't they gorgeous?"

"Mmm." Mandy Atkins sniffed the shaggy blossoms and then held them at arm's length to admire them. Her gaze passed from the flowers to Lisa, who stood tall and willowy in her midi-length tweed skirt and emerald green sweater. Her cunningly cut straight dark red hair fell in a fringe over her white forehead. Beneath the fringe, dark eloquent eyebrows slanted above hazel eyes that twinkled and danced, their expression indicative of the warm lively nature of their owner.

"You're like one of them yourself," Mandy remarked impulsively. "Earthy and exotic at the same time."

Lisa raised her eyebrows in surprise, and unusual color stained her high cheekbones.

"I don't mind being considered exotic even though I'm not, but I think I draw the line at earthy," she said, glancing down at the clean straight lines of her body outlined by the clinging sweater and skirt. "Do I look as if I grub in the earth for a living?"

"I didn't mean it like that," replied Mandy with a chuckle as she began to place the flowers in a big stoneware jar. "For me earthy means rich browns, glinting greens, burning bronzes, russet reds—your colors."

Lisa's ever changing eyes deepened to brown as their expression softened, and she put an arm around her friend's slim shoulders and hugged her.

"Thanks for the compliment. I should have known you meant color. Have you done much today?" she asked, waving her hand in the direction of the pottery.

Mandy sighed and grimaced. "Not as much as I would have liked. It seems to take ages to throw off the effects of flu. Aren't you home early?"

Lisa twisted away restlessly and walked to the big bay window to stare out at the gray November sky.

"Yes. Hatton and I had a disagreement, so I walked out," she said in a taut voice.

Hatton's Limited was a company that designed and manufactured women's clothing. Lisa had worked there for two years ever since she had left the College of Art. The company was well-known for its original and stylish clothes and for the high quality and finish of its articles. Lisa, who had been trained in dress design, had been considered extremely lucky by her friends when she had landed a job with the company, but her association with her immediate superior, Richard Hatton, the chief designer, had been stormy and marked by frequent clashes of temperament, culminating in her walkout this afternoon.

"Are you going back?" asked Mandy curiously. Possessing a fairly placid temperament, she was rarely surprised by the actions of her warmhearted impulsive friend.

"Not even if he comes and asks me on his bended knees," replied Lisa fiercely.

The thought of the impeccable, slightly supercilious Richard Hatton on his knees in front of Lisa was too much for Mandy's sense of humor, and she began to laugh. "You can hardly expect him to do that," she said.

"Why not?" demanded Lisa, swinging around, her eyes ablaze with strong emotion. "That's where he'd like to see me. Nothing would please him more than to see me groveling in the dust apologizing, asking him to give me my job back and admitting that he was right after all."

"You didn't tell him he was wrong?" exclaimed Mandy. "That was scarcely tactful of you."

"He wasn't tactful with me, so why should I be tactful with him? He criticized one of my designs and I told him it would sell like hotcakes. So he asked me what I knew about marketing. I told him and he didn't like it. Yet if the suggestions and criticism had been made by Johnny Holmes or one of the other men he would have listened and considered them. He's like so many men. He won't accept a woman as being equal to him in intelligence and ability. He thinks women were created only to have babies, keep house, be ornamental and provide comfort for the male of the species after his hard day's work."

"Well, aren't we?" interrupted Mandy provocatively, her eyes twinkling with amusement as she realized her friend was mounted on her favorite hobbyhorse, the rights of women.

Lisa flashed her a scathing glance. "You know very well what I mean. We're capable of much more, and that should be recognized. Richard Hatton assumes that because I'm a woman I must be incapable of logical thought, which irritates me because I want to be judged by my abilities, not because of my sex."

"And to think I once believed you were in love with him!" sighed Mandy mockingly.

"I was never in love with him," asserted Lisa vehemently. "For a while I admired him for his creative ability, but...."

"That soon wore off and was no substitute for love," suggested Mandy puckishly.

Lisa frowned. "I'm not sure I know what's meant by love. I only know I couldn't love a man who has as little respect for women as Richard Hatton. Love is only possible where there's equality," she said quietly, turning to lean her forehead against the cold windowpane and looking down into the dank tree-lined street of the Manchester suburb where they lived.

"How I hate November," she murmured. "'No fruits, no flowers, no leaves, no birds—November!' Who wrote that?"

"I think it was Thomas Hood. I prefer Scott's description," replied Mandy.

> "November's sky is chill and drear
> November's leaf is red and sear,
> All grey and crimson."

Then snapping out of her dreamy mood Mandy added, "I'll go and put these in water and put the kettle on. There's a letter for you from Scotland. It's on the mantelpiece."

Lisa continued to lean against the windowpane not seeing the branches of the plane trees that lined the street. The argument with Richard Hatton that afternoon had sapped a great deal of her strength and courage. It had been hard to defy him, especially when she remembered that only twelve months ago he had represented for her all she had admired and respected in a man, or so she had thought.

But she had defied him. She had stuck to her convictions

and as a result she was free again. Free of his overbearing demanding ways, free to design as she wished. No longer were her emotions in thrall to his every whim. She was her own woman again, like her Great-Aunt Maud.

The thought of her mother's aunt reminded her of the letter, and she went to the mantelpiece, took the envelope down and stared at the spidery writing. It was from Maud Roy, that formidable spinster who years ago had preferred to break off her engagement rather than go through with marriage to a man for whom she had lost her respect.

Tearing the envelope open, Lisa began to read the letter. Aunt Maud had wasted no time on pleasantries but had got straight to the point.

I have been ill, seriously ill, and I'm not likely to get better quickly, if at all. There is one in this village who likes to think I'm already on my last legs and that I'm ready to give in to his demand to sell my property to him. Three times I've sent him away with a flea in his ear. I've told him that when I've gone there'll be yet another Roy taking my place here at Breck House. It's the only argument that stops him, the only one he'll respect, since he's a stubborn clan-conscious Scot like myself.

But last time he was here there was a skeptical glint in his eyes and I could tell he didn't believe me.

This morning when I looked out of the window I saw him on the land below the shore road. He was measuring. I'm afraid he might build there and spoil my view. I could understand his attitude if he were an "incomer" to the village, but his family has been here since the Vikings came plundering along the coast and he should know by now that we Roys hold fast to our own possessions.

Come and see me if you can, Elisabeth, for Christmas and the New Year's holiday, so that I can show the rascal that there really is another Roy to whom I can bequeath my property. It's a long time since you were here. I'd love to see your bonny face....

Mandy came back into the room carrying the big jar of flowers. She set it on a low table and then stood back to admire the effect of the dark red blooms against the background of pale Wedgwood-blue wall. She glanced at Lisa and was surprised to see the glint of tears in her friend's eyes.

"Bad news?" she asked gently.

Lisa shook her head slowly as she pushed the letter into its envelope. "Not really. Aunt Maud hasn't been well. She wants me to go and see her. Poor old lady, she feels she's being harassed by someone and she needs the support of another Roy."

"How long is it since you last saw her?" asked Mandy.

"Six, almost seven years. It was just before mother and dad left for Jamaica. Mother and I went alone." Lisa paused, swallowed and then continued in a rather desolate voice, "Sometimes I think mother had an intuition that she wouldn't be coming back, because she insisted on taking me to Ardmont. Daddy couldn't go at the last minute because he had work to do. After mother died I always intended to go and visit Aunt Maud again, but somehow I spent the holidays doing something else, either flying out to stay with dad or taking trips to Europe."

"Well, there's nothing to stop you from going to see her now," remarked Mandy. "From all accounts you haven't a job, although it's my guess Richard Hatton will be on the phone this evening using all his charm to persuade you to go back. Why don't you go and have a holiday with your aunt? The change of scene might help you to unwind and to decide what you're going to do next. Kettle must be boiling."

She hurried out of the room, and Lisa began to pace the floor with long swinging strides, arms folded across her chest. Mandy's suggestion had fallen on fertile soil. Already in her imagination she was on the ferryboat crossing the wide Firth of Clyde, looking over tumbling sunlit water to the entrance of a narrow strait—or "kyle," as it was called in Scotland—that separated the island of Boag from the mainland. The strait led to the village of Ard-

The Taming of Lisa

mont, an old settlement dating back to the time of the Vikings, well-known as a yachting center and seaside resort, as well as the home of what had once been a flourishing tweed industry.

Another leap of the imagination and she was in the tall gray house sitting beside Aunt Maud listening to her vigorous voice as she talked about the Roy family, of which she was the only survivor. Then she was out of the house striding across the moors at the back of the village, lingering along the shore watching the yachts swinging at the moorings or envying the crew of one as sails were hoisted and it left its mooring to sail down the kyle to the distant sea.

It would be pleasant to go for a few weeks and stay in that place of summer calm in the midst of winter. It would be good to talk to her mother's only relative, to sleep in the room beneath the eaves where her mother had slept as a girl and to walk where she had walked.

Mandy returned with the tea tray just as the telephone rang.

"You answer," said Lisa quickly. "It might be Richard."

"What shall I say to him?" asked the unperturbed Mandy.

"Tell him I'm out. No, tell him I've gone away, far, far away, and at the moment I've no intentions of coming back," replied Lisa recklessly.

Having made the decision to go to Scotland, Lisa did not find it difficult to make further arrangements. A friend of Mandy's desperate for comfortable accommodation and genial companionship was only too pleased to move into the flat. A telephone call to Aunt Maud informed that lady that her great-niece would be with her soon, and in a few days Lisa stood, as she had anticipated, on the top foredeck of a ferryboat as it plunged and wallowed through four-foot-high waves across the wide firth.

The weather was far wilder than Lisa had expected. There was no resemblance between this crossing of the firth and the one she had made almost seven years previously. Today the wind tugged at the tweed cloak she was wearing, pulling it away from her body, and icy dampness penetrated her sweater and skirt. She was glad she was wearing a close-fitting knitted hat to protect her head.

Yet for all the wildness of the wind Lisa had no intention of leaving her position. She stood where she was looking over the wintry waste of water to the distant misty islands, a rather odd-looking figure in her billowing cloak and streaming, brightly colored scarf, drawing the attention of the only other passenger who had ventured up onto the top deck.

This passenger was a small boy of about seven years of age. He was warmly dressed in long tartan pants and a navy blue duffel coat. From beneath the hood of the coat a tuft of blond hair stuck out. When he had first come up on deck he had gone up to Lisa and had stared at her for a while, but she had been so engrossed in looking out to sea that she had not noticed him. Then he had gone to play on the wooden-slatted seats, walking along each of them and jumping off the ends. When he had tired of that he had disappeared down the companionway, the steep stairs that led below. He appeared again about fifteen minutes later and sidled up to Lisa to stare at her while he sucked a lollipop someone had given him.

This time Lisa noticed him and glancing down met the wide innocent stare of dark blue eyes set on either side of a shapely freckled nose.

"Are you a witch?" he asked.

She smiled at him. When she smiled two dents appeared in her cheeks on either side of her mouth and her hazel eyes twinkled warmly. "What makes you think I am?" she countered.

"You're wearing a cloak, and witches often wear cloaks, and you don't mind the wind."

"I'm not a witch. I wear a cloak because I find it warm and comfortable. I do mind the wind, but I'm not going to let it stop me from staying up here and seeing where I'm going. You see, it's a long time since I was last here and I don't want to miss anything."

He nodded with a quaint grown-up air as if he understood, and then with that casual manner that children often assume, believing that all adults know exactly what they are talking about, he said, "Sarah doesn't like the wind and she wouldn't come up here. But daddy likes standing up here."

Lisa looked around the deck. There was no one else there. Then she looked down at the boy again and thought that if she had a child like him, so fair and beautiful, she wouldn't let him wander about on the top deck of a ferryboat in bad weather because he might slip between the railings and fall overboard.

"Where's your mummy?" she asked, thinking she might take him to his parents.

"In Tasmania," he said carelessly. "We left her there."

Lisa felt a little deflated by his answer but persisted, "Isn't anyone traveling with you?"

"Yes, daddy is. He's in the bar with Sandy. They're drinking whiskey. I've just been to peep at them. Sarah's there, too. I haven't seen her before. She's very pretty. Yesterday I saw Santa Claus in a big shop in Glasgow." He looked around the deck and then leaned closer to whisper, "I don't think he was really Santa Claus. I think it was someone dressed up to look like him. I pretend I believe in Santa Claus because daddy likes creeping into my bedroom on Christmas Eve to leave presents on my bed."

Having made this important confidence he gazed at her solemnly for another minute, all the time licking his lollipop. Then he gave her another sweet smile and said, "I can see you're not a witch. You're too pretty. Bye!"

He went scampering across the deck to the companionway and disappeared again, and Lisa was left to wonder about a father who liked playing at being Santa Claus yet who preferred to drink whiskey in the bar of a ferryboat with a pretty woman, leaving his child to wander about unattended.

But her thoughts did not linger with the unknown parents of her recent companion because the ferryboat was entering the strait, an arrow of wind-ruffled gray pointing the way between the pale sage-green slopes of the island and the bracken-covered shores of the mainland.

With a quiver of delight she recognized certain landmarks. There was the big white house, gracious and serene, set back from a small beach of yellow sand overlooking sweeping lawns and backed by the tawny brown of deciduous trees and the bottle green of conifers. There, on the other side, was the small gray church with its tiny pointed steeple, crouching close to the shore.

As the strait grew narrower and the hills crowded closer she noticed the wind did not buffet her so much because its full strength was cut off by the land. The ferryboat slowed. Ahead four small islands appeared as blobs of burnt-sienna brown in a swirling mass of gray water. They divided the kyle into two passages, and Lisa recalled having visited one of the islands with her mother to see the remains of a fort that had been revealed by an archaeological dig that had been taking place when she had last visited her aunt. She knew that the whole area was a historian's delight because so many battles had been fought there from earliest times right up to the seventeenth century.

The ferryboat took the northern passage, passing close to one of the islands on which a red-and-white beacon was situated. Once through the dangerously narrow passage the boat turned southward, and there, opening before it, was the western part of the strait gradually widening between dark masses of land, a pathway to the blurred distant horizon.

Picking up speed, the ferry chugged fussily over to the west side of the kyle where granite cliffs topped by wind-bent Scotch pines overhung the water. Eventually the cliffs gave way to a wide bay, around the edge of which houses huddled to form the village of Ardmont.

Lisa remembered the village as a place of white and color-washed cottages and stately Victorian villas that had twinkled in the sunlight of early summer, bright among the green foliage. But now all the houses were a uniform gray and looked as if they were about to be pushed into the water by the sodden brown moors that stretched behind them up to the granite crags of the mountains.

As the ferry approached the long snout of pier thrusting out into the strait, Lisa hurried down to the main deck to find the embarkation gate. She stood near it watching the members of the ferry's crew throwing warps and expertly tying the ferry to the pier before they pushed out the gangway and allowed passengers ashore.

"Good afternoon. Am I right in thinking I'm addressing Miss Elisabeth Roy Smith?" said a man's voice nearby. It was a soft, pleasantly modulated voice and pronounced the letter *r* with that rolling sound peculiar to the Scots.

Lisa turned to look in surprise at a tall thin man with smiling gray eyes and sand-colored wispy hair who stood beside her.

"Yes, I'm Lisa Smith," she replied.

He held out a long-fingered hand. "I'm Sandy Lewis. My parents are friends of your aunt's. You probably don't remember, but we met briefly when you came with your mother a few years ago." The gray glance swept over her admiringly. "There have been a few changes in us both since then," he added with a hesitant but charming smile.

"Of course I remember you," said Lisa, placing her hand in his. "Your father has a sheep farm and you were full of ideas about resurrecting the old weaving industry to make tweed out of locally produced wool."

Pleasure glinted in his eyes as he responded to her sincere interest. "That's right. You might be interested to know that I managed to put my ideas into practice. We're actually producing a good-quality tweed. I'm just back from Glasgow, where I've been trying to make new contacts for selling the stuff. Dad will be here to meet me and, I expect, to meet you, too. He rang me up last night to tell me you'd be on this boat and to look out for you. Unfortunately I didn't." His grin was a little sheepish. "I was detained by an old friend."

"In the bar?" suggested Lisa dryly.

His thick sand-colored eyebrows shot up in surprise. "How do you know? I didn't see you in there."

"I wasn't. But a small elf in a navy blue duffel coat informed me that his daddy was in the bar drinking with someone called Sandy."

"Och, that would be wee Johnnie Lamont. How did he come to be talking to you?"

"He thought I was a witch."

"The wee devil!"

"Oh, I didn't mind, but I was rather concerned about him wandering about on his own on the top deck in that wind as we crossed the firth. He's so small. He could easily have slipped overboard."

"I suppose you're right. Fraser lets him do pretty much as he likes. Here, let me take your bags. I can see dad over there by the family town carriage."

Lisa looked in the direction he was pointing. A tall man wearing a Burberry coat and tweed hat was pacing beside an extremely well-preserved elderly Daimler.

"You go over to him and I'll follow with your luggage," instructed Sandy.

She did as she was told and was soon shaking hands with Hugh Lewis, who had the same gray eyes as his son set under fierce sandy-colored eyebrows. His hair, however, which showed below the edge of the greenish tweed hat, was white.

"Och, I'm glad ye've found each other. That's fine, just fine," he boomed. "Ye've fairly grown, Elisabeth, since I last saw ye. Sorry I was to be hearing about Barbara's death. Aye, but ye're her spitting image, only a few inches taller. And I'm thinking ye've a look of Maud about ye, too. Ye haven't got that determined tilt to your chin for nothing. Come away with ye and sit in the front with me. Maud's waiting for us. We've been promised tea and some of her home-baked drop scones for doing this wee service, Sandy."

"Good," replied Sandy, who had been putting Lisa's cases in the trunk of the car. "Shall I drive?"

"Ach, no. Ye can sit in the back and listen to Elisabeth and me talking."

"I'm glad to hear that Aunt Maud is able to do some baking," said Lisa as the car turned right onto the road that wound along the shore. "I was expecting to find her unable to get about."

"Well she canna' do much and she has to take great care. Maisie Weir goes out every morning to give her a hand and to clean through the house, and of course the district nurse and the doctor both call on her regularly."

"Move over to the left, dad," warned Sandy quietly. "You're out in the middle of the road."

"It's my road, isn't it?" barked the older man, and Sandy laughed.

"That's the way country people talk around here, Lisa," he explained. "They drive in the middle of the road because they're convinced no one else is going to be using it. It can be quite unnerving after driving in the city among law-abiding citizens."

"You hold your tongue, lad," retorted Hugh Lewis. "I helped to pay for this road, so it's mine."

Nothing had changed, thought Lisa, looking out at the neat privet hedges that marked the limits of the gardens of the Victorian houses to her left. The road was still barely the width of two cars.

From behind came the sound of a car's horn.

"Here he comes," murmured Sandy. "I told you to move over." Hugh Lewis made no effort to swing the steering wheel but kept the car in the center of the road. Glancing at his face, Lisa saw that it was stiff with pride and that there was a wicked blaze in his eyes when they looked in the rearview mirror.

"Damned arrogance!" he muttered as the car behind hooted again. "Thinks he owns the place!"

The driver of the car behind sounded his horn again and Lisa turned curiously to look past Sandy through the rear window. All she could see was the top of a black car that was so close to the Daimler that if the big car should stop suddenly there would be a crash.

"Well, since he bought that row of cottages at the back you have to admit he does own a sizable portion of the village," Sandy was saying mildly. "He was telling me when we were having a drink on the ferry that he'd like to buy The Moorings."

The car hooted again and it seemed to Lisa that the sound was derisive.

"Come on, dad, move over," Sandy said impatiently. "Stop being so stubborn. If you don't he'll take a chance and move out, and heaven knows what might happen."

"Let him, and good riddance," growled the older man stubbornly. Glancing out beyond him, Lisa could see why Sandy was worried. The road ran close to the shore, and any car overtaking at speed might run off the road onto the muddy beach.

"But he has the boy... and... Sarah with him," persisted Sandy.

"Humph, has he now?" remarked Hugh with another eagle glance at the mirror. "What's she doing here?"

"She's divorced her husband and has come to live at home for a while." Sandy's voice was flat and dull. Lisa looked at him sharply. His mouth was grim and there was an expression of sadness in his eyes.

"All right, I'll get out of his way," grumbled Hugh suddenly. "But mind you, it's only because he has the child with him. The poor wee laddie can't help having a delinquent parent."

He turned the steering wheel and guided the car closer to the hedges. The car behind accelerated and passed them with an acknowledging hoot on its horn. Lisa saw a boy's face at the front side window and beyond it the bulk of a man's body, had a brief glimpse of the perfectly chiseled profile of a woman sitting in the back of the car, and then it was past and bumping down the road in front, careering along as if furies were after it.

"Drives too fast, too," muttered Hugh Lewis.

"What do you mean by 'delinquent'?" asked Sandy. "Seems to me Fraser does his best to look after the child with little or no help from anyone around here."

"There's many a woman would be glad to help mind the child if he weren't so difficult and if his father were less arrogant," snorted Hugh. "What's he want The Moorings for?"

"Well, the Morrisons don't want it, you can be sure of that. George has been wanting to sell for some time. He needs to get away to a drier climate, he says. Fraser thinks it's time Ardmont had a decent hotel, so he's thinking of buying the place, converting it and putting a manager in."

"Damned interloper," grumbled Hugh Lewis. "Coming

The Taming of Lisa

here and turning the place upside down, thinking he can put people out of their homes just to serve his own ends."

"Now, dad, that's going too far. You can't call him an interloper. After all, he was born here and his family has been building boats here for generations. As for selfish ends, it seems to me he's helping the community as much as himself. The output from the yard has doubled since he took it over. He's employing more men. He tells me he has thirty working there this winter, some of them incomers admittedly. But the yard has given the village new life when it was in danger of becoming a place where only old people lived. As a matter of fact, it's helped my business considerably. Yachtsmen's wives often have money to spend and they like local produce."

"By buying you a drink he seems to have bought your loyalty, too," jeered Hugh. "I'd no idea you were so friendly with him."

"Fraser bought my loyalty a long time ago," said Sandy quietly. "You can hardly expect me to ignore someone with whom I went to school and who once rescued me from drowning down at the point."

"Humph, I'd forgotten that."

"I thought you had," said Sandy dryly. Then turning to Lisa he said with a grin, "Take no notice of our bickering, Lisa. I like your cloak."

"I designed and made it myself."

"It would look good in one of our tweeds."

She flashed him an interested glance. For all he was so quiet and self-effacing he had the same stubbornness as his father and she liked the way he had defended the man who had once saved his life.

"I'll take you up on that," she said. "When can I see some tweeds?"

"Anytime. Come to the mill someday and see the wool being dyed and spun."

"I'd like to see it being woven, too, if I may. For the past two years I've been designing clothes for a fashion house in Manchester and I'm interested in all sorts of fabrics."

A shrewd gleam lit his gray eyes. "Then you might be

just the person I've been looking for," he murmured. "Here we are at the Roy ancestral home."

They had reached the end of the village. Ahead loomed the gray sheds of the boatyard and beyond them the cliffs. Hugh Lewis swung the car out into the middle of the road in order to spike the entrance to a narrow rough road that rose steeply on the left leading to the tall gray house set back from the main road. The car took the hill reluctantly, puffing and panting, its wheels churning over granite chips, and eventually came to a gasping stop beside a small iron gate set in a stone wall.

"You go on to the house and we'll bring the luggage," said Hugh, and needing no second urging Lisa swung out of the car, opened the gate and walked along the red gravel path to the glass-paneled front door of the house. She rang the bell and then turned to look at the view from the doorstep.

It had changed. No longer was it possible to see up the kyle as far as the narrows. A big gray shed adjacent to the road effectively blocked any view to the north. However, it was still possible to look right down the sloping garden to the shore road and beyond that to the kyle and the green hills of the island of Boag sloping down to the curve of Black Rock Bay. Nothing had been built as yet on the land below the shore road.

Glancing at the big shed again, Lisa realized at last who had been harassing her Aunt Maud, and who wanted to buy Breck House. He was the same man whose arrogance and impudence aggravated Hugh Lewis, who had once saved Sandy from being drowned. He was Fraser Lamont, boatbuilder and the delinquent parent of the child she had met on the ferry.

The door behind her opened and she turned to find her aunt standing there. A tall gaunt woman in her late seventies, Maud Roy was dressed in a tartan skirt and green sweater, and she was leaning on a knobby walking stick. Her long-jawed, rather austere face softened into a smile and her deep-set brown eyes lit up when she saw Lisa, although she made no gesture of affection.

The Taming of Lisa

"Ach, so you're here at last. Aye, it's a bonny face ye have, but you're o'er-thin for my liking," she said abruptly in a harsh voice. "But they tell me it's the fashion to be lean."

She glanced along the path. Sandy and his father were coming with Lisa's cases. "It's grand to see you, Sandy," called Aunt Maud. "It's a long time since ye came visiting. Come away in. The kettle is on and the scones are buttered."

The view outside might have changed, but inside the house was the same. As she entered the big sitting room Lisa noticed with pleasure the familiar pieces of furniture; the huge mahogany sideboard on which the platters and chafing dishes belonging to an antique silver dinner service glinted in the light from the fire that leaped with orange and blue flames in the cavernous fireplace. Before the fire was a table formed by a Benares brass tray set on top of carved legs. On the mantelpiece above the fireplace blue-and-white Chinese ginger jars held pride of place. In one corner of the room there was the same corner cupboard containing odds and ends of ivory, small china figurines and tiny silver spoons and saltcellars. And at the big bay window the same starched long lace curtains hung crisp and white.

Sandy and his father stayed for an hour drinking tea, devouring buttered scones and exchanging gossip and wisecracks with Aunt Maud. As they left Sandy extracted a promise from Lisa that she would ring him up as soon as she found time to go and see the mill. Overhearing him, Aunt Maud was enthusiastic about the idea.

"That sounds grand, Sandy. If you can interest the lass in something maybe she'll stay longer than the month she's promised to me and then yon rascal will realize I mean what I say when I tell him I can't sell this place to him because there's a Roy to follow me."

"So that's how you've been keeping him at bay," remarked Sandy.

"Aye, but I have a feeling in my bones he's going to get the better of me one day by building on that land beyond the road. It's an ideal place for another slipway."

"But surely ye can claim ancient rights," said Hugh Lewis angrily. "Damned if I'd let him get away with it."

"I've tried," said Aunt Maud a little wearily. "I asked my lawyer, Murdo Menzies, to write to him. A lot of good that did! I had a visit from the Town and Country planning people. They told me that as long as the building doesn't take any light from my windows I can't claim anything. It's too far away from me to do that."

"Looks as if he's trying to squeeze you out," said Hugh.

"Over my dead body," replied Aunt Maud grimly, "and not even then."

Later when the long red velvet curtains covered the lace ones and made a semicircle of warm color at one end of the sitting room, blotting out the dark windy December night, and the firelight leaped cozily, illuminating Aunt Maud's fine-featured angular face, Lisa learned more about her aunt's fight to keep Breck House.

"I've had many fights in my time, Lisa, to keep my independence, my house and my land, and I've won all of them. But I'm getting old and this struggle has taxed my strength. Yon man is young and tough, and for all he has the charm of the devil, he's as hard as nails."

"But who is he and where has he come from? Mr. Lewis says he's an interloper, but Sandy says he was born here and went to school with him," said Lisa.

"He's a Lamont, and that family has lived in this place for generations. Boatbuilders all of them, sometimes successful, sometimes not. This one's father, Charlie Lamont, was unsuccessful. He was no businessman and was near to bankruptcy when he was drowned."

"How did that happen?"

"An accident when he was taking a yacht out to its mooring. The boom swung over, hit him on the head and he fell overboard. He sank like a stone. Fraser was twelve at the time. His mother sold the yard to a syndicate of Glasgow businessmen who were interested in yachting. She took Fraser and his sister, Anna, to live near her own people in Glasgow. I'm thinking it was enough to break the boy's heart, taking him away from here, from the home and the

The Taming of Lisa

boats he loved. But I've since discovered he couldn't possibly have had a heart to break."

"When did he come back?" asked Lisa. "He wasn't here when mother and I visited you."

"No, he wasn't. He came back five years ago from heaven knows where, bringing the boy with him. He says the lad is his son and they tell me there's a family likeness. No sign of a mother. It seems that when he left school Fraser apprenticed in boatbuilding and when he'd finished his apprenticeship he emigrated to Hobart in Tasmania, a great yachting place, so I believe."

"Do you know why he came back?"

"For all I dislike the man I'm willing to suggest that it was the pull of his homeland that brought him. Anyway, he had money and had no difficulty in buying the yard back. It had changed hands several times in recent years. No one had been able to make a success of it, partly because of bad management and partly because of lack of local knowledge."

"Judging by the new sheds and his desire to buy Breck House, I gather Mr. Lamont has been successful," observed Lisa.

"Aye. From the moment he arrived he talked of nothing but expansion, of wanting to build more boats and store more boats. He knows his business all right. He's clever at designing and during the past few years he's built up a clientele of wealthy businessmen. But he can't extend to the north and west of his property because of the cliffs. There's only one way, and that's why he wants my land. Three times he's come and offered to buy me out, and three times I've refused. Last time was hard because I'd been very ill and I was tired. But I kept thinking of all the Roys who had lived on this land and I kept thinking of you and I couldn't agree. So he said he'd try to get permission to build on the land beyond the road."

Lisa frowned into the fire. "Who owns the property to the west of you?" she asked.

"That's the Morrisons' guesthouse. It's called The Moorings."

"Sandy told me that the Morrisons want to sell it and Mr. Lamont is thinking of buying it and converting it into a hotel."

Aunt Maud's face registered shock, which was followed quickly by anger. "The devil!" she hissed. "The wily devil. So he'd box me in! As if he didn't own enough property in this village. He bought the row of cottages on the other side of The Moorings so that he could offer accommodation to anyone coming to work for him. Ach, how can I stop him from boxing me in like that?"

She leaned back in her chair, her eyes closed and her face drawn with pain. Lisa watched her anxiously, trying to think of a way in which to help.

"He'll get it," muttered Aunt Maud. "Who else would have the money available around here to buy the place and convert it? Somehow we must stop him, Lisa."

"Have you any money?" asked Lisa.

Aunt Maud opened her eyes, surprised at being asked such a direct and rather impertinent question by the young woman sitting opposite her, whose hair glowed with a copper sheen in the firelight and whose wide-set eyes danced and glittered with life.

"A little," she replied. "Why do you want to know?"

"Have you enough to buy The Moorings?"

"I doubt it. I should think the Morrisons will want a good price. Yon rascal will give it to them."

"Where did Fraser Lamont get his money?"

"There's one story going around that he married for money out in Tasmania, and that when his wife died she left him everything she had inherited from her grandmother."

"How convenient for him that she should die," observed Lisa dryly, who was disliking Fraser Lamont more and more. "If you like I could ask daddy to lend me the money to buy the place."

"But what would you do with it?"

"I could continue to run it as a guesthouse, or like Mr. Lamont I could turn it into the good hotel he seems to think Ardmont requires. Why should he get all the profit?"

Aunt Maud stared at her and then her brown eyes began to twinkle and she started to laugh, and before long she and Lisa were laughing together.

"Ach, Lisa, you're a lass after my own heart and I think I knew that when I wrote to you. I was feeling so low, lower than I've ever felt in my whole life, when I learned that I could do nothing to stop him from building in front of me if he wanted to. I felt sorry for myself, thinking I had no one to turn to. But now you're here and I'm beginning to feel better. I haven't laughed like that for years," said Aunt Maud.

"I'm glad you feel better. Together we'll show Mr. Lamont we Roy women aren't to be treated lightly. Anything he can do we can do better. Would you like me to write to daddy?"

"Not yet. I've another idea at the back of my mind that might work. I'll have to have a word with George Morrison, though. We'll invite him over one evening for a drop of whiskey. There's nothing George likes better than a drop of the malt."

WHEN SHE HAD SEEN HER AUNT TO BED Lisa went to the small bedroom that had been her mother's. Strangely enough it had none of the charm that it had possessed those long summer evenings more than six years ago. Now it seemed cold and austere and she was glad that there was an electric convector heater she could put on to warm the chilly air, and that someone had thoughtfully switched on the electric blanket in the bed.

Snuggling down into the warmth and listening to the wind howling around the house, shaking the window and clattering the slates on the roof, Lisa thought back over the day's events; of Johnnie Lamont with his sweet smile and big blue eyes, neglected and ignored by his father, who preferred to drink whiskey with Sandy and a certain lady named Sarah. Who was Sarah? She had meant to ask Aunt Maud, but they had been so busy planning ways in which they could foil Fraser Lamont in his attempt to buy The Moorings that she had forgotten to ask.

Lisa yawned suddenly and turned over on her side. Delicious waves of drowsiness swept over her. The buffeting of the wind and the sea air had both made her sleepy and she had no desire to lie awake puzzling over the identity of a woman she had never met. But as she drifted off to sleep the last image that flashed across the dark inner screen of her closed eyelids was of Sandy Lewis's face, set in lines of sadness when he had mentioned that Sarah had divorced her husband.

CHAPTER TWO

CLEAR SPARKLING MORNINGS with the kyle a ribbon of blue satin contrasting with the bleached winter-rimed grass of the island of Boag. Calm sunny afternoons with the distant mountains lavender colored, their summits iced with white. Deep purple gloamings after an orange sun had slipped below the horizon. So day followed day during Lisa's first two weeks as an anticyclone brought a cold fine spell of weather to the district.

Contrary to her expectations she did not find time heavy on her hands. There were Aunt Maud's two dogs to be walked three times a day, a chore that Lisa enjoyed because it gave her the opportunity to explore the countryside and the village again. Since Aunt Maud did not rise until midday, Lisa also had the chance to try her hand at housekeeping and cooking, both of which she had always left to Mandy when she had lived in Manchester. Admittedly Mrs. Weir still came to do the heavy work once a week, but there were still beds to make, washing to do and dusting, and although she found that sort of work dull she enjoyed cooking because it was creative.

She also enjoyed shopping in the village, and it was one day when she was in the village general store that she met Mrs. Morrison for the first time.

The weather had changed. It was pouring rain so Lisa had gone to the shop in Aunt Maud's small car. In the store she waited for Mrs. Ferguson, the proprietress, to serve the woman before her, half listening to the conversation that was taking place as she looked around the crowded shelves.

"There you are, Mrs. Morrison, that's you," said Mrs. Ferguson as she packed a final purchase into the woman's shopping basket. "Ach, it's a terrible morning."

"It is so. And I'm having to walk—the car is in the garage for repairs. Good thing our Gavin is home."

"When did he come?"

"Yesterday. He'll be here until after Hogmanay."

"Aye, it's fine to be a schoolteacher with those long holidays. Is Marjorie home, too?"

"No. She's better off where she is. Well, I'll be on my way."

Lisa made her few purchases and hurried out of the shop to the car. Soon she was driving along the shore road, windscreen wipers clacking noisily, tires swishing. Ahead of her she could see the robust figure of Mrs. Morrison. It did not take long to overtake her and to pull into the side of the road. As the woman approached the car Lisa reached over, opened the door and called out, "Can I give you a lift? I'm going to Breck House."

"That's very kind of you, miss."

Mrs. Morrison showed no hesitation about getting into the car and dumped her shopping basket on the back seat before she settled down in the seat next to Lisa.

"You're Miss Roy's niece," she observed chattily. "I've seen you out walking the dogs, and George, my husband, told me he met you when he was over seeing her the other day. How is she keeping?"

"She's up and down, sometimes well and like her old self and sometimes very poorly," replied Lisa.

Mrs. Morrison nodded her head sagely as she loosened her wet head scarf. "Aye, that's how it will be for her, poor soul. She'll be glad to have you with her, one of her own kin. There's no one like your own kin when you're in trouble or ill," and observing that she had a sympathetic listener Mrs. Morrison launched into a recital of how many times she had found her "own kin" had stood by her in time of trouble, finishing by quoting the example of her daughter, Marjorie, who had been found a job by her uncle in Glasgow when living in Ardmont had become too much for her.

By that time they had reached The Moorings, a big sprawling house built of gray granite, and Lisa had not been

The Taming of Lisa

able to say a word. As Mrs. Morrison took her basket from the back seat, however, Lisa slipped in an innocuous question.

"I hear you and your husband would like to leave Ardmont, too. Have you had any more offers for the guesthouse?"

"No. Only the one. A good offer, too, but George isn't keen to sell to Mr. Lamont for some reason. He doesn't care for him, not since Marjorie—" She broke off abruptly, then started again, "But as I say to him, what has liking a person got to do with selling a place? If I could have my own way I'd sell it to Fraser Lamont tomorrow. As it is I can see us waiting for years for another good offer."

"How much are you asking for it?" asked Lisa bluntly.

"Fraser has offered fifteen thousand pounds. I won't let George sell for less, you can mark my words. Well, thank you again, Miss Smith. Give my regards to Miss Roy, and season's greetings to ye both."

Fifteen thousand pounds! Fraser Lamont must be flush with money if he was able to offer that much for a dilapidated guesthouse. Either that or his credit must be good, thought Lisa as she garaged the car and made her way through the slanting rain to the house. There had been no time to ask Mrs. Morrison why George Morrison did not like Fraser Lamont. And then there had been that curious remark about her daughter, Marjorie.

Where would she find out about Marjorie Morrison? She decided she would ask Sandy when she saw him that afternoon when she went to see the mill. Maybe she would ask him about Sarah, too.

Ardmont Mill consisted of two big asbestos sheds. In one shed were the carding machines run by electricity into which the dyed wool was fed to be prepared for spinning. As always, fascinated by the change brought about in the fiber by the action of carding and spinning, Lisa watched the virgin wool, dyed golden yellow, emerald green, emerge as long single threads of yarn ready to be sent to the weavers.

"What lovely colors," she murmured. "Where do you get the dyes?"

"Some of them are vegetable dyes just as were used in the old days," explained Sandy. "For instance, the root of the iris plant makes pale yellow bog myrtle this deeper gold. Heather tips give a light green and crotal, which is a rock lichen and grows only in clear unpolluted air, makes a rusty orange. Of course we use synthetic dyes, as well, especially in the winter when the dye plants can't be gathered."

"Who weaves the tweed?"

"The villagers in their own homes. My mother is a weaver. In fact it was seeing her carrying on the traditional industry of the area, spinning on a foot-driven spinning wheel and using the handloom, that made me think of reviving the industry as a cottage industry that might keep villagers from moving away to the towns. Dad lent me some money and I received a government grant to build the sheds and erect the machinery. I persuaded some of the older women of the village to get out their looms, and so we started. Gradually we've been able to replace the old handlooms with modern steel foot-powered looms that go faster. Now we have thirty weavers of both sexes and several apprentices among the young school-leavers."

"What's their rate of production?"

"In a week a good weaver will produce two to two and a half tweeds; that is a strip of cloth eight yards long by twenty-eight inches wide."

"You must feel very pleased to think you've achieved so much in such a short time."

"It's nice of you to say so," replied Sandy with his charming diffident smile. "But there's something lacking. We don't sell as much as we should. I feel our tweeds could be as well-known as the Harris or Bute tweeds. I was hoping they would put Ardmont on the map again as a tweed-producing center. I know what I'm doing when it comes to spinning and weaving, but I don't seem to have the knack of selling. No gift of the gab, I suppose," he added, his smile becoming self-disparaging. "We'll go up to the farmhouse now. I'd like you to meet my mother and to show you some tweed she's just woven. I'm hoping you'll accept a length of it to make a cloak to your own design."

The Taming of Lisa

The Lewis farmhouse was built on a grassy knoll and commanded a fine view of the widening kyle as it flowed south. It was an old house and possessed fine examples of mullioned windows, stone vertical bars dividing the panes of glass. At the back of the house a big room acted as a studio where Mrs. Lewis worked at her loom, watching the shuttle as it shot back and forth automatically. She stopped when she saw Lisa enter the room with Sandy, and came forward to be introduced.

"Sandy tells me you're a dress-designer," she said. "I'd like your opinion of this tweed I've just finished. D'ye think the blend of colors is right or are they all too positive?"

Lisa lifted some of the cloth in her hand. It was light and yet firm and possessed a faint sheen. The colors were her own. They were the burning bronze and the glinting green so aptly described by Mandy combined with a brilliant yellow in a traditional check pattern. As a cloak for herself it would be perfect.

"They are positive," she agreed. "But on the right person it'll look great." With a quick twitch she released more of the cloth from its roll and draped it around herself. "Worn as a coat or a cloak with the right accessories it would be perfect."

Sandy and his mother stared. The color of Lisa's hair and eyes seemed to be intensified by the colors of the tweed.

"You're right," said Sandy. "It's perfect."

"If only—" began Mrs. Lewis, and stopped short.

"If only what?" he demanded, turning on her as if expecting her to disagree with him.

"I was thinking how wonderful it would be if Lisa could design a suit to be made out of one of our tweeds and model it for an advertisement to go into one of the Scots magazines. It would be grand publicity."

Touched by the softly spoken suggestion, Lisa smiled as she tossed the tweed back onto the table.

"I could certainly design something, but as for modeling, you'd be better with someone who is trained and possibly well-known."

"Like Sarah," said Sandy quietly, and his mother gave him a sharp worried glance.

"Who is she?" asked Lisa.

"Lady Popham. She was Sarah Chisholm before she married Sir Jack Popham. You may have heard of her," replied Sandy.

"Yes, I have. I've seen and admired her photograph many times. Do you know her?"

"Her parents came to live at Creddon Hall at the top of Loch Creddon about ten years ago," offered Mrs. Lewis when her son seemed disinclined to answer Lisa. "That reminds me, Sandy, did Fraser tell you that Mr. Chisholm wants him to do the alterations on the big yacht he's bought?"

"It was on that basis that Sarah introduced herself to Fraser in the bar on the ferry," replied Sandy.

"D'ye mean to say she didn't know him already?"

"You seem to have forgotten that Sarah hasn't been in Ardmont for almost eight years," snapped Sandy impatiently, "and she's only returned now because she isn't wanted elsewhere."

"Is it as long as that?" murmured Mrs. Lewis placidly. "My, how time flies, and now it's time for tea. Ye won't mind having it in the kitchen, will ye, Lisa? Hughie will be in from the barn and he'll be wanting to have a wee crack with ye about Maud."

It was almost an hour later before Lisa had Sandy to herself again and that was only for a few minutes when she was leaving. It was still raining and she asked him to sit next to her in the car.

When he raised his eyebrows in surprise she giggled and murmured, "Don't look so astounded and shocked. I only want to ask you a question. It wasn't possible in there with your parents present."

His surprise vanished as understanding dawned and he slid into the seat beside her and shut the car door.

"Now you've roused my curiosity," he said. "What do you want to know?"

"Why did Marjorie Morrison leave Ardmont, and why does George Morrison dislike Fraser Lamont?"

The Taming of Lisa

Sandy gave a low whistle. "The answer to that is rather spicy, and I'm glad you've asked me and not some busybody from the village, because probably the story I'm going to tell you isn't at all true."

"Why isn't it true?"

"Because Marjorie Morrison happens to be one of the biggest prevaricators I've ever come across."

"Well, come on, tell me. What is she *supposed* to have done?"

"It isn't a case of what she's supposed to have done, it's what she said Fraser did. You see, when he came back from Tasmania, Johnnie was not quite two and still needed looking after during the day. Marjorie had left school a year earlier but had done nothing very productive except to work as a waitress in the guesthouse during the summer months. So when Fraser asked around for someone to mind his child, Marjorie was pushed forward by her mother, thinking it would be suitable employment for the girl."

"Did he employ her?"

"Yes, for three months. Then suddenly he gave her the sack."

"Why?"

"Being Fraser, he never told anyone why. He just told her to clear out and he brought in an older woman to live in and be housekeeper and baby-sitter."

"What did Marjorie do then?"

"Well, her father gave Fraser hell but returned home, so I've been told, a very chastened man, having been told a few home truths about his daughter. For a while all was quiet and then the rumor, a very ugly one, began to spread. It had its origin, as you might guess, with Marjorie, who told someone who told someone else, and so on, that while she had been working for him Fraser had made several passes at her and had also made what she considered to be improper suggestions. She made out that he had sacked her because she had refused to comply with those suggestions."

"And you didn't believe her story."

Sandy shook his head. "Not on your life. Nor would you have done if you'd known Marjorie. Nor will you when you meet Fraser."

However, it was some time before Lisa met Fraser Lamont and was able to judge for herself what sort of a person he was. Meanwhile she built up an image of him based on the opinion of Aunt Maud only slightly modified by what she had learned from Sandy and from the boy she had met on the ferryboat. She imagined him to be a burly granite-faced individual with an overbearing manner who went his own way regardless of others.

One day after Christmas she was returning from her afternoon walk with the dogs when her attention was caught by a movement on the narrow shore. The two red setters, also noticing the movement, began to bark and strain at their leashes, pulling her across the road in the direction of the shore.

At once she saw that two boys were attacking a third smaller boy and even as she watched one of them flung the small boy to the ground, squatted on top of him and taking him by the shoulders began to bang his head against the ground. Shocked and sickened by such violence, Lisa stood stock-still as she saw blond floppy hair bounce up and down on the small boy's head.

Then she burst into action. Sensing her anger, the dogs bounded forward yelping and snarling. The two bigger boys looked around, stood up and ran off. Lisa shouted after them but doubted if they heard her because of the noise of the barking setters.

Quickly she knelt beside the blond-haired boy, who was struggling to his feet. She recognized the dark blue duffel coat and the dark eyes that gazed up at her solemnly. His face was grazed and he had the beginnings of a black eye.

"They thought you were a witch," he said. "That's why they ran."

"Who were they?"

"Doug Pettigrew and Jimmy Fox."

"Why were they fighting with you?"

"They called daddy a rude name, so I punched them, and then they began to punch me."

"But they're bigger and older than you."

"I know."

"Then why did you punch them?"

"I told you. They called daddy a name. They'd no right to do that because he isn't what they said. I know." His blue eyes filled suddenly with tears, which he tried in vain to brush away with dirty grazed knuckles. "They hurt me," he blubbered, and Lisa lost her heart for the first time in her life to a seven-year-old boy.

When he was a little calmer and had accepted the use of her handkerchief he agreed to let her walk home with him to find his father.

"He won't be in the house," he explained, waving his hand in the direction of the comfortable whitewashed villa that was situated on the rising ground at the back of the boatyard, surrounded by an untidy garden. "He might be in the office, or in one of the sheds. My name is Johnnie."

"And mine is Lisa."

"He might be a bit cross 'cos I've been in another fight, so you won't mind if I keep holding your hand, will you, Lisa?"

"No, I won't," she replied, squeezing the hand in question, while in her mind she rehearsed the short sharp reprimand she was going to give Fraser Lamont when she met him concerning the welfare of his son.

Passing the canvas-covered yachts laid up for the winter, they crossed the muddy boatyard to a fairly modern wooden building. Johnnie opened the door and they went into a room furnished as an office, on the walls of which the plans of various yachts were pinned. At a desk sat a middle-aged woman typing. When she saw Johnnie and Lisa she peered over the top of her spectacles and said, "Ach, what have ye been up to now?"

"He's been in a fight," drawled Lisa in her haughtiest manner. "And I've brought him home. Would you please tell me where I can find Mr. Lamont?"

The woman stared at her severely. "Ach, I canna be disturbing him now. He's talking to a very important customer. Leave the bairn here with me. He'll be all right."

"I'll do nothing of the sort. What I have to say to Mr.

Lamont is just as important as his customer, so I wish to see him personally," retorted Lisa, conscious of a draft on the back of her legs, knowing that the outer door of the office had opened behind her and that someone had entered.

"Then you shall be seeing him personally in a few minutes," said a man's voice behind her, a voice through which a thread of laughter ran, tantalizing and elusive. "Jeannie, will you please show Miss Smith into the other office? I won't be long."

Lisa whirled quickly, but she was not quick enough. The door banged shut as he stepped outside again. Going to the window, all she could see of him was the back of his square-shouldered figure as he bent to speak to someone in the driving seat of an expensive-looking car.

Johnnie tugged at her hand. "That was daddy," he whispered. "We'd better do as he says."

Lisa turned and caught the tail end of a superior smile on Jeannie's face as she stood up, opened the door to the inner office and simpered, "This way, please, Miss Smith."

As she walked past the smirking Jeannie into the other office, Lisa could not recall having felt so foolish in her life before. The fact that the man she had come to reprimand personally had recognized her, even though her back had been turned to him, and had called her by her name, when she had no idea what he looked like, made her feel at a disadvantage, which was a new and unpleasant experience.

Anger that he had placed her at a disadvantage swirled in a hot flood through her. She stalked over to the window of the office, which looked out over a motley collection of boat trailers and other yachting equipment. Johnnie, forgetful of the need to hold her hand and seemingly happy to be in his father's office, went to the desk, where he began to play with some drawing instruments that had been left there.

Words, critical and disparaging, had formed in Lisa's mind and were ready to be spoken as soon as Fraser Lamont opened the door, and as she heard the sound of his approaching footsteps through the outer office she tensed, ready to attack at once.

The Taming of Lisa

The door opened and she spun around to face him. Surprise dispersed her anger momentarily and had the effect of gagging her so that instead of speaking she stared in silence.

Far from being the burly granite-faced individual with the overbearing manner that she had imagined, he was handsome, blandly polite, and humor showed in the quirk at the corner of his mouth. About thirty-four years of age, not much taller than herself, he had a compact lithe physique that even his rough working clothes of tough denims and dark turtleneck sweater could not hide. He leaned easily against the closed door and returned her gaze with blue black eyes that took in every detail of her face.

"Now, what can I do for you, Miss Smith?" he asked pleasantly. Then Johnnie turned to look at him and the dark eyes shifted their glance away from her face to that of the boy. He lunged away from the door to squat before his son and touch with gentle fingers the purple mark beneath Johnnie's right eye.

"That's a beauty, Johnnie," he murmured. "How did you get it?"

"Doug Pettigrew hit me," replied Johnnie, blinking rapidly, trying, Lisa guessed, to prevent tears from spilling out again.

"There were two of them, both bigger than he," she interjected quickly. "One of them was lying on top of him gripping his shoulders and banging his head on the ground. When they saw me coming they ran away."

Fraser stood up and faced her. The humor had gone, leaving his mouth a straight line above a square determined chin and making his eyes look almost black. "You interfered," he snapped.

Was he suggesting that she had no right to interfere? Lisa tilted her chin as her original annoyance returned. "I went to stop it before any serious damage could be done to Johnnie," she snapped back.

He stared at her curiously and consideringly before turning to Johnnie and asking curtly, "Who started the fight?"

Johnnie looked up at him, his eyelashes fluttering and his lower lip trembling, no doubt wishing that Lisa was holding his hand. "I did," he quavered. "They called you a rude name, so I punched them."

The man's face softened slightly and humor touched his mouth again as he looked down at the boy. "It was brave of you to defend me, Johnnie, but try to remember never to get into a fight unless you're sure you can finish it. Both those boys were bigger than you and could have hurt you badly. It was silly of you to take them on. Now, off you run to see Mrs. Dobie up at the house. She'll bathe your wounds and do something about that eye."

Lisa felt her antipathy to the man rising several inches higher when she saw Johnnie's eyes fill with tears and his chin wobble ominously as he cried out, "But I don't want to go and see Mrs. Dobie! I want to stay with Lisa. She's kind."

"So is Mrs. Dobie."

"No she isn't, only when you're there. She's rough and she hurts me and she's always saying 'tut, tut.' I hate her!" blurted the boy.

"That's not true, Johnnie." The man's voice was wearily patient, as if he'd gone through this scene many times before. Yet the whiplash of authority crackled in it when he added, "Now, go to the house, at once."

Johnnie hesitated, his tearful eyes turning to Lisa hopefully, but in spite of her antipathy to his father she knew enough about dealing with children to realize she must not oppose a parent's authority in front of the child, so she smiled and said, "Go along, Johnnie. I expect I'll see you again soon. I take the dogs for a walk every afternoon."

His eyes lit up and his tears vanished miraculously and his sweet smile appeared. "Do you think I could come with you?" he asked.

"Anytime you like."

"Johnnie, get going," prompted Fraser sternly.

With a wary glance at his father the boy ran out of the office and through the outer room, banging the door of the building behind him. Fraser closed the inner door on the sound of Jeannie's typing and turned to face Lisa once more.

The Taming of Lisa

"Thank you for going to his rescue," he said coldly. "I doubt if your interference was necessary or wise. If he picks a fight he should be prepared to finish it. He has to learn to fight his own battles without assistance from others and also to learn when not to pick fights."

Pride. Oodles of it, thought Lisa with a sudden flash of insight into the character of the man. It was there in the set of his straight shoulders, in the direct glance of his dark eyes and in the hard line of his shapely mouth. Oh, no wonder he and Aunt Maud did not see eye to eye.

But anger was bubbling up again, anger that Johnnie should be made to suffer because of that pride.

"And next time he gets into a fight defending your good name and I happen to be passing, you'd prefer me to walk by on the other side of the road, I suppose," she exclaimed furiously. "Oh, yes, I get the message loud and clear, Mr. Lamont. You brook no interference. But hasn't it occurred to you that Johnnie wouldn't get into a fight if he weren't neglected and ignored? And if you think he's the sort who can fight to the finish without any help you're going to be very disappointed in him. He isn't like you!"

She knew instantly she had made a mistake, because instead of reacting angrily he leaned back against the door, folded his arms across his chest and stared at her with narrowed eyes.

"Isn't he?" he drawled. "You know me so well, then? I find that surprising, because as far as I know this is the first time you and I have met."

His bland insolence prickled under her skin, making her squirm inwardly as she realized that her knowledge of him was based entirely on hearsay and he knew that. But she allowed none of her discomfiture to show and returned his gaze steadily as she replied, "That's true. This is the first time we've met, yet you knew who I was even when I was standing with my back to you."

Humor was back, softening his mouth, glinting in his eyes.

"I recognized the dogs tied up outside. And surely by now you are aware that every newcomer to the village is discussed in full by the villagers," he explained. "Your knowledge of me, like mine of you, must be based entirely on the opinions of others. Yours, I surmise, is colored by your aunt's comments, and since there's no love lost between her and me, quite naturally her opinion of me is not particularly good."

"Neither is the opinion of a few others," she retorted airily, thinking of Mr. Lewis's forthright comments, and she was pleased to see she had scored a point as his dark eyebrows twitched together in a frown of displeasure.

"How long are you staying in Ardmont?" he asked brusquely, changing the subject.

"Until Aunt Maud is better," she fenced, not wanting to give anything away.

"She'll never get better. She's dying."

The curt brutality of his statement took her breath away. "How do you know?" she gasped.

"It's common knowledge. The whole village knows. Do you mean to tell me no one has had the guts to tell you yet? Haven't you seen Doc Clarke?"

"Not yet. He comes tomorrow."

"Then I'd like to suggest to you that you ask him for the truth about her condition. You will probably get a shock, but the truth is often shocking, and that's why people shy away from speaking it," he said coolly. "Why have you chosen this time of year to come and stay? It's not the usual time for a holiday."

His sharp direct questions and the autocratic way in which he had told her what to do when the doctor called irritated Lisa, but with an effort she controlled her irritation and answered patiently and honestly, "I came because she wrote and asked me to come. I happened to be free because I hadn't a job. Aunt Maud said she wanted me because I'm the only surviving Roy."

"But your name is Smith," he said sharply.

"It is, but my middle name is Roy, and my mother was the only child of William Roy, Aunt Maud's brother. She used to live at Breck House before she was married."

Horizontal lines creased his forehead as he searched his

The Taming of Lisa

memory. "I think I can remember her. She had red hair, too," he said. Before she knew what she was doing Lisa was touching the strands of hair that showed below the front of her knitted hat.

"It isn't red," she defended, rising easily to the taunt.

"I expect you have a fancy name for the color, but it looks like red to me, and Roy means 'red' in Scotland," he replied imperturbably. "Why hasn't your mother come to see her aunt?"

"She died a few years ago."

"I see." He drawled the words and his eyes narrowed again, the dark lashes almost meeting, hiding any expression. "So when Maud dies you'll expect to inherit Breck House. Is that why you're here—to make sure the will is made in your favor?"

This time she made no attempt to control her temper. "No, it isn't," she flared. "I had no idea Aunt Maud was dying when I decided to come, and although I know of no reason why I should answer your impertinent questions, Mr. Lamont, I'd like to make it clear that I came because I want to help her, because she's my only living relative on my mother's side and—"

"Very commendable," he jeered.

"Oh," she raged, "don't you ever have a kind thought for another person?"

"Not often. In my experience sentiment is a waste of time."

"So everything you do is governed by self-interest," she accused.

"Usually."

She could not be sure, but she thought she saw humor glint again in the depths of his eyes as he answered laconically. However, the expression was so brief and his mouth had not changed, so she decided she had imagined it.

"And I suppose you'll do anything to get what you want," she persisted.

His gaze lingered consideringly on the fronds of red hair, on her glinting hazel eyes and then on her generous passionate mouth, before he murmured, "Anything."

His cool appraisal combined with the quiet way in which he spoke sent a thrill of alarm through Lisa, and for a moment she had a strong sensation of having been caught in a trap from which there was no escape. Somehow she must get away from him out of the trap and into the fresh free air.

"I don't wonder there's no love lost between you and Aunt Maud," she remarked. Then coolly pulling on her gloves and swinging her long scarf over her shoulder, she walked toward him. He did not move. Standing before him, tall and slender, her eyes almost on a level with his, she said firmly, "I don't think we have anything else to say to each other, so I'll leave. Good afternoon, Mr. Lamont."

Still he did not move nor did his gaze waver. She was so close to him she could see a jagged scar on his face below the right cheekbone. It must have been a fairly recent wound because the marks left by the stitches were still very plain.

"I've one more thing to say," he replied smoothly. "I'd rather you didn't encourage Johnnie to go walking with you in the afternoons. There's enough tittle-tattle goes on in the village without you and me providing more food for rumor to thrive on."

"I'm afraid I don't understand," said Lisa stiltedly.

"Once it is known that you and Johnnie are friendly it won't take long for someone to suggest that there's more in your friendship with him than is obvious."

"You mean that someone will think you and I have some sort of clandestine relationship?" she asked, the color deepening in her cheeks.

"I do. If you were older, middle-aged, I doubt if any suspicions would arise. But as it is you're young and...." He paused and his gaze flicked over her face again before he continued with an impish grin, "And almost beautiful, in spite of the red hair."

Thoroughly confused by the compliment as well as by the humor, Lisa gaped. Then she remembered what Sandy had told her about Marjorie Morrison. Anger that this man should place her in the same category as a simpleminded

The Taming of Lisa 429

adolescent who had probably made a fool of herself by becoming infatuated with her employer chased the color from her face and made her eyes spark dangerously.

"And so you would deprive Johnnie of a little friendship and companionship just because you're afraid I might make up stories about you?" she hissed.

"You see what I mean? You've been a few weeks in the place and already you know it all," he said, unmoved by her anger. "You're quite right—that is the reason for my concern. I wouldn't want the blame for your loss of reputation to be placed at my door, Miss Red Smith. So stay away from Johnnie, if you please. Good afternoon."

He swung the door open just as the telephone on the desk rang. Without apology he went straight to it, and Lisa was left to make her exit unnoticed. As she left the room she heard him saying, "Hello, Sarah. I was hoping you'd ring. Tell your father I've made all the arrangements and should be in London on New Year's Eve. We could meet...."

The door crashed to behind her, helped on its way, she suspected, by a hefty kick from a seabooted foot.

Head held high, cheeks flaming, Lisa stalked through the outer office wondering how much Jeannie had heard through the thin partition wall. Outside the building she untied the waiting dogs. The sun had already slid behind the hills at the back of the village and the winter twilight was chilly with the promise of a frosty night to come.

As she skirted the shrouded yachts she spared a quick glance for the lighted front window of the white house where Johnnie would be receiving attention from the rough Mrs. Dobie.

Poor Johnnie! How she wished she could have tended his wounds. He was so much in need of love and attention. Not that she doubted his father loved him in his own fashion, but she guessed that the tough proud man with whom she had just crossed swords and who had admitted that he thought sentiment to be a waste of time had little time to spare to give Johnnie the care that a mother would give him. He was too busy expanding his business at the expense of other property owners in Ardmont or making arrangements to meet beautiful photographer's models for that, thought Lisa a trifle waspishly.

And yet he had had the nerve to tell her to stay away from Johnnie because he did not want any gossip. As if she cared for gossip! If he thought she was going to do what he had asked and ignore Johnny when she met him out walking, he had underestimated Lisa Roy Smith. She would walk and talk with Johnnie whenever she liked, giving him, she hoped, a little of the love and guidance she thought he needed. No one, not even a man as forceful as Fraser Lamont, could stop her from doing what she considered to be right when she recognized the need of another human being.

Such was her resolve as she returned to Breck House from the boatyard that day, but she had little chance to keep it immediately because Aunt Maud had a slight heart attack and had to be put to bed. Lisa called the doctor and learned from him that Fraser had not been completely accurate when he had suggested that Aunt Maud was dying. Apparently she had had a mild stroke earlier in the year about which she had not informed Lisa.

"Of course, she might live another couple of years or the next stroke might be a severe one and completely paralyze her or kill her," said the young doctor as he pulled on seaboots and then put on an oilskin and sou'wester. As most of his practice was spread out along the shores of the kyle and Loch Creddon he made many of his house calls by speedboat, and his noisy vehicle was a familiar sight on fine days as it roared past the village, sending up fans of spray.

"She'll have to stay in bed until she recovers from this attack. I'll tell Nurse More to look in every day until she's better," he added before he left the house.

Lisa found the plump, pink-cheeked district nurse a welcome visitor. She was always calm and smiling even though she had so many calls to make, checking up on the elderly people as well as on the young babies, and for the first time Lisa realized how dependent on the nurse such people were, especially in an area as remote as the Ardmont peninsula.

Now that she knew the nature of Aunt Maud's illness she was very glad she had been free to come when the old lady had written to her, and for the present she had no intention of leaving Ardmont and returning to Manchester to look for another job. While Aunt Maud needed her she would stay.

CHAPTER THREE

On New Year's Eve Sandy Lewis called in to ask after Aunt Maud once he had finished working at the mill, and when Lisa told him that she would be staying he looked pleased.

"Your walking out on your boss that day seems to have been fortuitous for me as well as for your aunt," he said as he sipped the tea she had made for him.

"Fortuitous for you? In what way?" asked Lisa, wishing he would be more direct in his approach. She knew he was shy, but there were times when his kid-gloved manner toward her was irritating. He treated her as if she were an article made of delicate porcelain instead of a healthy young woman with a mind of her own.

"Well, I've been thinking," he began diffidently, then added hurriedly, "I hope you won't think I'm pushing, Lisa, in asking you this... and you can refuse, you know."

"Sandy, come to the point," she urged gently. "I'll be the one to decide whether I refuse or not once I know what it is you want me to do."

"The point is—I need you," he said in a rush.

"Oh, Sandy!" she gurgled. "This is so sudden!"

"Ach, not in that way," he said testily, not seeing the humor of the situation. "I mean I need your ability and flair for designing clothes, your eye for good color combinations. That cloak and skirt that you've made from the tweed I gave you show off the material to advantage. If you would design more outfits like that and we could have made them up and advertised I'm sure our sales of cloth would increase."

"Have you spoken to Sarah Popham yet?" asked Lisa.

His gray glance slid away from hers to the fire and his mouth tightened.

The Taming of Lisa

"No," he said.

"Why not?"

"Because I don't think she would help us."

"You mean you don't want to ask her to help," she guessed shrewdly. "Don't you like her?"

He stood up suddenly and placed his teacup and saucer down on the Benares-ware table.

"Frankly, I can't see what she has to do with the matter we were discussing. Will you or won't you design some more outfits? You could choose the colors for the tweeds and they could be specially woven."

"Yes, I will, Sandy, if that's what you would like, because I'm not happy unless I'm designing clothes, but it doesn't matter what I do, it won't get you anywhere unless you have some good publicity in the more expensive magazines, as your mother suggested. And Sarah Popham might be able to help you to get that."

He turned his back on her and walked over to the sideboard where he picked up one of the many Christmas cards still displayed there. Lisa watched him, sensing the emotional turmoil her mention of Sarah had roused.

"At this very moment I expect she's meeting Fraser Lamont in London," she said carelessly.

He replaced the card carefully in the position he had found it and turned to face her. "How do you know?" he asked.

"I heard him making the arrangements with her one day when I was in his office."

"What were you doing there?" he queried with a lilt of surprise in his voice.

"Oh, I rescued his boy from a fight and took him home."

"And gave him a piece of your mind for neglecting his child," he suggested with a smile.

It was Lisa's turn to be surprised. "How do you know?" she challenged back.

"I met Fraser just before he left for London. He has a stand at the boat show and he's had to take Johnnie with him. The day of the fight Mrs. Dobie gave notice because

Johnnie kicked her while she was trying to attend to his black eye, so there was no one to look after him while Fraser went away."

"But what will a child like that do at the show?"

"Stay on the stand, I expect, with Fraser, or wander around getting into mischief. Who knows? Maybe Sarah will try her hand at looking after him."

"I would have looked after him here and he could have continued to go to school when it starts next week," asserted Lisa, temporarily forgetting that Fraser had ordered her to stay away from his child.

Sandy chuckled. "Can you imagine your Aunt Maud's reaction if she found you giving shelter to the son of her archenemy?" he remarked.

"But surely there's someone in the village who would have taken him. Your mother doesn't seem to dislike Fraser as much as some others I've met."

"Mother would, but then she would have to contend with my father. And then there's Fraser's attitude to take into consideration. Since the episode with Marjorie Morrison he's been very wary about asking anyone in the village to mind Johnnie. Of course the best arrangement would be for him to marry again and provide the child with a stepmother."

"Sarah Popham, perhaps," she suggested, watching him closely. "Aren't you jealous when you think of them meeting tonight in London?"

"No. I don't begrudge Sarah any happiness if she can find it with Fraser or anyone else. She's had a very unhappy time lately," he replied rather stiffly.

"So you do love her," probed Lisa.

"I used to be in love with her," he said rather wistfully. "I asked her to marry me, but she wanted to go away to London to make her name as a model. Who was I to stand in her way? I had nothing to offer. She was fascinated by the jet-set way of life with which she came into contact and married Jack Popham—his third wife!"

"More fool she," observed Lisa. "Well, if you won't ask her to help you by using her contacts and influence, I shall.

The only problem is when and how can I meet her? Do you think she'll be back from London?"

"Yes. I should think she went only to be with her mother and father while they went to the boat show. She wouldn't want to stay at Creddon Hall by herself. She isn't really interested in boats."

Lisa's eyes narrowed thoughtfully as she tried to see into the future. "But she might become interested if she thought that was the only way of holding a man who has attracted her," she murmured.

THE NEW YEAR OPENED QUIETLY. The weather was mild and by the middle of January Aunt Maud had recovered sufficiently to come downstairs for the afternoons. Her mind as needle-sharp as ever, she sat at the window of the sitting room and watched the waters of the kyle change color as the sky above changed, also.

"They don't seem to be building anything yet down there near the shore," she said one afternoon when Lisa came in from her walk. "Perhaps he hasn't been able to get permission after all. Or perhaps he's run out of money."

"Oh, I shouldn't think so. Johnnie was telling me yesterday that his father received many orders for fiberglass yachts at the boat show," replied Lisa.

"You've been seeing a lot of that child recently," grunted Aunt Maud.

"Yes, I meet him on his way home from school when I'm out with the dogs," said Lisa coolly.

Aunt Maud gave her a glance that expressed plainly her disapproval.

"Does his father approve?" she asked.

"He doesn't know. At least I don't think Johnnie has told him."

"And I can tell you why. He knows his father wouldn't approve. I don't approve, either. Do you realize, Lisa, you're encouraging that child to practice deceit toward his parent?"

"I can't see why anyone should disapprove of my talking to him. He's a very intelligent and sensitive boy, and he doesn't get enough attention. Actually I was thinking of bringing him here one day to meet you. I think you'd enjoy his company. And it would do him good to meet you and find out that you're not the old witch he thinks you are."

Aunt Maud stared at her haughtily for a moment, undecided whether to be offended or not. Then she broke into one of her delighted laughs. "Is that what he thinks I am?"

"Yes, he thought I was a witch when we met on the ferry coming here because I was wearing a cloak. But he thinks you're the sort of witch who has a caldron that you stir when you want to cast spells, and at the moment he believes you've cast a spell over George Morrison so that he won't sell The Moorings to a certain person."

"Whatever would make him think that?" demanded Aunt Maud sharply.

"He overheard his father say to George when they met one day, 'So the old witch has you in her power, too, has she?' Aunty, have you been threatening George in some way?"

"I? Threaten?" exclaimed Aunt Maud. "I'd never do such a thing! I merely suggested to George that if he dared to sell The Moorings to Lamont I'd let the whole village know that his daughter was a liar as well as a thief."

"A thief? Are you sure?"

"Of course I'm sure. She came to work for me once. I was sorry for the lass. Then I began to miss little things—small items of jewelry, little ornaments, then some money. I had George over and told him what I suspected and agreed to keep quiet about it because he said he would deal with her. She denied everything."

"Then if you know she told lies you don't believe what she said about Fraser Lamont."

"No, I didn't believe it. Whatever else I might think about the man, I couldn't believe he was lecherous. He's too open and direct in his manner for that."

Lisa thought of blue black eyes that regarded her directly and honestly, of a square-jawed, fresh-complexioned face and of the pride expressed in the set of straight shoulders and the hard line of a well-shaped mouth. As Sandy had said, once she had met Fraser she could not believe the story told by Marjorie Morrison, either, but she was pleased to hear her aunt express her disbelief, too.

"Well, I must say I didn't realize my only aunt was a blackmailer," she teased, referring to Aunt Maud's hold over George Morrison.

"I've no objections to his selling to anyone else," said Maud huffily. Then, changing the subject adroitly, she asked, "Have you heard from your father yet?"

"Yes. He says he hopes to get some leave soon because he's due for a change of commission, but he doesn't say when."

"If I know anything about Frank Smith he'll let you know the day before he is due to arrive and expect you to drop everything and run to meet him," remarked Aunt Maud. She sighed suddenly and gazed out at the waning sunlight. "Yes, I think I'd like to meet that little boy. His paternal grandmother died some time ago, poor soul, and the other one, whoever she is, doesn't seem to have much interest in him. Bring him tomorrow."

Next afternoon when they reached the end of the narrow lane leading to Breck House, Johnnie surprised Lisa by asking if he could come with her to see the old witch.

"Yes, you can. As a matter of fact she wants to meet you," she replied.

"Really?"

"Really. And if she likes you she might ask you again and show you some of her treasures."

"What sort of treasures?"

"Interesting things from places like China, India and Japan."

"Has she any puzzles or games?"

"I believe she has."

"Then I'll come."

"You won't be able to stay for long, Johnnie," Lisa warned. "She's an old lady and she's been very ill, so she gets tired easily. Also, I expect your housekeeper will be waiting for you."

"We're managing without one," he said, with that odd little grown-up air he sometimes assumed.

"Then who is doing the cleaning and the cooking?"

"Daddy. He's a good cook, better than Mrs. Dobie, and he lets me help him. But he isn't very good at cleaning and there's a lot of dust. Sarah came to see us the other day, but she only eats, she doesn't cook. She says she can't. Don't you think that's silly, Lisa? A lady who can't cook? She wouldn't be much good as a mother. All mothers cook and clean."

Out of the mouth of a seven-year-old boy, thought Lisa with a private grin. Here was the traditional male outlook that women were made to cook and clean and look after children. Yet from all accounts he had not learned it from his father, who considered himself capable of doing all those things without any assistance from a woman.

Johnnie's first visit to Breck House went off without a hitch. Both he and Aunt Maud were on their best behavior. The visit was repeated the next day, then there was a pause because of the weekend, but on the following Monday he came again and continued to come every school day after that. Sometimes he talked to Aunt Maud as she rummaged through her boxes of "treasure" or played simple card games with her. When she was tired he stayed in the kitchen with Lisa, who showed him how to use poster paints and a paintbrush, having discovered he liked nothing better than to create fantastic pictures.

Whether he told his father what he was doing during the hour after school, Lisa did not ask, as she did not want to spoil the pleasure he seemed to derive from visiting her and her aunt.

One afternoon toward the end of January, when the days were beginning to lengthen, Johnnie and Lisa were so absorbed that they forgot the time and realized with a shock that it was almost half-past five, long past the time when Johnnie usually left. Lisa hurried him out of the house and down the brae and went with him into the boatyard, thinking that if Fraser were angry she could do the explaining and spare the boy a little of his father's wrath.

As they approached the steps of the white house a woman got out of a car that was parked nearby and came

The Taming of Lisa

toward them. She was of medium height, slim and elegantly dressed, and had long curling honey-colored hair.

"So there you are, Johnnie," she said in a high-pitched, slightly shrill voice. "Your father has gone to look for you."

"I've been at Lisa's house and Aunt Maud gave me this," said Johnnie, holding out a model of an elephant carved in ebony complete with ivory tusks.

The woman ignored both his answer and the elephant and stared curiously at Lisa. "Are you Lisa Smith?" she asked, her speedwell-blue eyes taking in every detail of Lisa's clothing.

"Yes, I am. You're Sarah Popham, the model, aren't you?"

"I'd have been mortified if you hadn't recognized me," laughed the other. "Mrs. Lewis was talking about you to me only this afternoon. She says you design clothes. I haven't time to talk about this now—I was just going to drive home when you appeared with Johnnie, but I'd like you to design something for me to be made in one of the Ardmont tweeds. Could you come to lunch next Friday?"

"Yes, I think so," agreed Lisa, her quick mind leaping ahead, thinking how she could use this surprising turn of events to advantage, not only for herself, but also for Sandy.

"Fraser is coming then to talk to daddy about the yacht he's bought, so perhaps he could bring you over," said Sarah. She looked past Lisa toward the entrance to the yard. "Here he is now, so you can make arrangements with him."

Lisa turned to glance at the approaching man while Johnnie dashed up the steps of the house, flung open the front door and disappeared.

"Johnnie was quite safe after all, Fraser," said Sarah sweetly. "He was with Lisa and her aunt."

Fraser ignored her and walked straight up to Lisa. She could see by the fading light that anxiety had sharpened the angles of his face and had drawn new lines about his mouth.

"I thought I told you to stay away from Johnnie," he said sharply to her.

He spoke as if Sarah were not there, as if there were only the two of them standing in the shaft of yellow light that slanted through the swiftly falling dusk from the open doorway.

Lisa's chin came up and her eyelids drooped haughtily as she reacted to the reprimand in his voice. "He asked me if I would take him to see the old witch one day. I couldn't refuse a request like that. He's been coming every day. They get along very well and it's good for both of them. Today we were so busy we forgot the time," she replied coolly.

Some of the tautness went out of his face and his mouth twitched humorously. "The old witch," he repeated softly. "I'm afraid he learned that from me."

"Fraser—" Sarah's voice was slightly pettish, as she resented being ignored "—I have to go now. Lisa is coming to lunch next Friday, too. You could bring her, couldn't you? About twelve-thirty?"

Fraser slanted her a cold glance. "Lisa has the use of her aunt's car, so she doesn't have to depend on me to drive her to Creddon Hall," he said, making no secret of the fact that he was not to be regarded as a chauffeur for anyone who wished to go to the hall.

If she had any pride, real pride, she would have walked away there and then, thought Lisa to herself. But she did not move.

Sarah shrugged. "Oh, well, have it your own way. If you want to come separately that's fine with me. Your aunt should be able to tell you how to get to the hall, Lisa. It isn't far, and by then I should have some tweed from Mrs. Lewis. Goodbye for now."

As she passed Fraser on the way to her car she glanced up at him rather coyly. "I don't suppose it's any use asking you to walk to the car with me, see me into it and close the door for me?" she purred provocatively.

"No use at all," he answered with a grin.

"No one could ever accuse you of being a ladies' man, Fraser," Sarah grumbled with a return to her earlier petulance.

"And that's the way I like it," he returned equably. "Good night, Sarah."

With a petulant twitch of her shoulders she went off to her car and Lisa made a move to go. With a quick side step Fraser blocked the way.

"Don't think you're going to get away so easily," he murmured threateningly. "I've something to say to you, Red Smith."

As Sarah turned her car toward the entrance of the yard, twin shafts of light swept over them.

"Come into the house," ordered Fraser curtly.

"Do you think that would be wise?" asked Lisa with a touch of mockery. "If anyone sees me going in with you there's no knowing what they'll think. Remember the village tittle-tattle?"

Sarah seemed to be having difficulty with her car, because it was still there, its engine idling.

"If you don't come in and explain what's been going on after school for the past week or so, Johnnie will probably get a belting for lying," said Fraser quietly.

"Oh, no, you wouldn't," objected Lisa anxiously. The car was now moving forward slowly.

"Wouldn't I?" he scoffed. "You forget he's my child and I'm responsible for disciplining him. He knows he should come straight home after the school bus has dropped him in the village and that he gets punished if he doesn't obey my instructions. This time I've a feeling he isn't wholly to blame for being disobedient. His story is that he's been staying behind to help the teacher and coming on the usual bus. But since he has no money for his fare that's barely credible, and now seeing you here with him this evening makes me think you're behind all this. Well, are you coming in or not?"

"I'll come," she said resignedly, noting that Sarah's car had at last reached the entrance of the yard and was turning out onto the main shore road.

"But there are other ways of punishing a child without resorting to physical violence," she added.

"I know. I find them quite ineffectual, and my patience is wearing a little thin," he grated, closing the front door behind them. Then raising his voice he called out, "You can come out of hiding now, Johnnie, and do a little explaining!"

Taking off his jacket, he flung it over a chair in the hallway and said abruptly, "Come into the kitchen. I have to get a meal ready, and while I'm doing that you can tell me why you decided to ignore my request to leave Johnnie alone and why you've been enticing him up to Breck House."

"I haven't enticed him!" she denied hotly, sitting down on a kitchen chair and watching him take dishes and cooking utensils out of cupboards and drawers, then move across to the table to twitch the cloth straight, brush off the crumbs made by another meal and begin to set it with cutlery. The room was far better than she had imagined. It was bright and clean, and although it was not exactly tidy, there were no dirty dishes about. "I told you he asked if he could come and see Aunt Maud," she said, continuing her defense.

The glance he gave her was skeptical as he left the table and went over to the refrigerator, opened it and took out some eggs, which he proceeded to break into a mixing bowl.

"He wouldn't have asked if he hadn't been seeing you regularly and become used to you. You see, I know him rather better than you do. He doesn't ask favors of strangers," he said, and began to whisk the eggs.

"That's one way in which he's like you," observed Lisa calmly, noticing how deft and efficient were his movements. He had obviously had plenty of experience in whisking eggs.

"What makes you think that?" he asked, giving her a sharp glance.

"You didn't have to take him to the boat show with you. I would have looked after him for you, but you didn't ask me because you didn't know me well enough," she replied.

He stopped beating the eggs and turned to the cooker to switch on a hot plate.

"Whereas you're so clever you can assess a person's

The Taming of Lisa

character before you've even met him," he said with a touch of sarcasm. "Yes, I am cautious about strangers, especially where Johnnie is concerned. I have reason to be. Now what do you hope to gain by encouraging him?"

"Oh, I suppose it's because you do everything out of self-interest that you think everyone must do the same," retorted Lisa angrily. "I don't hope to gain anything. I met Johnnie on the boat coming over here and I felt concerned about him because he had no mother and apparently you didn't care a hang what happened to him."

He had reached into a cupboard for a heavy frying pan, and before turning to place it on the cooker he gave her another skeptical glance that did nothing to soothe her anger.

"I don't expect you to understand for one minute," she seethed, "but what I'm telling you is the truth. I thought I could help him by meeting him and talking to him after school, and when I discovered there was no one here in the house for him to come home to—not even Mrs. Dobie—I thought it would do no harm to take him up to see Aunt Maud as he asked. She said herself he seemed to have no grandmother so that perhaps she could provide that lack in his life."

He had his back to her now and was heating butter in the frying pan. All she could see was the straight proud set of his shoulders and the way his thick brown hair had a tendency to curl at the nape of his neck. When eventually he turned back to the bowl of eggs, she noticed that his mouth was set in that hard straight line, giving nothing away, and that his eyes were hidden as he looked down at the bowl rather than at her. He gave a final whisk to the eggs, picked up the bowl and turned back to the cooker, having said nothing. He poured the contents of the bowl into the pan and stood and watched the result, apparently far more interested in his cooking than in anything she had to say in her own defense.

From the hallway came the sound of a stair creaking as someone stepped upon it. Lisa guessed that Johnnie was creeping slowly down on his way to make an explanation.

"Have I answered your question?" she asked Fraser.

He did not seem to hear her because he did not turn around, nor did he answer, being too engrossed in his cooking.

"Mr. Lamont," she persisted, because it was most important for some reason that she should make him understand that her interest in Johnnie was purely altruistic, "have I answered your question? Do you understand now why I ignored your request to stay away from Johnnie?"

This time he heard her or, at least, he acknowledged that she had spoken, because he half turned and gave her a narrowed sidelong glance.

"Yes, you've answered it, in a way, but I'm not sure I understand your motives yet. I wouldn't like him to develop too much of a liking for you, because he'll be upset when you go away."

"But I'm not going away. I'm going to stay and look after Aunt Maud, and there's a possibility that I might go to work for Sandy Lewis."

At that point Johnnie burst suddenly into the room. He was still in his duffel coat and he was clutching his ebony elephant in his hand. He went straight up to Fraser and held up the elephant for him to see.

"Miss Roy gave me this," he said breathlessly, hoping to divert his father's anger by drawing his attention to the gift. "She isn't an old witch, like you said, she's just an old lady. You—you're not cross with Lisa and me anymore, are you?"

Fraser crossed his arms over his chest, leaned against the sink unit and looked down at the child. His mouth twitched a little with amusement, but he put on a pretense of frowning severely.

"Yes, I am. But not as cross as I was. Next time you decide to go visiting Miss Roy on the way home from school it would be better if you told me instead of making up stories about staying behind at school to help the teacher, and then I'm not so likely to rush off and make a fool of myself looking all over the village for you. You know the rule, Johnnie. You come straight home from

The Taming of Lisa

school and report to me when I'm here before you do anything else."

Johnnie's long eyelashes fluttered down over his eyes and his mouth quivered. "Yes, daddy," he muttered. Then with a quick change of mood he looked up again and said impulsively, "Can Lisa stay to supper?"

"Would you like her to do that?"

Johnnie nodded his head vigorously, his eyes shining hopefully. "She's a very good cook," he said. "I had some of her scones this afternoon."

"You're lucky," remarked Fraser with a touch of dryness in his voice. "Next time you have tea out you might think of me and hide some of those scones in your pockets. I haven't had a decent homemade scone for years." He glanced across at Lisa and added, "Will you stay and share our supper?"

She had a great longing to stay, to help prepare the meal and to clear away the dishes afterward and then to put Johnnie to bed and possibly read a bedtime story to him. It was a most extraordinary desire and it frightened her.

She stood up quickly. "Thank you for the invitation," she stammered, with less than her usual poise. "But I think it would be wiser if I didn't stay." Then she saw mockery gleam in Fraser's dark eyes and she continued hurriedly, "Aunt Maud is alone and she must be wondering where I am."

"Then of course it wouldn't be wise for you to stay," he agreed blandly, ignoring Johnnie's loud protest, and Lisa had the impression that he was relieved by her refusal and immediately felt a most unusual resentment that he should accept it so easily.

"Then can I go to Breck House again tomorrow after school?" persisted Johnnie. "Miss Roy said she'd teach me how to play dominoes. Please, daddy."

"No." The refusal was uncompromising.

"Why?" wailed Johnnie.

"Miss Roy doesn't like me much and I wouldn't want you to be a nuisance to her."

"He isn't a nuisance," began Lisa impulsively.

"I still don't want him to go to Breck House," was the icy reply, accompanied by a supercilious glance that told her quite clearly that Fraser resented her interference.

Tilting her chin, she moved toward the door. "Watch the omelet, Johnnie, please," ordered Fraser, crossing the room to Lisa's side. "I'll see Miss Smith to the front door."

"Oh, don't bother," she said airily. "I know you don't like to be regarded as a ladies' man."

He raised an eyebrow at her. "All right, be independent. See youself out," he said softly. "But don't blame me if you fall down the steps in the dark. Good night, Red Smith."

As soon as she closed the front door behind her she realized what he had meant. The thick door cut off all the light from the hallway and it was a while before her eyes became accustomed to the darkness. Although she went carefully she miscounted the steps, found there was one more than she had thought, on which she tripped, lost her balance and fell to her knees.

"Talk about pride coming before a fall," she muttered to herself. "That should teach you to refuse to be escorted to the front door in the future, Lisa Smith!"

She got to her feet and was glad to find that the ankle that had turned under her would take her full weight. It would have been very humiliating if she had been forced to ask Fraser for help.

How right Sarah had been when she had said no one could accuse him of being a ladies' man. He made no concessions to the so-called weaker sex. Lisa guessed that he always spoke to a woman as he would speak to a man, using no cajolery or flattery to soften his approach, and if the woman did not like it she could lump it. When she thought about it that was how she had always wanted to be treated, as an equal, no holds barred.

The wind moaned eerily and a few flakes of snow drifted into her face, brushing her skin like icy feathers. She pulled her hat down more firmly and buried her face in her scarf as she hurried up the brae to Breck House, wondering why Fraser had been so adamant in his refusal to allow Johnnie

The Taming of Lisa

to go again to visit Aunt Maud. He had said it was because he did not want the child to be a nuisance to someone who did not like himself, which meant his pride was stepping in there, but she had a suspicion that there was another reason and that it was closely connected with her.

Next morning she went to the mill to tell Sandy that she had at last met Sarah.

"We met by accident at the boatyard. She's invited me to lunch next Friday and she wants me to design some clothes for her, to be made from Ardmont tweed, so I might be able to do a deal with her, and persuade her to model the clothes for advertising purposes."

"I hope you can," said Sandy. "Come up to the farmhouse and see the tweed that mother is weaving for you. It's going to be superb."

So once again Lisa spent an enthralling morning admiring Mrs. Lewis's handiwork, which included a new tweed for which she herself had chosen the colors, the delicate mauves and pinks of a winter sunset as seen reflected in the water of the kyle.

It was as she was leaving that she noticed the two sheepskins, stretched on wooden frames for curing, lying in a corner of the room. Touching the white curly wool, she asked Sandy whom they belonged to.

"They're Sheila's, my brother Hugh's wife. She had a fancy for a sheepskin jacket and I said I'd get one made for her. Curing and tanning them is as far as I've got with them."

"I could dye them and make a jacket for her," offered Lisa.

"You could?" He looked surprised. They stared at each other across the frame as the same thought struck both of them. "Lisa, do you think you could design sheepskin jackets as well as tweed clothing?"

"I could dye the skin one of the colors used in a tweed and match them in an outfit," she replied excitedly. "Do you think Sheila would let me have these skins to experiment with?"

"I know she would. But what are you going to use for dye?"

"I'm going to use green ink," announced Lisa. As Sandy had once said, it did seem as if her quarrel with Richard Hatton had been fortuitous. Here in Ardmont she felt at home in a way she had never felt in Manchester. She guessed that the feeling was closely associated with the fact that she was no longer tied to Richard's routine. Here she was free at last to realize her potential as a fashion designer and Sandy's undisguised enthusiasm for her designs had acted as a spur to her inventiveness. Yes, she thought, she could be very happy living here in Ardmont, designing for Ardmont Tweeds Limited occasionally and for other companies later when her designing ability became known.

Full of this idea, she went straight into the sitting room when she reached Breck House to tell Aunt Maud. She found her sitting in her usual high-backed wing chair staring out of the window. It was not until she was close to her that she saw that the old lady was shaking with rage.

"Why, aunty, whatever is the matter?" she asked anxiously, afraid that such anger might bring on another heart attack.

"Matter? *That*'s the matter." Aunt Maud raised her stick and pointed with it. On the land beyond the shore road adjacent to the water a group of men were unloading from a lorry the girders and frames necessary for building a shed. "Have you no eyes in your head, lass?" barked Aunt Maud. "Didn't you see them as you drove along the road?"

"No. I was thinking of something else. Mr. Lamont must have received permission to build after all."

"Aye, he must. As soon as I saw them I rang up. He wasn't there. Jean Bridie told me he'd had to go into Kilbride to the school about that precious brat of his. So I told her that as soon as he came back I wanted to see him up here, and that he was to bring me proof that he has permission. He's taking his time to come, though. I suppose he thinks he can ignore me now that he's got his own way."

"Maybe he has other things to do," said Lisa soothingly.

"Are you sticking up for him?" demanded Aunt Maud.

The Taming of Lisa

"No, but I don't think he'll ignore you. He isn't afraid of you."

"That's the trouble," grunted Aunt Maud grudgingly.

It was almost three-thirty when the doorbell rang. Lisa answered its summons. Fraser looked much the same as when she had seen him the previous night. He was wearing the same sweater and pants, but instead of seaboots and a windcheater he was wearing polished brogues and a tweed jacket. In one hand he held a buff envelope, and he did not reply to her greeting as he stepped into the hallway but went on to the sitting room as if sure of his way. She hurried after him and was surprised to hear him greet Aunt Maud quite pleasantly, as if they were old friends instead of enemies.

"Good afternoon, Miss Roy. How are you today?"

"I've felt better, Fraser Lamont. Looking out of this window this morning did not improve my state of health. So you got your own way after all."

By way of answer he held out the envelope to her. She snatched it from him, pulled out the letter it contained, read it, then made a frustrated exclamation as she pushed it back into the envelope and handed it back to him.

"I can't understand these county people. One minute they're saying they don't want anyone to build an eyesore to spoil the countryside and the next they're giving permission to someone to erect ugly sheds on common land."

"The shed that will be built there will be no worse than Ardmont Mill, which sticks up at the back of the village like a sore thumb, and that land isn't common land. It has belonged to Lamonts for more than a hundred years, as I was able to prove to the county council, since I still have the original deeds of ownership showing the boundaries."

"Then why didn't your grandfather or your father build on it?" demanded Aunt Maud.

"Because they didn't need to. They had no wish to expand. My grandfather was able to support his family and keep the business going by turning out about seven yachts a year. My father, as you know, failed miserably. I don't intend to follow in his footsteps," said Fraser grimly. "These days the yachting business is much more competitive, and to survive you have to mass-produce boats as well as build the traditional wooden ones. I have many orders for fiberglass boats this year and I need that shed. Now if you'd been sensible instead of sentimental you'd have sold me your property and then you wouldn't be sitting here complaining about your view being spoiled, although when your hedge grows up in the summer you'll hardly see the shed."

All the time he was speaking Aunt Maud did her best to interrupt him, but he ignored her attempts by raising his voice slightly above hers until he had finished what he wanted to say. Then he turned to her and said with a cheeky grin, "Your turn now."

"If I'm sentimental you're as hard as nails, and rude, too, not letting an old woman speak!" she spluttered.

"I was always taught that it's rude to interrupt when someone is speaking," he replied coolly. "You *are* sentimental, you know, keeping an old house like this that's damp and riddled with woodworm, hanging on to a big garden that you can't afford to have tended, all because of 'false pride in place and blood.'"

"Humph, quote Tennyson at me, would you? False pride indeed, and I suppose you think you have none?" retorted Aunt Maud.

"If you'd sold it to me in the autumn when I offered, you could have gone to live in a pleasant flat in Largs or Rothesay, and then perhaps you wouldn't have been so ill."

"I've told you before, I intend to hand this house on to another Roy," muttered Aunt Maud. "And you needn't think you're going to squeeze me out by buying The Moorings. I've told George Morrison not to sell to you."

"Well, you can take the pressure off him now," returned Fraser, who did not seem at all surprised by her admission. "I've changed my mind. Now that I have this—" he held up the envelope "—I'm not so desperate and I can afford to bide my time. I hope you're satisfied now that what I'm doing down there is all legal and above board."

"Yes," admitted Aunt Maud grudgingly. "But that doesn't mean to say I'm pleased, so you can tell that brat of yours he needn't bother to come up here again. The sight of

The Taming of Lisa

him reminds me too much of you and you remind me too much of your grandfather, and when I think of what both of you have done in your time to me...." She paused, breathing heavily, and Lisa moved close to her, anxiously.

"It wasn't my idea that Johnnie should come here anyway," said Fraser softly. "Goodbye, Miss Roy. If you should change your mind and decide you'd like to sell, just let me know."

Without a glance at Lisa he walked out of the room. Her conscience pricking her about Johnnie, she went after him, catching up with him as he opened the door.

"I'm sorry about what Aunt Maud said about not wanting to see Johnnie again," she said. "I hope he isn't too upset about not coming."

He shrugged his shoulders carelessly. "He'll get over it," he said curtly.

"Like you did when your mother sold up and moved away from here and when your wife died, I suppose," she snapped angrily, annoyed by his hardness.

She could tell by the sudden blaze in his eyes that he was offended by her personal remarks, but he made no effort to retaliate.

"There's nothing to stop me from seeing Johnnie on his way home from school. Neither Aunt Maud nor you can stop that," she continued, goaded by his silence.

"You won't see him today," he returned coldly. "He's in hospital at Inverey."

"Why, what's happened to him?" she whispered, fear curling round her heart.

"He had an accident in the school playground. He has a concussion." He recited this information without showing a flicker of emotion.

"Oh, I'm sorry," said Lisa helplessly. She wanted to offer comfort and sympathy, but his attitude gave her no encouragement. She wanted also to rush off to the hospital to see Johnnie. But she had no rights where he was concerned, none at all. Yet she could not help trying. "I'll go and see him," she announced.

"No." His refusal came out like a pistol shot.

"Why not? Maybe I can help him?"

He gave her one of those narrowed skeptical glances that made her blood start to simmer.

"If you want to help you'll stay away from Johnnie," he said cryptically, and went through the door, closing it behind him sharply, leaving her gaping at the bunches of grapes that patterned the Victorian glass panel of the door.

CHAPTER FOUR

WITH ALL THE EASILY ROUSED EMOTIONALISM of the old and the ill, Aunt Maud was very upset when Lisa told her about Johnnie's accident, and for the rest of the afternoon she bemoaned the fact that she had called the child a brat and had said he wouldn't be welcome at Breck House anymore.

"I wouldn't have said it if I'd known. I only said it because I wanted to annoy his father in some way. Fraser is so hard that it's difficult to find weapons with which to hurt him. I thought perhaps the bairn was his weak spot and that if I hurt the child I'd hurt the man. Do you understand, Lisa?"

Lisa nodded, thinking of her own feeble attempts to annoy Fraser. Perhaps it was true after all; he was hard all the way through and nothing could touch his heart.

"You must ring up and inquire about the bairn every day," said Aunt Maud. "Find out if we can send something to him to show that we remember him."

"Yes, I'll do that," agreed Lisa. "Aunty, what do you think he meant when he said he could afford to bide his time?"

"I think he meant that he can afford to wait now until he can get what he wants, and we know that he wants Breck House. Promise you won't let him have it when I've gone, Lisa."

"Couldn't you make some legal arrangement covering that?" asked Lisa. "I'm sure Murdo Menzies could write something into your will. I would feel much happier and safer if you did that."

"That's a good idea. I'll get Murdo to come and see me." She sighed wearily. "Still I'd like to know what yon rascal has up his sleeve. Do you think you could find out?"

"I'll try, but I can't promise I'll find out anything. Mr. Lamont isn't exactly well-disposed toward me for some reason, so he isn't likely to tell me any of his plans for the future. But sometimes he talks to Sandy, so maybe I can learn something from him," replied Lisa comfortingly.

As Aunt Maud had instructed her, she rang the boatyard every day for news of Johnnie. Every time Jean Bridie provided the information in a cool impersonal voice. Lisa often wondered whether the primly spoken woman was briefed by Fraser about what she should or should not say about the child's condition, because she supplied only the briefest answers to Lisa's persistent and concerned queries.

"Yes, he had a fairly good night and is as well as can be expected," was her usual answer, which always had the effect of setting Lisa's teeth on edge.

One morning, irritated by the treatment she was receiving and convinced that Fraser was behind it, she asked Jean Bridie whether it would be possible for her to go to the hospital to visit Johnnie, as she had a gift for him. Although pushed slightly off balance by the unexpected request, Jean had an answer.

"Ach, no, miss, that would never do. Ye see, the doctors say rest is the only cure and the excitement caused by visitors will do the bairn no good at all. Even Mr. Lamont isn't visiting him."

Frustrated by Jean's sparsely worded answers and horrified by what she considered to be inhuman behavior on the part of Fraser in not visiting his child, Lisa rang the hospital immediately and asked for information about Johnnie, only to be told coolly that since she was not a relative of his they could not divulge any information to her about him.

Thoroughly roused by now, Lisa decided to drive over to Inverey, the county town twenty miles distant from Ardmont where the hospital was situated. Once she was there surely they could not refuse to tell her how he was, or at least to let her leave some fruit for him?

However, she was forced to change her mind about going as the result of a rather strange telephone conversation with Sarah Popham that left her shaken and bewildered.

Sarah rang up to remind her of the luncheon party that would be taking place at Creddon Hall the next day.

"I hope you haven't forgotten about it?" said the model in her shrill voice.

"No I haven't. I've plenty to show you and to tell you," said Lisa warmly, thinking of the different outfits she had drawn for Sarah to appraise and also of the success she had had with dyeing the sheepskins.

"Oh, good. I'm so bored I could scream. I talked to Fraser earlier this week and he assured me he's still coming. It will be a change to have some stimulating company."

"Did he tell you about Johnnie?" asked Lisa.

"No. He didn't say anything about him and I make sure I never show an interest in the child because I know Fraser doesn't like it."

A strange chill swept over Lisa. She felt she was on the brink of learning something she would prefer not to know.

"Doesn't he? Why not?" she asked through stiff lips.

"Because he's tired of being pestered by women, some of whom he's employed as housekeepers and who have fancied themselves as Johnnie's stepmother. They used the child to approach the father, if you get what I mean."

"How embarrassing for him," croaked Lisa, whose throat was suddenly dry.

"Yes, isn't it? But it's to be expected when you think how attractive he is. For myself I'd just loathe it if he thought like that about me, so I've decided never to ask about Johnnie or to show an interest in him, not that I need to use that form of approach with any man," said Sarah with a smugness of attitude that Lisa found totally out of tune with her own feelings on the subject. "Now tell me what's happened to Johnnie."

Subduing a strong inclination to bang the telephone receiver down and cut the conversation short, Lisa swallowed and answered as evenly as she could. "He had an accident and he's in hospital. Concussion."

"Oh, dear! How frightful, and how terribly inconvenient for Fraser having to go and visit him. He's so very busy at the yard just now. But then I expect you've been doing the visiting for him. You're so very fond of Johnnie, aren't you?"

The saccharine quality of Sarah's voice only emphasized the taunt implicit in her words. Lisa had no doubt about how Sarah Popham regarded her friendship with Johnnie.

"Yes, I am fond of Johnnie," she replied as coolly as she could. "I expect Fraser will tell you about the accident when we come to lunch tomorrow."

"Perhaps. But I wouldn't count on it. He and I have much more interesting subjects to discuss," replied Sarah with a coy little giggle. "Bye for now."

Lisa did not bang the receiver down. She laid it gently and carefully in its cradle and stood for a minute in the dimness of the hall, breathing hard in order to control the sudden surge of rage that shook her.

So that was how she appeared to Fraser Lamont—as a pestering woman who was using his child to ingratiate herself with him. The conceit of the man. The egotistical conceit! And Sarah Popham saw her in the same light. Probably they had discussed her and had laughed about her.

The injustice of it all made her blood boil again, and it took all her self-control to stop herself from marching out into the cold windy night down to the white house at the back of the boatyard to tell Fraser Lamont in no uncertain terms what she thought of him. Above all she wanted to make it quite clear to him that marriage with a man who had already been married and who had a child, or with any other man, was not in her plans for the future at all. And even if it had been she would never have stooped to using his child as a means of ensnaring him. She did not regard men as prey to be snared. Marriage was the culmination of love, and love could exist only where there was respect and equality.

Eventually she simmered down and went back to the kitchen, where she was dyeing the sheepskins with green ink. As she had expected, the leather, being porous, readily absorbed anything liquid, and the ink had produced a soft sage green reminiscent of the fields during the wintertime. When she turned the white wool of the outside of the skin

The Taming of Lisa

back against the green she was pleased with the contrast and began immediately to sketch a full-length coat with a close-fitting bodice and slightly flared skirt in which the white wool showed in two bands down the front fastening.

While she sketched, her mind went back to her recent conversation with Sarah. Now that she was calmer she could see that it shed new light on Fraser's attitude toward herself, and she began to understand his caution and his warning to her to stay away from Johnnie. He had been protecting himself, but not knowing her very well he had not realized that his adamant attitude had made her want to make friends with Johnnie all the more.

But she could not have him thinking she had had an ulterior motive in making friends with his child. She would have to prove to him in some way that she was not like that. She could not have him thinking badly about her.

Lisa's pencil slipped as she realized the direction her thoughts were taking. She stared at the black streak the pencil had made. Why should it matter to her what Fraser thought about her? She did not give a button for his opinion. Even so, it would be better if she did not go to visit Johnnie while he was in hospital, and when he came home she would go very carefully indeed. She would not like to be responsible for increasing Mr. Fraser Lamont's conceit of himself.

THE NEXT DAY she took the dyed sheepskins and the drawings she had made to the mill to show Sandy. He was very interested in both and suggested that they go into the sheepskin-coat business together.

"Or we can make it a family affair. The farm can supply the skins, you design the coats while I find someone to do the cutting and the sewing," he said.

"Yes, I've been wondering about that," replied Lisa. "We need someone to cut and sew the suits, too. I can make my own clothes, but I'm not really a dressmaker or a tailor. Do you think Sheila would mind if I took these skins to show Sarah Popham today? I've a feeling she might be interested in them."

"I'm sure Sheila won't mind."

"I wish you were coming with me."

"In some ways I wish I were, too, and not for the reason you're thinking," he said with a smile. "Seriously, Lisa, you'll be far better at that sort of thing than I am. In fact if I could persuade you to become a partner in the firm I'd leave all the public relations to you as well as the designing."

"Fraser is going to lunch today, too," she said.

"He'll be going to talk yachts to Harry Chisholm, I expect." He shrugged indifferently.

Lisa took a deep breath in order to control her impatience with him. "I just don't understand you, Sandy Lewis! You say you're in love with Sarah, yet you make no attempt to approach her."

"I said I used to be in love with her," he corrected mildly. "Now I'm not so sure. She's obviously attracted to Fraser. He presents a challenge because he has no time for women. I only hope in her pursuit of him she doesn't get hurt again. He's pretty impregnable."

"I've noticed that. Have you any idea why?" she asked casually.

"No. I can only guess that he loved his wife so much that when she died he grew an extra-hard shell to cover up his hurt, or his marriage was a mistake and turned him off women. He's never talked about it—in fact he's never mentioned his wife. We can only assume he was married because he came back with Johnnie."

"So you're not going to do anything about Sarah?"

"No. I tend to be a fatalist. Maybe she isn't for me. Maybe I'm going to find someone else with whom I can share my life, and possibly that someone is here in Ardmont, right under my nose."

Slightly disturbed by Sandy's final remark, Lisa left the mill and went to collect Mrs. Isabel Ramsay, a friend of Aunt Maud's who had agreed to stay at Breck House while Lisa was over at Creddon Hall. A widow who lived alone on the other side of the village, Mrs. Ramsay was an active member of the Women's Rural Institute and an indefatigable churchgoer. She and Aunt Maud had very little in common except their schooling and their love of Ardmont, but these two common interests had been enough to keep them good companions in their old age.

The day, which had dawned fresh and clear, had clouded over by the time Lisa picked up Mrs. Ramsay, and rain began to fall steadily, a gray curtain blotting out the island, stippling the sullen water of the kyle with big drops.

"Ye'll be needing to take care on the road to Creddon," warned Mrs. Ramsay. "The clouds come down low over the high parts and sometimes ye canna see where ye are going. And watch out for the bends. Keep well over to your left. Not that there'll be much on the road this time of the year."

Leaving in good time, Lisa did not hurry along the shore road as it wound up to the top of the cliffs beyond the boatyard. It seemed to her that Aunt Maud's car, which was not in the first flush of youth, panted a little as if it disliked making such a strenuous effort, and she was glad that the road flattened out for a few miles so that she was able to drive slowly and glance out occasionally at the northern arm of the kyle. Although it was blurred with rain she could just make out the small islands at the narrows. Immediately below, the entrance to Loch Creddon opened up and soon the road began to rise again in a series of bends, some of which took the car right to the edge of the cliffs and some of which took it inland under a canopy of tall trees from whose branches raindrops dripped, drumming a tattoo on the roof of the car.

Up and up the road went so that the loch below was no longer a mass of moving water but appeared like a solid sheet of dull steel reflecting only the gray of the heavy clouds hovering above it.

As the car rounded what Lisa had hoped was the final steep bend and was faced with yet another incline, its engine failed to pick up when she changed down to second gear for the long haul up. Slowly it chugged up, but as it approached the top she could see steam issuing from under its hood. Fortunately there was a lay-by at the top and she was able to guide it off the road and to a stop.

Having first discovered how to open the hood from a small booklet that she found in the glove compartment, Lisa stepped out into the clinging mistlike rain. The fact that steam had been coming out meant, she knew, that the engine was overheated. She supposed that the climb had been too much for the car's age and condition. To go on would be to ruin the engine forever. The only answer was to allow it to cool and possibly to find some water to put into it, all of which would make her late for lunch.

Vaguely she looked around to see if there was any water, and then grinned when she saw it streaming down the rock beside her. But although she searched the inside and the trunk of the car she could find no container in which she could carry water.

Then she heard the sound of a car's engine. It was coming from the direction of Ardmont. Relief seeped through her. Soon she was able to see the car as it took the slope much faster than hers had. It would not be long before it was near enough for her to signal. She stepped out and waved her long green scarf. The approaching car slowed down to a stop, a door opened and Fraser Lamont appeared.

"What's wrong?" he asked.

"Overheated engine," Lisa explained, thinking how attractive he looked in suit, shirt and tie with his rather unruly brown hair well tamed for once.

He gave her a slight disparaging glance, strode over the the car, lifted the top of the hood, peered underneath, grunted, then closed it with a bang.

"Better leave it here to cool off. You can come with me," he said brusquely, nodding in the direction of his own car. "Get in."

"I've some things in the back of this car that I must take with me," she said hurriedly. She pulled forward the driver's seat of Aunt Maud's car and reached into the back seat for her drawings and the sheepskins.

As she backed out she banged her head on the top of the doorway, a blow that made her feel temporarily dizzy and

The Taming of Lisa

also tipped her hat forward over her eyes. Intending to turn and thrust the things into Fraser's arms and tell him to put them in his car, Lisa found that he was already sitting in the driver's seat and apparently had no intention of helping her.

Tottering slightly, she walked over and tried to open the door of his car that was nearest to her. In the effort she dropped some of her drawings on the ground. Rage that he could sit there and let her struggle sizzled within her as she tried once more to pull the door open. This time she succeeded, and she thrust the sheepskins through the opening, saying between her teeth, "Here, put them in the back seat." Then she bent to pick up her mud-streaked drawings. When she saw the state they were in she could have wept. She was tempted to hurl abuse at the man who sat waiting for her. But when she looked at him and met the slightly mocking gaze of his dark blue eyes she changed her mind quickly. If she were rude to him he was quite capable of driving off without her. So she placed the damaged drawings in his outstretched hand and said meekly, "Do you think I should lock Aunt Maud's car?"

"Please yourself," he returned carelessly.

A great help he was, she thought rebelliously as she straightened her hat and locked the two doors. "Please yourself." If that was the only answer he could give she must make sure never to ask him for advice again in future.

As soon as she was seated and the car door was closed, he started the engine and drove off. The small high-powered car took the next incline with ease. Feeling damp after her brief stay out in the rain, Lisa sat taut and upright, looking straight before her, determined not to be first to break the silence. In fact she did not care if she never spoke to him again.

Her companion, however, had made no such resolution, for they had not gone far before he said easily, "It was a pity you dropped your drawings. I hope they aren't spoiled. They look interesting."

Although she longed to tell him that it was all his fault the drawings were damaged and that if he were a gentleman he would have helped her move the things from Aunt

Maud's car to his, she did not answer. She did not even look at him.

"Are they your reason for going to lunch with Sarah?" he asked politely.

"Yes." Brief to the point of rudeness.

"Are you a dress designer?" he persisted quietly.

"Yes."

"That must be why you look so rakish."

Lisa turned sharply, opened her mouth to object hotly to his description, then closed it when she saw the quirk of amusement at the corner of his mouth.

"I meant the word as a compliment, using it in its nautical sense," he explained smoothly. "A rakish ship has fine lines that show to advantage when it's well maintained. Your clothing, which I presume you design yourself, flatters your height and your slender build."

She had forgotten that he was a designer, too and as such would have an interest in good design in fields other than his own.

"Odd that we should have something in common, isn't it?" he remarked, as if he had read her thoughts, and she moved uneasily, looking out at the dark dripping leaves of rhododendron bushes that lined this part of the road. The car was going downhill now, swishing around bends as they approached the flatter land at the head of Loch Creddon.

"You're not usually so short of words," taunted Fraser. "Are you saving your conversation for the lunch table? Perhaps I should warn you that you'll not get a word in edgeways. Both Bunty and Harry Chisholm are great talkers. Another word of advice: if you're going to design for Sarah don't argue with her, just listen and then do what you think best. She's like her father. She knows a lot, has many ideas but is most impractical."

"Thank you for your advice, Mr. Lamont," she replied coolly. "I'll try to bear it in mind."

"I bet you won't," he retorted with a laugh. "You'll go your own way and be damned to me—which reminds me, you haven't asked me about Johnnie yet."

She stiffened in reaction. "I don't intend to," she replied.

"Why not? Why the sudden loss of interest? Is it because you found it wasn't getting you anywhere?" he jeered.

It would be dangerous to hit him while he was driving, thought Lisa grimly, but that was the action she felt like taking. Instead she gritted her teeth and hissed between them, "You're quite right. I decided the price I would have to pay to become his stepmother would be too great. I'd have to put up with you as a husband."

"Ouch!" he exclaimed mockingly. "You hit hard, Red Smith, but perhaps I deserved that one."

"It was nothing to what you'd have received if you hadn't been driving," she asserted. "You know very well I'm still interested in Johnnie. I've phoned Jean Bridie every morning since he went into hospital. But I won't have you thinking that I'm interested in him because I want a husband. Marriage is well down on my list of priorities for the future."

The silence that followed was not pleasant. Glancing at him out of the corner of her eye and noting the hard line of his mouth, Lisa felt once more that strange tremor of fear that she had experienced in his office the first time she had confronted him and wished it was possible to jump out of the car and run away from him.

The road was now bounded on either side by a low stone wall behind which stood tall trees. Twin gateposts appeared. Fraser swung the car between them and drove up a wide drive at the end of which stood a graceful gray building. He stopped the car in front of the entrance and Lisa prepared to get out.

Her hand was on the door handle when he spoke so pleasantly that she turned to look at him in surprise. He was leaning one elbow on the steering wheel and was watching her, his eyes narrowed, their expression unreadable.

"Thank you for speaking your mind," he said. "Now I have no doubt as to how you feel I must apologize for having been suspicious of your intentions. Shall we wipe the slate clean and start again?"

This tendering of the olive branch confused her so much that Lisa could only answer stiltedly, "If you wish."

"Then I'll begin by telling you that Johnnie is being discharged from hospital tomorrow. He's still having a few dizzy spells and he won't be able to go to school yet. But he can stay at home as long as he doesn't indulge in too much activity. It's going to be hard keeping him entertained and in one place."

"You could drop everything you're doing at the yard and look after him for once," she pointed out.

"What makes you think I'm not going to do that anyway?" he retorted. "Just because I don't go off the deep end and get all emotional every time he's hurt doesn't mean to say I don't know where my responsibilities to him lie."

"You didn't visit him when he was in hospital," she hissed. "I suppose you didn't think that came under the heading of responsibilities?"

"You know everything, don't you?" he observed sarcastically. "I didn't go to visit him because I was obeying the doctor's orders. There wasn't much point in going anyway because when I was able to go he was usually asleep." He broke off suddenly and then added with a rueful smile, "We're not doing very well with our clean slate, are we?"

He was right. Ever since she had agreed to wipe the slate clean she had snarled at him. If he had been guilty of suspecting her intentions she had been just as guilty of prejudice, of allowing other people's opinions of him to sway her judgment.

She looked up, ready to apologize, and met the blue blaze of his eyes as, no longer narrowed in speculation, their gaze lingered appraisingly on her face. He had not touched her and he did not touch her now, but for the first time she was aware of physical attraction flaring flamelike between them and understood at last why she felt that desperate urge to run away.

With a great effort she looked away from him down at her wristwatch. "We're late," she muttered, and opening the door she scrambled out of the car as fast as she could.

LISA WAS ENTRANCED by Creddon Hall, which was really a castle. Its clean uncluttered lines and quaint turrets expressed in pale gray stone appealed to her sense of design. Its setting, too, was perfect. Situated on the banks of the river that flowed into Loch Creddon, backed by the smooth curves of Creddon Hill and surrounded by woods of spruce and larch, it was shown to advantage.

Inside simplicity combined with every modern convenience was the keynote. In the entrance hall bare stone walls were an excellent background for the crests and trophies that hung there. Stone walls dominated the long dining room, a pale contrast for the antique oak dining furniture and the collection of bronze shields that decorated the wall facing the long latticed windows.

Bunty Chisholm, Sarah's mother, was a plump pretty woman who came originally from the north of England, and it was not long before Lisa discovered that she was the driving force behind the restoration and preservation of the castle, which had once belonged to a sept of the Campbell clan and had at one time been a rallying point during various battles that had been waged in the area between the Campbells and other clans.

Harry Chisholm, on the other hand, was a small vigorous man from whom Sarah had inherited her speedwell-blue eyes. He was, so Lisa learned from Bunty, the managing director of his family's company, which had been making pickles and preserves for many years.

Both were adept at putting their guests at ease, although Lisa noticed that the other guest, a young man who sported the latest in male hairstyling and clothing, was nervous. His name was Peter Wright and he was a free-lance photographer and close friend of Sarah's.

Sarah, who was dressed in a long woolen shift that clung to her figure, its simplicity relieved by several gilt necklaces, was in an impish mood. During the meal Lisa wondered once or twice whether she would get any business done with the model that afternoon. Her main aim seemed to be to draw Fraser's attention to herself by flirting with Peter, but in that she was failing miserably, because

Fraser was patently uninterested, being too absorbed in listening to his host talking about his new acquisition, a schooner he had bought in Portugal.

"It'll be the biggest hereabouts," Harry Chisholm was saying clearly. "Bigger than Ranald's. I'm tired of my brother-in-law sailing into the same anchorage and dropping his hook and seeing his topsides tower above mine. When I was in Portugal last year I saw this one and liked the look of it. Of course, it was still carrying cargoes. Wait until you see it. Beautiful ship."

"No good to windward," murmured Fraser. "You won't win many races in it in this part of the world."

"Won't, eh? Well, I suppose you know what you're talking about. That boat you designed for Ranald is certainly a winner. Well, I've bought it now and I want you to do the alterations."

Lisa did not hear Fraser's reply because Mrs. Creddon leaned forward at this point to inform her that "Ranald" was Ranald Gow of the well-known whiskey company and the husband of Harry's sister.

The meal came to an end. Harry took Fraser off to his study, Mrs. Creddon excused herself and Sarah slumped visibly. Looking considerably relieved, Peter Wright leaned back in his chair and lit a cigarette. Lisa came to the conclusion that if she did not take the initiative her visit to Creddon Hall would have been wasted.

"I've left my drawings in the car," she said, rising to her feet. "Shall I bring them in here to show you?"

Sarah came out of her trance, blinked and asked Peter for a cigarette before she answered. "No, we'll go to my sitting room upstairs. I keep all my stuff up there. When you've got your drawings come straight up the main stairway, turn right at the top and it's the second room along the passage."

They all left the room together and as Lisa went to the front entrance Sarah and Peter went upstairs. It was still raining outside and she ran back from the car in order to prevent the drawings and sheepskins from getting wet. She paused in the hall to glance through the drawings, placing the most badly marked ones at the bottom of the folder.

The Taming of Lisa

When she entered Sarah's sitting room Lisa had the distinct impression that she had interrupted an argument between Sarah and Peter, because as she appeared Peter left Sarah standing in the middle of the room and flung himself down in an armchair, a sulky expression on his face.

Sarah's face was pink and her blue eyes expressed hurt, but she smiled when she saw Lisa and came forward to take the folder of drawings from her. She showed immediate interest in the sheepskins and insisted on looking at the drawings of the coats Lisa had made. Since they were the mud-spattered ones Lisa drew them out with reluctance.

"I'm sorry they're so messy. I dropped them when I was taking them from my car and putting them in Fraser's," she explained.

"Oh, you came together after all," said Sarah sharply.

Quickly Lisa explained why Fraser had given her a lift.

"That was very clever of you," sighed Sarah, gazing down at the smudged drawings. "I wish I were as clever as you. Nothing I do seems to attract his attention. Yet he gives you lifts and invites you into his house. No, don't bother to deny it. I saw you go in that day we met at the boatyard. That's why I was so nasty to you on the phone the other evening."

"Do you want his attention?" asked Lisa curiously. Never having wanted to deliberately attract a man's attention, she was rather revolted by Sarah's attitude.

"Of course she does," drawled Peter from the depths of the armchair. "She can't stand it when a man ignores her. She'll go to any lengths to attract him, even to the extent of flirting with me. Look, Sarah, my love, Fraser Lamont might be every young girl's dream of a he-man, but I didn't come all the way from London to help you net him. I want to know if you're interested in modeling for me again."

"Oh, you know I am, Peter, but...." Sarah threw her hands wide in a dramatically helpless gesture.

Sensing that her moment to strike had come, Lisa snatched up the nearest drawing of a tweed outfit, grabbed one of the magazines she had noticed in a rack and went over to Peter.

"We—that is, Ardmont Tweeds Limited—are very interested in Sarah's modeling for you if she can model clothes like this and appear in magazines like this," she said.

Peter took the drawing from her and studied it, then stared at the page of fashion photographs she showed him. As he returned them to her his dark eyes appraised her curiously.

"You'd make a good model yourself," he murmured. He sat forward, put out a long slim hand and turned her face sideways. "Good profile and interesting coloring. Why not model the clothes yourself? I'm more than willing to photograph you."

Aware suddenly of Sarah's dislike of his sugggestion, Lisa moved away from him. "Because I don't want to become a model and because we need good publicity fast," she replied calmly. "Sarah is well-known both as a model and a personality. She has a way of making a rag look like a ball gown."

"Oh, do you think so, Lisa?" chirruped Sarah, enjoying the flattery. "How nice of you to say so. Would you really like me to model your designs?"

"Yes, I would—as long as they're made of Ardmont tweed."

"To help Sandy Lewis," said Sarah, her blue eyes narrowing shrewdly. "Strange...I never thought he would be the type to attract you. He had a *tendresse* for me once. Did you know?

"Yes, he told me."

"Did he now? I wonder why? It would be rather fun to do something for him," drawled Sarah. Then suddenly she clapped her hands together and swung around on Peter. "Just think, Peter, you could use Creddon Hall for a background." She turned and rushed over to the table, scrabbled through the drawings and went back to him with one showing an elegant suit in gold-and-brown tweed. "Imagine me in that against the postern gate—with daffodils blowing at my feet."

Peter studied the drawing and then looked up at her, his eyes crinkling at the corners in an amazingly affectionate smile. "You're right," he agreed. "You'd look great, Sarah." His dark gaze passed on to Lisa, the expression changing from one of affection to one of dawning respect. "You certainly have a fresh approach to the old standby, the good Scottish tweed. I wouldn't be surprised if the industry doesn't take a new lease on life when high society sees pictures of Sarah Popham in one of your creations."

"You'll help, then? Both of you?" asked Lisa breathlessly.

"Yes, for a fee, of course," replied Sarah. "I can hardly wait for those clothes to be made up. Who's going to cut and sew them? You'll have to be careful. Some people can make the most awful mess of a perfectly good design."

The rest of the afternoon passed quickly as the three of them planned which of the designs would look best made up. Lisa found that once Sarah had agreed to model the clothes she was sensible and had no hesitation in telling Lisa how to go about the business of publicity, so that by the time Fraser sent word to say that he would be leaving, several long-distance telephone calls had been made to advertising managers with whom Peter had contacts, and arrangements had been made for advertisements to be placed in several magazines.

"Did you have a successful afternoon?" asked Fraser politely as he drove through the gates and turned the car in the direction of Ardmont. The rain had stopped and the sun had appeared, a disk of pale yellow no bigger than the moon.

"Far more successful than I had hoped. It was lucky that Sarah had Peter Wright staying with her," answered Lisa, and went on to explain what happened.

"Is Sandy thinking of taking you into partnership?" queried Fraser.

"I think he would like that, although I'm not sure whether I want to be tied down in that way. I'd really prefer to free-lance as a designer; you know, get commissions just as you do for yachts."

"That's a chancy business," he remarked. "You have to be very good if you're going to keep the wolf from the door."

"You've made it," she pointed out.

"But only since I came back to Ardmont to a business that was already established. And I don't make my living from my designs. I make it from building boats, any sort of boat, by maintaining them, storing and mooring them, and by occasionally transporting them."

"Are you going to transport Mr. Creddon's schooner for him?"

"Yes, I am."

"How?"

"By sailing it. What other way?"

"I thought it might come by freighter. Won't it be cold and stormy sailing at this time of the year?"

"Probably. It usually is," he said with a grin. "But you must remember this schooner has been until now a freighter itself, and it has two hefty diesel engines in it to push it along, so it won't be necessary to sail all the time."

"Will you go for it personally?"

"Did you imagine I'd sit in the office down at the boatyard and twiddle my thumbs while someone else brought it?" he scoffed. "I've been sailing other people's boats since I was a lad, and one of the reasons why I'm in the business is that I enjoy sailing and the sea. I wouldn't pass up a chance like this for anything. There's only one problem. Harry wants it here by March so that we can start on the alterations he wants done to the layout below decks, and I haven't found a suitable housekeeper yet to take Mrs. Dobie's place, at least not one whom I'd like to leave Johnnie with while he's still shaky after that accident."

Now was her chance to rush in and say she would mind Johnnie for him, but she hesitated. His change of attitude toward her since she had told him she was not interested in marriage had put her on guard. She was fast discovering that when he stopped being a hedgehog he could be a pleasant companion.

The charm of the devil. That was how Aunt Maud had described it, and she was beginning to understand what her aunt had meant. There was charm in the brief flash of his smile, in those sudden direct glances that he gave her when

The Taming of Lisa

she was least expecting them, in the odd, offbeat compliments that he occasionally handed out. And because it was used so rarely and because it was allied to a ruggedly handsome face and a lithe muscular physique, such charm was dangerous and powerfully effective. He would use it, she decided, when he wanted something badly.

It was difficult to quell her natural impulse to offer to look after Johnnie, but this time it had to be done. She would wait and see what happened for once, instead of rushing in.

Aunt Maud's car was where they had left it. To Lisa's relief it started when Fraser turned the key in the ignition. He maneuvered it for her so that it was facing Ardmont to make sure that the engine was running smoothly.

"Seems perfectly all right to me," he remarked as he stepped out of the car. "Are you sure you didn't pretend it was boiling just to scrounge a lift with me?"

"I would never stoop to such a trick," she returned haughtily, taking her place in the driver's seat.

One hand on the door handle ready to close it on her, he looked down at her. It was another slow considering glance, lingering on every feature of her face, causing the blood to tingle beneath her skin. Again she felt as if he had reached out and touched her and yet he had not moved.

"You rise beautifully, Red Smith," he mocked, banged the door shut and walked away to his own car.

CHAPTER FIVE

FIRED WITH ENTHUSIASM after her discussion with Sarah and Peter, Lisa lost no time in going to see Sandy the following day. Although it was Saturday and the mill was not working he was there, showing around a young woman whom he introduced as Ina Scott, a skilled tailor who worked in Glasgow, home for the weekend to visit her parents. She had called at the mill that morning to ask where she could buy some tweed, and knowing her trade Sandy had had the presence of mind to invite her in and to ask her if she would be interested in working for him.

"I won't deny I'm interested," she said to Lisa. "I'd like fine to come back and live in Ardmont, I'm that fed up with the city, but d'ye think ye'll be having any business?"

"We have it already," said Lisa triumphantly, and proceeded to tell them about Sarah's demands for some clothes that she would model for them. Then she showed Ina the drawings of the suits. The woman bent over them and then exclaimed with delight.

"Could you make them fairly quickly?" asked Sandy.

"I could that," agreed Ina, her big brown eyes sparkling in her smooth cream-colored face. "I wish I could start now."

"Why can't you?" demanded Lisa.

"Och, well, I'd have to give notice to my firm," Ina began cautiously.

"How long?" asked Sandy.

"A week, or I'll forfeit my wages."

"Forfeit them," said Sandy with uncharacteristic recklessness. "I'll make them up to you."

Ina looked from him to Lisa, biting her lower lip uncertainly. "I know you, Sandy Lewis," she said at last, "and I think I can trust you, but I'm not so sure...."

The Taming of Lisa

"You can trust me, too," put in Lisa quickly. "Think, Ina, if you do as he suggests you won't have to go back to Glasgow tomorrow. You'll be able to work here during the springtime instead of in the grimy city."

"I'll pay good bonuses, Ina," said Sandy.

"Och, the two of ye have me in such a tizzy I'm not knowing what to do," complained Ina laughingly, her hands over her ears.

"Then go home and think about it," suggested Sandy. "If you decide to join us come out to the farm on Sunday afternoon for tea. Lisa will be there. She's bringing her great-aunt—you know Miss Roy, surely."

"Aye, I know Miss Roy. Are you her niece's daughter, then? I didna' ken that. But it makes all the difference."

Sandy nodded, smiling as if he understood her obscure statement. "Yes, Lisa is almost but not quite a local," he said.

"Then I'll away now, Sandy, to think about it, and I'll be letting ye know."

Ina turned up at the farmhouse on Sunday afternoon and shyly joined the company there. The problem of finding someone to make the suits for Sarah to model solved, Lisa spent most of the following week making patterns from her designs and helping Ina to cut out the material. She found the dressmaker a merry good-hearted girl, quick and methodical in her work. The daughter of one of Sandy's weavers and the foreman at the boatyard, she would have become a weaver herself if she had not been tempted by the superficial attractions of city life to leave her hometown.

"Och, ye ken how it is when you're young, Lisa," she confided. "Ye want to spread your wings to find out if the fellows in the city are any better than the ones at home. And then I used to think Ardmont was a dreary place in the wintertime. There was only fun in the summer when the holidaymakers came. We had to go all the way into Kilbride if we wanted to dance, so off I went to Glasgow to be apprenticed to a dressmaker."

"Do you find Ardmont any different now?" asked Lisa. "You seem glad enough to come back."

"It's changed a wee bit for the better. The mill and the boatyard have brought some of the younger people back and some newcomers, too. Have ye met Mr. Lamont from the yard yet?"

Lisa admitted that she had.

"My dad and my brother Wally both work for him. Wally was apprenticed to boatbuilding under dad when the syndicate owned the yard. He had just finished his apprenticeship when it was closed down and both he and dad were out of work for a while. Aye, but they were glad when Mr. Lamont came back and got things going again. They both like him and won't hear a word said against him, and believe me, there's been some funny things said, what with not knowing who is his wife or where she is."

"I thought she was dead."

"That's what some say. But nobody knows for sure, because he's never talked about her, and he isn't the one you'd ask questions of, so they tell me."

"No, he isn't," agreed Lisa quietly.

THE POSSIBILITY that Fraser's wife might still be alive bothered Lisa intermittently all day. The week had been so busy that she had not been able to do anything about Johnnie. But the boy had often been in her thoughts, and as she drove home that evening she remembered him telling her that they had left his mummy in Tasmania.

Acting on impulse, she drove straight to the boatyard instead of turning up the brae to Breck House. It had been a bright boisterous day with sunlight glinting on the flurried water of the kyle and pageants of purple-and-white clouds rolling across the sky. As she walked over to the white house the wind twitched at her scarf and lifted the skirt of her cloak.

The front door was opened not by Fraser, as she had expected, but by a tall plump woman. Lisa recognized her at once as someone she had seen several times in the village.

"Is Mr. Lamont in?" she asked.

"Och, no, miss. He's awa' on the morning boat for Gourock."

The Taming of Lisa 475

"Oh. I really came to inquire about Johnnie."

"He's doing fine, but he's sleeping just now. Ye wouldn't want me to wake him, would ye?" said the woman anxiously. "He carried on that much after his dad had gone that he exhausted himself."

Lisa took a swift inventory of the woman. She looked clean and wholesome enough and kindly, too. Johnnie could not possibly come to harm with her.

"No, don't wake him," she said. "I'm Lisa Smith. I live in the house up the brae."

"I recognize ye. Ye're Miss Roy's niece. I'm Ellen Dixon. I said I'd look after Johnnie for the week. He was at his wits' end looking for someone to mind the child while he's awa' to Portugal."

"Well, I won't stay now, Mrs. Dixon, but if you should need any help with Johnnie please don't hesitate to ring me up. He knows me and we're good friends."

"Thank ye, miss. Maybe ye'll call in and see him then. It would help take his mind off his dad's being away. Poor wee soul, he's bound to be upset. His dad is the only family he has, although I'm a wee bit sorry for the man, too. It can't be easy being an only parent, for all he seems so strong and competent."

It was a new slant on Fraser, Lisa thought as she sat later in Aunt Maud's bedroom sketching a new design. She had never considered the difficulties he must face being the only parent of a lively sensitive child. How had he felt leaving Johnnie with Mrs. Dixon? Did he worry about the child while he was away? Lisa shook her head. She was putting feelings where there were none. Fraser was as hard as nails. He must be if he could go away so soon after Johnnie had been ill, just because he wanted to sail a boat across the sea.

"What are you muttering about?" asked Aunt Maud, rousing out of the light doze into which she had fallen. She had not been well that week and Lisa had had to ask the district nurse to call again. "You're getting as bad as I am for talking to yourself!"

"I was wondering how Fraser can bring himself to leave

Johnnie and go away for so long," replied Lisa, and went on to describe how upset the boy had been when his father had left.

"Och, don't be fretting over the bairn. Agnes Dixon is one of the best. He'll be fine with her. I wouldn't put it past the little rascal to play up when he knows his father is going away. Aye, it's a hard job rearing a child single-handed. He should get married again."

"Maybe he hasn't found the right person to marry."

"Humph, shouldn't be difficult. There's many a woman would be glad to look after a child in return for home and security. It would give the child a sense of security, too, when his father goes away, instead of having to adjust to different baby-sitters."

"Probably you're right. But these days a woman doesn't have to marry to get a home. And what about love—doesn't that come into it?"

"What's wrong with a marriage of convenience? Often they turn out better than the sort based on so-called love," growled Aunt Maud.

"Why did you never marry?" asked Lisa.

"Because the man I wanted to marry preferred someone else, that's why."

"But I thought you were engaged to be married."

"Aye, I was," sighed Aunt Maud. "To John Lamont, great-grandfather of your wee Johnnie. So now you know why I can't stand the sight of yon rascal Fraser. He's the image of John when I was engaged to him."

THE WEEKEND PASSED QUIETLY. The Lewises came for tea and Sandy and Lisa took the dogs walking on the moors.

"Your aunt doesn't seem very well, although I can tell she's easier in her mind," said Sandy as they stopped to lean against an outcrop of granite and gaze down at the view.

"Yes, she does seem less harassed since Fraser told her he had no intentions of buying The Moorings now. I wish I knew what made him change his mind. All he would say was that he's no longer desperate for space since he re-

The Taming of Lisa

ceived permission to build that new shed and he can afford to bide is time."

They both stared down at the shed, which was now ready to have its roof put on.

"My father and Miss Roy have made Fraser appear like a monster who would devour Ardmont in one huge swallow," murmured Sandy musingly, "whereas in actual fact he's only a man trying to do his best to improve his business and help the community. If Ardmont is to survive there have to be changes, but the older people here can't accept that. Don't let your outlook be affected by theirs, Lisa. Fraser needs all the friends he can find."

"What makes you say that?"

"Sometimes I have the feeling he's very lonely. Unlike me, he doesn't have the help of a family—or a very pretty partner."

"Two partners," she chipped in, laughing. "Remember we have Ina now."

"How could I forget her? No, Fraser's done everything on his own without anyone's help, and I admire him for it. I couldn't have done it without encouragement and a helping hand—like this one." Sandy lifted her gloved hand from her side and pulled it through his arm. "Shall we go on, Lisa?"

She knew he was referring to their walk, but she had a sudden fear that perhaps he meant more, that he wanted her to go on with him through life, giving him a helping hand.

Her wild freedom-loving heart jibbed at the idea. Making a pretense of having to pull her hat on more securely, she removed her hand from the crook of his elbow and turned away to whistle up the dogs.

"We're ready to have a fitting with Sarah now," she said as she fell into step with him again, knowing that a conversation about the business would be safe ground. "Would you mind if I ask her to come to the mill tomorrow?"

"I don't mind your asking her, but she won't be coming because she isn't at Creddon Hall. She's gone to Portugal with her father. They flew there yesterday. I met Mrs. Chisholm at church this morning and she was telling me."

"That's where Fraser has gone," she said, and her voice sounded strangely flat and dull.

"So I believe. Looks as if he might have found a stepmother for Johnnie sooner than anyone expected, doesn't it? Sarah is very hard to resist when she's persistent."

"Don't you mind?"

"Not at all. Why should I when I have you—and Ina, of course," he laughed, taking her hand in his again, and this time she did not pull it away.

HER CONSCIENCE PRICKING HER with regard to Johnnie, Lisa called in to see him on Monday afternoon. The weather had calmed down temporarily and the day was mild and sunny. Already coltsfoots were appearing shyly through the dead leaves under the hedges, and snowdrops nodded their dainty heads in the garden at Breck House. Spring was on its way, slowly, inexorably. There would be a few setbacks between now and May, but nothing could stop the steady climb of the sun up the sky and the gradual wakening of nature.

Johnnie looked better than she had expected and seemed quite happy with Mrs. Dixon, whom he called Dixie. He talked for a while about his stay in hospital and the fun he had had with his father before Fraser had gone away. Then, turning large reproachful eyes in her direction, he said, "Why didn't you come to see me before? I thought you were my friend."

"I am your friend, Johnnie, and I always will be. I couldn't come because I've been busy...."

"That's what daddy said when I asked him. I thought perhaps you hadn't come because you were afraid of him. You needn't be afraid, you know. He's quite kind when you get to know him."

Hiding a smile, Lisa promised to call the next day and to bring the dominoes.

She called every day after that, but on Thursday Mrs. Dixon met her with a worried expression on her face.

The Taming of Lisa

"I've just heard from Jeannie that Mr. Lamont has been delayed. The boat isn't quite ready. It means he won't be back until next Wednesday and I told him I could only stay until Monday."

"Can't Jeannie mind him?" suggested Lisa

"Not really, miss. She has her own family, and between you and me, Johnnie doesn't care for her all that well."

"Where do you have to go on Monday?"

"I'm going to Gourock on the boat, to stay with my daughter's bairns. She's going into hospital for an operation."

"Then don't worry about it. If Mr. Lamont isn't back by then I'll keep Johnnie with me."

"That's a load off my mind. He's such a sweet wee laddie that I wouldn't like to upset him any more than I need. I can see that he likes ye and that he'll feel happy with you. By rights he should be going back to school by Monday. The doctor says there's no reason why he shouldn't."

Lisa decided not to tell Aunt Maud that she would be looking after Johnnie until Monday came because of the possibility that Fraser might be back. But when she heard that the weather forecast for the Channel and the Irish Sea on Sunday evening predicted gale-force winds, she guessed that the schooner from Portugal would not be dropping its anchor in Ardmont Bay on Monday, so she went down to see Johnnie off to school and to assure him that she would meet him that afternoon, then went to break the news to Aunt Maud.

"You'll bring him here to sleep," insisted Aunt Maud.

"No, I thought I'd go down there."

"And have all of Ardmont gossiping? I'll not have you sleeping in Fraser Lamont's house. Besides, I need you here."

Johnnie was delighted at the idea of sleeping at Breck House and quite happily helped Lisa pack his pajamas, clean clothes and a few toys. In the small bedroom under the eaves next to Lisa's he was a little bothered by the sound of the wind as it soughed around the house and rattled the slates, so she stayed with him for a while and told him about her mother, who had lived at Breck House and had slept in a room just like his.

"I'm sleeping in it just now, and I often think of her and one of the poems she used to say to me," she said.

"Say it to me," demanded Johnnie.

"I remember, I remember
The house where I was born,
The little window where the sun came peeping in at morn,
He never came a wink too soon
Nor brought too long a day...."

Lisa's voice trailed away and she did not finish the verse from Thomas Hood's poem because Johnnie had fallen asleep.

All the next day the wind blew and when Johnnie went to bed anxiety was obvious in his strained eyes.

"Does the sun really peep in your window in the morning, Lisa?" he asked after she had said the verse of the poem at his request.

"Yes, it does. In this one, too, I expect, because they both face east."

"I didn't see it this morning because the sky was all gray and cloudy. Do you think the wind will stop blowing soon?"

"I hope so."

"I wish daddy wouldn't go sailing," he sighed plaintively, voicing the anxiety that was uppermost in his mind, and to take his mind off the subject she said another poem to him.

IN THE NIGHT Lisa woke in sudden fright to the sound of Johnnie's voice calling her. She found him sitting up in bed sobbing.

"I dreamed that daddy was drowned," he cried.

"Dreams often go by opposites, Johnnie. I expect he's quite safe in harbor somewhere," she murmured comfortingly as she straightened the bedclothes.

She sat on the bed holding his hand and when she thought he had gone to sleep she would have crept out of

The Taming of Lisa

the room, but his hand clutched at hers and he whispered, "Don't go away."

So she lay down on the bed beside him and listened to the wind howling, her eyes wide in the darkness as she thought how awful it would be if Fraser were drowned at sea as his father had been drowned when he was a boy.

LISA WAKENED SUDDENLY. Her feet were cold because she had fallen asleep beside Johnnie without any bedclothes over her. She lay for a moment blinking drowsily at the chink of pale light that appeared at the curtained window, trying to make out what was different.

Then she realized how quiet it was. The wind no longer rattled at doors and windows searching for an entrance to the house. The early morning was peaceful and slumbrous.

Suddenly, outside in the garden, a bird began to sing, a vigorous flutelike song. Another joined it, chirruping merrily as it welcomed the dawn, and soon the whole garden was alive with song.

Lisa slipped out of bed and tiptoed to the window to pull one of the curtains aside. Dawn had broken in the sky above the dark hump of the island of Boag and pale light was reflected in the water of the kyle, was still flecked by little foam-topped waves churned up by the recent wind.

Everything looked as it looked every morning. But there was one difference, a difference that set her heart thumping unaccountably and caused a flush to stain her cheeks. Dark against the water, nodding at its anchor chain, its two masts swaying slightly as it shifted on the changing tide, was a big black schooner.

Lisa did not question the impulse that sent her scurrying from Johnnie's room to her own. There she flung off her nightdress and hastily donned pants, tunic and shoes. Taking a belted suede jacket from the wardrobe, she pulled it on and dashed down the stairs along the hall and out of the house. The chilly morning air stung her face as she ran down the path, flung the gate wide and rushed out onto the road.

As she hurried she was conscious of a wonderful exhilaration. No wonder the birds were singing! She felt at one with them. Her heart was singing, too.

"My heart is like a singing bird." How well that poem described how she felt this morning. But why?

Perhaps she would find the answer in the rest of the poem if she could remember it. Her run slowed to a walk as she searched her memory, and she came to a full stop outside the entrance to the boatyard as the last line of the first verse of the poem leaped to her mind. "Because my love is come to me."

Ridiculous! That might have been the reason for Christina Rossetti's heart's being like a singing bird, but it was no reason for Lisa Smith's joyous mood, because she had no love to come to her.

Then what was she doing here at the entrance to the boatyard at six o'clock on a chilly March morning?

She had come to make sure that Fraser was really back home and to tell him that Johnnie had cried for him in the night. She had come to ask him to reassure the child as soon as possible. That was the only reason.

But she could have waited. She could have had breakfast first before telephoning cautiously and sedately. There was no need for this headlong rush.

She took a deep breath of the fresh cold air in an attempt to calm her singing heart and to quell her suddenly tumultuous thoughts. When she had recovered a semblance of her poise she walked through the yard up the steps of the house and inserted the key that Mrs. Dixon had left with her in the lock of the front door.

The key turned, the lock slid back and she opened the door and entered. The house was quiet and yet possessed that indefinable atmosphere that a house has when there is someone in it.

She peeped into the kitchen. There was no one there. Coming back into the hallway, she peered up the stairs. She would look in the big bedroom that Johnnie had told her was his father's to make sure Fraser was there and then she would go as quietly as she had come.

Upstairs all the doors were closed except one. She went

over to it and peeped round it. In the pale morning light coming through the uncurtained window she could see quite clearly a tumble of dark hair on the pillow and the hump of a body under the bedclothes.

Backing out carefully, she pulled the door after her. To her consternation it creaked a little. She stood perfectly still hoping that it had not awakened Fraser, but her hope was unfulfilled.

"Is that you, Johnnie?" His voice sounded sleepy, benign. She did not answer or move, feeling sure he could hear the silly thumping of her heart.

"Johnnie—" this time the whip crackled "—come in here."

She put her head around the door and said as coolly as she could, "It's me—Lisa."

Fraser sat up quickly. The bedclothes fell away from his shoulders. A few days' growth of beard made an Elizabethan buccaneer of him. The top buttons of his pajamas were undone so that an expanse of chest was revealed. His generally disheveled appearance made him seem vulnerable, more approachable.

Just how wrong she was about that was shown when he leaned back against the headboard of the bed and said coldly, "Since when have you had the run of this house?"

How like him to put her in the wrong, she thought furiously, and her heart stopped singing abruptly.

"I—I came to make sure you're really back home and that the schooner out there isn't a figment of my imagination."

His eyebrows drew together in a perplexed frown. "Why?"

"Because Johnnie is at Breck House."

"What is he doing there? Have you kidnapped him again?"

Recalling his jeer that she rose easily to baiting, she quelled an urge to retort rudely and answered with forced patience, "Mrs. Dixon couldn't stay any longer. She had to go and look after her daughter's children, so I said I'd mind him. There was no way we could get in touch with you to ask your permission."

Reacting to the touch of acidity in her voice, he gave her a sharp glance. "It would seem I'm in your debt," he said stiffly. "What does Miss Roy think of having my brat under her roof?"

"It was her idea that he should stay at Breck House. She didn't want me to sleep in your house—as if that would have mattered for two nights."

"It would have mattered, especially since I was back about one o'clock this morning," he replied gravely.

"Didn't you look in Johnnie's room?"

"The door was closed and I assumed he was asleep and didn't want to disturb him or Mrs. Dixon. How is he?"

"He's well, but he was very upset last night when he heard the wind howling. He had a bad nightmare. He dreamed you were drowned. Will you come to see him and assure him that you're alive?"

"Give me fifteen minutes and I'll be over at Breck House," he said brusquely. He flung back the bedclothes and Lisa retreated hastily, closing the bedroom door behind her.

As he had promised, Fraser was no more than fifteen minutes in following her to Breck House, having dressed in his usual working clothes but not having stopped to shave.

Lisa's gaze lingered on the dark stubble of beard as she let him into the house.

"Johnnie won't know you like that," she murmured.

His fingers rasped against his chin as he rubbed the beard with one hand.

"Yes, he will. He's seen me with a beard before, in fact more with than without. Where is he?"

Lisa led him up the stairs, coping with an unfamiliar pang of jealousy as she realized there was so much of his past life that she did not know about.

Johnnie was awake, blinking drowsily in the dim light of his room. His greeting to his father was ecstatic, and Lisa stayed in the room only long enough to pull back the curtains and see Fraser rumple his child's hair and speak to him in a cheerful familiar way that must have chased away all the boy's doubts and fears.

Downstairs again she busied herself with the preparation of breakfast, deliberately keeping her thoughts on her plans for the day. She would try to contact Sarah, who must be back at Creddon Hall by now. She hoped Sarah had not forgotten her promise to model the suits.

When she heard Fraser descending the stairs she went into the hall.

"Like some breakfast?" she asked casually as he reached the bottom stair.

One hand resting on the newel post, he turned to look at her. "The way to a man's heart?" he queried.

"Not at all," she retorted, forgetting she mustn't rise to his baiting remarks. "I'm merely being neighborly. Anyway, I don't believe you have a heart, and even if you have the way to it must be strewn with sharp tacks making the approach to it most unpleasant, designed to deter the most determined and well-intentioned female, and not to be bypassed by the offer of ham and eggs, rolls and marmalade, coffee—"

"Say no more," he said, holding up a hand. "That's my favorite breakfast, provided you substitute tea for the coffee. As you assure me that you're well-intentioned, I accept your offer."

Slightly suspicious of his mockery, Lisa turned away into the kitchen and he followed her.

"Do you know, you rant almost as well as Miss Roy," he said easily as he sat down in a chair at the table. "Have you been taking lessons, or is it a hereditary vice of the Roys?"

About to set a full plate in front of him, Lisa opened her mouth to retaliate, saw the twinkle in his eyes, closed her mouth again and set the plate down with exaggerated care.

"No more than I suspect that a tendency to tease and tantalize is a hereditary vice of the Lamonts," she said. "Is Johnnie getting up?"

"Not yet. I told him to stay put for another hour. He seems tired after his restless night," he replied, and began to eat.

"You must have had a very rough trip," she commented,

sitting down opposite him. "We've had strong winds here for two days."

"I've known worse," he answered carelessly. "Fortunately we reached Campbelltown before it began to blow really hard, so we were in sheltered water all the way from there to here last night."

"Was the weather bad in Lisbon, too? Was that why you were delayed?"

"No. Harry and Sarah seemed to think it was necessary to throw a couple of parties for their friends and acquaintances before we left," he said, and grinned reminiscently. "Sarah reminds me a little of Holly."

"Holly?" Lisa was puzzled.

He drank some tea before answering her.

"Johnnie's mother. She liked a gay time. The more people and parties the better."

Liked. He had used the past tense, so Holly must be dead. Almost holding her breath for fear she might destroy this moment of unexpected confidence, Lisa searched her mind for some way in which she could persuade him to tell her more about Johnnie's mother.

"Is Johnnie like her?" she asked gently.

"Yes. In more ways than one. Apart from his eyes he has her coloring," he replied, "and like her he's a little timid, afraid of the wind and the sea and of storms."

His mouth had taken on an unfamiliar scornful twist, as if he could not understand such timidity in a child of his.

"Did you love her very much?" probed Lisa, still gently daring.

He flashed her a surprised glance, then his mouth tightened into the usual proud straight line and she prepared herself to face a stinging retort.

"A woman's question," he jeered. "And the answer is I don't know."

"But you must know," she challenged. "You married her. Don't people usually marry for love?"

"So I've been told." His eyes and mouth were skeptical. "I didn't have time to find out. When I first met her Holly was pretty, fun to be with, hospitable. She was the only daughter of wealthy parents. I was lonely, a stranger in a strange land. She wanted to be married, so we married, against her parents' wishes. That was mistake number one. They cut us out of their lives."

"Why?"

He shrugged broad shoulders. "They didn't say. I guess it was because they didn't consider me good enough for Holly. I was only a poor immigrant struggling to make my way in the boatbuilding industry in Hobart, whereas Holly was the daughter on one of Hobart's leading citizens, who had a private income of her own left to her by a doting grandmother. To their way of thinking no man was good enough for her."

He stopped talking to finish eating. Lisa gazed at his lean weather-beaten face, thinking how much good breeding and pride of race were responsible for the clear-cut angles of nose and jaw, the fine wide sweep of brow above intelligent direct eyes. The rest, the lines of humor and those of determination, were the product of his character. Oh, yes, Fraser Lamont, whether poor and struggling in Hobart, or successful and his own boss in Ardmont, was a man good enough for any woman, no matter how wealthy her parents might be.

"They thought you were a fortune hunter," Lisa suggested softly.

Humor glinted briefly in his eyes as he looked at her. "Perhaps." He shrugged noncommittally.

"What happened?"

"Their treatment of her made Holly very depressed. Then we had Johnnie, which was mistake number two. Apparently she should never have had a child—a fine thing to find out after the event! She died twelve months after we'd been married, leaving her private income in trust for Johnnie when he comes of age."

"I'm sorry," whispered Lisa, slightly shocked by his curt emotionless explanation of tragedy.

"Be sorry for Johnnie, not for me," Fraser replied

coldly, pushing her sympathy away. "He doesn't know what it's like to have a mother."

"And you like the world to think you don't mind not having a wife," accused Lisa sharply.

He leaned back in his chair and eyed her narrowly. "I'd like to know just what lies behind that remark," he challenged.

"Dislike."

"Of me?" He didn't seem unduly perturbed by the possibility that she might dislike him.

"Dislike of your abominable pride, which won't let you admit that you loved Holly and regretted her death, or that you need someone to be a mother to Johnnie. You're so afraid someone might pity you."

The color put there by exposure to strong winds and inclement weather seeped away from his face, leaving it taut and pale. For a few seconds his eyes blazed blue murder at her and she leaned away from him, thinking he might strike her.

But his anger was short-lived. His eyes narrowed again and black eyelashes hid the expression of violence. Rising to his feet, he pushed the chair carefully under the table and stood looking down at her.

"You know you should be careful what you say, Red Smith," he drawled, "or I'll be getting the wrong impression again. Such interest on your part in me and the way I should or shouldn't feel might lead me to think that you're angling to be Johnnie's stepmother yourself, in spite of what you told me the day we went to Creddon Hall."

Appalled that she had left herself so wide open for such a crack, Lisa could only stare up at him, her heart no longer as light as a bird's, but heavy, heavier than the customary lead.

"Thanks for the breakfast," he was saying crisply, "and for looking after Johnnie. Perhaps you wouldn't mind seeing him off to school for me. I've a lot to do today, as we must get the schooner out of the water before the weather deteriorates again. Tell Johnnie to come to the yard when he comes home and I'll see him there."

The Taming of Lisa

He had gone before she had recovered. Then, urged by the desire to explain, to apologize for what she had said, Lisa hurried after him and reached the front door, only to have it slammed in her face. She opened it. All the glory of the sunrise, orange and rose-tinted cirrus cloud fanning out against the azure sky above the dark hump of Boag, blazed before her eyes.

The iron gate clanged as Fraser swung it shut behind him. Lisa ran to it and leaned over it.

"Fraser!" she called, and knew he must have heard her. He did not look back but continued to walk steadily down the narrow road along which she had run so blithely only an hour earlier. And something about the set of his shoulders and the determined thump of his feet on the surface of the road made her realize the futility of following him. It was quite obvious he wanted nothing to do with her.

IF SARAH MENTIONED FRASER'S NAME AGAIN, she would scream, thought Lisa, later the same day. As she had hoped, the model had returned to Creddon Hall and had been quite willing to come to the mill to have the clothes made for her fitted. She had been at the mill for over an hour now, standing patiently while Ina fitted skirts and jackets, or sitting and smoking while an alteration was made to an article.

And all the time she had talked about Portugal and the fun she had had there with Fraser. Several times Lisa had tried to change the subject, conscious of Ina's pricked ears, knowing how furious Fraser would be if his visit to Portugal with Harry Chisholm and his daughter became the subject of gossip all over the Ardmont peninsula. But inevitably Sarah returned to her favorite theme.

"Is that the last one?" she yawned as she stepped carefully out of a skirt and handed it to Ina. "Good, that leaves me time to drive down to the slip to see if the schooner is out of the water."

She dressed quickly in her own clothes, a close-fitting jumper with a mandarin collar, flared pants and high-heeled shoes.

"I wanted to sail back," she announced as she attended to her makeup.

"I thought you didn't like sailing," said Lisa.

"I don't, but I'd have put up with anything to come back with Fraser. However, he wouldn't hear of it. He says he doesn't like having a woman on board and that he'd prefer to find me waiting here, looking decorative. I didn't press him because I know I'm decorative and that I like nothing better than being in the forefront of a reception committee, especially if there's someone like Fraser to be welcomed."

"It's a pity you weren't at the boatyard about one o'clock this morning, then," said Lisa with an acidity that surprised even herself.

Her tone was not lost on Sarah, who pouted a little as she replied, "Well, I couldn't help that. He told me he wouldn't be arriving until this afternoon. How was I to know he'd get here sooner? But better late than never. I'll go and welcome him now."

She went off and for a while there was silence in the room. Lisa stared out of the window, recalling the welcome Fraser had received from herself. Hardly a hero's welcome, she thought with a grin. They had circled each other verbally, like two angry cats spitting suspicion and snarling home truths. Yet when she had set out for the boatyard she had been so full of gladness because he had come back safe and sound. Gladder than a singing bird.

"So that was Sarah Popham," said Ina. "I canna say I'm impressed."

"She's very good as a model," replied Lisa.

"That's as may be," said Ina grudgingly. "Seemed to me she was laying it on awful thick about her high jinks in Portugal."

"You won't repeat anything she said, Ina, please? Mr. Lamont would be very annoyed if it became the subject of gossip in the village."

"No, I won't. I'm not a spreader of exaggerations."

"Exaggerations?" repeated Lisa, a mystified expression on her face.

"That's what I meant by her laying it on thick. Och, ye're

awful innocent when it comes to dealing with other women, Lisa. She was exaggerating and extending everything that happened while she was in Portugal. I've heard a lass do it before when she's wanted to impress another lass and make her jealous. She'd make out she'd had such a good time with a fellow when if the truth were known he'd been quite uninterested in her."

"But who would Sarah be trying to impress today?"

"Well, it wasna' me, I can tell ye that, because I dinna know Mr. Lamont," said Ina with a grin. "Could only be you," she added as she went out of the room.

Had Sarah been exaggerating her relationship with Fraser, wondered Lisa as she went back to Breck House in the clear light of late afternoon. Had the model intended to irritate her and make her jealous? Because if that had been her intention she had succeeded. For a while in the room at the mill she had been swamped by a green tide of jealousy because Sarah had danced with Fraser, had laughed with him and had been asked by him to be decorative and waiting for him when he returned from sea.

Why should she feel jealous, an emotion she had rarely experienced in the whole of her life until now? And why should Sarah Popham want to make her jealous? There was nothing between herself and Fraser to make Sarah think she had competition.

Nothing? Could she be sure of that?

She lingered in the front garden enjoying the softness of the air and the warmth of the sunlight, pretending she was more interested in the crocuses just showing purple and yellow through the grass than she was in the two figures inspecting the new shed. Sarah's honey-colored hair gleamed in the sunlight as she swung it back from her face, and the top of her head reached just to Fraser's shoulder.

Nothing between herself and Fraser! What about the flare of attraction she had felt coming back from Creddon Hall? What about the anxiety that had racked her during the night when like Johnnie she had imagined Fraser drowned? What about her singing heart that morning? But what about the slanging matches they had had? Didn't they prove something, too?

Never heard of the couples who expressed their love for each other in verbal warfare, she argued with herself. Like Beatrice and Benedick in *Much Ado About Nothing*, who had loved each other against their wills?

It couldn't be true. She couldn't be in love. She didn't want to be in love, and certainly not with a tough self-contained character like Fraser, who had admitted he had not known whether he had loved his first wife or not.

No, this feeling was foolish, the sort indulged in by romantic ex-schoolgirls like Marjorie Morrison, unworthy of the freedom-loving independent woman she knew herself to be, and it must be squashed at all costs.

However, during the next few days Lisa had little time to indulge in the feeling. A cable arrived from her father stating that he had three months' leave and that he intended to spend some time with her at Breck House. He would arrive at Prestwick Airport the following Saturday morning and hoped that she would meet him there.

"Just like Frank Smith," grumbled Aunt Maud. "Always last minute. Thinks we have nothing better to do but wait about for him to come home on leave. Expects you to drop everything and run to meet him. You'll have to go over on Friday and stay the night in Prestwick. You'd better ask Isabel to come and stay the night with me."

"That's the day Peter Wright is arriving. He's going to photograph Sarah at Creddon Hall. I promised I'd take Ina there on Saturday to make sure the clothes are fitted right," said Lisa.

"It might rain," comforted Aunt Maud, "then they'll have to postpone the photography. They'll just have to manage without you for once. It'll not do them any harm. Sandy Lewis is beginning to depend on you too much lately. He's making a lot of demands on your time."

"Oh, I don't think of him as demanding. I like designing for him. He's so appreciative."

"Humph. Doesn't do to be at a man's beck and call, as you should know. He'll start getting ideas if you are."

"Such as?" prompted Lisa, who was always interested in her aunt's views on the opposite sex.

"He might start thinking you're in love with him. Are you?"

"Good heavens, no!" exclaimed Lisa. "Whatever makes you think that?"

"The way you've been behaving lately. Reminds me of your mother when she first knew Frank."

Alarmed by Aunt Maud's shrewd observation, Lisa jumped to her feet and walked over to the window. The new shed was now covered by a roof. She could see Fraser standing, hands on his hips, his head tilted back as he talked to one of the men still working on the roof. The sight of his straight compact figure made her pulses race and the blood burn in her cheeks. She curved both hands around her face in an attempt to cool it.

"What have I been doing that's odd?" she queried in a slightly creaky voice.

"Just what you've done now. Jumping out of your chair for no apparent reason. Staring out of the window. Standing in the garden absentmindedly stripping my lilacs of their new buds. Rising with the dawn and rushing off down the road. Och aye, ye needn't deny it, lass—I've watched you and I've heard you. And what's more, you get into the middle of a sentence, then forget what you're going to say and go off into a dream. Sure sign of being in love."

"Did my mother really behave like this when she met dad?" asked Lisa softly.

A small figure had joined Fraser, a boy with blond hair who tugged at his father's sweater to get his attention. Fraser looked down at him and a few seconds later they walked away from the shed toward the yard.

"Aye, she did," sighed Aunt Maud. "You're like her in many ways. More generous than I ever was. I hope no man ever takes advantage of you."

"Do you think dad took advantage of mother?" asked Lisa, a dangerous edge to her voice. She loved her father dearly, and even her liking for Aunt Maud would not allow her to stand by and hear him vilified.

"No," replied Aunt Maud smoothly. She could be diplomatic when she wanted. "But I think you should be on guard against those who might take advantage of your generosity and use it for their own selfish ends."

When Lisa told Sandy that she would be unable to go to Creddon Hall, he offered to go himself and take Ina with him.

"I'll do anything for you, Lisa," he said lightly. "After all, that's what a partner is for, to share the load."

"But I'm not a partner yet."

"That's true. I wish you would decide to join us. Working with you has made all the difference to me. But you must know that. Seeing you here, listening to you talking enthusiastically about design, has given me a new fresh outlook on life and on the tweed industry." His faintly self-disparaging smile, which never failed to rouse her desire to take him by the shoulders and shake him out of his lack of self-esteem, appeared. "I was in danger of becoming slightly sour, not having known success in either business or love. You've changed all that."

Have I, she wondered uneasily, her gaze flickering to the door of his office as she contemplated escape.

To her relief the door opened and Ina stepped briskly into the room. Over one arm she was carrying a tweed suit.

"I thought ye'd like to be seeing the first one," she said, her brown eyes flicking from Lisa's face to Sandy's and back again, as if she sensed a certain tension between them. She laid the suit on the desk and stood back proudly to admire her own handiwork.

"It's perfect, Ina," said Lisa. "Just imagine how marvelous it's going to look on Sarah."

"Aye, I'm looking forward to seeing her in it. What time d'ye want me to be ready on Saturday morning?"

Lisa explained that Sandy would be going to the castle instead of herself, and was surprised to see a gleam of warm pleasure light up Ina's eyes.

"Och, then that's just fine. And what time would ye be wanting to leave, Sandy? Sure and I never thought I'd ever be going to Creddon Hall as a guest with the owner of Ardmont Mill to see me own sewing being photographed,'' exclaimed the little seamstress, and while she and Sandy made their arrangements for Saturday Lisa slipped out of the room, thankful that once more she had avoided a serious personal conversation with Sandy.

CHAPTER SIX

THE BOEING 707 in which Frank Smith had flown across the Atlantic Ocean landed on time early on a bright blustery March morning. He came through the door from the immigration and customs department, tall and spare, impeccably dressed as always, the white flashes in his dark well-groomed hair emphasized by the tan he had acquired during six years in the Caribbean. When he saw Lisa he dropped the hand luggage he was carrying, put his arms around her and held her closely for a moment.

Within two hours of his landing they were standing together on the top deck of the yellow-funneled ferryboat as it transported them across the Clyde, admiring the view of the mountains of Saddleback and the Cobbler to the north and the dark jagged peaks of the island of Arran to the south.

Frank did most of the talking, telling her about various experiences during his work with the British Trade Commission in the Caribbean, and it was not until they were passing the low-lying craggy islands at the narrows of the kyle that Lisa told him about Aunt Maud's poor health and how the worry over keeping Breck House had brought her low.

"Why is she worried?" asked Frank calmly.

"Wait. You'll see in a few minutes as we approach Ardmont pier," replied Lisa.

And he did see and stared in amazement at the mushroom growth of sheds at the boatyard that seemed from this point of view to be encroaching on Breck House, trying to push the old house off its land.

"Good Lord!" he exclaimed mildly. "Looks as if the yard is booming. If I'm not mistaken that's a new fishing vessel being built over there. Didn't know they built stuff like that. Who owns the place now?"

"A man called Lamont."

"Oh, so it's back in the family. Can't be Charlie Lamont. He was drowned more than twenty years ago, before you were born. Nice chap. Not much of a head for business—too kindly. He was always ready to do someone a good turn. I hired a dinghy from him that time I spent a holiday here when I first met your mother. He had a boy, tough little blighter, afraid of nothing. Could sail anything."

"He's still like that," drawled Lisa. "He's the Lamont I'm talking about. But I'll let Aunt Maud tell you about him."

Later that day Frank lounged before the fire in the sitting room at Breck House and listened to Aunt Maud, who had made an effort to come downstairs to greet him, as she complained about Fraser Lamont.

"Do you know, I'm thinking I preferred it when I knew what he was going to do," she grumbled finally. "Then I could take action to block him. But this recent idea of his to bide his time until he gets what he wants is more worrying. I feel like a mouse being played with by a cat, wondering where he's going to pounce next."

"I'll go and have a talk with him while I'm here," said Frank. "Pump him a bit—diplomatically, of course, I can see why you're concerned, Maud, but I'm afraid you can't stop the march of time and progress."

"You call yon sheds progress?" she demanded.

"I'll admit they're not beautiful and I know it would be ideal if places like Ardmont could remain untouched. But if they're to be viable communities in this day and age they have to move with the times. There's a great demand for yachting facilities in these parts and you can't stop the man from cashing in on it. Personally I think he's to be admired for coming back here and making an effort to revitalize the industry," replied Frank equably.

"But why does he have to do it at the expense of my peace of mind?" growled Aunt Maud. "I've looked out at the kyle and at the isalnds for years, and now what do I see? Huge sheds blocking my view, and if he has his way he'll be on the other side, too, squeezing me out. Lisa thought of putting in an offer for The Moorings to stop him from buying the place."

"Oh, indeed? And what were you going to use for money?" asked Frank with an amused glance at his daughter.

"I was going to ask you for a loan," she replied honestly.

"Don't you like Lamont, either?" he asked idly.

"I...I..?" began Lisa, appalled to hear herself stuttering hesitantly. She looked up warily to find she was being watched closely by two pairs of eyes, one sharp and disapproving, the other indulgently amused. She felt the color drain from her face as she realized she was not prepared to divulge her opinion of Fraser to either her father or her aunt.

"I think it's time we had a hot drink," she added, recovering quickly, and springing to her feet she sped from the room.

Although aware that he was very observant and extremely alert, Lisa found her father's presence at Breck House very comforting. Having spent all his working life in the British civil service in various trade commissions that had taken him to many different parts of the Commonwealth, he had developed a calm and collected attitude to life, totally lacking in prejudice. He was interested in everything and everyone, yet he rarely passed judgment on anyone.

While he was staying in Ardmont he was determined to see as much of his daughter as possible and so was not averse to accompanying her to the mill to be introduced to Sandy and Ina and to be shown around.

Ina was still full of her impressions of the day she had spent at Creddon Hall, and while Sandy was busy explaining the methods by which the wool was spun and carded she took Lisa aside to tell her all about the photographic session.

"Och, wait till ye see the photos, Lisa," she said.

The Taming of Lisa

"They're going to be super. Sarah was right—the castle is a perfect setting for that type of clothing. We had a lovely time. Mrs. Chisholm gave us lunch and in the afternoon Mr. Lamont came. He was out to see Mr. Chisholm about the alterations to his schooner, and he brought his little boy with him. He was very interested in what we were doing. Och, I canna think when I've enjoyed meself so much. He's very nice when ye get to know him."

"Who is? Mr. Lamont?"

"Och, no, I mean Sandy, of course, although I can see why Sarah is keen on the other. He had a silent self-contained strength that would appeal to some women."

"But not to you."

"No. I like a man to be gentle and to treat me as if I'm something precious even if I'm not. There's nothing better for a woman's morale than to be treated like that, and mine certainly received a boost yesterday," said Ina with her gay laugh.

From Sandy, Lisa supposed, with a faint feeling of uneasiness. She could imagine the simple practical Ina falling in love very hard with the first man who treated her gently, and she hoped she would not be hurt by Sandy, who, she was beginning to realize, had a tendency to reach out for the unattainable when it came to women.

Sandy's view of the visit to Creddon Hall was slightly different from Ina's. As Lisa was about to leave the mill he drew her aside to glance at the layout of a brochure he was going to have printed.

"It's about the tweed and the sheepskins. We'll need somthing like this to send out when we receive answers to the advertisements that will be appearing soon," he pointed out.

"Did Sarah agree to model sheepskin coats, too?" asked Lisa.

"I couldn't get a straight answer from her," he replied with a touch of irritation. "She kept flirting with the photographer, and then when Fraser turned up she behaved as if she were out of her mind."

"And how did Fraser react?"

"Oh, with his usual indifference, which only had the effect of goading her to further idiotic behavior. And then to crown everything Johnnie, who was very disappointed when he found you weren't there, kicked Sarah."

"Why?" asked Lisa, astounded by this evidence that her blond favorite was not always the sweet-tempered child she believed him to be.

"I felt like cheering when he did it," answered Sandy with a surprising touch of viciousness. "She deserved to be kicked for making a most unpleasant remark about you. Anyway, Fraser reprimanded him and took him off. Sarah stormed into the castle with Peter Wright following her, and Ina and I came home for tea at her parents' home."

Lisa could not help smiling. His "Ina and I came home for tea" sounded so cozy and normal.

"It seems I missed an eventful afternoon," she murmured. "What was Sarah's unpleasant remark?"

Sandy looked distinctly embarrassed and began to shuffle papers together, avoiding her eyes.

"Something about Johnnie needing to take care where you're concerned, that you were only friendly with him because you wanted to use him to get close to his father—and a lot of similar rubbish. None of us there believed a word she said. It was just spite." Sandy looked up from his papers and smiled diffidently at her. "I hope you'll bring your father to tea at the farm on Sunday. My parents remember him well and would like to meet him again. You and I can go for a walk if the weather is good. I've a great deal to say to you, Lisa." He glanced around the dusty office and added, "This isn't the time or the place."

The expression in his eyes should have boosted any woman's morale and set her heart thudding hopefully, thought Lisa. But the only effect it had on her heart was to make it flutter like that of a wild bird determined to preserve its freedom.

"Time and place aren't important, Sandy," she said. "It's what is said that matters."

He gave her an impatient glance. "I can't agree," he replied. "There's something I must tell you and I don't want anyone else listening. It's important—to me, at any rate, and I hope it will be for you."

Well, at least she knew what to expect when she took a walk with Sandy on Sunday next, thought Lisa with a touch of amusement, and knowing she would be able to take avoiding action and not give him an opportunity to declare himself. She was sure he was not in love with her but was only temporarily attracted to her because she was different and because she had helped him. She was beginning to understand now what Aunt Maud had meant when she had suggested that Sandy might be getting ideas. The more she helped him the more he would make demands, gradually assuming that she was there just for his benefit and eventually taking her for granted.

"Pleasant enough chap," said Frank suddenly. "He should go far with someone cracking the whip behind him. Has the basis of a fine little industry there."

"And who do you think will crack the whip?" asked Lisa as she steered the car along the shore road. The water of the kyle was placid and serene, pale lavender color shading to deep tones of violet and indigo under the cloud-streaked sky.

"That little nut-brown maid might be the one," mused Frank.

"You mean Ina?"

"Yes, I do. Unless you're thinking of taking him on yourself."

"If by 'taking on' you mean marriage—nothing was ever further from my mind," replied Lisa. "I could only marry for love, and love is possible only between equals."

"And you haven't met yours yet, I take it," teased Frank, amused by her reaction. "Yes, now that I come to think of it whoever tames your wild heart will need to have a strong hand as well as a loving one."

Lisa glanced at him sharply. Shades of Beatrice and Benedick again! Wasn't it Beatrice, when learning that Benedick really loved her, who had said:

> And Benedick, love on; I will requite thee;
> Taming my wild heart to thy loving hand.

She was about to question her father, to ask him whether those were the lines he had in mind, when he turned from his contemplation of the kyle and the shores of Boag and said, "You're right, of course. Love is possible only between equals. There's nothing new about that, as anyone who has been happily married and believes in marriage will tell you. But be careful, Lisa, that your love of freedom and independence doesn't prevent you from recognizing your equal when he comes along. I wouldn't like you to miss him as Beatrice almost missed Benedick." He glanced out of the window at a small boy dressed in navy blue who was trudging along by the hedges, stepping into every puddle left by the recent rain, and who looked up hopefully as he heard the car approach. "Who's that?" asked Frank.

"Johnnie Lamont," replied Lisa, bringing the car to a halt just ahead of the smiling Johnnie, who came racing up and peered in through the window at Frank. "We'll give him a lift."

Frank opened the door, smiled at the boy, stepped out of the car, and swung his seat forward so that Johnnie could climb into the back seat.

Pink-cheeked and breathless, Johnnie started to talk as soon as the car started forward.

"I've something to give you, Lisa," he said, waving a rolled-up piece of thick paper. "It's a picture I made at school today."

Lisa, who had noticed his unfastened coat, his undone shoelaces and his wild spiky hair, wondered if he had been fighting again.

"Thank you, Johnnie. That's very kind of you. I hope you haven't been in another fight," she said.

"Oh, no. Jamie and I have been rolling down the grass bank at the back of his house."

"Jamie?" queried Lisa.

"Jamie Carruthers. He's my new friend," he announced importantly. "His dad works for my dad."

Frank turned and looked at him, held out his hand and introduced himself. "How do you do, Johnnie. I used to know your dad when he was a boy."

"I'm seven," replied Johnnie after solemnly shaking hands. "Was he as old as that when you knew him?"

"Older. About ten or eleven, I'd say."

"Have you been to see him?"

"Not yet. But I'd like to. I'd like to look at some of those yachts he's got in his yard."

"Come now," said Johnnie generously, having taken one of his instant likings. "I'll show you round," he added, assuming his own special adult manner. "You too, Lisa?"

Lisa shook her head as she stopped the car at the bottom of the brae. "Not now, Johnnie. You get out and take Mr. Smith while I put the car in the garage." She unrolled the picture he had given her as he scrambled out of the car. It was a brightly crayoned drawing of a daffodil growing in a plant pot. "Thank you for the lovely drawing. I'll put it up on the wall in the kitchen at Breck House and then I can see it every day."

"Show it to Miss Roy, too," instructed Johnnie as he walked off with Frank, hand in hand, in the direction of the boatyard. Lisa sat and watched them for a minute before putting the car into gear and swinging it in the direction of Breck House.

She had decided not to go with her father and Johnnie to the boatyard, partly because she knew Frank wanted to talk to Fraser by himself and partly because she did not want to see Fraser. No, that was not exactly true. She was afraid to see him—afraid of that excited bubbling feeling that she experienced whenever she laid eyes on him. It was a feeling she attributed purely to physical attraction, to the time of the year. It would pass, she hoped, with the spring. Meanwhile she would help it on its way by playing safe.

The biggest problem was Johnnie. How to see him and remain friends with him without laying herself open for more sarcastic gibes from Fraser, punishing remarks—she could not forget— occupied her thoughts daily.

When Frank returned from the boatyard he seemed quite satisfied with his meeting with Fraser.

"I can't understand why you don't like him," he said to Aunt Maud. "He seems a reasonable intelligent sort of chap to me; ambitious, hardworking, knows where he's going. No need for anyone to crack the whip behind him," he added with a sidelong glance at Lisa.

"You're right there," commented Maud dryly. "It's the other sort of handling he needs—a good hard pull on the reins to stop him from overreaching himself. He'd buy up half of Ardmont if he could."

"I think you're wrong," said Frank. "He just wants a bit more elbowroom, and when he has that he'll be content." He produced his pipe and began to stuff it with tobacco, a favorite tactic of his when he did not want to be drawn into an argument.

"Och, it's just like you to side with him," sneered Aunt Maud. "What else did you find out?"

"Nothing very much. He showed me his fiberglass workshop and then took me to see a hull being built in the traditional carvel style. I was pleased to see he's keen on keeping the old boatbuilding crafts alive even though he's gone in for mass production. Craftsmen like Willie Scott and his son are worth every penny they earn. I told him something of the boatbuilding I'd seen being done in the Caribbean. Then he showed me the ocean racer he's just finished for some chap who's interested in being chosen to represent the United Kingdom in the Admiral's Cup series. If that yacht's successful it'll boost Lamont's business no end."

"Och, never mind all that," interrupted Aunt Maud irritably. "Did you get out of him what his next move concerning Breck House is?"

Frank gave her a slightly disdainful glance, as if her impatience offended him. "Good heavens, no! That will take time. I have to win his confidence before I start doing that. He was cagey enough as it was when he remembered who I was and my relationship to you and Lisa." Again he flicked a sharp shrewd glance in the direction of his daughter, whose cheeks suddenly glowed red for no accountable reason. "But I'll be seeing him again," continued Frank placidly. "The boy is a useful contact. Jolly little chap, but nervous and far too attached to his father. It's a pity he hasn't a mother."

"Fraser isn't the first man to bring up a child on his own these days," said Aunt Maud gruffly.

"Nor the last. But I got the impression today that he's feeling the strain a little."

"Oh, why?" The question was out of Lisa before she had time to think, and her father gave her another curious glance.

"He seemed unnecessarily irritable with the boy. Of course it could be that he has some problem on his mind," he replied.

IN THE DAYS THAT FOLLOWED Frank was often down at the boatyard, apparently fascinated by the activity there. He had taken over Lisa's former self-imposed task of meeting Johnnie as he came home from school, and Lisa was glad to let him do so, as it eased her conscience a little where the boy was concerned.

With regard to Fraser's having a problem on his mind that was making him short-tempered, she wondered whether it was connected with Sarah. If he was in love with Sarah and wanted to marry her, Johnnie's dislike of the model could create an almost insurmountable difficulty.

She was encouraged to think she was right by Sarah's own behavior when she came to the mill one day, bringing with her two friends who were staying at Creddon Hall for a few days and who were interested in the tweeds. Sarah showed off all the time, taunting Lisa about eher friendship with Johnnie and her relationship with Sandy. Her whole manner was brittle in the extreme, as if she were on the verge of a nervous breakdown or hysteria.

"She's got it in for you, right enough," muttered Ina after the model and her friends had left. "She's fair wild about something. My guess is that she doesn't like ye being so friendly with the wee Lamont laddie when she knows he loathes the sight of her. She's afraid ye might cut her out with his dad."

Lisa laughed. "As if I would or even could! I hardly ever see the man," she said

That wasn't exactly true. She managed to catch a glimpse

of Fraser every day somehow, using every means she could think of to see him and not be seen—peeping from her bedroom window to watch him walk to the new shed, taking the setters for walks along the paths that climbed the hill at the back of the boatyard so that she could look down and see him crossing the boatyard. One day, greatly daring, she walked right past the entrance to the boatyard hoping she might see him giving instructions to the men working on the big schooner. He caught sight of her and paused in what he was saying to the workman leaning over the high stern of the boat. His eyes flicked over her in a quick, slightly surprised way before he turned his back on her, deliberately, to continue with what he had to say.

And she had gone on, her legs strangely shaky, vowing to herself she would not pass that way again when he was there.

Secretly astounded by her own behavior, Lisa found she could not help it. For once natural instinct was having its way with her, pushing aside the dictates of her will no matter how hard she tried to assert that strong and highly developed faculty.

Sunday came around once more, a clear calm day. Walking with Sandy along the long rocky snout of land from which Ardmont got its name, she told him of her suspicions regarding the situation between Fraser and Sarah in order to prevent him from telling her the "something important" that he did not wish anyone else to hear.

"You could be right," he murmured, giving the matter his usual grave consideration as they paused at the end of point of land and looked out across the sea. On distant land hazy blue mountains basked serenely in the pale spring sunlight. The water twinkled happily and rushed at the shore in a series of merry little waves. "Sarah, of course, won't have any idea how to deal with a young boy like Johnnie," continued Sandy, then stopped abruptly and stiffened as he looked past her. "Better change the subject quickly, Lisa," he warned quietly. "Someone else has decided that today is a good day to walk round the point."

She turned slowly. Coming along the shore toward them were three familiar figures—Sarah and Fraser followed by a

The Taming of Lisa

dawdling Johnnie. As soon as he saw Lisa, Johnnie broke into a run, overtook the other two and dashing up to her held out a fistful of shells for her inspection.

Compared with his boisterous greeting of Lisa the four adults' greetings seemed remarkably constrained. With a cool nod and a politely spoken, "Fine day for the time of year," Fraser walked on indifferently.

Sarah, however, did not possess his composure or his understanding of Johnnie, who would have followed his father eventually. She paused and said in a superficially sweet manner, "Come along, Johnnie, dear. Lisa doesn't want to be bothered with those silly shells. She's taking a walk with Mr. Lewis."

"You do want to look at the shells, don't you, Lisa?" said Johnnie, looking up at her appealingly, and she saw bewilderment and hurt in his blue eyes and that his lower lip was quivering.

"Yes, I do," she replied, unable to resist that look, ignoring her initial intention to play on Sarah's side and suggest that the boy go with the other woman.

"Johnnie, hurry up," insisted Sarah peevishly.

"No. I don't have to do what you say," returned Johnnie. "I want to stay with Lisa and go for a walk with her."

"That's all very well, laddie," interposed Sandy mildly, "but Lisa and I happen to be going in the opposite direction to your father and Sarah, so it can't be done."

Sarah glared at him exasperatedly. "Can't you see, Sandy Lewis, that it would be more helpful if you changed your mind and walked the other way? Then he'll come without any more fuss," she said, and Lisa waited tensely for his reply.

"Well, I suppose we could do that," he replied obligingly. "Would you mind, Lisa?"

Thinking that he would have even less chance to tell her "something important" now that Sarah was there, Lisa let her glance stray in the direction Fraser had gone. He had stopped walking and was waiting, hands in his pockets, staring out to sea.

"No, I don't mind. You go ahead. Johnnie and I will follow," she replied absently. Sandy looked a little taken aback by her easy acquiescence, but before he could suggest any alternative Sarah had linked an arm through his and was saying gaily, "Come on, Sandy. It won't be the first time you and I have walked along this shore together."

They went off, and Fraser having noticed that they were approaching turned and began to walk slowly in the direction of the village.

Johnnie looked up at Lisa with a conspiratorial grin that showed his two new, slightly crooked top front teeth.

"Now I've got you to myself," he said triumphantly. "Oh, look! A little crab. Help me catch him, Lisa."

It took some time for Lisa to persuade Johnnie that they were not going to catch the crab that day, and by the time they reached the end of the village Sandy and Sarah had disappeared and only Fraser was there, leaning against the gate set in the dry-stone dike that divided the Lewises' farm fields from the shore. He watched them come, a rather forbidding frown on his face.

"You two have taken long enough," he said reprovingly as he straightened up.

"Where are the others?" asked Lisa, trying to appear indifferent to this unexpected encounter.

"Sandy invited Sarah to tea at the farm. He said to tell you to follow them over the fields." He jerked his head in the direction of the path on the other side of the gate.

"Didn't he invite us to tea, too, daddy?" asked Johnnie brightly. "I'd like to go to the farm and see the animals."

"Yes, he did, but I refused on your behalf," replied Fraser curtly. "The way you've behaved this afternoon you don't deserve to go to tea anywhere."

Johnnie's shoulders slumped, and tears of disappointment welled in his eyes. Lisa decided it was time to interfere.

"Oh, why don't you come? I'm sure Mrs. Lewis won't mind. There's always plenty to eat, and Mr. Lewis loves to show off his barns and his equipment," she said persuasively.

The glance Fraser gave her was both cynical and hostile.

"Can you imagine Hugh Lewis sitting down at his own table in comfort with me as his guest? Or Maud Roy enjoying her afternoon out having to face me across the teacups?" he asked derisively. "No, thank you. I would rather not go where I know I'm not welcome. Come on, Johnnie. It's a long walk back through the village."

Without a word of farewell to Lisa he turned away and set off. Johnnie hesitated, looking up at Lisa. Realizing the boy was not following him, Fraser swung around. "Johnnie!" he called harshly.

"I want to go with Lisa to tea at Sandy's farm," the boy said stubbornly.

Watching anger sweep darkly across Fraser's face, Lisa recalled her father saying he thought that Fraser was feeling the strain of being an only parent, and before he could threaten the child she said softly to Johnnie, "Go with your daddy, Johnnie. He'll be all alone if you don't."

The boy gave her a puzzled glance, but went obediently and pushed his hand into Fraser's, turning to look back over his shoulder and call, "Goodbye, Lisa."

She watched them go, her heart twisting painfully as she quelled an urge to go with them. It seemed more right and natural that she should be going with father and son, making three instead of two. But she was expected for tea, and if she did not turn up everyone would wonder why she had not returned with Sandy.

As she walked across the field she wondered why Sarah had deserted Fraser and had gone to tea with Sandy. Had she accepted Sandy's invitation in an attempt to pique Fraser? Was that why he had been so curt and hostile?

Certainly the model was on her best behavior during tea, although occasionally on looking up Lisa surprised Sarah staring at her with something of the same hostility Fraser had shown, and she wondered what she had done to arouse such enmity. Nothing as far as she could tell, except to get on too well with a little boy called Johnnie.

The thought bothered her for the rest of the evening, and try as she might she could find no answer to the problem apart from leaving Ardmont altogether. Perhaps she should go with her father when he left. Perhaps if she went Johnnie would turn to Sarah, using her as a substitute for the friend he had lost.

But such answers did not please her. She did not want to leave Ardmont, and as it turned out she could not leave, nor could her father, because Aunt Maud had a severe stroke that left her paralyzed down one side, making it necessary for her to have constant attention.

March was going out like a lion, flinging a series of violent squalls at the village, tossing the tops of the trees, flattening the grass, snatching slates from roofs, tugging at the canvas covers of the yachts. Watching the wild weather from a window one day Lisa was sure the roof of the new shed down by the water would lift right off and fly away as she watched it ripple and pucker, only to have her view completely obscured suddenly by rain that hit the pane like a tropical torrent, sluicing down the glass noisily.

Later the same day she sat with Frank in the sitting room listening to a performance of Brahms's Fourth Symphony being broadcast from Glasgow by the Scottish National Orchestra. Leaning back in her chair, Lisa allowed herself to be swept along on a wave of romanticism caused by the bittersweet melodies.

Then through the sound of the music she became aware of an alien noise, the shrill burr-burr of the front doorbell. She glanced at Frank. He had heard it, too and stood up to turn down the volume of the radio. The bell sounded again.

"I'll answer," he said. "Whoever has come out on a night like this must be in need of help or slightly crazy."

He was back in a few minutes, leading a small boy by the hand. It was Johnnie, his duffel coat open over his pajamas, his feet bare, his blond hair dark with rain, his face streaked and blotched with crying.

"A young man to see you, Lisa," announced Frank quietly. "I think he's in trouble."

Lisa was out of her chair and kneeling before the child in an instant, propelled there by love and concern.

"Oh, Johnnie, what have you done?" she asked anxiously.

The Taming of Lisa

"I've run away from home," he muttered shakily, and promptly burst into tears.

It took a while for Lisa to pacify the sobbing child. When the flood of tears came to an end and he leaned against her, exhausted and shaken by sobs, she was able to push him onto the padded stool by the fire. Her father, who had left the room as soon as Johnnie had burst into tears, returned with a towel to dry the child's wet hair and a small tray bearing a glass of milk and some biscuits.

As he sipped the milk and munched biscuits, some of Johnnie's composure came back and gradually Lisa was able to prize out of him his reason for running away from home.

"Have you been telling lies again and has your father been punishing you?" she asked gently.

"No." The expression in his big eyes was reproachful.

"Then why have you run away?"

"To punish him."

"Why? What has he done wrong?"

"He says he's going away again." He shuddered suddenly with sobs.

"To fetch another yacht?"

"I don't know. He says he'll be away more than a week."

"And you don't want him to go?"

"No. I hate him going away. I hate boats and sailing. I wish he did something else."

"But building boats and looking after them is your father's work," interposed Frank rather sternly. "He likes doing it. You can't expect him to change his work just because you don't like it. He has to earn his living and feed you and clothe you, and he's doing that in a way he knows best."

Johnnie turned to look at him, only half understanding this strange adult outlook.

"I—I wouldn't mind if I could go with him, but he says— he says—" here Johnnie gulped as tears welled again in his eyes "—he says I have to stay at home and go to school, and he'll get someone to look after me. I asked if he would ask you, Lisa, and he was very cross and said he wouldn't... and sent me to bed. So I ran away."

"You didn't run away far, young man," remarked Frank with a touch of dryness, and Johnnie gave him a timid glance and huddled closer to Lisa.

"Well, it was windy and wet, and I'm frightened of the wind," he defended himself weakly, "so I came to find Lisa."

"That was the right thing to do," she comforted him, her thoughts straying to the man down at the white house behind the boatyard, whom Sandy had once described as being lonely and needing all the friends he could find. "But we'll have to tell your father that you're here. He'll be very upset in the morning if he looks in your bedroom and you aren't there."

She glanced at Frank, who nodded and slipped out of the room to use the telephone in the hall.

"He'll be very cross," whispered Johnnie. "He's been cross for days, ever since he came back on the big black boat. I don't think he likes me anymore and wishes he didn't have me...."

"I'm sure he doesn't think anything like that," said Lisa with a confidence she was not feeling as she recalled her own suspicion that Johnnie's dislike of Sarah might be coming between the model and Fraser. "I expect he's worried about something and that's making him short-tempered."

Johnnie did not look in the least impressed by her suggestion, although he leaned his head against her shoulder and stared into the fire. They were unaware of the passage of time as they talked about the pictures they could see in the flames, and both of them turned rather guiltily when the door of the room swung open behind them and Fraser walked in. From the door Frank looked at Lisa and murmured, "I'll go and relieve Mrs. Ramsay. She's sat with Maud long enough tonight."

Fraser was breathing deeply as if he had run up the brae. Above the rolled neck of his dark sweater his face was pale and strained-looking and his eyes burned blue as he glanced briefly at Lisa before going to stand over Johnnie and ask abruptly, "Why, Johnnie?"

"I didn't mean to stay away—not forever. I just wanted

to frighten you," the boy blurted. Bursting into tears again, he flung himself at his father, clutching him around the thighs.

"Well, you succeeded," Fraser admitted with a grunt of laughter as he sat down on the stool and pulled his child between his knees. "But why?"

"Because you wouldn't ask Lisa to look after me while you're away. I won't mind your going if I can stay with her."

Over the boy's blond hair Fraser looked at Lisa, his eyes wary.

"You could have asked me, you know," she said softly. "Why didn't you?"

"You know damned well why," he grated between taut lips. Then the expression in his eyes softened as their gaze lingered almost hungrily on her face, and once again she had that peculiar sensation as if he had touched her. "If you like you can blame that abominable pride you once talked about," he added more gently, with the faintest glimmer of a smile.

Suddenly her legs felt weak and her head swam as if she were intoxicated. The confused feeling forced her to sit down in the nearest chair, and that was a mistake, because the stool Fraser was sitting on was near to the chair and she found her face was on a level with his, too close for comfort, so that she had to lean back.

"I suppose you didn't want to ask me because if I agreed you would be in my debt," she accused in a squeaky voice most unlike her own.

"Something like that," he drawled rather vaguely, looking away from her.

"Where are you going?"

"To a yacht builders' conference in Essex, and then I was hoping to go over to Holland to visit a business associate."

"How long will you be away?" she asked, trying hard to be practical as he glanced at her again.

"About ten days."

"Don't you ever worry about Johnnie when you go away?" she queried. "Supposing you were in an accident, or were drowned when you're bringing a yacht here. Don't you wonder what would happen to him without you?"

"Yes, I worry," he answered sharply, frowning. "More than you realize, perhaps."

"But not enough to stop you from going," she accused.

"He kicked up such a shindy this time that I'd more or less decided not to go, although it would mean losing contacts and probably contracts," he replied with a touch of impatience.

"Just because you couldn't swallow your pride and ask me to look after him," she scoffed gently.

He looked away from her again, his mouth tightening stubbornly. Johnnie, who had been resting quietly in his father's arms but had been listening to every word, moved and muttered, "Can I stay with Lisa, daddy, while you go away?"

"That's for Lisa to decide," replied Fraser smoothly, pushing the boy away from him and rising to his feet. He picked up Johnnie's duffel coat from the floor and handed it to the boy. "Here, put this on and we'll go home," he ordered gruffly.

Lisa sighed and shivered. The moment of strange intimacy so shattering and revealing to herself was over. Fraser had withdrawn behind his usual impassivity after having cleverly passed the decision on to her, avoiding having to bend his stiff neck and ask her to mind his child.

"Very clever of you, Mr. Lamont," she jeered quietly and saw the corner of his mouth quirk with amusement. "When would you want to leave Ardmont?"

"On Friday."

Lisa looked down at Johnnie's expectant face and knew she could not refuse the appeal in his eyes.

"Then when you come home from school on Friday afternoon, Johnnie, come straight here. I'll be waiting for you," she said, smiling at him.

Fraser stared at her with narrowed eyes. "You're sure?" he asked. "Won't you have enough to do? I hear that Miss Roy is very poorly."

"My father is staying longer. He will help."

The straight line of his mouth relaxed as he caught Johnnie's upward hopeful glance.

"Well, son, it seems as if you've got what you wanted after all," he said lightly. "But you needn't be thinking that running away will always get this result. Shall we go home now?"

Johnnie's smile was evidence of his restored faith in human nature as he went with Fraser to the door.

"I've a feeling you've got what you wanted, too, Mr. Lamont," drawled Lisa, unable to resist the temptation to provoke him as she followed them out into the hall.

Fraser swung around and gave her a level look that set her pulses leaping.

"Not quite," he replied. "My wants are more complex than Johnnie's and will take some time to achieve. Keep in touch with Jean Bridie. She'll know my movements next week and will let you know of any change of plan." He glanced down at his son's bare feet and finished, "You can't walk home like that."

He squatted down, and Johnnie, apparently knowing what to do, climbed onto his back, twining his arms around his neck. Fraser put an arm under each of Johnnie's legs, which were spread across his back, shifted the child more securely on to his back, then stood up. Lisa opened the front door for them and lingered there after they had gone, peering out into the stormy night. She thought she could hear Johnnie chuckling as his father ran with him down the road and she smiled to herself as she closed the door. Johnnie had got what he wanted, but his father's wants were more complex. She imagined they were like Romeo's:

> More fierce and inexorable far
> Than empty tigers or the roaring sea.

But what were they?

She knew that one was the acquisition of more land to extend the boatyard. Was marriage to Sarah another? Either because he loved Sarah or because marriage to her would be advantageous in a way that his first marriage had not been.

Sarah's parents were wealthy, well connected and certainly would not cut her off if she married a Lamont, whose genealogy, while not aristocratic, was probably longer than that of a Chisholm.

Impatient with the direction her thoughts were taking, she went back into the sitting room. The empty glass and the scattered biscuit crumbs were the only signs that Johnnie had been there. But Fraser's presence seemed to linger, a bulky ghost in dark clothing with damp curling hair and blue black eyes which occasionally looked at her as if they liked what they could see.

Too much imagination, that was her trouble, Lisa berated herself angrily as she knelt in front of the fire and picked up the poker to stir the glowing embers. She flung another log on the fire. It caught immediately and sparks flared up against the blackness of the chimney. Staring at them, Lisa was shaken suddenly by the memory of her own reaction to Fraser's physical presence in the room. Did such confusion mean she had fallen in love with him after all?

"Lisa?" Frank had come into the room, startling her. She jumped to her feet, feeling her heart pounding in her ears. "I think you'd better call Dr. Clarke. Aunt Maud has taken a turn for the worse."

AUNT MAUD died on Friday morning just as the ferry taking Fraser to Gourock left the pier. Lisa was glad that Frank had stayed longer at Breck House because he was able to see to all the arrangements for the funeral, which was a simple affair held at the small church in the village and attended by all Maud Roy's friends and acquaintances, who gathered later at Breck House for refreshments. When they had all gone Lisa and Frank discussed Maud's will. Apart from a few small bequests to friends such as Mrs. Ramsay, she had left everything else including the house and a small annuity to Lisa on condition that the house would not be sold during Lisa's lifetime and never to a Lamont. If Lisa attempted such a sale she would automatically forfeit both the house and the annuity, which would both be turned over to charity.

"She really disliked the Lamont family, didn't she?" said Frank. "I wonder why?"

"I believe it had something to do with Fraser's grandfather, John Lamont. You know she was engaged to him at one time?"

"Yes, I knew, but I never knew the reason for her breaking off the engagement."

"Well, Mrs. Ramsay told me that someone in the village told Aunt Maud that John was seeing another young woman on the sly. She was furious and decided to confront him with the information. Apparently he was a very proud man and would neither deny nor admit that there was any truth in the story, so Aunt Maud broke off the engagement. A few years later he married someone else."

"So that's why she never married," said Frank. "Just as well, if she had so little faith. You know, I can't help thinking she's left you stuck with a white elephant. This house isn't exactly comfortable. Of course, you could always let the place to someone, I suppose, when you want to return to Manchester."

"But I'm not going to return to Manchester. I haven't any work to do there and I have here. Sandy has just received orders for tweed suits designed by me, and then there's the sheepskin side of the business to be developed later this year. I'm staying here."

"Well, you must suit yourself, of course," said Frank mildly, giving her a shrewd assessing glance. "But the cost of upkeep on a place like this will be considerable. I doubt if the annuity will cover it."

"Then I'll take in lodgers in the summer. Bed and breakfast," she said.

"Yes, I can imagine the advertisement," he answered with a laugh. "'Come and stay at Breck House, plumbing suspect, drafts considerable, wonderful view of boatyard.' Well, I think I'll love and leave you for a while and depart for London and warmer climates. I'll let you know where I'll be going after my leave is over. I'm hoping for a position in Whitehall. Time I settled down."

Frank left on Wednesday's boat, and after seeing him off

Lisa walked slowly back along the pier. The day was warm and sunny. In the gardens of the staid Victorian villas clumps of daffodils and narcissi nodded in the faint breeze. April was in, that most tender and cruel of months when desire leaped in the blood and memory stirred painfully. Not the best time of the year to die, Johnnie had said when she had told him about Aunt Maud, and now, looking around her, she could not help but agree with him, because today Ardmont, the kyle, the distant mountains and islands all looked their best. Colors were deep and clear, sharply delineated. The sea was indigo blue speckled with white-crested waves, edged by the pale curves of sandy beaches above which emerald-and-ocher fields were crowned by bottle-green woodland that gave way to bracken-brown moors and pale mauve rock. It was days like this, coming after the periods of interminable storm gray, that made Lisa realize why Aunt Maud and others had stayed to live in this remote peninsula, made her understand why Fraser had returned. For here there was peace and unspoiled beauty.

At the mill she found Ina in one of her tizzies. The April issues of two magazines carried advertisements of Ardmont tweeds showing Sarah slim and elegant wearing the suits designed by Lisa, and already Sandy had received several telephone inquiries.

"Och, I'm so excited I could do a jig!" exclaimed Ina, who was capering around the office, much to Sandy's amusement.

"I'm beginning to wonder how we're going to meet any orders we might receive. You can't possibly make all the articles of clothing, Ina," he said. "You'll need help. Do you know of anyone who would come and work here under your supervision?"

"Not offhand. But I'll make some inquiries among me friends in Glasgow."

"I'll have to hire someone extra to work in the office, too, to answer written inquiries and to organize the mailing of brochures and goods," continued Sandy with an air of suppressed excitement after Ina had left the room. "And all

The Taming of Lisa

thanks to you, Lisa. You'll have to become a partner now. I can't afford to let you go."

"Well, I'm not thinking of going anywhere. I'm staying in Ardmont. You've only to ask me, Sandy, and I'll do more designs," she replied.

"But you must be paid. If you won't join the company we'll have to arrange something else on a commission basis. Supposing I think about it, discuss it with mother and dad, who are the other directors of the company, and then see you one evening next week? It's so difficult to discuss anything here with the noise of the machinery and people coming and going all the time. If you'd come up to the farm one evening...."

"That isn't possible. You forget I'm looking after Johnnie, and he goes to bed at seven. Why don't you come to Breck House instead?"

He frowned and looked rather dubious. "Well, I suppose it will be all right. I wouldn't like anyone to think..." he began diffidently.

"Oh, come off it, Sandy. You wouldn't have hesitated to come if Aunt Maud had been there upstairs in bed."

"No, I wouldn't. But it's different now. You're alone and—"

"Listen, these days a man can go calling on a girl who lives alone without anyone thinking wrong things. Why, in Manchester—or any city—"

"Yes, in the city, but not here, Lisa. The people here are still very conventional in outlook," he objected seriously.

"Sandy, if I were a man and you wanted to do business with me would you hesitate to call on me in the evening?" she challenged.

"No, I wouldn't," he admitted.

"Then will you please forget my sex and treat me as an equal if you want me to design for you?"

"I'm not sure that I can," he said slowly, staring at her with puzzled eyes.

"Try," she urged. "Or otherwise I can't join your company."

CHAPTER SEVEN

LISA SPENT THE WEEKEND gardening and walking with Johnnie. He was good company and she realized that when he returned to his own home Breck House would seem empty and lonely. There would be no Aunt Maud to talk to or listen to. Although she had not lived with her for very long Lisa missed the old lady's caustic comments and often found herself staring at the big wing chair placed in the window of the sitting room, in which her aunt had liked to sit, with a feeling of sad regret, wishing that she had come to Ardmont more often to visit her.

But she would not feel lonely for long, she vowed to herself. Being alone was part of being independent, of being free. She had plenty of inner resources to fall back on so that she need never feel lonely. Aunt Maud, herself independent and heart-whole, had made it possible for her to be independent. She was free in the full sense of the word; free to develop her potential as a designer and as a woman.

As a woman? Her thoughts stumbled over the phrase. How could she in all honesty say that she could develop fully as a woman on her own? How could she fulfill her destiny as a woman without the love of a man? Deliberately Lisa willed herself not to think such treacherous thoughts, conveniently ignoring the fact that she had lain awake several nights since Fraser had left Ardmont, wondering where he was and what he was doing, imagining what their next meeting would be like and wishing that there were not so many barriers between them.

Sandy came on Tuesday evening just as a sliver of a new moon appeared over the hump of Boag, silvering the small clouds that drifted near it and winking at itself in the pallid water of the kyle. He stayed not more than an hour and all the time he seemed ill at ease. But at the end of that time Lisa had consented to become a partner in Ardmont Tweeds Limited and also to be chief designer.

Sandy spoke of nothing else but business, and Lisa decided that this was the "important thing" about which he had always wanted to tell her and was relieved. When the clock struck nine he rose promptly and said he must be on his way. Lisa went with him to the front door and they stood together on the doorstep for a few minutes admiring the sheen of moonlight on the sleek water and talking in a desultory fashion about the future of the mill.

Then with a suddenness that took her completely by surprise, Sandy bent and kissed her on the lips. It was a brief kiss, shy and featherlike, but it left her in no doubt that he would have liked to make it longer and more demanding if he had considered it the time and place.

"To seal a bargain that I hope neither of us will ever regret in the hopes that it will lead to a more binding relationship," he whispered. "Good-night, Lisa."

He went quickly along the path, and her amazed farewell was said to his back. The gate clanged after him and she heard the granite chips of the roadway crunching beneath his quick feet as he went down the brae.

"Very interesting," observed a masculine voice through which a tantalizing thread of laughter ran, and she whirled around. Fraser was standing only a few feet away from her, the crisp crest of his hair and the clear-cut angles of his face easily discernible in the moonlight.

"What are you doing here?" she demanded, thoroughly confused by the sight of him.

"I came to call on you and to offer my condolences, having only just heard of Miss Roy's death. I was about to press the doorbell when the door started to open and I heard you and Sandy talking. I ducked to one side and was treated to the sight of him giving you a good-night kiss. Almost as good as going to the cinema," he scoffed.

"He was sealing a bargain," she retorted. "I have agreed to become a partner in Ardmont Tweeds."

"First time I've seen one business partner kiss another one," he mocked.

"I didn't expect you until tomorrow," she said, deciding to ignore his gibes.

"Sarah drove me down from Glasgow. She left me at the bottom of the brae. It's a pity we weren't a little later, then she could have given Sandy a lift home," he said dryly.

"Oh, so you've been with her after all," she accused.

"I'm not quite sure how to take that," he drawled, coming closer. "What do you mean by saying I've been with her in that tone of voice?"

"Someone told me that she was away, too, in the south of England and on the Continent, and I thought—"

"Not very nice thoughts," he interrupted sharply, and she felt as if he had rapped her on the knuckles. "No, I have not been with Sarah for the past ten days. I met her at Abbotsinch Airport this evening and she offered to drive me down here, so I accepted. It was she who told me about Miss Roy. I'm sorry. You must miss her."

"Yes, I do."

There was silence between them. It was so quiet Lisa could hear the distant swish of waves on the shore and the quacking of nesting ducks among the reeds on the islands. She kept her eyes on the shimmering path of moonlight. She was afraid to look at Fraser when she knew he was looking at her.

"Last time I returned home you invited me to breakfast," he murmured. "I hope that this time you might invite me in for some supper. There wasn't time to eat on the way here. Also, I have something to ask you and I would rather ask it behind closed doors."

"I expect it could keep until tomorrow."

It had been one thing inviting Sandy into the house, but it was quite another to invite Fraser while he had such a peculiar effect on her senses.

"I expect it could, but my appetite can't," he replied. "There's nothing to eat in the cupboard at my house. Would you have me go to bed hungry?"

He was beguiling her, using his voice, his physical nearness, his knowledge of the purely feminine instinct to provide food for the homecomer to get his own way. The change in his approach disconcerted her and she found it impossible to refuse.

"Come in," she invited, and turned into the house.

In the kitchen Lisa found cheese and crackers. Wondering what to offer him to drink, she came across a bottle of beer left by her father. She placed it with an opener and a glass tankard in front of Fraser, who was already sitting at the table and helping himself to the cheese. He gave her a grateful glance and she noticed that now she could see him properly he looked weary. Dark lines were scored under his eyes and his face looked thinner. Whatever had caused the strain before he had left Ardmont had not been lifted by his trip to Essex and Holland.

"What do you want to ask me about?" she asked, watching him pour beer into the tankard. When the bottle was half-empty he stopped pouring to offer her some.

Discovering that her throat was dry, she nodded and fetched a glass for herself, then held it out for him to pour the rest of the beer into it. Then she sat down at the table and helped herself to a piece of the Dunlop cheese and began to nibble it, thinking how much more natural it seemed to be sitting here in the kitchen with Fraser than it had been to sit with Sandy in the sitting room.

"I want to ask you about this house," said Fraser. "Who owns it now?"

"I do. You knew Aunt Maud was going to leave it to me."

"That was what she said to stop me from asking her to sell it to me. It didn't have to be true," he replied cynically.

"Well, it was," she replied shortly, bracing herself for the question she guessed would come next.

"Will you sell it and the land to me?" he asked curtly.

"No. And even if I wanted to I couldn't."

"Why not?"

"By the terms of the will I can't sell it, and certainly not to a Lamont."

His eyes narrowed unpleasantly and she had an awful

feeling he was going to say something nasty about Aunt Maud. But he didn't. Instead he finished his beer and then attacked the cheese again.

"I see," he said slowly. "Can *you* build on the land?"

"I don't know. It didn't occur to me to ask the lawyer."

He ate more cheese, and judging by the frown on his face he was thinking hard. Gradually the frown faded and when he spoke it was to ask casually, "Has Johnnie been good?"

Relieved that he had decided to leave the subject of Breck House, Lisa launched into an account of Johnnie's behavior and doings.

"He seems to have had a good time," commented Fraser. "And so do you. It's a relief to hear that he didn't have one tantrum or keep you up several nights on the run."

"He would only do that if he felt insecure. Every time you go away you upset his very precarious sense of security, because you've always been the one stable person in his life. If he had a mother he would react to your absences quite differently because she would provide the security and the stability, too. Even the same baby-sitter would be able to do that. But you've used so many different people," said Lisa forthrightly.

"Do you think I don't know that?" he snapped. "I've tried in many ways to be both mother and father to him, but having a business to run makes it difficult. And then either he takes a violent dislike to a baby-sitter or they take a dislike to him or to me—I'm not sure which. Short of not going away at all, I can't think of any way out of the problem, and if I don't go away occasionally the business will suffer."

"You could marry again," said Lisa quietly.

"Whom would I marry?" he said with a touch of bitterness. "It has to be someone Johnnie likes, otherwise I would just be creating a hell for three people."

He stared broodingly at the empty tankard, and Lisa's mind flicked to Sarah. He must want to marry the beautiful model, as she had guessed, but Johnnie was in the way.

"Wouldn't you have to love her, too?" she queried.

"Respect would be all that was necessary," he replied coldly, "and she wouldn't have to mind when I wanted to go away on my own."

Slightly chilled by his answer, which made it clear that he would consider a marriage of convenience for Johnnie's sake, Lisa sharpened her claws for an argument on the relative rights of women and men.

"Would you mind if she went off on her own occasionally and was independent?"

"Not at all. I would welcome such an attitude. It would make me feel easier in my mind. I value my own personal freedom so much that I'd hate to be responsible for curbing another's. I couldn't stand the sort of woman who would cling and weep every time I wanted to go away. It's that more than anything else that has put me off marrying again."

Had Holly clung and wept, wondered Lisa. She was suddenly sorry for the pale ghost of the girl who had been pretty and gay and just a little timid and who had possibly bruised herself against Fraser's rocklike hardness.

"Not all women cling and weep," she retorted.

He cocked a satirical eyebrow at her and then grinned. "Meaning that you don't, I suppose," he said, leaning back in his chair. He stretched his legs under the table and folded his arms across his chest and looked at her in that slow considering way that always made her skin tingle.

"You know, when I think about it, you'd suit very well," he drawled. "Johnnie likes you and you like him. You're sufficiently independent not to make any demands that I couldn't meet; you wouldn't cling and weep. In fact, if I weren't aware that marriage is low on your list of priorities I would ask you now to marry me for Johnnie's sake."

It seemed to Lisa that all the blood drained back to her heart, making it overfull, ready to burst. Her face white, her eyes dark pools of greenish light between long dark lashes, her hair a burnished red helmet beneath the glare of the electric light, she faced him across the table, wishing that there was some way in which she could throw his challenge back in his face. It would serve him right if she took it up, she thought furiously.

Aloud she said, "You mean a marriage of convenience?"

"All marriages are convenient in some way or other," he replied smoothly. "This one would be convenient for Johnnie and provide him with a mother he would like to have."

"And how would it be convenient for you?" she asked in her coolest voice, although her eyes were blazing with anger.

"I wouldn't have to worry about him while I was away, that's all."

"And how would it be convenient for me?" she asked finally.

"That would be for you to decide, of course," he replied, and stood up. "But it's merely a passing thought I had, because I know you have every intention of remaining unmarried, that being the fashionable thing for women to do these days, apparently."

Lisa's reaction was impulsive and irrational. Aware only of an overwhelming urge to surprise him, to shake him out of his bland assumptions about her, she rose to her feet and swept around the table to stand before him, her head held high.

"On the contrary, Mr. Lamont," she said coolly, looking him straight in the eyes, "for Johnnie's sake even I would give up my single status. You're on."

"What do you mean?" The sharpness of his voice and the widening of his eyes gave her a fleeting moment of pleasure and triumph. She had called his bluff and for once he was disconcerted.

"I mean that you can go ahead and ask me to marry you and I'll accept your proposal. You see, just lately I've changed the order of my priorities. You've made your suggestion at the time when marriage is first on the list."

He stared at her in silence, but it was impossible to assess his feelings because now he had himself well under control.

Then he began to laugh, quiet laughter that sent alarm flickering along Lisa's nerves. It was as if he were laughing

The Taming of Lisa

at a joke he had no intention of sharing with her, and she had a suspicion the joke was on her.

"Well, that's a change of attitude," he scoffed.

"No more of a change than in yours," she retorted. "I seem to remember that at one time you had no use for women who made friends with your son."

"That was before I realized that he liked you and that your liking for him had nothing to do with me," he replied more seriously. Then giving her a sharp glance he added more crisply, "All right. I'm asking you to marry me, Red Smith, the sooner the better for Johnnie's sake, because I have to go away again at the beginning of May to bring a yacht over from Ireland. Would May the first suit you, before the registrar? It isn't long since Miss Roy died, so I'm sure you won't want a church ceremony with all the trimmings, and I'd prefer a quiet quick affair myself because I'll have to go away the same day."

Vaguely, as if in a dream, Lisa found herself agreeing while she smothered an image of herself floating down the aisle of the village church in a white dress that she had designed herself. Within minutes she was standing on the front doorstep exactly where she had stood with Sandy only an hour previously. The moonlit night was mild, the air heavy with the scent of lilac. Ducks still quacked among the reeds and in the distance a dog barked.

"A night for bargains to be struck and sealed," said Fraser derisively. "I'd seal ours, but that would be making an unnecessary demand on you. I'd like to see Johnnie before he goes to school tomorrow. Will you send him down, please?"

Lisa wondered why she should feel so disappointed that he had decided not to seal their bargain in the same way that Sandy had.

"No, you come to breakfast instead," she invited impulsively.

He looked at her, and smiled. It might have been a trick of the moonlight, but it seemed to her that his smile had a faintly wicked, triumphant quality.

"You're on," he said, and turned away to walk down the path.

IN THE NIGHT Lisa remembered that smile of Fraser's. He had looked, she decided, as if he had won a victory. It was at that point that she got out of bed and opened the door of her room, determined to go downstairs and phone him even though it was two o'clock in the morning and tell him that she had changed her mind again, that she was not prepared to marry him for anyone's sake. But she had not gone downstairs. Instead she had paced the bedroom, pausing now and then to stare out at the sky darkening above the island as the moon slowly slid out of sight.

Why had she suddenly ditched all her dearly held principles about love and marriage and had agreed to marry Fraser Lamont for convenience? Convenience to whom? To Johnnie and him. But what was there convenient about such a marriage for her? Nothing as far as she could see. And yet the decision to marry had been hers. Why?

Because with all his talk of how she fitted the bill exactly for the position of Johnnie's stepmother, Fraser had dangled a tempting bait before her and she had risen, as he had known she would.

Lisa cringed and squirmed in bed as she realized how easily and readily she had risen while her will had been in abeyance.

She could not go through with it. Now that she had recovered her wits, she realized it. She could not have people like Sarah Popham pointing at her in scorn, and she would tell Fraser so when she saw him at breakfast.

In the kitchen as she prepared the meal she went over all she would say to him. She would tell him that he did not have to marry her if he wanted her to look after Johnnie. She would do that anytime he asked.

Johnnie was already downstairs in the dining room playing Aunt Maud's old tinkling piano—or at least pretending he could play it. The front doorbell rang and she heard him scamper through the hall to answer it, his shriek of delight when he saw his father, and her heart started to pound. Nothing would make her go out into the hall to greet Fraser. He could find his own way to the kitchen.

It was a while before he appeared and she had just fin-

The Taming of Lisa

ished frying eggs when the kitchen door burst open and Johnnie rushed in and flung his arms round the top of her legs.

"Lisa, daddy says you're going to be my mummy. Is it true?" he demanded.

She looked across the room at Fraser, who stood just inside the door watching her narrowly. No sleepless night for him, she thought, noting that the lines of weariness and strain had gone from his face.

"Lisa, it is true, isn't it?" whispered Johnnie urgently. Looking down at him, she could see doubt and disappointment dawning in his wide eyes.

"If your father says so it must be true, mustn't it?" she replied rather uncertainly.

"Oh, goodie!" Johnnie danced around the room. "Wait till I tell Jim that I'm going to have a real mummy like him!"

"Johnnie," cautioned Lisa, flinging an exasperated glance at Fraser, "I don't think you should tell anyone just yet."

But Johnnie was deaf to her remark. "And Miss Hargraves, my teacher, will be pleased," he continued gaily. "She's always saying I look as if I need a mother to look after me."

At this rate the whole village, the whole peninsula would know by noon, thought Lisa helplessly, and glared at Fraser as he took his place at the table.

"Devil!" she mouthed silently at him, remembering rather belatedly Aunt Maud's warnings about him, and he had the insolence to laugh openly at her as Johnnie rattled on about the numerous people who would be pleased when he told them that he was going to have a mother.

"Would Miss Roy have been pleased, too?" he asked suddenly, and Lisa thought how horrified Aunt Maud would have been to learn that her only surviving relative, on whom she had depended to keep Breck House out of the hands of the Lamont family, had agreed to marry a Lamont.

Again she glared at Fraser and received an amused glance in return.

"Of course she would," he said smoothly to Johnnie.

"When she was younger she wanted to marry your great-grandfather."

"Why didn't she?" asked the boy.

"He decided to marry someone else," replied Fraser easily, and Johnnie was silent as he tried to work out this new puzzle.

"Do you know where Frank is?" Fraser asked Lisa.

It took some time to realize he was referring to her father. "Yes, I do. I had a letter from him yesterday. He's staying with some friends on the Riviera."

"Then I'd like to suggest that you send him a cable asking his opinion and possibly his permission before we inform the registrar."

Lisa was surprised. His whole approach to the matter had been so unconventional so far that she had not expected him to even think her father had any say. She was just about to declare that she didn't need Frank's permission to marry when she remembered suddenly that Fraser had married Holly against her parents' wishes and had regretted his action. So she said meekly, "Yes, I will."

It would help, she decided, to have her father's opinion and would give her some much needed breathing space before the notice of the forthcoming marriage was posted in the window of the registrar's office in the nearby market town of Kilbride. But as she telephoned the cable she wondered who was listening on the local switchboard. How right Fraser had been when he had once told her nothing could be done in Ardmont without the whole place knowing about it!

As soon as she could she went to the the mill to tell Sandy before he heard the news from the grapevine. To describe him as being surprised was to underestimate his reaction. He was flabbergasted and sat for a while, silent and staring. Then he stood up and went to look out of the office window to hide the expression on his face.

"I can scarcely believe it," he croaked at last. "You said nothing of this last night."

"I didn't know because he hadn't asked me. He came to see me after you'd gone."

The Taming of Lisa

"But you must have had some inkling, some idea of what was in his mind? A man doesn't suddenly propose marriage. He has to lead up to it in various ways."

Lisa was silent. How could she explain to Sandy or even expect him to understand Fraser's mocking challenge and her own reaction when she hardly understood them herself?

"Would it have made any difference to your offer of a partnership to me if you'd thought I was going to be married?" she asked.

He came back to the desk and looked down at her. "Of course it would. You must see that, Lisa. As a married woman your loyalties will be, must be, to your husband first. Any business commitments will come afterward."

"I don't see it that way," she argued stubbornly.

"What about Fraser? What does he think? Supposing I want you to go away on business for the company, what would he say then?"

"He would let me go, just as I would let him go. I wouldn't have agreed to marry him if I hadn't known he would let me do what he does himself."

Sandy looked thoroughly puzzled. "Sounds more like a business partnership than marriage," he said.

"But don't you see, that's what marriage should be—a partnership between equals," replied Lisa, slightly astounded to realize she was defending her future relationship with Fraser.

Sandy rubbed a hand across his head, making his fine reddish hair stand up spikily.

"No, I'm afraid I don't see. Marriage for me is loving and caring for someone."

"And as long as she loves and cares for you and keeps her place in the home and cooks your meals and washes your clothes and is there when you come home from work you're prepared to go on loving and caring for her," said Lisa tartly. Then seeing a rather sad disillusioned expression cross his face she blurted, "Oh, I'm sorry, Sandy. It's obvious your ideas and mine on this particular subject don't coincide. I couldn't be that sort of wife. I—I'm too wild a bird to be happy caged."

"Yes, I can see that now," he said with a touch of dryness, his eyes suddenly very clear. "I hope you'll be happy, Lisa. I'm sure that in choosing you Fraser has done the best for his boy. I know you're fond of the child and that he responds to you. It's just that it happened so suddenly, when I'd thought Fraser was looking in Sarah's direction and she was hoping...."

Lisa didn't hear the rest of his sentence because a flash of insight flickered through her mind like lightning, illuminating a good reason for accepting Fraser's proposal. Once Sarah knew Fraser was marrying her, she was bound to turn elsewhere, and why shouldn't the model turn to Sandy, who had waited all these years?

"Now it's your turn to hope," she said softly.

"Perhaps," he replied rather heavily. "Now, about these new inquiries for tweed suits, I was thinking we should make up some samples of the tweeds available to send out to prospective buyers."

Lisa turned her attention to business, knowing that in some way she had hurt him, and it was not until she saw Ina later that she learned how.

"I must say ye're a sly one," teased Ina, having already heard the news somehow about the forthcoming marriage. "Ye never let on even when I talked about Sarah having it in for ye. Now I know why she did. When's the wedding to be?"

"Soon. Probably the first of May."

"Och, the man's in a hurry and no mistake!"

"It's for Johnnie's sake. He needs a mother," said Lisa defensively, wondering how many times in the next few weeks she would be trotting out that reason.

"Aye, I can see that, but there must be a bit more to it than that," said Ina with a knowing twinkle in her eyes. Then as she saw no answering humor in Lisa's eyes her ripe red mouth made a round shape of surprise. "Ye're never telling me that you and he are marrying for convenience?"

"Yes, I am. There's nothing wrong in that, is there?"

"Well, I'll be blowed!" Now the shape of Ina's eyes

matched the shape her mouth had made. Her face sobering, she jerked her head in the direction of Sandy's office. "The boss isn't any too pleased. He's been walking around all morning with a face like a wet week. I canna help feeling a wee bit sorry for him, especially after what ye've just told me."

"Why should he be miserable? I've told him I'm still willing to be a partner in the company," replied Lisa with a touch of impatience.

Ina shook her head slowly as if she considered Lisa less intelligent than she had thought. "I've never met a lass like ye, so sophisticated on the outside and so innocent underneath. It's not that which is upsetting him. Have ye not noticed he has a fancy for ye himself, and now by promising to marry yon Lamont ye've dashed all his hopes?"

"But he loves Sarah—or used to."

Again Ina shook her head. "Not since you came to Ardmont, he hasn't. Och, the poor lad! It's more than a body can take—to love and not be loved in return twice in his life," she said with a sniff and a glint of tears in her eyes.

It was no use her thinking she was helping Sandy by marrying Fraser, thought Lisa ruefully as she walked the dogs later that afternoon. What she had tried to avoid had happened. He had been in the process of falling in love with her ever since she had stepped ashore with him last December, she realized as she cast her mind back over their friendship. The invitations to tea at the farm, to go walking when it was fine, the number of times he found excuses to talk to her in his office at the mill, his wanting her to be a partner in the company—they had all been part of his slow shy approach and had culminated in the kiss he had given her last night to seal a bargain that he had hoped would lead to a more binding relationship.

She should have known that a man like Sandy, extremely conventional and slightly old-fashioned in his attitude toward women, would never have made such approaches if he had not wanted more from her than she was prepared to give. But having been brought up to be natural and at ease with the opposite sex and to regard herself as any man's equal, she had not realized that he would read into her naturalness with him a depth of liking for him that had led him to hope for more.

"Cooee, Lisa!" Johnnie's voice was shrill and carried on the still soft afternoon air.

She looked around. He was chugging along the road behind her, coat flapping, hair flying. When he reached her he smiled up at her and asked breathlessly, "Are you still going to be my mummy?"

"I—think so."

"Goodie! I was afraid you might have changed your mind."

Remembering how close she had been to changing her mind that morning, Lisa blushed rather guiltily and Johnnie noticed. His smile faded and he looked reproachful.

"You—you wouldn't change your mind, would you, Lisa?" he whispered.

"No, I wouldn't do that."

"Cross your heart and hope to die?" This was something he had learned recently from Jim.

"Cross my heart," she repeated.

She was caught, she thought, caught in a trap of her own making; caught by an affection-starved child who looked up at her with his father's eyes. And although, like a wild bird, she had made several attempts to be free of this trap, they had not been very vigorous or determined attempts.

"Are you coming to make our supper tonight?" asked Johnnie.

"No, I'm not."

"But you should if you're going to be my mummy."

"No. Not until I'm living with you, and not always then. Your father is a very good cook."

"But mummies always make the supper. Jim's does," he wailed.

Lisa realized that this was something she must get straight before she went any further.

"Just because I'm going to be your mummy doesn't mean I have to do everything Jim's mummy does. I expect

I'll get your meals lots of times and I'll always be there when your daddy isn't. But sometimes I won't be there, and then your daddy will look after you as he does now. Do you understand?"

He stared at her solemnly before he nodded his head. "As long as you're there most of the time. I don't want you to be like Jim's mummy. She's fat and she hasn't got eyes the color of mountain pools when the sun shines on them—"

"Like what?" Lisa interrupted, astounded by this flow of words.

He squirmed a little and then repeated what he had said, adding defensively, "That's what daddy said they were like when I asked him what color your eyes are 'cos I didn't know. He said they were green and brown like the pools in the mountains where he goes fishing sometimes. And he said your hair is the color of the leaves of the copper beech tree in the garden at Creddon Hall. Lisa, don't you like what he said?"

"Yes, yes." She found she was shaky and breathless. "Yes, of course I do."

The likening of the color of her hair to the leaves of the copper beech tree was very different from the scornful "Red" that Fraser had once used and that he persisted in calling her, and hearing his opinion of her coloring second-hand from his son gave her an odd feeling of having eaves-dropped on his most private thoughts, thoughts that she would never have suspected him of having.

Possessing this new knowledge of her future husband made her look forward to seeing him again. She expected him to come to Breck House to discuss the arrangements for their marriage in more detail, but he did not come and she did not see him for two days. Remembering rather belatedly that it was to be a marriage of convenience in which the usual rules of courtship did not apply, she realized eventually that he would not call to see her unless it was absolutely necessary.

Consequently she started to look for excuses to go to the boatyard to see him and found a very useful one in the arrival of a cable from her father in answer to the one she had sent him. Frank had been brief and explicit.

Delighted with your news. Proceed with my blessing.

His reply surprised Lisa. Frank was not the sort of person who went in for transports of delight, being very reserved when it came to expressing his emotions. She had realized that during his stay in Ardmont he had formed a good opinion of Fraser, but she had not thought he had known him long enough to consider him seriously as a prospective son-in-law.

The day was damp and gray, and down in the boatyard an aggravating little wind whipped around the corners of the big sheds, blowing the wood shavings and pieces of cardboard about and snatching at the canvas coverings of the yachts. From the sound of one shed came the noise of an electrical saw. Peering into the shed Lisa's attention was caught by the beautiful workmanship and rakish lines of the yacht being built in there, and she stood for a moment rapt in admiration for the smooth planking of red gold mahogany curving from bow to stern.

On the slip another yacht was ready to be launched. It also possessed the fine lines of the one in the shed, but it gleamed with new paint and on its bow its name glittered in gold-incised lettering: *Madrigal*.

Fraser stood near its high bow in characteristic pose, hands on his hips, head tilted slightly back as he watched the boat slip gradually backward into the gray wind-flurried water. Then it was afloat, swinging on the current, looking slightly ill at ease until its engine started up and one of the men on board took the wheel and steered the stately yacht away from the slip toward the black mooring buoy that bobbed a few yards away from the slip.

"I like her lines," said Lisa. "Who owns her?"

Fraser turned sharply to look at her, not having heard her approach. "She belongs to Ranald Gow, Harry Chisholm's brother-in-law," he replied brusquely.

Meeting his eyes suddenly, Lisa remembered his descrip-

The Taming of Lisa

tion of hers. If hers were like mountain pools in the sunlight, his were like the sea on one of those perfect days of sun and wind, deep indigo, mysterious and yet somehow inviting.

She blinked quickly, conscious that she was turning pink and that he looked faintly amused.

"Do you want to see me about something? If so would you mind being quick? We have two more yachts to launch."

"Isn't it a bad day for launching?" she stuttered, wanting to show an interest in his work about which she knew so little. "I mean, the wind must be a nuisance."

"It isn't perfect, but it will do, and at this time of the year, with so many owners demanding that their yachts be ready by the end of April or even before, we can't afford to waste time," he explained patiently. "Now, what can I do for you?"

She held out the cable, telling herself she must not be hurt by his brusqueness and apparent lack of pleasure in seeing her. Theirs was a business arrangement and there would be no room for being hurt of taking offense. If he was busy she must state what she wanted and get out of his way quickly. But she could not help wishing he had smiled at her.

He handed the cable back to her after reading it. "Well, that puts us in the clear with regard to your father. Kind of him to be quick in replying. Now we can go ahead and inform the registrar. We have three clear weeks before the first of May, which is all that is required." He slanted a derisive glance at her. "Know of anyone who might object?"

"No one. If my father had been against it would you have backed out?" she challenged.

"Would you?" he countered.

"That isn't a proper answer."

"It's all you're getting now. Think you could give Johnnie his supper tonight? I'd like to stay down here until these boats are in the water."

"Would you like me to put him to bed, too?" she queried with mock meekness.

"It would help," he replied curtly, and walked off into one of the sheds.

Johnnie was very pleased to have Lisa prepare his supper. He insisted on having it in his own home and so Lisa went there reluctantly. Once inside the house she was rather appalled to see the state it was in. The living room was thick with dust, and books and newspapers were scattered everywhere. The dining room, a dim dusty room, looked as if no one had entered it for years. In the kitchen dirty breakfast dishes were still on the table. The whole ground floor of the house looked dismal and uninviting on that gray April day.

She stood in the middle of the kitchen wondering where to start. She could not possibly prepare and serve a meal in such conditions.

"It's worse upstairs," volunteered Johnnie, who was watching the play of expression on her face.

"Worse? It couldn't be. Hasn't Mrs. Wilson been to clean this week?"

He shook his head solemnly. "Mrs. Wilson is ill, so she can't come, and daddy's been too busy to bother with housework."

Slowly Lisa took off her coat. "Then you and I are going to work very hard the next two hours, Johnnie Lamont," she announced.

Later, as the light died slowly in the western sky, Lisa finished reading a story to Johnnie, tucked him into his bed, kissed him good-night and went downstairs, thinking back to that night in January when he had wanted her to stay for supper and she had longed to stay and see him to bed. Well, her wish had come true in a very unexpected way.

Downstairs in the living room she flopped into a deep armchair and yawned. Never had she felt so tired. Since she had entered the house almost four hours ago she had washed dishes, scrubbed the kitchen floor, changed the sheets on two beds, and grateful because Fraser had had the sense to install an automatic washing machine, she had loaded it with all the dirty clothes she could find. She had cleaned the bathroom, vacuumed as much as she had time

The Taming of Lisa

for, prepared a meal and eaten it with Johnnie, made him have a bath and seen him to bed.

In all that time Fraser had not put in an appearance at the house. Occasionally glancing out of the window, she had seen him crossing the yard and had noticed at least one other yacht take to the water. She assumed that he would stay down there until the third one was safely launched and moored for the night. He would be like that, she thought sleepily, working right through until a job was finished before he relaxed and came home to eat.

Now she knew why she had rebelled for so long against the idea of marriage. No woman used to freedom and independence as she was could do the sort of work she had just done willingly. Only for love would a woman submit willingly to such slavery. Only for love.... Her head dropped against the hard stuffed back of the armchair and she slept.

She was on a sailing boat for the first time in her life. It skimmed over indigo blue water, its sails like white wings spread out from the mast. She lay on the foredeck watching the ripple of the bow wave, happier than she had ever felt in her life. Then from behind her Fraser's voice barked an order. She obeyed immediately. More orders came, fast and furious, sending her scurrying from one side of the boat to the other until she was breathless, bruised and bleeding. The orders stopped and she turned hopefully, expecting a reward. But he wasn't looking at her. Beside him sat Sarah, laughing up at him, and while Lisa stood transfixed he bent his head and kissed Sarah....

Lisa opened her eyes. A shiver ran though her body. She was crouched in the armchair in the dark room and she felt cold. Uncurling herself stiffly, she stood up and shook her head to clear it of the stupid but vivid dream.

The front door opened. "Fraser? Are you there?"

That was Sarah's voice calling. Running her fingers through her hair, Lisa went out into the hall and switched on the light. She could see Sarah standing outside the door.

"No, he isn't here yet, Sarah," she called. "Won't you come in?"

Sarah came in. She was as immaculate as ever and her mouth was as tempting and provocative as it had been in the dream.

"Since you ask me, yes, I'll come in and wait for him," she drawled, and the ice in her voice put Lisa on her guard. "I've a few things I want to say to you."

They went into the living room, but neither of them sat down. They stood eyeing each other like two cats about to start a fight.

"I've just been talking to Sandy," said Sarah. "He's not happy about this arrangement between you and Fraser. It was the first I'd heard about it because I've been busy helping mother entertain some guests. Is it true? Are you and Fraser going to be married?"

"Yes, it's true."

"So I was right after all! You're no better than those other women who made friends with Johnnie with an eye to the future. Only you were more clever, besides being attractive in an unusual way. You pretended you weren't interested in marriage. And of course the fact that the child likes you must have weighed heavily in your favor. Still, I'm not as convinced as Sandy is that Fraser is marrying you for Johnnie's sake. I think he has a much more ingenious and subtle reason."

Lisa, who had been congratulating herself on her self-control in the face of Sarah's spiteful insults, looked up sharply.

"Oh? What is that?" she asked.

Sarah's lovely eyes narrowed cunningly and then their gaze slid away, avoiding Lisa's direct glance. With her hip-swinging walk she swayed up and down the room a couple of times before she answered.

"The annoying thing is I think I might have put the idea into his head," she said at last, coming to stand in front of Lisa again.

"How did you do that?"

"I gather from Sandy that Fraser proposed to you the night he arrived back from Holland, the night I drove him home. Is that right?"

The Taming of Lisa

"Yes, it is."

"Well, on the way down I told him about Miss Roy's death and that you owned Breck House, and I suggested that the time was ready for him to make an offer for it."

"What did he say?"

"Only that he had already thought of that. Did he make an offer?"

"Yes, he did. I had to refuse to sell because of the conditions of the will. He wasn't pleased," said Lisa hesitantly, recalling the unpleasant expression on Fraser's face when she had told him about Aunt Maud's will.

"And soon after that he asked you to marry him?" persisted Sarah, her eyes glinting with devilry.

Lisa did not reply at once. She was thinking of that moonlit night when the scent of lilac had been heavy. Had Fraser proposed marriage to her or had she suggested it to him? She found she wasn't sure anymore.

"Yes, I believe he did," she replied vaguely.

"Then there you are," said Sarah, flinging her arms out wide in a dramatic gesture. "It's as clear as day. He wasn't thinking of Johnnie at all. He was thinking that if you were his wife you could hardly refuse to give him permission to build on your land, especially after you'd been married to him for a while. He wants to marry you because he wants Breck House."

CHAPTER EIGHT

HALF AN HOUR LATER Lisa sat at the kitchen table in Breck House and held her aching head on one hand while she wiped away salty tears with the other. She was still shaken and alarmed by the bout of weeping that had overtaken her as soon as she had reached the house. Not for years had she wept like that; like a tired, disappointed child.

But why the disappointment? Pushing lethargically to her feet, she went over to the sink, filled the kettle and plugged it in. She would make some tea, that cure for all upsets of the mind. She only wished she had someone to share a cup of tea with—Ina, perhaps. But she would have to drink it alone. The price of independence, she thought with a grimace, was having to deal with problems alone.

As she reached into the cupboard to get out the tea caddy Lisa answered her own question. She was disappointed because she was afraid Sarah's suggestion that Fraser wanted to marry her because he wanted Breck House was true. Thank heaven she had had the presence of mind not to betray her disappointment to Sarah, who probably would have reveled in it. Keeping her cool, she had said to the model in as steady a voice as she could muster, "But of course I know that. You don't think I'm such an innocent to enter into such an arrangement with a man like Fraser blindly without knowing what he's about? It's his business and mine, not yours or Sandy's."

And then while Sarah was still staring at her wide-eyed and a little shocked she had added, "Would you mind waiting for Fraser here? There are some things I must attend to at Breck House and I don't like leaving Johnnie alone in case he wakes up and is frightened. Fraser shouldn't be

The Taming of Lisa

long. You might tell him too that his supper is in the oven keeping warm."

Then she had swept out of the house and had not stopped running until she had reached the friendly comforting darkness of the old house on the brae.

It hadn't been a bad performance, she thought, but she hoped Sarah had stayed until Fraser had arrived because she had a feeling he would not be pleased if he found Johnnie alone. However, for all she had been able to hide her hurt from Sarah, she was still left with this awful suspicion that Sarah had been right, and that she had been blind when she had said she would marry Fraser, having forgotten the occasion of their first meeting when he had said he would do anything to get his own way. That laconic "anything" had included marrying her.

What should she do? Confront him with the suspicion and see how he reacted?

The kettle boiled and she poured boiling water into the teapot, pretending that the globules of moisture forming on her cheeks were caused by the steam, and were not the tears.

"Lisa!" Fraser's voice was sharp, and she almost dropped the kettle. She put it down carefully and spun around to look at him. He stood in the entrance to the kitchen from the hall. His eyes and hair were very dark against the unusual paleness of his face and she had the impression he was very angry about something.

"How did you get in?" she stammered foolishly.

"How do you think? Through the front door. I knocked twice and when you didn't answer I tried the handle and found the door was unlocked. Were you deliberately ignoring my knocks?"

"No...no. I didn't hear them, or the doorbell." How foolishly she was behaving, like a child caught in the act of doing something she shouldn't.

He was coming across the room toward her. He would see the tears on her cheeks, and he could not bear women who wept.

"Would you like a cup of tea?" she asked desperately, turning to the cupboard where the crockery was kept.

"Yes, please, I would," he said, and to her relief he sat down at the table. "I came to thank you for cleaning up the house. I'm afraid it was in a bit of a mess."

"Why didn't you tell me Mrs. Wilson wasn't cleaning for you? I'd have come and tidied up."

"I never thought of asking you," he replied easily. "After all, we aren't married yet."

"Oh, so you'll expect me to clean up as a matter of course when we're married?" she retorted, feeling a strange lift to her spirits as she reacted automatically to his teasing, and he grinned appreciatively although his eyes narrowed observantly as she moved toward the table and he was able to see her face clearly.

"It will be entirely up to you whether you clean it or not," he returned, and then with concern deepening his voice he asked, "What did Sarah say to you?"

"Then she did wait for you? I was hoping she would, because I didn't want to leave Johnnie— Oh, have you left him alone? Will he be all right, I mean...?"

"He won't come to any harm for an hour while you tell me what went on between you and Sarah. It must have been unpleasant if it's made you cry."

"Me?" she exclaimed jauntily. "Oh, I never cry."

"No? Then why is your face all blotchy and why are your eyelashes spiky? It can't be some new form of makeup," he said dryly.

"It isn't blotchy," she protested, and went to peer in the mirror above the sink. "Oh, yes, it is," she muttered, looking quickly away from her reflected face. She picked up the teapot, crossed to the table and began to pour into one of the cups.

Clear hot water came out of the spout!

"Red Smith, you are in a bad way," Fraser mocked gently. "Sit down and I'll make the tea."

Lisa collapsed into the nearest chair, put her elbows on the table and clasped her head in her hands. Behind her she could hear the kettle boiling again, the tea caddy being

The Taming of Lisa

opened and closed, the water being poured into the pot and then the click of the pot's lid as it was put in place.

Fraser came back to his chair and put the teapot on its stand.

"It will be infused in a few minutes. I can't stand unbrewed tea. Please note for future reference," he said.

"There won't be any future for us," Lisa replied, looking at him. He raised an eyebrow at her as he slid down in his chair, hands in his trouser pockets, and stretched his legs under the table. His hair was ruffled and dark stubble blurred his chin. The color had returned to his face and he no longer looked angry. He looked more like a man who had worked hard all day, had enjoyed his work and was now ready for some relaxation—and some fun. Judging by the gleam in his eyes, the fun was going to be at her expense.

"Because of what Sarah said to you?" he prodded.

"Yes."

"Are you going to tell me what she said or am I going to have to shake it out of you?"

She was a little alarmed. He had never touched her once in all their strange association, and the thought that he might take hold of her now and shake her made her feel dithery. She was not sure how she might react.

"She said that you want to marry me because you want Breck House," she replied hurriedly. "Is that true?"

"To a certain extent, yes, it is true. The thought had crossed my mind some time ago," he said smoothly. "Does that make any difference to you?"

"Of course it makes a difference! You deceived me. You didn't tell me that was why you wanted to marry me," she said furiously.

"I have many reasons for wanting to marry you and I haven't told you all of them—yet. I just dangled in front of you the one that I thought would interest you at the moment—and you bit," he explained coolly.

He picked up the teapot and poured. The fluid flowed in a golden brown stream into a cup. Disconcerted by his answers, Lisa stared at the big hands performing the homely rite of pouring tea and adding milk so efficiently.

They were strong hands. Were they also loving hands capable of taming a wild heart?

Fraser pushed a cup and saucer in front of her together with the sugar bowl and asked if she had any biscuits. "I enjoyed my supper," he said, "but there just wasn't enough of it."

When she had found what he wanted Lisa sat down again and began to sip her tea.

"So Sarah came to cause trouble, did she?" Fraser observed. "She must have been annoyed about something."

"She was. About you and me getting married. She said she'd been to see Sandy and he was very upset...."

"I thought he might be," he put in quietly. "In fact it was his interest in you that pushed me into taking action sooner than I might have done."

"That and Aunt Maud's death," she suggested acidly.

"Another contributing factor," he drawled, and over the top of the cup that he had raised to his mouth his eyes glimmered with amusement. "Did it never occur to you that I might marry you for your property?"

"No. Because I know very well that it remains my property by law no matter whom I marry, and you can't make me give you permission to extend the boatyard onto my land."

He was smiling to himself as he poured more tea into his cup, that faintly wicked triumphant smile. "That's very true," he agreed. "Then why are you all steamed up about Sarah's suggestion?"

Lisa became very interested in the tea leaves at the bottom of her cup. The reason for her being steamed up, as he called her behavior, had just flashed through her mind and she did not want to admit it as yet, least of all to him.

"I don't like being deceived," she said rather weakly.

"Is that all?" He sounded very skeptical.

"It may be funny to you, but to me it's important."

"And because I haven't told you everything about myself you want to back out?" he asked.

"Yes, I do. I don't think I can go through with it," she replied in a choked voice, still peering into her cup as if she could find solace there.

The Taming of Lisa

"So just because a jealous woman vented her spite on you you would let Johnnie down," he accused quietly.

The cup clattered as Lisa placed it hastily in the saucer.

"Oh, you—you—devil!" she exclaimed. "You know I can't do that to him."

"I hoped you couldn't, because I would have had a hell of a time explaining to him," he admitted. "Can I assume then that we go ahead as planned?"

"Yes," she muttered, not looking at him.

"You know, I suppose, that Sarah was also wild because she discovered that Sandy Lewis had fallen out of love with her and that she blames you?"

"He isn't in love with me. He only thinks he is," she answered.

"Tell that to Sarah. One of the reasons why I proposed marriage to you was that I hoped to divert your attention to me so that he would get over his infatuation with you and remember she was around. But she seems to think it's too late. That's why she ripped into you tonight," he said.

"Oh, and that was one reason why I agreed to marry you, too," she admitted. "I thought that when Sarah realized you weren't available she would turn to Sandy and...." Her voice faltered to a stop as she realized what she had just done. She had admitted to having an ulterior motive for marrying him, too.

"Nothing to choose between us, is there, Red?" he gibed, rising to his feet. "It's time I went home. I'll pick you up tomorrow early in the morning to drive into Kilbride and get this business with the registrar fixed. Don't bother to come to the door. I saw myself in, so I can see myself out," he added, turning to her as she moved to his side.

His unexpected turn brought them very close together and Lisa stepped back defensively.

"Perhaps it's time I sealed our bargain, too," Fraser said. There was a mischievous twinkle in his eyes and she retreated again, being brought up short by the table. She did not want him to kiss her because she was afraid that they both might find out too much about her real feelings concerning him.

"Don't make me hate you, Fraser," she warned him, hoping to deter him.

But he was not deterred. He stepped after her, reached out a hand, grabbed the edges of her knitted cardigan near the throat and pulled her forward.

"That's a risk I'll have to take," he replied with a laugh, and kissed her firmly on the mouth. She was just thinking that there was nothing shy and featherlike about this possessive kiss when fireworks seemed to explode in a shower of sparks behind her closed eyelids and immediately all her resistance collapsed. But she had no chance to respond because he moved away, and before she had opened her eyes he was in the hall and calling out, "'Night, Red. Sleep well. See you in the morning."

SURPRISINGLY ENOUGH she did sleep well, better than she had for nights, and she was ready and waiting when he came to pick her up to drive into Kilbride. They took Johnnie with them to save him from going on the school bus, so there was little opportunity for conversation between her and Fraser on the way there. As they came out of the office Fraser saw an acquaintance of his waiting by the bus stop who wanted to catch the ferry from Ardmont to Gourock, so they gave him a lift. When they dropped the man at the pierhead Lisa got out of the car, too, because she wanted to go to the mill. With a wave of his hand Fraser drove off to the boatyard, and judging by the faraway expression on his face his mind was already taken up with the day's work ahead of him and Lisa Smith was the last person he thought of.

At the mill Lisa found the atmosphere extremely uncomfortable. Sandy was sad and vague, and Ina was silent and reproachful. Anyone would think she had committed a crime in consenting to marry Fraser for convenience, thought Lisa impatiently as she walked home. If the two of them had gone around holding each other's hands and gazing into each other's eyes, swearing undying love, everyone would have been delighted and there would have been messages of congratulations from all sides. As it was, only her

The Taming of Lisa

father seemed pleased. From Sandy she had received reluctant good wishes, from Ina reproaches and from Sarah spite.

She had to admit to feeling a little guilty about Sarah and Sandy. She felt she must make amends somehow. Eventually she decided to go to see Sarah, having first phoned to make sure that the model was at home.

She was greeted over the phone by Bunty Chisholm, who promptly invited her to lunch, saying that she wanted to see Lisa about a suit she would like her to design.

Lisa accepted the invitation and an hour later set off in Aunt Maud's old car. Driving along the road, high above the twinkling water, she recalled the last time she had come that way and the car had boiled on the hill. Today was quite different. Spring was in the air. The sun was shining and visibility was good. She could see right down the northern arm of the strait to the distant hills of Ayrshire.

Stopping the car in the lay-by where Fraser had found her that wet winter's day, she got out to stand and stare for a moment. Far below her the narrow stretch of fertile land that bordered the strait was being plowed by a bright red tractor. Beyond the freshly turned earth the water was translucent green changing through amethyst to deep, deep indigo and then to black in the shadow cast by the tall conifers that grew on Eilean Glasa, the Gray Isle.

On such a day Lisa's spirits should have been high, and although they had a tendency to float that way when she remembered Fraser's kiss of two nights ago, she kept having to subdue them, telling herself that it had meant nothing to him. He had merely been indulging his sense of humor, making fun of the way Sandy had sealed a bargain. It had not been a loving tender embrace even though she had had an inclination to respond to it.

When she reached the castle there was no sign of Sarah, and for the first half hour she spent a pleasant time with Mrs. Chisholm, being shown various parts of the castle. When eventually they returned to the long lounge that looked out over lawns that swept down to the River Creddon, Sarah was there, slim and lovely in a plain green dress, lounging in an armchair sipping sherry. She shot a sulky glance in Lisa's direction while Mrs. Chisholm poured sherry for herself and her guest.

"What are you doing here?" she demanded.

"Lisa has come to see you, dear," said Bunty sweetly. "Although I thought I'd take the opportunity to have a little chat with her myself. Well, here's to you and Fraser, Lisa. I'm so very pleased for you both and so is Harry." She raised her glass in Lisa's direction and then sipped a little of her drink. "We'll have lunch in the morning room and then I'll leave you two together, because I have to go into Inverey. It's my turn of duty at the hospital."

All through lunch Bunty kept up a flow of conversation about her voluntary hospital work so that the awkwardness between Lisa and Sarah was not noticeable, but when she had gone Sarah made no attempt to hide her hostility.

"If you've come to ask me to model more clothing for you, you can forget it. I don't want to have anything to do with you, or with Fraser—or with Sandy Lewis," she added.

"That isn't why I've come," replied Lisa, suddenly seeing Sarah for what she was—a very spoiled child. "Although I think its's very foolish of you to take that attitude toward Sandy, who hasn't done you any harm ever, in spite of the way you treated him years ago. I've come to explain that I didn't deliberately set out to make him fall in love with me, as you seem to think, and to tell you that he isn't in love with me anyway."

"But he was so upset about you and Fraser. He kept on saying he couldn't believe you were like that."

"He was upset because he had found out that I was different from what he'd expected. He'd built up an image of me as his soul mate, his partner for life who could do no wrong and who would rush to do his bidding and transform his life for him. He has some very old-fashioned ideas about women. He treats them as if they're something precious, yet expects them to be subservient at the same time. That's a tall order."

Some of Sarah's sulkiness vanished and she looked at

Lisa with interest. "I suppose you're right, and that's what I found so restful about him when I came back in December, met him on the boat and found him just the same, very courteous and a little shy. But he didn't show any signs of still being in love with me and I was piqued," she said slowly. "So I tried to attract his attention in the only way I know how, using the one available man, Fraser, whom I found attractive, too. It didn't work."

"No, it didn't work with either of them, did it? You can't bear a man to ignore you, can you, Sarah?" commented Lisa.

"No, I can't." Sarah jumped to her feet and began to stride up and down the room. "Oh, what a fool I am! Peter warned me. Peter's always warning me, has been for years. He warned me about Jack. I should take more notice of him because he's nearly always right. He knows me so well. You get to know a person very well, you know, when you're with her every day, for hours, taking her photograph."

Before she realized what was happening Lisa was listening to Sarah's confidences about Peter Wright, about the awful things he did and said to her, the way he pushed her around.

"Mother would have a fit if she knew," finished Sarah with a sudden giggle.

"But you really like him to behave like that, don't you?" said Lisa. "You'd rather have that than no attention at all."

Sarah looked surprised. "Yes, I suppose I do like it. It's better than that casual please-yourself attitude that Fraser has toward women. How do you put up with it?"

"I must be going," said Lisa evasively, not wishing to admit that it was his casual attitude that made her prefer Fraser to Sandy.

"Oh, must you go? Just when we were beginning to understand each other," complained Sarah petulantly. "That's what I've missed in my life, having a girl friend to talk to. I'm sorry I was bitchy to you the other night, but everything seemed to pile up inside me. You seemed to have had all the luck with the only two eligible men in Ardmont without so much as lifting an eyebrow, without trying even, and I had to get at you somehow. Forget what I said earlier about not wanting to model the tweeds. Anytime you like."

"Only if Peter Wright is the photographer. You wouldn't look quite the same if he weren't there to push you around and be rude to you."

Again Sarah looked surprised. Then she giggled as understanding dawned on her. "Do you know, Lisa, I think you're right. Thanks for coming."

Vaguely pleased at the outcome of her interview with Sarah, Lisa wondered what to do about Sandy. If he was going to behave as he had after Sarah had let him down eight years ago, he was going to ruin his life. She sensed his discomfort at her presence in the mill and knew that she would have to take drastic action soon. She could not work under such conditions any more than she had been able to work for Richard Hatton.

One morning Sandy's melancholy, deferential treatment of her got on her nerves so much that she turned on him and said crisply, "It's no use, Sandy; I can't be a partner. It's—it's like being a prisoner. I can feel my creative urges dying for want of air. I'm stifled. I shall have to break the contract."

"But what about the designing you were going to do?" he complained anxiously. "You can't let me down like this."

"I'm not going to let you down," she replied desperately, wondering how she could make him understand. "But I will if I'm tied. Can't you see I have to be free to design properly? Once I feel that I have to design because you're dependent on me I can't do it. Let me free-lance and I'll never let you down."

He stared at her consideringly. "Och, very well," he muttered resignedly. "I suppose I was a fool to think that I could ever tame you. But I'm beginning to think Fraser is going to have his work cut out keeping you in order."

"I shouldn't waste time worrying about him," she retorted tartly. "He's more than equal to the task. But there's

The Taming of Lisa

something I have to tell you and I'm going to tell you here no matter who is listening in. There is someone in this village right under your nose who would make an excellent partner in your company, far better than I would be because she's practical and levelheaded. She'd also make that partner for life you're looking for. But because you're her employer and the manager of the mill, she thinks you're completely out of her reach. Being the warmhearted person she is she'll be content to adore you from a distance while remaining your faithful employee. Think of all that love going to waste, Sandy, while you sit here yearning for the unattainable. There, that's all I can say, except to apologize for not living up to your expectations. But I'm only human, not a goddess to be worshiped or a slave to run to your bidding."

While she was speaking his face had gone red and then white as he'd reacted to her words, but the melancholy had gone.

"Don't apologize," Sandy said gruffly. "I'm human, too, and just as much to blame. I realize that. You see, I was so afraid of Sarah when she came back that I turned to you. I should have known better. I wonder if you're right about Ina."

"Well, there's only one way to find out. Surely you know the truth of the saying about faint hearts by now, Sandy Lewis," Lisa retorted as her parting shot.

It gave her a great feeling of satisfaction to play at being fairy godmother. She had done her best to make amends to both Sandy and Sarah, and she was sure that now she had pointed out to them that Ina and Peter were their natural partners they would both take some action in the right direction instead of yearning after someone totally unsuitable.

CHAPTER NINE

TIME WAS PASSING in a blur of April showers and calm sunny periods. Buds were swelling and birds were nesting. A gradual change was taking place as the new growth of grass began to assert itself in field and garden. Blackthorn bushes were ablaze with tiny white flowers and hawthorn hedges were showing bright green tufts as leaves burst out of the fine spiky branches.

Another change was also taking place as more yachts were launched and took up their positions at their moorings. They brought movement and color to Ardmont Bay as they swung slowly around every time the tide ebbed or flowed. Winter with its wild storms and moments of frosty brilliance was over, and soon the village would be full of summer visitors.

The boatyard buzzed with activity. Most afternoons Lisa met Johnnie as he came home from school, gave him his supper and put him to bed because Fraser was so busy. The only time she saw him was when he returned to the white house for his supper after Johnnie had gone to bed, and then she left him with hurried instructions about his meal and went back to Breck House to sew the suit she was making to wear on the first of May.

Not once did Fraser make any effort to detain her, to talk to her about the day's events or to ask her what she had been doing. His usual reply to her excuse for leaving was an absentminded nod of agreement before he disappeared upstairs to wash off the grime of the day.

At first Lisa did not mind such casual treatment, being only too glad to make her escape. It was all part of the arrangement between them, she reminded herself, that neither should make any unnecessary demands upon the

The Taming of Lisa

other. Fraser had a deadline to meet where his work was concerned, and she could understand his being absorbed in that work because she behaved like that herself when she was working on a design.

Still, it would have been pleasant if he had invited her to stay with him while he ate his supper or had shown appreciation occasionally of what she was doing for him.

He never did, and the first of May loomed up with nothing more said about the arrangements for their marriage. And although Lisa knew that the announcement was still in the window of the registrar's office and that both Sandy and Ina had been asked by Fraser to be witnesses, she began to wonder if Fraser himself had forgotten that he was to be married.

The thought occurred to her as she watched him on the last day of April supervising the launching of Harry Chisholm's big schooner, which had now been renamed *Sea Saga*, the fifth of Harry's boats to be given that name. She felt a sudden freezing of her heart and acknowledged ruefully that she would be unable to bear it if Fraser had forgotten.

The big black boat slipped into the water, creating a miniature tidal wave that swept up over the shore and onto the road. Fraser turned with a triumphant grin and shouted to her, "That's the last. Now we can get married!"

Suddenly embarrassed by Wally Scott's grin and the amused cracks made by some of the other men, Lisa turned and walked away into the yard, where Fraser caught up with her.

"Don't tell me you'd forgotten," he jeered.

"No. But I thought perhaps you had," she retorted.

"And that worried you?" he was quick to ask.

Her step did not falter and she kept looking straight ahead, refusing to rise to his baiting.

"Not really," she lied coolly. "If that's the last boat to be launched this week I suppose you won't be working late this evening, so perhaps you'll be able to put Johnnie to bed. He'll be pleased if you do, because he hasn't seen much of you this week."

"Fair enough," he said, equally cool and casual.

"What time shall I see you tomorrow?" she asked.

"Ten o'clock at the registrar's. I want to be back in Ardmont to catch the eleven-thirty boat for Gourock. I'm taking Wally and young Weir with me to sail the boat back. You bring Ina with you tomorrow and I'll take Sandy."

Was ever a marriage arranged so casually, thought Lisa as she walked up the brae to Breck House. Perhaps she ought to call it off now because to continue might bring heartbreak for herself. Her hands clenched at her sides. This was the nearest she had come to admitting that the impossible had happened and that she, of all people, had fallen in love with a man who was quite obviously not in love with her.

Next morning was fine and clear. The sun was there behind a film of gray haze that covered the sky. Later it would break through and the day would be warm. Lisa dressed in the new suit. It was a soft shade of blue and had a long straight skirt that had a slit in it to allow for freedom when walking. The jacket was waisted and had wide lapels and under it she wore a blouse of frothy white lace. On her head she placed a wide-brimmed hat, but as she picked up her matching white gloves and handbag she realized she hadn't any flowers. Tears pricked her eyes suddenly. It was her wedding day and no one had thought to provide her with any.

Ina arrived in good time and together they drove through the village and out onto the moor road that wound inland to Kilbride. Half an hour later they walked into the registrar's office, where Fraser, looking remarkably spruce in a finely checked tweed suit, was waiting with Sandy. As Lisa walked in he came to meet her and presented her with a small posy of violets.

Unable to look at him because emotion at the sight of the dark velvety petals of the shy delicate flowers threatened to overcome her, she asked, "Where did you find them?"

"Under the hedge in my garden," he replied, "I'm afraid I forgot to order any others, so I was up with the lark seeing what I could find. They're a little early, due to the mild weather we're having."

The Taming of Lisa

Touched by the gesture, Lisa could only thrust her gloves and bag at Ina to hold while she pinned the posy to the lapel her jacket with a brooch she was wearing, and then followed Fraser into the room where the brief ceremony was to take place.

Within an hour they were back in Ardmont walking along the pier toward the yellow-funneled steamer that was ready to leave. Ina and Sandy had left them and had gone to the mill, and Lisa had only a thick gold band on her finger and a posy of violets pinned to her jacket to remind her that she was married.

"You don't know what a relief it is to know that Johnnie will be with you," said Fraser. "It will make all the difference to going away. He wanted to stay off school and come with us to the registrar's office, but I wouldn't let him. I said that it was something strictly between you and me."

"Did he object?"

"Of course he did. He seems to have a fixed idea that you are entirely his property. You'd better start putting him right about that before it starts causing trouble."

"Why would it cause trouble, and with whom?" Lisa asked with an air of innocent surprise.

He grinned down at her as the boat's siren wailed to warn passengers not yet aboard that it was about to depart.

"That's something for you to puzzle about while I'm away," he said. "I should be back Thursday night sometime if this weather holds, just in time for Harry's schooner party."

"Schooner party? What's that?" asked Lisa, finding it difficult to hurry in her long skirt.

"We're invited to go with the Chisholms with about seventy other people on a cruise up Loch Creddon so that he can introduce his latest and biggest boat, not only to all his friends and relations and business contacts, but also to all the other boats he's owned. It's a crazy childish idea and only Harry could get away with it. Didn't I tell you?" he shouted to her as he stepped aboard.

The gangplank was pulled back, the embarkation gate was closed and the steamer began to sidle away from the pier.

"You never tell me anything!" yelled Lisa across the intervening strip of water and saw him laugh as he turned to talk to the two men from the yard who were going with him to fetch the boat from Ireland.

That night Lisa slept at the white house in the spare room next to Johnnie's. There had been a few slightly confusing and embarrassing moments when Johnnie had insisted that she move into his father's bedroom straightaway. In answer to her calm statement that she preferred the spare room he trotted out his usual argument. "Jim's mummy sleeps in his daddy's room. Jimmy says all mummies sleep with daddies."

"Yes, I know," Lisa answered. "But, you see, this is slightly different. Your daddy isn't here and I think I'd better wait until he comes home."

To her relief Johnnie seemed satisfied with this answer and helped, or rather hindered, her in the process of making up the spare bed, but she began to wonder after a while how much of the conversation would be relayed to Jim, thence to Jim's mother and thence around the whole village.

The spare bed was not very comfortable, having lost most of its springiness and having developed a hollow in the middle out of which Lisa had to climb in the morning. She decided after the first night that as soon as Fraser returned she would have her bed from Breck House moved into the room. She was quite sure that there was not the slightest chance of her being invited to share Fraser's room, as she had suggested to Johnnie.

She did not have much time in which to ponder the strangeness of her situation because the day after Fraser left she met Bunty Chisholm and was soon involved in the preparations for the schooner party.

Bunty, neatly dressed in navy blue trousers and anorak and wearing short yachting boots, was crossing the boatyard when Lisa met her. When she asked for Fraser and was told that he'd gone to Ireland she looked astonished.

"But you were only married yesterday," she exclaimed. "Why aren't you on your honeymoon?"

The Taming of Lisa

Completely nonplussed by this question, Lisa found herself blushing and muttering about Fraser's having to fetch a boat from Ireland immediately, or lose a client, and about it being difficult to go away on a honeymoon because of Johnnie.

"Well, I could mind Johnnie for you. There's nothing I'd like better," said Bunty. "I'm very fond of children. I only wish Sarah would settle down and present me with a grandchild. She's gone to London to see Peter—she wants him to come to the party. She seems very attached to him, but Harry and I find him a little strange. What do you think, Lisa? I'd hate her to make another mistake."

"I think Peter understands Sarah," replied Lisa cautiously.

"Well, I suppose that's a step in the right direction. I'm just going out to the yacht to see that everything is all shipshape for Saturday. I'd be glad if you'd come with me. You might be able to make some suggestions."

And so Lisa set foot upon a sailing yacht for the first time in her life. Fascinated, she stood and looked up at the two masts, the foremost one slightly shorter than the thick solid main one. Glinting gold in the sunlight, they soared up against the blue of the sky.

Then she went below down the neat stairway and was amazed at how much space there was. The original stowage holds had been converted into a comfortable living accommodation. There was a huge saloon furnished with comfortable settees and an extending table. It had fitted cupboards and bookcases and there were even framed pictures on the paneled walls. Further exploration revealed a big galley with every modern convenience for cooking, several small bedrooms with comfortable bunks, a toilet and a washroom complete with shower. Looking around admiringly, Lisa now understood why the carpenters at the yard had been working overtime.

"We're very pleased with the conversion," said Bunty as they returned to the big saloon. "Fraser has done a good job. Now when we arrive at the anchorage at the top of Loch Creddon on Saturday I think we'll serve a buffet luncheon. There'll be about six other yachts besides this one, including *Madrigal*. Harry wants to serve champagne only as it's a sort of celebration of his forty years of sailing, and I thought we'd start with smoked salmon and follow that by various cold meats and salad, with fruit and nuts to follow. What do you think, dear?"

Helping Bunty plan the party took up all of Lisa's spare time that day and the following day, and Thursday arrived without her realizing it. It was a fresh blustery day with a strong southerly wind blowing up the kyle; a wind that would flow Fraser back home.

The thought excited her and she found herself looking forward to his return, but by ten o'clock at night when the wind had died down and the kyle was calm once more there was no sign of the yacht he was bringing.

Lying wakeful in the narrow humpy bed, Lisa hoped nothing had happened to delay his return, and she was just beginning to doze off when she heard the front door, which she had purposely left unlocked, open and close. The sound was followed by the thud of rubber seaboots being dropped in the hallway, and immediately she tensed and her heart began to beat faster. There were more noises from below, the sound of the kitchen light being switched on and off, followed by the switching on of the landing light. The stairs creaked as Fraser walked slowly up them and she heard the soft pad of his feet on the bare wooden floor of the landing. The handle of the door to his bedroom rattled as he turned it and then there was a profound silence after he had opened the door.

Then to her surprise she heard the sound of his feet coming across the landing toward her open door. Against the yellow oblong of light his form was a dark silhouette as he stood there looking in. Lisa found she was incapable of sound or movement. He stood there for about a minute, then moved away. A few seconds later she heard his bedroom door close and she let out the breath that she did not know she had been holding and let unexpected disappointment have its way with her.

The next day Fraser was up and out in the yard before

The Taming of Lisa

she arrived downstairs, but he came back to have breakfast with Johnnie. He was just the same, Lisa thought, saying very little about the trip across the sea from Ireland, answering Johnnie's questions absently and, judging by the lack of questions on his part, having very little interest in what she might have been doing. When Johnnie had left to catch the school bus, he went upstairs to shave, and it was when he came down to the kitchen again that she asked him about moving the bed from Breck House.

"Please yourself," he replied maddeningly. "It's your bed."

"Thank you very much," replied Lisa, thoroughly irritated by his lack of interest. "But I'll need help to move it. Do you think...?"

He looked at her then and the coldness of his expression repelled her slightly. What had happened to the man who had given her a posy of violets that he had picked for her from his garden?

"If you want one of the men to help you shift it you'll have to wait until next week," he said curtly. "They'll all be too busy today."

He went out of the room and soon she heard the crash of the front door as he slammed it behind him.

For a moment Lisa stood biting hard into her lower lip, telling herself that it had been silly to indulge in hopes and longings while waiting for his return last night. She must always remember that she was there for Johnnie's sake and that she must not make any unnecessary demands on Johnnie's father.

The day took its course. She went once more with Bunty Chisholm to the schooner to make sure all the preparations for the party had been made. She took the dogs for a walk, met Johnnie and made supper. Fraser was no more sociable at this mealtime than he had been at breakfast and only spoke to her to tell her when they would be leaving to go aboard *Sea Saga* in the morning and to give instructions on the sort of clothing she and Johnnie would require. Then after he had seen Johnnie to bed he went back to his office, saying that he had some drawings of a new yacht he wanted to finish so that he could show them to one of Harry's friends who would be present at the party. After looking out the necessary clothing and sitting for a while on her own watching TV in a desultory fashion, Lisa went miserably to bed, wondering what she had done to offend Fraser so soon in their married life.

When she looked out of the bedroom window next morning she was glad to see that the water was calm. A slight mist hung over it and was still there, clinging to her hair and sprinkling Fraser's hair with glittering drops of moisture as he rowed her and Johnnie out to the schooner in a dinghy.

On board she waited for the arrival of Bunty and Harry while Fraser rowed back ashore to bring Willie Scott, the foreman, and his wife aboard. Within half an hour there were about twenty people on board, including an elderly man called Skip Burnett, who had taught Harry how to sail. With the Chisholms Sarah and Peter arrived, bringing with them a tall fair young man whom Sarah introduced as her cousin Brian Sutcliffe.

"Look after him, Lisa, will you?" said Sarah. "He's from your part of the world and he sometimes feels lost among these clannish Scots."

Soon *Sea Saga*'s decks were thronged with guests. The men were mostly interested in the rigging and the marine equipment on board, and the women spent their time admiring and exclaiming over the more domestic details such as the size of the galley, the comfort of the saloon and the convenience of the shower in the bathroom.

The mist thinned and as it cleared the sun came through. A light breeze blew from the south.

"Perfect, perfect," crowed Harry. "Just what we need. We'll hoist every sail and run up Loch Creddon in style."

Most of the men aboard being sailors themselves, there were many willing hands and soon all sails were set. The mooring was cast off and *Sea Saga* slipped gracefully through the water, a big black bird with white wings, passing Ranald Gow's big yawl, which cast off its mooring almost immediately and followed the schooner up the kyle.

The Taming of Lisa

But by the time they had reached the islands at the narrows the pleasant breeze had died away, and as *Sea Saga*'s bow pointed to the entrance of Loch Creddon the engine had to be started. Ahead lay five other boats, all of them becalmed, and as the schooner approached Lisa could see that three of them were called *Sea Saga II, III, IV*.

"I rowed the first *Sea Saga*, all fourteen feet of her, out into Loch Creddon this morning and anchored her," Brian told Lisa as he leaned beside her on the bulwarks and watched the pine-clad slopes of the north shore of the loch slide by.

Having discovered she came from Manchester, too, he had stuck to her like a winkle to a rock. It wasn't so much a case of looking after him as trying to lose him for a few minutes, thought Lisa. And to make matters worse Johnnie, resenting Brian's attempt to monopolize her attention, had behaved badly several times; so badly, in fact, that he had already drawn Fraser's ire and had received a sharp setdown. At the same time Fraser had given her a reproving glance, obviously blaming her for his son's bad manners. Not that he had much time for noticing what either of them was doing. He was too busy talking to old acquaintances, giving advice to Harry on the handling of the schooner and sharing jokes with Sarah.

By the time they reached the head of the loch it was past noon. The weather had turned warm and muggy, and Brian commented that he wouldn't be surprised if there was a thunderstorm.

All the *Sea Saga*s were tied up alongside each other with the most recent acquisition in the middle, its two masts towering above the others. The other boats anchored nearby and soon all the guests were swarming onto the schooner to help themselves to the champagne and the food that had been set out in the saloon.

After having collected some food for herself and Johnnie, Lisa took the boy up to the bow of the schooner. For once they had lost Brian and she hoped that Fraser might join them. But he did not appear. And why should he, thought Lisa disconsolately. Last time she had seen him he had been having a perfectly enjoyable time with Sarah.

Suddenly without appetite, Lisa set her plate on one side and leaned against the bulwark, steeped in misery, only vaguely aware of the laughter and gaiety of the people around her. Below her the water looked dark and turgid, having none of the colorful clarity it possessed on a sunny day. Above, ragged gray clouds circled menacingly and on the shore the trees, through which she could just glimpse Creddon Hall, soughed suddenly as a wind from nowhere whipped through them.

Johnnie had found a piece of rope and was pretending to fish. He had climbed onto the bulwark and was balanced precariously on his knees, leaning over to look down into the water. Lisa was just about to warn him to be careful and to grab the back of his jersey when the very thing she was trying to prevent happened. He fell overboard into the water.

"Daddy!" he shrieked, then his mouth was promptly filled with water and he sank.

Lisa's only thought was that Fraser would hate her if she let his child drown. Kicking off her shoes, she clambered onto the bulwark and dived into the water just as a clap of thunder resounded around the hills.

Water came up over her head in a smooth green wave and the shock of its terrible icy cold penetrated her clothing. She surfaced quickly and looked around for Johnnie. Rain was falling, hitting the water with big drops, and thunder rolled ominously again. Lisa saw Johnnie dog-paddling madly and she struck out in his direction. She thought she could hear voices calling to her, but the sizzling sound of the raindrops as they hit the water faster and faster in a deluge made it difficult for her to hear properly. The sodden weight of her wet clothing was pulling her legs down so that she could not kick effectively. Spitting water out of her mouth, she looked around to see if she was anywhere near Johnnie. Something hit her on the side of the head and she lost consciousness.

CHAPTER TEN

THERE WAS A PAIN in her chest and every time she took a breath the inside of her windpipe felt as if it had been rubbed raw. Knives seemed to be sticking into her stomach and it heaved suddenly with nausea.

A familiar voice said, "She's coming round now."

Lisa opened her eyes and looked straight at Fraser. He was kneeling beside her, bending over her. Behind him she could see the trees moving in the wind. Rain dripped on her face and thunder rumbled distantly. She realized that she was lying on the ground and that she was wrapped in a thick blanket, with another blanket lying over her. Turning her head, she found Sarah on her other side, also kneeling and looking at her with anxious blue eyes. Her honey-colored hair was soaking wet and hung in damp tails around her delicately molded face.

A pain throbbed on the side of her head and memory came back with a rush. Trying to sit up, she demanded hoarsely, "Where's Johnnie?"

Fraser pushed her back. "Take it easy," he ordered sternly. "Johnnie's fine. Brian and Bunty have taken him to the castle."

"What hit me?" she asked, raising a hand and feeling the bump on the side of her head.

"A lifebelt that some idiot threw to you. You sank but fortunately came up again. Sarah and I were able to grab you and bring you ashore and apply artificial respiration while Brian and Bunty rescued Johnnie. As soon as Brian comes back with a car we'll take you to the castle and put you to bed," Fraser said brusquely. His face was pale and dour, and his crisp hair had been flattened by the rain.

"Mother will look after you," said Sarah comfortingly.

"You're very wet," Lisa murmured.

"Not as wet as you, dear," grinned Sarah. "The heavens just opened after you went over the side. Poor daddy, I'm afraid his party is spoiled. Here comes Brian, I think. Will you be able to walk to the car, Lisa?"

"I'll carry her," said Fraser. "Thanks for your help, Sarah."

"Don't mention it. I was glad to help. It wouldn't have done for you to have lost her after being married only for a few days. I'll go back to the schooner now and tell everyone you're all right and try to cheer up poor daddy."

She rose to her feet and walked away. Raising her head, Lisa watched her push off a dinghy that was pulled up on the small beach at the head of the loch, step into it, sit down and begin to row.

"I'm too heavy for you to carry," she said weakly to Fraser.

"Be quiet and do as I tell you," he ordered, and she had to bite her lip to control an urge to burst into tears. She had very nearly drowned and he showed not the slightest bit of emotion.

Following his terse instructions, she stood up with his help. Her head swam and she was glad of his support. Wrapping the two blankets around her, he heaved her into his arms and started to walk toward the car that was just stopping at the end of a rough road a few yards away.

"Never do that again, Lisa," he burst out suddenly.

"But I was afraid that Johnnie would drown," she quavered.

"You nearly drowned," he retorted in a tight voice. "Never jump into the water to rescue anyone until you're sure there's no other form of rescue available. Today there were plenty of dinghies and plenty of people capable of manning them and rescuing Johnnie. There was no need for you to fling yourself after him fully clothed. The water was quite calm and he's able to keep himself afloat in such conditions. Didn't it occur to you that I'd taught him how to take care of himself if he ever fell overboard?"

He was angry. She could feel the anger throbbing through

The Taming of Lisa

him; see it in his white face and darkened eyes—angry because she had tried to rescue his child. If she had not felt so weak she would have slid from his arms, told him he was an ungrateful beast and made her way to the car on foot. But all she could do was turn her face against his chest so that he would not see her tears, and mutter into his damp sweater, "I did it for you."

Two hours later Lisa was in bed, wearing one of Sarah's nightgowns, in one of the guest rooms at Creddon Hall. She had been examined by Dr. Clarke, who had been called in by Fraser to make sure that she and Johnnie had escaped serious injury, and then she had been ordered to go to sleep and had been left alone. Since she had an overwhelming desire to sleep she turned on her side and slept almost immediately.

When she awakened the sky outside the narrow latticed windows was dark. No noise from other parts of the castle penetrated the thick door of the room and for all she knew she could have been quite alone in the building. The feeling of having been deserted persisted, giving her a sense of panic.

Where was Fraser? Where had he gone when he had left her after telling her to go to sleep? Was he in the castle or had he returned to the schooner? Moving cautiously, she eased herself up in bed and stretched out a hand to her right. After groping for a while she found the switch on the bedside lamp. Rose-colored light filtered through the big parchment shade, dispersing the gloom and restoring her spirits a little. Lisa leaned back against the pillows and looked around. The room was circular and she guessed it was in one of the turrets. Its predominant color was rose pink and the furniture seemed to be made mostly of rosewood that gleamed warmly in the soft light.

In a mirror above the dressing table opposite the bed she could see herself reflected: a pale wedge of a face topped by spiky red hair; eyes wide and dark; shoulders surprisingly creamy where they appeared out of the scooped neckline of the nightdress. She looked vulnerable, a little lost, not at all the independent, self-contained person she tried to be.

Irritated by the image, she threw back the bedclothes. She would get up and assert her independence. She was just about to swing her legs out of bed when the knob of the door turned. Startled, she pulled the clothes up around her and watched the door open and Fraser appear.

He must have been back to Ardmont, because he was dressed in a tweed sports jacket, dark trousers, a shirt and a tie. He walked across to the bedside and stood looking down at her.

"Have a good sleep?" he asked.

"Yes, thank you. I was thinking of getting up."

"Don't bother. Stay where you are. Doc Clarke said you wouldn't feel back to strength until tomorrow or even the day after. Are you hungry?"

She nodded. If he had married her for love he would not be so matter-of-fact, she thought rebelliously. He would have taken her in his arms, kissed her and told her how glad he was that she had not drowned. Instead he stood hands on his hips, his eyes dark and unreadable, his mouth a straight line, giving nothing away.

"Bunty thought you might be, so she's having a tray prepared for you. I'll go and get it," he said.

As he went toward the door she experienced again the panicky feeling at the thought of being alone. It was so unusual that she sat up, clutching the bedclothes about her.

"How is Johnnie?" she asked, in an attempt to detain him.

"Fine. He's fast asleep in the room above this," he replied, and went out of the room, closing the door.

She was alone, frighteningly alone. She could only assume that it was shock that had produced the feeling and she determined to deal with it. She would get up, put on the long pink quilted dressing gown she could see lying conveniently on a chair and sit at the small writing table that was set beneath the window. Lying in bed she felt too weak, incapable of coping with the man who was her husband. However, when she stood up eventually she felt remarkably dizzy and had to sit down on the edge of the bed quickly. Her head had hardly stopped swimming when the door opened again and Fraser came in carrying a laden tray.

"Where do you think you're going?" he asked as he placed the tray on the bedside table and turned to survey her.

"I thought I'd eat sitting at the table over there," she said, very conscious of his interested glance at her bare legs and feet, which showed below the hem of the short nightdress.

"And you couldn't make it," he observed dryly. "Well, back you go. This tray has legs on it and will fit across your legs and act as a table, so you'll be quite comfortable. I'll fix the pillow for you."

As he reached behind her to plump up the pillows and set them against the headboard she protested, "I'm not an invalid!"

"For the time being you are," he replied firmly.

Soon she was settled comfortably with the tray in front of her and was eating the thick broth that Bunty had sent with fresh rolls and butter. Satisfied that she was going to eat, Fraser walked over to the window and looked out.

"What time is it?" asked Lisa.

"About eight-thirty."

"Is the party over?"

"Yes, it ended with the thunderstorm. Harry decided to take the schooner back to Ardmont. I came back here with him because Bunty asked me to stay the night so I could be near you and Johnnie."

He pulled the rose-patterned curtains across the window and immediately the room took on an intimate atmosphere. Lisa leaned back with a sigh, having finished the meal, and he came across to remove the tray and put it on the bedside table again.

"You look better now," he commented. "Not so big-eyed and frightened."

To her surprise he sat down on the side of the bed quite close to her. As always his nearness tormented her and she looked away to the other side of the bedroom. On the curved wall there were some small pictures and she peered at them, trying to make out whether they were original paintings or reproductions.

"Those are very pretty pictures, but I don't think they merit being stared at so intently," murmured Fraser mockingly. "What's the matter?"

"Nothing."

"Don't lie."

"Do I have to share my inmost thoughts with you as well as a bed tonight?" she asked querulously.

"You don't have to share anything with me, least of all a bed," he retorted acidly. "You made your thoughts on that aspect of marriage to me quite obvious when you decided to move into the spare room in my house. Don't worry, I can sleep with Johnnie tonight. He's in a bed three times too big for him."

The harshness of his reply startled her and made her look at him. He was not looking at her. He seemed more interested in the pattern of roses on the Chinese carpet. There was a bitter curve to his mouth and he was frowning. Lisa recalled the way he had hesitated on the threshold of the spare room that night he had returned from Ireland and realized suddenly that he had been as disappointed as she had been that night.

Realization broke the bonds she had imposed on her love. She wanted to reach out and stroke away the frown and the bitter curve and to tell him he did not have to sleep with Johnnie.

"I know it's a pretty carpet, but I'm sure it doesn't merit being stared at so intently," she ventured, a quiver of amusement in her voice.

His head jerked around as if pulled by a puppeteer's string. His eyes were wide with surprise, but when he saw she was smiling he smiled, too.

"You're right. It doesn't," he replied. "I much prefer to look at you. I've always liked looking at you."

Struck with a sudden uncharacteristic shyness, Lisa had difficulty in returning his gaze.

"So I'd noticed," she answered as lightly as she could.

"In fact that's one of the reasons I married you. I thought it would be pleasant to have you around to look at."

"Then why didn't you tell me?" she asked shakily.

"I thought it was a reason that wouldn't appeal to you," he replied provocatively.

"Were there any other reasons for marrying me that you thought might not appeal to me?" she asked.

To her consternation he stood up. He was going to leave her alone again.

"Yes, but I'm not sure whether this is the time to tell you. You've had a harrowing experience and should rest. I'll take the tray downstairs."

As he stretched out his hands to pick up the tray she reached up and caught the nearest one. It felt strong and warm, a hand you could cling to when you needed comfort. But he didn't like clinging women who wept, she thought as tears welled in her eyes.

"Please tell me, Fraser," she whispered.

His hand closed around hers as he looked down at her. "I need much more encouragement than that. You see, I have that abominable pride to settle with," he replied.

That pride behind which Lisa now realized he hid all his hurts and disappointments. She stared up at him wondering what she could say or do, and all she could think of saying was the truth that was uppermost in her mind because her own pride had ceased to be a barrier.

"Please don't go away and leave me here alone. I know you don't like women who cling and weep, but I don't think I can spend tonight by myself after all. Please stay, Fraser. There's no one else in the whole world I'd rather be with than you."

He sat down on the side of the bed again, released her hand and grasped her roughly by the shoulders.

"Do you mean that?" he demanded. "And if you do are you prepared to take the consequences of what you've just said?"

Smiling through her tears, she reached up and put her arms around his neck and placed her damp cheek against his.

"I mean it. And I'll be glad to take the consequences. You see, I love you," she whispered.

Some time passed before she was able to speak again.

She asked, rather breathlessly, "Have you settled with your pride yet?"

She felt more than heard Fraser's familiar grunt of laughter as he held her close to him.

"I think so—with your help," he murmured into the curve of her shoulder. "Thanks for saying it first."

"Saying what first?"

"That you love me. You see, one reason why I asked you to marry me was that I'd discovered I'd fallen in love with you, much against my will."

Amazed by his confession, she had to ask questions. "Oh, when?"

"Is it important to know exactly when?" he laughed.

"Yes, because I'd no idea you loved me until now. You've been very secretive about it."

"I could say the same for you," he jeered softly. "I was attracted to you from the moment you set foot in my office, but I struggled against the feeling, partly because I distrusted it and partly because of pride. If you knew how many of my own words I've been eating recently!"

"I've had the same problem," she laughed. "And I thought it was Sarah who was causing the strain. I thought you were in love with her and couldn't marry her because Johnnie didn't like her."

"It was your association with Sandy that had me bothered, and when I came back and saw you kissing on the doorstep I knew that I had to do something. I thought that if I could persuade you to marry me I'd be able to teach you to love me once we were living together. So I stooped pretty low in my own estimation and used Johnnie as bait."

Lisa was silent, thinking once again how easily she had risen to his bait. How well he knew her, far better than she knew him. But he had let himself be guided by love and now she knew his was the loving hand that had tamed her wild heart.

"I think I began to understand your behavior a little when you gave me the violets," she said, watching him walk across the room to the mirror to straighten his tie and subdue his hair. "But you were so cross and distant when

The Taming of Lisa

you came back from Ireland that I began to have doubts again. I thought that you didn't want me after all, but just a mother for Johnnie."

"Not want you?" he exclaimed, turning to glare at her. "How do you think I felt when I found you sleeping in that old lumpy bed in the spare room?"

"Well, how was I supposed to know where I should sleep? You never told me," she retorted, glaring back at him. "Then you've been perfectly beastly today, flirting with Sarah and being angry with me for trying to rescue Johnny."

"So I was flirting with Sarah, was I? What about your behavior with Brian? He scarcely left your side, he was so fascinated," he gibed. "Since you mention it, I was angry because you almost drowned before we'd had our honeymoon!"

"Oh, are we going to have a honeymoon?" Lisa asked innocently.

He came across to the bedside table, picked up the tray and gave her an amused sidelong glance.

"Of course. I planned it before I went to Ireland. Beginning tomorrow, if you're better. I've borrowed a small sailing sloop from a friend and we're going cruising among the Western Isles. Didn't I tell you?"

"You never tell me anything," she complained to his retreating back as he walked to the door. "I know nothing about sailing."

"You'll learn fast enough," he said as he opened the door.

"But supposing there's a storm? Sarah said you don't like having a woman on board if there's a possibility of a gale."

He turned and looked at her, and her skin began to tingle.

"Depends on the woman," he replied laconically.

He was going, leaving her alone again, after all they had just said and done. But it wouldn't do to cling because he might not come back if she did.

"Will you be coming back ... here ... tonight?" she asked, trying to sound casual.

"I'll always come back to you, Red," Fraser said softly. "Remember that. See you later."

He went out and closed the door. Lisa leaned back against the pillows, her heart gladder than a singing bird's because at last it had been tamed by love.

TAKE THESE 4 FREE

Harlequin Romances

as advertised on TV

Thrill to romantic, aristocratic Istanbul, and the tender love story of a girl who built a barrier around her emotions in ANNE HAMPSON'S "Beyond the Sweet Waters" ... a Caribbean island is the scene setting for love and conflict in ANNE MATHER'S "The Arrogant Duke" ... exciting, sun-drenched California is the locale for romance and deception in VIOLET WINSPEAR'S "Cap Flamingo" ... and an island near the coast of East Africa spells drama and romance for the heroine in NERINA HILLIARD'S "Teachers Must Learn."

Harlequin Romances ... 6 exciting novels published each month! Each month you will get to know interesting, appealing, true-to-life people ... You'll be swept to distant lands you've dreamed of visiting ... Intrigue, adventure, romance, and the destiny of many lives will thrill you through each Harlequin Romance novel.

Get all the latest books before they're sold out!

As a Harlequin subscriber you actually receive your personal copies of the latest Romances immediately after they come off the press, so you're sure of getting all 6 each month.

Cancel your subscription whenever you wish!

You don't have to buy any minimum number of books. Whenever you decide to stop your subscription just let us know and we'll cancel all further shipments.

Your FREE gift includes
- **Anne Hampson** — Beyond the Sweet Waters
- **Anne Mather** — The Arrogant Duke
- **Violet Winspear** — Cap Flamingo
- **Nerina Hilliard** — Teachers Must Learn

FREE GIFT CERTIFICATE
and Subscription Reservation

Mail this coupon today!

In the U.S.A.
1440 South Priest Drive
Tempe, AZ 85281

In Canada
649 Ontario Street
Stratford, Ontario N5A 6W2

Harlequin Reader Service:

Please send me my 4 Harlequin Romance novels FREE. Also, reserve a subscription to the 6 NEW Harlequin Romance novels published each month. Each month I will receive 6 NEW Romance novels at the low price of $1.50 each (*Total–$9.00 a month*). There are no shipping and handling or any other hidden charges. I may cancel this arrangement at any time, but even if I do, these first 4 books are still mine to keep.

_____
NAME   (PLEASE PRINT)

_____
ADDRESS

_____
CITY   STATE/PROV.   ZIP/POSTAL CODE

Offer not valid to present subscribers
Offer expires October 31, 1982   BP059